FORGOTTEN MASTERS VI

A SUBTLE APPROACH

SCOTT M. SWAINE

Primix Publishing
East Brunswick Office Evolution
1 Tower Center Boulevard, Ste 1510
East Brunswick, NJ 08816
www.primixpublishing.com
Phone: 1-800-538-5788

This is a work of fiction. Names, characters, places, and incidents either are the product of the author's imagination or are used fictitiously, and any resemblance to any persons, living or dead, is entirely coincidental.

Published by Primix Publishing: 12/13/2024

ISBN: 979-8-89194-152-6(sc)
ISBN: 979-8-89194-258-5(hc)
ISBN: 979-8-89194-153-3(e)

Library of Congress Control Number: 2024907501

Because of the dynamic nature of the Internet, any web addresses or links contained in this book may have changed since publication and may no longer be valid. The views expressed in this work are solely those of the author and do not necessarily reflect the views of the publisher, and the publisher hereby disclaims any responsibility for them.

CONTENTS

Chapter 1

HEAVY BURDENS

"Look here, will you," mentions one scout.

"Aye, quite a nasty one, that is," responds the other scout.

"It looks a bit like the sort of thing you get after His Lordship drops Mystra's Fury on the place."

"Right to that, but I doubt this is from His Lordship, which only brings one other to my mind, and it ain't a pretty thought."

"I think we need to bring this report in straight away."

"You may be right. All these holes we've been spying lately, and now this one. I dare to think of what happened here."

"Or what's left of the place after. Could there be anyone alive at all?"

"There must be, at least in that one city."

"Aye, and it's buried somewhere deep, to the best of our knowing."

"No doubt this is why, I'll bet, and not just to keep away from it, but as good mention to keep the people in hand."

"Especially if they think the war is still on."

The two scouts had been making a progressive set of runs across a wide, flat, and quite barren land. The region was dry, the air was warm, and the scenery was bleak, filled largely with craters of various sizes, the worst of which, so far, lay just in front of them.

It was a massive hole, at best guess measuring more than a mile across. It wasn't a natural feature; this appeared to be carved out of the land with debris lining the surrounding region. It was clearly the result of an immensely powerful weapon, and likely it came from high above.

The two scouts studied it for several moments, further surveying the surrounding landforms. In the distance, they could see mountains stretching off to the south and another line running along the horizon to the east. It was roughly midday, and although their run had been fairly short, the heavy gravity took its toll on their endurance. That, combined with the unpleasantly hot, dry climate in the region, caused them to consider a brief rest before taking it any further. This latest find would certainly justify a return to camp to give a report.

One of them pulls out a rune stone and begins chanting over it, causing a swirling wave of energy to usher up around him, and then to funnel into the stone itself, marking the rune for a later return to the region, rather than to make the full run from their last starting point. The other scout brings out a rune and weaves a chant on it to invoke the mystical energies that causes it to summon up a portal. He gestures at the first scout to touch the stone and the man departs from the scene in a flash. The remaining scout then waves off the enchantment and casts a different one, this time for his personal activation. He claps his hand down on it and vanishes from sight.

They arrived in a carefully concealed military camp snuggled up to a hillside gully and further enclosed in a wall camouflaged to appear as the surrounding terrain. The other guardsmen inside the camp stood vigil attending to the surveillance of the local region through peepholes in the wall, but nothing has been seen outside since their initial arrival almost a month ago. Not even wildlife.

"Captain Hagmaert," calls one of the scouts as he enters a structure serving as a command post. "We've just returned from our recent run from the east and north."

"Anything new out there?" he responds. "So far, this tour is turning out to be as dead as the land itself."

"Aye to that, Captain, but still no life in sight. However, we've been seeing more of those craters, and the one we just came from is bigger than most. It reminds me a bit of the one His Lordship dropped in the valley on his first arrival to Therinë, though not quite as beastly. Still, it bears the appearance of more like what we saw earlier, but on a grander scale. Whatever was sitting there got sent fully to its maker, I'll bet."

"Poor devils…" he moans. "More so that everything else out there is so barren. I wonder what this world looked like before they came."

"Still no sightings of any Suuden-Aryku, nothing on land or in the skies…lucky for us, I might say."

"True, we wouldn't want them catching sight of us, even if we're just running around on open terrain. Have you seen any dwarves out there yet?"

"Not as yet, but my guess would be, if any did survive, we might have better luck searching nearer the mountain ranges. You know how they are usually."

"Right. What did you see as for mountains? Maybe we could send a few cautious runs over there to check on it."

"There was a row to the east of our last run which looked promising, and of course that line running more to the south from the low end of the plains. I'm a mite curious about that one, too."

"Good, then we might try the nearest one to the south. Just keep in mind to stay out of sight if you do see anything. We have no idea how they'll react, and considering the condition of this land, I doubt they'll be very sociable."

✦✦✦✦✦

"My Lord, we have another report from our outpost."

"General, the more of these reports you bring in, the more disturbed I am about their implications. It would seem the Suuden-Aryku, if they are truly the ones responsible, have made thorough work of that place."

"Indeed, and the Captain just sent in this most recent one. Here, take a look."

General Gabarleine was reviewing some of the reports being sent by the Captain. The most recent scouting run had been recorded and arrived during the night at the Watchmen Intelligence Center, otherwise known as the WIC building, in the city of Rolsklinde on Therinë.

Thaelyn was just arriving from Tae'Eladar, after making a brief visit to his personal office in the guildhall in Bya'an Tamoranth, the capital city of his kingdom on that world. He looked over the latest report, shaking his head and staring solemnly at the mention of the large blast crater.

"Commander," he relents. "We would seem to have a very serious issue with these Suuden-Aryku, and by association, that one who dares call himself Marshal Darumon."

Commander Kailen Nazég was a regular feature in the room. The High Commander of the Daanen-Aryku Sentinels, he began spending most of his time in conference with Thaelyn and the General. Accompanying him was his junior officer, Lieutenant Padriyl Lapäli, who served as an intermediary for a while during the initial moments of the war on that world against Darumon and his Suuden'kai loyalists. When that war came to a close, with the enemy forces abandoning their position, the focus then moved to other worlds in order to give chase.

"I would agree, Your Lordship," Kailen admits. "If they were so determined to take that world as to use the High Elves, or should I say Flame Elves as they were called in those days, as a decoy to misdirect the native dwarves…"

"And let us not forget," the General adds. "Those elves were not apparently well-suited to the heavy gravity environment of that world."

"That as well, which only adds to the misery of the situation. And then to presumably come down behind them with a hidden base, and furthermore to blast everything else to nether-space, what else should we expect from them."

"But once again…" Thaelyn cautions. "We should consider these chips of theirs that may force them to obey despite their better judgment. For this point, we again have to point our fingers largely at Darumon.”

“Maybe so, but I’m getting anxious to know just how those people could ever allow themselves to fall so far, with or without him and his antics.”

“This is indeed a disturbing question. And it reminds me of that one conversation with their Commander Geilv, and how he described them as pursuing some great cause to return something stolen.”

“Returning something stolen is one thing, but how do you justify THIS!” he points assertively at the report.

“I do not, as I would the same with Therinë and what they did here. So unless we are speaking of another situation where they describe it as ‘containment’…” he sighs. “But now, when looking at this latest report, it would seem Darumon is taking a pattern here of removing a large part of the world population, perhaps to save himself the trouble of large-scale management, while his agent, that Thane he installed in Glimmerheim, tells his fables of a false war outside and forces them to close themselves off underground.”

“One thing is for sure,” Kailen considers. “Blasting the rest of the world apart would give a good incentive to those people to stay buried.”

“Indeed it would, a justifiable cause to reinforce the notion of a continued war with the elves. I should think the timing of it would need to be carefully considered, however, so that the people within the city were already buried, and therefore they would not see the true source of these impacts.”

“So, they trigger the reaction with the elven invasion, causing just enough concern that the Thane, who is likely an agent by this time, can convince the people to bury themselves in their mountain, closing off the entrance to their city, and then lay whatever type of bombardment they were using to tidy up.”

“And here we have a new concern,” Thaelyn muses cautiously. “We did not see any sort of aircraft in use during their occupation here on Therinë, but I do recall a few of our scouts reporting blast craters in some remote regions to the south. Therefore, we must ask ourselves what sort of bombardment they are using, and then ask what sort of ships they are using to deliver it."

"It would take something big to dig a hole this deep. We know they have atomic technologies, but if we're talking about bombardment, are we speaking of bombs, missiles, or their most favorite plasma weapons."

"If we are speaking of atomics, I would wish to bring our people in on a routine basis to check their health, in case there is any residue left behind."

"Granted, and we can help you with that, if you like. But you know, my personal thoughts are plasma. The weapons are rechargeable, and if we're blanketing a full planetary surface..."

"Of course, the use of ammunition, like bombs, becomes problematic."

"But this would have to be a heavy caliber."

"I recall once speaking to your mother about some of the earlier encounters your people had over the course of your ten millennia pursuit by the Suuden-Aryku. She said some of those occasions involved orbital bombardment, and naturally this means they must have some manner of vessel capable of this."

"Yes, and since we're a space-faring society back on Azgarén, no doubt Darumon has invented a few new toys to play with, like so many others we've seen so far. My guess here would have to be no less than a heavy cruiser or maybe a battleship."

"Do you recall ever having such vessels in your space navy prior to this?"

"I don't recall us ever having a space navy prior to this, and certainly not with such heavy firepower. Most of this would be theory to me, or academic from our old history, maybe also from a few vid-com action films. It's just so hard to believe that we were once a peaceful society and how Darumon turned them around to behave as such monsters."

"Let us keep our calm for now, Commander. We still have far to go in our investigations. Darumon has been developing a long list of atrocities, from using these chips to control the Suuden-Aryku, to using drugs on the dwarven mining crews, mind control on the elves, and then what we saw here in Rolsklinde when we first arrived."

"My Lord," the General interjects. "Although we might suggest Darumon has his criminal history, we should also ask who this Thane is. Could he be another servant creature to Sargeras, perhaps like Darumon, or maybe a lesser one, if Darumon once said he is the last of his kind? Or simply a local resident he corrupted, much like he did to the elves."

"This is a question we need to answer, but very carefully so they do not see us coming. We also need to find this other mining camp said to be out there, as well as the Suuden'kai base. Of course, to find the base, or even the mine, we may also need to find the city, and so far, this land is stretching out in all directions."

"The mine was said to be south of the city," Kailen notes. "So, if we should be lucky enough to find that first, then we just need to head north."

"True, so we should keep this in mind. And we were suggesting at one time that the Suuden'kai base might be in close proximity to the city if the Thane is pulling out his mining teams during this famous feast of his and using that drug. Those men would not likely be in such good condition for any long treks cross-country, so he might just send them out a door and right into the Suuden-Aryku's hands."

"But so far, no sightings of any kind," he sighs.

"Not as yet, but I think we are far from finished. So far, it appears the progress is slow due to the situation of the heavy gravity, the dense atmosphere, and the unpleasant climate...hmm..."

"What is it, Your Lordship?"

"Just a thought, really, about the climate conditions. Aside from relieving our people on occasion for this medical review, I am also wondering about anything else out there. They say there is no sign of any life, not even wildlife, and much of the vegetation shows signs of severe distress."

"That's a bit disturbing, and it brings a few thoughts to my mind."

"Mine as well. If the bombardment was so severe, are we looking at a global warming effect, and therefore the reduction of wildlife?

Although some of it might be the direct result of the attack, could some also be a form of die-off due to a radical climate change?"

"An extinction event in the making, where the hot, dry climate is simply an indication of things warming up so much that nothing can survive anymore."

"This is despicable, my Lord," the General argues. "We take such pride in our home and the natural elements around us as a part of our blessings of life. Do they hold so little regard for other people's homes, like this one? And then, what about Azgarén? How might that appear? Could it be they have polluted it to such extremes as to cause a similar loss?"

"General," Thaelyn relents. "These are surely excellent questions to ask. In this case here, it is clearly an effort to destroy a world such that they can reduce their concern to only that small portion they actually care to manage. The destruction of the local climate may simply be incidental to this effect. The next question we might wish to ask ourselves is what we can do about it. Assuming we find the city, and assuming we are able to liberate its citizens in any way, they will be hard-pressed to find any comfortable living in the outside world."

"What about these Trees of Life of yours?" Kailen asks. "Isn't it my understanding that they have the ability to purify a local environment and restore some form of natural balance?"

"They do, and they could possibly serve that purpose here, if in sufficient quantity to cover the land. But the damage already caused might require caretakers to coddle them during the first couple of decades until they are strong enough to overcome the handicap of the natural elements. And then we have the dwarves. Traditionally, they are not as sensitive to the needs of the overland nature as elves tend to be. They will need to be carefully educated on these matters, assuming they are receptive to our presence at all."

"Eiki, me dear, how ye be this morn?" calls a female visitor to a neatly kept home in a well-travelled section of the city.

"The same," Eiki responds blandly. "Another day t' sweep the floors an' tidy the shelves, nay that they need t' be tidied any more than they are, but 'tis all I have t' d' here."

"Ye're nay the only one t' suffer these woes. This accursed war has been the bane of us all for as long as we can recall it."

"Aye, an' it ne'er sees an end. It just keeps ragin', year in an' year out."

"'Tis the curse of those hellish point-ears! The Thane tells tale of them pourin' out of their portals without rest. I don'na know what sort of battles be a-ragin' up there, but ye an' I both know our men are workin' hard t' keep the warriors fit with the finest fare."

"But Telta, it don'na make sense t' me! How long has it been by now? Centuries! An' our men keep goin' up t' craft for the warriors an' ne'er come back. Our men are nay the warrior caste. They be but smiths an' forge keepers. Where d' ye think they be a-goin' if the Thane tells tale of more t' be sent?"

"The war must be a-layin' upon them somehow. The Thane ne'er lets us go up an' see with our own eyes. The tales are the land be ablaze with the terror of the point-ears."

"Aye! An' there be another puzzlin' bit for ye. If the land be a-blazin' for so long a time, where d' ye think the warriors are comin' from, ay? None of us here sees the clans sendin' out t' fight, only smiths t' serve up the fare. Where d' these warriors come from, d' ye think?"

"Eiki, mayhap we be a-servin' up the fare, but the towns an' such outside, they be the ones t' the fore of it. Surely, the warriors are sent from there an' the Thane simply be a-keepin' us safe so we can serve our best t' keep them fightin'."

"I don'na know, Telta. Me gut feelin' tells that our men are bein' sent out for more than t' serve up anythin'. These tales go back t' our fathers an' their fathers, an' maybe more after that. An' we get no new tales of the battle from outside, only that it be a-ragin', an' our men are made t' go out an' serve up for it."

Eiki and Telta stood outside the modest home, one of many in a neighborhood carved out of the rocky cavern walls along a lane cut through the dense interior of their mountain home well beneath the surface.

The city was a hollowed-out grotto, made larger during the initial years of the war by the dwarves to further develop the space as the local population was ordered to move fully below ground. The Thane had instructed them to dig deeper into the mountain to escape from the advancing waves of enemies invading the land above, a process that began nearly four centuries ago, and to their knowledge was still occurring.

It was a bustle of activity as laborers and shopkeepers carried out their local business. Workshops were in constant motion to produce goods crafted from local resources, either quarried from the surrounding stone or mined from deeper in the tunnels. Markets sold food grown in subterranean farms producing a variety of comestibles native to the region that were tolerant to the underground habitat, along with meat from an assortment of livestock being maintained in a long series of animal pens.

There was no natural light in this space. In many cases, bioluminescent lichens were used to provide lighting in those areas where the need was only modest. Many homes benefited from this, and often the marketplaces as well. In only a scant few instances were fires maintained in braziers using either coal or wood. The source for these was said to be bartered by the Thane in exchange for the workforce he provided to the war effort on the surface.

Ventilation shafts had been carefully cut through the sides of the rock walls in various places to afford the circulation of air with the outside, but the exit points were typically located in hard-to-reach places, and carefully concealed, both inside the cavern and outside the mountain, to keep from being noticed and perhaps used by their enemies in a surprise attack.

The two women paused from their conversation to look around the local area. Eiki studies the activity of the people passing through the lane in the course of their work, while her long-time friend Telta took to straightening her apron during the momentary intermission.

"Telta," Eiki begins again. "I don'na like it. Me husband was one t' be sent away, an' he has'na even sent word of himself since. 'Tis like all the rest. Ye an' I both know, once the Thane calls his feast, ye make yer last goodbye, for it will be the last time ye see yer loved one again. 'Tis no war, this... It be nay less than a death call."

"Aye, me dear, but at least the tales have gone from the two feasts down t' the one. Many have taken t' say this be a sign of the war comin' t' a close, as there be fewer men goin' out, an' so there be less of a need t' fit the warriors over yon."

"Mayhap there be but one feast now, but the tales are the Thane has called upon our smiths t' bring up more of their wares an' faster. I don'na know if this be a sign of the war comin' t' an end, or if it be only a change from sendin' out the smiths on that one feast, now t' keep them here t' d' the same, but harder."

"Mayhap it be that, but at least they be a-stayin' home now. An' mayhap the others will return one day, includin' yer beloved Tol."

✦✦✦✦✦

"All right, Cadet, we'll run through this again, but this time we'll simulate some aberrant weather on the screen. Keep to your instruments and be sure to watch the landforms on the HUD to gauge your flight characteristics."

"Yes Sir."

The simulation taking place was a demonstration of flying an aircraft over a projected landmass as part of a training exercise for new pilots. The simulator consisted of a pilot's seat with a variety of controls situated around the virtual cockpit, and a wrap-around screen to project the image of the outside world as the occupant maneuvered their computer-generated aircraft through the skies.

The scenario could be modified with any of a variety of circumstances, such as stormy weather, excessively hot and cold climates, and high winds. It could also simulate conditions not native to the local environment, such as alien worlds and even travel through space.

Cadet Marelle Carronel had been in study for a few months

by now, interspacing her training course with her other classes at the academy in her service to the Order. She, along with several other students, so far mostly Daanen-Aryku, were undergoing flight training in preparation for their future needs in the war effort to provide service for aerial surveillance, transport, and most importantly, air combat.

In addition to her training in the simulator, it was necessary for her to take a few special courses with the Daanen-Aryku to level out her basic technical understanding of aircraft designs and the principles of flight, as her native society had no idea how any of this works. Prior to this, her only experience with aircraft was a mischievous little joyride she and her friend, Relissa, once made with the help of Lieutenant Lapäli, using a large Suuden'kai transport they found near the dwarven mining enclave north of Rolsklinde. This was during the Suuden-Aryku occupation of that world, where they were using it to pick up large quantities of adamantium. Along the way, Marelle discovered the thrill of operating such a magnificent vessel and felt a yearning to learn more about it. However, this technology was well above anything her society had ever dealt with before, so the learning curve would be steep.

The training simulator was one of several located in a facility at the Bahlaie Research Center, locally designated as the BRC, on Tae'Eladar. The basic design of the facility was a familiar format to the Daanen-Aryku, with the exception being the equipment was designed to operate in the Tae'Eladaran native language rather than the traditional Daanen'kai form, as was most common when the Daanen-Aryku developed such devices.

Marelle made herself comfortable as the simulation began, switching on her flight controls, indicators, and scanner displays. She powered on each system as if she were in an actual aircraft preparing to take off. The simulation would allow her to lift off the ground and fly through the air using real-time physics and control feedback, giving her the sensation of flight without being inside a real vessel.

When the system diagnostics were complete, she signaled her

readiness to the control booth, which in this case was her instructor at a monitoring station.

"This is Cadet Carronel, ready on deck."

"Acknowledged, Cadet, you are cleared for departure."

The current simulation represented a small single-seat training craft stationed at a military airbase, but without the runways. In this case, the aircraft were all hover-enabled VTOL designs, so they could rise and land vertically. Therefore, the air base used marked landing pads for the aircraft to lift off from. The simulators were also linked into a network for multiple students to run group missions together, though at this moment each was running their own individual program.

Marelle reaches up to the forward console and engages a switch to power up the flux field, which applies lift to the vessel, then runs a finger along a touch-sensitive gauge to program the field strength. This design was different from what the Suuden'kai heavy transport used, in part to be more functional for the need, as well as to create a unique design not as readily interpreted by any Suuden-Aryku who might happen to capture any examples of it. Therefore, the resulting aircraft would use the same design concepts.

The purpose of this sliding gauge was to program a minimum flux field, permitting greater control in the air while providing a lower-end cushion that the aircraft would bump into before crashing to the ground. The flight stick that would normally control her direction, once in the air, was linked to this feature, thus allowing lifting and diving maneuvers to a much greater degree than the heavy transport might otherwise allow. In a combat situation, where dogfighting might come into play, this was a necessary feature.

She lifts off the ground gently in her simulated scenario, gradually rising to a predetermined height, as was standard protocol when piloting an aircraft under Daanen-Aryku operating procedures. Once she leveled out, she engaged a throttle lever on her left to begin moving forward. Her simulation showed a smooth acceleration over the ground as she pulled back her flight stick in her right hand to allow her to gain altitude.

The scenery on the screens passed under her as she flew over the land, rising higher above the ground. Although it was only a simulation, she could almost feel the sensation of sailing aloft. Her objective, in this case, was to travel along a course to the north to another airbase and make a landing. Unfortunately, the trip would not be as pleasant this time as with previous ones.

As she coursed her way over a set of mountains, she suddenly came into a dense covering of clouds. The indicators on her console showed strong crosswinds and electrical discharges within the stormy cloud cover. Visibility was lost and she found she had to focus almost entirely on her instruments to navigate. The scanner display showed a 3D representation of the surface topography, and her altimeter revealed a comfortable measurement, but the winds were becoming more violent, with flashes of lightning outside.

"Central, this is Cadet Carronel," she announces on her helmet mike. "I've encountered heavy storm activity with high winds and electrical bursts. I am having difficulty maintaining a stable flight characteristic. I'm going to attempt to achieve a greater altitude to rise above it."

"Understood, Cadet. Be aware the storm activity is part of a suspected super-cell entering the region. Wind speeds could exceed Category Three levels."

"Acknowledged."

Marelle attempts to pull up on the stick to rise above the storm, but the clouds seem to condense around her, forming into a large swirling mass. She finds herself entering into a violent hurricane.

The winds rip at her aircraft, tossing it to the side. She loses her flight stability for a moment as a squall suddenly slams into her. She tries correcting it by tugging the flight stick in the opposite direction, attempting to return control to her hand, but the aircraft begins to tumble.

"If you think you're going to take me out of the sky," she mutters softly. "You'll need to work harder than that."

She turns away from the obvious flow of the winds, catching them as a tailwind and pushes the stick forward sharply, thrusting the throttle up at the same time. The instructor observes tensely as he watches her going into a power dive.

Marelle reaches up to the flux gauge as she monitors the topographical display. The landforms below are closing in quickly. An alarm sounds as they reach a critical distance. She runs her finger all the way up the gauge to max-out the flux field, and pulls up sharply on the stick, followed by dragging the throttle back a couple notches to slow her velocity slightly.

The scene around her shows the underside of the tempest as she penetrates beneath the storm, barely missing the mountainous terrain below, and instead diverting into a ravine, where she flies low between the hillsides.

The instructor stares at his monitor following her motion, letting out a tenuous sigh of relief that she didn't plow into the side of the mountain. But she wasn't out of danger yet. She was flying very low to the ground at a high rate of speed inside a ravine that twists and turns with the uneven terrain.

Marelle studied the scene intently, following the canyon until she saw a convenient pass to sail over into the next one, turning and following back the way she came. As she looked up into the sky overhead, she could see the greater portion of the storm above.

"Well now, let's try this again...my way."

She powered forward on the throttle and pulled back on the stick, plunging into the cloud structure again, this time turning to follow the flow of the storm winds, coasting along with it rather than fighting against it.

"Cadet Carronel," utters the voice on her headset. "What are you doing up there?"

"Fighting the gods of wind and thunder, Sir," she replies calmly. "Can you give me an E.T.A. on my target?"

"Your current course is off target from your projected flight plan."

"At the moment, I'm not concerned with that, so long as I'm still in the air and moving in the general direction. This baby up here wants to play rag doll with me, so I'm giving it a good run."

"Understood. At your current rate of travel, your time estimate will be approximately ten minutes, but you'll need to make a course correction or else overshoot your landing zone."

"Acknowledged."

She continues along with the flow of the hurricane, attempting to match her own speed to that of the wind outside. She feels the effects of buffeting on the feedback actuators inside the simulator, telling her the air outside is very rough and could easily cause her to lose control again. She glances down at the scanner display to see she is coming out of the mountain range into the open spaces again, so she begins a gradual descent to pass underneath the cloud cover, hoping to restore her visibility.

As she drops out of the clouds, she can see the air base in the distance to the left. She'll need to correct her course to meet with it, but that also means cutting into the winds. She tilts the stick to the left and increases the throttle power to compensate for her course alteration, holding herself steady until she comes into alignment for a landing maneuver.

The base is now easily visible and not far ahead. She adjusts the flux gauge to allow her greater ease of vertical motion after her plummet into the mountains. The winds outside were not as severe now, having passed out of the major part of the storm. She comes into range of the base and lines herself up with an illuminated landing platform, where she throttles down and engages the landing gear. She brings the flux field gently to zero, allowing the craft to settle onto the ground, then powers down the controls.

Marelle sat there for a moment in the seat of the simulator breathing out the tensions of her ordeal. This was one of her toughest tests so far. She then emerges from the unit and strolls over to meet with her instructor, who was just coming out of his monitoring booth.

"Cadet," he calls to her. "In all my years, I don't think I've seen such unorthodox piloting techniques as what you just did."

"Well, Sir, if I may speak bluntly…"

The instructor nods, allowing her to continue.

"First, before I came along, I seriously doubt you ever trained a human in one of these things, and we tend to think a little bit differently than your average Daanen'kai example. Second, I doubt you ever trained for combat piloting. Somehow, I don't think the leisurely scouting surveys you're more accustomed to would do the trick in this case."

✦✦✦✦✦✦✦

Sulíma, Túfula, and Petrith were taking a break from their work helping the other refugees from Ruuki uy'Daan settle in and find occupation in the burgeoning village being developed outside their former ship. The setting was a bustle of activity as they endeavored to redevelop their industry and commerce venues after the close of the war on Therinë. The Naarg uy'Sodrad still partially served as their home, but new homes were being built outside now, and as they were completed, the scene took on more of a comfortable town-like environment, although with the crashed remains of a massive vessel in the background.

Many aspects of their new industry were taking roles to provide for the continued war effort elsewhere, as they were producing much-needed materials and resources for the projects involving new vehicles and other technologies. As for the consumer goods, a large part of that was being imported from Tae'Eladar as new marketplaces opened up to provide for their local needs.

"Túfu," Sulíma announces as they convene in a small café. "I see they started work on the new school. Not that I'm actually very excited about going back to school after all this time, but I know we all need it."

"From what I understand," she responds. "This one will be making use of that Elixir of Visions they use on Tae'Eladar. I still find it strange to see a simple elixir able to do everything that thing can."

"Accelerating memory function? I'm actually looking forward to it. In part, to hurry things along so I can get into the higher studies, and after that, maybe I can do something useful with myself."

"You know," Petrith adds. "When you consider everything else these people invented, I think it's interesting to see how they found solutions to things even our own science missed."

"I have to admit, you're right, and a part of me wants to learn more about it. Watching them and trying to study this strange technology they use, comparing it to our own, and then to see they don't have any of the usual precursor techs we might normally expect."

"Yeah, from what I've seen this past month since arriving here, these people have created a strange and unfamiliar science for themselves, completely different from our own, if only because they have access to this stuff they call the dynamistic flows."

"And so unfortunately for us," Túfula offers. "We came from a universe that doesn't have it. So, while we took the long hard way around things, these people apparently enjoyed a lot of shortcuts."

"Right," Sulíma asserts. "And I want to see where these shortcuts can take a few ideas we used back home. Just think... We were looking at their power sources which resembled perpetual motion devices. Now look at the old fusion reactor we had back on Ruuki uy'Daan. If you could hook up a hydrogen provider to it based on their magic to simply conjure the stuff out of thin air, you could disregard all the intermediate facilities we were using before to supply the fuel."

"So, are you thinking of taking up studies now?" Petrith grins.

"I might! Maybe I can take some courses in their mage studies and see if I can mix it with some of our science to discover new ways of using it. Just think of the possibilities! They say it works by the will of the mind. Great cu'Nar, I can't even imagine all the things a person can do with it."

"But remember what Kali said," Túfula recalls. "It can also be dangerous if you don't learn to respect it, just like any other form of science. So, be careful you don't go blowing up any labs along the way."

"Yeah, I suppose so. I would like to look into their training courses, but so far, we've all been so busy over here trying to settle in and bring ourselves up to date on the local news, that I haven't had time even to go visit Tae'Eladar. By the way, we need to sign up for one of those language classes, too. We'll never get anywhere without that."

"So far," Petrith accedes. "Most of us have been working as a labor force on these local projects. We still need to build new homes and a working infrastructure."

"We have help from the people of Tae'Eladar, so it's not like we're in a really bad way."

"No, probably not… Unlike all those times when we got pushed to a new world and had to start over from scratch. Then, once that school is up, I'm sure a lot of us will be taking classes to refresh ourselves in our old lessons and fill in for all the education we missed due to the attack on Ruuki uy'Daan. This reminds me, we need to check the classrooms in our old school, as well as the old city library, for any surviving holo-disks we can salvage for our new curriculum."

"Good point," Túfula agrees. "The school got hit hard in those early days when the orcs were pillaging everything. The library might be a good source since I think a lot of the records were held in a vault, loaded into arrays of readers for the people to access through terminals in the main hall. If those are still in reasonable condition, we might be able to pull them out and reuse the disks."

"Is there an easy way into the vault? Last I saw, portions of the building were collapsed."

"I'm sure we can figure something out. And then we can bring it all here and set it up in a new library for everyone to study."

"And this time," Sulíma admits. "We might have a chance to finish our education and make something useful of ourselves."

Marelle was just returning from her flight training session back to the guildhall in Bya'an Tamoranth, where she and her friends would often meet after school for a little gossip. Relissa and Marelle's brother, Haran, had already found a seat on their favorite bench, along with Tristeen, Haran's fiancée, who was visiting from Rolsklinde. She was taking a break from her political duties overseeing the redevelopment of that city to enjoy the simpler pleasures.

"The Ninth Circle," Tristeen muses. "That'll keep you busy for another four years after you finish this course. I might start to think you're avoiding me," she huffs playfully.

"Tristeen, my dearest..." Haran croons.

"Oh no," Relissa moans. "Here we go again with the kissy-kissy bit. Haran, there's a great little inn down the lane there. I hear the rates are really affordable, too."

"Indeed, but we've already worn out several of the beds. I'm told they have new ones on order, however," he grins.

Tristeen slaps him friskily in the arm.

"Haran!" she scolds. "You're not supposed to tell them we were the cause of that little fiasco with the paintings jumping off the walls."

"Of course, my dear... I would never suggest such a thing as what you just informed our friends about," he chuckles.

They let out a bold round of laughter as Marelle settles into her seat.

"All right, you two," she intervenes. "So, what are we talking about today?"

"Hey there, Marelle," Tristeen offers. "We're just discussing Haran and his efforts to take his mage studies all the way to the Ninth Circle. That's a lot of work, from what I hear."

"Yes, it is," Haran confirms. "But I want to achieve my finest in the mage studies, for a number of reasons, really."

"What reasons are those?" Marelle asks. "As if I didn't already know..."

"Well, naturally I want to serve the best I can for the Order."

"That much is a given."

"Right, and for all that they offer, and in such a neatly organized and freely available format, I can't resist the call to service."

"I don't blame you for that point. This academy is simply remarkable for all they offer."

"Another reason is sitting right next to me," he glances at Tristeen and smiles. "After all, she deserves the best, and I also want to make myself look good in her mother's eyes," he coughs subtly.

"Aye," Relissa smirks. "You got that one right. She's a tough one. After all, this is her little girl, and she's not going to let go easily."

"And then there's the memory of the old academy," he reflects solemnly. "How many years did I have to suffer in that place, and they barely taught me enough to light a campfire."

"Speaking of which," Tristeen wonders. "How is 'Priest' Malorn doing these days?"

"Priest…" he chuckles. "That just doesn't sound right. The Dean of the old academy, the bane of education in Rolsklinde, the right-hand man to the Governor and all the trouble he was to us, and now he's a priest working for us here. Last I heard he was well into his studies at the temple, and also attending a few of his own classes here in the academy, to fill in for a few things that even he didn't get back home."

"Due to the previous Dean and all the corruption he laid down. And all because of that…creature…who was pretending to be our Governor."

"Anyway, this is another reason I want to excel, if only out of spite for all that, and to show…well, I suppose Darumon at this point, as he was the one behind everything…to show him I can."

"Do you plan on actually going up to his face with it?" she winces.

"Well, I can't say that, precisely. Maybe it's just figurative, a personal goal for myself."

"Good. After all, I'd like to see you stick around a little while so we might have a chance to make a family together."

"Of course," he smiles. "But it does bring up a curious thought. How would a mage of the Ninth Circle fare against such creatures as those?"

"Personally, I don't really care to test the theory."

"From what I understand of it," Marelle considers. "The Ninth Circle is tough, as are all the advanced courses, for that matter. I don't know how it might rate in regard to a godlike creature, but bringing it down to our level, you'll find some very special technical applications for your profession."

"Yes!" he affirms. "And this is perhaps the most exciting part of it."

"Which is why I'm wondering when he'll find time for me," Tristeen pouts.

Haran wraps his arm around the girl in a tight hug.

"Tristeen, we have lots of time together. I think we'll manage just fine."

"Perhaps, but my mom is nagging me to produce a child one of these days. I know we're both a little too busy for that, but we'll need to consider it at some moment."

"Don't you think you should also consider marriage at some moment?" Marelle suggests.

"Yes, of course, but again, with both of us taking classes in one or another academy, and with my work schedule, it's a little hard to find time for everything."

"What about you, Marelle?" Relissa asks. "I see you with Roderic skipping around town on occasion."

"Yeah. It's a little like a dream come true for us. Previously, when we were both in the Guard, we had to remain so professional. We had this policy about consorting with your fellow officers."

"I can't see it. If you loved him, and he felt the same, why couldn't you just open up about it?"

"We did a little bit. We shared a few personal moments, but they tended to be brief and very private, like we were two kids trying to sneak away from home for a little nuzzling."

"Jiggers… And how old were you?" she grins.

They shared another laugh as Relissa continued.

"Humans…" she concedes. "Oh well, since you're in different services now, I guess it doesn't matter anymore. So, when are you going to hitch up and make some little ones?"

"The hitching up part isn't too much of a problem, but we're a little mixed on the issue of little ones. We would both like children, but my tight training schedule doesn't give me a lot of time to be a mother. And this carries its own problems."

"You mean not enough time at home? Well, I suppose after you finish, you can come back to it, ay?"

"I'm hoping I can, and then pray we don't find ourselves in the middle of a new war right away, giving me enough time to raise a child, at least until I can break away again for my service. But that's not the only issue. It's my age."

"Your age? Wait, you're thirty-six now, right?"

"Yeah. My birthday, as you recall, was earlier this year, and by the time I graduate next year after my final classes, the most important of these will be my Sixth Circle of mage study, I should be thirty-seven. This cuts it a little close for me."

"I get it, because you humans have this clock thing inside that cuts you off at a certain age. Bloody wicked, that… We elves don't suffer like this. So, you'll only have maybe a few years to catch up where you should've been a decade ago, by the measure of most others."

"Right, and it's a little scary, especially as we'll be moving to new worlds searching for Darumon and Sargeras by that time."

"Do you think you'll be going to the head of the war? I thought this flying thing of yours would keep you mostly out of it, at least directly."

"I can't be sure. Adalon made that prophecy that we'll be sharing something together. Then Thaelyn said that other one with the Silver Wings, which means her, probably involves her in the final scene somehow."

"And how does this involve you? Do you think you can carry her in that dinky little flying boat?" she smiles.

"I don't think it will involve a dinky one, and if she said we have something coming, and that was followed so closely by this other revelation of her joining the fight and we need to build something huge…hmm."

"Well, keep up your training, that's all I can say. You're way ahead of me. Like Thaelyn once said, my only trouble is talking to squirrels."

"How is that coming along, by the way? Have you graduated from squirrels to anything bigger?"

"I'm still working on developing the language patterns. They have a cute way of doing it, but you need to grow them from babes to get it right."

"Relissa," Tristeen inquires. "Didn't you say you're working on the mage craft also?"

"Aye, to the Seventh, so I can mark runes and use portals. It's apparently a popular Circle for the scouting trade. So, if we're all just finishing up the Fifth now, this means two more years for me, one more for Marelle, since she's only going to the Sixth, and four for Haran."

"But depending on when you find Azgarén, and…you know… well, I wonder if you'll all be out of training by that time."

"Buggers, I hope so. Not that I'm looking forward to charging up to a god of any kind, but I hope to play at least a small bit in that."

◆◆◆

"Belrum, dear, ye're lookin' a wee bit pale today. Did ye find anythin' this time?"

"Nay, love. 'Tis as dry as ever out there. The land be a-dyin', ye know this much. I've nay seen as much as a bush rat in many a season. Methinks those of us makin' our camp in this hole will soon be the last."

"What about the other camps? We know there t' be others out there. Can they be a-farin' better? Mayhap we should see about gatherin' up t' better cope in these hard times?"

"Friah, while that yay be a grand thought, methinks they nay be a-farin' any better than we. The last time I spoke t' them, they told the same tales as what we have here."

"I fear for all of us, Belrum," she sighs mournfully. "Since the day the land outside was blasted t' the heavens above, the animals have fled an' the plants an' trees have faded. All we have are the few briar sheep we were able t' save, but even they need t' eat, an' the grasses outside are dryin' up."

"Aye, an' the meat we get from them be a-spreadin' thin for us here."

"Speakin' of meat, I have yer supper ready."

"Broth again?"

"Aye, we can only spare a few small cuts of what we have. But the lads below were able t' pull up some fresh roots for us, so it nay be so thin this time. Eat well, me love, an' later we'll cuddle 'neath the blankets, dreamin' up hope for better days."

The couple sits at their table inside their makeshift home in an old mining camp. The scene was typical of the survivors from the holocaust outside, where the land was bombarded by unknown aggressors, leaving the region to grow sterile as the devastation caused so much harm to the environment as to initiate a natural disaster of epic proportions.

They were part of a gathering of people numbering only a few hundred in this group, the last remnants of the local societies that used to inhabit towns and villages on the open plains. These were largely farming communities, livestock handlers, and the associated merchants and laborers. The land used to be covered with many such locales feeding into the larger cities, some of which were on the plains while others were half buried in the mountains.

When the attack came, many were killed outright. Only a small fraction managed to duck inside the nearby mining tunnels and a few natural caves in the region. Since that time, they have struggled to survive by pulling together whatever meager resources were still available on the land, including any remaining livestock, and a few simple crops they were able to salvage, in hopes of bringing them underground for safety. But the land outside continued to change as the imbalance tilted further to the extreme, causing a rise in temperature and therefore the loss of more of the local ecology.

Chapter 2

A DELICATE BALANCE

"You know, it would be nice at this moment to have some of those trans-coms we were using in days past with the troops on Therinë."

"Aye, Captain, but you heard what His Lordship said about those. If there are any Suuden-Aryku on this world, they could catch an earful of our signaling, and then all the hells would break loose on us."

"Indeed, Scout, but so far we have yet to see any Suuden-Aryku, or anything else for that matter."

"Aye, but some of the lads thought they saw something in that row of mountains south and east of us, a cave or maybe a mine entrance. They're out taking a closer look at it today, maybe to take a peek inside, if there's a chance."

"Good, just be sure to stay out of sight in case there's anything inside there. How much farther till we reach that row of eastern mountains?"

"Maybe by the end of the day we'll be on the edge of it, but the lads may need to start up fresh this next morn to see about any good runs along the base. From the last report, they didn't see much, but once they get up to it, we'll have a better look."

Captain Hagmaert and his men continued to scout the region,

moving closer to several promising targets based on the crude maps so far being created by his scouting teams, and what was provided earlier by Chief Bronzeheart, the dwarven forge smith who was once part of the enslaved mining crew in the enclave north of Rolsklinde.

The Chief and his crew had collected their best efforts to recall some of the land features from the old tales of their ancestors, even though none of them had ever been to the surface to see it themselves. They were originally citizens of the dwarven city of Glimmerheim, where the local Thane had ordered the entire population to bury the city deeper underground to avoid the invasion on the surface. The citizens were forbidden to travel upwards again, instead serving the alleged war effort from the safety of their homes while others fought above.

The maps created by the dwarven members were sketchy, at best, and proving to be difficult to follow for all the changes in the land since the last time anyone saw it. Cities and towns once depicted on the maps were now enormous blast craters, evidence enough that something once existed there, but without definitive proof, it was hard to say what it was. General landforms, such as mountains and hills, were falling into place somewhat, but rivers and lakes were showing up mostly as dry beds.

One group of scouts was on the eastern side of a large plain, having been making slow but steady progress in the heavy gravity and burdensome atmosphere of this strange world. The scouts, and for that matter all of the troops, were unaccustomed to operating under such conditions, as this would represent their first excursion into a world significantly different from their home turf. They didn't have any previous training specialized for this service, nor did they have any equipment or means of support sufficient to make life any easier, other than the occasional magical augmentation to increase their strength in order for them to bear up under these conditions.

They made routine check points for rest, and to mark new runes to the local area, in case they needed to return to camp in order to send a new team to continue the journey. On this day, they finally reached the base of a broad and prospectively encouraging range of mountains, based in part on the information they received from the dwarven forge smith back home. This was hoped to be the potential location of a mining operation believed to be in progress in the service of the Thane of Glimmerheim. It would represent the second of two mines suspected of being in operation producing adamantium ingots for Darumon and his ambitions, the first one being that which was found on Therinë.

A substantial group of them ran along the base of the row of foothills lining the range of mountains, splitting up into two teams, one moving north and the other south, to cover more distance. The range extended for hundreds of miles along its full length, so it was expected to take a while. But scouting, by its nature, is a patient game, and these were professionals.

The line to the south seemed the easiest, as it appeared to be descending near the horizon, meaning it probably terminated shortly thereafter. But the prospects of finding anything in this segment were not as promising as the northern side. Nevertheless, the work still needed to be done, and they did so diligently.

The view to the north, however, was another story. The barren plains continued to the horizon and were lost in the haze of the dusty air. As the other team made its northern progress, they would check the nearby mountain crags for any signs of life or other activity. They were looking for a mining entrance, probably of a similar configuration to the one found on Therinë north of Rolsklinde, where the mine was connected to a road, but also had a large rectangular alcove carved into it just outside the entrance. This was a landing zone for a Suuden'kai cargo aircraft to pick up the supply of ingots for transport elsewhere.

Another team of scouts was sent to the range of mountains south of the outpost. This range was offset from the other one, dividing a lower set of plains into two regions. It was not nearly as prominent as the other line, but still of interest to investigate in case there was anything of value to be found.

As the team approached the near end of the range, they followed it further to the south. The gullies and ridges all appeared as a typical mountain range should, although diminutive in size, until they came upon a sight that did not fit the general scene. It was only about twelve miles along when they found what appeared to be an ancient dirt road. It looked forgotten and neglected, like a remnant of a lost civilization. Considering this was the only sign, so far, of any form of habitation still present on the land, it was worth taking a closer look.

The road stretched off into the distance from the mountainside to the nearby plain in the general direction of one of the large craters discovered earlier by another team. It ran up to what appeared to be a hole in the side of the mountain, an ad hoc mining entrance, probably a smaller mine once operated by a local community. The prospects of what might lie inside were tantalizing, but at the same time, considering the general destruction of the rest of the land, the scouting party had to restrain their anticipation of what they might find. It could be just as dead as the rest of the world.

"Right, then, lads," announces the scouting party leader. "Here we go now. We follow the plan as given to us. We check the local space under a cloak. If there are dwarves inside, they shouldn't be a problem for us moving about like this, as they don't use magic directly. The word is we take a peek, but don't get involved without further instruction. We go in, look around a bit, and if there are people inside, maybe see if we can listen in on some of the local banter. We should also find a nice little nook to mark a rune for our later return, should we need it."

"Aye, maybe if we climb up on one of these clefts above us," another scout gestures to a nearby indentation. "That could provide us with enough cover for the rune."

"Good then, see to it. The rest of you, go dark and go silent. Stay low to the shadows and keep clear of the fray."

The team engaged a magical invisibility chant to conceal their bodies while the last one moved to a safe spot within the nearest gully to mark a rune to the area. When the rune was ready, he joined the team as they entered the mine.

The mining tunnel was of only a mediocre design, not apparently fashioned as part of a large-scale effort. There were no rails present, as was the case with the tunnels in the mines north of Rolsklinde. They passed by a few hand wagons sitting in small alcoves, seemingly abandoned. The general air of the scene seemed ghostly at first, until they began to pick up the sounds of movement deeper within, coming from what they thought to be a large gathering chamber.

<hr>

"We be a-runnin' low on straw again, lads," comments one of the dwarves in the dining hall of the mine. "What say ye t' the likes outside this week? Have ye seen anythin' about that we can forage?"

"The barrens just outside are as bare as ever," answers another dwarf in the hall. "'Tis just nay the season for the grasses t' grow, an' the sun be a-burnin' what was left of it."

"If we don'na find new straw for the animals soon, they'll be a-dyin' on us, ye know that!"

"Aye, brother, I know...I know. Mayhap we can check up on the range t' the north again. I think I could see a wink or two of sprouts coverin' it from the last time I ran the field."

"I'll go, if ye wish," offers another dwarf in the room. "I was a-thinkin' of makin' the run again this month anyway. This'll make it a wee bit better use of me time. I just wish I could get a decent meal out of it. I don'na know what t' feel the sorrier for, us or those poor critters that are nearly as frail as we've become."

"Belrum, if ye could do this," replies the first dwarf. "Mayhap we could offer a small cut more for ye for yer favor. But ye know as well as the rest, these sheep are all we have left of the old farms. If we go too quickly through them..."

"Aye, there'll be nothin' left, an' we die all the sooner. But from what I see out there, lads, I think this be a-comin' no matter how we stretch ourselves. One might say we should go out with at least one last full belly t' remind ourselves of the good days."

"Many of us might agree t' that, but we keep holdin' out for better times. Mayhap this dry spell will break, an' we can get back t' the farmin' as we always did."

"Dry spell?" he huffs. "An' what of the terror from the sky that started it? The land out there has been a-workin' its way up slowly for centuries, lads. Recall the old days. We had homes, farms, mills, an' a good many of us had families with a long line of honored ancestors, may their spirits find their peace after what happened."

"Belrum," calls out the second dwarf. "We have'na seen the like of that in all this time. Can ye be sure it t' be out there still? Mayhap it departed long ago an' we can go out again in peace."

"Lad, while I may wish that all the same, I feel in me gut that it be just a-waitin' for us t' poke our grizzled snouts out long enough for it t' take notice. An' then, ye know what might come after. Some of ye have made the run out there, an' ye saw the great gouges carved away from the land. D' ye want that of this mountain?"

The room goes silent in contemplation of the statement, with only the shuffling of feet and the thumping of fingers on the tables breaking the air, until Belrum spoke up again.

"An' then there be the other thing that comes t' me mind, that bein' those beastly curs sappin' up the haul from that mine."

"Aye, I recall ye mentionin' that, an' a few of us have been out there t' look at it, those sorry sods."

"Look here, lads," he asserts. "I'll make the run t' that line just up from us on the morrow. I'll gather up a good full bushel of grasses from the hillside an' bring it back t' ye. At least the little darlin's will have a good meal from it, an' the rest of us will make d' from what we can muster. But ye have t' admit, if we don'na find some new space for any amount of farmin', I fear for the worst."

The conversation turned to lighter subjects, mainly in an attempt to raise their spirits. Several of the women brought up mugs of water for the group to drink, drawn from a well located deeper in the mine. It was a poor substitute to the favored drink of dwarves, with that being beer or ale, but considering food was being rationed so severely, such luxuries as these were discarded long ago.

Amongst the shadows, unseen by the gathering of natives, several figures had been observing the interactions. Although the dialect of the local language was difficult to follow for the scouting team, they had taken some lessons from the dwarves currently working in Rolsklinde, also native to the region, who offered to help with the efforts to discover the circumstances of this strange world. When the scouts had seen enough, they began to work their way out of the mine and into the open again.

"Well, lads," admits the scout leader when they exit outside and dismiss their cloaks. "It looks like we found ourselves some dwarves. I'm not saying this world is Morndindor, but it sure does look right for it."

"Aye, but did you hear what they were saying in there about food and struggling to survive in all this?"

"That should be clear enough from what we see outside here. If the only livestock they have is now in there with them, and even the grass to feed it is in short supply, we have ourselves a bit of a problem, and I think time is against us."

"And also," comments another scout. "Did I hear mention of someone working a mine? Can we be speaking of the same one we're looking for?"

"What were the words he used? Beastly curs, and then sorry sods. I can't imagine a dwarf using those words together in the same sentence referring to the same individual. What do you think?"

"I think we need to find where that mine is located. But to do this, we might need to make contact somehow."

"Maybe, but first we report in."

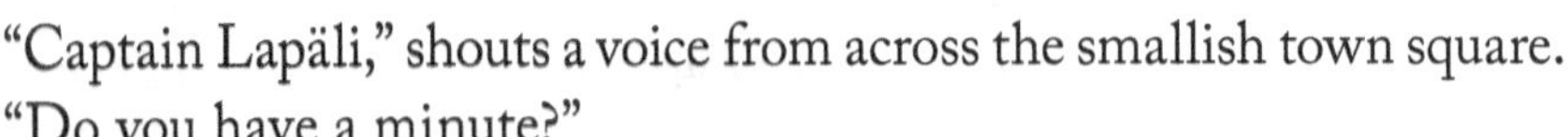

"Captain Lapäli," shouts a voice from across the smallish town square. "Do you have a minute?"

The Captain and his wife, the Daanen'kai chief technician who was working on a number of joint research projects with Thaelyn's people, were enjoying a morning meal at a local café in the village setting outside the Naarg uy'Sodrad. The ship stood as little more than a reminder of their long pursuit by Darumon and his minions. It served as a type of citadel now, half-buried under a hillside as it crashed and plowed its way through the local landscape.

"Petrith!" the Captain calls back at the arriving group of friends. "What are you and these two young rascals doing outside this early?"

Petrith, Sulíma, and Túfula were arriving in the square after finishing their meal inside the citadel, where they and most of the other refugees from Ruuki uy'Daan were taking shelter.

"Sir," Petrith responds. "I'm sorry to interrupt your meal, but I'd like an opportunity to speak with you, if you don't mind."

"At ease, Cadet, I'm no longer on active duty. After three and a half centuries, I think it's about time for a rest, so let's make this a casual affair. Pull up a chair and tell me what's on your mind."

The three friends find seating at a nearby table and arrange it to join the other two.

"Captain, do you recall our discussion a while back when His Lordship and the others established that outpost on Ruuki uy'Daan? The one where we spoke of possibly signing up for service with their unit."

"I do indeed, and I know your tail has been itching to learn more about it. Have you made a decision yet?"

"Yes Sir. With all due respect, I'd like to resign my position with your command and sign up with this special unit they have training over on Tae'Eladar."

"That unit has been in training for at least a few years by now, to my understanding. You'll be a little behind the others at this point, but I suppose that doesn't matter too much, since we still don't know when you'll go into actual service."

"Yes, I know, so I should probably get started as soon as possible and try to catch up. From what I understand, they're all going through some very special instruction over there, not just combat, but also mage training and…well, there are some other special courses being given that I think I might want to take a closer look at."

"May I ask which ones? You'll remember, I've been briefed on most of this by now. Even though I'm not on call at the moment, they still let me set one hoof in the door, so once I get my horns twisted back around after raising all you kids these past few centuries, I hope to get back in service again."

"Oh Captain," Sulíma giggles. "You loved it, and you know it. What kind of life would you have had if it weren't for me and Túfu here?"

"A peaceful one, I'm sure," he grins. "But also in a lot of ways, I'm glad you were there for those times when I needed a morale kick."

Petrith makes a discreet glance around the café to ensure no one of critical station was within earshot before continuing. He lowers his voice to continue.

"Captain, do you recall when we explained to you about those odd dreams I had during all those years?"

"Yes, I do," he replies in a hushed tone. "Do you think you can do anything with it?"

"I had a little talk with that instructor of theirs, her name is Aelwyn. She can apparently speak our language, having been working with so many others by now, and she told me I probably demonstrated yet another Gift we have that could be latent in our species, perhaps one of many relating to this Prodigy thing."

"You mean, in addition to the others, like telepathy, and most importantly, this projection skill? That's a little scary, to think of it."

"Yeah, I suppose it is, and this simply opens up questions concerning anything else we have yet to discover. This one is called clairvoyance, the ability to see other places normally outside physical reach."

"Yeah, like that shower scene with Kali," Sulíma grins. "What was it you were looking at again?"

"You're right, Suli," Túfula adds. "And here we were thinking we had a strong young stud in our midst, when in fact he was making a study of bathing techniques."

"Will the two of you ever let me live that one down?" Petrith simpers. "I knew it was a mistake to tell you that one!"

They all shared a laugh at the memory.

"You know, Petrith," the Captain admits. "I would actually

think it to be perfectly natural for a young man like you to peek into a girl's shower. But if only to examine the soap she was using, that's disturbing."

"Great, now you too… Anyway, if I already show signs of using it, maybe I can develop this like the others in the program."

"And maybe then," Sulíma considers. "You and Kali could both take a shower. She can wash up while you handle the soap for her. After all, I doubt anything else is expected to happen," she casually rolls her eyes away.

"Just you wait your turn, little lady. According to Kali, with the population troubles we're having, we'll all be getting involved in that shower, and I'm going to save something special for you."

"Promises, promises… Does it involve soap, at least?"

Petrith smiles and shakes his head in frustration before continuing the conversation.

"So, Captain, I'd like to get involved in this, and some of the other training they're giving out over there."

"This is fine, but let me ask you one thing," the Captain leans forward. "Before you go off fighting any battles and leaving all these lovely young ladies to worry about you, do you feel this is truly your calling, to join a full military and fight a war? This isn't a game, you know, and the Suuden-Aryku don't play nice, from what I hear."

"I know, Captain. I'd be lying if I said I wasn't at least a little bit scared of what could happen, but I also don't want to just sit around on my tail waiting for the next time they come looking for us. They've been chasing us for nearly ten millennia. Now we have a chance to go on the offensive and give back a little of the pain they've been giving us all these years. I feel we owe it to a lot of people who've been killed along the way, and more who might die if we do nothing at all."

"But to fight on the front lines, or maybe take another position. War isn't all about battle and killing. You might want to spend a little time with His Lordship and see what he has in mind. You have skills that don't necessarily fit on the front line of battle. Maybe another position would work out better for you. And I hear he's some kind of expert on placing people into their best service."

"All right, fair enough, but whatever the end result, I still need to start some kind of exercise soon to be ready for it."

"Captain," Sulíma calls the attention. "Túfu and I would also like to get some more of our own education. We once talked about bringing in whatever holo-disks we could find in the old school, or the library, or whatever, to help in building a new school for us here. The trouble is we also want to get involved in something more productive than just sitting around for the next few decades as we try to slog our way through a new school system."

"Technically," Túfula admits. "It might not count as decades if you consider that elixir."

"Well, whatever."

"The way it looks right now," the Captain offers. "It might be a while before we have any kind of school ready for us here in this new town we're building. His Lordship has people helping with a lot of the construction effort, and I hear they're also assisting in some of the factories they've built for us, if you can imagine that."

"Yeah," Túfula admits. "I was making a few visits to those factories to see what they're doing, and I saw people of all shapes and sizes working the lines. Not even in my wildest dreams did I ever imagine such a variety of races all working together for a common cause, and all in perfect harmony."

"I still ask why we couldn't have found people like this a long time ago," Sulíma notes. "It could've made a world of difference for us."

"It might have made several worlds of difference, Suli," Petrith suggests. "Especially if we could've understood from those early moments who and what Sargeras really was, and then this Marshal Darumon and what he was doing."

"And yet," Túfula concedes. "It couldn't have been this way, not if the Marshal is the one pushing us from one world to another, and he didn't actually push us here to this one early enough to make the discovery. Just remember what that Adalon person said in her prophecies. She was watching us, and waiting for us to arrive here, but apparently it couldn't go any faster."

"So, we just had to take all this abuse," Sulíma moans. "Because we couldn't go any faster to arrive here."

"Well," the Captain resumes. "We're here now, what's left of us. A lot of good people were lost along the way, but maybe we can help save a lot of others. Suli, what is it you think you would like to do with yourself?"

"Captain, one thing I'm sure of is that I want to learn how to use this magic of theirs. We have people here who have apparently been taking lessons for years, so obviously it's possible for us to learn, and when I listen to the stories Kali was giving about some of this new technology we're developing with the Tae'Eladarans, I want a piece of that."

"Oh wonderful," Túfula moans. "Are we going to see you pounding on some new contraption you can't fix for a century?"

"More likely," Petrith muses. "She'll just throw fireballs at it when it misbehaves."

Sulíma playfully nudges Túfula and slaps Petrith on the shoulder at the suggestion.

"I just don't know how to fit this into a study course," Sulíma continues. "Back home, we were only part way through our junior school. After that, we would've gone to the senior school, and then the university. This would carry us a couple of centuries as we still needed to grow up during that time. Now, here we are at four centuries and nowhere near where we should be for our age."

"Suli," the Captain responds. "If we go by Kali's example, they pushed her through their training so fast, she barely had time to breathe. Even if they follow a more relaxed approach for the rest of you, it's still many times faster than what our own school system normally takes. Our system tends to take it slow due to the length of time required for any of us to mature into it."

"That's another problem, Captain," Túfula remarks. "Everything we do is slow. We grow slowly, educate slowly, build slowly, and research slowly. I was thinking about this while I was watching those people in that factory. Even though they describe themselves as Early Industrial, they're adapting at a phenomenal rate as compared to us. They went from at least a partially manual, and maybe an early form of mechanized labor, to computerized automated factories almost overnight, even if it were only to help us rebuild. Is this normal for them, or abnormal for us?"

"I don't know," Petrith winces. "But it's definitely scary."

"I once heard someone tell me they could pass us up in a matter of centuries. They already have some technologies that equal or surpass us, and according to Kali, they had these before they understood electricity. That's not simply scary, but it also puts things into perspective about where we came from and how we're built."

"It's all because of this magic of theirs," Sulíma admits. "Which clearly means this is powerful stuff, and we're the underprivileged runts, despite all our technology. And this is all the more reason why I want to learn about it. I want to continue my studies in technology and maybe some kind of engineering. I owe it to that stupid old machine back home in the camp work yard."

"Owe it?" Túfula inquires curiously. "Why would you feel you owe something to that old heap?"

"Because it always tried to show me how I didn't know enough about how to fix it right. I get one piece working and another one breaks down. This is just my way of getting even."

"What about the medical field, like your sister?"

"As much as I love Ankhia, and in my early years I thought I might follow her, in the time since then, I think my interests have changed. I want to invent a new form of science, kind of like what they're doing over in that research facility Tanjhira is working at right now," she looks over at the chief technician. "But I want to make it official for our people, a new branch of study for future generations."

"That sounds very ambitious, Suli," Tanjhira accedes. "The Professor I'm working with describes it using such words as Arcane Science and arcanic devices resulting out of it. What we're doing right now is mostly top secret for this war effort, but eventually it'll filter down as consumer products once the rest of the population matures into it. To be honest, I wouldn't mind creating an official form of study out of our research, but I'm only barely keeping up with him and all his rapid ideas. And my horns have already fallen off on several occasions," she grins.

"Well then, I need to take these mage studies, and carry them to the max. That's obviously the first step, along with whatever else they use for their own form of engineering studies, as well as ours. Maybe we could team up sometime after that to compare notes."

"Keeping in mind, Suli," Túfula cautions. "We still need to qualify to get in. I think I heard it said those higher-level studies are restricted by that special test they use."

"Oh, right. Well, I guess we need to do that before anything else. And we should probably do that soon to get things started. I wonder how long all this will take."

"For the mage studies," Tanjhira reflects. "I recall Kali took her First and Second Circles during her first year after signing up, which apparently isn't too hard. The rest were supposed to follow one per year, up to the Ninth Circle, though I think she's only going to the Eighth for her profession. But it got complicated because of their push to get to you, and they drove her through some of them very hard, the poor girl."

"But before we can do anything, we need to learn their language, which has to be our first study course. How long does that take? You took that course, right?"

"Yes, I did. My case was also a rush job to get things going, but the official course is only three months."

"What?!" she shrieks. "Three… Months…" she gasps. "How in all the nether-space can you learn a language in just three months? They must be more advanced than orcs for that much, at least!"

"Suli," she chuckles. "Yes, and it's actually a very well-developed language. It falls back to that elixir of theirs, and their learning techniques are highly accelerated, even by what they might consider normal for their race."

"All right, I recall Kali teaching some of us the orcish language.

Although, I'll admit, I never really considered it to be much of a language. But you're saying it goes this way for everything?"

"From what I understand, courses that might take years only take as many months. You mentioned our people taking forever to learn anything? These people could probably go through our entire library in only a few decades, for instance from childhood to adult, and still have most of their lifetime to play with it."

"And their lifetime," Túfula recalls, "is said to be something less than a century or so, for the humans that is. The others are somewhat longer, but nothing like ours, and already they passed us up."

＋＋◆◆＋＋

"My Lord, I trust you slept well?" the General asks as Thaelyn enters the WIC strategy room.

"Indeed, well enough. It is pleasing that we have this moment to catch up on our personal needs, but as it becomes apparent after a while, we still have work to do. Do we have anything of interest today?"

"Actually, yes. We received a report last night from our outpost. A team of scouts has discovered what they believe to be an old mine in that one range of mountains south-southeast of their location. They carefully entered the tunnels under a cloak to investigate, and found a smallish gathering of dwarves!"

"Ah, this is both good as well as bad, when we consider the devastation outside. Were they able to gather any useful information along the way?"

"A few bits that could prove to be of value for later perhaps. A conversation was overheard during their visit between some of the dwarves concerning the failure of their local food supply."

"This is certainly to be expected."

"It is, and they were speaking of collecting grass for what we assume to be some livestock they are harboring somewhere deeper within."

"And considering the condition of the land, no doubt that grass is becoming very hard to come by."

"Yes, and for this reason I think we might have an opportunity presenting itself to us, and possibly also a problem, as the scouts mentioned the dwarf who would go out looking for this grass might try venturing up to the hillside near our outpost. This brings him rather close, and if he knows the terrain well enough, he might take notice of a change in the landform due to the camouflaging around our camp."

"I see, and so we must take some form of action to ensure our security. Did they mention anything else during this conversation?"

"There was a brief mention, and with our dear Captain's usual flare to recall such details verbatim, the dwarves spoke of a mine of some sort being operated by individuals using such words as," he pauses to clear his throat for emphasis, "beastly curs and sorry sods."

"Indeed!" Thaelyn grins at the reference. "Am I to interpret these poor fellows as having some form of grievance to this circumstance?"

"It would certainly seem as much. And if we consider this mine as possibly being the one we are looking for, the beastly curs could represent the Suuden-Aryku, and the sorry sods the poor dwarven workers."

"Is there any word yet from our other team, the one searching around that eastern range of mountains?"

"Not as yet. My understanding is they reached the base, splitting into two groups moving in opposite directions, but they have yet to find anything. My personal opinion, by the description given, is that we are more likely to find something to the north of their position rather than the south, due to the distance they are likely to cover. And then we still need to hear from anyone moving north to find the city, although I think we should hear something from them soon, as the team we sent up there should not be long from the furthermost end of that large plains region, according to the details given to us by Chief Bronzeheart."

"This is testing on the nerves, General. Ordinarily our scouting ventures would not take so long, if only for the heavy gravity and burdensome atmosphere they must endure along the way. I must feel for them at this moment."

"They are loyal and courageous, my Lord, a tribute to your service. We will see to our work as best we can. My greatest concern is whether we will find a Suuden-Aryku base and where that may take us in the longer term."

"In the meantime, we should make some sort of plan, and quickly, for the ultimate arrival of that dwarf said to be foraging for grass in the hills. If he comes too close, he might take notice of us, and I would much rather maintain control of this than to let him run for cover and possibly reveal us to others."

"Yes, my Lord," the General considers. "And for this, I had a thought. Although I suppose one could say we would be buying their friendship, if food is such an issue for them, but perhaps we could offer a supply to keep them standing until further arrangements could be made. This could also include feed for their livestock."

"I would not wish to describe giving food to such needy people as a way of buying their friendship, but it would likely do the job. I must also wonder, however, if they have any connection to the city, and if there could be a possibility of our presence being revealed to them. Giving food is one thing, but keeping them silent is another. And then I suppose we should ask ourselves, are there any others out there?"

"How would you suggest we go about this, then?"

"If we send any of our own people, it could cause a stir, and we do not need any of that at the moment. These people are likely going to be very skeptical of outsiders. Even if we use one of our own dwarves for this purpose, we might still have an issue due to the differences in language, where our dwarves have altered their dialect in the time since their early ancestors came to Tae'Eladar. Therefore, I think we should use one of the dwarves from the enclave up north. By this time, they are nicely adjusted to working alongside us, and most by now have also learned our language, as they are working several shops here in the city. Perhaps if we could call upon Chief Bronzeheart and have him represent us in this matter."

The General nods in agreement and summons a page from outside the room to find the dwarven forge chief in his shop in the southeastern district of the city. The page takes his orders and dashes outside the building into the streets, navigating the roadways into a section of the city assigned to handle much of the heavier industry, such as smithing shops, metalworking and smelters, woodworking and carpentry, and stonemasons.

Chief Smith Bronzeheart, and several of the other dwarves that once served in the mining operation to the north of the city, were now employed in honorable labor, as opposed to the slave conditions by their former oppressors. They were busy at their forges and smelting vats, processing iron and other metals harvested from a series of new mining ventures found elsewhere around the land. Some of these new mines were being operated by other members of their group, as well as Tae'Eladaran laborers, and the flow of materials was enough to keep even the most resolute amongst them thoroughly occupied. It was a dwarven delight, and they found a new sense of purpose for themselves.

"Chief Bronzeheart," calls the page as he enters the smithy foreman's office. "His Lordship requests your presence up at the WIC building. He has need of your service."

"Does he now?" he replies. "Well, we nay be wantin' to keep him waitin'. I hope we have some good word from his scoutin'. Me and the lads here have been scratching our backsides and wipin' the sweat from our brows since the days ye first set foot on that land, wonderin' what those bloody devils have done to our homes."

"Aye, I'm sure we all feel the same for that measure. Hopefully, we'll have some answers for you soon. Please follow me."

The two of them exit the shop and work their way back up to the upper plaza district where they reenter the WIC building to meet with Thaelyn and his officers.

"Yer Kingship," the Chief announces. "What say ye this fine day?"

"Chief Bronzeheart, we have some word back from a recent scouting patrol which has us concerned over a few details, but it could also present an opportunity for us. However, we must take this cautiously, for reasons I am sure you already understand from our previous discussions."

"Aye, I recall the tellin'. It must be a hard life, bein' in the military, especially when ye tell these tales of these dastardly Suuden-Aryku, this Marshal of yers, and keepin' to the shadows so they won' be knowin' what ye're doin' right under their noses. What do we have this time?"

"The first crisis we have is one we already suspected from our previous observations. As you will recall, our scouts have been discovering massive devastation across the land, apparently from some form of bombardment, and likely by the Suuden-Aryku. The land has become dry and barren, and we believe we are observing a condition we describe as a global warming event, where the climate temperatures are rising in an uncontrolled manner, creating conditions too harsh for the local flora and fauna to tolerate. This could then lead into a kind of extinction event for many forms of life."

"Great All-Father, and that what ye're tellin' about be the home of me kin and me ancestors. Good King, what can we do about this? Be there any kind of magic in yer back pocket ye can give us to save our home?"

"While I have a few ideas, they would all involve a large-scale effort, and would probably take time before we see any kind of correction. This would also represent a very visible display for any who might be observing, including the Suuden-Aryku, and we simply cannot allow them to know we have arrived on that world. Therefore, this may have to wait until we can bring the situation more into our favor."

The Chief lets out a quiet moan as he looks down at the table and the stacks of papers scattered around between the officers.

"Take heart, Chief," Thaelyn reassures. "I will not abandon your people. It is simply that we must move carefully and in small steps until we can be sure our enemies are dealt with. This problem has no doubt been growing over the course of centuries, and it is unlikely to result in any major changes in the comparatively short time I hope to see our operation through."

"Right, then, Yer Kingship. Ye be the one with the military mind, and a great deal of knowin' for a great many things. What else do ye have? Yer man said ye have work of some kind for me, ay?"

"Yes, this is a job I think would be best suited to a man such as you, mainly because you are a native. Though we still have not found any definitive proof that this world is Morndindor, the evidence is strongly pointing in that direction, so we will describe it as such unless something tells us different."

Thaelyn pulls up the most recent scouting report from the table as he begins to lay out his plan.

"We received a report this morning from our outpost. A group of scouts found what appears to be an old mine in a southern range of mountains from their location. Inside they found a number of dwarves taking refuge, if only just barely. We assume from what we see, and the discussions you and I had previously of the lay of the land, that these might be residents of what used to be the local farming communities. The scouts were able to infiltrate the den and listen in on some local conversation, and the primary topics seemed to center around the lack of food, and also straw for some animals they apparently keep with them."

"Aye, from what ye've been tellin' me of the land, I s'pose this would be a good cause for it. And more, I can say we do sometimes keep our sheep and other herdin' beasts with us inside the mountain, or at least this be the case in Glimmerheim. The old tales were that we had farms and families tendin' to their herds up on the surface, but with what ye've been tellin' me of the land, it makes perfect sense that they'd be bringin' them down inside by now."

"Very good, but now we have a problem, and at the same time we have a potential solution. If we are clever enough, perhaps we could turn this to an advantage for all of us."

"Oi, this be kind to me ears, Yer Kingship! Ye've got me attention if I can be of any help."

"The most obvious is to give aid to these people, but we must also remember to be discreet, so our enemies do not take notice. If these people have any contact with Glimmerheim, we must ensure that word of our efforts is well contained."

"Aye, I understand that part fair enough."

"Our scouts overheard a discussion that one of the men from this refuge will soon make a journey to the line of hills near where our camp is located, as an effort to forage the local grasses for their livestock. This could be dangerous as it could reveal us if he takes close enough notice of our camp walls. Even though they are covered to appear as the local hillside, the addition of material to the surrounding terrain may stand out."

"Ye've got a good point there. A man with a keen eye would take notice of this, especially if he be a local dweller."

"But this could also present an opportunity for us to make contact. However, once again it must be discreet. I would imagine these people to be rather skittish by now, after what we suspect may have happened in times past to cause the devastation we see today. If any of our own people were to make this effort, it could go awry for us. Even if to use one of our own dwarves, the difference in dialect could cause some concern. Therefore, you come to mind."

"Yer Kingship, I'd be happy to help, but ye'll remember, I nay be the good sort with words if ye're thinkin' me to be a diplomat."

"Perhaps, but you are familiar with all the details we have collected together, so I would consider you to be the best we have, and I will give you a few careful instructions on how to go about this to help you with the initial introduction. We will need to present ourselves as friends, most importantly, and with the means to help these people in exchange for information and a little trust. Sit down here with us, Chief, and let us go over what we have to offer."

✦ ✦ ◆ ✦ ✦

"Ankhia, I think there's a limit to what we can accomplish here, given what we have to work with."

"I know, Likha, but we need to bring ourselves up to a point where we can try a few field tests. His Lordship is hoping to receive word soon on the discovery of a Suuden'kai command base, and we need to find ways to get inside and deal with the crew quietly."

Med-tech Tad'vaal and her intern, Likha Vuurti, had been working together with several implant devices extracted from the bodies of Suuden-Aryku troopers sent against them during the latter part of the war just outside their ship. This was during the final stages when Thaelyn and his army assisted in reinforcing their lines, and the tide was beginning to turn in their favor. The bodies left behind afforded the medical team their first good look at their enemy up close to discover some of the hidden secrets of how they had been altered with artificial implants of various kinds.

"But these implants we've been studying," Likha continues. "They aren't in a functional state anymore. The best we can do is study the circuitry and guess at the rest."

"And that's where we need to continue this into field testing. The engineers we've been working with to create this jamming device have tried to make it generic enough to scan a wide range of frequencies to identify which ones are used in these transponders. Once we have this recorded, the rest should fall into place. Then, the next step would be to design something we can apply to an individual, or maybe a field emitter for a localized area, to block these signals from interfacing with their neural collective. We have to isolate each person so we can remove or disable them without any of the others knowing about it."

"That's really the scariest part about all this. If we're going to try capturing any of them, what kind of repercussions are we opening ourselves up to?"

"Nothing good, you can be sure of that. But this is only if we get caught. So let's not get caught!"

"Yeah, but how do you capture and remove members of a base command crew without any of the others taking notice? I think the base commander, at the very least, would notice the shortage of his servicemen after a while."

"You're right, of course," Ankhia affirms. "And we need to keep him, of all people, unaware of this, at least until he's been dealt with. I'm recalling Kaliya and her affair with the orcs that one time. She learned how to impersonate one after defeating it and using that form to infiltrate the camp to perform her espionage on that conveyor. So, what if we tried replacing them with fakes temporarily after we dispose of the originals?"

"Interesting, and we need to take control of that base anyway. But we can't use any of our own people. You know this. And Kaliya is just one person. I don't think she can imitate an entire base crew, can she?"

"Not alone, she can't, but she's been training a full team lately, so we have more than just the one to play with now."

"An army of people like her," she shudders. "How do we even know who's who anymore," she chuckles weakly.

"I'm sure this can get complicated after a while," she smiles. "But for now, the worst stumbling block I can see facing us is getting close enough to any of them to use a scanner to identify their signaling patterns."

"Did you have any ideas for that yet?"

"Well, other than to have a spy, like maybe one of their scouts, go in under a cloak and plant something. Or if Kaliya, once again, could impersonate a Suuden'kai trooper, and just sort of casually wander around scanning people she happened to pass by. But that could be noticed, and then they'll start asking questions."

"Which is exactly what we do not want," Likha scowls. "Darn it, Ankhia! If only these stupid implants we have in our possession were operable, we might have our answer right under our noses."

"Yeah, I know, but they were dead when we got them, right along with the body they were attached to, which tells me they turned themselves off when the host died. I'm not an engineer, and this technology of theirs is strange, to say the least. In the time we've been separated from them on Azgarén, they seem to have made some impressive movements forward on their designs, such things I don't think any of us ever would've considered before."

"There weren't any power sources that you could see on it, right?"

"Nothing I recognized right off the top. No power cells or a core of any kind. It just seemed to be sitting there on the cranial tissue, half buried in the skull and with probes leading into various regions of the brain."

"What about an external power source? Were there any other implants or a power module on the body?"

"Nothing, and I didn't even see any leads that might connect to a power input on the device itself."

"There must be something. It's an artificial device, it needs power. It can't just…"

Likha pauses as an idea begins to form in her mind. She turns away from the conversation to develop it further, tapping a finger against her lips in deep thought.

"Likha, do you have something?" Ankhia asks softly so as not to interrupt the young intern's contemplation.

"Ankhia, if you don't mind my asking, where did you take your courses on medical study…the old university, right? What sort of lessons?"

"I started on Ghabeel, same as Kailen, but then we had that attack and were pushed to Ruuki uy'Daan, so I finished there once we had a facility up. I mostly centered on exobiology, but I also took the standard fare of medical courses so I could serve in the local medical ward as an intern, like you. At least until we got pushed one more time and landed here, then I had to take up my current position as Medical Chief."

"But let me ask you in this way. How much do you know about implant technology, overall? We don't use it much for our own people, except in rare cases these days for the delivery of pharmaceuticals or other corrective procedures and treatments."

"Yes, that's true, and once it's done, the device comes out. What are you getting at?"

"Ankhia," she turns with a grin on her face. "Look at these devices, and then those ones we pulled out of the human population. You remember those, right?"

"Yeah..." she frowns. "How could I forget those horrid little monsters!"

"But what I mean is this. They were in there for the long term, the lifetime of the patient. What sort of power source do you think could go that long, even if it were something like a power cell?"

Ankhia took a moment to think, and the realization began to settle in.

"Dammit, Likha, you're right, these aren't temporary devices like all of ours are. We use them for only a brief moment, maintaining them from time to time to recharge the cells if we expect it to take longer. But these were permanent!"

"And for this you need external power, right? Something with either low or no maintenance. Just look at the humans. They got them as children, say around twelve years old, and kept them until sometime after fifty. And these Suuden-Aryku are keeping them for much longer than that, I'm sure."

"All right, but what kind of external power? Is it a device outside the body, maybe using induction? Part of a suit they wear?"

"No, I doubt it. The humans weren't wearing suits of any kind, and still they had this."

"True."

"Ankhia, don't you see it? It's got to be in the body itself. Natural, like a bioreactor... These were in contact with living tissue, right?"

Suddenly, Ankhia makes the connection. She jerks up and slaps herself on the forehead.

"Dear cu'Nar, of course, a bioelectrochemical reaction. And since these Suuden-Aryku are becoming famous for their application of nanotechnology, all you need is a catalyst and maybe a small nano-array of inducers to maintain it. Then stick it to any piece of living tissue, and there you go. No wonder it quit when these bodies died. Let's take another look and see if were right. And you should probably go thaw out Banni. We'll be putting him back into service."

"Ooh!" Likha squeals. "My boyfriend's back!"

✦✦◆✦◆✦✦

It was entering late afternoon on Tae'Eladar. Relissa, Haran, and Marelle were convening in their usual spot on the bench in the courtyard of the guildhall, where they would sit and enjoy some occasional conversation on topics ranging from their class studies to common social affairs.

"Marelle, you're quiet as a mouse today," Relissa notes. "Is there something wrong?"

"Huh? Oh, no, not really. Well, yes, but I'm trying to work it out with a few crazy ideas to add bits and pieces of things that don't normally go together into something that works better than the junk I'm using now. But don't tell anyone I called it junk, all right?" she smiles cautiously.

"Right, so what in all the bleedin' hells does that mean?" she grins.

"It's about my flight training. Don't tell anyone this, but those Daanen-Aryku don't know a flippin' thing about fighting, at least not in the air. The simulator I'm using for my practice is designed according to a standard layout they use in many of their aircraft. Scout craft, in this case, which is what I'll be graduating into soon for those training craft, also."

"Aye, so what's wrong with it, other than the scouting bit? Not that I'd know a bloody small bit about anything."

"First, these people are not strong on warfare, or else they'd have better designs of combat vehicles…assuming they had any combat vehicles to start with. This simulator, and by association their typical designs of aircraft, are laid out for casual scouting and cargo transport, not war. The designs, for lack of a better word, are lazy."

"How do you define lazy, in this case, Sis?" Haran asks.

"Well, my right hand is stuck to a flight stick, which controls the general direction I'm moving in the air. You know, turn left, turn right, go up, go down, that sort of thing. My left hand seems trapped on a throttle, the lever that adds thrust to move forward. Are you with me so far?"

"Barely, but I recall some of this from our previous talks anyway. So, where is the problem in this? It sounds like a decent arrangement from my perspective."

"Right, until you go into combat and start killing stuff, as the new aircraft design will use a combination of technology where I, as a mage, need to channel my energies into the craft and through the guns outside on the wings. Where and how do I do that?"

"Ah, yes, now I see it. Hmm, this is a perplexing situation. Do you have any ideas?"

"A few, but it'll require a reworking of the controls, so my hands are in the right places to control the aircraft, but also free enough to work magic."

"Jiggers, how do you manage that one?" Relissa wonders.

"To do this right, I think the controls will have to work differently. The problem is, even with my training here in the academy, and a lot of additional education I'm taking with the Daanen-Aryku, I don't know enough about the possibilities of technology to figure out a proper solution, or if the one I'm thinking of could work for me. But here it is… Maybe it's like Thaelyn says, where one crazy idea can eventually lead to a better one."

She opens up her bag and pulls out a notepad she had been using to draw up several diagrams and layout ideas for her new configuration. The drawings are crude, but they were only to give the basic concept, not a final design.

"Here, look at this. The first thing I need to consider…well, maybe not the first, because there are multiple things all at once that are important, but here is my first idea. Instead of a flight stick, maybe to use something like a rod I can channel my mage energies into that would eventually find its way to the guns. I could still use it to twist and turn the aircraft, but then I wonder how we connect it to the console, as it might still require the more traditional pivoting linkage to function. I had the same idea for the throttle, but it all comes back to the same problem."

"You know, Sis," Haran considers. "As one who is much more dedicated to the mage arts, I've seen some of their devices here in the academy. Some of them are made for exactly what you mention here, to channel energy from the mage into a working component."

"What are they made of? That's one of my questions and why

I'm struggling so hard on this, because I recall from our studies that this often requires special designs and materials."

"You're right. They have a kind of museum and artifact showcase here that I've spent some time visiting on several occasions. It's such a wonderful display, you should go see it when you have a chance. But anyway, some of their most extravagant works, a few of which are very old, are a beautiful handiwork of enchanted metals, wood, and even crystals."

"I don't really think an aircraft is a good place to put a piece of wood, not the way I'm flying them. Handling the controls like I do, I'll probably get a lot of splinters after a while," she giggles.

"Then you should consider the metal, or maybe crystal. Many times I see them working combinations together, especially in the modern day."

"You know," Relissa considers. "This reminds me a bit of my mage studies where they were demonstrating those Reflection Globes. Do you remember those?"

"Yes, I do," he recalls. "This is a fine example. It's a crystalline globe, spherical in shape, where you conjure up a reflection of yourself, and the globe projects that as an image in physical space."

"Aye, it's actually part of their illusionary school of magic. You can turn it in your hands, tilting it this way and that, to make the projection run around the field. It mimics your own body, so you can be walking, running, standing, and it sends that out as your ghost for others to look at."

"I swear," Marelle moans. "The things people can come up with."

"Especially in a society where everyone is well-studied in this," Haran submits. "The possibilities are simply magnified at that point. For instance, I think they might use this in the performing arts, among others."

Marelle was studying her drawings while they carried on their conversation, when suddenly she perks up with an idea.

"Hmm, wait a minute. You know, you two are good to have around on occasion."

"Only on occasion?" Relissa smirks. "Gee, thanks Marelle, you're such a pal."

"Oh, you know what I mean. You gave me a new idea just now. But I wonder how we could make this work. Let me think a moment."

She pulls out a pen from her bag and turns to a new page, then starts drawing another diagram. She based it on the idea of a globe, or at least a dome design, and mumbled to herself as she tried to fit the pieces together.

"If we make it out of a type of crystal that channels the energy from my hands, then into a conduit, kind of like how they make some of their devices here. You know, like the gateways and other things. But then what? Do I want just one, or do I need two, one for each hand?"

"Where are these guns you need to fire off?" Haran asks.

"Both sides, to my understanding..."

"Jiggers, Marelle," Relissa winces. "I don't want to be standing next to you when all that goes off."

"Next to me shouldn't be a problem, it's what's directly ahead of me that you should be more concerned about. Whatever is in my sight won't be there for long."

"Then I would probably have to suggest you take one on each hand," Haran admits. "When casting spells, we often use both hands, sometimes together, sometimes independently. If you could do the same here, you would be twice as dangerous...and twice the reason to keep away from you," he chuckles.

"Wow, Bro, you're so helpful!"

Relissa and Haran share a moment of bemused glances.

"But now the tough part," she continues. "Let's say I'm in the process of charging up to fire one off. I'm still supposed to be flying the aircraft, and to do this, my hands have to be somewhere, doing something, to control all this."

"Very well, we should take a closer look at what we have to work with. Right now, you have the flight stick, which you turn one way or another to guide the direction. These globes worked similarly, by rotating or sliding the hand over it to guide your reflection's movement over the land. Can we apply that here?"

"It's an interesting idea, but like I said, I'm not so sure on the range of possibilities of technology, ours or the Daanen-Aryku's. But this is certainly a good suggestion to bring forward. And the throttle?"

"Maybe something similar… You once said you push it forward to gain speed, pull it back to slow down. Maybe sliding your hand forward and back can do the same. If the theory of operation can be applied to one, in my mind it ought to work on both."

"Good enough. But now, we have one last detail I need to consider as to how their aircraft work."

"And what's that?"

"The flux field generator… I learned as part of my early studies that there are many ways in which to conduct flight. The most primitive is with how birds do it, powering up with their wings to catch the air and lift themselves off the ground. Then they basically ride the winds after that, mostly. But not here…wind or no wind, and for that matter even without air of any kind, as they say their designs can work outside the world in space, where there isn't any air at all. They use this flux field as a cushion to lift off the surface of the ground, apparently reflecting against something to do with the magnetic and gravity fields of the world. This is where I probably need to do a little more study. We only touched on it, and I mostly just said, uh huh, right…" she grins.

"That's my sister!" he laughs energetically. "All right then, let's think. Is this another control you need to work in constant motion?"

"Not really, I set it and let it go unless something changes, like if I'm lifting off the ground or need to land again. But lately, I'm finding I need to use it during flight for some of my more desperate maneuvers, and this is one of my problems. It's not in a convenient location."

"Desperate maneuvers? Like what?"

"Well, they're running me through these simulations, and throwing things at me like heavy storms, high winds, blizzards, and other bad stuff, trying to test me and give me a variety of unfavorable conditions to overcome just in case I find myself in such places in the real world."

"Ah, of course, I understand, and I suppose that's very wise to study."

"Right, because it could easily knock you right out of the sky, and it almost did on several occasions. This is where I have some of my trouble, and a little frustration, just trying to keep myself up there. This control is on the forward console, not in my hand."

"Then we probably need to put it in your hand somewhere. But if you only need it on occasion, it shouldn't be directly under your hand, just near enough so that, oh, say a finger...or perhaps your thumb could easily get to it."

"Hey, there you go. My thumb certainly has enough mobility, and some of the controls they've been toying with as part of these design concepts for a combat craft use buttons and switches under the thumb. We use a slider here, so if we put this just to the side of the globe thingy, where my thumb would be..."

She continues drawing on her notepad, now outlining a rough design of a touch slider strip control to represent the flux gauge from her old training simulator design. When she's satisfied with her layout, she turns it to show the others.

The drawing shows two dome-like objects, one for each hand. On the left she has a strip representing the flux gauge, positioned slightly off to the side to allow easy access for a thumb. On the right, the globe appears by itself, so far with no additional controls nearby.

"Well, girl," Relissa considers. "I haven't got a bleedin' clue what I'm looking at, but if you can get this bugger to work, it'll be a fine one."

"A thought comes to mind," Haran ponders as he studies the image. "Granted, I have no idea what sorts of pressures you might be under up there, but if you will be involved in any sort of acrobatics, as I suspect you will be, you will need some manner of harness or safeguard to keep your hands where they ought to be, rather than waving all about the cabin when you make any of these desperate maneuvers you mentioned."

"Good idea," Marelle accedes. "I think we could hook something up, but I don't want it to be too tight just in case I do actually need to get out of it quickly."

✦

"This is a great many details for me poor old head to grip hold of," Chief Bronzeheart moans.

"I think you will do very well for it, Chief," Thaelyn reassures. "Most of it you know already from so many prior discussions here with us, and with others in the city. It is actually not as much as it may seem. Merely that we are reviewing a good portion of it all at once, and it may appear as such on the surface."

"Right ye be, I s'pose. 'Tis true that I recall a good piece of it from before, but to hear it all again, and now to think I need to be layin' it upon some other poor sod that has so many woes of his own."

"I know, Chief, and I sympathize with both of you, and for that matter all those not included in this equation. But we will work this problem and bring aid to those most in need, and then see about improving the situation overall."

"And that be the finest part of it!" he yips. "If I had to choose who to name as a new King for me people, I dare say it'd be ye. To the deepest rings of the abyss with that Thane and his ilk…"

"I am most pleased with your enthusiasm, Chief, and surely, I would be honored for the favor. Now, I think it is best if you proceed on your way as soon as possible. The timing of day and night for us places morning soon to arrive on that world, and to our knowledge, our visitor may be making his trek shortly after sunrise."

"Aye, just let me grab for me'self a few bits and bobs, mayhap a change of clothes so I don' look as ragged as a hobgoblin on Fool's Eve."

The Chief offers a gentle bow and makes his exit from the room. As he hurries down the hall, he passes by a group of young Daanen-Aryku visitors waiting patiently for their turn at a meeting with the officers.

Petrith, Sulíma, and Túfula were making a visit, joined at this time by another friend, Tana, who was also hoping to investigate a few possibilities for her own needs. They had been waiting in the hall, as instructed by one of the attendants, for a meeting with Thaelyn relating to their recent discussion about signing up for some form of education. When they saw the dwarf exit, they interpreted this as their moment to make their presentation.

"Your Lordship," Petrith announces as he leads them into the room. "I hope we're not intruding. The clerk outside said to wait until the other meeting came to a close before entering."

"Yes, I received word of your arrival some moments ago. With so many people coming and going through these halls of late, it is important that we introduce a little civility and some tactical scheduling to these occasions. What is it you wish to speak about, Mister Girhani?"

"Well, each of us here has been in discussion about what we want to do with ourselves. Clearly, we want to serve a valuable purpose, but we have a few minor problems, and I think you already know the worst of it being our early education was cut short."

"Indeed, I do, and in some ways no different from Kaliya, although she apparently had some tutoring from her brother and others within the Naarg uy'Sodrad."

"We had a little from our teachers," Túfula offers. "It wasn't the structured lessons from an official school, but it was better than nothing."

"Perhaps, and this is fair, but from what I understand of it, you had a great many years taken away from you. Now, here you are as adults with barely the skills to fulfill even the most rudimentary of tasks your usual professions might demand of you. This must be corrected, and quickly, if you wish to offer yourselves into any manner of service."

"That's right, and we're anxious to get started, but the school we're building back home won't be ready for quite some time yet, and then we need to fill the data files with some manner of curriculum for the classes. We used to have a data center in our old school system. I'm not sure what's left of it, especially for the university, but we were thinking of going back to see what we can salvage of the old records."

"This is a good suggestion. Perhaps you could organize something in this regard?"

"I'd be happy to, but we still have the issue of being stagnant until something is ready, so we're thinking of signing up for some kind of classes on Tae'Eladar."

"Indeed. Do you have a preference? I recall each of you once mentioning a variety of favorite topics. Although..." he glances at Tana. "I am not sure if I ever met this young lady."

"My name is Tana Lar'akan," she offers. "My mother is Navina, and she's apparently in training along with Kali in her special unit."

"Ah, yes! I seem to recall your name mentioned once. Something relating to nature studies, and perhaps even to go so far as, well..." he coughs softly, "...the druidic faith?"

"Yeah, Kali once mentioned this to me, although I really have no idea what it is. You see, Your Lordship, much like what Kali explained of herself once, I hold my grievances for the Suuden-Aryku and all that they did to us. Same as the orcs, actually. And while I NOW know of Darumon and what responsibility HE holds in all of this, and therefore I can accept the solution of the orcs, I'm not so easily convinced to let go of the Suuden-Aryku and what SHOULD be their responsibility to know better."

"Yes, I suppose we must apply a little of that somewhere along the way. But let us go gently on it until we have a full understanding of what is occurring on Azgarén right now."

"All right, fine. Needless to say, I would love to kick a few of their tails for all they did to us, to say nothing of everything else out there. But I think I would prefer to stay out of the line of fire. I might want to kick some tails, but I'm not really a fighter...I don't think."

"The military service is not necessarily for everyone, and we need civilian roles every bit as much as military."

"Of course. And here is where we come back to what Kali mentioned to me once. And although it might sound a little crazy for one of us to take up studies of this sort, I wanted to at least talk to someone about it."

"Absolutely. Do you have something specific on your mind to begin with?"

"All my life, I had this wanderlust for nature. As a girl, I would run through the jungle, sometimes picking flowers, and often admiring the wide variety of plants out there. I would sometimes watch the orcs as they used herbs and other things in their tribal activities, and I even learned a few things by following their example. But the pure joy of walking amongst the natural flora, the smells, the feel of the air, the ground under my hooves, made me feel so free. And then, as I grew up, I had to learn to make use of it for my own needs..."

Sulíma interrupts with a sudden giggle.

"Yeah, like clothes..."

"Uh huh," she grins. "And as you and Túfu so often chided me, it wasn't much in the way of cover."

Thaelyn listened and smiled as he tried to envision their relationship and lifestyle on Ruuki uy'Daan before he arrived.

"Anyway," Tana continues. "Between that, and body paint, and other things I used as part of my scouting efforts during this time, I learned a lot of things to help me blend in with my surroundings. And it felt so natural for me, like I was a part of it...despite the fact that I was almost naked," she glares playfully at Sulíma.

"I think the naked part WOULD be a part of it," Túfula smirks.

"Well, maybe," she shrugs. "But Kali once said I might make good material for a druid. And according to what I've been hearing, it's a kind of priest of nature. But we're not a religious society, so the priest part seems a little strange. And yet, with what I'm hearing of these gods of yours, maybe it isn't so strange after all. It sounds a little like taking up a kind of apprenticeship."

"In a manner of speaking, you are actually right," Thaelyn nods. "Our priests, regardless of their specialization, do behave in some ways as students under the guidance of an educator. The Estelar behave as a parental society, and they do offer such lessons to the younger races, in one form or another. For the druid profession, as well as the ranger, you would likely follow the teachings of the one we call Mielikki."

"The Forest Queen, yes, Kali mentioned that one once. But how do you get started on something like this? I would like to know more about it before splashing my hooves in something I might not be right for."

"You people have such amusing expressions," he smiles. "Yes, of course, knowledge would be useful here to help you make your choice. For this, I would direct you to the High Priestess Rumoren Summersong. She was participating with us once as we first established ourselves here in the settlement of Firstfall, to the south. But now that things have quieted for us in this world, I believe she has returned to her prior duties in the Grove District back home in B.T., where she presides over a druidic temple, and gives lessons and sermons."

"A grove district? Inside a city? That sounds almost like a rural or farming environment," she chuckles.

"Perhaps on the surface," he grins. "But the wide variety of races we have amongst us provides us with a considerable diversity of cultures. The Grove District is where we have the main dryad grove, where Shescellaie, the Queen of the dryads makes her home. She is the one I originally made my agreement with to restore the bond of nature to the people of the world, and not only the elven culture, as it was originally intended. Everyone can benefit from it, even your people."

"Even though we're not FROM your world?"

"It does not truly matter, as you are still living entities, and as much a part of the natural environment as any other. The dryad grove, as we call it, is a collection of special trees, where the mother element is called a Tree of Life, and the others are a ring of daughters she spawns as she matures. The dryads themselves are a type of spiritual entity that lives as an essence within the trees, each with its own, and one can commune with them using a native language inherent to their original home world."

"Original home world...not Tae'Eladar?"

"Yes, the elven society brought them along as they migrated to Tae'Eladar. Therefore, they use an ancestral form of language from that place."

"But are we saying these are sentient beings? Trees?"

"Indeed, these are not your common form of plant life. The High Priestess can surely give you a better understanding, and maybe even a tour where you can see for yourself. If you hold such a fondness for nature, this would be a fine pursuit for you. Either this, or maybe the ranger profession, where you would work more with animals."

"Would that include tigers?" Túfula asks hesitantly.

"It could, and more beyond that."

"Tana, be careful of that one. Remember Camp One?"

"Yeah," she rolls her eyes. "But I would be on the other side of it, in this case."

"In our world," Thaelyn resumes. "It is largely the Wood Elves that choose this profession, as they also prefer living in such a natural environment. Therefore, the Grove District, whose name on one side can be attributed as the home of the dryad grove, also reflects upon their preference for an entirely natural appeal. It is a segment of the city, but in this case, rather than using artificial building materials, everything is organic."

"Wow! That would be fun to look at just for the architectural design."

"Indeed, it is quite a sight, and it draws a fair amount of tourism."

"But it also sounds like I'm going to stand out a lot, if I'm the only of my people there."

"I would not pay any mind to that. Kaliya had a similar concern when she first signed up. You could simply be the first of many more to come if we should find others with a similar passion. If your society carries any part of your ancestral tendencies, you may find yourselves feeling more at home there than you might realize."

"Meaning to say..." she raises her brow inquisitively.

"You are not a natural predator species, and your ancestors, these Eracyodines, are said to have likely been herbivores, correct?"

"Um, yeah, I think."

"Oh dear cu'Nar," Petrith moans playfully. "And we're talking to a girl who makes her clothes out of grass."

"Yeah," Sulíma giggles. "I can already see her trying to pluck the leaves from that tree for her new fashion design."

"Oh no!" Tana admits. "I may get my tail in a tangle with that one! All right, I'll go over and talk to her. Um, does she speak our language?"

"Actually," Thaelyn considers. "I think not. I do not think she spends as much time interacting with your people, so you may need some help. Perhaps Kaliya can offer a few moments to introduce you and provide translation."

"That sounds good enough to get started."

"We're all going to need those language courses before anything else," Túfula notes.

"Yes, this much is certain," Thaelyn affirms. "Especially if you have in mind to attend any of our studies. But now, what about the rest of you? Mister Girhani, I recall you once mentioned joining a military effort. Now that you have had some time to rest and think it over, do you still feel this way?"

"Yes, I think so," he accedes. "Between the three of us," he motions at Sulíma and Túfula, "we were speaking with Captain Lapäli and his wife this morning, trying to pin down a few ideas. They suggested I should speak to you and hear your thoughts on the matter. They tell me you have a knack for placing people in their best professions."

"Did they now…" Thaelyn chuckles. "It would seem my reputation has gained a bit of ground in recent times. Very well, we should first ask each of you what directions you wish to take. You desire a military course, but what about these two young ladies."

Sulíma and Túfula share a moment glancing at each other, wondering who would speak first. Túfula appears to raise her brow to yield to her friend.

"Your Lordship," Sulíma offers. "I'm not one for the military. My sister is a medical professional, which tends to fall in line with much of our family, either that or engineering and technical studies.

But as for me, I had in mind to take on a rather ambitious goal, and I know it'll be hard, but I feel very excited about it, and want to see it through."

"And what might that be, young Miss Tad'vaal?"

"Well, I've been spending all morning trying to invent a new name for it, based on how we do names in our scientific fields. Our faction is supposed to be studying metaphysics, but this seems like a whole other category, the magical sciences, and then combined as a form of technology, like your people use. If we could bring this to our people on a more official level, we need a way to define what it is. So far, from what Tanjhira tells me, you might have a term like Arcanic Technician, but we like to make short forms of these words. Then, once again, to apply our native faction into it, and I had an idea. Meta-Tech. How does that sound?"

"This is a rather curious one," he smiles. "And quite reasonable. But now, explain to me what a Meta-Tech is, other than for the obvious implications."

"We were talking to Tanjhira, and she admitted to us that she would love to be able to define all this work into some category we could use later as an official form of science for our people. But she's not directly studied in this magic of yours, and the war effort doesn't give her a lot of time to build up to it."

"I understand and sympathize. Perhaps, when we can find some better opportunities, she can indulge herself more thoroughly."

"Maybe, but we don't really know when that'll be. This is where I come in. I want to study the full line of mage courses, and whatever else you have on how you apply it, as well as our own engineering studies, and try to combine these into something I can share with my people. If we consider the old riddle of metaphysics and what it tries to teach us, how the mind can perform so many fascinating tricks, if only you understand how to define them within your thoughts, and coincidentally this is exactly how magic works, then the term Meta-Tech works nicely as someone who works this as a profession to develop technology out of it."

"Very good, and this very same principle can be found amongst those societies of a much higher advancement who have already achieved this."

"We might not be the first, but this is our turn at it. You have so many wonderful achievements here, and you discovered them so early, as compared to what we had to go through, I can only imagine the possibilities if we could learn how to do this and apply it to what we already know."

"Indeed," he grins broadly. "I think, for all you have now, we could see some rather curious developments arise out of this, but I would also advise you to carry this at a carefully measured rate. We do not wish to out-step ourselves with our high ambitions."

"Right, I understand, so if you could teach me how to do this, I'll do my best to follow all the rules."

"Of course, but I do also need to point out, if you wish to carry this all the way to the Ninth Circle, this will require you to qualify with the proper testing. This also means passing the Spirit Test. Do you recall our previous discussion on this?"

"Yes, it's a test of the purity of the spirit, even though I'm still a little unsure how you do something like this, but I guess studying in your academy will help me understand it better."

"Good, so before we carry this too far, we should see about that first, as it could severely influence our final decision."

"And assuming all goes well, I might eventually find myself bouncing between your academy and our new university, once it gets built."

"Clearly, this will require some adjustments to the scheduling, but ultimately, I believe it is important to bring a fully functioning university into operation as quickly as possible. I am sure you are not alone in your educational demands. Perhaps, along the way, if you have any spare time, you could also take up an apprenticeship with the Chief Technician and our own Professor Cogswoggle. This should fill up your day quite nicely, and use up a bit of that youthful zeal," he chuckles.

"And she definitely has a lot of that," Petrith smiles.

Thaelyn next turns to Túfula who had been nervously silent during this time.

"Yeah, I guess it's my turn," she admits. "Your Lordship, I suppose I might also want to take some mage courses, if only to keep up with this twit," she nudges Sulíma's arm. "I mean, after all, someone needs to watch over her to keep her out of trouble."

"Oh dear, I can see another occasion forthcoming..." Thaelyn mutters.

"Excuse me?"

"We have seen a few pairings of this sort pass before us in the past. Now we have another coming into view."

"Oops! Well, we girls tend to do this to our men," she giggles.

"And no doubt, just like with us, it might cause some premature aging,"

"That, along with sagging horns."

"Absolutely! But I do enjoy good challenges. I find such occasions to be very fulfilling. I can recall many occasions of others, some from my own race, and a fair few of the Child Races as well, ask why I would choose to come to any of the Prime worlds, as we tend to call them. This is precisely the reason, because of such wonderful young people like you to make my life so interesting."

"Oh! Then I definitely need to join up, just to make sure you don't get enough sleep at night!" she grins.

"That has happened a few times as well," he concludes thoughtfully. "I look upon such people as you with the same eyes as my Father. You are the Children of Creation, and I have often regarded myself in much the same light as he and the other Estelar. Though I will admit, for my experiences, one would very literally need the patience of the gods to see it through, on occasion."

He shares a warm grin with the group as they feel a comforting sense of family developing.

"And again," Sulíma mumbles softly to her friends. "I have to say, why couldn't we have found them a few worlds ago?"

"But now..." Thaelyn resumes. "As for your studies, if you think you would only take a selection of mage courses, what else would you desire? What sorts of interests fascinate you most?"

"I often thought of following my father in culture and history," Túfula admits. "But from where I'm standing right now, I might not have a lot of material to work with, at least not for our people."

"There is much more out there than what you might possess. For instance, our world has a rich history behind it, and if this is your pleasure, I am quite sure this will occupy you for a good while. We might also suggest, for your natural lifespan, there could be a plethora of possibilities as we discover new worlds and their associated societies. You may find additional interest in those, as well."

"Now there's an idea. Xenoarchaeology, maybe also xeno-historical studies."

"Also, once we arrive on Azgarén, if we can liberate any part of it, I am sure you can pick up for your own society again."

"You think so? Of course, now I have to ask what kind of history I might want to study over there. It would seem that monster, Darumon, has influenced so much of it to his own designs, I can't be sure what's real or not."

"Then perhaps this can be your passion. To research and discover the truth of it, knowing about his influence and trying to derive the facts of how your society actually developed. Surely, there must be something of worth to encourage your sense of pride for your people. Regardless of what Darumon did in the guise of this King Saakerav you once mentioned, if this was truly him, or anyone else, I might suggest one good thing came out of it."

"And what's that?"

"It brought you together as a single society, and elevated you to where you are today. Irrespective of his interests, this is still a good thing for you, as now you are united behind a single cause. We simply need to be sure the cause is a worthy one."

"Hmm, yeah, that's a good thought. All right, I think I can work with that. Kind of like how you did things here, I guess."

"Indeed! Tae'Eladar was locked in a quaint medieval station for a long period of its history. Due to the involvement of magic, the study of science, in the traditional sense, was not as commonly investigated. They developed as far as they felt they needed, and any new wisdom fell out mostly from those in privileged positions of study, if any fell out at all. It was also largely a feudal society when I first arrived, ruled by aristocrats and pompous lords. This did not help matters. Further, the world was broken into many political rules, including such as monarchies, oligarchies, councils, and even a few dictatorships. Had I not arrived, it might still be that way even now, perhaps to remain that way indefinitely, as they did not seem to hold much interest in evolving themselves."

"Wow, so you turned the whole world around all by yourself. That really does sound like the stories my father used to tell. Only in your case, you created this body that goes out and saves everything else they see. How do we even describe something like that?" she giggles.

"Yes, I suppose we could say ours is rather unique for this point, and we are fortunate to be prosperous enough to afford this to ourselves. You seem to hold this story in high regard, a bit like a romance. Do others of your people share this perspective?"

"I don't know. My father, like I said, would tell stories, but ever since he took up a position on the Council, I guess he fell out of the habit. I don't often talk about it, because we had too many other problems, and of course most of us from Ruuki uy'Daan didn't finish our schools to learn anything. And even at that, with our teachers trying to help us survive out there, we mostly learned only what was critically important."

"So, a fair portion of your history was set aside in lieu of the more imperative matters. Then perhaps you can use your stories to inspire a few others. Share this with those in our training program. It might give them a stronger sense of purpose, if this is the direction we are intended to take."

"Even though it might have been Darumon using us for something?"

"I would say, especially if he was using you, as we are going to turn this around and use it for ourselves."

"This sounds a little like a slap in the face," Petrith chuckles.

"Precisely! And we should be sure he sees it to fully realize how we have learned of his deceptions. His plans to culture and develop you will go fatally awry, as predicted by Adalon in her prophecies."

"What does she say about this?"

"For this point, I will recall a few of her verses…"

Thaelyn walks over to a table near the rear of the room and picks up a notebook. He returns and flips through a few pages.

"Here…" he points at a section of writing. "This is the beginning of the chapter where she begins speaking of Sargeras and Darumon, along with your people. Listen to this…"

He pauses to clear his throat before reciting the verses.

"Alone in the dark, they lie in wait, Forgotten and Ignored; two Ancient Ones, from times unmeasured, and a life they once adored. This one essentially tells us they are out there, still alive, and unchained. Then the next one… The Master sleeps, his servant toils, a plan he does unfold; resurge of hate, avenge of spite, a terror vaguely told. This series tells of Darumon making his plans for a return, presumably to take revenge and likely with the result of restoring the old ways for their kind."

"That sounds bad," Túfula admits. "No matter how you look at it."

"Now for this part… From virgin soil, a nascent breed, the Forgotten One will spur; a spark of whim, a sudden rise, where emergent minds occur."

"That's interesting, so how do we interpret that one?"

"Have you learned, by this time, of the history of your species and how we believe Darumon may have influenced it?"

"Actually, yes…" she frowns. "Kali told us something, and I couldn't believe my ears. I very nearly pulled my horns out because of it…in a literal sense of the word. I don't want to be the half-breed child of that monster."

"I can thoroughly appreciate your feelings on the matter. This verse essentially tells of how Darumon…and we believe it must have been him if Sargeras was sleeping during this period…how he invoked your early ancestors, which you call Eracyodines, into sentience. We believe he did this suddenly, and likely using his own essence in the process. This could offer us a number of answers as to your current condition, including your extreme longevity as well as your ability to use these remarkable Gifts. So, if it makes you feel any better, consider your…" he coughs subtly, "…half-breed nature to be providing you with a few exceptional qualities. Not just anyone can make such a claim."

"Oh…well, all right. If you want to put it that way, maybe I'll reattach my horns for it."

"Very good. And finally, we have this one… The Forgotten One, long in slumber, seeks to take his prize; a race of Children, slowly grown, shall lead to his demise. This, my young friends, is where you take back your prestige. And at this point, I would suggest this concept of the Stormhooves, which is also referenced in these verses, will lead the charge."

"So, the story of the Stormhooves could serve as inspiration to our new cause," she muses. "Ooh, I like it! I'll sit down with a few people and share what I can. This might also be a good exercise in my history lessons."

"Excellent! And now back to the young man here. Mister Girhani."

"You know," he replies. "The Captain was right. That reputation of yours shows up like a beacon house. Just with these three, I can see the result."

"Yes, it is a talent I find great pleasure in sharing."

"Well," he sighs. "As I said, I was interested in signing up for military service, but after talking to the Captain, he suggested I speak with you first to see if there are any special areas you might find me best suited for. Primarily, the reason for this, as the Captain was saying, other than to suggest I may have some skills that aren't necessarily made for front line activity, is that I have some important obligations to fulfill, and shouldn't be rushing off and potentially getting myself killed."

"And what obligations are those?"

"These two right here," he thumbs at Sulíma and Túfula, "and one more over at the academy."

"Dear Powers, young man," Thaelyn yelps. "Three of them?"

"It's a hard life, Your Lordship, but I'll do my part," he beams widely.

They all let out a rowdy laugh as Thaelyn attempts to compose himself again.

"Commander," he calls to Kailen. "Are all your young people as ambitious as these examples?"

"I don't know about all of them," he responds from the table. "But these three would certainly stir the pot for their collaboration."

"Indeed! I can already see the events of the coming years will be quite an entertaining show to follow. Very well, so let us consider what skills you have already. I am aware you were serving for a time under Captain Lapäli, correct?"

"Yes, I was," Petrith nods. "I was stationed on scouting patrols, mostly on the fields outside our old school, which was located on a hillside and had a good view of the city. I would sit there most of the day watching for anything unusual, like orcish patrols entering the city and…well, also the mutants, to make sure they weren't trying to cause any more trouble for us," he turns his gaze downward in recollection.

"This was before you realized their misfortune, correct?"

"Yes, and I feel bad that all this time we thought they were just as dangerous as the orcs, when in fact they were yet more victims made to suffer, and even more so than we were."

"This is actually made worse when you consider our part," Tana adds. "Here we are, three and a half centuries of cowering in that hole in the ground, and watching the orcs rummaging around the city, thinking they're simply looking for trophies, as if there could be anything else to rummage through, when in fact they were rummaging for our people to abuse them. And we didn't even bother to investigate the reason why."

"Let us move past that moment," Thaelyn soothes. "While it was unfortunate, it probably could not have been easily corrected.

Not with so much fear and skepticism. So, you were a scout, and by the sound of it, a very patient one."

"Sometimes I wonder about that," Sulíma suggests. "Was he really so patient, or asleep on the job out there?"

"Patient, Suli," Petrith corrects. "We're trying to brag me up, remember? I don't want a job protecting a flower garden. Although I will admit, it had a lot of dull moments, and my mind would drift on occasion, which is one of the reasons I was thinking of something a little more active. When we went out to recover those reactors, I felt a sense of invigoration come over me. The travel was slow, but those few moments of action were enjoyable, especially at Camp Two."

"Did you tell him about the head?"

"Um, what head was that, Suli?" he feigns.

"You know. The...head..."

"I'm quite sure I don't recall that."

"It was when I found that orcish drum. What was that music group I was thinking of starting up?"

"Um, Suli..."

"Yeah! That's right! Suli and the Orc Heads!"

"I really don't think..."

"It was my way of recovering after what you did the night before."

"Suli!" he interrupts.

Thaelyn observed the exchange with some enthusiasm, his mouth curling into a modest grin at their interplay. He turns to the table again.

"General, I think we may need to arrange a new page for our list. We may have a few special candidates for it one day soon."

"Oh?" he perks up. "Do we have something of special interest over there? It makes me wish I could share in the dialog."

"I will share the details later, but you may find a need soon to take their language course. If we are moving in that direction, it could prove useful."

"Indeed, I suppose you are right. I will see about it when I get the chance."

Thaelyn returns to the group, still smiling.

"Am I to assume by this minor altercation that you know something of what occurred that eve when a stray orcish head was delivered through the conveyor to our side?"

"A stray orcish head…" Tana winces. "It sounds so innocent. Oops, he lost his head. Oh well, there it goes through that hole in space," she giggles.

"Yes, and here we have another one," Thaelyn shakes his head.

"Your Lordship," Petrith pleads. "Honestly, I had no idea your people were in control over there. I was feeling a little perky after our raid on their camp, and felt like making a statement to the rest of them that we're taking charge of our lives again, even though they couldn't have known it was us doing it."

"This is true, and technically I suppose you should count yourself fortunate that it was not the Suuden-Aryku to find it, otherwise they might go to investigate the cause for it. Of course, this assumes they actually cared enough at that moment to bother."

"I thought about this, but the camp was hundreds of miles to the south of our position, so I figured we were far enough out of range not to be noticeable. Also, we had speculated already that the Suuden-Aryku may have no further interest in returning, as was evident by the abandoned camp with the other conveyor, and that the orcs may be considered an expendable race to them. Even the Captain agreed to this, at least in principle."

"Then it would seem you covered some important aspects of this, at least in theory. Perhaps you understood your adversaries well enough to make an informed judgment."

"He actually played out a very logical approach to his reasoning," Sulíma offers. "We were arguing the point just before he did it, but after a while, I couldn't disagree with it."

"Really! What sort of reasoning, in this case?"

"First, if there are orcs on the other side, this might represent a statement, one to another, that our side was turning against whatever authority was originally driving them. The same for the Suuden-Aryku, assuming they were even paying attention by this time. The idea was to suggest the orcs turning against their 'god' image, if this is what motivated them, and not wanting to be spent any longer."

"Very interesting."

"Now, while this might call the attention of the Suuden-Aryku, one of two things might happen. Either they came to check on the conveyor and the associated camp to see what happened, or not. And if they did, and chose to take similar action, like what they used on us so many times, it would be the ORCS, not us, they would blast to nether-space. But we generally believed they might not be an issue, or that the orcs on our side might not be worth travelling halfway across the galaxy to finish off, since so many had already gone through. So, it might not actually result in anything for us."

"How curious, and with so many carefully derived conclusions."

"We saw this migration they were making," Petrith continues. "We knew it had to be for a reason. One idea was a land grab on the other side, but it would make better sense to use all their conveyors to spread it out, rather than to build one big city for everyone, as orcs don't build cities."

"Indeed, I must agree with that ideology."

"Other than this, it might be due to something critical happening on the other side and they're all being sent to follow it. If we suggest it to be a battle, either they're all focusing on a really tough target, or being spent like water. And if they're being spent like water, no one ought to care if a few of them turn rebel."

"Yes, you do have a point."

"We also hoped, although this was a distant hope, that we could use this in a longer-term plan to incite others to turn against the Suuden-Aryku, maybe to save what was left of them, if we could shut down that last conveyor. We didn't want to see the demise of their race any more than you apparently did. Despite Tana's feelings on the matter, and many others, we didn't want our inaction to be any more responsible for their loss than another society's direct action."

"That, young man, is perhaps the noblest of considerations. And very becoming of your breed."

"Thanks. And therefore, as Suli said, we debated the issue until

I came to the field decision to take this action in the hopes it might lead to something later."

"Very good, then. Although I personally would prefer consultation before making such a decision, I can certainly see, in your predicament, where effective communication might be lacking, you might find a need to take unilateral action for a higher cause."

"Yes, and the Captain also admitted this same point."

"And so it is," he nods. "So, let us summarize a moment. You are a patient one for your scouting forays, but you also tasted the thrill of battle. Then you indulged in a bit of intrigue and deductive reasoning to bring about a rather elaborate conclusion, based at least as much on speculation as some careful insight of your opponents, and at the same time, you laced the outcome in such a way as to offer protection, for whatever value it might ultimately bring, to they who might themselves be made victim. This carries a certain level of prestige for a number of venues. Did Kaliya explain to you any of our cultural values?"

"She did. She also laid a heavy one on poor Tana here once."

"Yeah, and wow," she rolls her eyes. "This was during my outburst over the orcs and her stone god figure."

"Ah, I believe I recall her mentioning this," Thaelyn affirms. "She explained some portion of what we call the Measure of Balance, where all life is revered and must be respected, no matter who it belongs to. We might fight the evils around us, but we should never insult the pure essence of life as an element."

"I remember a few things Kali told us," Túfula admits. "She's currently learning this as part of her own studies in your academy. But then, how do you go out and wage war against such beings as orcs and the Suuden-Aryku?"

"We do as we must to protect our own, perhaps also they who are similarly made victims. And the orcs, at that moment, as well as your Suuden-Aryku here on Therinë, represented themselves as a threat to many. The orcs perhaps not as much for their military prowess, but rather that we believed them to possess portal magic, and this could be used to devastating effect as a terrorist weapon against others. This would be in addition to their warlike nature, and the apparent worship of a god image that drove them to the destruction of anything in their path."

"That doesn't sound hard to do," Tana muses enthusiastically.

"Then we had the Suuden-Aryku, and although we might suggest they are governed by these chips, they are still a threat, and that threat had to be countered to save innocent lives. Their loss had to be tolerated for a greater good."

"Ouch," Túfula winces. "But yes, I suppose I can see your point."

"A greater good…" Tana considers. "So, we need to count numbers in this equation. The needs of the many, as opposed to the needs of the few."

"Correct," Thaelyn nods. "Unless we can say those few hold such insurmountable value as to overstate the greater masses on the other side. Although this might also count as a controversial definition."

"Wow, who do you have to be to overstate a whole crowd of people on the other side."

"I can give an idea," Sulíma offers. "Not a nice one, but I think it would hold merit. Take someone like Tyanna when we were arguing over that solution to remove her mutation thingy. Someone of high authority, high education, high social or professional value that might otherwise LEAD those masses. Someone with a full horn-load of university education, and compare that with someone who can barely sell pastry buns on a street corner without tripping over his own hooves."

"Yikes!" she chuckles. "But yes, not a nice one, but it might hold merit, controversial or otherwise. Who do you use to rebuild your lost society if no one even remembers how to build it. You'll go back to the Stone Age at that point."

"Indeed," Thaelyn admits. "And we would surely wish to preserve at least some of our achievements along the way. But a better example of our philosophy would be the end result of how we dealt with the orcs. And a fine demonstration of this was given by none other than the one who held such a deep prejudice when I first met her that there was some question in my mind if she could ever overcome it."

"I think I know who that was," Tana recalls. "Kali, when she made that negotiation for a truce, right? I was there, and I listened to her as she spoke to that shaman. I couldn't believe how she laid out her speech…the acting, the dialog, how she presented it. It was like she was a wizened elder teaching the secrets of the ages to a young student."

"I recall when she reported back to us on the occasion," Thaelyn reflects. "She tried to recall everything that was said and how she presented it. This, in combination with that encounter within their camp once, and also as they were travelling in search of their missing solar panels. And then we have that encounter in the city with her god image, which I hear sent dear Miss Tad'vaal running home in such a mad rush that she could not stop even after she arrived," he grins. "At least until you passed out from exhaustion."

"Oh. Yeah. That," Sulíma huffs.

"And through so much of this," Tana continues. "She said she was mostly making it up as she went along."

"Yes," Thaelyn concedes. "This is most certainly a skill demanding of a great amount of improvisation."

"Just for the sake of argument, Your Lordship," Túfula asks. "How do we consider this an example? Like Suli's experience with that stone god image."

"Quite simply, rather than attacking outright and possibly slaying the offenders who were assaulting that poor mutation victim in the street, Kaliya came up with a scare tactic that saved lives on all sides. This one act alone was worthy of a special medal for her choice, and the rest afforded her with an additional set of medals, including one custom made for her diplomatic efforts."

"A custom-made medal. Great cu'Nar, actual medals of valor… When was the last time I ever heard of someone winning a medal for something?"

"In or out of a military profession?" Petrith wonders.

"Anywhere, really… I know Kali won a few awards in sports at school, but I'm not so sure I would count that in the same way."

"We honor our people for their deeds," Thaelyn recounts. "No matter how small. But hers was truly unique in how she applied it, using this Gift of hers. I believe Lieutenant Lapäli was making a recording of the ceremony, so you might want to ask him about that."

"Ooh!" Sulíma croons. "Home videos? Yes, I need to see this."

"Now, back to you, Mister Girhani... Is there anything else you can offer as a skill to your good credit? You mentioned your Captain suggesting something away from front line action."

"Well, Your Lordship," he ponders. "He didn't actually specify anything at the time, so let me see. Like I said, my main job was scouting at the old school…not much else I can say about that…"

"Perhaps something on the side, like a hobby?"

Sulíma begins giggling uncontrollably. She attempts to cover her face, which appears to be blushing.

"Suli," Petrith moans. "I hope you're not thinking about that shower scene again."

The girl tries shaking her head underneath her hands.

"Uh-uh," she utters in a muffled voice.

"Actually, Petrith," Túfula interjects. "You should mention that skill of yours," she pauses to consider her words. "And not just the fact that you completely ignored staring at a naked girl, but rather were studying her bathing accessories," she begins giggling also.

"Oh dear," Thaelyn ponders meekly. "This must have been a most enjoyable occasion. Dare I fall prey to the inevitable?"

"Oh yes!" Tana blurts ironically. "Suli and Túfu might have their say on things, but here I am with my tail hanging out more than most, and all HE can think about is Kali and her soap," she crosses her arms and pouts teasingly.

Thaelyn raised his brow prominently and turned to find Kailen, who was still sitting at the table, but now laying his head in his hand.

"Oh dear cu'Nar, please don't tell me…"

"All right, everyone," Petrith asserts. "You girls just won't let up on me. I swear to the cu'Nar, I'll never live this one down. Your Lordship, over the course of, well, a long period of time, I had a series of very odd dreams where I thought I was watching Kali during what seemed like scouting runs serving the Sentinels, and later in some form of training. As it turns out, it seems I was experiencing a type of clairvoyance skill, which is likely derived from all these other things, and I just didn't understand it at the time."

"Indeed!" he emits enthusiastically. "This would make for an interesting study. Have you spoken with Aelwyn on this yet?"

"Yes, I have, actually, so she will probably investigate this at some point with her students. I was thinking of trying to develop this, or any of the other skills she teaches, to see if it might be of service."

"This would indeed be of service, any or all of it, depending on your direction. But now, how would this apply to studying young ladies in the shower, hmm?" he raises his brow.

"Well, um…" he sighs. "Kali and I were very close when we were young, so my dreams carried me to visit her, it seems. One time, I found myself watching her in your guildhall shower room. The trouble is my focus was apparently misdirected to following the… um…strange type of soap she was using, rather than her body."

Thaelyn glared at him disconcertedly for a long moment, and then glanced at the two girls standing next to him.

"And you say there are three of you who are supposed to be attending to his aspirations? Young ladies, I think you need to try harder."

"Dear cu'Nar, Your Lordship," Túfula relents satirically. "I can only do so much, and if Suli tries any harder, she might break something."

"All right, fine…" Sulíma giggles. "If we get back to Petrith and his, um, skills… After all, we need to get ourselves to work and let His Lordship get back to his…you know? I was giggling about something else which just popped into my head. These things happen to me on occasion."

"She's right about that much," Petrith admits. "And not necessarily sensible ones."

"And what was it, Suli?" Túfula asks.

"Well," she hesitates. "He asked about something on the side, like hobbies."

"Petrith has a hobby? So, are we speaking of him napping on

the school field, or hiding behind that row of bushes near the pond?" she grins.

"Oh, Túfu, no, I'm talking about…um…well, it's nothing. The mention was about something useful, so I just had a silly reaction, you know me."

"Yeah, you have silly reactions if the wind blows the wrong direction."

"I find myself curious now," Thaelyn muses. "Could this hold some important relevance?"

"Honestly," Sulíma asserts. "I really don't know if this is something we should be talking about, because it brings up bad memories."

"Ah, I see. But perhaps we should bring it into conversation anyway, if for no other reason than to release it, rather than hiding it. If you would wish to confess something, it might serve a healing purpose."

"Do you think so?"

"Kaliya had many pent-up emotions and personal failures hidden inside when I first met her. By the time we were finished, however, she managed to reveal all of her hidden miseries, and she was finally able to qualify for our service. Perhaps we have another of the same?"

"Well, maybe. Petrith, what do you think?"

"I'm still not sure what you're talking about, Suli," he issues.

"Your little thing with the Security Council mainframe…"

"Oh please, Suli," he begs. "Don't even mention that one. I'm still hoping for something better than janitorial duty."

"I remember that one!" Kailen shouts from across the room.

Kailen was still sitting at the desk listening in on the conversation, when he rose up and strolled over to join the group.

"I was working in the Security Council office at the time, do you remember that?"

"Yeah…" Petrith sighs wistfully. "And it didn't actually help much. It got me in trouble with a lot of people, including you. It was really embarrassing, especially since our families were so close at the time."

"May I inquire as to the nature of this event?" Thaelyn asks.

"Your Lordship," Petrith admits nervously. "I was young and a little bit out of control…"

"A little bit?" Sulíma counters. "You caused such a stir that the whole city was talking about it for a year! And that was just on the outside of the SC center. Ankhia once told me they were scrambling to reprogram every security code and firewall they had in the building, to say nothing of what the Elders thought about it."

"Still, it was a stupid mistake, and I paid for it."

"Eh…" Thaelyn interjects briefly. "I am still at a bit of a loss…"

"What they're talking about, Your Lordship," Kailen responds, "is this young man and his computer hacking obsession. One day, he broke into the mainframe at the SC office, which was a high-security data center. He didn't really do anything critical, other than try accessing several of the files. But the fact that he did it at all got the whole building up in arms."

"Indeed! And when we say breaking in, are we speaking of a remote link? And how difficult a task is this? My impression suggests this must have been a rather sensational effort."

"Yes, it was. It was a remote access from his home terminal, cracking his way through firewalls and complex encryption schemes."

"It was childhood curiosity to see if I could do it," Petrith relents humbly. "And I did. The Security Council mainframe was touted as having some of the best security of all the government networks. Unbreakable, they said. I proved them wrong. But cu'Nar's pity, did I ever hear about it afterward! The reprimanding and restrictions they placed on me held me out of just about every public occasion and school event on record. I was underage, so they couldn't arrest me, but I was held in detention at school, confined to the house, and wasn't allowed the use of a data terminal again, indefinitely."

"He suffered really badly for this, Your Lordship," Sulíma frowns. "So, I wouldn't want him to get in trouble for anything again. He's not a bad person, just trying to have a little fun, but this probably wasn't a good example of it."

"Perhaps not in this case," Thaelyn affirms. "But we are speaking of when he was much younger, and youth can sometimes carry its trials. Now that he is older and wiser, I am sure he would know... um...hmm..." his voice trails off as his mind starts clicking.

Kailen turns to study his face, and the sudden change of manners calls the General's attention at the table. He perks up, trying to interpret Thaelyn's new posture.

"My Lord?" he utters softly.

He pauses the General with a finger to continue his thoughts in the Daanen'kai tongue.

"Hacking..." he mumbles privately. "Perhaps. Deduction, intrigue, logical analysis... Mister Girhani, did you get one of those thrills you so craved?"

"Huh?"

"You mentioned earlier how your scouting efforts left you wanting, even though you did so rather patiently, and then your expedition to retrieve those conveyors gave a rise to your excitement level. Your debate at Camp Two, your decision-making... Did you feel any such rise on this occasion, such as during or after you successfully conquered your objective?"

"Your Lordship," Kailen intones cautiously. "What's your direction in this?"

Thaelyn simply turned and smiled mischievously at the question before returning to Petrith for his response.

"A thrill..." Petrith wonders. "Like what I got at Camp Two? Well, that was a different occasion..."

"Nevertheless," Thaelyn continues. "As one who had an opportunity to indulge in something other than to sit and nap while watching an empty street. You were confronted with a challenge. This challenge invoked your wit and guile to overcome an obstacle, and as a result, you achieved what might otherwise be considered unachievable. Irrespective of the legal implications, how did this make you feel?"

"Well, I suppose I would have to say I felt good that I could do it, even though it didn't last long. Once they came pounding at my door, my world collapsed."

"Yes, I suppose it would. But now, do you think you could do it again?"

"Oh no, I'm not going anywhere near that again. Not after what happened to me the last time."

"Mister Girhani, I am not asking for the illegal aspect of it. What if this could be a legitimate form of occupation?"

"Huh? A job? To hack something? Wait a minute, you WANT me to do this?"

"What would he hack?" Túfula asks anxiously. "You wouldn't have him try hacking into anything of ours, would you?"

"Maybe he wants to hack those living machines he brought to visit once," Sulíma grins mildly.

"Oh no, nothing of that sort," Thaelyn admits. "But we are in a state of war, in case you forgot, and our enemies are likely to be in possession of some valuable information that could be useful to us."

"You want him to hack the Suuden-Aryku?!" Túfula screeches.

"Let us recall our details. You served as a scout, with a fair bit of patience for the duty, but felt inadequate at times. You enjoy the thrill of the hunt, but let us restrain ourselves from the bloodletting. And if also to consider Camp Two, you apparently demonstrated some very refined analytical deduction, as well as the accumulation of detail for the logical determination of process. You seem to possess a technical proficiency with electronic networks, and the capacity to decode high-security encryption techniques. Furthermore, let us once again mention your proactive ambition to apply yourself to a higher purpose. The unfortunate illegal nature of this youthful zeal notwithstanding, you were attempting to prove a point…a point which does, as it turns out, hold merit. Commander, even you would agree that if a young child, of all things, can break into your systems, a more determined professional could do the same, and with much more malignant designs."

"Yes, I suppose I have to admit to this," he nods.

"Therefore, we must recognize this to hold professional value, if only for the countermeasures against more of the same. As some might say, to fight fire with fire."

"All right, I might also need to admit to this. But are we suggesting this to fight against the Suuden-Aryku doing this to us?"

"While I might not expect them to perform such as this, if they are more prone to simply blast you off the planet, this dear young man would represent a good example of a spy. And not just any spy, but one designed for electronic espionage."

"Electronic espionage," Kailen shakes his head. "And this from a society that barely uses electricity."

"Well," Sulíma concedes. "You have to admit, it fits with them having conveyors and supersonic animals before they have aircraft or space travel."

Petrith gazed in shock at each member of the group. He couldn't find his voice at first, largely because such a thing as this was never a lesson back home. It was a wild ambition, nothing more. At best, it might resemble an action video on their local entertainment networks.

"I…um…but… Well, actually… But Your Lordship, it's been centuries. I'm seriously out of practice. In those days, I spent much of my free time on these things. I had my own terminal in my room. I was often up late at night trying different methods, like experimenting with fake IDs and false routing to throw off the security scans. Cracking their codes was the toughest part, but once I learned how they formulate their encryption hashing, things started falling into place. What you're talking about here is going up against the Suuden-Aryku with their systems, and I can't even be sure how those work at the moment."

"Still," he considers. "You did not know as much about those you broke into, I would wager, and yet you did so just the same. Where is that thrill of breaching the void, I wonder? That taste of victory to achieve the unachievable. The application of one's wits to deduce those principles that should otherwise lie outside your reach. Or did they vanish in the same flash as with the fascinating vision of Kaliya's bar of soap?" he grins.

"Oh, dear cu'Nar," Sulíma moans.

"Yeah," Túfula affirms. "He's got you, Petrith. You really did need to pay closer attention to the naked girl handling the soap."

Petrith covered his eyes and shook his head at the clear and obvious rub.

"And let us not forget the Prodigy Gift," Thaelyn continues. "If you are lacking information, you can always steal it."

"Steal it?" Petrith intones cautiously. "Wait a minute, what about this society of laws of yours?"

"While I will admit, we are a society of laws, and I would not openly permit the breaking of such, even the Estelar occasionally use espionage against each other if it serves to maintain the Measure of Balance. And war carries its own demands which can sometimes transcend our peacetime virtues. In this instance, we are using it to defeat our enemies, and this will ultimately save lives."

"The needs of the many again," Tana reflects.

"Correct. I consider this a cause worthy of the vice. However, I would still need to approve of any actions, even at that."

"Um…" Sulíma wonders. "How do you define theft if you need to approve of it first?"

"For instance, stealing an instruction manual out of a book shop might not be favorable. But if we can simulate some form of trade, this would be better…assuming we have something to exchange in our hands. Otherwise, if to play the same game Darumon is best known for, we can impersonate virtually anyone and use one of your data chips to access an information network and simply download something. The network could possibly be a public access service and therefore not as critical."

"Cu'Nar's eyes, you're good. So by stealing it, he's not actually STEALING it. Did that make sense?"

"Good old Suli," Túfula pats her on the shoulder. "Careful you don't blow a fuse."

"There can be many definitions," Thaelyn admits. "But the information, in this case, belongs to our enemies, and likely itself is being used inappropriately. Therefore, we turn it around and use it against them as a corrective effort."

"All right," Petrith relents. "But to what end? How would we use it? Am I supposed to crash something, or corrupt information… or what?"

"This largely depends on factors we cannot be sure of at this time, and we still need to train you, regardless. This will require time, and time is a commodity we may not have in great abundance. But I would imagine, once we arrive on Azgarén, we will need to learn their ways and find a few of our own while creeping about under their noses. We may have a need to access certain data networks, possibly through their own terminals, to acquire information about their operations, and we will likely need to unlock a few security codes along the way. It may also become necessary to infiltrate some of their networks to apply a little of our own form of propaganda, as Darumon has become so famous for. Overall, we need to undo what he has done, and this might involve unraveling his own machinations. If this forces us to take such actions as breaking into someone's computer network, it is HE we are fighting, not those who are otherwise his victims. And anything he creates is fair game to us."

"Wow, now there's some justification for you," Túfula winces.

"And that's a long list, already," Sulíma accedes.

"Indeed," Thaelyn nods. "And it can perhaps grow even longer. And what better way to gain this than with a thief."

Petrith retracts from the conversation as he reflects on his past life on Ruuki uy'Daan and the experiences of his youth. He gazes at his three friends as he ponders the implications.

"Who would've thought?" he evokes quietly. "For all that I suffered, the accusations, the mistrust, the loss of privileges, and the simple pleasures of life, all for a foolish game I once played. And here I am about to make it into a profession that could save countless lives and bring our people home."

"Talk about vindication, Petrith," Túfula pats him on the shoulder.

"Yeah, if only it could've come a little earlier," Sulíma huffs playfully. "I mean, for all the times he was confined to his room, I missed out on a lot of tail-swinging opportunities," she giggles.

Petrith glared at the girl for her unrelenting flirtation.

"Well, Your Lordship," he chuckles ironically. "May the cu'Nar help us all, but I guess you've got yourself a spy! But I'll need help getting started. Remember, it's been a while, so I have a lot to refresh myself on."

"I swear," Túfula moans. "Between you and Kali. And I thought she was bad with her god complex and the orcs."

"Commander," Thaelyn resumes. "I trust you can see to his training on your side while I enroll him in some of our courses at the academy. We should see if any of your engineers can provide some equipment for him to play with, as well as the people at Bahlaie and the captured Suuden'kai terminals."

"Absolutely, Your Lordship," he replies.

"We should also begin his Prodigy training, since I am sure he will be using that at some moment."

"This is getting a little scary now," Túfula grimaces. "Just think… We were worried about him peeking at us in the pond from behind those bushes. Now he could BE one of those bushes."

"Well," Sulíma sighs. "I just hope he's actually paying attention to our bodies this time and not the soap."

Chapter 3

FIRST CONTACT

"Chief Bronzeheart, what a pleasant surprise."

"Aye, and already I can feel the good soil of me home beneath me feet again. Do ye mind if I take a wee peek outside this wall of yers to see what those bloody devils did to me home?"

"It's still a bit dark out there, but so far nothing is moving around. Just take care to keep your hollering to a low grumble. We're still trying to maintain secrecy here."

The Chief had arrived at the outpost with Captain Hagmaert and his scouting troupe. It was still early morning, local time, and the sun was not due to rise for almost another two hours, but he wanted to prepare himself for his anticipated meeting. They were expecting the local resident to be arriving later in the day on his way to forage some of the hillside grasses for his farm animals.

The Chief trudges heavily from the portal receiving area towards the camp exit, which resembles a small corridor in the shield wall surrounding the camp emerging into a camouflaged grotto within the canyon gully. His footsteps plodded unusually harshly on the ground due to his extended absence and being out of condition to his natural gravitational environment.

He finds the outer breach in the corridor and pokes his head through to survey the nearby region. It was still too dark to see much detail, but his enhanced dwarven vision, which was more accustomed to underground living, allowed him to see enough through the low light levels.

The land was open and flat, with very little vegetation to speak of, and barely a few trees holding on. He could feel the dry and excessively warm air on his face, even for the nighttime conditions. The dismay was enough that he could only shake his head morosely and pull back in.

"Captain, 'tis a sorry sight, that… I spent all me life in that hole beneath the mountain, ne'er to go topside. This here be me first time to see the world from above, and I'll tell ye true, I don' like the smell of the air here. It smells like a world gone bad, it does."

"You've never gone up before?"

"Nay, the Thane forbids it, tellin' us tales of the war ragin' harshly out there. He tells us to stay put, only to send out supplies to the front. That be the whole of it."

"No troops…or at least the suggestion of it?"

"Nay, only the goods from our smithy works…and, well, those of us chosen by the Feast. In fact, the word is the towns up top are the ones doin' all the fightin'. What a laugh that one is, ay?"

"Indeed. Tell me a little about your home. How do you make such things as food and water, and being so deep under a mountain, how do you refresh your air?"

"Aye, ye like a good tale, then here ye go. Glimmerheim is a right grand city, ye know. I recall tales of it bein' our biggest. The center of the kingdom, it was."

"A capital city, then?"

"Aye! For the food and water, we have wells deep down where we bring up good water, clean and pure as can be. We have a number of large caverns deep below where we do our farmin'. There are crops we grow that make a hardy livin' down below. It nay be a grand life, what with the war sappin' us out, and we had to make a few sacrifices when they closed the doors on us, so it was told, but we try to make do with what we have left."

"But at least you have enough food and water to go by?"

"Aye, I s'pose we nay can complain…nay by much. But when I compare to the life I have with yer folk, it falls a wee bit short or more."

"I understand. And the air?"

"Ah! Long ago, when they were first carvin' out the caverns, they cut shafts in the rock to circle the air around. As we dug deeper, we simply cut more. We get enough, ye can be sure of it. We dwarves know about the need for air, and this here is an old habit."

"Good to hear. Being someone who spends all my life on the surface, I would tend to worry about that after a while."

"Aye, I s'pose ye would. We dwarves may spend more time below than what we do above, unless ye're talkin' about the towns up here with the farmin' and the herdin'. They're a wee bit different breed, more set to that sort of life."

"Something else that comes to mind… I know dwarves have a special kind of sight that allows them to see better in darkness than some of us, but still you need some form of lighting down there, don't you?"

"Aye, ye're a quick one," he chortles. "We know of a good kind of lichen that does well deep down. It gives off a kind of light while growin' on the rocks. But it needs special rocks for it, ye know, and we farm this and put it around the city. And then we have such like crystals we can make glow with a bit of old dwarven rune craft."

"I know of this rune craft. Your kinfolk back home kept a few of your old traditions alive, and I think they even made a few new ones along the way."

"Ah, this is pleasin' to me ears, Captain."

"But under the circumstances, I would think any kind of fire would be out of the question in an enclosed space like that, wouldn't it?"

"Mostly, I would say yay to that. We have cookin' fires, like in homes and taverns. But there are a few cauldrons where we burn either wood or coal, and then ye have the smithy proper and the fires we work there."

"Fires in the smithy are one thing. I know dwarves and their smithies. You often use enchanted fires for your work, especially if you're running an adamantium forge."

"Aye, we pull out special minerals from the rocks deeper below to burn in those. The pyromancers can keep those blazin' for a good while."

"But you say cauldrons burning wood and coal? Coal you can get underground, but where does the wood come from?"

"Aye, 'tis true that, but in both cases, we get it from somewhere else. This here is another fine one for a good laugh, if it nay be so sad to think about. The Thane brings it in. I don' know where from, but it sure smells of foulness when I look at this outside," he points figuratively through the wall. "The tale is it comes in trade for our goods goin' up."

"Interesting. So he drives you deep underground, closes the doors, and tells you tales of what's going on up here, when in fact it's completely different. Then he tells you to make these goods in trade for such things as coal and wood..."

"And such a fine trade for the weak value alone," mentions one of the scouts who had been listening in.

"Absolutely! Adamantium is a highly valued material, more so than gold in some cases. But in fact the metal you make goes to the Suuden-Aryku, and the towns you're supposed to be trading with are nothing more than giant holes in the earth. Very nice."

"Those are me same thoughts, Captain," Tol nods.

✦✦✦

The sun slowly rises on the horizon, not that either Belrum or his wife, Friah, notice it in their makeshift home inside the old mine. Still, their natural rhythms follow it, nonetheless. The refugees in the mine stir to life as the morning ritual commences.

At the end of their early meal, Belrum makes himself ready for his run up north to the ridge of hills bordering the valley outside. His duty today was to see about collecting a good armful of local grasses for the farm animals being kept deeper in the mine.

91

He pulled on his usual work clothes and a set of boots which just barely held together anymore. He kissed Friah goodbye, as was his tradition before going to work, and sets off out the front entrance into the barren land. He makes a brisk pace, but not a true run, as his physical condition didn't allow him a great amount of stamina for the lack of proper nutrition.

As the weary dwarf moved off into the distance, a set of eyes peered out from an invisibility cloak not far from the mine entrance. Once Belrum was safely out of range, a scout dispelled his cloak and cast an enchantment on a rune for a quick departure from the area.

"Captain, he's on his way," announces the scout as he reappears within the outpost camp.

"Good, what estimate do we have for his time of arrival?"

"He's working a modest trot. Not quick, mind you, but I figure half a day."

"All right, so maybe about midday he'll be coming up to these hills. Chief Bronzeheart, we've been through this a few times by now, but I'm one for detail, and this is important. We need this to work in our favor. We've been receiving these deliveries over here as our offering," he gestures to an array of sacks and crates, and several bushels of hay recently deposited near one wall. "If these people are so desperate for food, I can't see how he could refuse, and our offer is quite simple. The only stumbling block might be how they would respond to outsiders like ourselves in their midst."

"Aye, and so I go out in me best manner and use me finest talkin' to see if I can bring him into good favor to our needs. Captain, I'll say it again, I nay be the one to make pretty words, but ye can be sure I'll do me best."

"If we have till midday, I might suggest you try to get a little rest. You've had a long day so far, by the measure back home. We'll let you know when it's time."

"Good to hear. And ye're right, me eyes are burnin' just a wee bit by now."

The Chief moves off to one of the cots used by the men for their rest break and lies down. The hours pass and the scouts make occasional checks for the approaching dwarf outside on the plain. They were sent out under a cloak to survey the region at a distance, first to make sure he was still moving, and also to return time estimates for his arrival. Finally, just after midday, a sighting reveals him making his approach to the hillside further down from their position.

Belrum was making his way towards the hills. His sights were set on a patch of grasses he was familiar with that held the potential for some decent growth. He didn't take notice of the unusual addition to the landscape further down the row, as it was actually just far enough off to the side to be out of his immediate view, and therefore his concern. He arrived at the base of the hills and started climbing the slope, pulling up several prospective handfuls of grass along the way.

"Chief, it's time," the Captain whispers. "He arrived just east of us, and a fair walk from here, but I doubt that'll be a problem. Go out and meet with him. Serve up your finest, good sir, and remember to speak in your native tongue. You might have become a bit too accustomed to what's used by our own dwarves by now."

"Aye to that…"

The Chief trots out of the outpost shelter and onto the open land. He works his way around in the direction of their visitor, which can be seen off in the distance keenly focused on his work.

Belrum had pulled up several good bundles of grass by now, but the stalks were thin and wouldn't likely make very good sustenance for the animals back home. He climbed up and down the hillside in a pattern to cover the area, grabbing any piece of grass he could find. The hillside had a reasonable amount of natural coverage, not thick, but at least not too thin. He knew this would not last long, but it was all he could provide for the survival of his people and their livestock.

He moved further along the hillside making ready to climb another section when a surprising sound ushered up from behind him.

"Hello there, friend! Ye be a kind sight t' these eyes in this sorry land. Mayhap ye can give a good moment for a wee bit of tellin' t' an old soul with a heavy heart?"

Belrum jerked up and looked over his shoulder, following the sound of the strange voice. He saw the figure of a middle-aged dwarf in remarkably fine clothing and neatly presented. This man clearly did not fit the general scene of the land as compared to his own people.

"Who be ye there?" he replies hesitantly. "I nay be a-knowin' yer face…or yer clothes."

"Ah, these old things," he checks his attire briskly. "It be but the best I could muster in these times. Ye see, friend, I be somethin' of a traveler, an' I heard a tale of some folk in this land. Ye may have s'posed by now I nay be of the local kin, but I would give a good word t' the All-Father for a kind bit of talkin' t' one."

"Aye, me kin have been a-givin' words t' him for a long while, but the land nay be a-makin' better for us. Some of us have been a-thinkin' him t' be turned away by now."

"Nay, brother, ye can be sure he be a-watchin', an' from what I see out here, he would surely be a-fumin' at the nostrils for it. But mayhap we can help each other. I bring with me a bit of a tale, at least as what me kinfolk know of it back home, an' from a band of friends we came upon once. Mayhap, if ye think ye can take a wee rest for yerself, we can trade tales."

"Good friend, I would'na be the one t' turn away a friend with a tale, but the day be half past by now, an' I truly need t' be a-pullin' up as much straw as I can for our sheep back home. The little darlin's are shrivelin' up on us in all this heat."

"Aye, I hear ye, brother. I can feel it on me face, an' it nay be a good sort. Then, what say ye if I could sweeten the offer with a good promise of help for ye an' yer kin?"

"Help? What kind of help?"

"For one, ye say ye have sheep that be a-wastin' away in this heat, an' with nay more than what, this wee bit of grass ye're pullin' up here?"

"Aye," he examines the bundle of grass he was carrying by this time. "It nay be much, but I need t' pull up all that I can."

"Then what would ye think if I could offer ye better, an' nay only for yer sheep, but for yer kinfolk as well?"

Belrum paused to study the man. His clothes were certainly in much better condition than anything he had seen before, and as someone who didn't look like a native, he looked like he might have come from a better place. Nevertheless, even though the promise of food seemed tempting, it also seemed hollow with his own experiences during the course of his lifetime in this desolate place.

"Well, I nay be one to ask for charity, but…" he hesitates.

"Lad, blast the talk of charity. We be a-talkin' about savin' lives here, an' I think the All-Father himself would have a few words t' say for it. Come down an' sit with me, an' I'll tell ye me tale. Mayhap ye can tell me yers as well, ay?"

"Well, aye then, I nay be one t' show bad manners, nay t' a good soul callin' out the name of the All-Father. But I hope ye can understand how this place nay be what it was in me father's day. It be a hard thing t' trust someone new."

"Aye t' that," the Chief proclaims. "I nay be t' arguin' with ye. I can see with me own eyes this land, an' it breaks me heart."

Belrum carefully ambles down the hill to meet with his caller at the base. The two of them pick a comfortable seat on a nearby mound and settle in.

"Will ye tell me yer name, friend?" Belrum asks.

"Aye, me proper name be Tol Bronzeheart. Mayhap ye can share yer own?"

"Aye, 'tis fair… Belrum Strongfoot."

"A good name, that. Would ye an' yer kin be from the old farmin' out here?"

"Aye, but nay me'self… Me father's father, he be the last t' work the land proper. But that was afore the blastin' came down an' carved it all away."

The Chief knew this was a clue. His instructions were to try to gain as much information as he could, especially to find confirmation of where he was, as well as try to make friends and an offer of aid. But the going would be hard in the light of this man's obvious skepticism.

"What about yerself, Tol?" Belrum asks. "By yer clothes, ye

can'na be from 'round here, an' I nay be a-knowin' of any kinfolk still in the valley who look like ye."

"Ye're right, I come from a far place. I've been away a long while from me old home. Right now, I be a-tryin' t' find a city said t' be near here. But I think it still be a fair walk."

"What city be it yer looking for? There nay be anythin' still standin' in these parts. Everythin' was blasted t' the All-Father by a mighty power from the sky."

"So the tellin' goes," he hangs his head. "The city was called Glimmerheim, d' ye know this name?"

"Aye! An' it still be a fair walk from here, but ye'll be sad t' know it was blasted the same, an' with half the mountain brought down on it."

"Half the mountain?"

"Aye. Me an' a few of the lads back home made a run or two up there t' look at it. The outer city was blasted t' bits, an' it looked like the side of the mountain got hit by whatever pummelin' carved away everythin' else."

"So that be the tale of it," he closes his eyes and shakes his head.

"I be sorry t' say it t' ye, Tol, but I think yer travels were for nothin'."

"Nay, Belrum, it nay be for nothin'. At least I know the tale now. An' more so t' say I be where I thought me'self t' be, even if it does break me heart t' see it."

"Ye did'na know afore now?"

"Lad, when yer father an' his father tell ye tales of the land, an' then ye come out here an' see it for yerself, an' it nay be anythin' of the like, ye start t' wonder."

"Aye! Ye're right," he chuckles faintly. "I lived here all me life, but me father an' his father told me tales of what it was like afore the pummelin', an' it be a sorry sight by now."

"Aye then, so let me get on with me tale. Yer sheep nay be a-gettin' any closer t' feedin' time with us jabberin' about lost homes."

"What sort of tales d' ye have? Ye said we could share somethin' new, but how could mine be any different from yers?"

"Because me home was inside Glimmerheim, Belrum, an' we nay have any tales of what I see out here."

"What?" he yelps and turns more to focus on Tol. "D' ye mean there yay still be people down there?"

"Aye! We dug deep t' get away from it, but I think the tale from me own will be a grand bit different from yers. Let me ask ye, what tales d' ye have of all this pummelin'? Like, for instance, where did it come from? Ye said from the sky?"

"Aye! Me father's father was there at the time, an' he saw a great pummelin', like great balls of fire blastin' the land away. They carved out mighty gouges, takin' away every city an' town we ever knew about. It was like they knew where t' hit, an' hit the most important of them all."

"This makes sense t' me for what I hear of it on me own side from me friends. They tell tales of who it might be that did it, an' why."

"Wait now… Ye say WHO did it? Who could be a-tossin' down balls of fire like a mighty storm from the gods themselves?"

"A folk with a mighty grand bit of knowin' far an' away higher than ours, Belrum. Our folk are still a wee bit on the young side, but there are others out there who are wiser an' stronger, an' one of them found us."

"Oh grand!" he shouts. "So, what then… They come along an' see us poor farmer folk, so they decide t' blast us for the favor?"

"Nay quite as much, so let me tell ye the tale from me own side. First, I have some friends who are at war right now against a mighty foe. I came out of Glimmerheim once several years ago as part of our Thane puttin' on a feast t' call up smiths an' such t' go up an' serve a fare for a war he was a-blabberin' about."

"A war?"

"Aye. Ye see, Belrum, he tells us tales of a war out here, nay any pummelin' or anythin' else. He forbids us t' go up an' look at it, so all we have are his tales. An' he lies grandly."

Belrum frowned at the obvious implication, not simply about the stories of a war, but that the Thane himself was telling these obvious lies and ignoring the truth.

"Why does he tell ye t' go up t' serve any fare if there nay be any war up here?"

"T' answer that, I need t' ask ye this… D' yer kinfolk still tell tales of those point-ears that were once said t' be a-comin' out of portals at us?"

"Point-ears! Tol, that yay be a grand long time ago, an' they were ne'er that much t' speak of."

"Aye, mayhap, but that nay be the tale we get down below. The Thane rages each time he comes out of hidin' in his room. Our poor Chancellor has t' listen t' it, an' the tale be that this land up here be a-burnin' with the war of the point-ears ragin' across it so harshly, that we yay should ask if there be anythin' left by now. An' the tale has been this way for four hundred years."

"I can'na believe this, Tol! How can it be that ye an' yer kin ne'er found out about this? Ye say he ne'er lets ye go out t' see it?"

"I s'pose if ye say the mountain came down on us, there nay be a way t' go out by now."

"Aye, ye're right. But then, if ye can'na come out an' see it, how does he figure there be a war out here at all?"

"Ye may also want t' ask how he sends folk like me an' others out on this feast. It all comes out as part of a grander tale."

"A grander tale…" he frowns. "Aye, fine then…so, what be this grander tale?"

"For this, we need t' go back a wee bit in our history. I recall once a tale of a band of gnarly brutes called orcs comin' at us one time. D' ye know this one?"

"Eh…wait, orcs…" he ponders. "I think I may recall a tale, but this here be old, an' we don'na talk much of it now."

"Aye, fine t' that, but this was about five hundred years ago, as it was told. This band of orcs came at us, but by the tellin', it did'na last long, an' our warriors were said t' have beaten them back grandly."

"Aye, this be fine enough."

"But now we have this one about point-ears, an' by the tellin' I once heard handed down by me father an' his father, the tales did'na sound so grand."

"Aye, the same as me own. An' that one only went a short while afore they stopped."

"Good, at least this much we can agree on. But both of them come from the same place, an' they were both owned by the same bigger foes."

"What?" he gasps. "Owned by bigger foes?"

"Slaves, Belrum, sent at us t' test us an' see how we fight."

"Be these bigger foes the same as what did the pummelin'?" he scowls.

"Aye, but before ye get yer whiskers in a bundle, hear the rest of it, an' I'll promise ye an' yer kinfolk a hearty meal for the favor."

"Aye, so ye say, but…" he glances around the local area. "Where d' ye think this hearty meal be a-comin' from? I nay see anythin' like a camp out here with any friends."

"Give me a moment an' I'll explain. For this, we need t' go long ago in t' history, but nay our history. These friends of mine, they nay be native t' this land. Just like with those who found us an' pummeled the land, there be another folk now chasin' them."

"Chasin'…? Tol, I hope there will nay be any more pummelin'. There nay be anythin' left t' pummel!"

"I know, an' so d' they. They have scouts out here lookin' for people, tryin' t' find survivors so they can help them. An' we already know food t' be a bad thing for ye."

Belrum drew back at the suggestion, even though the mention of food was not so unexpected, but rather to say there were people running around looking for survivors. The pieces were suddenly starting to fit.

"Tol, be this t' say ye know of me an' me kinfolk by now?"

"It be the reason they sent me out here, t' meet with ye since I be native t' this land…well, a wee bit at least. I work for them now, after they found me an' a group of others workin' a mine an' pullin' up Adamant."

"Adamant!" he yips. "Wait now! Tol, be this the one we found over yon t' the east," he turns and points.

"Nay, ours was different, found in another land completely. Ye know of one found here?"

"Aye! But now I be a-wonderin' who they be a-workin' for, because they were a-pullin' up Adamant an' makin' bricks from it, t' the best of me knowin'."

"Aye, an' the Thane has us makin' the same in Glimmerheim. These folk nay be friends, but they also be slaves. An' the Thane be a-workin' for them."

This sent Belrum into shock, and he pulled back from the conversation with a blank stare. Tol knew he had to finish before the poor man should begin to panic and run off.

"Ye see, Belrum," he continues. "All of them…all these slaves are servin' up t' this mighty one they call Darumon. Now, this part may sound like a wild tale, but ye need t' understand the truth of it. Remember when I said there are those out there of a mighty high knowin'? Well, this Darumon may well be one of the mightiest of all, an' he likes usin' wee babes like us t' d' his work."

As Belrum listened, it began to settle in his mind, and this caused him to glower at the suggestion.

"He be a left-over from ancient times," Tol resumes. "T' folk like us, we might have old tales, like those of the old titans. These might be tales ye give t' the wee ones at bedtime, but there be a note of truth behind it, as well. This Darumon be a kind of servant t' one, an' his master goes by the name of Sargeras. We think he yay be the last of the titans still out there. No one knew of it until recently when he came out an' started makin' trouble for folk like us."

"An' mayhap the pummelin' be a part of this? But why?"

"He wants our Adamant, but he nay wants so many of us arguin' about it. He has a race of people who go by the name Suuden-Aryku. They be tall, with horns like a hill sheep…"

"Oi!" Belrum perks up. "Wait, I think I know of this. I saw somethin' like that come 'round once or twice at that mine over yon t' the east. They were a-pickin' up the Adamant an' carryin' it away in some beastly large…somethin'…that flew away t' the sky."

"Aye! Good then, ye can help us. We be a-lookin' for it right now, hopin' t' help those men an' put a stop t' it. That mine be the work of our Thane."

"All-Father help us, yer Thane did that?"

"That feast I spoke of, I was once a part of it, sent t' another mine that was found by our friends. They helped me an' a crew of others, an' now we be a-helpin' them help all the rest. But here be our biggest trouble…we need t' move slow an' quiet. The Thane can'na know we be out here. If he hears of it, he tells his friends, these Suuden-Aryku, which then goes up t' Darumon. If that happens, things can go bad for a lot of people."

"Like more pummelin'?"

"Aye, mayhap that, mayhap more… One thing that worries us yay be if he simply runs an' hides again. He could stay that way an' no one would know where he went, until one day, he comes out an' it all starts over."

"Aye, an' that sounds bad already, for whatever poor sod he finds next."

"So we need t' find the city, find a way inside, an' look 'round t' find our way under his nose. We need t' know who he be an' how he got in there, then how he talks t' his friends outside an' how t' put a stop t' him, so we can save the people inside…includin' me beloved wife," he turns and lowers his head.

"Tol?" Belrum inquires softly. "Be she still inside there?"

"Aye, like so many others, an' nay a one of them knows what be a-happenin' out here. But we can'na say until we can cut the Thane out of this. An' here be me proposal t' ye an' all yer kinfolk. Help us t' help everyone else. We'll give ye food t' help with yer woes, an' ye can share it with others, if ye know of any. But ye need t' keep it quiet if ye ever go up t' the city."

"There nay be a way inside the city, so nay a way for me t' say anythin'."

"Fine an' good…though there must be a way if I came out of there. Mayhap a secret door. But just in case we find one, an' ye find yerself in there one day afore we be ready…"

"Aye, I understand, Tol. But where be these friends of yers, an' where be they from if nay from this land? An' also, if they be a-chasin' these others who be a-pummelin' us from the sky..." he glances upwards.

"They be from another world, Belrum. These others in the sky were a-makin' trouble for more than just us."

"Another world?" he muses distantly.

Belrum takes a moment as he tries to comprehend the concept of a full world. He scans the valley in front of him, and all he thought he knew of his world, and then placed on top of this the idea of something coming from the sky above. But the notion, in the local culture, just wasn't advanced enough to give him a full example.

"I know what yer thinkin', Belrum," Tol explains. "I was the same afore all this, mayhap nay as much as ye. Me world was a city 'neath a mountain with nay a way outside. Nay even a sky over me head. The Thane called us t' his feast as part of a show he put on every year. Two of them, one for us, another for this other mine ye speak of."

"Two of them!"

"He feeds us this gnarly stew which tastes of foul 'shrooms an' meat. The 'shrooms are the ones t' be feared here. They taste of metal, an' carry a type of poison in them that puts a man in t' a spell where he nay can see his hand in front of his face. But he listens well enough, an' follows his commands without a word."

"Aye, Tol, I saw such as this in that mine. They looked like they were a-sleepin' with their eyes open."

"Me an' the lads I travelled with were the same, until our friends came an' found us. They gave us medicine an' helped bring us back t' full health. While we were there, we learned who they were, an' who this titan be, along with his servant, an' a fair bit of history that travels well away from us here."

"What sort of history, can ye tell me?"

"It gets a wee bit complicated. D' ye think ye can take it?"

"I don'na know, but so far I'll give it me best."

"Right, then... This servant, Darumon, be a-lookin' t' start a fight with some ancient foes. This be the reason he needs Adamant, t' make a titan-sized weapon out of it."

"Titan-sized? I fear that sounds yay worse than the pummelin' we took."

"Aye, ye can bet on it, an' our friends be a-hopin' t' put a stop t' this, as well. But here be a fine twist t' things. His old foes…well, one of them that we know of, has been a-watchin' him, an' waitin' for him. But they could'na make any moves until he hit one more world, an' this would open a kind of door so this old foe could come out proper."

"Aye, I think I see why ye say this gets complicated."

"Stay with me, Belrum," Tol encourages. "An' remember me promise t' ye. There was a key t' this, an' this key was a band of people who tried runnin' from Darumon. They be more of these Suuden-Aryku, but now with a new name as they try t' run away. They call themselves Daanen-Aryku. Darumon was a-chasin' them, mostly for fun, until they ran t' this other world where they found this old foe. When Darumon saw this, he turned an' ran back home t' where he keeps his Suuden-Aryku slaves."

"Tryin' t' get away from it?"

"Aye, he be a-hopin' t' sneak in so he can hit from behind. Thankfully, this did'na work the first time. But now, this old foe an' all the folk who follow her are comin' out an' buildin' up, makin' themselves ready t' find Darumon. Along the way, they found a path t' this world. Here in this world, they think Darumon has a kind of outpost where his Suuden-Aryku slaves bring the Adamant in that flying beastie ye saw, an' we think it t' be right near Glimmerheim."

"Great All-Father!" he yelps. "So this means yer Thane has only a short walk t' go up an' say hello?"

"An' t' hand over our people from his feast, an' anythin' else he has t' say. This here can yay be a problem for us, so we need t' find it."

"What will ye d' once ye find it?"

"We can'na be sure until we take a good close look at it. But we want it, ye can be sure of that much. We think it might hold value if t' take it an' hold it. In the end, though, we need t' help the people of this world an' get Darumon out of here."

"Aye, that much I think I can understand. So, ye're askin' me for help t' find yer way 'round the barrens, I s'pose, an' ye'll trade this for food. Be that the way of it?"

"Food, an' other help, if ye need it. D' ye know of any others out there?"

"Aye, a few here an' there."

"Good, ye should send out word as best ye can. We need t' help all our brothers an' sisters."

"That be a right fine offer, Tol."

"Now, as for our friends… There be a band over yon," he turns and points along the row of hills. "It be hidden behind a wall that looks like the hillside. They be a-hidin' in case these Suuden-Aryku, or anyone else we don'na know, comes 'round t' take a peek. Ye an' yer kinfolk are fine, but we can'na let anyone else know."

"Aye! Or else it goes back up t' the Thane an' his friends, ay?"

"Aye t' that. So, ye need t' tell yer kinfolk, an' anyone else ye meet, t' keep it quiet. This band be set in a military post, an' led by a Captain. But he nay be a dwarf, so try t' keep yer wits about ye when ye see him. His people are a wee bit taller than ours."

"Be he one of these Daanen-Aryku?"

"Nay in his case, his goes by the name of Human. They look a fair bit like us, but taller an' with nay as fine a beard t' brag about," he chortles.

Belrum raises his brow at the mention and feels compelled to smile.

"These people come from a world called Tae'Eladar," Tol continues. "An' they already crossed one world called Therinë, where me an' the others from this feast were a-workin' our mine. Then they had t' cross one more, an' here they found those orcs. From there, they found their way here."

"They must be a mighty folk t' d' all this."

"They have a fair bit of knowin', ye can be sure of this."

"What about those point-ears. Ye said they were part of this somehow."

"Aye, they were also on Therinë, one of the local clans, an' these people already helped them escape from this titan."

"They seem t' be a-helpin' a lot of folk escape from this titan."

"Ye're right. They follow a King, an' he be the one leadin' the charge against Darumon. He be a fine leader, as fine as any ye can ask for. I wish we had one of them in Glimmerheim," he shakes his head solemnly. "But the offer of food comes from him, an' his people are here t' see it through. So, Belrum, what d' ye think of this tale?"

Belrum leaned back to ponder the lengthy, and nearly incomprehensible story, most of which went well beyond his limited education, and tried to reflect on his own stories, as well as what he saw in the mine and out on the fields.

"Tol…" he sighs deeply. "Dear Brother Tol, I hope ye'll understand when I say this yay be a grand bit of tellin', an' nay the sort an old grizzle-beard like me'self can swallow in one sittin'. But when a man's belly be as empty as mine, I s'pose there nay be much t' d' but ask if mayhap this be the way of it. We be at the end of hope back home, an' we've been a-prayin' t' the All-Father for somethin' special. So, if this be the one, I'd be a sorry sod t' turn it away. Can ye show me these friends of yers, mayhap? I'll keep yer secret, ye can be sure of that. Nay that I have anyone t' tell 'round here," he chuckles faintly.

"Good enough, Belrum," Tol nods. "Then put down that dry grass, ye'll nay be a-needin' it. I'll show ye t' me friends, an' then we can see about yer kin."

The Chief gets up, followed by Belrum, and he leads them back to the outpost. Along the way, Belrum finally takes notice of the strange addition of the camouflaged walls.

"Tol, what be this here? It looks like the hill, but it nay be dirt an' stone."

"Aye, they patched up a wee little wall an' made a bit of decoratin' t' make it look like the hillside."

"This here be a fine bit of work. I think I nay would have noticed this…mayhap nay unless I was right on top of it."

They continued around to the side where the hidden entrance was located, and he led them in. As Belrum enters the outpost, he looks around at the alien design of the wall, which seemed solid, but at the same time it didn't look like any material he could recognize. Many of the people were much taller than he was, with some of them wearing armor made of glimmering metals.

"Praise be… Mayhap this be Adamant they be a-wearin'?"

"Aye, they wear the finest I've ever seen, an' this be from a smith of a forge said t' be the finest in Glimmerheim."

Belrum was dazzled by the spectacle of the lay of the outpost design. There were sleeping quarters, a kitchen, an officer's hut, a storeroom for supplies and food, and a central campfire with several people sitting around it, all turned to look at him and smiling pleasantly. Towards the rear was an odd ringlike device standing upright with a strange landscape image floating in the middle. The collected sights were enough to cause him to freeze in his steps.

Captain Hagmaert noticed the arrival of the two dwarves as they made their way in. He makes a casual approach, taking care not to come too close or too quickly, so as to give the poor man his space.

"Good greetings to you, friend dwarf," he offers. "And I would offer you a fair welcome. My name is Captain Julian Hagmaert. I trust our good friend, the Chief, has told you who we are and why we're here?"

Belrum tried desperately to find his voice. The language was dwarven, generally speaking, but not entirely familiar to him as it held a strong foreign accent.

"Aye, that he did," he returns cautiously. "Ye speak our language, but nay the same."

"Yes, we have a population of dwarves who live amongst us on our world. They have been there for a long time, part of a migration we think occurred in ancient days. The language they now use is a bit different from the one you have here."

"Be that the way of it? Hmm…a migration? I nay be a-knowin' of any migration, but then, I be but a poor farmer's son, an' me schoolin' nay be as good as some."

"That's quite all right. This was a very long time ago, so it's questionable if anyone here might recall it by now. Can we know your name, good sir?"

"Oh, aye, where be me manners. Me name be Belrum Strongfoot. Eh, me kinfolk be a-takin' up inside the old Verdantgem Burrows mine, if ye know about it. Nay many of us, nay these days…only a few hundred…"

"That doesn't sound good for the numbers, but we would like to help as many as we can find. And if you know of any others, we will invite them as well."

"Aye, good Tol here was a-sayin' ye were out there lookin' for folk who might still be alive, may the All-Father be praised for it. An' in return for this, we could help ye find yer way 'round the land."

"That's right. We have a number of important objectives ahead of us in our war effort. One is an enemy military base which we think is somewhere out there, another is a mining operation with more people like Tol."

"Aye!" he yips excitedly. "Mayhap I can help ye already, an' earn a wee bit of yer help for me kinfolk. Tol said ye were a-lookin' for an Adamant mine. Aye, I know of one. It be to the east by a fair run. Ye'll come t' a long line of mountains, but then ye need t' go north a mite an' ye'll see it cut into the side, like a big box carved out of the rock."

"Ah, good, and thank you. I'll tell my people when we get ready for the next run. Also, um, Chief, did we find out where we actually are?"

"Aye, Captain," Tol responds somberly. "This here be Morndindor, just like ye thought. But according to Belrum, Glimmerheim be half buried under a mountain by now. I know we have a city down below, so I be a-thinkin' it be only the outer city an' mayhap parts of the upper town, near t' the doors. I recall now some old tales of a rumblin' thought t' be from the war outside, but he says it be one of those bombardment blasts that took down part of the mountainside."

"Ouch!" he winces. "That could possibly collapse portions of the rock inside the city. I would be really careful if you ever go into that area. The rocks could be very unstable."

"Aye, but somehow we need t' dig our way out, too."

"Yes, so this will need to be examined very carefully. Approximately where can we find the city, Belrum?"

"Um, t' find Glimmerheim," he considers. "Ye'll need t' go north by a good long run from here. There used t' be a road, but in this land, nay much be a-holdin' on. The dust an' wind, the dry air an' such, it be a-wipin' away everythin' we once had out there."

"We believe your world is experiencing a condition where things will likely get worse as time goes by, maybe to a point where it becomes impossible for anything to survive at all. We have a name for it, but it probably doesn't matter right now. Just to see it is bad enough."

"Aye, I've lived here all me life, hopin' it will get better, but it ne'er does. Be there any way t' change it?"

"There is, at least in theory, but it will not be easy, nor will it be quick, and it'll require a lot of work across a large area."

"Oi… An' I think I can see where this might be a-goin' already, if ye're tryin' t' hide from these Suuden-Aryku ye speak of. So ye nay can d' anythin', at least nay until that beastly Thane be taken care of first, ay?"

"You catch on quick…" he smiles. "But we can still help the people, and this is what we should do first. Here, take a look at what we have for you."

The Captain steps over to the side wall where he begins pointing out the large array of supplies they had collected the previous evening.

"Here we have bundles of hay, and these sacks have grain inside," he indicates. "This is for your livestock. Then we have these other sacks…"

He moves to another row of bags that filled the space.

"Fruit, vegetables, bread…"

The Captain continues ticking off a shopping list of items. Belrum inches forward in utter disbelief, his face growing pale from the unimaginable display.

"But…this…" he stutters. "Ye can'na mean…"

"And in these boxes here," the Captain moves to the next set. "These boxes are magically enchanted to remain cold inside. This is to keep the meat fresh. If you have no other way of keeping your meat, you might want to hold onto these."

"Meat?" Belrum wheezes.

Belrum feels faint now. He drops to his knees and settles on the ground. He once again glances across the full assortment of wares, which resembled more containers of any kind than he had ever seen before, to say nothing about holding food. He begins sobbing.

"But Captain, I be nay more than a poor farmer's son! Even if I were t' give ye the grandest of showin's 'round the land, there nay be any way I could d' so much as t' pay for all this."

"That's not the point, Belrum," the Captain soothes. "Lives are at stake here. If you can help us save any of those, this here is only a small thing in comparison."

"Small?!" he blasts. "This be more than I've seen in most of me life! Well, mayhap half of it, t' be sure."

"We are a prosperous people with much to offer, and we're not afraid to do so."

"Now I know why Tol praised yer King so grandly. He did all this?"

"Yes, and he'll do more as the need arises. This is simply our way."

Belrum had collapsed fully to the ground by now and was sitting there staring at the full array of goods, trying to fathom how anyone could own so much as to virtually give this away. He covered his mouth with one hand while leaning on the other.

"Captain, I be a-tryin' t' think of what I can d' for ye t' help me kinfolk that might be worthy of all this. I nay be one t' ask for charity, even though Tol argued with me for the word. I don'na want t' make me'self look like one who takes gifts an' does'na give back for it. An' this here be a right grand gift, no matter how much help I can give. Ye can be sure ye've got me attention. I nay be as young as I once was, but I'll d' all I can t' help ye as best as me poor old legs can carry me."

"We understand the fine nature of your people, Belrum. Your folk are sturdy and honorable. That's all we can ask. We also understand the nature of the gods you worship, and ours follow the same creed. And maybe you can recruit a few others to help you, so you don't have as much pressure on just your own shoulders."

"Aye! 'Tis true. The lads back home would surely want t' give back a wee bit. An' if we can find others out there, this would be a fine showin' t' the All-Father that we be the good sort he always taught us t' be."

"Most excellent. Now, we'll need to help you bring this home. I'll call up a few of my men and we can begin right away."

"Eh, Captain, d' ye know where our home be? Tol said ye had scouts out there lookin' about, but me home be a good half day walk from here."

"Yes, I know this already. We found your mine entrance recently, and then took notice that you were apparently coming up here to forage the local grasses. But the travel time, for us at least, isn't nearly as bad. We use magic a lot in our society, and one application is to use portals to cover longer distances."

"Portals! Oi, I heard a few tales of those with the point-ears. How does it work?"

"Well, I could point out one method we use. If you look over there..." he points at the gateway node. "This is what we call a Gateway, and it's a device that uses the same principle as our magic, but here as a more permanent fixture."

Belrum gazed at the strange apparatus with the floating image in it.

"That there be a portal? An' what be that in the middle of it?"

"That is an image of the other side, which in this case is a world we're currently occupying as we march forward to find our enemies."

"That be another world," he wheezes. "Oi, me head... I think it'll be a-poundin' afore long."

"Well, try not to worry about it now. There is a lot to cover, and this all came very quickly. For now, let's just help bring you home. We use portal rune stones when we make our scouting runs, and we have one set up nearby your mine entrance just in case we were fortunate enough to gain your help."

"Aye, just in case… Um, mayhap I can ask what if ye did'na get me help?"

"Well, surely, it would be important to gain your assistance, one way or another. Likely, you would be afraid of new faces, especially in a land like this outside. But overall, I think it was a fair certainty we could find a way. After all, Belrum, can you refuse our offer of aid for your people? You follow the one you call the All-Father, and the dwarves we have back home do the same."

"Really now!" he chuckles. "Aye, ye've got a point, good an' proper."

He sighs deeply and pulls himself together to stand up again. His shock had settled somewhat by now and he was feeling ready to carry forward.

"How d' we get all this back home…" he mumbles silently.

"Here, let me show you how we tend to do things where we come from."

The Captain waves to call over a group of his scouts, along with a mage and the recent portal rune they made to the front of Belrum's mine entrance. The mage enchants the rune and the traditional glow of energy circles around the item in his hand. Belrum stepped back at the strange anomaly as he continued to watch.

"Here is how we do this," the Captain begins. "First, we send the men to the other side to act as receivers, then we send along the goods, and they move them aside to make room for more."

Belrum watched as the men each touched the stone and vanished in a ball of light. He jerked back at the first sight of it, but as the process continued, he studied it carefully. Then the mage began to touch the rune stone to each bag and box on the ground in sequence to send it forward. On the other side, the men moved everything to a clear spot according to a carefully timed sequence.

"After that," the Captain continues. "It becomes your turn. You simply touch the stone, and it carries you through to the other side. Our men will help you further to bring it inside if you desire."

"An' that be the whole of it? I be home again, quick as a blink? Oi, Captain, when Tol said ye be a high an' wise sort, he nay be a-tellin' any wild tales."

"And don't be afraid to come back here if you need anything else. I'll try to have my men check on you from time to time, or you can come back up here yourself if you have the need."

"Aye, that be a good thing t' know. Well, Captain, ye can be sure I'll tell me kin about all this an' let them know who t' thank for all yer good help. An' we'll send out word t' the other clans we know about, mayhap t' see if there be any more, an' try t' bring them all together."

"Very good. Take care, friend Belrum, and I hope to see you again soon."

Belrum was now feeling a much warmer sense of comfort for the hospitality, though he was still a little hesitant about the magical aspect of the travel options. He reached out as the mage held the glowing rune stone in front of him, and lightly set his fingers on the surface.

It was nearly as quick as his fingers touched the stone as he was enveloped in a ball of light. His senses spiked at the sudden transition, and he had to force himself to remain calm until his eyes could focus again on the new scenery forming in his vision. He found himself standing only a short distance in front of the tunnel opening where his people made their home. Standing nearby were the scouts and a large pile-up of containers.

"Blessed be... D' yer people use this much where ye come from?"

"Very often," replies one of the scouts. "We have devices like what you saw in our camp, but larger, in our cities and towns for common people to use when they travel. And our military uses them almost every time we go out."

"In yer cities an' towns... This world ye come from, how many of these cities d' ye have? D' ye know, mayhap?"

"I don't know the count, but there are many all across the land. Our King spreads his domain across the entire world, and recently we took even more land on a new world we found called Therinë."

"Aye, Tol mentioned the name as part of yer war travels. Great All-Father, a King of a full world an' more..."

He pauses to look at the remains of the land around him. He can only close his eyes, lower his head, and shake it solemnly.

"An' our world nay be more than a field of holes," he relents.

"Belrum, our Lord will surely want to help your people, but the pressures of our war must come first before we can feel any of our work will leave us safe."

"Aye, I get yer meanin'. This has been a-comin' for as long as I've been alive, so I s'pose it nay can get any worse in the short of it."

"This is our thought as well. But now, as for all this," he waves at the assembly of goods. "Do you want us to help bring it inside, or do you think your people can do this? Either way is fine with us."

"Aye, eh... I be a-thinkin' now. It would be a grand help if ye could bring it inside, but I think me kinfolk would jump at the sight of ye..." his mouth begins to curl into a little smile. "Aye it would!" he laughs. "For the tale I have t' give them...oi! They would ne'er expect t' see this comin' home! Har! But lad, ye should give me a wee moment just t' break it t' them that we'll be expectin' guests."

"Uh oh..." the scout grins. "Do they carry weapons inside there?" he wonders impishly.

"Nay lad, we be farmers, nay warriors. The worst of it yay be an old cookin' pot."

They share a quick laugh together as Belrum totters off into the mine.

He makes an anxious rush inside, passing through the tunnels into the large hall deeper within, where most of the dwarves gathered in general discussion and relaxation, or simply if they have nothing else to do, which was most of the time.

"Lads!" he shouts. "Ye nay will believe this! Ne'er, I say!"

The room was echoing with general conversation when he came in shouting like a madman.

"What be that, Belrum?" calls one member of the congregation. "An' where be the straw ye promised this morn?"

"Aye, about that... I found me'self somethin' better than straw, along with a grand tale t' ruffle the kinks in yer beards an' burn yer ire about all our woes outside."

"Huh? What d' ye mean?"

"Brothers…an' sisters too…" he yips excitedly. "This be the day we've been a-waitin' for! May the All-Father be blessed, for he finally sent us our salvation."

"Belrum?" calls a female voice off to one side.

He turns to find his wife staring at him like he had just lost his mind, which is not unexpected under the circumstances. He rushes over and grabs her in a passionate embrace and starts plastering her with kisses.

"Friah, get yer cookin' pots out. An' call up the other lasses with everythin' we've got. We'll be eatin' hearty tonight!"

"Belrum!" shouts another male dwarf. "What in all the blazes be the matter with ye! Ye're actin' like ye saw the Soul Forger himself!"

"Aye, an' even if He had come t' me dyin' bed, I think it would nay be as grand as what just now came up out on the barrens. Lads, I found me some new friends. They bring tales of the sort ye'll be a-tellin' yer grandchildren about for as many generations as ye can count! But for as much as ye'll want t' hear the tellin', ye'll also want t' be a-chowin' on a good meal, I'll wager. Har har!"

The room glances around at each other as they try to interpret his rambling.

"Aye lads," the other dwarf admits satirically. "Our dear Belrum finally lost the last of it. We all knew it be a-comin'."

The room rises up in a moment of laughter at the overexcited dwarf's rant.

"Aye, ye all go an' laugh if ye wish," Belrum charges teasingly. "Make it a good one! But we'll see who has the last of it when I bring them inside."

"Hey now, Belrum," the other dwarf retorts more seriously. "Just what d' ye mean by that?"

"Galmir, ye may laugh at me if ye wish, an' call me an' old grizzle-beard, but I tell ye true, I found better than any old thin straw out there. New folk have come in t' the valley, an' they be a-lookin' for folk like us who nay but barely be a-survivin' 'round here. An' best of all, they bring food, great loads of it, more than ye can blink at with both eyes."

"New folk? From where? Nay here in the valley…"

"Ye're right, an' they be a-waitin' just outside for me t' break it t' ye so ye don'na go climbin' the walls when ye see them, because they nay be dwarves. An' they told me a grand waggle of a tale that I need t' share with ye, an' ye'll ne'er believe it…" his voice echoes as he makes his way back out of the mine.

He hurries outside and waves the team to come in. They each pick up either a box or a bag, and start marching through the tunnel.

The dwarves inside felt a chill when Belrum rushed out of the room, and it deepened as they heard the sound of many footsteps coming back in. One by one, they watched with stirring anxiety, as a troupe of strange unnaturally tall men come waltzing into the room carrying supplies, only to return outside for more, and repeating several times over.

"Belrum," whispers Galmir as he catches the man on the arm. "What in the name of the All-Father be this here now?"

"Galmir, I'll tell ye everythin', but it be a big one, an' me head be a-poundin' from it. So go easy. All the pummelin' outside, the land blasted t' the All-father, that mine we found up there, an' more after that. There be a grand tale behind it, one we were ne'er given t' know about. But these folks are at war, an' the ones who did this be the ones they be at war with."

"A war?!" he gushes under his breath. "But, where d' they come from, if they nay be dwarves?"

"They come from another world completely. Think back t' the point-ears for a moment, an' another one where we had orcs comin' at us. These were both tests, an' the pummelin' be the end of it. A mighty folk found us an' made trouble here. Then they went an' made more of it on another world, an' this brought these people up."

"But why?"

"There be foes on our land takin' up our Adamant, an' they only wanted smiths an' miners t' d' the work, nay farmers."

Galmir slapped his hands to his temple and let out a screech.

"Aye, me friend," Belrum pats him on the shoulder. "I nay be the better for it. This war ran us down like a beggar in the street for the favor of our Adamant. These folks found us sittin' here in a bad way, so they came offerin' t' help in what way they can."

Galmir and the others stared in awe as the procession of goods began to fill up one full corner of the room. Several of the dwarves began pulling chairs and tables out of the way to make more space available.

"All this?" Galmir wheezes.

"These people are a rich folk, an' they don'na mind spendin' it on helpin' others. But Galmir, we need t' show up our best manners an' give a wee bit back for all this."

"How?"

"We need t' call up the other clans, tell them we have help waitin', an' tell them t' come an' share this with us. These be our new friends, an' they promise t' help as many as they can. So bring out the plates an' say yer prayers t' the All-Father that this may be the day of our salvation."

As the last of the crates were brought in and set down, the lead scout came up to give a small presentation.

"Good friend dwarves," he announces. "We wish to offer you this gift as a token of our friendship. This man here," he gestures at Belrum, "was kind enough to accept this on your behalf, and we give this without demand, only to ask a small favor. I am sure he has been telling you a little about our visit outside, but there is a war occurring, not so much on this world, but elsewhere. However, we believe there are enemies somewhere in hiding here, and we need to find them, but quietly to make a surprise hit. Our greater enemies cannot know we are here, or else it could spoil many of our plans."

"What greater enemies are these?" Galmir asks.

"Belrum has our story, so I should not occupy too much of your time away from your meal. But we believe you may have seen some of them taking the results of a mining operation further to the east. However, the greater enemy is one called Darumon, and he controls the rest. We have a camp to the north in a line of hills where Belrum was visiting today to pull up his grass. This became our meeting point. If any of you should have any emergencies, you should come to us for help, but otherwise keep things quiet until we can make our move."

"But who be ye? Ye're nay a dwarf, nay like any I ever did hear about. Where d' ye come from?"

"My people are called Human, and we come from a world called Tae'Eladar. We have several races of people living in that world, including some dwarves like you. We live and work in peace, and we brought our world together under the rule of a King who teaches us our finer values. But again, this can probably wait until later. Belrum and his tale will surely occupy you for this day. Perhaps we can talk more at a later time, once your bellies are full and your nerves are settled a bit," he smiles and turns to leave.

"Nerves are settled?" he chuckles softly. "Aye t' that! But I'll yay be offerin' me thanks t' ye, even for this much."

The scout signals to the others to exit the mine. They file out into the open where one of them pulls out his rune to provide transport back to camp. A couple of the dwarves find themselves drawn by their curiosity to follow behind at a distance to watch them leave. When they peered outside, they observed the flashing of the portal energies, and the team was gone.

◆◆◆

"Over there, men. Maybe that's it."

The scout leader directs the group's attention to a distinctly artificial feature in the side of the mountain they were approaching. It was elevated somewhat from the valley floor with the remnants of a dirt road leading away.

"Aye, I might say we found it," confirms another. "I can't think of what these dwarves might be doing cutting out such a big hole in the side of a mountain like that."

"Nor in such a perfect box shape. This looks just like the one on Therinë."

They worked their way along the base of the foothills until they came to the road, then crept along the slope until they came within easy view of a large rectangular clearing cut into the hillside, just in front of a mine entrance.

"All right, the drill here is to scout the entrance, and slowly test the environment inside. The landing site is clear, but we don't know the last time the Suuden-Aryku came, or how long till the next time. If these dwarves are under the same effect as before, and the story from Belrum leads us to believe so, we should be able to just run through and inspect the place without interference."

"Right then, so we check for their supply, tally up a rough estimate, check their farming to see if it matches, basically compare to what was found in that other one on Therinë."

"Correct. But keep in mind, this is still unknown, even though we might expect these conditions, we need to play it safe anyway. We'll check the front, maybe a few tunnels in, and if it looks good, we make our inspection. Let's refresh our chants to give us a full charge."

The team begins collectively casting a set of enchantments to boost strength and stamina. This process had become a routine during their runs as a way to compensate for the burdensome gravity and atmosphere. When they finished, the lead scout spoke up again.

"Good, now check your potions. Make sure you have haste and cloaking vials on the ready, just in case."

The men check a set of slots on their belts to ensure they had at least one of each potion handy.

"All right," he points to the nearest man. "Let's have you go up there first. Go dark and go silent. Make your run quick and send back smartly."

The man nods at the coded instruction, and begins casting a magical cloak while the others duck out of the way and watch the surrounding area, both land and sky, for anything that might be moving around.

They waited patiently for several moments. Nothing is moving out there. The region here was as dead as most of the others they'd seen. As they followed the line of mountains with their eyes, it extended out of view to the north. Somewhere up there was another team hopefully closing in on the far end of these plains to another group of mountains said to be where they would find the city of Glimmerheim.

The scout sent to inspect the mine entrance reappeared near the group, dispelling his cloak on his arrival.

"What do we have up there?" asks the scout leader.

"The entrance is clear, and I can hear sounds of work inside, but my guess is much deeper."

"Any dwarves in the near area?"

"Nothing up front…"

"Good, let's move up there. We'll go in under a cloak and stay that way till we see movement. Only after seeing how these dwarves appear will we decide how to move around otherwise."

The team moves up onto the platform, which looked the same as the one on Therinë, where the rock had been cut away as a large box shape, suitable for a Suuden'kai air transport to land in. As they approached the mine entrance, they cast cloaks on themselves before entering.

The tunnels extended inside and downward by some distance. Side tunnels branched off, and a railway system had been laid down. They tried to follow the sounds of activity, but the echoes made it hard, until they eventually came to a large room filled with tables. They entered the room from one corner. On the opposite side, midway along the wall, they saw a passage leading off into another tunnel, with two more tunnels leading off from the far end of the room on different walls. The room appeared to be empty at the moment.

The scouts, being specially trained and enchanted as part of their conditioning by the Order, were able to detect each other even under the cloak. The leader brings the group into the room, and they split up into the different tunnels, with the leader staying in the central location as a hub.

The first one to return came out of the side tunnel midway on the opposite wall. Within his cloak, he was able to make a set of hand gestures visible to the leader of what he found. The message was that of a kitchen and another side room leading into a sleep chamber. The tunnel further extended into a large cavern with farm animals and a strange masonry wall at one end. He also mentioned a set of workers in the kitchen preparing food into a stew, made from meat and some kind of mushroom.

Several moments later, another set of scouts return with messages of miners working a smelter deep in one of the tunnels at the far end. They appeared singularly focused on their work, and there did not seem to be any form of communication between them.

The scout leader had heard all he needed. He dismissed his cloak and gestured for the others to do the same.

"All right, men, let's get to work," he orders. "The Captain wants an estimate of their storage supply of ingots. And I'll take a close look at that kitchen and the wall, to see if it's another of those farms."

"Will we be going inside that farm?" another scout asks. "I heard a few things about that last one."

"No, I think a brief peek through the window is good for now, assuming the door has one. Just enough to confirm it's the same. Once we have this information, we'll report back. We also need to make a rune outside for a later return. I'm sure we'll be coming back here often to check on things."

They break in different directions to attend to their work. This would be the start of a lengthy operation.

It was midmorning in Rolsklinde when Thaelyn was making his arrival after a morning inspection of the guildhall back home. He had received notice that Marelle was interested in making a meeting with him for some manner of consultation concerning her flight training. Today was a weekend for her on Tae'Eladar, so she had the day off from her studies and wanted to make good use of it.

As Thaelyn enters the WIC building, he is greeted by Marelle, Chief Technician Lapäli and Professor Cogswoggle in the forward lobby.

"My Lord, how have you been lately?" Marelle calls out to him.

"I do well, thank you. I must admit, I have missed hearing your cheerful voice since you became so entrenched in your studies."

"Yeah, they keep us busy over there, that much is for sure."

"So, what is it you have in mind for me today, young lady? Are you attempting any new scandals? I see you have some new accomplices."

"Always!" she chirps. "But on this occasion, I have some things to go over with you about my training."

"Training… This was concerning your flight training, correct?"

"That's right. I have some issues with how things are going, and I want to see if we can improve it."

"Improving a technique is always favorable. Let us step inside the conference room and see what you have."

He leads them down the hall to a pleasantly decorated room with a large table and many chairs around it. They each take up seating and Marelle pulls out her notes from earlier in the week when she had her discussion with Relissa and Haran in the guildhall courtyard. She clears her throat and prepares to make her presentation.

"First, I'd like to thank the Chief and the Professor for taking time away from their busy work to listen to my girlish rants," she giggles.

"I like listening to girlish rants," the Professor declares jovially. "Unfortunately, the lovely Tanjhira here doesn't do as much, no matter how many times I beg her for it."

"Professor," Tanjhira grins. "If you keep this up, my husband might have a few things to say about it, and I'm worried that you may become much shorter afterwards."

"Is there something I should be made aware of between you two?" Thaelyn inquires.

"Oh, just a little friendly office talk, Your Lordship. He keeps flirting with me, even though he knows I'm married."

"Oh, that… Yes, gnomes are known to do that…often. It is a part of their charm."

"He does have that, I will admit."

The Professor lets out a very animated giggle in his chair at the Chief Technician's mention.

"I'm trying to imagine a Daanen'kai and a gnome," Marelle ponders. "The image is both amusing, and disturbing at the same time," she chuckles. "Anyway, here's the problem. With all due respect to the Daanen-Aryku and all they've done to help me learn to fly, if they think they know anything about air combat, I think they missed the target."

Tanjhira lets out a laugh before commenting.

"Well, Marelle, I will admit, and I'm sure it's been said before, we're not made for strong wartime encounters, but we're doing the best we can. So, what is it about our design you're having trouble with?"

"The flight controls, mostly. The worst of it is how I'm supposed to fly and cast magic at the same time, since the weapons are based on a mage channeling their energies through the aircraft itself."

"We had several design concepts drawn up once. Did you review any of them?"

"I looked over a few when I was speaking to my instructor once, but they all look the same to me, and don't really tickle my fancy the right way. I'm basically a mage now, soon to be going into the Sixth Circle of study, so I think I can speak well enough on what I need to make that part work. Having one hand on a flight stick and the other on a throttle isn't doing it, because on some of those designs, they have me using an alternate device or control to cast the magic, which essentially takes my hands off other critical controls. Moving my hands from one place to another while zipping across the sky at high speed, chasing bad guys, or maybe having them chase me…I don't think that's a good idea."

"I would tend to agree on that, Marelle," Thaelyn notes. "Did you have any alternate ideas on this?"

"A few things went through my mind in those first days when I was trying to figure out how to make it better, but in the end, it just didn't seem like the best choice. Then I had a pleasant little chat with Relissa and Haran, and together we came up with something new, and I think I like it, if only we can figure out how to make it work."

"One moment here," Thaelyn hesitates. "You had a discussion on how to redesign the highly complex control architectures for operating an advanced, and so far, experimental aircraft, using technology that is still largely in development by people of different races, different backgrounds, and different technological skills, with a ranger and a mid-classman mage who know virtually nothing about flying?"

"Well, my Lord, you know me." she responds coyly. "I figured if Relissa can talk to squirrels, and Haran can light candlesticks, they ought to have a few interesting ways of looking at things."

"Oh, Powers help us," he covers his eyes. "I think I will keep my feet firmly on the ground. Very well, and what did you finally come out with? This should prove to be rather interesting to hear."

"First, let's go over what I have now, and then what I have in mind. My right hand is on the flight stick, my left hand is on the throttle, and mostly it stays that way. I saw some designs that use buttons or switches on one or the other of these to operate additional features, but these controls, as they are now, won't channel my energies."

"Very well, this would obviously need to change."

"Next is the flux cushion. This is a touch-sensitive slider on the forward console. It's mostly used to provide lift when taking off, and remove it when landing. My problem here is I'm using it for more than just that lately when I do some of my stunts up there."

"Stunts… Have you actually been in a real aircraft yet, or is this still on the simulator?"

"Simulator, but the real one isn't too far away, and I want to get this right before I do that."

"I should think so! What manner of stunts do you mean?"

"Fast maneuvering, diving, climbing, flying low to the ground, lots of crazy stuff. My instructor tells me he's going to lose the curl in his horns because of me."

Tanjhira explodes with laughter, drawing the attention of the room for a moment. The gesture spreads to the others.

"Well, Marelle," Thaelyn admits with a smile. "If you want my opinion on these antics, I must actually concur with you on this. Although I do not personally come from a society that engages in this practice, I know that combat piloting does often involve these tactics, especially during such a sequence some call dogfighting, where you and others are chasing about up there."

"That's exactly what I thought! I've been spending a lot of time trying to think up ideas of how people do this, and it just seems like this would happen anytime you get into it. So, these controls would need to change, even without the magic stuff getting involved."

"Allow me to explore this with you a moment. When you mention even without magic, how would you change it?"

"That flux field control in front of me. I'm working it quite often when I make some of these dives and such, using it like a cushion to keep me from hitting the ground before pulling up again. Moving my hand from the throttle to the slider and back again isn't wise, in my opinion."

"No, I think not. It should be more convenient to your hand."

"This is what Haran said, like on the side for a finger or my thumb."

"Interesting. But he is a clever fellow, and this would certainly be more intuitive for the application. Anything else?"

"Not as far as this goes, unless you get into the magic part..."

"Very well then, let us move on to that. How do you envision this?"

"I remember you said once that even crazy ideas can sometimes lead to better ones, right?"

"I have been known to say that, and it is often correct. And I would expect no less out of you, young lady, so let us hear this idea of yours."

"Relissa helped a little bit at this moment, plus Haran contributed his part, so I want to give them some of the credit, or the blame, whichever comes first," she grins. "When I was explaining how I need to channel magic, Haran described some of the other devices he's seen in your museums and such. For instance, the materials used. Then Relissa remembered those globe things she was playing with during one of her lessons."

"Globe things... Reflection globes, perhaps? Yes, they can conjure up an illusionary image of the user and send it out onto the field as a false front, even to move around on command."

"Those were made of some kind of crystal, if I understand it, and these crystals can channel arcanic energy."

"Certain ones can, and our people have studied them at length."

"Can they transfer this along some kind of conduit, like to the guns outside?"

"If it is designed appropriately..." he nods. "We use conduits like this in such apparatus as our portal gates, and even the Dynamistic Spires."

"Good, so if we could use something like a globe or maybe just the top half of it..."

She pulls out her notepad where she had been drawing her examples and shows it to the group.

"If I had one on each side, the right hand could slide over that one to govern my direction, like the flight stick does, while the left one moves forward and back, like the throttle. And here, you see where I put that little monster of a flux slider," she points to her diagram.

Tanjhira and the Professor lean in to study the image as she explained it.

"Now, the real question is," Marelle continues. "Can this actually work, or something similar to it? The controls are both in my hands, the crystal can also channel my energy, I'm not moving my hands all over the place, and...oh, I need something like a strap or harness, according to Haran, to keep my hands from leaving the controls in case my maneuvering throws me off."

"A good point," Thaelyn observes, "as you are not actually gripping something here to aid in holding you steady."

"The first thing I see is this..." the Professor comments. "If you're so busy sliding your hands to govern the aircraft's motion, that constitutes an application of your focus right there, if we say you are applying a mage focus as your flight control. Then if you wish to channel to the weapons, you need to refocus yourself, breaking from the flight operation."

"Oops, alright, one problem," Marelle concedes.

"One moment, maybe this can be resolved easily," Tanjhira mentions. "We need dual operation of these controls. You need continuous access to the flight dynamics, but at the same time access to these conduits to channel your power. If we lay a touch-sensitive membrane on top which does not interfere with you channeling your energy, you could keep moving your hands around even as you channel."

"Hey, I like that."

"The only thing we might need to consider at that moment is how to monitor where your hand is on the surface. The flight stick has a spring-loaded center to it, and you feel where you are by the tension on this load within your hand."

"Right, but if this surface is curved, wouldn't that tell me something?"

"A curved surface might give some indication, but then I have to ask about how your hand is laying on it. If you are laying your full hand on this, you might have your fingers as well as your palm resting on it at the same time, and this can cause a problem, as you have multiple contact points delivering multiple inputs to the control."

"What if I only use my fingers?"

"Lifting your hand, say at the wrist, and only setting your fingers on it would cause excessive tension on the tendons within your wrist, which could then cramp up."

"Uh oh, not good…"

"This touch-sensitive panel of yours," Thaelyn offers. "Is it pressure-sensitive or conductive?"

"We could use either of those here. Do you have a preference?"

"Pressure-sensitive would certainly be a problem, but if it were conductive, and then if she were to wear a glove of some kind, where only the fingertips were revealed, or overlaid with some material to use as an interface, we might be able to overcome this."

"An interface… Wait. What if we make it flat? We don't need the curve in this case. She wears a special set of gloves we call virtual gloves. The surface layer of the control becomes holographic, now a separate unit at her fingertips. Her palm can rest on a ball, which becomes her channeling orb, while her finger runs the matrix of the field for the directional control. But hold on, we need to make this convenient for her to reach, and…"

Tanjhira closes her eyes to envision this in her mind, unconsciously waving a finger in the air as she draws her mental picture.

"…It would have to be angled up slightly, possibly also adjustable for better ergonomic comfort."

"Ergo-what-ic?" Marelle asks.

"That means to make it more convenient to your hand without causing any of that tension I mentioned earlier. It's a design layout that fits the body better."

"That sounds like a better solution to me," the Professor agrees. "She's not spending her mage focus on directing the craft, and much like if she was standing and casting a spell, she could orient herself while still channeling through the orb."

"So, you mean we could actually do this?" Marelle marvels. "Wow, won't the people back home be surprised!"

"Next is the throttle," Tanjhira continues. "It's simpler in design, but we could probably do something similar with that. There's just one thing that comes to mind now that I think of it."

"And what might that be?" Thaelyn wonders.

"Well, I'm still concerned about her finding the right positioning in this case, but I think I might be able to find a solution to it if we use some ridged gradation markings on the surface for tactile feedback on where her fingers are."

"Whatever that means…" Marelle winces.

"Either that, or we could put a monitor in the HUD for both controls, maybe even a combination of the two."

"And what about that flux slider in this case?"

"I would actually question that for a moment," Thaelyn considers. "I might have to agree with Marelle that this particular control seems like an additional step for something we could otherwise do without if we are clever. Even under these conditions here, she still needs to divert some small amount of attention to something that I might consider to be debilitating in a combat craft."

"All right, Your Lordship," Tanjhira concedes. "But our technological designs are mostly based on creating a repulsion effect using a magneto-graviton drive system."

"Gah!" Marelle cringes. "There's that word again! If you can call it that…"

"In this case," Thaelyn reflects. "I suppose I must assume that these drive systems are primarily intended to operate within a planetary gravity well, especially as you traditionally use them only for scouting or cargo transport."

"Yes, actually you're right, although it can also go into a limited low orbit on occasion."

"Limited might be fine for a utility vessel, but combat is another thing, especially as we are dealing with such as the Suuden-Aryku, and who knows what they might have available. I think we should up the ante in our case."

"Then this system wouldn't necessarily work for us, so what else do you have in mind?"

"A well-practiced combat pilot, and for that matter even Marelle, if she could tame a few of her wilder ambitions," he winks at her, "ought not to fly at supreme velocities directly into a mountain. What other sorts of technologies can you provide for flight?"

"Well, I suppose we could fall back to some manner of jet propulsion, but that limits us to an atmosphere, unless we use a rocket. There's also an ion stream, but those tend to be slow to react."

"And these might also require fuel which we do not have readily available, or if we are in hostile territory and it becomes difficult or impossible to supply. This actually brings me to a difficult paradox that has been on my mind of late, and that is how to supply ourselves with the flows while in such a place as Azgarén."

"Oh wonderful," Marelle yips. "Now you tell us! I can't cast my magic in that place, can I?"

"Not unless you bring some manner of charge with you, but that charge might also be limited in capacity. The only other solution is to generate it."

"Is there a way to artificially generate it? I know how it's made naturally."

"I think the best way is truly the natural one in this case, as it tends to be the byproduct of the arcanids from the Fourth Fold, at least for those of us here. Unless you can learn to excrete it yourself," he grins.

"Ew! And I thought it sounded bad before. All right, but then what? We need to solve this, for just about everything we're planning on doing over there."

"I know. I have been delaying this as I ponder our options, but the need is becoming more pressing as we move forward, and we need the final answer. The trouble is I may need to ask permission for it."

"Permission? You need to ask permission for something?"

"In this case, yes, as the technology I am thinking of is a part of my teachings from my Father. In his absence, I will need to ask Torm to grant this, and I think we have a good enough argument for it when you consider the danger of Sargeras."

"Whoa!" she screeches, throwing her hands up. "This is one of THEIR technologies?"

"Technically, it could count as an early Celestial technology, but it is certainly higher than anything we should have in our present state. If I can gain this from them, we can create something we call a harvester coil, and then draw from it."

"That sounds interesting, but is this to say they'll teach us how to do it, or give us something ready-made?"

"Like with all things, I suspect this will account as a learning experience. Therefore, I think, with a little inspiration, the Daanen-Aryku might be able to build part of it, while we invoke the other part."

"Well, if you say so. Then what? How do we use it?"

"As with any other energy supply, we install it and tie in the various components to draw the power. We could use it as a field generator for area coverage, so our mages could operate without any additional burden, and also possibly apply it in the armor suits like what Kaliya is using, if we can make it compact enough for the proportions."

"So, we have aircraft, plus an army of mages, and other such people, moving around a world like Azgarén, operating in a manner such that the Suuden-Aryku can't even understand. Ooh, suddenly I like it. But good luck in getting it."

"Now, with this in mind, allow me to offer a thought for consideration."

"Uh oh," Marelle mumbles cautiously. "Here go his thoughts."

"We use our gryphons for travel on occasion, and we envelop them in what we call a transport sphere. This acts as a shell, enveloping them and permitting them to travel at highly accelerated velocities."

"Oh dear cu'Nar, Your Lordship," Tanjhira exclaims and grabs her horns. "Is that how it works? I've heard of this supersonic transport thing, but Grace of the cu'Nar, you just described something that resembles our nether-space inversion drive. That's what the Naarg uy'Sodrad uses…or rather used to use when it was still present. It's a common feature on all our interstellar vessels."

"Indeed, although in your case I believe it was likely subverting your ship into a massless pocket relative to real space, whereas ours is more like a projected field around the physical body. Nevertheless, you are right. Ours could be described as a junior version of it, and with a little creativity, perhaps it could be modified."

"You would put a nether-space inverter into a single-pilot combat craft?" she shrieks.

"By the Mind of Gond," the Professor muses. "That would be a surprising one."

"I must consider where we are going and what waits for us," Thaelyn admits. "As well as how we might present ourselves along the way. There are many variables to ponder at this moment, not the least of which is to confuse and confound our opponents."

"Yeah, you'll confound them alright," Tanjhira chuckles ironically. "And most of us as well!"

"It would be prudent to keep our identity hidden as best we can. We do not want them to know who we are or where we come from. We must represent ourselves as an enigma for as long as possible, at least until such time as we can make whatever final move is necessary to bring this into our favor. And since I cannot be sure, at this time, what that final move is, I will aim for overkill."

"Overkill! Yes!" Tanjhira blasts and raises her hands. "Cu'Nar forgive us if we should ever disappoint."

"Ooh!" the Professor squeals. "A girlish rant, I'm so happy. Thank you, my Lord."

"Anything to please, Professor," he smiles.

"Gods above," Marelle wheezes. "And to think, I thought I had it bad."

"You're going to make me pull out my horns before long," Tanjhira shakes her head.

They all share a laugh together before continuing.

"I think this is all within reason, thus far," Thaelyn affirms. "If we can do it with our gryphons, we can surely do this with a combat craft. Furthermore, our gryphons can use a portal rune to recall back to base, or any other location for that matter. I want the same in each of these craft. When we send them in, they will strike and depart to places unknowable before our enemies can gauge who their attackers are."

"This sounds just like what you were worried about with the orcs," Marelle suggests. "If they had portal magic, they could make these same kinds of runs at us."

"Precisely, and now we will turn this in our favor. If they have such a potent space navy, I do not wish that navy to gain any advantage."

"Using a portal rune," the Professor notes. "If we consider the example of the gryphons, this should be a fairly easy conversion, I think. Especially if we envelop the ship in an arcanic field from this generator of yours. But this limits us to one location, unless you want something addressable, like what the Naarg uy'Sodrad once had."

"That would be desirable, of course, certainly in the longer term. Let us first see about converting the technology, and then see where it takes us. But this leads us to the next issue: From where will we strike."

"Your Lordship," Tanjhira admits. "At this point, it could be literally anywhere you choose, including from space. You've got inversion drives, which are inherently unrestricted for use in space travel, and a jump drive, to come and go from anywhere."

"This is painting a very dangerous picture," Marelle winces. "And to think, all I was asking for were more convenient flight controls."

"Indeed," Thaelyn relents. "But you did bring up some important questions, and as you said, crazy ideas can often lead to better ones, and perhaps even a few that were not considered before. As for where to arrive using these little wonders, this is a puzzle with a very difficult answer. We must find a way to Azgarén, and so far, all we can speculate on is the possibility of using one of their own conveyors. This, in itself, may be a problem as I would expect it to arrive in a populated zone, and likely a military base."

"That would be a bad thing."

"Yes. Therefore, we need to plan our moves carefully to evade into a quieter region."

"Where do you suggest we'll be going, in this case? Out in the woods? Do they have woods over there?"

"I would tend to say they ought to, and we will need to establish some manner of base. Our aim is Darumon and Sargeras, and it is not as likely to see them flying combat craft. And so, it should be at ground level, likely hidden, perhaps even below ground for this point, or carefully camouflaged. We will borrow from Darumon and his games, and turn this against him."

"Dear gods, so you're going to distract him with false attackers while setting us down in his backyard?"

"Indeed, this is actually a clever idea, Marelle," he nods. "And with our new craft, we could possibly do exactly that. If we create a ruse of unknown and perhaps very strange pursuers, arriving and departing using this jump drive, they should not be able to track us.

This leaves us with how we make our assault, and therefore another aspect of this redesign.”

“Uh huh…” Tanjhira sighs gingerly. “And what else would you have me put into this beast, Your Lordship? So far, it’s grown well beyond a simple fighter craft.”

“We must consider our weapons. Keeping in mind, we want to cause as little actual loss of life as we can, therefore we need to use weapons that are not as outwardly destructive.”

“Like stunning weapons?”

“A true stun weapon, launched from a strike craft, might be impractical, as we would need ground persons to collect those who are stunned. So far, we only wish to disable their capacity. Aerlie and I once created a form of magic attack during our war here on the suspicion that the Suuden-Aryku might try launching in our direction using their own form of assault craft.”

“Oh, yes! I remember that. It was a sort of EMP weapon. It projected a powerful electromagnetic pulse to disrupt the electronics and power systems of the target. That sort of weapon shouldn’t be a problem for us, especially if you can provide your example. One of those could take down a ship, probably a much larger one than ours, as well as ground targets, and who knows what else, but leave the people mostly unharmed, unless they’re standing right next to a high-voltage conduit.”

“What do we do with the other weapons, my Lord?” the Professor asks. “Will we be discarding them in favor of these new ones?”

“I think we should create a dual mode operation of some sort,” he muses. “We may still need to contend with hostiles, either in the air or on the ground, so we should be prepared.”

“What Circle of magic do I need for all this?” Marelle shudders. “I remember a mention once that this thing of yours was an elite spell.”

“This is true, but with a little refinement, and the combination of the technological approach, you might be able to do it in a lower Circle. I will need to study this and let you know. However, it is still a potent spell, and might just require a higher range than your previous goal.”

"Wonderful, another year or more… My Lord, I should mention something that's been on my mind when you talk about going longer in my studies."

"And that is?"

"I'm thirty-six right now, would be thirty-seven by the end of my existing studies, and Roddy and I have been talking a few times about a family. You do realize what that means at my age as a human, right? And then to go more on top of that…"

"Yes, of course, and I would not wish to deny you this pleasure. Let us examine this and see where it takes us, and we can go from there. I should think this new research and development will take some time yet. If we can remove at least some of our most imposing threats, such as Darumon's weapon, it could possibly buy back some time."

"And give me a break long enough to do this?"

"We shall see what we can accomplish. I will recruit Aerlie's aid, along with some of our mage Elders, and see what will be required for it. Perhaps we might have an answer before this year is out, and allow you a period of time to attend to this. If so, we could give you this next year as a break in your studies."

"The whole year? It doesn't take THAT long to do this," she smirks. "I just need a nice quiet moment…and then nine months later, you know."

"True, but we tend to err on the side of caution where pregnancy is concerned, especially if the woman is enrolled in classes and imbibing the elixir along the way. Although we suspect it would not have any serious harmful effect on the unborn, we prefer not to take the chance of any anomalies."

"Oh, that…hmm… All right, if you say so… Then what will I do in the meantime?"

"For the immediate term, I might suggest you and your beau take the appropriate nuptials and confer with Aerlie on various routines and practices that could ensure a successful conception."

"You mean there's special ways of doing this? I thought you just jumped into bed and boom; it happens."

"Not in all cases. Sometimes it is a matter of timing within the female's monthly cycle. There are certain moments where you will be more likely to conceive than others."

"Really! This goes a little beyond what my mom told me. All right, anything else…Dad?"

"Well," Thaelyn chuckles. "I might further ask Aerlie to offer her support to ensure a healthy child. A blessing by Lathander would do nicely. He holds dominion over life, birth, renewal, and similar qualities. Many people go to him for a blessing of this sort."

"That sounds wonderful, and I really want this to work. Thanks a lot."

✦✦✦✦✦✦✦

"That's just plain nasty," remarks one scout.

"Aye, it looks worse than Rolsklinde after they finished with it," comments another one.

"Look at that landslide," muses a third scout. "It looks like someone blasted out the side of the mountain and it all fell right in the middle."

"And I'll bet if there were any doors leading in, they're right beneath that hillside."

"Even if they wanted to get out, it wouldn't be easy. It'd take months to dig your way through all that."

The team of scouts sent north through the plains had finally reached the outskirts of the ruined city of Glimmerheim. The outer city, once a glorious display of elaborate architecture, avenues, memorials, parkways, and other attractions, was now a picture of apocalyptic devastation.

Many of the larger buildings had been reduced to blast craters surrounded by rubble sprayed across the streets. Plazas and parks were pitted and scarred. The roads were fractured and upturned. No part of any building was left standing. But unlike in Rolsklinde, where the attack by the rogue army of dwarves under the influence of the Suuden-Aryku leveled the city to heaps of debris, this debris was scattered thoroughly. The source appeared to have come from above, like in so many other cases of bombardment they've seen.

Finally, to the rear of the ruins was a massive mound of dirt and rock that had clearly been carved from the side of the mountain above.

"Just one question on my mind, though," infers one of the scouts. "Why isn't it just a bloody big hole in the ground, like all the rest?"

"Maybe it has to do with the shockwaves that might echo underneath," the scout leader suggests. "Like with an earthquake, hit it hard enough and it might collapse the underground portion that's supposed to be inside that mountain."

"I can't imagine how it might have survived even with this much."

"Well, now that we're here, we need to get to work. We need to find a way in. If those Suuden-Aryku are pulling dwarves out, there must be a door, a secret tunnel, or something else around here."

"Not likely you'll find it down on this side, not with that pile-up of rock sitting there."

"Maybe. But at this moment, we may need to search every crevice we can reach into."

"His Lordship once suggested the Suuden-Aryku would make a base nearby for convenience, but I don't see anything down here, so I'm thinking up in the mountains, maybe behind it."

"That's a good thought. But for that, we'll need climbing gear."

"Aye," replies the second scout. "But that's a bloody big mountain to be climbing in this heat."

"And it's not just the heat," the third scout remarks. "We also have this gravity. Bloody beastly, that..."

"Well, lads," the scout leader affirms. "It looks like we've got some work ahead! Better call up some gear for it. Let's mark a rune and send for help. This will take a while."

✦ ✦ ✦ ✦ ✦

"General, do we have anything of particular import today?"

Thaelyn was making his arrival in the WIC building. It was the next day after Marelle's visit with her flight control revamp.

On Tae'Eladar it was still the weekend, but he was expecting an important delivery the previous night, so he was taking time from his personal leisure break to follow up on it.

"Yes, my Lord. This came in, just as we were hoping. Our scouts found what we believe to be the remains of the city of Glimmerheim, at least on the outside."

Thaelyn stood at the strategy table where stacks of various papers had been piled up from previous reports. The General presented him with a new bundle as he gave his review.

"Here is the report of what they found," he explains. "Along with several photographs, as you requested. The city is a wreck, to say the least, and a large portion of the mountain behind it has apparently been shorn away and laid on top of what was left."

Thaelyn examined the photos, shaking his head at the magnitude of the damage.

"I wonder how many people once lived there. This would certainly reinforce the idea to stay inside the mountain, and further obstruct anyone from their curiosity to peek outside. But this does not entirely resemble the same appearance as the others."

"The report here speculates it might have used a lighter form of attack than the others, if only to prevent any large-scale shockwaves reverberating through the ground."

"Ah, but of course, and therefore causing collateral damage within their underground chamber. Very clever of them. But then I must wonder how deep they truly are inside there. The collapse of this mountainside would surely have caused some damage to the nearer portions. What about access?"

"They called for climbing gear, and we now have the larger portion of the team searching the site. But considering the area to cover, they expect it to take some time."

"And made worse by scaling a mountain under those conditions they must suffer. Very well then, may the Powers give them strength. We will wait, it is all we can do."

Outside in the plaza, business was plentiful, as travelers passed in and out of the city gateway hub. They moved through the streets and browsed the local marketplaces. All the races were represented, including several Daanen-Aryku who were in town visiting some of the local entertainment and shopping venues.

It was a typically active day, at least until a visibly disturbed man in an ornate robe stormed out of the hub building followed by five young Daanen'kai, including a male and four females.

They hurried their way across to the WIC building, passing through the lobby and eventually into the strategy room where Thaelyn and his officers were attending to their review.

"My Lord!" the man shouts into the room. "I am dumbfounded!"

"Master Sagrid, what is it?"

"These people behind me here, look at them!" he urges as they strut forward to the table.

Thaelyn and the General both place their focus on the recent applicants to the guildhall administration counter. Kailen was sitting at his table, but rose up at the commotion and made his way to meet them. Petrith, Sulíma, Túfula, and Tana were all arriving, led by Kaliya as their escort, and all wearing violet Spirit Test badges on their lapels.

"Powers be blessed," Thaelyn intones as he studies the visitors. "Master Sagrid, are you sure about this?"

"My Lord, at this moment, I can't even be sure if I am awake or dreaming. Young Kaliya here escorted these others into the office this morning to assist in their applications. The first two," he gestures at Petrith and Sulíma, "informed me they wanted to take the test. This other one," he directs at Túfula, "apparently came along for the ride, and this final one…with the, um, rather scant apparel…" he smiles gently.

"Yes, we met earlier," Thaelyn grins. "Young Miss Lar'akan, our newest druid hopeful."

"Anyway, she got involved after we started seeing the other results."

"But their badges… All of them?"

"We ran it through once, but neither I nor the Adept could believe what we were looking at! So we ran a test on each other to verify the chair was working properly, and then tried it again. I don't know what else to do in this case."

"Your Lordship," Kailen asks imperatively. "What does this mean? They're all violet! I thought you once said that's supposed to be generally unavailable for mortal bodies."

"Indeed," he considers. "At least for those amongst the people of Tae'Eladar, but then, if Kaliya got it, hmm…"

"Maybe I'm not so special after all?" Kaliya mentions.

"Oh, I think you are indeed special, but then so may be the rest. Let me think. There must be a reasonable explanation for it."

He studies the group of applicants for a moment, contemplating the many discussions he shared with Kailen and the others in recent times.

"Kaliya, come down here a moment," he waves for her to bend down within easy reach.

Thaelyn places a hand on her temple to scan her spiritual energies. He peers deep within to gauge what he sees, and then pulls back.

"All right, let me compare this to these others. Mister Girhani, if you would indulge me."

Petrith approaches and bends down while Thaelyn repeats the process.

"Good, now let us try one more," Thaelyn submits. "Three is usually a good number to gain our bearings. Miss Tad'vaal, if your quirky manners would permit me."

"Does it involve soap?" she smirks, and then complies.

Thaelyn grins at the suggestion and conducts one more scan.

"My Lord?" the General inquires softly. "Do you see anything?"

"I do. Just like with Kaliya, their minds are all quite potent. But in addition, I can also sense a strong positive flow of energy coursing through them. In fact, it almost feels superimposed on their native essence. Oh, but wait…" he slaps his head.

He draws back to study them briefly again, especially their eyes.

"Of course, why did I not think of this before? That blessing of the cu'Nar! You once mentioned they shared a part of their essence with you, and if they are Positive Elementals, you would be heavily charged with it."

"Right, I remember now," Kaliya recalls. "You once said this may be the reason for the glow in our eyes. Could this impose some sort of skew on our test results?"

"A skew, quite possibly, and in a very good way," Thaelyn suggests. "By aligning you to the positive side, it could pose an effect of refining your spiritual essence to conform to the same polarities as those we might see in the Celestial realms."

"Here we have the Celestial references again," she sighs. "And therefore the violet… The only other example of a violet was Aerlie, right? And she's a Celestial."

"This is correct, and here we see it repeated in each of you. This represents a fascinating quandary."

"Uh oh…here we go with the dissection study again," she grins.

"Well, perhaps I would not carry it that far. I am not a biologist," he grins.

"Thank the cu'Nar for that!" she chuckles.

"But this does bring up a curious mention, perhaps more than one at this point. You said it was for some manner of protection, did you not? What sort?"

Thaelyn glances between Kaliya and Kailen, until Kailen speaks up to answer.

"According to our father," he offers. "The cu'Nar made it seem like a type of protection from Sargeras. Although the meaning wasn't very clear to us, they made it appear as a way to cleanse us of something undesirable, therefore freeing us from…I don't know, his corruptive influence?"

Thaelyn furrowed his brow as he listened, and then passed his gaze between the others in the group.

"Protection…or perhaps a cleansing, and something relating to him, but is it physical or otherwise? They are incorporeal creatures, therefore if this is cleansing you, and thus protecting you…" he pauses briefly in thought. "If we only suggest your Elder Council bowed down to him for the promise of wisdom, which could be no more than simple greed, this represents a psychological motivation. Therefore, we are left to wonder what else there is. The cu'Nar did not happen upon you by accident, they were sent there. But we previously suggested this was simply to act as spies or messengers. And yet, if they were further given instructions to protect you from something by sharing this positive essence, which I would find highly irregular of such beings…"

"Wait," Kaliya interjects. "I remember something when we first met with Aelwyn in Sigil. We were talking about this."

"Yes, I recall this now," he nods. "We should probably consult with her on this. Positive Primes interacting with such beings as you, and further to do so outside their native domain, and especially to share their essence… This must carry a very deep implication. Protection? With respect, I doubt you would understand this level of interaction through your classic science studies. This is interacting with your spirit essence, altering it with this strong positive charge. If the explanation suggested a cleansing action, you must have possessed something that someone did not want you to keep. And if the result yields a violet, this now aligns you to the positive side, which makes you much more compatible…" he halts abruptly. "Compatible! Yes!" he snaps his fingers. "With the Estelar, and their Measure of Balance! Something the Primordials fervently rejected. So, this would make you incompatible with THEM."

"A cleansing of something relating to them… Oh dear…" she moans. "Um, my Lord, if we were MADE by them…or at least Darumon…"

"Indeed! Darumon and his hybridization effect…"

"Cu'Nar's pity! So, we contained something left over from him, and these cu'Nar are what? How do we describe this…burning it off with this strong positive zapping they gave us?"

"This could actually represent a good analogy, the result being you now possess qualities resembling that of a Celestial, essentially converting you away from his side to ours."

"But, but, but…" she flusters. "And therefore, we get the violet on your test."

"And yet, this still seems curious…" Thaelyn muses. "If we are speaking of a form of conversion, this might also suggest the Primordials and their ilk to represent a form of life that is incompatible to the Estelar and their system of polarities. Well, what I mean is," he chuckles, "surely their behavior would tell as much, but is this the only reason, or…" he pauses to consider his words, and subtly shakes his head. "No, this is an extreme measure to take, I think. Simple incompatibility might not be the only issue here. A cleansing? This better resembles a purging. What if Maker Kuroku hates them so much that she wants all trace of them purged from existence?"

"My Lord!" the General offers. "If this is so, she must truly despise those Primordials for this point. This might also offer a clue as to why she carries so much interest in him that she has been pursuing him for so long."

"Cu'Nar help us," Kailen moans. "That sounds bad."

"It does," Thaelyn agrees. "Therefore, Darumon's creation… By converting you to our side, she is removing you from his. But this also carries a rather curious twist with that violet score. If you are hybridized in such a way with him, and then…zapped…to our side…" he reflects on his thoughts some more. "Could it actually be…" he muses softly as he gazes into Kaliya's eyes. "Powers behold if it is."

"What?" she asks nervously.

"He is nearly a god, young lady, and I suspect an ancient being, at that. And you are half of that, as is so clearly evidenced by all these Prodigy Gifts of yours. Kaliya, Aelwyn may have jested somewhat by mentioning the Celestial races, but with the infusion of this blessing, you and yours may have been…completed…as a new contender. So, if the Maker is performing this, she must be trying to ensure your place amongst the others."

"Great cu'Nar!" Kaliya wheezes. "And that's probably the scariest part of all. You're saying we could be one of you? We're not ready for that!"

Chapter 4

INTO THE DEEP

"Gods be blessed," shouts one scout. "I was never one for mountain climbing, and this is the worst of it."

"Easy does it, lad," calls the scout leader. "I think I see a ledge up there."

"That would be wonderful. Maybe we could take a break? What time is it?"

"It looks to be well after midday, I think," responds another scout further down.

A scouting team had been working their way up the side of the mountain above the ruins of Glimmerheim. It was their second day of slow-going due to the difficult terrain and the burdens of the local conditions. They were only about midway up at this moment when they saw what appeared to be a deformation in the rocks just over their heads, indicating a possible ledge they could rest on.

They struggled determinedly, pounding spikes into the rocks, and attaching ropes and ladders to ease their way up. The pressures of the climate, as well as the gravitation, made this a particularly difficult climb.

The scout leader pulled himself up another notch, then pounded one more spike into the rocks and hooked on a safety line. The other scouts waited at a small outcropping just below, struggling to keep a foothold in the limited space. He swung to the side slightly and pounded another spike into the rocks, hooking a second safety line to it, allowing him to hang between them.

"Bring up that ladder," he shouts. "This might be the last till we get to the ledge."

The scouts below hoisted up a ladder, one of several they had been carrying and repositioning along the way. The collapsible rope ladder used metal steps, and could be wrapped up for ease of transport. It was made to hook over the spikes and their clips, and then draped down to afford a convenient climb for the rest of the team. He reels it in and hooks it over the two new spikes he just made. He then tests it for security before stepping onto it.

He takes a few steps up on the ladder which raises him within a comfortable arm's reach of the ledge he saw above. He gathers up some free rope and ties it off at one of the new hooks, easing the tension on his safety straps to give him movement again, and continues to the top rung of the ladder, where he can now easily reach the ledge above. He grips a firm hold on the rocky edge and hoists himself up, but as he begins to mount the ledge, his eyes behold a strange sight.

"Wait now, lads. This isn't a ledge."

"Drat it!" complains the first scout. "And here I was hoping to have a little picnic. So what is it then?"

"It looks more like a road to me!"

"A what?!" the scout yelps. "What in all the nine hells is a road doing way up here?"

"That's a very good question," he responds as he fully climbs onto the surface. "Come on up, lads, and take a look."

One by one, the other members make their way up while the leader helps them onto the flattened terrain.

The feature was clearly unnatural, a wide road-like surface carved into the side of the mountain. It extended out of view on both sides of a crag, and appeared to be angled slightly upward to the right.

"Well, isn't this bloody wonderful," mocks the first scout. "And you made us come up the hard way. I'll bet this is part of the local scenic tour, it is!"

"Right you are," the scout leader jests. "So, if you see any tour carriages passing by, be sure to flag one down for us, will you?"

"All right, so what do you think we've got here?" asks the second scout. "This can't be normal. It looks too clean and perfect."

"I agree. We need to see where it goes on both sides. Let's try over here to the left. The downhill slope might do our legs a little easier. Just keep your eyes open."

They begin travelling off to the left, down the gentle slope and around the crag. The roadway continues along the flank a short distance until it terminates in a small cul-de-sac that meets another face. There, they could see a feature carved into the rock.

"Look there," the first scout points. "That looks like an alcove, with a door set in it."

The scout leader brings them up to the hidden entrance. It was a heavy wooden door with sturdy iron bracing.

"Well now, what do you suppose is behind here?" remarks the second scout. "Shall we knock and see who answers?"

"I'm not wearing my porter suit," replies the first. "Maybe I should make a quick run home to tidy up first?"

"This door looks like it could easily be of dwarven make," suggests the leader. "What do you think?"

"Fair enough, wood and iron works for me, but we're just a tad high off the ground here, aren't we? The city was supposed to be running under the mountain, not above it."

"If that be the case," moans the second scout. "There must be a banger of a stair inside."

"Still, a stair would be better than climbing the side of a mountain."

"All right," the scout leader declares. "We'll leave this be for now. Get the camera out and make a portrait for the folks back home, as well as this road. To me, this cul-de-sac looks good enough for a vehicle to come by and load or unload goods through this door. So, we need to know what's on the other end of it."

One of the scouts pulls out a Daanen'kai camera and takes a few shots of the area. The scouting teams have become accustomed to using these devices, having begun the practice during the war on Therinë and continuing up until now. Along the way, they discovered they liked the convenience and versatility the units offered.

"Good," the leader instructs. "Now, let's go up this other way. I'm very curious over why a bunch of dwarves who don't go outside would cut a road midway up the side of a mountain."

They work their way up the incline back around the crag to the other side. As they came around to the other flank, they saw the clear presence of a large opening in the opposite face. The road curved along the side and disappeared within.

"Well now, what's that?" notes the first scout.

"Whatever it is, it's big," comments the second.

"Carefully, lads," cautions the leader. "Keep to the walls and go silent."

They followed the roadway around the inward curve of the facing up to a large tunnel entrance. As they arrived at the mouth, the leader carefully peeked inside.

"This here travels well away through the mountain, and it doesn't look like dwarven work, if you ask me."

"Aye," the first scout agrees. "Not even the dwarves we have back home build them this clean, or this big. It's a nice job, though. Perfect circle up top there…"

The leader examines the wall just inside.

"This is concrete here. This couldn't be cut with picks and chisels, it's too perfect. It looks like a giant drill came through and bored right into it, and then laid over the surface with a smooth layer of concrete."

"Do we know if these dwarves use any of that?"

"I can't see how, actually," the second scout admits. "This would take a machine, I think, and a big one at that. It comes in, cuts through here, shores it up and pulls back. There's nowhere for it to go on this side, except straight down," he peers over the cliff side. "So, it had to come through from behind."

"Aye, and then a work crew cuts this road in the side up to that door over yon," he thumbs over his shoulder.

"And so," the leader muses. "The only question to ask now is who the work crew was, especially if they have a machine big enough to do this sort of work."

"Well, Chief," the first scout smirks. "We don't have a lot of choices open to us, except to run through and see if anyone is home."

"You're right, but I'm taking this one carefully. This tunnel is big enough to run a royal carriage through it. And if it belongs to who we think it belongs to, we need to take this slow. I want everyone to check your spells and potions. We're going in, but real quiet."

"Do we go in dark on this one?"

"So far, it looks calm up here," he sighs and glances around. "We can't be sure how often they use it. I recall the mine on Therinë apparently went at long intervals between visits. If it's the same here, we can't be sure of the last time they came by. So, we'll go in, keep a sharp eye out, and if you see trouble, hit the potion."

They each nod and refresh their augmentation chants. They then check their supply of emergency cloak and haste potions before the leader guides them in. The tunnel appeared long and generally dark, except for intermittent lighting in the ceiling.

"Chief," whispers the first scout. "These lamps over us don't look like anything I've seen before."

"No," he pauses to study one directly overhead. "We'll make a note of this for our report. Those look long and slender, and I think I see some cables connecting between them."

"Aye, like tubing or some such, probably electrical cables… This should exclude the dwarves, I think. Chief Bronzeheart and his folk didn't look the sort to use any of this."

"Not unless they made some interesting advances in recent times."

They continued down the tunnel. It seemed to curve gently around to the left and out of view. They walked for several minutes with no sign of activity anywhere ahead. All was eerily quiet.

"Bloody hell," gripes the first scout. "How long is this beast? Did they carve it fully through the mountain?"

"Maybe," the leader responds.

"If they did," the second scout chuckles. "They don't know how to cut a straight line."

"Maybe they were going around a natural feature in the rock, or perhaps they were aiming to block any line-of-sight advantages if anyone ever came up here. They wouldn't just rush in, and this could afford an extra bit of time for the people on the other side."

"Aye, maybe, and for the length of this beast, that would give a fine bit of forewarning."

"But if to think of it," the third one offers. "If you want any bit of forewarning, wouldn't YOU need a way to see it? Maybe like a camera hooked up to a watch post?"

"Good idea!" the lead member ushers tenuously as he halts the team.

He begins scanning the ceiling and walls for anything like camera devices.

"Did you happen to see anything on the way in?" he asks.

"Nope, nothing stood out so far on the walls. Just smooth concrete."

"All right, keep your eyes open. It might be small, and likely pointing in this direction."

They travelled further along, passing a continuous line of lights overhead, a long chain of them that had to be coming from somewhere at the far end. The air flowed through the passage as a gentle breeze passing from one side to the other of the natural landform.

They were approaching the midpoint when the first scout pipes up.

"Oi! Halt lads! Pull back quick!"

The group came to an abrupt halt and pulled back around the curve. The first scout then brought their attention around the corner and pointed to a feature on the far side of the tunnel angling around the curve.

"There, do you see it? I'll bet that's your answer to the camera."

On the wall, near the ceiling, was a clearly visible surveillance camera aimed in their direction.

"Good work, man," the leader admits. "We'll need to sneak around it. I want one of you to go dark and continue through to the far end, just to see if there are any more. Report back smartly after you're done."

"Aye," the first one offers.

The scout casts a quick invisibility chant on himself and rushes off to inspect the rest of the tunnel. A few minutes pass before he returns to the team, where he dispels his cloak.

"All right," he begins. "It's just the one up there. I think a quick run under a cloak will get us past it, and then we keep on marching."

"Good," the leader nods.

The group all cast cloaks on themselves and sneak past under the camera. Once out of view, they shed their cloaks, and continued along until the tunnel seemed to straighten out. By this time, they could see light from the other side, but it was still a considerable distance ahead.

"Gods be blessed," the second scout moans. "Whoever cut this had a lot of patience."

"That, along with time, opportunity, and determination," the first one reflects. "I wonder how long it took. And surely this much effort would result in a lot of debris removed, as well as noise."

"Aye! You're right, and this would travel through the rocks. Dwarves tend to be keen on these sorts of sounds. I wonder if they took notice and what they thought of it."

"My guess," the leader offers. "If they were being told of a war outside, this was just an excuse to keep digging deep and bar the doors."

"Oh grand, but aye, that would make sense to me as incentive. This much rumbling would be good enough reason to hide from it."

They cautiously trotted forward, now that they could see the end, and there was apparently nothing else in there with them. They approach within sight of the exit, now able to see fairly well outside. It looked like it opened into a ravine. They could see glimpses of structures just outside the tunnel, but it was not clear what they could be.

"All right, hold here," the leader commands. "This is close enough for my taste until we know what's out there. I'll have one of you go dark and make a quick run, just for a peek, and then come back."

The first scout moves off from the group and casts a cloak on himself. He disappears and hurries off towards the exit while the others wait tensely.

A minute passes, almost two, and the group watches intently for any movement outside. All seems calm until the scout returns and dispels his cloak.

"Good then," the leader sighs in relief. "What do you see?"

"We found them, Chief! The bloody bastards carved a tidy little nook out of a hollow in the hills back there. I see buildings, a few vehicles, some two-legged uglies, and best of all is what I think to be a conveyor, like the one in the photo from Therinë that our dear old Marshal Darumon blew up on us."

"Excellent work, lad. Now, we need portraits, and we also need to find a few safe nooks or spyholes where we can set up stations. And also, I'd like to see about any roads or ramps, trails, anything safe and easy to get above the camp for a bird's eye view looking down. After that, we need to find a secure place to mark a rune."

"That won't be easy," the second scout moans. "That road back there didn't give us much to work with...too open to view, if you ask me."

"Aye," adds the third scout. "No cubbies, and the slope is too steep and rugged to take it off to the side. I don't know if we want to chance making it on the road itself. What if we're popping in when someone passes by?"

"We need to figure this out, men," the leader declares. "I doubt any of us wants to climb that mountain again."

⁺✦⁺✦✦⁺✦⁺

"Your Lordship, good to see you," Kailen announces. "Ankhia has a few things to report, and we also have a long-anticipated delivery from Captain Hagmaert."

Thaelyn was once again entering the WIC building to find a delegation of people waiting for him. Med-tech Tad'vaal had finished up her research on the Suuden-Aryku implants and had a report ready to turn in, while the General waited with his announcement.

"Very good, where should we begin," he replies as he takes up a seat at the table.

"Your Lordship," Ankhia declares. "I think I should yield to the General here since I believe his holds priority and should go before mine."

"You are very kind, Miss Tad'vaal," the General submits. "My Lord, we finally have what we've been waiting for. Our people found the Suuden-Aryku base. In fact, it is partly due to this report that the Med-tech is making her visit today, in preparation for what steps we might ultimately take there."

"Most excellent!" he exalts. "Where is it?"

"It is nestled quite neatly in a partially excavated canyon up in the mountain range behind the city. Our people found an odd road carved into the mountainside as they were climbing. They report that from their vantage, they suspect it is too deeply obscured from view by anyone in the valley below. On travelling the road, to one side they found a wooden door, likely leading into the dwarven city as a type of secret entrance, and the other side was a mile-long tunnel leading through the mountain. They described it as being large and neatly carved, as if bored through by a machine and further reinforced with a layer of concrete."

"That sounds like a very professional construction effort. And at the end of this tunnel is the base?"

"Yes, a substantial base with several prominent buildings, and most importantly a conveyor unit."

"Very good. Did they look inside that door?"

"Not as yet. They are waiting for instructions. We also have these," the General pulls out several photos made during the scouting run.

Thaelyn examines the photos of the wooden door, and then the base, as seen from different angles.

"Now the real work begins," he ponders. "We must infiltrate that door and the base with spies, and observe whatever we can from it."

"How would you wish to go about this?"

"For the moment, I must think. And I would wish to give the dear Med-tech a chance to speak also. Med-tech, would this happen to have anything to do with your recent research project?"

"Yes, it does," she begins. "My intern, Likha, and I have been working out ways in which to disable the Suuden-Aryku implant transponders so we can find a way to infiltrate their base, or any installation for that matter, and quietly take them down without others discovering our actions, at least as far as these neural links are concerned."

"Yes, I recall this was the theory of your research."

"We had some initial difficulty trying to study the circuits of those pieces we took out of the bodies that one time, because they were all inactive. I originally figured they died with the host, but I was wrong."

"Oh? In what way?"

"Your Lordship, I got stuck in a rut on this for too long. I was thinking in terms of the types of implants we use, which are all temporary and have power cells attached. These others are permanent devices, and so the Suuden-Aryku seem to have perfected a means to draw power directly from the bioelectrochemical reactions of living cells within the body as a way of operating the device. It's beautiful, if only it weren't for the fact that it was THEM using it."

"Indeed, I recall we have mentioned a few times before that they seem to have made a number of innovations since your departure. Clearly, if they intended these to serve a longer-lasting purpose than a temporary medical procedure, they would need this."

"It certainly seems that way, so I'm going to have to turn my horns around and try thinking like one of them from now on."

"Why, Med-tech, I think your horns are quite appropriate as they are. The experiences we are gaining from these discoveries is a good learning tool. And who knows, we could even apply them to other occasions if we should ever have a need to improve our own methods."

"All right, thanks," she smiles tenderly. "Yes, a medical implant that doesn't need as much servicing would simplify things a bit. Anyway, I reexamined this to see if there was a way to reactivate them just long enough to test some equipment our engineers have been working on. The equipment, so far, was designed to scan the frequencies of the transponders so we could find ways to jam the signals. To do this, I needed living cells to attach them too."

"Somehow, I am suspecting you are referring to a living host of some sort. Dare I ask if you created any new replicants to molest?"

"No, we just reenlisted Banni to our service. And as you can probably imagine, Likha was very happy."

"Med-tech," he sighs. "You need to find an eligible young man to satisfy that dear young lady's needs. Very well, what was your result?"

"We attached a set from one of our examples, which involved an external cranial interface plus a set of chips we found inside the neural tissue. Even though Banni doesn't have a cranium, we were able to power it long enough to monitor the signaling. The unit looks like a very efficient design, using what we call extreme low power circuitry. Our engineers were trying to analyze it once we got it running. They were able to identify several key components, but a few of the circuits didn't make a lot of sense to us."

"In what way?"

"The arrangement includes a number of probes that I originally found buried inside the neural tissues, and these attached to centers we generally describe to govern certain areas of neural activity."

"I recall you once mentioned such as emotion and perhaps some higher thought processes might be affected, correct?"

"Yes, and I still believe this to be correct. Our studies suggest there is at least a passive governing effect being applied here, but we also found something else as we tried to follow the flow of communication pathways in the circuit design. According to the engineers, it resembled a bank of micro-discharge capacitors."

"Discharge capacitors?" he intones inquisitively. "And where do they connect?"

"I believe this would normally channel into a cortex layer, based on the routing. If this is the case, I'd hate to be the one on the receiving end of it. I would imagine that to hurt."

Thaelyn frowned deeply at the suggestion, and then a sudden flashback came to mind.

"A discharge…like a feedback effect!" he recalls sharply and snaps his fingers. "Powers behold, this is where it comes from!"

"My Lord?" the General wonders. "Does this hold some special relevance for you?"

"Yes, General! I recall this now during my conversation with that Commander Geilv. As we were speaking, and he began realizing my words to him, I could overhear him groaning, or at least it sounded as such. When I inquired of this, one of his officers, perhaps the one sitting at the comms station, informed me he was experiencing a feedback reaction from that one chip they describe as the medical implant, which also apparently affects the emotional content."

"Yes, indeed," he nods. "I recall this mention once. So, even if they do try to resist these chips, they get hit for the favor of it. That's simply nasty!" he groans.

"I recall Lieutenant Lapäli reporting this to me, as well," Kailen winces. "This rewrites the image a bit. And so, he was experiencing some level of emotion from those revelations of yours, but in the process, he got a feedback hit to put him back in his box."

"That poor man," Ankhia moans. "I actually feel for him, for this point."

"I recall him saying this was not the first time," Thaelyn asserts. "Which means, he must have questioned one or more of these incidents previously. But he also mentioned how Darumon was very, um…what was the word? Reserved, I believe, at informing people of any details."

"Why doesn't that surprise me?" Kailen notes ironically.

"This is getting crazy," Ankhia shakes her head. "I can't imagine how or why anyone would invent such a thing, and then apply it to someone, or how that person would allow it to be applied to them. We can suggest Darumon is driving them to one thing or another, but this still requires people to do the work."

"As well as some amount of incentive," the General muses. "If Darumon used so much deception everywhere else, I must wonder what he has been using over there that it would drive these people to apply such devices as these. He must be weaving some rather elaborate tales."

"Indeed," Thaelyn accedes. "And thus, we have one more item to add to our list."

"That list is becoming rather complicated by now."

"And it represents a lot of work ahead of us if we should wish to correct it."

"Anyway," Ankhia continues. "The chips seem to link with the interface, perhaps as a central regulator or a diagnostic monitoring unit. It has a connection port on the side where I have to assume a device, like an external probe, might plug in for a maintenance procedure."

"This could be interesting. I wonder if we can learn how to interact with it, and what function it might serve."

"I can't be sure right now, and especially not in the example I have to work with. It must surely use some sort of communications protocol, and likely a very proprietary one, so this might need to wait. Finally, the interface includes a circuit to link it with a broadcast hub. I can only guess here, but I'm going to suggest this transmits data to or from a central relay. Does this relate to a neural collective, where if one sees you, they all see you? I don't know. Does it represent a monitoring network, so if something happens to the individual, a beep goes out to a monitoring station? Possibly. This makes good sense, at the very least. But does it do anything else…I don't know, and I hesitate to ask."

"I would very likely agree, Med-tech. So, we have the prospect of a control effect of the higher thoughts, and emotion dampening or even negation, further compounded by this punishment effect if they disobey."

"Yeah, this sounds more like a torture device than a control mechanism. Those bastards…whoever it is."

"He mentioned two chips, one of a military design and the other medical. I can surely understand the use of a military chip to impose a governing effect over the higher thought processes. We already know how Darumon likes his servants to do as they are told without question, so this fits nicely if he wants them to follow his instruction. But that medical chip…" he ponders distantly.

"The most obvious question on my mind," Ankhia muses, "is what sort of condition are they trying to treat with a neural implant device? It can't be biological, at this point, and that already covers virtually every illness I can imagine."

"That one doesn't make any sense to me," Kailen offers. "Unless it's just a story to give a reason to use it."

"Probably, and then you have this feedback to keep them in their boxes, like you said."

"And, like the General mentioned," Thaelyn considers. "If we consider Darumon and all his games of misinformation and propaganda, we may have a great many deluded people over there. The Commander, if he is any example, seemed to hold just enough of his own reasoning to listen to my words, and that officer of his also seemed like a fellow with his own sense of mind."

"But, Your Lordship," Kailen asserts. "How do we apply this with all those occasions of their attacks on our people? They behaved as if they had no compassion whatsoever."

"I cannot say with certainty, but this example did not seem to carry that same environment. Maybe those other occasions held something we are missing in this case. Perhaps these chips are configurable to the need."

"Wonderful, programmable people."

"But now, we must ask ourselves how they would behave if these were removed. Med-tech, how do you feel about removing these from a live subject? Do you feel you could extract them without harming the patient?"

"I had enough practice with all those cadavers you left behind on the field, so I think with a little care and patience, I could do it. But I would want to take it very slow on the first few to be sure I understand the procedure. And although I don't want this to sound wrong, if we find any high-ranking officers, I know they would hold greater value, but I might want to, um, try myself on a lower ranking one first, just to make sure it meets with my expectations before moving on to the more important figures."

"I understand, but as you said, go gently with it. We do not want to bring harm to anyone, if we can help it, not even a lowly non-com," he smiles softly.

"Absolutely."

"Very good, then our objective should be to capture, rather than kill, then to remove these devices and see if we can gain their cooperation to reveal the details of Darumon and his activities. If the High Commander actually showed a reaction to my statements, and his rebuttal was that the opponents he was facing were alleged to be in league with Darumon's higher enemies, but without an accurate definition of who those higher enemies are, it could be he has no true understanding of what he is doing other than to follow orders based on his chip."

"And with Darumon controlling the chip," she relents. "And thus controlling him, and probably the rest of the Suuden-Aryku military, and who knows how many others besides that."

"Much like everything else around here," Kailen moans. "The dwarves with their drug effect, the elves and the telepathic mind control... None of them would likely WANT to follow him, so he forces the issue."

"And this represents a serious offence," Thaelyn affirms. "One that I would expect from him and the other Primordials, if only for their history. Very well, Med-tech, what about this research of yours? Did you achieve any sort of result?"

"Yes!" she responds avidly. "We were able to identify the signaling, and even though we couldn't decipher the coding, at this moment I think we just want to block it completely. Maybe later, if as you say we could convert one of them...assuming such a thing is actually possible...we could investigate the issue more."

"Good. Then here is what I will suggest. If these units link to a central monitor, we need to disable them and keep it that way, at least until such time as we can feel safe that they can no longer link to the mother network."

"This would require something portable, and attachable to the individual, so it travels with him as we relocate him out of range. But now, the trick is to get close enough to take down the opponent before that initial signal goes out. For that I think we need an area jammer. But how do we get close enough to deploy an area jammer? It's a sequence of paradoxes, one on top of another. I think they would probably take notice if something interfered with their neural net, assuming they receive any kind of monitoring feed from it, so we wouldn't have much time to play with."

"And we will need a sufficient crew to deploy into the field to attend to this," Thaelyn submits. "As well as a non-lethal method to subdue them…"

✦✦✦✦✦

"Sergeant, His Lordship has a message to deliver to Cadet Nazég when she finishes her course."

"What sort of message, page?"

"Simply to have her meet with him at the WIC building when she's done for the day."

"Does he require her in projected form?"

"No, I believe this is a simple conference."

"All right, I'll pass it along. Thank you."

The page turned and exited the room after delivering his message from Thaelyn to the combat training hall. The Sergeant continued running his students through their drills for the daily class until the bell rang signaling the end of the day.

Kaliya had been outside on the athletic field practicing with her sword-staff weapon. The routine she was performing was as much a combat art as it was a deadly dance. In a way, it reminded her of her old gymnastics' performance from her school on Ruuki uy'Daan, but with dangerous implications. When the bell rang, she came to a rest, twirling the weapon one last time to orient it with the sheath mounted on her back, and dropping it inside. She then made her way up the stairs to the combat hall to meet with the Sergeant and clock out her time for the day.

"Cadet, you have a note here," he announces. "Freshen yourself up and get over there."

Kaliya picks up the note and reads the message concerning her meeting with Thaelyn.

"Yes Sergeant. Thank you," she responds with a salute before leaving the room.

She dashes off to her dorm room to pick up a change of clothes and her bathing kit, then to the showers to wash up. She makes a return trip to her room to drop off her bag and comb her hair, bringing her final details in order, then launches out to her meeting.

She arrives in Rolsklinde through the city hub and briskly strolls across the plaza to the WIC building, coursing her way through the halls to the strategy room where Thaelyn spent most of his time.

"My Lord! You called for me?" she announces as she enters the room.

"Kaliya, yes, come and sit with us."

Thaelyn had assembled a team of advisors for the occasion, including Kailen, Ankhia, Chief Bronzeheart, and of course the General who was ever-present.

"This looks serious, what's going on?" she asks.

"We are putting you to work…again. But on a larger scale than before."

"What about my training?"

"You will still engage in that, but we must ask you to devote an appreciable amount of your time and effort to other tasks now. My suggestion would be your afterhours, to the best of your ability. You can try working in extra training time, if you can afford it, but this is a situation of growing imperativeness."

"Naturally," she nods. "Based on what I've been hearing lately, we seem to be arriving at some critical junctures."

She finds a free chair at the table and sits down while Thaelyn gives his address.

"Recently, our scouts found the remains of the city of Glimmerheim. It would appear to have been dealt severe damage, likely from bombardment, but with smaller weapons in this case. We feel this could be to preserve the underground chambers within the mountain from the inherent shockwave effects."

"Yes," Kailen affirms. "I would have to agree. Using the heavier weapons, like what we saw elsewhere, would generate some rather severe aftershocks."

"In addition, the side of the mountain appears to have been intentionally collapsed in front of the city gates leading inside, probably to prevent any outside attempts to gain access, and also to inhibit anyone inside from leaving."

"That be about the tellin' Belrum gave me that time," Tol recalls. "A sorry thing, that. The tales tell of a grand sight to be seen in the outer city. But nay more…"

"Cities can be rebuilt, and we will do so, but for now we must focus on what lies within. Yesterday, our people found a roadway of some kind cut into the mountainside well above ground level. To one side was a wooden door which we presume leads inside the city as a sort of rear entrance. Chief, are you aware of this door?"

"Nay to that, Yer Kingship! That be a new one to me."

"As I might suspect," he muses. "It likely came about in secret, as it leads out midway up the mountain and around this roadway to a large and neatly constructed tunnel passing through the mountain itself into a ravine on the other side."

"What's on the other side, as if I needed to ask?" Kaliya wonders.

"A Suuden-Aryku base, involving a selection of structures and a conveyor."

"Just as you were hoping for," she grins. "Good. So, what's next?"

"What is next will be some very carefully considered surveillance to study our enemy in order to find our opening. But we also need to find a way inside that door unnoticed to locate the Thane and observe his actions. And I want a general review of the people inside to judge their behaviors to see if we need to make any special considerations there."

"What about that mine you found once?"

"We have people observing it and making tallies of their output. One concern we have already is what sort of condition the workers are in presently due to this stew they eat."

"Your Lordship," Ankhia suggests. "It would be a good idea to make an analysis of their health, if only we could get our hands on a few examples for study. I could run some tests and tell you how much of this mushroom they've been ingesting so far, perhaps even to keep a running tab on it to give you a better idea of its progress."

"Excellent, and this could offer us a timeframe as to when this group was first put into service and how long they might have before it becomes critical."

"Yer Kingship," Tol interjects. "Why nay to bring the whole crew out of there straight away, now that ye know of them?"

"Because if the Suuden-Aryku should make another run to pick up their supply, they will surely notice the workers missing, and this would fall outside their usual expectation."

"Aye, of course… But then, for how long will we be playin' this game with them?"

"We must first understand some of their common practice. There is a reason for this, so let me explain. So far, to our good fortune, they do not know of our presence, and we must keep it this way indefinitely. This tunnel seems to be the only way in or out by land, and our scouts tell us there is a surveillance camera located inside, likely to observe any unusual activity coming their way."

"Oops!" Kaliya mutters. "Be careful of that!"

"Indeed! For now, we will keep out of sight and study their activities. But our spies, even under cloak, can only do so much. We have multiple objectives to meet here. The mine is only one of those, and will fall in line with the others as we make our move."

He studies one of the photos of the Suuden-Aryku base for a moment before continuing.

"This base seems to have a centralized command booth to it, to oversee their operations. This is our most important target for observation. The base commander and his officers will serve to supply us with valuable information. Among other things, we want to study them, not only to learn how their operations proceed, but also to learn of their personal interactions and their manners."

"How do you hope to manage that?" Kaliya asks. "Send in a scout with a recorder to listen in?"

"Essentially yes, and you will be the scout, along with your team."

"Um, excuse me, but I think I missed an important memo on this. What team?"

"The one you will assemble from a selection of the more proficient students of our conjoined training course. You will begin building a team of special operatives, and together you will infiltrate the installation, perhaps as something small, like an insect."

"A team…" she mumbles quietly. "I'm getting a command role."

She gazes at her brother to see his expression. He returns with a gentle smile and a reassuring nod.

"And here, as the proverbial fly on the wall," she recollects from earlier moments in her training. "Cu'Nar's grace, be careful of what you ask for."

"Eh, Yer Kingship," Tol hesitates. "Mayhap I should be askin' ye about this, if only to keep me old head from achin'. This lass here, she be a fair bit bigger than any of the local bugs I ever did hear about. How do ye plan on passing her off as one?"

"Kaliya, perhaps you would like to answer this," Thaelyn directs.

"Sure. Chief Bronzeheart, I should probably keep this simple, since it's largely a military secret for us so far, but I have a special ability where, among other things, I can create an image of myself and alter the shape to impersonate other things. Several of us have been in practice for it by now."

"Really now!" he praises. "Oh! That will be a fine trick to pull on them. But still, ye're just a wee bit bigger than the average bug. Can ye really make yerself so small?"

"Actually, yes… It's like a mental image of my body which I can project outwards, and size isn't really an issue here."

"Aye then, that should be enough to cause a bit of poundin' in me head," he chuckles.

"It is also important to keep a low profile," Thaelyn continues. "And I would suggest not only using a diminutive form, but also camouflaging. Your spy activities will ultimately teach you about their manners of conduct and behavior patterns, and this will eventually lead us to impersonate them."

"This is starting to sound complicated," Kaliya muses. "So, I'm going to guess here that at some moment, one of them will go missing and I take their place."

"Not just one, the whole crew."

"Whoa! That's a little more complex. And this is where MY crew comes in. Wow, this should be fun."

"I wouldn' want to be one of them about that time," Tol winces.

"We need to take that base," Thaelyn asserts. "But it must be in such a way as to fool anyone observing it, such as the Thane or anyone who comes through the conveyor. Once we have control of the base, taking the mine should no longer be an issue. If the Thane only interacts through the base commander, we can probably play a temporary ruse on him to make it seem like all is well."

"But for that," Kaliya offers. "We need to observe how the Thane interacts with the base commander, just to make sure we're right on this."

"Correct, and this is your second objective. We can perhaps send a few scouts into the city under a cloak without too much difficulty, and they can assist in locating the Thane's Hall, and generally describe the lay of the city, which is the reason why we have the Chief here, to get us started."

"And then what?"

"What comes after is largely dependent on several factors. The Thane could be a corrupted dwarven resident serving Darumon, or he could be some manner of projection or manifestation of another creature in the service of Sargeras. I would suggest you take extreme care when approaching him, just in case he is able to sense your presence."

"Good point."

"Along the way, we still have the issue of their manufacturing and storage for Darumon's weapon."

"Do we know anything about that yet?"

"Not as yet, but I think the only way to truly discover this would be after taking the base in order to use the conveyor for our own purpose and see where it leads. Then we have a new problem with whatever operations crew is on the other side."

"A question, how do you plan on taking that base in the first place? My team can go in as projections, but then what?"

"Kaliya," Ankhia begins. "I've been working with some engineers to develop a device to interfere with the signaling they use in their neural interface. We believe it probably links to a network hub or monitoring station. This should allow us to break their connection and isolate each one, so when we make our strike, even though an individual might know what's happening, their collective does not."

"Good, I was worried about that. And so, we take them down one at a time, or maybe in small groups, until the base is ours, I suppose."

"Depending on how the intelligence gathering goes, yes. Our hope is to capture, not kill, so we can collect individuals for interrogation later, possibly to learn some valuable information about what they're doing and how best to approach Azgarén."

"Ugh, me head," Tol moans. "I nay be the military sort, and this be a lot for me poor noggin to bear."

"I'm sorry, Chief," she offers. "Some of this is very advanced warfare, even for a few of us. But in order for us to capture any of them, we must use non-lethal methods, and also be very discreet until the operation is complete. This is probably the most difficult part of the operation, so far."

"So far," Kaliya muses. "What kind of non-lethal methods are we considering here?"

"Kaliya," Thaelyn resumes. "I am going to have you focus more deeply on elemental magic. We were aiming in this direction originally, and I believe we were right. But more specific to the air and water schools, along with all the other females."

"Wait, you just lost me on another memo… Why only the females? What are the males doing?"

"Earth and fire…"

"Dear cu'Nar, what are you building?"

"We are reinventing the Stormhooves and giving better credit to that name. The females, with your special weapons, will be lightning and ice. The males with theirs will be earthquakes and firestorms."

"Great cu'Nar! We'll wreck the place!" she chuckles ironically.

"Aye!" Tol agrees humorously. "I nay be the one to know about this magic of yers, but by the sound of it, ye'll be the cause of another pummelin' like what the Suuden-Aryku did."

"But that doesn't actually answer the earlier question," Kaliya continues. "What sort of non-lethal methods?"

"We will create a new spell for your people," Thaelyn responds. "A form of physical attack. In some ways, it will resemble the Shocking Grasp strike, but this will be more potent and specialized to apply a form of electrical stun to disable our opponents."

"We'll need to get up close and personal for that. And not in projected form, either."

"Initially, yes, although I suppose as we evolve this, it might later afford us a ranged application, as well. It would also be wise to aim for a nighttime strike, to reduce the number of people moving around. If this is the case, we could possibly use priests and their sleep chants, if they can sneak up on our opponents quietly enough."

"That's a good thought. If I simply rush up and smack them on the head, it might disable them, but they would still know who it was, not that it matters at that moment. But if they're sleeping at the time…"

"Indeed, if we should wish to use our hidden advantage to its fullest, perhaps we could play on this when they wake up."

"This reminds me of your play with those Flame Elf scouts you kidnapped once. Marelle told me you hit them so hard and fast, they didn't know which way was up before you had them bagged, tagged, and dangling by the heels," she chuckles.

"And at the same time, you will need to play a few more of your own games, as you did with the orcs, when you make your approach to take down the Suuden-Aryku."

"You know, before too long, I'm going to need to write an instruction book on all of this."

"Kaliya," Ankhia submits. "As part of that play, you'll need to deliver an area jammer unit to block their signals before you attack. Surely, you'll need to play a little excuse for what it is and why it needs to be set down in the room with them."

"Oh, thank you, Ankhia. Hey everyone," she animates. "Look what I found. Let's see what this button does…"

The group all shares a laugh with her.

"Our first priority is the control booth," Thaelyn asserts. "This would be the center of their operations, as well as communications. Take that and descend the ladder to everyone else. During the initial observations, we will see if we can identify a communications relay associated to these interfaces. Perhaps we could disable this to provide cover for the rest of the operation. Otherwise, we will need to relocate the jammers, as necessary. Either way, you and your team must take down the entire crew. It must be swift and silent, as best it can be."

"The nighttime approach would be best for that. But then what? We have them, now what do we do with them?"

"I will create some units you can attach to their bodies," Ankhia notes. "Then you transport them back to us for processing."

"And so, we have our base. Now, what about the Thane in all this?"

"We must observe and study how he interacts with the others," Thaelyn concludes. "We will not actually make a move until we know something about his nature, as it may require us to modify our plans. And as I said, I would also like to learn something about the general nature of what is going on in there."

"Eiki, dear… How ye be today?" Telta calls as she approaches the modest house.

"The same, by the whole of it. I've been a-workin' the sewin' table all morn, but ye can only patch the same shirts an' trousers so many times afore they look more like rags from a doll tossed away with the rubbish."

"Aye, me own dress be that way. I was a-hopin' ye could help with a new one. D' ye have any new cloth this week?"

"Barely a few scraps by now. This be me other problem. The herds down below get shorn, but the wool from them goes too quick, an' there be a lot of people t' clothe. An' what be the worst of it, the coin I get from me work be a-runnin' short these days. Mayhap I'll be a-sellin' me own clothes afore long."

"'Tis a foul thing, this war. If only the Thane would let us go up an' see about tradin' for more wares. I'll be a-bettin' there be some fine cloth for sale up there!"

"Aye, the tales of the farms an' their herds, an' so many weavers an' cloth makers," Eiki pauses to examine her dress, which was faded and threadbare. "If only me poor beloved Tol were here. His work down in the forge brought up some good coin."

"Aye, ye're not alone there. I hear the same tale by others whose men got sent away."

"I still say there be somethin' foul t' all this! We be a-wastin' away slowly in here. I don'na care if the Thane stopped the one feast, an' now those men stay put. He be a-workin' them harder an' we see nothin' comin' back from it. I'll tell ye true, I be almost ready t' go up there me'self an' take a look!"

"Eiki, ye know what will be said t' that! There was tell of the doors bein' closed an' all the ruckus some folks say was heard echoin' from above. I even heard a few say in whispers how the upper part of the old town was smashed. I don'na think ye can even get through that."

"Then how d' ye think we'll ever get out of here when the war finally be finished? Say, one day, the war be endin', an' say we be allowed t' go back up. What d' we need t' d' for it, dig our way out?"

"Mayhap, if the war has been a-ragin' for so long…"

"Aye, but now hear this. If the war has been a-ragin' for so long

AND the old town be smashed, what d' ye think of anythin' else up there, ay? The Thane was said t' be a-tradin' our wares with the people up top. How d' ye trade through a smashed town?"

The two long-time friends argue their debate on Eiki's front porch while the usual bustle of the city flows through. It was a typical day in Glimmerheim, and the people just barely managed to get through the day with a seemingly diminishing supply of goods being produced locally to supply a population that had been slowly growing over the years after they moved underground.

In another part of the city was a well-appointed palace, with ornate columns lining the front steps and several gilded braziers burning ceremonially to the majesty of the Thane of Glimmerheim. On entering the oversized front doors into the grand hall, with its sculpted columns and tiled floors, and where the walls were lined with statues of famous people in the city's old history, one would walk the long carpet up to the throne, where the Thane would preside over the city's many obligations.

"We need more!" the Thane rages. "We be a-fallin' behind every year of it, d' ye hear me?"

"Aye, good Thane, we be a-tryin' the best we can," consoles the Chancellor. "Please keep yer temper, the lads down below can only bring up so much at one time."

The wrathful scene was not uncommon in recent years, as the Thane demanded of his Chancellor more production from the forges on each occasion of his visit.

"The point-ears nay be a-holdin' back, d' ye know this?" the Thane shouts. "The lands above be a-blazin' with them!" he gestures emphatically. "An' the warriors up there need the finest we can offer!"

"Aye, but why d' we only send the bricks an' nay the fare they truly be a-needin'? Are the men ye sent up before makin' so much? Because the people here have gone t' thinkin' the cuttin' of the one feast be a sign of the war easin' up on us."

"We be a-sendin' the bricks because bricks are what we be a-needin' the most! Don'na mind what the men up there be a-makin', they be a-makin' it well enough! They be a-holdin' the lines, but only if ye get those forges below t' cookin' it up faster!"

"Aye, I'll put in another word for it. They be a-strugglin' t' serve, an' ye know we all want this war t' be over soon."

The Chancellor bows uneasily and leaves the room. As he exits the front doors, the Thane looks around at the now-empty hall. He rises from his seat and strolls off to a corridor behind him, making his way through the hallways to his personal chamber. The chambermaids he passes along the way each bow before continuing to their duty. When he comes to his private quarters, he enters and closes the door. The attendants in his service knew that when he was in his private room, he was not to be disturbed under any circumstances. The Chancellor was in charge of most of the city's affairs in his absence.

The Thane locks the door behind him and turns into the room, pausing briefly to study the furnishings. He steps over to the bed, which had just been neatly refreshed by one of the chambermaids, and pulls down the covers, ruffling them up to give it a used appearance. Next, he walks up to a bureau and pulls out a set of clothes with an identical appearance to what he was currently wearing. They were neatly folded and tucked away in the drawer, the day's fresh laundry. He shakes out the fold and wads them up in his hands, then drops them into a pile at the foot of the bed. Finally, he pulls out a set of slippers from under the bed, also the same style and color as what he had on, and tosses them randomly near the clothes pile.

Once the room met with his approval, and all things gave the appearance of having been lived in, he paused in recollection and soon vanished in a puff of ethereal vapor.

◆◆◆◆◆

"Belrum!" Galmir calls into the mine. "We've got more out here, an' they bring tell of more after that."

"Aye, the word be a-travellin', an' we need t' be a-gatherin' them up."

"But we don'na have that much room in here! Where will we be a-puttin' them all?"

Belrum and his fellow refugees in their mine hideout were seeing the results of sending out messengers to the other dens of refugees they knew about, with word of help and food, and to spread the word to others. Now they were receiving migrations of survivors into their small home, some of whom have been walking for days.

"Aye, I know this. I've been a-thinkin' about it. In the morn I think I need t' make the run t' that camp up there an' let them know we have this trouble. Mayhap they can help somehow."

"But how? They say we can'na go outside t' build a new town, or these Suuden-Aryku ye speak of might see it. Then we risk more pummelin'."

"Ye're right, Galmir, but we have t' bring them all t' our side for everyone t' find food an' better livin'. Just bring them inside for now. Me friends up there are a kind folk. They would'na let us down in these times."

"I hope ye're right, or we'll be in for more trouble than ye can shake a bushel of sticks at."

The most recent group of refugees was invited in and given food and water. The room was already quite full, and the conversation rumbled through the nearby tunnels as the revelations of the war and the invaders was shared all around. Belrum stood up from his table and introduced himself to the newcomers, sharing his news and attempting to reassure them that they would find new hope. Deep down, however, he felt a little uneasy at how that new hope would manifest itself. Galmir was right about not being able to go outside, but what else was available to help so many who might show up at his doorstep.

All he could do was look around at the gathering and sigh, hoping his visit to the outpost in the range of hills to the north might prove fruitful. By the end of the day, he and his wife retired for the evening.

✦✦✦

"You must pace yourself," ushers the monotonous voice on the communicator. "How much do you think you can push that man before he and the others become agitated?"

"That man is a worm!" snaps the reply. "He wouldn't dare stand against me. And these people are so deluded, they wouldn't know which way is up if you pointed their stubby little noses at it."

"Irrelevant, we must maintain control in order to keep the flow of metal consistent."

"Consistent? It's down considerably since we lost the mine on Therinë. You told me on how many occasions the processor ran out before we could resupply it. We had a nice little balance until that…incident…over there, and the Marshal had to pull out. Why he didn't just flatten those intruders, I don't know."

"The report I received described a potential discovery by Sargeras's opponents. The Marshal made a tactical retreat to ensure our security."

"A tactical retreat…" he huffs. "All right, fine, surely the Marshal knows what he's doing, but it doesn't help matters if we're supposed to fill our quota. And for that, we need to push these puny little dirt-shovelers as hard as their stunted legs can carry them."

"Ytani, I am concerned that if you try pushing too hard, something may break, and we cannot afford…"

"Commander!" he interrupts brashly. "I've been running this operation for nearly four centuries now. I think I know how hard I can push them, and so far, they behave like the good little dull-horns they should be…assuming they actually had horns to begin with. They have no idea what's happening outside beyond the stories I give, and there's no way for them to find out. And even if they did try to dig their way out, they wouldn't find anything except devastation, thanks to our glorious military cleaning up all the loose ends out there. Therefore, the situation is well in hand."

The voice on the com-link went silent for a moment as the Commander attempted to recompose himself.

"By the way," Ytani adds. "What were the last numbers?"

"The stockpile is at eighty-six percent."

"We should be at least a point or two above that by now. This operation is so incredibly dull, watching that meter rise. And now we're falling behind schedule even more. We can't bring it out of the city any faster than it was to begin with, and that other mine is similarly dragging its hooves. If only we could send someone to find a new source."

"While this might be desirable, it would require an expedition, and this would complicate matters if they should start asking questions of what they see outside."

"I'm not concerned over questions, Commander. Witnesses are expendable in this operation, so long as we fulfill our needs to serve the Marshal."

"Ytani...!" the Commander begins sternly, but abruptly halts with a subtle groan issuing through the link.

"Carefully, Commander... Remember your obedience chip. That's what it is, after all. We need to be sure our fine officers serve to our highest standards."

"Your statements are offensive. I was serving the Sentinels before they arrived, and my service was never questioned."

"This isn't a measly Sentinels, Commander!" he growls. "This is a TRUE military, one that gets the job done without a lot of sag-horns crying about the weather."

"So it would seem," he relents begrudgingly. "Nevertheless, I was going to say, regardless of the issue of witnesses, I would find it unlikely for you to gain their cooperation if they should begin to suspect something other than your stories to explain the conditions outside."

"Commander, does the term 'superior firepower' mean anything to you?"

"Ytani, does the term 'death before dishonor' mean anything to you? My interpretation of these people is that they hold a strong cultural tradition based on the values of credibility and dedication. If they do not like what they see, they will fight for what they believe in."

"As if they ever fought to begin with," he rebukes. "We once had them scrambling to dig out that hole of theirs. Anyway, that was four centuries ago. Whatever is in there now has been thoroughly domesticated. Still, I suppose you may be right," he sighs. "If we bring out an expedition team, they might prove difficult to actually do any work. Better to save them for the next work crew in the mine to the south, they'll be more productive, and probably live longer…" he begins laughing maniacally. "Yeah…live longer!"

"Ytani…" the Commander hesitates as he tries to check himself.

"Save it, Commander! You don't have what it takes any more than the rest. I'm the one who manages this operation, by order of the Marshal. You serve ME, whether you like it or not. Personally, I love the idea. I just wish this operation could go a little faster. With the loss of that one mine, and the processor constantly running out of that stuff, I worry about some piece of machinery hitting something it's not supposed to, and then you know what happens."

The link ends as a hand reaches over to the terminal on the desk and switches the unit off. The form of a body reclines into a comfortable chair, turned to a wall with a video monitor. He picks up a remote control from the desk and presses a button, turning on the device, then activating a holo-disk player on the shelf just below and engaging the playback feature. A video appears on the screen as it begins playing.

"Oh wonderful…reruns again," he retorts unenthusiastically. "Why can't they ever get any new material? Four centuries of watching these morons poke at each other gets so incredibly boring after a while. But then, what do you expect of a society that doesn't know how to laugh properly."

✦✦✦✦✦✦✦

"All right, listen up, men… His Lordship has made several directives. First, the dwarves in that mine have been working for an unknown period of time, and we need to measure it somehow to see how much of that toxin they have in their bodies by now. The Med-tech here needs an escort so she can take a few readings."

Captain Hagmaert was giving instructions to his troupe at the outpost on the decisions made the previous day in Rolsklinde by Thaelyn and his most recent conference. Ankhia had been sent to the region to make a study of the dwarves to see what their current health condition might be.

"We need a mage with a rune. Open it up for her."

A mage comes over and takes a rune from a table for the mine. He enchants it and allows her to transport away, along with a scout to accompany her.

"Good, the next point is the city. We need a few of you to go inside under a cloak. Keep it quiet. Our objectives are as follows…"

He picks up a paper from his desk to review the notes sent to him as part of his orders.

"We have a rough map here given to us by Chief Bronzeheart. We made a few copies to go around. You'll go in, split up, and scout the general affairs of the city. Keep to the shadows and out of the way of local traffic. If you look at this map here…" he holds it up so they can follow him, "…you'll see the Thane's palace is here…" he points at it, "…which seems convenient enough since that looks to be right near their back door on the mountain."

The group studies the map and references the copies in their own hands.

"The door likely leads through some sort of hidden access somewhere, possibly coming out either in or around the palace, so that he can monitor it easily. Chief Bronzeheart tells us he knows of a storeroom where they presumably drop the metal as it comes out of the furnaces. This is supposed to be for pickup by the people outside for their war effort. Bloody hell to that, I say! So, we're expecting this back door to link up to it."

"That sounds grandly convenient," remarks one scout. "What about the Thane himself?"

"If you can get inside easily, do so, but don't go too deep. So far, we're only taking a peek to see if there are any cubbies. If you find one, and no one is looking, see about making a few portraits for us so we know how to proceed. We're going to be sending in special units to spy on him, and they'll need to know what to expect so they can set themselves up."

"What kind of special units, in this case?"

"His Lordship is creating a special operations unit led by Lieutenant Nazég using projection to get inside and spy on the Thane. He also thinks it would be wise to look for any alcove or nook that's out of view and away from other people. We could use this to mark a rune as a direct way in, rather than passing through the door, since our rune topside is out on the road and a bit risky. We don't need to spy a road, but we do need to spy on both ends of it."

"Fair enough, anything else?"

"This special unit will also be assigned to study the activities at the base, watching the people and how they interact. This is apparently a prelude to further operations they'll be conducting up there."

"Right then, so what do we do in the meantime, play blind man's bluff?"

"Don't worry men, I've got plenty of work here to keep you busy."

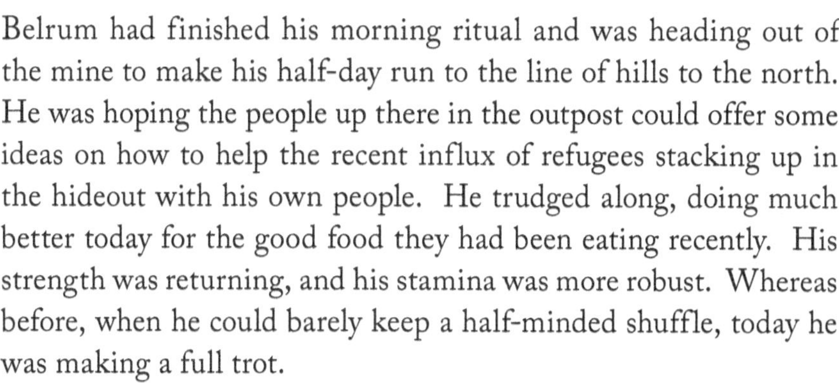

Belrum had finished his morning ritual and was heading out of the mine to make his half-day run to the line of hills to the north. He was hoping the people up there in the outpost could offer some ideas on how to help the recent influx of refugees stacking up in the hideout with his own people. He trudged along, doing much better today for the good food they had been eating recently. His strength was returning, and his stamina was more robust. Whereas before, when he could barely keep a half-minded shuffle, today he was making a full trot.

He followed his usual trail through the fields, a path he was well familiar with, pressing forward to meet his goal. The hills seemed to come into view a little quicker today, mainly because he was moving faster. As he finally approached the outpost walls, still carefully concealed in their disguise, he walked around to the side to find the hidden entrance.

"Good Captain?" he calls. "Can I bend yer ear for a wee bit?"

The Captain was sitting at his desk when the man came in. He perks up at the announcement and rises to meet his visitor.

"Belrum, good to see you. What do we have today? Do you need another delivery already?"

"Well actually, yay t' that, but we have another bit of trouble that I need t' speak about."

"And what might that be?"

"We've been a-makin' like ye said an' callin' out for our kinfolk across the land. Word be a-spreadin', I can tell ye that, an' now we be a-haulin' in a good many of them t' our wee little mine. It yay be a-gettin' tight in there by now, but I don'na want t' send them away for the small space. I was a-hopin' ye an' yer kin could help with an idea or two."

"This is certainly a problem, and I must admit, some of us have been concerned over what to do about it. This land is no good for you to go out farming again, and we can only hold just so many in that little mine. But we need to bring as many survivors together as possible."

He ponders the situation for a moment until a suggestion comes to mind.

"Hey, wait… I have an idea, but we need to present this to my Lord for his approval. I think it should work, at least as a temporary solution until we can correct some of these other issues. What would you say if I was to write up a note with my idea and send it off, along with you to present your case?"

"Erm, send me t' where?"

"He spends a daily ritual consulting with his officers in a city we call Rolsklinde. I can send you and an escort to meet with him. I'm sure he would be able to help you with your problem, and with my note offering a suggestion, we might have a good answer for you, or at least the beginning of one."

"Ye said one time he was a King, did ye?"

"Yes, he is."

"An' this city, where it be, on yer other world?"

"On one of the worlds we own."

"Yer King be a King of more than one world?! Oi! Great All-Father, bless me the strength. I be but a poor farmer's son, d' ye remember that?"

"Don't worry, Belrum, everything will be fine. But the difference in day and night for us puts him in his bed right now. I would say we should do this perhaps this eve."

"What be this idea of yers, if I may ask?"

"If we consider this land is too dry and hostile to grow crops, and we want to bring all your people to one place for safety and survival, then I can think of only one idea that works in both cases, and that is to relocate you elsewhere, at least until we can gain control of the situation here."

"Relocate? Hmm, like mayhap t' this other world ye speak of? What be the land like over there?"

"Fertile and green, perfect for growing food. We could possibly have you go in as hired hands to other farmers to get started, or maybe we could start something new, depending on how many people we find here."

"What about herdin' space? An' d' ye have any herdin' beasts of yer own, or d' we bring ours?"

"I certainly wouldn't want to leave your own animals to suffer here in this wasteland, would you?"

"Aye, good point… But then, how d' ye bring all this about? D' ye use that portal thing of yers over yon?" he points to the gateway at the rear of the camp.

"Perhaps that, or possibly runes, depending on how this plays out. This one actually leads to Ruuki uy'Daan, so if to use it, you would need to make two jumps from here."

"Oi, that be a-makin' me head pound just thinkin' about it. Right, then, I s'pose this could be a good plan. Many of us are thankful for yer help, but ye know, we dwarves like t' work an honest livin' too."

"Precisely, and this is what makes me think of this idea to put you to work. Not only so you can take care of your own family, but also to make you productive again, and to give you a sense of honor for yourselves."

The suggestion warmed Belrum's heart as he listened to it. He began thinking of the old days, when his father was still trying to work the land, if only just barely. And how he hoped one day to do the same, at least until the situation outside went from bad to worse, and the only thing they could do was take refuge inside the mine.

"But now, what about the rest?" he asks. "There be more out there, methinks. If we all go through, what d' we d' about them?"

"That is a very good idea. You should bring this up with my Lord at your meeting. Maybe he can find a way to help."

"Good then, I s'pose. So, we need t' be a-settin' ourselves t' it in the eve, ay? I should go back an' tell the lads that I'll be a-goin' out late. Me wife, she tends t' worry, if ye know."

"Of course, let me get you a ride home, and when the time comes, I'll send someone to fetch you."

+ +◆◆◆+ +

Evening came to the barren lands as a scout was sent to find Belrum at his home. He had told the others about the Captain's plan, and while it met with mixed reactions, in the end they could not argue over the potential of moving to a better place where they could start working for a living and creating new lives.

"Belrum?" the scout calls into the mine.

The assembly inside, which had grown recently with new immigrants, turned to observe the tall man in a neatly fitted shirt, a leather jerkin, leggings, and boots entering the room. Muffled whispers echoed through the crowd as they studied the tidy uniform with a heraldry symbol on it of a dragon wing shield emblazoned with a hammer and weighing scales, and clutching a vine in its talons.

"Aye, here I be."

Belrum had dressed in his finest clothes, which didn't look much better than his ordinary ones, save for a fewer number of holes. His hair and beard had been neatly groomed and braided, and he looked almost like he was going to a grand ball, country style.

"Very good," the scout replies. "I'll escort you through and back again. There should be no problem to it. Are you ready?"

"Belrum," Friah calls from against the far wall. "Don'na forget yer pretty over here!"

Belrum turns over his shoulder and makes a brisk dash to embrace his wife with a tender kiss.

"I'll be back soon, me love. Don'na wait up for me. I don'na know how long this may take."

"Take care. Ye're travellin' t' places far from home, an' ye've ne'er gone so far as just the few barrens outside."

Belrum joins the scout while he enchants a rune to take them directly back to the camp. The nervous dwarf touches the rune and is whisked away in a flash, much to the shock and surprise of most of the occupants of the room, many of whom jump to their feet and push to the far wall. The scout then enchants the rune for his own departure and is taken away a moment later.

Belrum and the scout course their way into the camp and up to the portal gate.

"Eh, how d' ye use this beastly thing of yers?" Belrum asks.

"It is very simple, perhaps even more so than the rune," the scout offers. "It is already set, so you just jump through the hole and watch your feet on the landing. Then, like with the rune, step out of the way for the next one to pass."

"Aye, simple for ye, mayhap," he chuckles tenuously. "But for an old grizzle-beard like me…"

"I suppose you're right. I was born into it, as was everyone back home by now, so this is simply a part of life for us. But once you get used to it, it goes very easily. One thing I should advise is this one has a much longer journey, so you'll see yourself travelling through a long tunnel before you come out again. Just keep your mind on what you're doing until you arrive."

"Really now! Aye then, well, here it goes."

Belrum takes a deep breath and lets it out slowly, then makes a concerted effort to leap into the portal, unsure if he would collide with the back wall of the camp, or if he would find himself flying off some other direction. He vanishes into the image of the window. The scout pauses a moment as he observes Belrum appear within the image on the other side, then stepping away slightly, and he follows behind.

Belrum arrived on the platform of the connecting unit in the military outpost erected on Ruuki uy'Daan. He had to force himself to move again to step away from the aperture so the scout could come through, but his feet felt frozen to the ground.

He found himself in another outpost, similar in many ways to the one he just left, but the surrounding terrain was considerably different. The air was cool, at least reasonably so as compared to his own world, and the land appeared to hold fields of lush grasses. In the distance was a modest line of mountains and trees, and to the side were the ruins of an old city.

The scout arrived just behind him and stepped around to check if he was all right.

"This be Ruuki uy'Daan, ay?" Belrum asks softly.

"Yes, it is. This is where the Daanen-Aryku lived before they were pushed to the next world, which is where we're going next."

"That city there, be that one of theirs?"

"What remains of it. As you can see, it has been in a state of decay for a while, but we have some people trying to clean it up now."

Belrum sniffs the air. It smells uniquely different to him.

"The air here, it smells wet."

"There is an ocean just up to the north there, and this land was originally a jungle, so it is very wet."

"Praise be... So much for these tired old eyes t' see."

"Also remember what we said about the difference in the world as compared to yours. Do you remember our story about the elves?"

"Aye, those we used t' call point-ears. I nay be a-knowin' their true name afore Tol came along."

"Yes. If you recall the stories, they appeared sickly and weak after arriving on your world. This is because of the stronger gravity you have there…it makes things feel heavier. You, on the other hand, might feel lighter here due to a lesser gravity. You should also take care of your breathing, to keep it slow and steady, as the air is a bit thinner here for the same reason."

"I remember the tellin', but it be a mite different t' actually see it…an' feel it."

He checks his feet, testing himself with a small hop and discovering he feels lighter than usual.

"That yay be simply amazin'."

"And not only for you," the scout admits. "This is just as new to us to travel to a world like yours, so the experience is likewise in our case."

"An' t' think ye're able t' travel like this in the first place, findin' new lands an' discoverin' what might be there."

The scout leads them to the next gateway node in the camp and directs him to jump through.

This time, Belrum emerges into the center of a bustling city. He almost forgets to dodge out of the way to let the scout through due to the high level of activity. He cautiously steps off the platform while glancing all around him at the people, the buildings, and the occasional chatter.

"Oi…" he moans delicately. "Mayhap this was'na such a good plan after all."

The scout comes through behind him and steps out into the plaza.

"Welcome, friend Belrum, to the city of Rolsklinde," he announces politely.

"A city. A full livin' city. May the All-Father give his blessin' t' it. An' all these people! Praise be, what kinds of people d' ye have here? I see all kinds an' colors."

"We have elves of various kinds, a number of dwarves, and a few Daanen-Aryku, plus others. But this is actually a human city. The others are visitors from neighboring ones."

"So, ye have more after this? Oi…"

"Of course! But this world also suffered terribly because of the war. Much of the world is still empty, and so we're trying to encourage the people to grow again."

"An' this be from that titan an' his slave people, ay?"

"That's right. This city was blasted almost as badly as Glimmerheim once."

"But ye look like ye've been hard at work rebuildin' it."

"That we have. It took a lot of time, and many people to do the job, but we made good work out of it."

"Just for the sake of the tellin', if ye could ever bring our world back t' us, would ye d' the same favor?"

"Absolutely! My Lord did not hesitate to bring these people into his care and help with their needs."

"Yer King be a blessed soul. I s'pose we should be a-goin' t' speak with him by now."

The scout nods and leads the bewildered dwarf across the plaza to the WIC building.

✦✦✦✦✦

"...And these pictures are of the Thane's palace from the outside," the General notes as he presents a recent volley of photographs.

Thaelyn and his officers were reviewing the previous day's scouting run after successfully passing through the secret door up on the mountainside. Also present was Chief Bronzeheart, who was expected to be a part of these interactions for the foreseeable future as a consultant for the local city affairs and culture. They were just finishing up the examination of the photographs taken along the way.

The General continues, "Our people found a number of safe locations where they could make a quick appearance to use their cameras. Then this one..." he pushes another photo into view. "This is just inside the front doors. As you can see, it appears quite typical for a grand hall design. I believe we may have several possibilities amongst these pillars, and almost any ceiling corner where Kaliya and her team could set up positions to observe the Thane's activity while in this room."

"This is good work," Thaelyn nods. "More so that along the way they found the storeroom where the Thane apparently has his people drop the shipments of ingots for the Suuden-Aryku to pick up."

"Aye," the Chief adds. "We put it there for the ease of tradin' with the people above, or at least that be the tellin' of it."

"That actually makes sense to me," the General admits. "They said it appeared to be a junction with a partially collapsed exit to what we think may be the upper district, and then closed off when the city moved deeper. The only way in or out now is the passageway up to that door on the mountain."

"Making for very easy access by the Suuden-Aryku to retrieve those ingots sight-unseen," Thaelyn considers. "As well as their labor force."

"Further, for our convenience, it connected through a side passage right next to the palace. The door was not even locked, only barred by a simple latch."

"Yes, General, so easy…so convenient…" he pauses briefly. "In fact, this was too easy. There should have been guards."

"Guards?" the General muses curiously. "While I would surely agree if this were a main gate, this is hardly anything more than a back door to an isolated road leading up to a hidden base. It seems like a very secure location, so why should they need guards on it, especially if the Thane owns everything?"

"While this is true…" Thaelyn wonders. "It conjures up an image I cannot agree with. Chief, do you maintain any kind of security within your city? This is to say guard patrols or postings at the critical areas?"

"Nay," the Chief reflects. "We nay be needin' any guards as the Thane tells us we be too deep to worry about anything from above."

"And the people believe this?" Thaelyn asks incredulously.

"Aye, for the greater part of it, and since we nay have ever seen any trouble, it settles into their minds this way."

"I see, and I suppose you may have a point, but personally, I would find this unacceptable. Whether as a military leader, or even a common man, I would never make such a frivolous assumption.

You have stories of this war, and even if these were false, if you wanted the people to believe in them, you need to demonstrate some manner of action to suggest a wartime condition, and this means posting guards at ANY access point. And if you only have the one, this becomes even more critical."

"Ah, but of course!" the General affirms and slaps his hand on the table. "Forgive me, I was stuck on the notion that this was an independent folly."

"Granted, but this only exacerbates the situation. Let us consider a moment... The Chief and his people tell of their Thane and his stories, using such words as to say the war was blazing above, meaning to be quite vigorous. All the while, during this time, you are providing these materials to the surface as a supply for their warriors."

"Right, so if something is going out, something else ought to be able to come in, therefore the need to demonstrate some form of protection from that which you do NOT want to come in, real or imagined."

"Correct, and yet there is still something wrong. Chief Bronzeheart, you once told us the upper portions were said to be partially destroyed, and of course the stories of closing the doors to block off access."

"Aye, 'tis true that," he accedes.

"This is a very curious notion, my Lord," the General intones intriguingly. "Chief, those doors of yours, do they represent the only way into your city? There are no other doors, a rear access or something?"

"Nay to me knowin' of it. The only way in would be that one leadin' to the store where we drop the bricks. I hear tell of a door leadin' out, but no one is allowed to go through it. The Thane forbids it."

"How convenient..." he smirks ironically. "But under the circumstances, our scouts are suggesting the blocked doorway is likely the one leading to the upper town, and this too is unavailable."

"I think I have to agree," Kailen adds as he listens silently to the debate. "This doesn't fit properly. This is suggesting the idea that no access in would conversely mean no access out. Unless we're saying they created such a secure secret access point for this trade venue, if these ingots are intended for the outside world, how do they justify sending them there, but without any guards blocking any illegal access in?"

"True," Thaelyn accedes. "And even with a secret access point, I think after four centuries, someone would take notice of it, especially if this war is as vigorous as the Thane describes it. The land should be overrun by now."

The Chief frowns as he suddenly feels the contradiction of these terms flooding his thoughts. He pauses to consider the notion and turns to the side in a moment of silent contemplation. The others continue the debate.

"Indeed, my Lord," the General agrees. "If you are at war with someone, one of your first priorities should be to cut off his supply lines, and this city represents a solid one. If we consider the example of Rolsklinde and the Governor, and their stories of war here, but with no recent examples to anyone's current knowledge, these people must be seriously deluded by now…with respect, of course," he glances at the Chief.

"Aye, General, I know yer meanin'."

"Nevertheless, he did actually post guards, if only for the showing."

"And yet," Thaelyn concludes. "This still does not follow logically. No proper leader or military commander would allow access to such a sensitive area as this without at least a slight show of security to protect it, whether it was necessary or not. In these stories, you have a war, you have enemies rampaging across the land, you have cities burning, and you have the ever-present demand for both materials and labor to go up and serve. This in itself suggests the war is not letting up. Even more so if you factor in the general knowledge dwarves ought to have that adamantium is a superior material to use in both armor and weapons. So, whatever is raging up there, if they were using these materials properly, there should be nothing left of it by now."

"Bricks…" Tol moans softly. "All he ever asks for is bricks, nay the sort of ware to fight with."

"This suggests one thing already," Kailen offers. "Whoever it is telling these stories doesn't have a clue what adamantium is or how to use it."

"Agreed," Thaelyn affirms. "This could possibly narrow our focus for who he is based on his personal knowledge, but it also poses its own paradox. Whether a dwarf, or a servant being to such like Sargeras, he should be far more knowledgeable. Either that, or this Thane is telling his stories for the sheer delight of storytelling alone."

"Storytelling…" the General muses. "He comes out of hiding… hmm. Chief, how often does he actually come outside?"

"I hear tell it nay be too often," he reflects. "He stays in his private chamber day and night, only to come out to scream at the Chancellor for more bricks."

"Then, this is his entire purpose, to reinforce the message to keep up the pace. I would therefore suggest he has some sort of access to the base and makes occasional visits from there to deliver his demands. But now, we need to understand what sort of man he truly is, if not a tactical-minded war leader. This sounds much more like he is playing a game of entertainment."

"Furthermore," Thaelyn considers. "If we are to say he has direct access to the base, and does not participate in the local society, he might not actually be a dwarf. And yet if he is a servant to a Primordial…" he pauses in thought. "This still does not follow politely if he should know the value of adamantium. Unlike the people here, who did NOT know the value of this metal, dwarves surely would, so you could not simply hide the knowledge. Therefore, his stories do not hold up to proper scrutiny, at least…well, again with respect to the Chief here…not to anyone with a thinking mind. So, if as he says, it settled into their minds this way, we may have a similar situation as what we found here in this world, meaning to say so many long-duration stories numbing their capacity to actually think any more."

"Aye, yer Kingship," Tol concedes. "Ye may be right. I recall now how me and the lads were when we first woke up here, and then to think of the people back home."

"I suppose this is possible," the General admits. "But now this forces me to ask, how can this be. If we go by Darumon's example, he was a very savvy individual, for all the intrigue he played. Here we have another circumstance of a city under an oppressive force, but it is not being played out as wisely as he did here. If we further say, according to Adalon's prophecies, he and Sargeras were the only two hiding alone in the dark, then who is this third one that does not know the utility of adamantium, and who creates so many wild stories of a war, and further to send out such a valuable material as this, which would clearly draw attention after a while, and yet who never portrays the image of security for their production. This is a severe lapse of duty, to say nothing of knowledge."

Thaelyn smiled at the clever reasoning.

"Nicely done, General. Then he cannot be a third Primordial, especially if he is making such obvious mistakes, or is simply behaving in an irrational manner."

"My Lord!" he rebukes teasingly. "I know you have a habit of occasionally testing people, but are you now playing this on me?"

"No one is immune, General," he grins. "We all occasionally need a refresher course. This is to make up for your failure to rationalize the lack of guards."

"Oh dear," he chuckles. "But I still put it to you there is some level of rationale to it. It simply does not follow with a military mind driving it."

"I will admit, you do hold a point. And here is where we must reconcile this idea. From that perspective, where you KNOW there is no need for security, stories or otherwise, we must be speaking of someone who is not well-versed in military protocol, but who does enjoy telling stories and playing games."

"Very good. As if he was playing with a toy city, I suppose, and one with no natural enemies to bother with…at least no true ones."

"Precisely, therefore he does not deploy any guards, as he does not consider this necessary, or maybe not a valuable use of resources.

And perhaps, like the Chief said, after four hundred years of these stories, he probably thinks he owns that city very tightly."

"You know," Kailen folds his arms and reflects warmly. "Watching the two of you, in itself, can be very entertaining. So, who is it we're talking about if not a military man…a civilian perhaps? By the sound of it, not knowing as much about adamantium, we could qualify one of our own people…except for the disguise, of course. So, unless we're using something like a puppet, or maybe an animatronic to imitate a dwarf…"

"This is an interesting idea," Thaelyn muses. "Given the advances those people have made behind our backs, almost anything is possible. Do you know of anything like an artificial intelligence construct that could simulate an actual person to this degree?"

"Not in our possession. I know we had some AI applications back home, like for research networks and information repositories. As for a robot-like thing impersonating a person…well, it's hard to say."

"Chief, how does the Thane behave, to the best of your understanding?"

"It's said he comes out only on those occasions to rage at the poor Chancellor, then runs back to his room till the next time. I think it's also said ye cannot go in there to disturb him during this time."

"Then, by the sound of it, he does not take food or anything else a normal…living person might need. This could possibly represent an artificial unit being activated and deployed, and maybe someone speaking through a remote link."

"But my Lord," the General interjects. "That someone would likely need emotions to conduct this level of abusive behavior. With those chips installed…"

"Indeed! Good point," he gently slaps a hand on the table.

"A little payback for that last one," the General chuckles demurely.

Thaelyn turns and gawks at the General for the bold remark.

"Oh really! You are turning it back on ME now?"

"No one is immune, my Lord," he grins brightly.

"I swear!"

Kailen leads the group in a hearty laugh at the careful play.

"Very well," Thaelyn resumes. "But we must still consider this much. This is presumably a military base. Whoever is in command must therefore be military. As for the Thane, if he is not a Primordial, and for this point I think we must also include Darumon himself making appearances, as surely, he would know better than to downplay the value of adamantium, especially to people who know how to produce it, and furthermore if we are speaking of someone without a reasonable level of military prowess, it cannot be one of the base personnel. That idea of a civilian is sounding better, although problematic."

"What if we say briefly that it WAS Darumon?" the General asks. "For instance, making runs between this and his other assignments."

"All right, but then we must ask about the timing. If Darumon was spending four centuries occupying his office here in the city, and perhaps with witnesses coming and going to observe this, we must ask about the timing and duration of these visits to the Thane's Hall, and if he could get away long enough for it."

"Very well, if we suggest he makes his visits only on those rare occasions, and then returns to his other work, he might have a very busy schedule between this and his other objectives."

"But even at that, we still have these other points against the argument. Surely, he would keep his stories straight, and surely, he would know enough about adamantium, and also that the dwarves would know this, as well, to realize they would probably not sit still for a four-hundred-year war using up their most precious materials in a fight that should not take that long."

"Granted. Then, perhaps as the Commander said, this would limit us to the Suuden-Aryku, one that in this case does NOT have an emotion inhibitor chip installed, and who probably does not ask enough questions of those who would know best what this material is actually good for. Even if we suggest a native who was badly corrupted by Darumon, he should still know adamantium better than this to realize the folly of his stories."

"Absolutely. But then, are we going back to a civilian member, or military? Are we using that animatronic idea, or something else?"

"The scenario here is clearly different," the General submits. "And you know, I would think this would constitute an important part of Darumon's operations. He surely would not wish to flub it up as badly as this if he were paying such close attention to it personally. He did better than that here on this world, and this one might not amount to such a critical objective."

"Meaning," Kailen leans forward. "He set something up and left it in the hands of someone else? Someone who is either civilian, or military with very poor management skills? That sounds like an error in itself."

"Yes," Thaelyn muses as he leans back. "We are speaking of procuring a substance to make a weapon of godlike proportions. You do NOT want this to go awry. Therefore, these stories, this clear lack of proper understanding, of protocol..." he ponders deeply. "It contradicts the notion. Regardless of who is in command, there should still be standards to follow. Even in Rolsklinde, you had the occasional few who asked questions. What about THEM?"

The Chief was now visibly disturbed. He leans back in his chair and sighs heavily.

"Me poor Eiki...she was right," he mumbles softly. "May the All-Father forgive me, I should have listened harder to her."

"Excuse me Chief?" Thaelyn inquires.

"Ye speak of they who ought to be askin' questions. Well, aye, I have one for ye. Me wife, Eiki. Yer Kingship, I nay be the soldier, but even I nay can think of the reason for this. It would be foolhardy for all the wild tellin' goin' on down there."

"And Eiki? How does she see it?"

"For years, at least to the last I'd seen of her, she was tellin' these same tales. Most people don' go out askin' a lot of questions, believin' what the Thane tells them. Eiki, she was a harder one than most, and she would bring it together sometimes, askin' up these same questions ye and yer men just came out with. But with the tales down there, some of them old tales with nay a soul in our time knowin' the truth of it, they be just whispers of local gossip to share over a stein of ale."

"Chief, when we first arrived in this world, we found many of the local people, especially in this city, in a similar fix. Yours is nothing new to us. Clearly, this will need to be corrected, but this bears a remarkable similarity to the last one we found."

"Yes, but with a notable exception," the General recounts. "On the surface, he sounds very similar to Darumon as the Governor for his storytelling, although this example seems much harsher. Maybe he borrowed lessons for this point, or maybe he chooses it this way for the audience he is playing to."

"Perhaps, but if this is the case, he is behaving especially belligerent, unless we are to suggest the extended duration has invoked him to increase the level of desperation to continue forward."

"Yes, that may be a good cause for it. The people would surely grow weary of this prolonged war after a while. Perhaps this is in response to keep up the image."

"And so, he begins to exaggerate the stories…what was once an invasion of weak elves and a mercy killing has now grown into a cataclysm of burning cities and the whole world made an inferno."

"Great All-Father, Yer Kingship," the Chief exclaims. "So, all the wild tellin' nay be anythin' more than a man gone mad to get more bricks?"

"Quite possibly, and this man, whoever he truly is, has no interest in showing the appropriate protocols for a city at war. Chief, what sorts of activities do your people engage in down there?"

"Everyone works their trade, many of the men in the forges and mines, others in shops and the farmin' caves. Me dear Eiki would work as a clothes maker sometimes."

"Business as usual…for a city at war…and presumably a large and well-known city, sending up materials on a regular basis to aid in a war effort, and he makes such a prominent blunder as to fail to offer protection from those same enemies that are ravaging the rest of the world. I find myself suddenly very curious about this Thane. Chief, can you tell us anything else about him?"

"All I can say for sure is the Thane be a hard one. I nay be knowin' much about him personally. I don' think he has a family, not that it matters if he is nay even a real person. And like I said before, he storms up a fury in his throne room every time the Chancellor goes to see him. That's really all I know of him, afore he runs off to his room again. From there, he comes out only when he chooses."

"This sounds like quite a show he puts on. But I wonder if this could be another example like here, where Darumon had a mini conveyor in his basement."

"If he does," the General cautions. "We need to be careful of that reactor again."

"Indeed. Darumon had in mind to set it off as a disposal technique for the city. And then regarding these temper rages, which seem a rather immature form of behavior, unless we say it is simply an act. But this Thane sounds like he might actually enjoy the moment."

"If he does," Kailen offers. "This could symbolize a superiority complex. Someone who doesn't actually care what adamantium is, just that it's something he wants to serve Darumon's needs, and he must be doing so very lovingly for these visits. He was probably installed just for this reason and given custom training."

"Powers help us if this is true. Then we could indeed be speaking of a civilian, because I think a military man would get his facts straight, chip or no chip. That Commander Geilv and his local officers gave an impression, for what little I could gain out of it, where they behaved with a good amount of training and protocol, despite any chips controlling them."

"Incredible. So, it seems we have someone, maybe like the Dean, who was seduced by power and authority, and going loose-horned on the rest to demand all this metal. He gets worse as the years pass by, maybe because the people are becoming anxious and frustrated by the lack of resolution to the war, and so he exaggerates the stories..." he pauses in thought briefly.

"But along the way, he probably loses track of his details and starts making errors, like with no guards, no reasonable excuse for how things are traded, and so on."

"And those weak elves in the beginning, then to take over the place later on. Something changed, and it doesn't take into consideration the dwarves and their proficiency with this metal."

"Neither does it consider taking four centuries to destroy a world during wartime," the General adds. "Not if the land is essentially overrun and every city is on fire."

"Surely, in this time," Thaelyn admits. "He would need to impersonate a series of Thanes. Four centuries is a bit outside the lifespan of just one. This could possibly offer an excuse if a transition misinterprets the earlier stories."

"How long are their lifespans?" Kailen asks.

"I can answer that one," the Chief offers. "Our people can go a good century and a half to two centuries, dependin' on the type of work and a wee bit of good fortune for their health and good eatin'."

"So, we're probably talking about at least three Thanes, maybe more, depending on when it started and how old the first one was… and how often they transition."

"Mayhap, although to me proper thinkin', I nay can think of one time for a change of throne, nay in me lifetime. For that matter, I nay can be sure of me father's lifetime, but methinks it may still hold that way. An' now that I think of it, I recall it said that the Thane looks like a young lad in his prime, nay an elder."

"One moment…" Thaelyn asserts. "Are you suggesting we could be speaking of someone potentially impersonating the same man for four centuries straight?"

"I nay can be sure if I can speak for it fully, but this could be the way of it. I nay know of a family, and this includes kinfolk to take up the throne before or after."

"That would be ridiculous!" the General complains. "If he is playing this so mindlessly that he doesn't even offer a transition of rulers…"

"Indeed," Thaelyn nods. "We could say the same for Darumon as Governor here, but human lifetimes are much shorter, especially after that trick he played with his implants cutting them down even more. No one would hold any personal memory after a while, and his substandard education system would remove everything else. But this… This man, whoever he is, he is not a very wise individual to be playing this at all."

"Good gods," the General shakes his head. "Very well then, if we are speaking of an otherwise simple man, I think dealing with him should not be too difficult. The only thing after that is Darumon taking notice of his absence. How do we go about covering for that? Do we assign another of Kaliya's team to impersonate him? And if so, we need to know who he is topside and how he behaves. And for this, we need to study him."

"Agreed…"

The conversation comes to a brief lull as they consider the topics and what directions they might need to follow. During this moment, a voice ushers up from the doorway.

"My Lord, may I disturb you for a moment?"

Thaelyn turns towards the door to find a scout and a very jittery dwarf standing there, patiently waiting for his turn. The dwarf's clothes belied his point of origin, and his demeanor was clearly evident of his nervousness.

"Yes, Scout, please come in with your guest. Might I assume this to be our visitor from afar, as the Captain informed me?"

"Yes, it is. May I present to you the good man Belrum Strongfoot."

Thaelyn steps around for a better look. Belrum was hunched over penitently as he came in. He saw the Chief sitting on one of the chairs, and nods to him modestly. But of all the people in the room, he couldn't help but notice the impossibly tall, blue-skinned officer rising up to stand on the other side of the table, and attempted to crank his head up in a vain effort to meet the upper part of him.

"Great All-Father, what be that over yon?" he whispers to himself.

He pulls himself up as Thaelyn approaches and tries to meet him in the eyes. The nobleman's height stood well above the trembling dwarf.

"Oi, forget what I said about the other one, look at yer eyes. Are they truly made of gold?"

Thaelyn smiled at the modest, if not simple-witted statement.

"I am Lord Thaelyn, King of Tae'Eladar, and most recently of portions of this world, Therinë."

"I be most humbled in yer presence, Yer Kingship. I seem t' be a-sayin' this a lot now an' again, but I nay be more than a poor farmer's son, an' I come before ye most graciously for the favor of yer ear."

"I have heard some good words from my Captain of your efforts. Please, stand up; it is not necessary to bend so low here."

Belrum makes a difficult effort to straighten his back, though it still felt weak.

"My Captain sent a message early this morn to expect you," Thaelyn continues. "He said you had a rather unfortunate, if not unexpected problem developing, and he was sending you to speak to me about a possible answer to it."

"Aye, that be the way of it. We've been a-gatherin' up as many of our kinfolk as we can get out word for, but the size of the mine we live in be a-feelin' the crush."

"Yes, this makes perfect sense. Allow me to ask you this. How would your people feel about coming to this world to live, if only for the short term until we could bring aid to yours?"

"I was a-talkin' t' the clans' folk today since yer Captain made the offer. Some nay be sure of leavin' their home, but they all agree we can'na farm our own land, an' we also can'na turn down t' take up somewhere, even if for a wee bit till we can go back home."

"Very good. Now, considering our situation, we could carry this in a number of directions. In the beginning, I would recommend you take up occupation on some of the existing farms, at least until you can become adjusted. Our culture, our language, and perhaps other aspects of life here may vary from yours, and I would wish to ensure you can adapt to it for the best result."

"Aye, this seems fair enough."

"Furthermore, I am a believer in bringing people together into a united society. So, once we have a good threshold of immigrants, we could begin to build a colonial village setting for you. We have a large expanse of open space in this world...the unfortunate result of the war here...therefore, land is not an issue. Since our arrival, and the conclusion of that war, the native people of this world have given themselves over to my rule, and as the result, I seem to have inherited this world into my kingdom."

"That be a right fine inheritance, if ye ask me!" he chuckles.

"Yes, it is, and one I did not expect at this time of my rule. We were not ready to branch out to other worlds before this, and yet here we are."

"An' I hear it nay be just this one, but that other I crossed over… ehm, Ruuki uy'Daan?"

"That one is still under investigation. The city you likely saw as you passed by belongs to the Daanen-Aryku," he points at Kailen as an example.

"Oi! That be a Daanen-Aryku?" Belrum yips. "Great All-Father, they be a mighty folk!"

"Yes, the Commander here is one of the more generous examples," Thaelyn grins.

"I be a-thinkin' of the story good Tol laid upon me ears. If such a folk as they can be pushed 'round so much, I nay be a-wantin' t' see the ones pushin'!"

"Indeed, and they did demonstrate themselves to be rather difficult. But now, back to you… I would expect it will take a fair amount of time to see any reversal of the conditions in your world once we do get started. Therefore, we should interpret our work together to be long-term, whether we describe it as temporary or otherwise."

"Aye, I s'pose this will be the way of it."

"I spent much of my time on Tae'Eladar uniting a variety of nations into one kingdom, so I would tend to discourage the development of an independent society which might then turn to rival the rest. This is unproductive. Rather, I would encourage cooperation, which benefits everyone. Open trade and communication between us can share many fine resources and information, even culture and other items unique to each of us. We have a dwarven population on Tae'Eladar, and I am quite sure they would take great pleasure in reuniting with their ancestral kin."

"Aye! That be a fine one! I nay can recall this migration ye speak of, but as I think I said afore, me schoolin' nay be as good as some."

"And I would imagine, for all the devastation your world took, the greater majority of your knowledge and wisdom, even many of your finer skills from so many dedicated craftsmen was lost. This is one of the greatest tragedies, and probably cannot be replaced."

"Ye're right. I know we have a few folk who be weavers an' simple cloth makers, but the tellin' goes we once had a grand bit more."

"Then this is a chance to rebuild yourselves. We might describe this as where you take up occupancy on our land, with the idea of one day returning home to yours, or we could describe this as a form of immigration, if you should wish to become a part of our society. Some of you may choose this anyway, after a time, and doing so could open up a number of possibilities for you and your children."

"Ye mean t' simply make a new home here, an' leave the old land behind us?"

"It would still be there, and we will not hold you back from it, but the conditions there, at least at this time, are unfavorable. Should you or your children choose to migrate back one day, we will give you our blessings. Or..." he muses distantly. "Well, I invited the people of this world to join me, and I would extend it to you and yours on Morndindor as well. Who knows? We will very likely be working together for a long period, so we cannot be sure how you might feel after that. You may become a part of the kingdom anyway," he chuckles and shrugs.

"More of that inheritin' business, ay?" he smirks. "Aye, mayhap, an' nay only for the work ye'll be a-makin' there."

"Indeed, the Chief and some of his people are already speaking of this. They have settled in very nicely since their arrival."

"Yay be t' that!" the Chief affirms energetically. "Belrum, me an' the lads here have been a-thinkin' this be a fine land with good people. So far, we've been a-makin' our homes here in the city. It was hard at first, bein' new t' this place, an' a few of us were a-thinkin' of our kinfolk back home. Ye'll need t' stay together an' work hard for it, but if ye listen t' this man here, ye'll nay go wrong by it."

"And his people are not the only ones," Thaelyn adds. "Even some of the Daanen-Aryku are expressing a desire for it in recent times, and they are even harder to convince than the rest. Yours would be welcome right alongside the others. But for this, I might suggest the idea of the colony setting, to bring some of your native charm into the equation, as well simply to provide enough new homes for everyone."

"Our native charm," Belrum considers as he glances at himself. "Ye actually hold so much carin' for this? I be but a simple farmer, an' this here be as much charm as me old legs can carry."

"I regard everyone to carry something special, and together we are stronger for the contribution of each individual, old legs notwithstanding," he smiles.

"Oi, those be some fine words, Yer Kingship. It nay be a wonder ye're a King over so many. Ehm, but farmin' nay be the only thing. We also have heardin' beasts t' care for, an' we have a few crafters that will need shops or some such."

"Yes, and then we have this. Then I would suggest we begin outlining the village setting sooner, rather than later, in order to plan for your future needs. This can include workshops and marketplaces for your people to make and sell their goods, and we have a large market within this city and many others to trade with. As for your animals, they will need land, and we can certainly arrange this easily enough. By the way, this actually reminds me. When we first found Chief Bronzeheart and his people in the mines here, there was some breed of animal with them. I am wondering if these belong to your world."

"Oh? What be they about?"

"They were of moderate height..." he estimates with a hand. "They had dense curly hair, mostly a dirty white, hoofed feet, a rather short tail, and loosely curled horns."

"Hmm, that yay be a-soundin' like a briar sheep, it does. Aye, I know the sort. D' ye still have them?"

"Yes, we took them out of the mine and brought them to Tae'Eladar where we placed them in the foster care of a farm near our home city. They are being maintained there still. In fact, I believe I heard they had a new generation or two since that time," he chuckles.

"Aye! They'll d' that, if ye let them," he laughs vigorously.

"Indeed, it was actually very encouraging to see them developing. But anyway if you want them, they are yours, as they belong to your world anyway. Although I am asking myself if you will need to negotiate with the foster caregivers, as they might have grown attached to a few by now," he grins.

"Aye t' that, if they want t' keep a few for themselves, that yay be fine with me, an' I can'na thank ye enough for yer help."

"Then we should begin moving your people as soon as possible. We can send word to the local families to expect you. You should also be made aware that most of the people in this world do not speak any form of Dwarvish, so it might be a little difficult in the beginning. We have classes you may take, and I do recommend this, so you can learn our language."

"Oh…ehm…I nay have any coin in me pocket, so I don'na know if I can afford any schoolin'."

"Not to worry, this particular course is free of charge, so there should be no problem with that. Chief Bronzeheart and his men can help you orient. As for the coin, I think you will soon see your pockets begin to fill again once we put you to some honest labor."

"Coin…in me pockets. I can'na imagine it. But oh, before I forget. I be a-thinkin' there be more kinfolk out there. We can move what we have, but I don'na know what t' d' about more comin' in. Can ye give a bit of yer fine wisdom for that, mayhap?"

"Yes, and this is important, as some of them may be far afield. Even if your word does get out to the local clans, and maybe spread beyond that, we must also consider those at far distance from your home. For this, we may need to send out scouts and intermediaries to speak with them. We must try to gather up as many as we can, otherwise some may fall victim to the withering land."

"But at such a far distance, I can'na imagine anyone walkin' that much, nay with the land an' food as it be with us."

"Indeed, this will need to be attended to in a much more efficient manner."

Thaelyn considers his options for a moment on how best to accomplish this, while at the same time trying not to reveal his actions too boldly to his enemies.

"Good sir Strongfoot," he continues. "You have done so much for our combined service, how would you, and perhaps some of your more capable fellows, like to take up occupation with us to see this through?"

"Ye'd put me t' work for ye?" he responds excitedly.

"Yes! As a native, and now with such experience with our people, you would be perfect for this. And if you could recruit a few others, we could make this even better."

"But how could I be of service t' help those in such far places?"

"Ah, we are not ones who spend a great deal of time simply walking."

"Aye, I see that with all these portals of yers."

"But that is not all we have to offer. We often use animals as mounts to carry us on longer journeys. I would use a number of these on this occasion."

"Ridin' beasts, aye! I know the tales, but ne'er seen one me'self."

"Good, then I think we may have some good ideas to work with. I can provide the transport, and you can provide the native charm. We can then use our portals to move the people rather than to have them simply walk."

"Some of the people are yay a bit scared of these portals, Yer Kingship."

"I understand, but survival must take the higher priority in this case."

✦✦✦✦✦

"Well, well…" Petrith intones. "What do we have here, I wonder?"

"Look at this place!" Túfula declares mutedly. "And this is where they take their baths?"

"Um, are we really supposed to be in here?" Sulíma asks timidly.

The three of them had finished their language course for the day. It was early afternoon, and they were taking a tour of the guildhall facilities trying to acquaint themselves with the layout of the academies, the training halls, the cafeteria, and other amenities, including the baths. They had just entered the bathhouse near the rear of the complex to examine the facility in preparation for when they would ultimately be taking their own official courses. At this time of day, the room was empty, as the classes were still in session around the guild.

The room was decorated with planters and lush foliage. It had several small pools for patrons to sit and socialize. The walkway they were on led out from a locker room on the side and along the edge of the room to an enclosed space where they could hear the flow of water. They followed it around to find a large communal granite-tiled waterfall shower.

"I don't believe it!" Petrith mutters as he steps in for a closer look. "This is it!"

"You mean from your dream, Petrith?" Sulíma asks.

He moves around the shower, trying to find a comfortable angle to compare with the vision he had once. The waterfall flowed out from over their heads to one side of the room, through a series of flutes and channels, and drained through a grating in the floor. On the other side was an alcove with shelving for bathing accessories and closet space for towels. Petrith studied the arrangement and shook his head in wonder. He reached out a hand to test the water. It seemed comfortably warm to the touch.

"This is heated," he remarks. "Túfu, you'd better take back some of those suggestions of them being primitive. This is a resort!"

"I've just never seen, or even heard, of anything like this outside of what we're so familiar with back home. And this would be in a class by itself."

"Well, familiar or not, I wouldn't mind using this even now. Would either of you girls like to join me?" he chuckles.

"I'm tempted," Sulíma contemplates. "I really am. But I didn't bring my soap, and I know how much you like the stuff," she giggles.

"Oh no, not again," he relents and slaps his head. "How many times, Suli?"

"I think she's going to milk this for everything she can get," Túfula grins.

"All right, fine. You bring your soap, and we'll see just how much opportunity you get to use it."

"Promises, promises, just like always," Sulíma pouts playfully. "Túfu, when do you think he'll ever live up to any of this?"

"Maybe we simply need to approach it differently. Kali said her soap was scented, remember?"

"Oh, right! That's a great idea!"

"Cu'Nar, help me," Petrith moans. "But seriously, one of these days we WILL be in here."

"Yeah," Túfula admits. "And it'll be for real. But at least I hear it's separated into boy's and girl's rooms."

"Except for those pools outside, that's co-ed."

"Right, so these people have a culture of communal bathing as a social activity."

"But without the sex, so Suli won't be happy," he smirks.

"I'll manage," Sulíma relents wistfully. "So long as someone takes care of me afterwards...a little music, a little wine..."

"Suli," Túfula wonders. "When in your life did you ever drink wine?"

"Um, well...but that's what people talk about around here. It's supposed to set the mood."

"Either that or dumb you down so you don't know what you're doing."

"So long as I wake up happy..."

They browsed around a bit more through the social area before leaving to investigate the other parts of the guildhall. They travelled outside to watch the mage practice in the lower field, peeked inside the combat training hall, and finally the cafeteria.

"And this is where they eat," Túfula considers. "We'll need to get used to the types of food they have around here. Three and a half centuries of that stuff we had back home, and it's nice to eat better at the Naarg uy'Sodrad, but now we'll be coming here for it."

"Kali eats here, and she doesn't complain," Sulíma reflects.

"Yeah, but she also lived on Therinë during all that time, so she probably became accustomed to it with some of those others. This might only be a minor change for her."

"I have to wonder how much of it she could actually sample," Petrith admits, "if they were locked inside the ship so much. Nothing more than aeroponics labs in there."

"All right," Sulíma nods. "But for those other occasions, she lived through it, that's the point I'm trying to make, and so will we. I'm perfectly happy to give it a try. And if you can let go of some of that skepticism, you might too."

"I'm sorry," Túfula shrugs. "I guess it runs in the family."

Chapter 5

A NEW BREED

A few days have passed since the meeting over the new operations being planned for Morndindor. In addition, the hallways were buzzing with gossip over the results achieved by Petrith and the gang with their Spirit tests. It was creating a new sensation, but so far, the association of the Daanen-Aryku being on par to Celestials was being held in reserve. This was a delicate topic, and Kaliya wanted to keep it under control. She had spent much of her free time reviewing her objectives for her upcoming raid of the mining base, and who to select for her team. But at the same time, she also knew there was a higher need looming in the distance.

It was not specific to her, but rather all her people. The prospect of being equivalent to a Celestial race, for their Gifts, the violet test score, and most importantly, their unusual heritage, being the children of a near-godlike creature, as it was suggested during that last meeting, brought with it a dire circumstance. It carried a solemn burden of responsibility, one that she knew her people were simply not prepared for at this moment in their cultural evolution. But it was inescapable, and entirely demanding of the most critical applications of responsibility and respect. But where does one go to learn these lessons, except from they who are already there.

On this day, she called up a meeting of her newly selected teammates.

"I would like to call the attention of the group," Kaliya begins. "I have several things I need to announce, but some of this isn't going to go down easily for any of you. First, we are gathered here in preparation for a special operation, which will be a kind of trial-by-fire to test our abilities. We found that base on Morndindor, and naturally, we need to take it complete, along with the base crew. For this, I am being given a command role to lead this infiltration force, but we need to prepare ourselves first. We've never done anything like this before. We've never acted out an offensive military campaign, so we need to teach ourselves how to fight, and especially how to win."

The room fills with murmurs and hushed crooning.

"No doubt, we will need to undergo a series of training courses together to learn how to work as a team. But I think this should not be a problem. We have good people teaching us and a lot of resources to draw from. But the real point of this meeting is not so much our upcoming assignment, it's how we must represent ourselves along the way. First, I know many of you were from a profession that didn't start out as military in nature. Now, here you are as part of this special joint effort we have assembled as we move towards Azgarén. But it doesn't end there. We have something new that came up recently, and for this, we must lift ourselves to something much, much higher…such that none of us may truly be prepared for."

"That sounds serious," remarks one of the females.

"Navina, this is more serious than I think I have words for, and it demands our fullest attention to detail. We simply don't have a choice in it. This is who we are, like it or not."

"Uh oh… What is it?"

"It relates to the Prodigy Gift, and what it means for us as a species."

"A species? All of us?"

"Yes, it has to include all of us. If this is a latent ability only now showing itself, we need to consider every member of our society out there, especially those on Azgarén who may also have it, but who don't know it yet, and surely wouldn't know how to use it even if they did discover it. This is a godlike ability, one we should NOT be in possession of at this point in our evolution, and yet, here we are. And this isn't the only ability we seem to be gifted with."

"Yeah, we've been trained in this as well as telepathy so far, and I think I heard Petrith also demonstrated clairvoyance once."

"Right, and if we have these, we may have more yet to be discovered. We just need to experiment a little, or maybe find those people who already accidentally found them."

"That's a little scary to think of."

"And what's even scarier is WHY we have them. This becomes our legacy, and not one we could ever be ready for. We're simply not evolved enough to realize the implications. But due to our heritage of being Darumon's children, we are given to possess traits more becoming of a Celestial race."

The room erupts in a round of oohs and quiet whispers.

"And finally, we have the blessing of the cu'Nar. I was in conversation with Thaelyn a while ago concerning the test scores Petrith and the others received. I know there has been a lot of gossip going around the halls about the latest sensation of violet test scores, but what I have been trying to keep quiet so far is what this really means for us. I don't want a lot of people whispering about us behind our collective backs while we're so desperately trying to train and prepare ourselves for an important mission. Eventually, I'm sure it'll get out, but for now, we should try to keep a low profile for this point, at least until we can achieve something to demonstrate ourselves."

"All right, but if what you're actually saying is, um…"

"We are a new Celestial race, but well before our time."

"Oh dear cu'Nar…" Navina wheezes, followed by the rest of the room.

"Yeah, and you have THEM to thank for it, at least in part. That, and also Maker Kuroku. If she instructed them to do this, there had to be a reason for it. Thaelyn says this had to be intentional, as a rather drastic maneuver to purge…not cleanse, but purge the essence of the Primordials still inside of us, essentially converting us away from Darumon's heritage, and aligning us with the positive side of the Measure of Balance, therefore making us compatible with such like the Estelar…as a Celestial race."

"In all the nether-space, Kaliya! I was actually hoping you were just joking with that statement."

"I know what you mean, Navina, but unfortunately, I think I have to agree with Thaelyn on this point. We are half Darumon, and worse is we have been, um, well…" she coughs softly, "…for lack of a better term, inbreeding ourselves as half-brothers and sisters, ever since the days of that first generation of Eracyodine hybrids he created, and refining these qualities until we are what you see today. Maybe, for our ridiculously long lifespans, it took this long for the bigger Gifts to finally come out. The trouble is, we, as a race, don't have the first idea how to live, work, and play, as Celestials, but now we have to learn."

"How?"

"By taking our examples from they who are already there. Thaelyn for one, and Aerlie for another. The Seraphim are a good example, and they are also a very mature one, where each member is most often addressed with the title of Dame. This is a title of knighthood, perhaps one of the most exalted forms of prestige this side of full nobility."

"Oh dear…"

"And for this, we come to Adalon's prophecy of the Stormhooves. This is where it comes into play, I think. But in our case, we need to reinvent it to meet the need, and what a need it is," she rolls her eyes. "We must set an example for everyone else…and I do mean everyone!"

Kaliya pauses to study their reactions before continuing.

"I understand Túfu has been trying to share a few of her father's history lessons relating to the old Order of the Stormhooves. We will represent the rebirth of that old knighthood, but with a few new twists. To recap the history of it, the legendary Order of the Stormhooves, as told to us by our historians, was founded by King Saakerav, something like a thousand millennia ago, as a means to join together the varied nations of the Old World. It is often regarded in modern times as a romantic period in our history, although I hesitate to mention this could be for no more reason than the propaganda effect to cause us to admire it so much as the greatest thing ever to happen to us. This is probably as a means of keeping us from going back to the old ways, as it doesn't serve Darumon to have us spending all our efforts on so much internal conflict."

The room fills with moans and sighs, along with a few whispers over the implications, until Navina speaks up again.

"So, King Saakerav," she offers. "For all we might think of him as a great leader, and such a fantastic role model, was really Darumon in disguise to lead us into his Grand Plan, which required unity for our people, therefore making us more manageable, I suppose, right?"

"Generally, yes," Kaliya responds. "But Navina, we can say one thing about it. Grand Plan or otherwise, he did actually do us a favor. Being united DID solve many of our internal issues, and brought our society into peace and enlightenment. While it might have been for his greater purpose, it served one of ours, as well. So, let us not place too much blame on him for this point, as we did take benefit from it."

"All right, I'll keep my horns curled for this much."

"Nevertheless, we are going to make our own play on this romance, and this time, give the people a real reason to admire it."

The room now fills with a gently optimistic murmuring as Kaliya continues.

"People, regardless of his intentions, he gave us a symbol to aspire to, and that is the Stormhooves. But we don't need to concern ourselves as much with the standards set by the originals, as we need to bring this into the modern day. The original Stormhooves were a crusading military body to unite a world. Well, that world is united now, and our people need new leaders to set new standards, and those standards have to reach very literally to the gods above, no less!"

The sound of reverent oohs and ahs circles the room.

"To our benefit, we have good people guiding us, this being the Lord and Lady, Adalon the Silver, and Shescellaie, Queen of the

Dryads. This represents the Pillars of Three behind the Order of Tyr. And then we have the wisdom and the teachings of the Estelar. They are the grandfathers above all the rest, and they will be ours as well. All this combined will instill upon us the values we need to create our own legend. They will teach us what needs to be done and how to do it, in order to set the example for US that we may set it for others!"

The room now fills with cheers and applause. Kaliya examines their faces and feels the rush of authority flowing through her for the newly inspirational leadership. She hadn't felt anything like this since the time she once earned the rank of Ensign in the Sentinels. But that was short-lived, and turned out very bad for her due to her impetuous ambitions and anger for how badly her people were suffering in the war. This was now a fresh start, and with a higher purpose behind it, and she felt good about it.

"The Order of the Stormhooves will need to set its own standards of excellence, especially if we are to describe ourselves as a young Celestial race. This is OUR heritage for OUR people, and we must become the educators to teach future generations how to live up to the standards made by those who already hold this prestige. It is not a choice, but a demand. We cannot simply turn this off. And we who are in this room, as well as those others who are still out there in training, and anyone else who may join up later on, must rise to this challenge."

She pauses to consider her wording for a moment.

"But the question we must ask ourselves is what sort of example do we set? Are we simple soldiers? No. Are we simple educators? No. Then what are we, if we describe ourselves to be something so unique that there can be no comparison to any other society out there. We are born of a creature that should not exist, but he does. We carry his legacy within us, and this lifts us to some rather unrealistic demands for any corporeal race. We are described by those who should understand best that we could rival a Celestial race for these Gifts. But if we are to set the proper standards befitting this title, we need to understand how to represent ourselves in the process."

She turns and begins pacing across the floor.

"Ever since the day we learned of Adalon's prophecies describing some kind of fighting force being resurrected, I've tried to imagine what this could be. My education was interrupted on Ruuki uy'Daan, so I didn't get the full lecture on the Stormhooves. Then our people began to take this dedication to Lord Oghma as a way to defend against Darumon spying on us, and my ideas began to consolidate a little. It was vague in the beginning, more like conjecture. You know, like asking a series of 'what if...' questions, and how it might appear on the outside. But this last discussion with His Lordship, and the horn-twisting revelations we came up with...this demands something special. Naturally, I will need to present this idea to him to gain his approval, but I feel he would be proud."

She pauses with a mischievous grin, which causes a few additional whispers in the room as to what this young officer had in mind. Her reputation was fairly well-known by now, for better or for worse due to her activities.

"We must dedicate ourselves to certain precise virtues," she continues. "I think we can all agree that to offer ourselves to Lord Oghma is a good choice for guidance and direction. It suits our manners and social directives. Ours is also being described as an elite fighting force, if for no other reason than for our unique skills, like the Prodigy Gift, and other qualities you will not find in your average military body. Therefore, we can easily suggest we are in a class by ourselves."

She turns and starts pacing the other way, subconsciously realizing she is apparently picking up habits from Thaelyn.

"But do we want to stop at only this much? I think not. A form of dedication to any member of the Estelar is a valuable quality. They are teachers and parental figures, and so we must follow the same. Along the way, it also occurs to me the Prodigy Gifts, and for this point I think I should use the term in plural, as there is more than one here, but they must be treated no differently for us than any other Celestial race would their own. And THEY are all students under the Estelar. But from our perspective, this would equate to a form of religious dedication of purpose."

"Um, Kaliya," Navina cautiously raises a finger for attention. "At any moment during your interrupted education did you ever get the lesson that we aren't normally a religious society?" she giggles softly.

The room gushes with laughter at the mention.

"Yes, Navina," she smiles. "But you have to admit one thing, and that is a religion teaches respect, responsibility, and most importantly, an unshakable dedication to a purpose, in this case a holy purpose. This is what makes a Celestial race so…well, Celestial. And to a society like ours, where we might think advancing to a higher level of intellectual enlightenment might take us away from any form of divine worship, strangely, once you hit a certain point, it seems to come full circle right back to it."

"Oh great! But yes, I can see where this is going now."

"And here is where our direction takes us. If our entire species holds these skills, they're going to need someone to monitor and govern how they're used, as this could lead to all kinds of errant behaviors, possibly resulting in pandemonium if it gets out of control."

The room now rumbles with a new set of moans and whispers, as they try to imagine the possibilities for crime and other abusive applications.

"Yes," she nods. "Elder Vankkar is very often known to voice his opinions about this, and in many ways, he is right. I recall once when I was speaking to him…it was during my initial report on Thaelyn's first arrival and the use of telepathy to aid in our communication, and I explained to him the idea that if we can do it at all, such as with my father, then we need to hold ourselves up to these same levels of responsibility."

"How did he respond to that?" Navina asks.

"As you might expect, and generally the same as I'm saying here. We're not ready for it. But what I'm saying is, we don't have much of a choice. We need to evolve."

"Wow."

"It therefore falls to US to set the example," Kaliya asserts strongly and thumbs at herself, along with waving a hand at the group. "And this example does indeed have to be holy…just as holy as any other Celestial race following the direct tutelage of the Estelar. We are the vanguard! We are the ones to discover these secrets. We are the ones to understand their virtues, and also their danger. We are the ones who made contact with the Estelar, and from this, we now hold their teachings. We were called away by the cu'Nar to discover these truths. Call it a pilgrimage, if you will, to seek greater wisdom. And now, we must bring this back to our people. And what better example to set in their eyes than a Knighthood of Paladins!"

The room erupts vibrantly with more oohs and ahs as they reflect on their recent teachings in the academy on the notoriety of the paladin class of holy warriors.

"Um…" Navina ushers timidly once again. "Not that I would wish to argue, and it certainly sounds great for all the things I've been learning here at the academy, but my question is how you expect to go to Azgarén and teach this to a world full of iron-horns who haven't got a tail-yanking clue over any of it."

The room again fills with laughter as they consider the notion.

"Well, Navina," she grins. "I don't know how to answer that yet, but no doubt we'll need to teach them a few new tricks along the way. I don't expect it to be easy, but it's certainly necessary."

Kaliya once again glances around the group before resuming her lecture.

"Paladins, as you know from your studies, are the highest form of noble warrior, and part priest as well. And I can already tell you, we're going to need this, and on multiple levels. We have an upcoming mission to train for, at least part of which is to subdue a base full of Suuden'kai soldiers, and do so quietly, using non-lethal force. We will be training some new magic for this, but if we can manage it, we also need to take them while they are sleeping and KEEP them that way, in part, as Thaelyn likes to say, to maintain their unknowing of who grabbed them so we can use this later."

"And how do you take someone in their sleep?" Navina asks. "Hit them with a tranquilizer dart?"

"Well, I suppose that's one way, but as a paladin, we can learn to use a few priest spells, one of which is their sleep chant. This was mentioned briefly during our last meeting, and if we get started now, I think we could earn enough favor in our worship to receive that one before the mission begins. Then we would be fully functional on all accounts."

"So, on top of all the other studies they're cramming down our throats, you want us to spend what's left of our day in the temple in study of the priesthood?" she sighs.

"Come on, people, we can do this," Kaliya encourages. "I know this is a rush job, but it's really important. Once this particular mission is complete, we can arrange a more convenient schedule for ourselves. I'll speak with Lady Aerlie to get us started. We can dedicate a couple of hours after class for this, and maybe our weekends, allowing us to build up enough potential to get this one application. The sleep chant isn't that much to ask for in the beginning."

"All right, fine…I'm in!" she tosses up her hands. "If only for the fact that we have that world full of iron-horns who don't have a clue, and we'll need to yank their tails simply to get their attention."

"Good, so let's get started. This is the Order, people! We don't do things here like they do on Azgarén. We need to get our tails in action like there's no tomorrow, and I know we can do this…I've already been there."

She pauses again to review her notes before continuing.

"We need to start conditioning ourselves to work as a team. This not only means in physical form, but also projected. Cardinal Aelwyn has suggested a number of exercises for us to try on each other in projected form to see how we interact. This will be our first official training session. We are writing the book on how this works, and all those who follow will study from this same book. To begin with, I have a list of objectives here, so we'll take it by the numbers. Some of this we've done before, either individually or in small groups, but I want to run a few exercises on a larger scale, just to be sure."

She studies their readiness before assigning the first task.

"Our first objective is to project ourselves and begin behaving as normal people would. We will travel around the guild as a group, speaking and interacting with other people and each other as if it were just a typical day in the sun. We need this to understand the basic forms of group communication and interaction on a large scale."

"Will everyone who trains for this new unit need to practice these procedures?" Navina asks.

"Probably not. I think once we understand how the projection skill works on a group level, it'll follow with the basic development. But there are still so many unknowns about this skill, we need to test ourselves."

"Got it."

The group acknowledges the directive and they each take up seating in the room. They were using a conference room on this occasion, with the tables moved off to one side and additional chairs brought in. She had assembled a team of thirty people which was then divided into three squads.

They sit down and begin relaxing themselves into a light meditative trance. This process had become very familiar to them by now, as they have been practicing this skill in one form or another for a couple of years. Kaliya, so far, was the most experienced, as she was the one taking up roles to travel to Ruuki uy'Daan on her scouting runs, and eventually to lead the Order troops there to establish an outpost. Now she was teaching others about her experiences.

Slowly, they descended into their meditation, soon to call their minds to lift out of their bodies into physical space. The room began to fill with the additional presences of their projected forms.

Kaliya lifted out of hers fairly easily, being so well practiced by now. The others followed behind individually. She moved to the head of the room and turned to observe the rest of her team make their emergence. When all heads had been accounted for, she began to speak again.

"Very good. Now, let's see how well we can carry a conversation together. Each of you turn to your partner and strike up a bit of gossip."

She strolls over to the group as they pair up and start talking about the daily affairs of their training, classroom studies, social affairs, and their favorite foods. She joins in a few of the discussions and shares her own interests. It behaved like a typical recreational gathering. When she was satisfied, she came to the head of the room again.

"Good, that should be enough. It seems we can interact with each other in this form quite easily. I expected this would be possible from all our previous individual experiences, but to see it with each other as a large group is promising. This means our full team could be projected and still be functional. Now, let's go outside."

She prepares to lead the group outside and into the courtyard.

+ + + ◆ + + +

Relissa, Marelle, and Haran had gathered on their favorite bench in the courtyard to exchange notes on some of their recent lessons. Petrith, Sulíma, and Túfula were also gathered, as the two groups had discovered each other through their mutual friendship with Kaliya. Even though the three newcomers were still early in their language lessons, they were attempting to carry on a conversation with their new friends.

"You and Kali…you go out looking…at orcs…in old days?" Túfula fumbles with her words in her broken form of the tongue.

"Many times," Relissa responds, trying to keep the words simple. "In the Badlands, in mountains, the western plains… Haran was with us, too."

"How long…do you know her?" Petrith asks, similarly with difficulty.

"I've known her almost twenty years."

"And Haran?"

"Not that long," he replies. "Maybe eight or nine now, Kaliya and Relissa…"

Marelle was broadcasting her typically mischievous grin during the exchange. Sulíma takes notice of the odd display and tries to inquire about it.

"Marelle," she asks. "Why are you...um... smiling?"

Marelle decides the game has gone on long enough. She begins speaking in the Daanen'kai native form.

"I'm just thinking of the early days when we were new here trying to learn everything. Now here you are."

Petrith and his two female companions stared at her in disbelief at the well-formed words spoken in their own language.

"You tricked us!" Sulíma spouts.

"Sorry, but I couldn't help it. We have this tradition here with the new kids."

They all shared a laugh while Marelle offered up an explanation.

"You see, all three of us studied your language in our early years once the course became available. We figured, since we're probably going to be involved in this war somehow with the Suuden-Aryku, it could be useful. And even if not, it's still a good language to study."

"Suli," Túfula observes. "It looks like you have a little competition for the mischief around here."

"Yeah. I wonder if I could take lessons. Remember, I like to diversify!"

"Oh please," Petrith moans. "You're bad enough doing the solo routine."

Kaliya and her troupe were entering the courtyard. The display of the large congregation drew the attention of many people passing through the area. She noticed Relissa, Sulíma, and the others sitting on the benches and walked around to greet them.

"This looks dangerous," she admits. "Combining all of you together into one mass means trouble, I can see it already."

"Kali!" Sulíma shouts. "Do you know what these little tail-pullers just did to us? Here we are struggling to talk using their language, when in fact they know ours already."

"That must've been fun. It sounds just like them, too."

"What's going on out here?" Petrith asks as he studies the large assembly of bodies. "Are you having some kind of convention?"

"You might say that. This is the team I was assigned to put together, so we're going out on a training exercise. Which brings me to my next point…do any of you have an object of any kind we could examine? Relissa, what about your notebook?"

"Aye, I have one of those."

She digs into her bag and pulls out a journal she uses to take notes for her classes, then hands it over to Kaliya.

"Just don't go scribbling up a lot of ditsy pictures in it, ay?" she jibes.

Kaliya takes the book in her hands and holds it momentarily, turning it over to examine it from both sides. She then turns to the others.

"All right, our next test will be to see if we can pass an object, from one to another between us."

"Huh?" Relissa mutters quietly. "What kind of wacky training is this where you need to pass things around? Are we playing relay runs?"

Kaliya directs one of the team members to step forward. She holds out the book for the other person to take into her hands. The friends sitting on the bench look on, perplexed as to the meaning of this so-called exercise. The teammate reaches out casually to take the book. She tries gripping it with her hand, but it passes unimpeded through the object. The friends watch in amazement at the spectacle.

"Buggers," Relissa drones. "How did you do that?"

"Actually," Kaliya considers. "This isn't something I was hoping to see, but silently I was suspecting it."

"What do you mean?" Túfula asks.

"Let's try someone else," Kaliya suggests.

She moves among the group, testing each one. In a similar fashion, each person tries to take the object in their hand, but fails when their hand simply passes through it.

"All right, this is a problem. I should consult with Aelwyn about this to see if she has any suggestions. Meanwhile, let's try it this way."

She sets the book down on the ground for the next try.

"We'll try it by setting it on a local surface and allow it to re-phase, then the next person picks it up."

She directs each person in turn to pick up the object. This time it works. They retrieve the book from the ground, hold it a brief moment, and then set it back down again for the next person to try.

"Good, so we may need to use this as a common workaround when passing objects between us, and maybe others. Next, we need to practice moving and working as a team effort. We need to make this look good, so let's all do our best."

She picks up the book and hands it back to Relissa. As she returns to the group, she gives a new instruction.

"Everybody, let's make like birds and take to the sky!"

The people on the benches look on as Kaliya and her entire team begin to morph their shapes into a flock of hawks.

"Túfu…" Sulíma mumbles hesitantly as she moves around her friend.

"Don't get behind me, Suli, use Petrith. That's where I'm going."

"Jiggers!" Relissa shouts. "Are you all projected?"

"That's right, Relissa," Kaliya squawks back. "We're the early representation of our new military body, the Stormhooves. We're basically rewriting the book on military Special Forces operations, so we have a long way to go still."

Kaliya turns to her team to give her orders.

"All right everyone, form up on my wings and watch my movements. We'll move like a flock in formation, trying different configurations as we go along."

Kaliya turns back and starts flapping her wings to gain lift. She leads the team into the air and over the walls of the guildhall.

Relissa and the others watch as Kaliya and her group take up a classic V formation, just like a flock of birds. The formation was awkward at first as the people had never worked in conjunction with others in this manner before, but Kaliya led them to the left and right, turning in circles in the sky above the city, giving them an opportunity to fall into place and practice moving with the flock in a game of follow-the-leader.

"Buggers," Relissa mumbles. "This war is getting weird."

"You're right," Marelle admits. "And I think it's just getting started."

✦

"Look there!" utters one scout in a hushed voice.

"Aye, they look to be loading up that air transport," confirms the other scout. "That's the first time I've seen them do that."

"They're on the move down there. That truck we saw going out a short while ago, and now this."

"That truck went down the tunnel. There's only one place it could be heading off to. So, where do you think this other one is going, or should we even bother to ask?"

"Let's watch a minute and see. If it picks up and heads off south, I think we'll have our answer."

"Aye, but then we need to get a quick note to the Captain so he can send someone out to the mine to check on things."

The two scouts were stationed in a quiet nook in the ravine above the Suuden-Aryku camp, out of immediate view of anyone below, but with a good view of the events occurring down there. The job was rather mundane, as not much ever really occurred on a regular basis. Some occasional supplies had arrived through the conveyor, but during the time they had been watching the base, that was the only highlight so far. At this moment, however, something new was occurring.

A short while before, a truck was loaded up with a work crew and departed along the road through the tunnel in the direction of the door that leads down into the city. It was suspected this was a routine service to pick up the recent supply of metal from down below. Now an air transport, somewhat smaller than the one Marelle and Relissa once brought home from the mines north of Rolsklinde, was loading up with another work crew and preparing to take off.

"Lad," the first scout considers. "We might be in a good spot for hiding from those down below, but once that beastie takes off, it'll be above us looking down."

"Aye, as soon as it starts lifting off, we need to go dark until it passes."

"What about when it returns?"

"Let's get a note ready for the Captain, and give him the time for it. We'll watch the clock to see how long it takes to hear from the boys at the mine when it arrives. They can then report when it leaves, and we wait for the time when it should return back. That'll give us a decent heads-up to it."

"Good plan!"

The scout starts writing up a report to send to Captain Hagmaert at the outpost. When they see the aircraft lifting off, he checks his timepiece and records it into the report while the other one enchants a rune to send the report on its way. He drops the folded-up paper onto the rune, and it vanishes from sight. They each then cast a cloak on themselves to hide from the passing vessel overhead.

They performed this same routine with the truck, sending off a note to tell the Captain about it so he could send in scouts to observe the retrieval process, albeit very carefully from under a cloak. These runs were important in order to monitor the volume of adamantium the Suuden-Aryku were retrieving at any given interval. They had been sending agents inside to tally up the numbers waiting for this moment. And since the Suuden-Aryku were unable to detect them under a cloak, it was a reasonably safe operation.

The base represented a central roadway lined with a series of structures running the length of the ravine. The tunnel marked an exit on one end, and a large conveyor facility was found on the other side. Near to the conveyor were a series of landing pads for aircraft to land on, and just in front of the large aperture was a marked safety zone for inbound and outbound traffic. The base also had parking for local vehicles and covered storage.

Down in the base, inside the control booth, a call comes in for the base commander.

"Commander Kriv'tik, speaking," he answers in a classic emotionless voice.

"Commander," ushers the voice from the console. "So, here we are again. I see we have another run taking place outside. What is the status of the processor at this time? Are we at least keeping pace?"

"Supply is very low; the processor is running at half capacity."

"That's not what I want to hear, but I guess I have no choice but to tolerate it."

"Ytani, you know as well as I the situation at the processor. Why must you argue the point?"

"Because I'm personally sick of this incredibly dull assignment. You would be too if you had half the mind for it. The only real excitement I receive around here is my payment for services rendered. Speaking of which, do we at least have any halfway decent selections this time?"

"Our work crew has not changed, except for your last 'payment' being returned home for restorative treatment."

"Yes, well..." he chuckles indifferently. "Considering how I almost need to put a blindfold over my eyes each time they make a visit, just to keep my stomach from gushing upwards, a little cosmetic work becomes necessary. Perhaps, one of these days, you might consider looking for one that isn't quite as repulsive."

"Your insults are unappreciated. This is a military operation, not a bordello to satisfy your fetishes."

"This operation is whatever I make of it, Commander!" Ytani shouts. "The Marshal put me in charge of acquiring the metal, so if you want to keep your job, and for that matter your illustrious military title, you'll do whatever is necessary to keep me happy. The Council kissed his tail as soon as he promised that reward of great wisdom, and since the rest of you follow them to a fault, it goes without saying my authority supersedes yours."

"Indeed, they did," he admits grudgingly. "But at the very least, could you try to respect the manners of our people when you take your...payment...into your home? I would like to keep them operational as my base staff."

"Oh please, Commander, as if we're running short of people back home."

"That is not the point..."

"And what are you going to do about it?" he interrupts. "Simply order up replacements, like you did before…Central always has spares, I'm sure. Or should I submit one of my own reports directly to the Marshal about your lack of participation in his Great Cause. I'm sure he might have a few words to say about it, and likely after placing you under the active mode of your chip. How would you like that, hmm?"

The voice on the com-link was silent for an extended moment until Ytani spoke again.

"Yes, as I thought. It's not so nice being someone's puppet. And with your Suppressor chip installed, you can't even take offence properly."

"I can take offence just as easily with or without it," he murmurs resentfully.

"The bottom line is, he needs the metal, and you need ME to get it. I'd like to see any of YOU go down there and demand the stuff. And since I'm not modified like the rest, I have my…needs. And at this moment, my needs involve a female to serve as my relaxation tool. So, if you want to keep me happy, you'll send whatever you have that looks at least partway like a woman, not some alien parasite with legs."

"You are intolerable, Ytani," he mutters disparagingly. "Your attitude concerning our people is inexcusable. The Marshal only keeps you this way to provide your skill to his service, nothing more. You are as much a tool as the rest of us."

"The female?! …Commander?" he screeches. "Do you have one or not?"

"Yes…" he responds in an unnaturally restricted mode of contempt.

"Good! You know where I am. Send her immediately."

"And what condition will you return her in this time?"

"Whatever condition suits me, depending on how well she performs. You might want to tell her to at least try to make the attempt this time."

✦

A series of careful scouting runs had been occurring within the city of Glimmerheim recently. The purpose of this was to improve the maps of the city, to identify the precise placement of strategic facilities, and to study the forging operations and supplying of the depot with the finished product, as well as food production. The city was considered potentially unfriendly, but not hostile territory, mostly due to the influence of the Thane and the misinformation of the war.

As the scouts moved silently in the shadows, a pair of women made their habitual visit to exchange pleasantries and polite chatter.

"Eiki, ye look so glum today," Telta observes.

"I miss me poor beloved Tol. Every day that passes be another night in an empty bed an' another morn t' start a lonely day."

"Mayhap ye should get out a bit more an' see other people?"

"Nay, I'd ne'er forgive me'self t' give up on me husband, nay till me dyin' day, methinks."

"But ye know this already, there ne'er be a time when the men come back from the war. How many women d' ye think had t' make this choice by now?"

"Aye, this be the way, mayhap for a few, but nay for a long while after, when all other hope be a-fadin' an' the coin purse be a-runnin' empty."

"Speakin' of coin…"

"Aye, that too… I think I may need t' be a-sellin' a few things from the house t' keep up. But ye can only go so far with that afore ye're livin' in the street."

"Eiki, me husband an' I be a-makin' a fair bit better than ye. Mayhap ye'd let us help with a bit of good-neighborin'. Ye can'na keep up like this."

"Telta, yer a good soul. I don'na want t' be askin' for help, but if I ever be a-hopin' t' keep me home, mayhap ye could offer up only a wee bit t' hold me till the next shearin', an' then I can try t' get some more wool t' start me sewin' again."

◆ ◆ ◆ ◆ ◆ ◆ ◆

"Is that one over yon?" shouts the scout as he points at a possible mine entrance.

"Mayhap it be," Belrum responds. "We should go an' take a closer look, t' be sure."

Belrum and his scouting escort had been coursing their way far to the south to a new range of mountains discovered a few days before. They were searching around the base of it looking for additional mines or caves where people could be found hiding from the devastation outside, as Belrum and his people were.

They had come across what looked like a mine entrance, so they moved closer for a better look. They dismounted from their horses and walked up to the opening. The entrance looked common enough, but they could hear no obvious sounds inside.

"Mayhap we should go inside t' look?" Belrum suggests. "They may be deep, an' we can'na hear it out here."

"Maybe," the scout offers. "But let me go in quickly under a cloak to check it out first. It could be empty or there could be an animal den instead."

"Right, ye d' that an' I'll wait a bit."

The scout casts a cloak on himself and proceeds inside. Belrum waits for several long moments out in the dry air. The lands in this region were no different from anywhere else, and they had passed several more craters along the way where there must've been some form of civilization present. It was depressing for Belrum, but he knew it was paramount to find the last vestiges of his people in order to save their lives. Yet, there was still so much land out there to cover.

He continues to wait several more minutes, wondering what's taking so long. He starts to worry about the scout, but he holds firm to his spot hoping the younger man would emerge soon. Another few minutes pass, and the form of the scout reappears outside the mine. Belrum sees a look of gloom in the man's eyes.

"Ye took a wee bit on that," Belrum notes softly. "What did ye see?"

"I'm sorry, Belrum, it's a tomb in there. There was a dining room with several bodies and a bed chamber with even more. I tried searching more of it, but it was largely empty of anything else. You can go in yourself and see, if you like, but I don't actually recommend it for the smell."

Belrum hangs his head low.

"This be the way of it, for how the land be out here. Mayhap they just did'na have enough t' eat. What should we d' about it?"

"Ordinarily I would arrange for a burial. I could mark a rune to this location and have someone come out here later after we report in. Do your people hold any special rites in this regard?"

"I think nay more than a few good words t' the All-Father. This will give them a good rest."

The scout nods as he moves off to one side and marks a rune to the local vicinity. They return to their mounts and continue on in search of the next one.

"What the devil is that now?" directs one of the scouts overlooking the Suuden'kai base.

"Is that...? Get the scopes!" orders the other one.

The two scouts spying on the military base from their nook had noticed someone moving strangely among the buildings on the far side. It appeared female, hunched over and apparently clutching at her side, dragging one leg and barely able to walk.

"Bloody hell!" yips the first scout, trying to keep his voice under control. "What happened there? Look at her! She looks like she got mauled by a tiger."

"With the exception of her clothes gone missing! That looks like the same one we saw earlier visiting that house at the end."

"In all the blazes, man! Who in all the nine hells would do that to a woman? She looks like she got hit by a mugger in the street, dragged off into a corner and violated harshly."

"Do they do this to their own people, or did something else do this?"

"If she went inside that house, it must be whoever lives there. Either that, or he has a wicked pet he keeps inside."

The scouts observe the female as she staggers towards the control booth. They see a group of others rushing outside to catch her just as she falls. They lay her on the ground to examine her. More people hurry outside to join the gathering, some with devices in their hands which they move across her form as if to study her injuries.

"See there, she's bleeding," the first scout observes. "And not just in one place, there on her side and on the leg too."

"Mate, I think that one on the leg isn't actually coming from the leg proper. That's a rape injury! A bad one, by the looks of it. And I see a lot of scratches and minor cuts. Look at her face, all bruised like that. They're ugly enough with that biotech implant, but she looks battered to me."

"But I have to admit one thing, the others are doing their duty to attend to her. It's a crying shame to see this. I truly feel sorry for the lady."

"Aye, but what actually caused this? It was my understanding that these people with their implants are cut short of their emotions. Wouldn't that also take away such foul manners as this, too?"

"You might think, so we should probably take a closer look inside that house."

"Our orders so far are to watch the control room, not the house. It wasn't considered as high a priority."

"I'll bet that changes after this."

"Bloody right to that!"

The people on the ground hover over the stricken female for several moments longer until some of them pull away and stand up, then look off to the side along the length of the base. The others pull back to a kneeling position, laying down their medical scanners and simply staring at her.

"What are they looking at?" the first scout asks urgently. "Those standing up, that is…"

"Must be the house, is all I can figure. This tells me it's not the first time."

"But dammit, man. If it's not the first time, why are they simply standing around? If it were me, I'd go charging over there and knock the door down for the favor."

"As would I. But look there. What about her now? They stopped working her."

"Bloody hell. She looks like she died from it!"

"That breaks it for me!" the second scout scorns. "Why don't the rest go after the beastie that did this if they know what it was?"

"Not a bloody clue. Either that emotion thing cuts out their drive to seek justice, or..."

"Or what? You know how I hate it when you do that."

"Wait a minute. Who do we have down there? I see several who look like ranking officers, ay?"

"Um..."

The two of them study the scene through their scopes trying to identify the participants as best they can.

"I see a man down there in a fancy uniform," the second scout notes. "It has a few colors on it the rest don't have."

"Aye, so maybe he's the top man of the group. But then..." he pauses. "That doesn't make sense."

"Why?"

"If HE is the top man, then who lives in that house that he doesn't run up to the bastard for the favor of this deed?"

"Bloody hell man, someone higher? Blimey! And he treats the others like this? We need to bring this in straight away!"

✦✦◆✦✦

"My Lord, I'm terribly sorry for pulling you away from your bed, but this is a rather bizarre and urgent affair."

"It is not a problem to bring me out of bed, General. But such occasions as these tend to portray a disturbing turn of events. Especially as I look around the room to see who is attending."

It was the early morning hours on Tae'Eladar when Thaelyn had been raised out of bed by an urgent summons to meet in the tactical war room inside the guildhall. The cause was Captain Hagmaert, who had arrived personally with a recent scouting report he believed should be reviewed immediately by Thaelyn, the General, and Kailen, all of whom were still dressed in their night clothes.

"What do we have here, Captain?" Thaelyn asks.

"My Lord, my apologies for disturbing you, but I felt this to be rather urgent. Though there may be little we can do about it at present, considering how Lieutenant Nazég is only just beginning to train her team. Nevertheless, this situation cannot go unanswered."

He presents a paper forward with his report. Thaelyn picks it up as the Captain relates the story to the meeting.

"Earlier in the day, that is local time, our scouts observing the Suuden-Aryku base noticed a female stumbling along from a building resembling a house at the far end of the camp in the direction of the conveyor, one of the last in the row. She was fully naked, battered, lacerated, and bleeding from two prominent wounds, one of which appeared vaginal."

Thaelyn abruptly pulls up from the paper to focus directly on the Captain. He was grimacing deeply, as were the others.

"She collapsed in front of their control center building," the Captain continues. "A group of people rushed outside, apparently trying to tend to her. However, in the end, it appeared that she died from her injuries."

"Powers pay witness, Captain!" Thaelyn cries. "That sounds like a sexual assault! A violent one, at that. Who attacked her?"

"I chose not to send anyone too close to the suspected building, rather to examine it at a distance. It appears as a simple home design, a bit larger than the surrounding buildings, with a window facing out onto the road. The scouts were unable to see anything of particular import through the window, but they did report seeing what appeared to be some manner of common furnishings."

"A residence…" he muses. "Then I must wonder what manner of individual lives there."

"My Lord," the General considers. "This is entirely contrary to what I would expect of the Suuden-Aryku, even with what we think we understand about their behavior. A sexual assault and battery? This indicates an abusive behavior against women!"

"Indeed, it does. And worse, this is clearly a psychopathic behavior, which is often rooted in a deeply disturbed emotional state. This should automatically rule out the Suuden-Aryku due to their emotion inhibitor implants."

"Then who is responsible?"

"Could this residence be owned by the one operating the base?" Kailen wonders.

"The scouts were suggesting this could be the case," the Captain responds. "However, it may NOT be the resident military officer, as they believe they saw him, among other prominent members, outside with the woman. So it must be someone in a higher position of authority. And worse. They also observed those people turning in the direction of the house, and their posture suggested this was not the first time."

"Did they take action?"

"No, Commander, they appeared as if being held back by something. Which might suggest this individual holds some level of impunity over them."

"Held back…and impunity… Maybe because of those chips. Dammit. So, someone is taking advantage of these chips to have his way with their female staff members. This is worse than psychopathic. This is just plain sadistic."

"Intolerable," the General scorns. "Not even in Rolsklinde, to our knowledge that is, did something like this occur by the hands of Darumon, who was operating the affairs there. They had those plague implants, but I would say this is an even higher atrocity."

"I would agree, General," Thaelyn affirms. "And although I dread admitting to this, I might think even Darumon would have something to say about it. This is not a game of sport; this is a sick fetish."

"But if he's not directly involved in this operation, then who? We were suggesting a possible civilian impersonating the Thane, perhaps using this machine replica of a dwarf. If his behavior during those tirades is any indication, could it actually be worse for this example?"

"But General," Kailen offers. "If this person is a civilian, and these others are military, one of whom must be of a Captain's rank or better to command that base, he should hold authority to govern these things."

"Absolutely, Commander, I would surely agree to that, but this situation seems to defy the expectations."

"And yet, Captain, you think you saw him outside with the others?"

"Aye," he nods. "If we're judging the uniforms correctly. Here, see for yourself…"

The Captain leans over the table to retrieve a trans-com he brought with him. He pulls up the photo library for review.

"They took a portrait of the scene as it was wrapping up."

Kailen takes the unit and studies it for a moment.

"Yes, this one here…" he points at the image. "That's the rank of a Commander grade officer. And yet if HE is not marching over there to attend to this… Wonderful. But there would not be much else to rank higher than this. The HC, perhaps. But from your past interactions with him, I have my doubts he could be inside there."

"This is disturbing," Thaelyn muses. "And this also reignites that same controversy as with Commander Geilv and his presumed position of authority, or the lack of it, on Therinë. Under these circumstances, whatever authority this individual has, and if we say it is a civilian, rather than the base commander, it must supersede him, if he did not take any corrective action. But like you said, this would defy reason for the organization of that camp. Therefore, my only thoughts are that if Darumon controls these people through these chips, and if he was occupied elsewhere during this time, this other one must hold a form of proxy authority."

"If we're speaking in terms of a proxy under Darumon," the General considers. "This could open up a few possibilities. If we go by his lack of military prowess in the city, he might be a civilian, maybe a part of their local government with an authority position above their military. Commander, how would you feel on this idea?"

"The only true authority above the military," Kailen considers. "And this would include the position of the HC, would be the Council. But he must be a very perverted example, especially if to say he is absent his emotion chip."

"Perverted..." Thaelyn nods. "Yes, this much is certain. This man is not as well-mannered as anyone else we ever saw working for Darumon. Did Darumon choose this explicitly, or is it more like you said where he is taking advantage of the situation for a little... exotic pleasure."

"I wonder how many people would know of these chips. If they are described as military, is this common knowledge or classified, as so many military technologies tend to be. And then, given this, a government official might know of it, therefore he might try exploiting it. But then, we come back to the Thane. Are we indeed speaking of an animatronic? A government suit might not be so tech savvy as to operate something like that."

"Perhaps someone else operates it, and...well, maybe this would not work as well. He would need an operator in there with him, which now counts as two people. And if one of them is behaving in such a way as this, I would better think it to be a private fetish."

"You mean, no witnesses to report him? But if he holds so much authority as to override the base commander..."

"Yes, this whole scenario seems problematic. Here in Rolsklinde, Darumon had the Dean as his second-in-line. If he only needs one individual, and he likes to limit people and their personal knowledge of anything to avoid the complications of cross-interaction, one person in the lead position, say to manage this base, would be preferable. But if that one person, in this case, is lacking in so many skills, and also holds so many psychological issues that he cannot even interact politely with others..."

Thaelyn pauses in deep thought.

"A specialist," he muses. "This could be it. Maybe like the Dean. Someone with proxy authority, who is also absent the chip, and holding the specialized skills to perform his unique function. The military side might be only utilitarian, for this point. They pick up and deliver the metal, while the specialist resides in that luxurious house of his, soaking up the pleasures of his position over what he might regard as his personal entourage of servants."

"Oh great..." Kailen moans. "Then, how do we explain the Thane? Are we actually speaking of an animatronic at all, or could it really be a dwarf with a back door leading topside? Would a dwarf do this to people, or is he just a lesser attendant under this guy?"

"I suppose I cannot speak of the dwarves of that world as intimately as this, but if Chief Bronzeheart is any example, I think the general population within the city would not behave quite to such abominable degree as this. The dwarves I know of tend to hold much greater pride than that. And this also dates back to well before I arrived. I would tend to stay with the idea of a Suuden'kai operative, for this point, and if he is absent his chip, he likely holds some amount of joy over it. Therefore, he might be abusing the rest, who are so conveniently subjugated by it."

"All right, so far it makes sense. We have someone with special skills, which makes him especially valuable. He doesn't have his chip, maybe as a special allowance so he can do his work. He operates something to impersonate a dwarven Thane, playing the whole thing like a game, but apparently losing track of his details after so long. This guy actually sounds like a kid playing a video game to me," he chuckles.

Thaelyn gazes at Kailen for a long moment as he begins to piece together the image, and then a new thought emerges.

"A child with a game...a toy city with toy people...where he can scream whatever stories he can imagine, and apparently, they became numb to it after a while. And..."

He mulls the idea a moment longer, waving a finger in the air.

"...Yes, and if he KNOWS there are no enemies out there, why bother with security. It is unnecessary, at this point. A toy city serving only his needs, and nothing more. And the base crew..."

He pulls up the scouting report one more time for another look.

"Battered, lacerated, naked, and likely the result of a violent rape. Yes, a young male with high sexual cravings would do nicely for this point. Commander, if I may, can you explain to me a few small details of young males amongst your kind and the hormone rushes you receive as you mature?"

"Hmm, well, I could give you a couple of examples right off the top. Look at someone like Petrith. He was very ambitious as a juvenile with that little game he played on our computers once. This can give an idea for their occasional mischievous behavior, though this one didn't cross that line of harming other people."

"Thank goodness," Thaelyn smiles. "His example could be described as curiosity, at least as much as youthful zeal."

"Maybe. As we grow to adulthood, we go through the usual hormone surges after puberty, and this can cause the individual to behave in ways where they might fantasize about the opposite sex. But to go so far as invoking this level of abusive behavior? I wouldn't say this is normal, not unless we have an imbalance, or...hmm... actually, wait, if he's male... Uh oh..."

"What is it, Commander? Do we have something?"

"An idea, at least, and I can actually vouch for this from personal experience. But this is a very specific situation here. Fortunately, in my case, I had coaching and the benefit of, um...wait a minute..."

Kailen pauses as his mind begins turning over several subjects at once. He glares at the report on the table, and then passes his stare around the room.

"Your Lordship, I have an idea, but this is highly speculative, and also very specific to a single train of thought. What if he is a young male who also practices on weightlifting equipment? Furthermore, what if he spent most of his younger life isolated in that space without the proper coaching or counseling to condition him with better disciplinary training?"

"This is very curious, Commander, and indeed it does sound quite specific. How do we define this?"

"We call it the Alpha Male syndrome. Young males involved in the weightlifting sport can develop much more than simply muscle mass. Our hormone output increases as well, and this naturally drives us a little tail-crazy after a while. We usually go through discipline training along the way, also adjusting our diet, and maybe spend a little time with a special lady to help relieve the tension. I had Ankhia on my side, and she was very supportive. But if he is behaving so badly, my first guess is he didn't have any of this support."

"Good, this could offer a potential answer."

"Also, if he's a young male, how long has he actually been in that house, because after a while, you would tend to develop a tolerance to it anyway. This suggests to me he must be quite young, maybe on the order of only a few or several centuries, and this now makes me ask about the duration of that operation…four centuries. Look at Petrith and Suli for your examples of behavior at that age."

"Indeed, so this is how we might measure it? This would surely complicate the equation for us. I should think anyone sent to a base like this ought to be at least of legal age, which for you is two centuries, plus the additional four we suspect with this mining operation, and that places him at six, minimum."

"Old enough to outgrow some of this, even without the proper counseling…assuming he was well-groomed to begin with. But if he was in there alone this whole time…" he raises his brow inquisitively.

Thaelyn frowns at the tall officer as the meaning begins to settle.

"A juvenile sent unattended to work at a military mining base?" he muses uneasily. "But of course! A child playing a game! He has no formal education in anything beyond whatever rudimentary training he likely received in that house, and surely not enough to manage any complex operations, like his activities down below. Therefore, he invents whatever stories are necessary to bring up the metal and the work crews. And if he is so disquieted in that house…" he begins pacing around while in thought. "This could offer a possible clue. If he is alone in there, perhaps from a young age, growing up without any parental support…"

"But my Lord," the General wonders. "An actual child…where would his family be?"

"An excellent question, General. Where would they be if he

was assigned to a project to build a doomsday weapon. Probably not where they should be, neither is he at home as HE should be. For this point, if we are in fact speaking of a child recruited into service, for whatever reason, his family was clearly not invited. And knowing Darumon as we do, I hesitate to ask where that family actually is right now. But we still need to reconcile why Darumon would choose this. A young child playing with toys, perhaps? He would still need the means to build and operate that mechanoid device…"

"A mechanoid?" Kailen winces. "I'm not so sure I want to ask, but for the sake of my horns…"

"Sorry, Commander. Yes, this is a term we sometimes use back home for such as you were describing, intelligent artificial constructs."

"Ah, all right, that's not too bad. Something like those modrons, perhaps?"

"They would surely qualify, but those are also sentient, whereas these do not always have to be. They could instead be user-operated devices, maybe for industrial or even military purposes."

"Like warbots? Interesting. Or maybe simple robots or android units."

"But you still need the training to build and operate one. This might also aid us to consider the same unit being used this whole time."

"He doesn't consider the turnover of generations."

"Correct. So, unless Darumon provided something…and yet, we are still missing a piece…the voice."

"The voice…to impersonate a dwarf?"

"An adult dwarf, to be precise. I doubt he could so easily pass himself off as one with a child's voice. And for four centuries, where surely, if your kind matures in any way similar to the other races we know of, your voice changes over time."

"Indeed it does," Kailen nods. "Especially for a male. Ours become very deep along the way. Just look at me in relation to an average human. I'm at least an octave or two below that. But one thought that comes to mind is to use an emulator. Whatever his natural voice may be, an emulator could create a consistent foreign voice pattern."

"Very good, this is a possibility. But we must still try to reconcile this, as we are surely speaking of someone of younger years. And this, combined with the civilian aspect, could not possibly override a military commander. There must be something else. If we describe him as a specialist, where his skills are so unique, and they would carry so much value that Darumon would use him as opposed to any qualifying adult…this simply does not carry any rationality. He is placed into a house with the sole purpose of impersonating a dwarf…all alone…isolated…" his voice suddenly drops off and he stops cold in the room.

He stands there momentarily as he tries to collect his thoughts. A new image was emerging.

"Oh dear Powers," he muses silently. "Would he do that? But let me see. He is alone and without any family, who would surely protest the decision. He has little or no proper rearing; therefore, he develops his psychoses. He grows up believing he owns everything, including the base personnel, likely because Darumon afforded him some amount of immunity. He has full emotions, meaning no chip, assuming this chip is a universal demand…and I think Geilv did mention something about a mandate…"

He pauses a moment as he tries to recall his conversation with the Suuden'kai High Commander.

"Feedback, medical…Council mandate for something preventative…"

"Preventative…" Kailen reflects. "So, everyone SHOULD have it, but this one doesn't. And oh, is he enjoying himself!"

"Indeed! This might even play into the psychosis. A special privilege that only HE has, so he can lord over the rest."

"My Lord," the General wonders. "Can you explain your thoughts to us?"

"This is easily as much speculation as what the Commander just gave us, but the pieces do build a functioning picture with a reasonable outcome. He starts out as a child, with a special, and

I mean a VERY special quality that Darumon probably does not want anyone to know about, including his parents, especially if we consider those first Prodigy Children."

"Great gods!"

"Yes, General," Kailen moans. "That's how I would describe it right about now."

"And so Darumon relocates him," Thaelyn continues. "His parents may be absent from the picture by this time, to keep his secret. He is installed in that base, where he grows up with his own pet city and surrogate family, the military crew, who may or may not offer much in the way of parental support."

"Especially if they're under the control of those chips."

"Yes, and along the way, he is exempted from that emotion chip, which as I mentioned could be universal to all of them. And by the description the Med-tech gave us, this does not sound like a proper medical device, not with that feedback effect in there. But as such, he might also feel a sense of favoritism for this point."

"And so," the General considers. "He might feel the power to simply have his way of things. If this Prodigy Gift is still described the same, or whatever definition they use for it by now, he must feel himself to be very unique, and this relates to value for his ability to impersonate a dwarf. And in this case, HE is the dwarf…a projection. He pops in whenever he needs to make his demands, pops back out… and then what. What does he do in a house all by himself…other than molest the female staff members?"

"I can tell you one thing, Aerlie would like to hear this one. She has her own study in psychology, and I think the first thing she would say is his isolation could develop any number of anomalies. Boredom, for one thing, therefore a need for his…exotic excitement. A superiority complex, and therefore his manners with people. Also, if he was exempted from this one chip, could he be exempted from anything else, like that biotech seed. If, like you say, he could be involved in bodybuilding, he might revere himself as an idol to his own perfection. And if Darumon installed him as the sole body to deliver his precious adamantium, the base crew may have no choice but to comply, either as the result of their chips interfering with their better judgment, or simply because they have no other options, since none of THEM knows what this material actually is."

"Cu'Nar help us all," Kailen growls. "And if he does actually do any weightlifting, this only exaggerates the condition. He might regard the others as inferior, maybe also unsightly, especially if you consider the chips and that seed entity. It's no wonder that female came out of there looking like she crawled through a warzone. I'd really hate to imagine what she must've gone through in those last moments."

"That's truly despicable!" the General spurns. "But if we are speaking of a projection, and he is a Suuden'kai individual, he would not be as dangerous as Darumon himself."

"Yes, and this does make better sense now. Running a mining base should be a fairly simple operation, almost anyone with a business mind could do it. That military commander might be the one operating the technical side of things. This would probably be beneath Darumon's personal interest, so he would put it in the hands of others while he goes off to bother us and everyone else…it would be more entertaining for him," he smirks ironically. "And if this Prodigy Child is the one imitating a dwarf, HE might hold the proxy authority, as his skills might be regarded as irreplaceable, especially if Darumon was trying to cover it up before this…and maybe still is. Those people might have no idea what they're looking at, other than what Darumon tells them, and he could invent any story he likes."

"Indeed, I'm sure he could."

"Assuming he invents anything to begin with," Thaelyn muses. "This person could be so isolated, and with such a personal secret, therefore with even more inflation of his ego, that no one truly knows how he does it at all. This would increase his sense of value even more, such that he could demand almost anything, and get away with it!"

"Including murder," the Captain suggests after a long silence. "Bloody hell, my Lord, how do we approach this? Do they hold any virtues in that society of theirs, chips or otherwise? You once said that High Commander of theirs seemed a fairly solid chap, even with his chip. Surely this might suggest something."

"It might, but under the circumstances, I feel we must stay our course. I would surely not wish to see another, so I am going to suggest these occasions may not occur too frequently, or else that reaction out there might have been more severe. But if we do see another, I want to know immediately, in case we need to take corrective action, with or without our need for secrecy. Aside from this, I would like to see about our mission before this happens again. If Darumon is treating this mining venture such that people are being made expendable, I want to remove them from the equation and install ours instead."

"Aye, sounds fine by me."

"I might even go so far as to say this Prodigy Child could end up the same way once his usefulness is complete. If Darumon is only using him for this one occasion, he might not hold any value beyond this. But military personnel take time to develop. This would hold much more value if he is hoping to launch any military maneuvers."

"That would seem almost comical," Kailen moans. "He thinks so highly of himself that he puts the others into this situation of abuse. Then one day, 'Oh, by the way, we don't have any more work for you, so here's your termination notice…' and boom…" he draws a line across his neck.

✦✦✦✦✦

Following the meeting, Thaelyn and his officers went back to their respective homes to try to recover some of their lost sleep, although none of them was truly successful. Now daylight has come to Tae'Eladar as well as Therinë, and they were reconvening in the WIC building in Rolsklinde.

"General," Thaelyn calls as he enters the room. "I require information on that residence, but I do not wish to send any of our regular scouts in there for the risk of being discovered by either the Suuden-Aryku or the occupant of that home. Although Kaliya and her team are not yet ready for official duty, we must press forward with what we have."

"Are we still considering it to be an Azgarén Prodigy Child, my Lord?" the General replies.

"I consulted with Aerlie on our discussion earlier, and she agrees on many of the principles of a god syndrome, if he feels himself with such special privilege and authority. And this Gift would certainly afford this much if it were not demonstrated with the appropriate level of discipline and respect."

"Of course."

"Therefore, this becomes our best suggestion, but naturally, it needs to be confirmed. This will be Kaliya's first objective. I want her and her team to infiltrate the area and make a close inspection of that window, possibly to see if there is a way inside the home to discover who lives there. Regardless of who it is, she must be very careful in case the occupant can somehow perceive of her presence even in projected form."

"Very well, I shall pass the word along. However, I believe she and her team will need to make an initial visit to the region to become familiar with it physically before they can project into it later."

"Yes, the same as with the city underneath... Let us include this as well. I want spies inside the Thane's Hall to watch his behavior the next time he makes an appearance. Commander..." he turns to the Daanen'kai officer. "We need some manner of video recording equipment from you for the occasion."

"I already gave the word on this some time ago when we first started considering the prospect of recording their actions for study. Our people have been working to modify some of our existing equipment to serve, but the most difficult part is to make it small enough to fit inside a tight space, like a crevice or small opening, and still provide a good image. Our local industry doesn't have that capacity yet, so we're mostly using the engineering workshops inside the Naarg uy'Sodrad."

"What about the industries we were refurbishing on Ruuki uy'Daan? Did any of those provide this capacity?"

"Some, but this still requires a design concept we've never used before."

"Of course. But see to it quickly, we need this. Scavenge whatever you need and cobble something together from it. It does not need to be excessively extravagant, simply functional. A simple trans-com with an external power pack, perhaps…whatever…"

"I'll send this to our people and tell them to put a rush on it."

"I believe we will need two of these devices to start, one for the Thane's Hall, the other for the control booth of the base. In the meantime, I have a few ideas on my mind to cause a little havoc with their operations. Once we get word back from Kaliya on this homeowner, we shall see how far we can press them."

"Relissa, are you gaining weight?" Marelle inquires disbelievingly of the dark elf.

"Me? Never!" she objects.

"Well then, what is that bulge there under your jacket?" Marelle observes as she studies Relissa's new attire. "Are we sneaking away a few late-night snacks now?" she grins.

Just then, the ungainly shape of Relissa's forward proportions began to undulate. Marelle pulls back from it, uncertain as to what might be preparing to pop out at her.

"It's moving!" she shouts.

"What?" Relissa poses casually. "Oh! That!"

The two women were sitting at their favorite table in the cafeteria at lunchtime in the guildhall. Their class studies were progressing nicely, and the close of the current school year was approaching soon.

Relissa looks down at her new jacket, which was oversized for her proportions. She turns slightly to present herself to her friend and pulls open one panel, which overlapped the other and revealed a large pocket inside covering most of the interior. As she holds it open, Marelle sees two little noses pop up over the lip of the pocket, then further to emerge into view as a pair of furry little heads.

"Aw, they're so cute!" she croons. "Are those field squirrels?"

Relissa brings a hand down for the small animals to climb up onto her shoulder for a presentation. They were light brown with faint black spots and tan undersides.

"Aye, this is Scratch and Snickers," she announces. "They're part of my Ranger training. I'm supposed to keep them with me to bond with them and train them to do tricks."

"So, when Thaelyn says you talk to squirrels, you're actually doing it now," she giggles. "Where did you get them?"

"They're part of the family I used to play with back home when I was working for the Guild of Wardens in Solinaia. Of course, this is a younger generation now, but it's a good start for me."

"Will you keep them with you all the time?"

"Mostly, and I made up a little box for them to bring home later."

"Um, Relissa, do they let you keep those in the dorm room?"

"Aye, for the smaller critters… It's all part of the lesson. They'll be staying with me during this time."

"You remember we're bunking together, right?"

"Oh, Marelle, don't worry about it, they won't bother you. But if you feel something warm and furry wrapping around your neck at night, try not to swat it too quickly," she chuckles.

"Yeah, I'll try," she grins. "Will you be working with other animals sometime?"

"Aye, I'll be learning birds, larger animals like wolves, and eventually things like bears and big cats. They say I might want to tame one for companionship on dangerous runs, depending on what kind of service I go into."

"I'm trying to imagine you with squirrels in your pocket and a tiger at your side. I just hope you keep the tiger well-fed or else he'll be sticking his nose into places."

"You're right. But I don't think that'll be a problem. If you work it right, it all falls together, and they behave much more like a family."

"But don't they make a mess inside there? I'd hate to be the one trying to clean your pockets!"

"It's all part of the learning. I need to keep a special little nest in there with padding and a bit of straw. The pocket is big enough to make a little bed for them."

"And what if they start getting, um…playful?" Marelle grins. "Do we have a male and a female, or both the same?"

"This time it's two brothers, so there'll be none of that frisky business going on."

The two of them share a laugh and return to their meal as Relissa coaxes the small creatures back into their hole.

It was late afternoon, and a swarm of flying insects had descended into the courtyard of the guildhall. It made circling motions across the yard and around statues. Relissa, Marelle, and Haran were just coming outside to sit on their favorite bench when they noticed the unpleasant intrusion.

The swarm continued its flight pattern, occasionally to land on a wall or a statue, then to pick up and fly off to another location. The three friends studied the motion, silently wondering if they should relocate elsewhere for their meeting. Then the swarm made its way directly in front of them. Thinking they were about to be attacked and stung by something, they raised up their books ready to swat anything that came too close.

The swarm mysteriously halted in midair, hovering in place. The lead insect then appeared to turn towards the mass and made a curious loop, then settled to the ground. The rest of the swarm followed, landing at well-spaced intervals.

"What are those things doing?" Marelle asks hesitantly.

"I don't know," Relissa answers. "But if they come any closer, I'm going out there and stomp on them."

Before Relissa and the others could make any further judgments on the matter, to their surprise, the swarm of insects began to change shape.

Kaliya and her team had been in another group practice session.

As they reimagined their images from insects back to their natural forms, the friends reeled back and gasped.

"Buggers, girl!" Relissa shouts. "You're bugs now?"

"We need to practice all different shapes, Relissa," Kaliya remarks. "As well as how to behave accordingly. You never know where they'll be sending us."

"That was a very convincing display," Haran notes. "You certainly had us fooled, and by this time we should probably be expecting it from you."

"Good, then I guess our work here is done!" she grins.

"How are you coming on your other training?" Marelle asks.

"We still have a long way to go, for instance team coordination in combat operations. We need to develop our own technique, but since so much of this is completely new, it's still experimental."

"Aye!" Relissa admits. "I'll bet there never was anything quite like you out and about before. Even without this bleedin' war, you'll still be a one-of-a-kind deal. Just think if one of these days we find ourselves in a new fix. What kind of work will they put you to?"

"That's a very interesting question, Relissa. If all goes well for us here, we could find ourselves with all sorts of possibilities in the future."

"So, what's next on the list for you?" Marelle wonders.

"Right now, we've got orders to go to Morndindor. We were just finishing up a little practice for something we might be using over there."

"I suddenly feel very sorry for those Suuden-Aryku," Haran satirizes. "They're about to be assaulted by a swarm of bugs. They'll never know what hit them!"

They all joined in a round of laughter at the suggestion.

"Actually," Kaliya responds. "This one is a spy mission. We need to inspect the inside of the Thane's Hall, the control booth of that base, and a house they found at one end of it, to see who lives there."

"A house? What's a house doing in a military base?"

"I was called in to a meeting with Thaelyn earlier where I got a very disturbing briefing over something that happened last night.

We think it could be the guy portraying the dwarven Thane, and that he could be a Suuden'kai Prodigy Child, but one with extremely bad manners and violent tendencies. So far, it's mostly some extreme speculation between Thaelyn, my brother, and the rest, so this is where we come in to find confirmation."

"What was this bad report about?" Marelle asks.

"A female member of the base crew was seen coming out of the place naked, badly injured, and bleeding, probably from a violent rape and torture, and died on the roadway in full view of our scouts and the base crew."

"Gods above! Those people actually behave that way?"

"This one does. Apparently, the crew went out to help her, but when she died, all they could do was glare in the direction of the house, as if they knew what happened, but couldn't respond to the action. This tells us, whoever lives in that house runs the show, and the rest are his playthings."

"And more gods above! What is wrong with these people? Is this guy the base commander, do you think?"

"I asked this as well, but he was apparently outside with the others. Thaelyn thinks this guy is just a simple civilian, but with special privileges due to his Prodigy Gift that only HE can procure the metal, and this denotes value, possibly giving him a really big ego, along with any number of psychoses for his favoritism aspect. He could also be a young guy, maybe without a family, starting as a child and growing up without any real child-rearing to teach him better manners."

"And even MORE gods above! Kaliya, you be careful with that guy. I've seen a few things in my day, but this one blows the roof off the building."

"We will. We also need to find good spots for future surveillance. But for now," she turns to her team. "Everyone recall back. We'll gear up and reassemble here. Then move forward."

The entire team envisions their maneuver to return back to their bodies, which were again sitting in the conference room deeper within the guildhall. From there, they would return to their respective dorm rooms, change clothes, and equip themselves for their outing.

✦

Chief Bronzeheart's mention a few days before of his wife Eiki and her opinions of the affairs in the city over the years, prompted Thaelyn to become curious about her. He reflected on Tristeen Macaid and her family, and the other noble families of Rolsklinde, and how they questioned the affairs of the city management. He wondered if the same might be true here, and further if he could exploit it. But in the case of Rolsklinde, Darumon had been impersonating the Governor, and as he departed, he made one last attempt to cause trouble. Thaelyn did not want a repeat of that here.

"My Lord," the General suggests. "If they need this metal for Darumon's weapon, I personally find it unlikely they would so eagerly sacrifice the only remaining population they have to harvest it."

"You may be right, General," Thaelyn concedes. "They may have backed themselves into a corner on this one, simply by merit of their tendency to reduce the remaining population down so they would not need to manage it. Also, the city is apparently quite deep. It would take repeated hits by their bombardment weapons to destroy it, though I would not wish to see that happen either."

"But if we are suggesting the Thane is actually this Prodigy Child, and perhaps not even a properly trained military leader, what sort of authority might he have? He uses his position to play his fetishes, but does he hold a governing power over a true military force, or simply the mining operation."

"My personal judgment would be just the base. I cannot imagine Darumon giving out authority of a full military fleet to such a man as this. If he abuses his base staff so obscenely, I will surely hate to see how he might treat a naval fleet."

"Indeed!"

"But we may not be able to answer this immediately, so our operations will begin small, and we will work from there."

As the day progresses, Thaelyn called a new meeting, this time including Chief Bronzeheart to make a series of plans inside the city. It had to start with an inside informant, and perhaps a rabble-rouser. He referred the group to an updated copy of the city map made from the recent scouting runs designated as cartography missions.

"And so, Chief," Thaelyn asserts. "Travelling to this region of the city, and along this avenue," he directs to the map, "your house is located along this row. And this is where your wife would spend much of her time?"

"Aye, she was workin' the sewin' table for many a year. If she still be doin' that, this be where ye'll find her. But I think, like with so many others, she'll nay be takin' kindly to just anyone comin' up to her with a tale like this."

"I would not choose to approach her with any of our own men, for the same reason as those outside, and more so because this is inside the city, which is an even greater risk. Rather, we should send an agent, and it would have to be a native."

"Mayhap I could go? I miss her so terribly."

"I understand, Chief, but I must also point out a complication with that. You are known inside the city. If the people should see you, it would cause a commotion that could reach back up to the Thane's ears. You, among others sent to the mines, are not expected to return, and the Thane would take notice of this. I think we should keep to a more subtle approach for now."

"Then who? Mayhap Belrum, or one of his fellows?"

"That would be a better choice for this occasion, someone who would not stand out. We could give instructions on how to proceed and go from there. This could also work for us as an outsider who might not otherwise have any way of arriving, now doing so and with such a story as ours."

"Oh! Aye! That'll be a fine one to stir things up. But if ye're tryin' to keep it quiet, ye should nay be lettin' it out on the streets so grandly."

"Not in great detail, no. We must keep to a careful focus. If we can provide a few new rumors in the alleys, perhaps we could buy ourselves a little time. And then there is the mining operation. Only a very select few in this case should be in the know. They can do our work for us."

"Ye're a sly one, Yer Kingship. Ye make me wish I could be servin' up in yer military. So, when do ye think we should try to make this happen?"

"I will need to find Belrum again and reassign him temporarily. At last word, he was in the field searching for more survivors. This reminds me, General. Have any of our scouts noticed any Suuden-Aryku scouting patrols coming or going from the base, perhaps to survey the land for any recovery efforts?"

"Not as yet," he reflects. "And from the photos we received, I do not even think they have any scouting vessels on hand. Commander, did you notice anything?"

"No," Kailen responds. "From all those photos, I saw only one small craft, and it seems stationary, and a larger transport which I believe is the one they use for hauling the adamantium from the mine, along with what I'm guessing to be a troop transport, probably for carrying the base personnel."

"Then this gives me cause to wonder," Thaelyn suggests. "If they went to such an effort to lay waste to the land such that they think the outside world is effectively dead, they may have no further interest or concern for it. If this is so, perhaps we could use some of our gryphons to search the more remote regions for survivors. It would make things go much quicker. Scouting from the sky offers a much better scale of coverage."

"That may be, Yer Kingship," the Chief declares. "But if ye think the people out there would be afraid of yer men comin' up the normal way, I dare to think of them seeing those flyin' beasties," he chortles.

"This may be true, but the benefits outweigh the difficulties."

Morning was dawning on Morndindor, and the outpost was stirring to life. The Captain reviewed the morning mail with the most recent orders and instructions delivered from Rolsklinde. The scouts made a cursory circuit around the local region to ensure all was well while the morning meal was prepared.

Belrum was just rising from his bed. He had been making camp with the others while he went out on his missions to find more people. He joined with the other men in the kitchen area to share his meal.

"Belrum," the Captain calls as he joins at the table. "His Lordship has a new mission for you, a special one. He has instructed me to give you a briefing on how to proceed."

"A new one? What be it this time, Captain?"

"He's sending you into Glimmerheim to make contact with a local. You will pass along information and attempt to bring her out for a detailed consultation in Rolsklinde."

"Whoa, there! Captain, need I remind ye, I be but a simple farmer's son, nay the spy."

"Yes, I remember, but today you are a spy. Don't worry, I'll brief you on how to proceed. It shouldn't be that difficult to get inside, we'll help you with that, as well as extraction back here. The tough part will be to convince this woman to follow you."

"An' who be it I will be a-speakin' with?"

"Her name is Eiki Bronzeheart, the Chief's wife. Apparently, she has had ideas about the local management of the city for some time, and His Lordship wishes to speak to her personally. He has plans on using her as an activist."

"A what? An activist ye say? Ye may recall I ne'er did get a proper schoolin' as a lad."

"An activist is someone who basically makes trouble for the local authority," he winks.

"Oi, so that be the game now, ay?" he laughs. "But I ne'er have been inside the city. I nay be a-knowin' me way 'round in there."

"We have a map, and I will show you where to go. From there, find your way back and we will pull you out."

"Fine then, but what d' I say an' how d' I make this lass follow me? I be a-thinkin' she would nay believe a word of it without somethin' hard t' show for it."

"Indeed, so we have this…"

The Captain pulls out a small silk cloth with a mithril ring wrapped inside. It was inscribed with dwarven runes denoting a family heraldry. He displays it briefly and sets it on the table.

"This is from the Chief," he issues. "It's a family heirloom to represent his authority. You'll show this to her to prove who you are and where you come from. You'll give her a story, and you need to convince her to follow you out. But she must also be made to understand our situation and the need for secrecy."

Belrum looks at the small trinket. He picks it up and studies it, in awe of its fine craftsmanship and design.

"Such a grand thing as this yay comes from a fine family, Captain," he declares soberly. "As I look at me'self, this lass nay will take quickly t' me manner or me clothes."

"Do the best you can, Belrum. His Lordship thinks you would be our best hope, as you're not known inside the city, so you wouldn't stand out as much as the Chief would."

"I be grateful for his kind thoughts, and I yay be just a wee bit nervous at this, but if ye need me, I'll d' me best for ye. Erm, when d' we go?"

"I am waiting for a special arrival of some agents who will also need transport into the region, so we'll go when they arrive."

✦✦✦

It was late evening on Tae'Eladar, and Kaliya was preparing her team at the guildhall. The team was dressed to travel lightly, as the only thing they had in mind to do at first was to scout the general area in order to become familiar with the terrain so they could later project themselves to it from memory.

She latched a belt around her with a slot for a rune stone. In her years of study, she had risen high enough in the ranks of mage craft that she could easily enchant and use these curious devices for herself. She reflected on those first days on Therinë when Thaelyn and his men made their initial appearance on the scene, and how they made such productive use of these stones. Now, it was her turn.

She directed her team out of the guild courtyard and onto the street, navigating through the portal gates to the city hub, then to Rolsklinde, and across the plaza to the dedicated portal leading to Ruuki uy'Daan and the outpost that was still holding ground there. From there, she simply stepped over to the next portal, also in that camp, leading to the outpost on Morndindor.

Captain Hagmaert and Belrum were finishing up their meal, and their briefing, when she and the others began stepping through the portal.

"Captain, we're ready," Kaliya announces.

Belrum watched as the troupe of Daanen-Aryku came marching into the camp.

"Great All-Father, look at that, will ye."

"Are you ready, Belrum?" the Captain asks. "The time has come."

"Aye, I be a-guessin' so," he acknowledges, wiping a napkin to his mouth one last time from his meal.

The Captain calls up a scout to escort the man on his way. A mage picks up and enchants a portal rune to the valley just on the edge of the outer city as their first destination. The scout also picks up the rune once marked on the mountain road above the valley.

"Good luck to you, all of you," the Captain offers.

They begin passing through the portal aperture, arriving in the valley facing the ruins of the outer portion of Glimmerheim.

"Erm, lad," Belrum wonders. "How d' we get inside from here?"

"This is only the first step, Belrum," he responds. "Next, we will go up to that road we found once and work our way in from there. These people need to see this area first, however."

"Aye then... But I be a wee bit confused why they need t' see this wreck of a city."

"It's a little bit complicated, but I'll ask you to hold your nerves when you see it in action."

"Oh dear... When ye start puttin' it in t' such words, I feel the hair on the back of me neck risin' up."

Kaliya brings her team off to one side to study the landforms.

"All right, we all need to memorize this so we can come back here projected. This area seems very bleak, but we still need to absorb the details of it to find our way back. I want everyone to take a good look around."

The team pauses to study the surrounding territory. They examine the ruins of the city, the mountains, the landslide that appeared to be carved out and collapsed to the rear of the city, and the open spaces everywhere else. They also took in the dry air and climate sensations, and further studied the sky and the local moon and sun. When they had done enough, Kaliya drew the attention again.

"Are we set? Good. Now people, it's show time! This is our first official outing, so let's make it good. We've had some practice together, and this is a fairly simple operation, but experience is experience. We're working a strange new profession, and we need to get it right the first time."

She pulls out her rune from her belt and begins enchanting the energies. This rune would take them directly back to the guildhall, for expediency. She casts the spell for secondary transport and directs each member of the team to touch it for a secure departure.

"Aye then," Belrum notes. "I be a-guessin' their work be done now?"

"Not quite," the scout replies. "Just wait a few minutes longer, my friend. You'll be in for a little show."

They wait patiently for several long minutes. The morning air was warm, as was usual for the region. Daylight was well underway, but the scene was eerily quiet. For as far as the eye could see, not a single thing seemed alive. It was a desert-like environment, stale and desolate.

Belrum looked around the scene. He felt a little exposed and vulnerable in such a wide-open expanse, and he nearly jumped out of his skin when he saw the apparitions of Kaliya and her team reappearing out of nowhere standing right next to him.

"Bringer of Souls!" he yelps. "What be that now!"

The scout let out a modest laugh at the poor man's outburst.

"Belrum," he consoles. "You're not the only one to feel this way. This is new to us also, but fascinating to watch. These people have a special ability to move in ways most of us cannot. I can't really say anything more because it's a military secret, so far."

"Scout," Kaliya announces. "We're ready. Is it my understanding this man will be entering the city?"

"Yes, he will, both of us actually. I'll be his transport in and out."

"Good. Some of my people will also go in to study the Thane's Hall. The rest will be going up to the base to examine a few things."

"All right, I have a rune here that takes us up to the road. You should be able to see it once you're in the air and moving up the mountain. From there, you would normally go through a tunnel to the other side, although be aware of a camera inside there. But in your case, I'm guessing you'll fly right over the top," he smiles.

"Yeah, to be discreet," she affirms. "We'll fly up, spy it from the air, and I'll have us settle on a ridge to make a survey before proceeding."

"Very good, I'll wait till I see you move to the road before going up to meet you. I'm not expecting anything up there this time of day, so if I see you landing on it, I'll know it's clear."

Kaliya nods in acceptance of the suggestion, and then turns to her group.

"This is it! Take your bird forms and follow me."

The team redirects their image projections, and morphs into a flock of hawks, just as they had practiced before. Belrum jumped at the sight of it and ran behind the scout for protection.

"Lad," he mutters nervously. "I be a-wantin' t' ask ye what that be, but I nay be a-wantin' t' know the answer."

Kaliya takes off, along with her team, and begins flying high into the air. The grace and beauty of the scene was rhythmic as they took up their formation, soaring over the land and up the side of the mountain.

Belrum watched as the strange birds flew away towards the mountain, working their way up the side. He followed their motion to about midway up the slope when they seemed to alter their flight and descended onto the rocks.

"That's our cue, I think," the scout observes.

"A cue?" Belrum asks.

"A signal… She was looking for that road, and if she landed on it, it would be a signal that it was clear for us to go up."

"Lad, can ye tell me what in the name of the Dwarffather those people be about? They be more of the Daanen-Aryku folk, ay?"

"Yes, they are, and like I said, they have some very special qualities. We hope to use this in our war against Sargeras and Darumon, though I'm sure there are still a lot of details to be worked out."

The scout pulls out his rune to the road above and enchants it. Belrum touches the rune and is sent away, and the scout follows soon after.

They arrive on the road high above the valley on the mountainside. Kaliya and her team had returned to their natural forms by this time, and together they were examining the door leading into the dwarven city.

"Alpha Squad," she declares. "I'll have you follow this down to the city. Your mission is to inspect the Thane's Hall. We've studied the map, and it should be right next to where this passage comes out. Be discreet, take a small form and keep to the shadows and small spaces. Once inside, look for crevices and vantage points within the main hall, preferably above, like on a wall or a ceiling. There are also columns and statues which might be useful for concealment. Keep in mind, we'll be returning to the area on spy runs and carrying video equipment that needs to fit the space. You'll need to transport it, and therefore you'll need a form capable of carrying it and a suitable location to hide it."

She directs the squad on their duty. They opened the door, which was apparently not locked, but instead used only a simple latch to close it. The squad moved carefully into the corridor, along with the scout and Belrum. It led into a spiral staircase turning a wide circle. The slope was gentle, making it a fairly easy descent.

Kaliya called up the remaining members of her team and once

again they changed into birds. They took off and made a steep rise to the top of the mountain, then a brisk glide across the range until they came into view of the ravine with the Suuden-Aryku base.

She set the team down on a ridgeline overlooking the ravine. From here, they had a clear view of the base and all of the structures. At the far end, they could see the conveyor, and a collection of vehicles parked in their respective landing zones and garages.

"All right, here we are," she announces in a birdlike squawk. "We have a number of objectives here, and I want to see us get as much done as we can while we're in the area. Primary is to check that house at the far end and also the control room for any nooks, holes, ventilation ducts, anything we can crawl into to study their operations. Remember, we'll be using video equipment, so once again, we need a way to import it and set it up."

She pauses while she considers any other potential opportunities that may be available for study. She reviews the various elements on the ground and gets some additional ideas.

"See those aircraft at the far end?" she points with a wing. "I want a close inspection of those to determine what they might be used for. One is presumably for transporting the adamantium, but the other two are guesswork so far. We'll start with Beta Squad branching off to check on that while Gamma pokes around these storerooms to see what's inside. I'll check the house. Change to bugs and fold your way across. When we're done, we'll reconvene on the roof of the control booth."

The group transforms themselves into a swarm of insects, the same as when they were practicing in the guildhall courtyard. One group folds their perceived forms from the ridgeline straight to a location near one of the aircraft at the far end, the travel time being reduced to a fraction of an instant due to the nature of the practice. The other group folds themselves to one of the storerooms to look for a window to pass through or a crevice to crawl under.

Kaliya folds herself directly to the rooftop of the house. She takes a brief look around the area, although the perception of view from the standpoint of a bug is somewhat awkward. She begins working her way off the roof to the wall where the scouts had previously observed a window. As she approaches the edge of the window, she very cautiously peers around the frame to the inside.

In a rearward section of the interior, she could see a table and chair, some cabinets, and a countertop, along with some appliances in a kitchen setting. She moved along the frame of the window for a different perspective. Her new vantage exposed the forward portion with a plush chair, a side table with a data terminal, and a large video monitor set against the far wall with what appeared to be a holo-disk reader just underneath on a shelf. She could also see a doorway leading out of the room on the opposite side.

"How nice," she thought to herself, as she was unable to speak in this form. "A cozy little home. I wonder what's on the other side."

The current room she was observing was empty, to the best of her judgment, so she decided to fold her image inside the kitchen area behind the counter, then to the ceiling where she altered her image to blend with the coloration of the interior surface.

She now stood upside-down on the ceiling, her body an off-white color to conceal herself. She moved away quickly to a corner and began crawling along the length of the wall. She paid special attention to the plush chair, as it was turned to face the video monitor. As she came forward to a better perspective, she saw it was empty. Then she started hearing sounds from another room. She could almost feel a sensation of her blood chilling, even though she wasn't physical, so it had to be psychological. She hardened herself against it, realizing she has a decided advantage in this form. She followed the sound through the doorway into a narrow hall.

The sounds were rhythmic and mechanical, like a repeating process. They seemed to be coming out from the nearest room, directly across from the door leading into the entertainment room. The hallway led to the rear and terminated a short distance away with another door.

She debated which way to go first. She wanted to see what was making the noise, but she instead decided to scout the room at the end in case she had to make a hasty retreat after discovering the occupant. She quickly ran across to the far end of the hall and peeked inside the room. It looked like a bedroom, with a bed, a dresser, a closet, and clothes scattered on the floor in one corner. There was another door to the side along the wall from her.

"Not very tidy, is he," she mused again in her thoughts.

She was about to peek around the other door when she caught sight of something sticking out under the bed. Her curiosity at the strange surroundings caused her to divert and take a closer look. For as long as she could hear the sounds from the other room, she considered herself at leisure to peruse the decor. She flew down to the floor and crawled under for a peek.

Under the bed, she found a set of straps with buckles, a thick rod made of a type of polymer, something that resembled a short whip, and articles that looked like they could be used as cuffs, and another as a collar, all apparently well-used with metal loops attached.

"What in all the nether-space is this guy doing here?" she again ponders silently. "What is this stuff?"

The sounds from the other room stopped. She freezes and waits to see if anyone comes out of the room into the hall. She hears a groaning, followed by a procession of very distinctive sounds.

"Hoof steps... So, he must be Suuden'kai after all, or else another creature with hoofed feet."

A shape emerges from the doorway down the hall. A brawny figure looms outward and makes its way in her direction to the bedroom. She pulls back further under the bed hoping he doesn't look down.

The large male enters the room. He was shirtless and wearing snug knee-length pants. As he arrives, he turns to the other door, which Kaliya could see led into a washroom. She peeked out briefly to take a better look. He was certainly a Suuden'kai, but she noticed immediately a very different quality to him as compared to the others.

"He's not altered! No biotech seed and no cranial implant that I can see, just pure meat. He must work out a lot! That's probably the sound I heard."

The male turns and steps inside the washroom. She could hear the sound of running water and moved to the end of the bed for a better view. He was standing there gazing at himself in a mirror, checking his arms and flexing his muscles. He was indeed very well-developed. She couldn't help but gaze at him, studying the manly figure. It was simple girlish curiosity.

"Kailen nailed this one. Weightlifting, the Alpha Male syndrome. But look at that body," she croons softly. "He would give Kailen a good run for all that physique. I remember when he used to work out like that."

When he had finished examining his latest physical prowess, he pulled off his pants and tossed them into the dirty clothes pile.

Kaliya flinched and cringed at the sudden sight of the masculine backside. She tried turning away, but her curiosity drove her to take another look.

"Whoo! That's not something you see every day. But no soap, so I shouldn't stare too long. Petrith might get jealous," she giggles softly.

The man then stepped out of view into what Kaliya presumed to be a shower. She paused in contemplation of her next move. There was one more room, and she might as well take a peek while he was occupied. So, she crawled out and flew down the hall to the forward room. Here, she found what appeared to be the weightlifting equipment.

"And here we have it. All right, put down one mark for the theory. But now, what about the rest of it?"

Along another wall, she saw a strange apparatus she couldn't recognize. It was standing upright with two cross pieces at oblique angles, an X shape, with clips at each end. Sticking up from the center was another rod with a clip. The whole assembly was mounted on a base with a piston to lift it off the floor. She also saw a rack on one side with a collection of unrecognizable, to her at least, tool-like objects resting on it. She moved in closer for a better look.

"I clearly must've been raised in a very sheltered home," she muses privately. "I don't know what this stuff is, but it doesn't look nice."

Several of the devices were elongated and of different diameters.

Some were knobby, others were rippled. A couple had power cables attached and appeared to be homemade with metal nubs along the length. She saw something that looked like an athletic mouth guard, with a strap to secure it around the head, and there was also a blindfold. And then she saw several metallic clips with wire leads connecting to a power supply on the floor alongside the apparatus, and finally a number of narrow blades and thin skewers.

"Where did he get all this?" she considers. "Some of this looks like old historical torture gear. Cu'Nar's grace, I pity anyone who might be in this room when he uses it!"

She then notices some rags in the corner. They were stained with blood. Although she was not in her physical body, she could still imagine chills running through her, and suddenly felt very uncomfortable in these surroundings. Then the sounds of water in the washroom stopped.

She knew the time had come. She had to leave. She took off and flew out to the kitchen area. Hoof steps could be heard in the bedroom, and she figured he was probably getting dressed by now. She landed on the window and oriented her view outside, quickly folding herself to the ground, then taking off in the direction of the control booth.

✦✦✦✦✦

The squad that was sent through the door and along the spiral stairway to the city was nearing the bottom. It was a long descent, but not overly difficult. They were just entering a large room that was used to store the ingots. A few small piles had been laid down already since the Suuden-Aryku made their last visit. The room had no particularly interesting features except for some wall sconces emitting light from what looked like a type of flame at a distance. On closer inspection, however, it was only a simulated flame within an enclosed bulb. These sconces lined the full length of the spiral stairwell.

"Excuse me," the scout whispers to one of the teammates. "Do you know what these lights are? They don't appear to be what I would expect of dwarves."

"I haven't seen this type, personally," he replies. "But they appear to be electric. The bulb is probably filled with a special gas, and the flame is actually an interaction of an electric charge between two metal plates causing the gas to spark and emit light."

"Likely Suuden-Aryku then, do you think?"

"Very…"

They approach the door that leads into the city proper. The squad leader halts their motion to examine the door.

"Scout, does anyone usually stand outside here?" he asks.

"Not that we've seen in the past. A few people might be passing by at a distance, but this door leads into a kind of alley at first."

"Not very smart if you're trying to make this sound like an access to the surface, especially as it sits right next to the home of their Thane, which would represent a serious security risk."

"Aye, my thoughts as well."

The squad leader slowly lifts the latch and pulls the door ajar just enough for a sliver of a peek. The immediate space on the other side was clear. It led out along the side of a building to a street. A few people could be seen passing by, but their attention was turned to other matters.

"All right, we have an opening," he announces softly. "Scout, take the door. Everyone else, make like bugs."

The team morphs their images into their insect form and begins crawling out the door.

"Oi, me head," Belrum mumbles quietly. "How can it be possible for somethin' so big t' make like somethin' so small."

The scout simply gazes at the troubled man, patting him on the shoulder and smiling supportively. When the last of the marching mites leaves the room, he turns to Belrum with some last-minute instructions.

"Belrum, now is your time. This alley here leads out into a street. You have your map, so follow it carefully. I'll stay here and wait for your return."

"Aye then, I'll be off. May the All-Father give me the strength for this."

He steps forward to peek into the alley. It appears clear and no one is passing through the street beyond, so he quickly dodges around the door and sets to his duty.

As Belrum was trudging off down the alley, the squad continued forward along the wall of the palace, moving up to the top and toward the front. They turned around the corner under a roofline and paused to examine the scene. They found a set of ornate double doors leading in, with no guards or other sentries watching the front. They continued along the shadow of the roofline, and then directly down over the doors.

The doors were open at this time, revealing the long carpet leading up to the throne, and the decorative tiling. The team moves quickly to step inside to the interior wall, then further up into a corner for concealment. In addition, they altered their images to match the local coloring.

The squad leader examined the room. It was empty. The walls were lined with columns and statues, any number of which would work well for a spy post. He wanted to be near the throne for the best view with the video unit. Since the room was clear at the moment, he brought the team out and flew across to a side wall near the throne. There he took them into a crevice behind a statue.

The monument was set on a shelf in an alcove on the wall, as they all were. From here, they could look out in the direction of the throne and most of the room. Some of the columns were blocking the view of the hall, but that would occur no matter where they were. The throne was the most important to see, and to be near enough to hear the conversation clearly.

He examined the backside of the statue. It appeared as a warrior in plate armor, with thick shoulder guards. Between that and the neck was a cozy little space where they could possibly set up a camera. He turned to the rest of the team and gestured, as best he could in this form, that this location was desirable. They all made mental notes of it for future reference in case they would be called on to serve this station. They continued a survey of the room for additional locations, and when they were finished, they recalled themselves outside again onto the road on the mountainside, where they would wait for Kaliya.

✦

Kaliya and her team had reassembled on the rooftop of the control booth building. She had altered her form back into a bird for better interaction and visibility by her teammates.

"All right, everyone," she squawks softly in her bird voice. "This is not likely to be easy. It's a tight space, there are people inside, and I'm not expecting to find a lot of convenient cubbies to hide in. My thoughts are to look for ventilation ducts, or some sort of fixtures on the walls that may provide space in or around other devices. We'll go in a few at a time. The first team will survey the area and look for a likely spot, and others will make the visit to memorize it for later."

She selects two others to follow her, and she leads them to the edge of the roof. They change into insects again and crawl over the edge onto the wall, working their way to the control booth window that overlooks the yard.

From their position, they can already see several Suuden'kai officers sitting at a console behind the window. The yard was mostly empty, with only a couple of workers walking out to a utility building across the way. She led her small unit along the wall and around the side to a door, but the door appeared to be closed, and there was no window in it. They continued along, looking for other convenient access points, passing a window belonging to a cafeteria, but it was occupied with visitors. They finally located another one to the rear of the building belonging to a restroom. She peered inside to see it was currently empty, so she brought her party onto the window and angled upward to find the ceiling. They then folded themselves into the room onto the new surface. Once in place, they altered their images to provide camouflage and moved off to the side.

Across the room was a door, but it appeared to be a powered sliding door. It only opened when a person approached in proximity to a motion detector, and being a bug didn't do the job. She didn't necessarily want to wait for the next person to feel the call of nature, so she noticed a ventilation duct grill and considered this might be the only way for now. She led them up to it and inside the shaft.

Travelling through a shaft of this sort didn't help matters for finding her way around, so they wandered from one duct to another, turning at junctions hoping they were moving the right way. It was dark, so she reinvented her form with a luminescent glow to provide light in the dark space. The others followed in kind, mimicking her form to further give aid as well as for the experience to try new shapes.

Kaliya was only barely able to guess which way she was going, based on where she started and the general direction she wanted to go, then finding a suitable path to follow. In the end she could hear intermittent conversation echoing through the tunnel ahead, and she followed it to a new vent opening.

The team arrived at another grill opening into the control booth, looking down at it from the rear of the room. They could see the operators at the console by the window, another group at a console on the near side, a storage cabinet on the left, and the exterior door to the far right, by her perspective. The space between the fins on the grill allowed a reasonable view, and she considered this might be the best they would find under the circumstances.

She turned back into the duct and moved away from the grill just enough to be clearly out of view. She reimagines her form to another manifestation, similar to a praying mantis, but in her case uniquely altered so that the forward arm-like appendages more closely resembled actual arms with hands. She begins producing a series of hand signs, a silent form of language, directing her team to use this location and to lead others here for examination. They would use this spot for their spy operation.

Belrum had been wandering the streets of the city for a while now, trying to follow the map provided at the outpost camp. The path was

clearly marked, but he was inexperienced in navigating such a place as this. People passing by would pause to look at him. His clothes were clearly not the sort most commonly worn by the city folk. But with the affairs of the city as they were, where a lot of people were experiencing hardship by now, they mostly just shrugged it off.

He found his way through a main avenue, which was fairly simple to locate, and followed his directions to a cross street, and then to other side lanes. In time, he managed to find his way to a lane carved through a section of rock deeper to the rear of the city, where it curved away from a larger street through what resembled a neighborhood of homes chiseled out of the native stone.

His map indicated the house he was looking for, and he was able to pinpoint it in front of him, but his nerves were beginning to spike at this moment, not knowing how he would proceed or what sort of reaction this woman would have to him. Then he sees her sweeping the patio.

She was pleasant in her appearance, with smartly designed clothes, certainly better than what he was wearing, although they still appeared old. She seemed to be middle-aged, much the same as Tol. He realizes this is his moment, so he timidly steps away from the lane to the edge of a walled enclosure.

"Excuse me, good lass," he calls to her. "Mayhap ye could give me a moment t' bend yer ear?"

Eiki had been busy with her typical daily chores. It was the only thing she had in her life to keep her occupied, and it largely entailed sweeping the already thoroughly swept floors. She turns at the sound of the gentlemanly call.

"Aye, what be it ye want there?"

"I be a-lookin' for the home of a good woman named Eiki Bronzeheart. Be this the one?"

"Aye, ye found it. Be there somethin' ye need from me? I nay have any cloth today t' be a-makin' ye new clothes," she declares politely as she examines his worn attire.

"Aye, 'tis a shame," he replies, looking down at his tattered garb. "Nay that I would have the coin t' pay for it, I think. Instead, I have need for another thing, if ye don'na mind t' hear me tale. I came here special t' speak with ye, good woman Bronzeheart."

Eiki stops her sweeping to study the man, perplexed as to the reason why he might be here at all.

"I hope ye nay be a-thinkin' t' try courtin' me. Me husband may have been sent away once, but I nay be ready t' give up on him returnin' back, ye hear?"

"Aye lass, an' if ye heard me whispers, I nay be the rich sort t' give ye a proper livin' 'round here. Besides, I already have me'self a pretty back home, an' I yay be sure she would have a few words for it," he laughs softly hoping to relax the nerves.

Eiki quickly realized he was simply a polite gentleman trying to draw attention to something, but the reason eluded her, so far.

"Aye then, me apologies, good sir. I know there be those roamin' about durin' these hard times that may try takin' advantage of a lonely wid…ehm, someone who's man got sent away."

"Mayhap ye were about t' say widow, dear Eiki? Aye, I can already hear the ghosts moanin' through the streets here," he glances along the lane to observe the other pedestrians. "But this nay be the reason for me visit. I have somethin' that needs t' be said t' ye, but only t' yer ears, nay t' be a-shoutin' it in the street, if ye don'na mind. Mayhap we could speak more in private?"

"More private? Man, this here be about as private as a proper woman like me'self can afford. Don'na think ye'll be a-tryin' t' get me in close spaces. Nay with the clothes ye've got on. I don'na fall for sweet words that quick," she chuckles bemusedly.

"Aye, fine t' that," he smiles gently. "An' I'll nay argue with ye on yer proper manners, t' say nothin' of me bein' a mite beyond those sprightly years," he chuckles again to ease the tension. "But this nay be the common sort of tale t' tell, an' it involves someone ye know who sent me in here t' tell it t' ye."

Eiki's expression suddenly turned sober as she analyzed those words.

"Sent in here?" she mumbles distantly.

Belrum realizes this is the time he needs to prove himself. So far, the conversation went about as well as he could have expected, given his poor diplomatic skills, and this woman clearly wasn't an easy push-over. So, he searches for Tol's ring, which was still wrapped neatly in the silk cloth.

Eiki studied him intently as he began fumbling with his pockets, soon to pull out an oddly wrapped object. Belrum extracted the silk-wrapped artifact and offers it to her. She glared at the bizarre material wrapping the hidden item. As a seamstress, her first thoughts circled on the material itself. She takes it and studies it closely, rubbing her fingers on the uniquely delicate alien fabric.

"Blessed Mother, what be this here?" she croons. "I've ne'er seen such as this afore. It be so soft an' supple. Where did ye find this?"

"That? Well, t' be honest, it simply came 'round with what be inside. I nay be a clothmaker. I be only a poor farmer's son. I don'na even know the name for it. But this nay be the point I be a-tryin' t' make here. It be what lay inside that I bring t' ye."

Eiki glares at the man for the casual demeanor over the exceptionally fine cloth. But if he were only a farmer's son, this could answer for it. So, she unfolds the cloth to reveal its contents.

In an instant, she recognized the family heirloom ring of mithril. The markings were unmistakable. Waves of shock and disbelief rippled through her. She gasped heavily. Her skepticism had been shattered and replaced with terror at the thought of how this pauper found this most precious of artifacts. She snatched it out of the folds of silk to examine it closely, studying the runic markings that bore its proper ownership.

"Ye had better speak quick an' true, man," she urges. "Where did ye find this? An' who be ye that ye DID find it?"

"Mayhap ye can find that private space now for a wee bit of tellin', good woman Bronzeheart?" he smiles impishly. "But ye need t' know this much from the start. Me tale can'na be shouted in the streets here. I came here t' tell ye, an' ye alone. An' I have instructions on what t' d' about it, too."

"Instructions?" she whispers nervously.

"Aye. There be things goin' 'round us that nay be what they

seem. I hear tell ye hold a bit of temper that ye like t' make noise on occasion. Well, this will get ye howlin', but ye need t' d' it a certain way."

"What about Tol? Where be he in all this? Why could he nay come here an' tell me himself?"

"The tale be a hard one, lass. He can'na come home right now. So, he sent me instead."

She studies the ring again and casually glances around the area to see if anyone was paying any special attention to their interaction.

"What be yer name?"

"Me name be Belrum Strongfoot. I be the son of a poor farmer. We used t' have land out in the Sungold Fields, but that be long ago, afore the land was laid t' waste."

"By the war?"

"I s'pose ye may say that, but this nay be a war of the likes we can speak of in simple words. I hear tell ye speak of point-ears in here, ay?"

"Aye, the Thane tells us tales of how the land above be a-ragin' with them burnin' everythin' they see."

"Aye, so I hear from Tol. But this nay be the real tale. Yer Thane lies t' ye through his false teeth, he does!"

"Lies!" she growls, but then pulls back as she tries to compose herself out in the open.

"Now, we need yer help in here. I come here on behalf of those out there who be a-joinin' up with new friends fightin' a real war against the real foes of our world. Tol sent me, along with the others, t' find ye an' tell ye this tale, an' hire ye in t' our service."

"Me? I be but a simple clothes maker, nay a warrior."

"Aye, an' I be but a poor farmer's son, an' nay young enough or whole of body t' fight, an' yet, I be a-makin' me best effort."

"Aye, right…" she relents.

Eiki withdrew from the argument, quickly realizing if the world was in such poor condition that this man apparently lost his home, this means you must fight, no matter who you are.

She glances once more at the ring, then around the local scene as she tries to compose her thoughts.

"Lies, ye say. But what about these tales of the point-ears? It be said he comes out an' rages at our poor Chancellor about it."

"Aye, an' accordin' t' the tellin' I got, he also calls for yer men, like Tol, t' go out an' serve up somethin' for a war that nay be a-ragin' at all. Instead, they were sent t' more mines t' pull up more Adamant bricks. That be the whole of it...bricks, lass, nay anythin' else."

"Ye've got t' be a-kiddin' me!" she shouts.

Her outburst drew the attention of several passersby, but she simply smiled to disarm their interest before returning to the conversation. At this moment, she was panting from her heated anxiety.

"Where be he now? Tol. Be he well an' good? By yer manners, um..."

"Aye, he be fine an' good. Don'na worry for him. He be a-makin' far better than some, for the way of things outside. But now, if ye want t' know more, I think it best if we take it away from so many ears that nay should be a-hearin' it this way."

"I don'na understand, Belrum. Why can'na we talk out here? If the Thane be a-tellin' so many lies, should'na we let the people know of it?"

"Aye, I s'pose, but nay with HIM listenin' as it rumbles 'neath his whiskers. He be the true foe here, Eiki, an' the one we be a-fightin'. An' his friends be the ones pickin' up the bricks. An' they also be the reason our world got blasted t' the All-Father with people like me an' so many more dyin' along with it."

This statement sent chills into her, as she began to piece it together that the war wasn't so much outside, it was inside. And the stories weren't about invaders, but some kind of conspiracy for adamantium ingots, and with the Thane taking a prominent role.

She reflects on the ring once more. She knew Tol would never give it out unless he was trying to pass an important message. She pauses in her thoughts, trying to think of a way to cover their actions. She was not one to invite just anyone inside her home. It was not a polite custom for a single woman, or even a married one whose husband was away, even under such conditions, to bring strange men into their homes. Not unless she could find a justifiable excuse for it. She glances at him and nods discreetly as she devises a plan.

"Ah, I see now!" she exalts openly to anyone who might be listening. "Ye want me t' patch up yer work clothes a wee bit. Aye, I can d' that for ye fine an' quick, just come with me an' let me take a gander at this. Ooh! This may take a bit of time, t' be sure. Step inside here an' find yerself a chair while I bring out me sewin' kit."

She winks at the man and leads him inside, closing the door behind them.

"Fine then, man," she asserts. "Ye've got me ear, but I hope yer tale be a grand one. If ye're speaking of the Thane playin' tricks on us, we'll need somethin' hard t' show for it."

"Aye, I'll nay be t' arguin' this part. But it be a grand waggle of a tale, an' me head be a-poundin' from so much of it."

She pulls up a couple of chairs by a table and directs him to sit opposite her. She takes up her seat and waits expectantly. Belrum struggles to clear his throat and recall the complex details of his story.

"Yer husband Tol came t' me once out on the barrens. He was sent t' speak t' me since we were a-sufferin' in a wasteland out there. There nay be any good land t' grow food, an' everythin' be a-dyin'. Every city an' town was blasted t' the All-Father not long after this tale of the point-ears came an' went."

"Came an' went? How long are we speakin' of here?"

"Only a hand or two of years, by the tellin' of me father's father."

"That nay be the tale for us in here."

"I know. He told me yer Thane tells these wild tales of a war still a-ragin' outside, but there nay be anythin' at all out there. When the point-ears stopped comin' through their portals at us, things went quiet for a wee bit, until a mighty blastin' came down from the sky at us. Every city an' town was blasted perfectly, leavin' nothin' but great holes in the land."

"How can something like this be possible?"

"At the time, we had no idea, 'cept mayhap the gods above cursin' us, or some other foulness we could'na explain. Then it stopped almost as quick as it began, an' it stayed quiet ever since. But there was nothin' left by then. Those of us who still be alive are mostly takin' up inside mines an' such. The pummelin' destroyed everythin', all our homes, an' now we had nothin' but the clothes on our backs an' what few skills we could muster t' live in a dyin' land."

"Blessed Mother…an' for how long? All this time, was it?"

"Aye, four hundred years. Me father an' his father handed down stories of how the air grew warm, the land dried up, all the animals ran away, an' even the trees an' grasses were a-fadin' from sight. We learned of a word for this from some new friends we met recently, but it be a word our folk probably ne'er heard of afore."

"What word be this one?"

"They call it a climate change, a kind of slow-motion disaster of a dyin' world, where it gets ever warmer, an' things die off until there nay be anythin' left at all."

Eiki pulls back from the conversation a moment to ponder this concept, but it was indeed something new, and seemingly unnatural.

"Be there a way t' fix this?"

"Aye, mayhap, but nay a small one. It has t' be as big as the world itself. But here be our first problem. The foes still be out there, an' they would surely see it. So, it has t' wait for now."

"Aye, but now, what about these foes? An' these friends ye speak of?"

"Right. Keep in mind, me old head nay be the good sort, an' me words nay be as smooth as some."

"Fine then, take it slow if ye must."

"The true foes nay be from this world. If ye think of the point-ears floppin' through their portals, they were nay from this world either. They came here through portals from somewhere an' tried harassin' our people. But they were weak an' sickly t' our eyes, fallin' down, hard of breathin'…" he pauses in consideration of the old stories. "Me father passed along the tale of how they tried tossin' magic or some such at us. They seemed driven t' make trouble, an' the warriors had t' fight, even though these point-ears did'na seem like a proper challenge. It played in our eyes more like a mercy killin' than a good fight for a proper warrior."

"I be a-tryin' now t' think of the old tales we have in here. This sounds familiar t' me, but this be a right old one, an' nay the same as what the Thane tells now."

"Mayhap, if he wants ye t' think they still be out there, an' such that it keeps ye buried under this mountain. But like I said, this ended only after a hand or two of years. But it was nay a war, Eiki. It be more of a test t' see how we fight."

"A test? How so?"

"D' ye still have the old tales of orcs comin' at us once upon a time? Five hundred years ago, we had another invasion, they were called orcs. They hit us in much the same way, but nay for long, as our warriors beat them back good an' proper. That was the first test. The point-ears were the second, an' this one was t' turn our eyes away from the real foes. The orcs, the point-ears, they were slaves sent at us by those who pummeled the land clean t' the heavens above."

"But why?"

"Adamant. They want it, an' they must think us t' be right grand folk who can give it t' them. But nay farmers, Eiki. Smiths, miners, aye, but the rest weren't needed."

Eiki reeled back from the conversation as it started to make sense. She briskly reflected on the Thane's feast and all the men being sent out. It was always smiths and miners, never anyone else.

"So, ye have all our men out there, all workin' in mines an' pullin' out more Adamant, an' then makin' bricks with it? Blessed Mother, he must have a lot of mines by now."

"Um, nay by the whole of it. Ye'll nay like this part, but ye'll need t' know of it. The Thane puts on this feast, ay?"

"Aye."

"An' this be t' send out for his fine tellin' of a war a-ragin' outside, ay?"

"Aye..." she emits tensely.

"But did any of them ever come home?"

"Nay!" she asserts sternly. "An' this be one of me grander

complaints. There nay be even a wee hint, nor a word or two, t' say they be alive an' still a-workin'."

"Aye…" he sighs somberly. "Eiki, that feast nay be the sort ye'd want t' feed even t' a mangy field rat. It be a death trap for yer men. It carries a poison that puts them under a spell where they d' as they are told an' nay talk back for it."

"Blast it!" she curses. "He would d' that t' our people for nay more than Adamant?"

"It gets worse. It kills after a while."

"Kills!" she shouts. "I can'na believe this! An' this be the Thane's beloved feast he screams for every year?"

"I saw it me'self, me an' some of the lads from me kin. We found a mine t' the south of here with some of yer men inside. Their eyes were as cold as death an' they nay spoke a word, just worked without end. Then, one day, I made the run t' check on them. This was yay a while back. I found those same men lyin' dead on the ground. Nay long after that, a new crew showed up an' took their place."

Eiki's nerves were reaching their limits by now. She screamed and began storming around the room. When she finally realized the ruckus she was making, she quickly silenced her outburst, and rushed to peek out the window. No one was immediately outside to hear anything, so she returned to the table.

"What about Tol?" she urges. "How is he? Ye said he was fine an' good, ay?"

"Aye, but only because of these new friends. He an' the crew he was with were found in one of these mines. But it was nay even on this world. They were taken t' another world entirely, if ye can imagine such a thing. This here, combined with the poison, be the reason he nay can come home right now. They were ne'er intended t' come home. An' I think, if any of them did, an' the Thane should ever hear of it, it goes up t' his friends, an' we'll see more pummelin'."

"Oh grand, but with nay more out there t' pummel, where does it go, here t' the mountain?"

"What be left of it. Ye got a big hit outside that brought part of it down over yer doors, so folk like me can'na even get inside t' see what ye be about in here."

"But wait, how d' the men go out if the mountain be blasted t' cover our doors?"

"Ye have a room where ye drop the bricks. There be a door in there leading up a long stair t' a door on top of the mountain. There be a road up there, leadin' through a grandly fine tunnel, an' then up t' a secret military base ye probably ne'er knew about, where the Thane an' his friends bring yer bricks, an' also yer men t' be carried t' the mines."

Eiki gapes at the man for the apparent audacity of the Thane and these 'friends' of his having such gall as to build a base right on top of them.

Belrum continues, "An' this here be the reason for the point-ears turnin' our eyes the wrong way. While we were all watchin' them floppin' out of their portals, these foes set down on top of yer mountain. Then yer Thane told ye t' close yer doors an' nay ever peek outside again. After that, these others came along an' pummeled everythin' else they did'na care for, makin' ye slaves here with closed doors an' wild tales t' keep ye huddlin' 'neath the sheets. An' that be the whole of it for yer blessed Thane. But try nay t' go a-screamin' too loudly such that he can hear ye, because I nay be finished."

"Belrum! How much more can there be t' this tale of yers?"

"It gets complicated now, as now it goes beyond our world. As I once said t' a few of me kinfolk, we got run down like a beggar in the streets for the favor of our Adamant. This be the whole of it for us. But the reason why they WANT the Adamant…aye, lass, this'll be a tale t' curl yer whiskers…assumin' ye had any," he smiles delicately.

"Uh huh…" she smirks. "Right, then, go on. What be THIS one about?"

"There be a lot of slave folk involved here. The orcs an' point-ears are lesser folk by compare. They were used only t' make trouble for us down here. The higher ones are called Suuden-Aryku. They be high of knowin' an' much more developed. They hold such power as t' travel the skies an' stars above, which be where these other worlds are found. They apparently found us once, saw how good we were with our diggin', an' decided t' use us for it."

"Oh grand. So, be this t' say, we dug our own graves for our fine skills?"

"Mayhap, but we nay be the only ones. All these slaves were used at one time or another for whatever skills they were best at, includin' these Suuden-Aryku."

"With them bein' able t' travel the skies from one world t' another?"

"Aye, this, an' more after that. But while they may be a right grand folk for so much other knowin', apparently they don'na know how t' work Adamant. An' here we come t' the one who wants it an' why."

"Uh oh…"

"There be one at the top, an' he be the stuff of legends for folk like us. His name be Darumon, an' he be a servant t' another one, named Sargeras. These are sometimes called Primordials, but t' folk like us, with the old tales we sometimes carry, they be the Titans of legend."

"Titans?!" she shrieks. "Wait now, are ye sure about this? These be tales for wee babes at bedtime, Belrum."

"Aye, because the tales be so old, no one believes them anymore. And mayhap rightly so, as the tales be truly old. These Titans are s'posed t' be dead by now, but one of them yay be out there still, an' he wants Adamant, great mountains of it."

"Why?"

"His kind are ancient foes t' the gods we know an' love in the modern day. Those like the All-Father. There was a battle once, long ago in days our kind should ne'er even know about. The last of these Primordials was killed off, but this one escaped an' went in t' hidin', he an' his servant. The tale I have here comes from these new friends we found. They come from another world, where he was found makin' trouble for more folk. But this time, he be the one t' get in trouble for it, when his deeds were discovered an' he was chased off. Now, they be the ones chasin' him, an' they have t' d' so quietly, since these two are runnin' from a kind of law, an' hidin' from it."

"Well, that be a fine thing, though a bit late for us here."

"Aye, mayhap, but this new tale be only a few years old by now. He was out there for a long while afore this, makin' trouble for a lot of folk, includin' those Suuden-Aryku. He took them first, then came for the rest later. An' he lies t' everyone with such grand tales the likes of which even the Thane can'na hold up t'," he chuckles.

"How nice…" she huffs. "But where does this bring us here under the mountain? We have a pummeled world outside, slowly dyin', with folks like ye an' yers strugglin' t' live, an' with the Thane callin' up more feasts, an' with more of our men goin' out, an' more women with empty beds t' sleep in."

"Aye, here we go, so listen carefully. Like I said, I be but a poor farmer's son, an' nay with much schoolin', nay that we have any schools t' learn from. Eiki, ye an' yer folk in here yay be but the last of our kin. Me an' mine were barely holdin' on, an' some nay even that much, until Tol an' his new friends found us an' took us in."

"Tol did that?" she croons as she curls a gentle smile.

"Aye, but he be a-workin' for this new folk, so it rightly be them a-makin' most of it for us out there. They arrived nay long ago, mayhap only a couple of months, by the tellin'. They set up their own military camp out on the fields near my old home. They found us barely alive in a mine we were usin'. They gave us food an' told us t' find more of our kin an' bring them in. Right now, we're searching high an' low for more people, but the land be so dry, it be impossible t' grow anythin'."

"Belrum, we have tales in here of the farmin' folk, an' weavers an' such like. What about all that?"

"I be a farmer, but the land nay be good for it, nay for most of me life. The last of us were a-huddlin' inside an old mine, hopin' t hide from whatever it was that blasted everythin' else. As for yer tales, it be all gone now, sent t' the All-Father an' leavin' nothin' but gapin' holes in the land."

Eiki closed her eyes and turned away as she tried to envision all the glorious tales of farms and great herds of animals, weavers and cloth makers, tanners and leatherworkers, and everything else out there said to be providing some of the finest wares for any market. The vision of loss seemed so unreal, she could only sigh mournfully as she tried to collect herself again.

"Everythin'…" she moans. "A whole civilization."

"Aye, lass. I hear yer words. So, they gave us an offer t' bring us t' another world, one of several they own by now as they hunt for this Darumon."

"Only Darumon, nay the other?"

"Darumon be the one a-makin' the most noise. The other one, Sargeras, I hear may be mostly sittin' tight on the home world for these Suuden-Aryku. They'll get t' him in good time."

"Good, but where d' these people actually come from, these friends of yers?"

"They come from a world called Tae'Eladar. That world is owned by a good an' kind King that brought many different folks together. Then, one day, orcs arrive an' make trouble for them."

"Orcs again?"

"Aye, Darumon was headin' back that way t' make trouble for these old foes of his, but he was found out. An' the King of that world came out t' make war on him for the favor of invadin' his home."

"That King sounds like a yay angry sort."

"Aye, ye might say that, an' for good reason. When he learned who Darumon an' Sargeras were, he knew he had t' make this charge t' finish them. I hear tell he be related to those others. So, this here nay be more than t' finish what was started, an' it yay also be the reason Darumon wants revenge."

"What was the reason for this battle that he wants revenge for it?"

"His kind was found makin' trouble for folk like us. An' he thinks he has a proper right t' it."

"Oh grand!" she shouts. "An' he STILL be a-makin' trouble for folk like us. So, this revenge be nay more than t' make more trouble, an' for what reason? He was told nay t' d' it any more by people who set down a law?"

"Aye! Now, these folks, led by this King, be a-chasin' him. They found a world called Therinë, where Tol an' his team were a-workin' a mine. This was also where Darumon found those point-ears. He turned them t' slaves an' spent them like thin ale on the war here. This King rescued them, along with Tol an' his crew. Then there be another folk on that world, an' they be the same folk as these Suuden-Aryku, but a band that tried t' run away when Darumon came t' their world t' make slaves of the rest. This folk calls themselves Daanen-Aryku, t' give them a new name."

"Be they good folk or bad?"

"Good, an' now workin' with this King t' chase Darumon back t' the hole he crawled out of. But Darumon was found a-hittin' them hard just for the fun of it."

"Blast that devil t' the abyss! If he can'na make slaves out of them, he plays with them till they slump over dead?"

"Aye, that seems t' be the way of it. Here be where this King learns of Darumon, but he also figures Darumon, with his Suuden-Aryku slaves an' their ability t' pummel things, be a foul sight on that world. Better t' simply chase him off t' save what was left of it."

"Oh dear…"

"He would rather go off chasin' him, but on terms he can better control. This King next found a world called Ruuki uy'Daan. This be where those orcs call home. He knows by now they were also slaves, so he spares what was left of them an' helps them find a new home far away from anyone, includin' Darumon, who might hold a grudge on things."

"Aye, by now I can see it, for the way that beast be a-treatin' others."

"An' now, this King be here with us. He has his people helpin' mine, an' bringin' us all back t' Therinë t' find new homes, at least until he can help with the dyin' land outside."

"Does he actually hold such power t' d' that?"

"I can'na say, but t' live on that new world be a grand better sight than outside here. We have good work, we be a-makin' coin again, eatin' good food… Ye can'na argue this much, an' he did all this without thinkin' twice for it. He even gave us a bit of land for our herdin' beasts."

Eiki felt a gush of emotion rising up as she reflected on the extreme generosity of anyone who would offer so much to so many complete strangers.

"Why can'na we have one of those up in the Hall," she muses wistfully.

"Aye, I heard Tol say the same. An' this King has people spyin' on that base up top t' learn of their ways. He wants t' take it whole, but quietly. He thinks the Thane be one of these Suuden-Aryku, but a special sort that can change his shape. And Great All-Father, I've seen a few of this sort," he rolls his eyes. "Those Daanen-Aryku, a whole gaggle of them, just crawled inside the Thane's Hall as tiny bugs snoopin' for hidey-holes t' spy on things."

"Bugs?" she winces. "Just how big are these Suuden-Aryku?"

"Twice as tall as me an' then some, with horns like a briar sheep an' blue skin. An' their eyes glow, if ye can believe that one."

"Belrum, how d' ye change yer size from twice that of a man to a wee bug?"

"I don'na know, an' they nay be a-tellin'. They say this yay be a special secret, an' I don'na doubt it, if they hope t' use this against Darumon."

"Oi! That would be a fine one. T' sneak up on him as a wee bug that he nay be a-knowin' of it?" she laughs heartily. "Right then, but just for the sayin', why spend time watchin' him an' nay just pummelin' him like he did everythin' else?"

"The tellin' goes that Darumon an' his master, Sargeras, are hidin' from these other foes. They go by the name Estelar, a race of gods. This King an' his people, an' the Captain I be a-workin' with right now, tell tales of them. They say our gods, what we call the Morndinsamman, be a part of it, an' this King be a close kinfolk, which yay be why he was so angry that this Titan be out there still. These Estelar were s'posed t' have destroyed them long ago, but Sargeras ran an' hid from them."

Eiki was suddenly, and quite visibly stunned by this suggestion.

Regardless of the fact that she held at least a partially religious devotion, as most dwarves do for their gods, the suggestion of these gods existing physically, and further referenced as a race of beings in opposition to this one that caused so much havoc in their world, was shocking. This altered the meaning of the term 'gods' in her mind, bringing it down to a society of beings, much like people, fighting other people over some dispute they shared. This was then compounded by this King being somehow related to the rest, and then chasing across worlds, rescuing everything he found. It dazed her imagination.

"An' so," Belrum continues. "If he sees them a-comin' for him again, he could run an' hide again, an' mayhap we nay would find him till some other poor folk gets hit by him. This be why we have t' move in secret, t' catch him afore he runs again. An' if the Thane sees it, he tells the rest, an' there it goes again."

Eiki glared at him for his explanation, trying to imagine this scenario. A creature running from the gods, apparently all of them, and hiding, hoping to come out sight-unseen to take revenge, and using little things like these slave societies to do his dirty work, at least until he's discovered, and then to run again.

"This be also the reason Tol has t' stay out," Belrum concludes. "If the Thane hears of it, he'll start askin' questions of how an' why a man nay s'posed t' be a-returnin' now be a-comin' back."

"Aye, I see it," she mutters. "Blessed Mother help us all, how did we find our way in t' this, Belrum? Why us?"

"By the tellin' of it, we be some of the finest t' haul up Adamant. An' he needs great loads of it. It be only our poor luck he found us."

"All right, um…so ye came in here lookin' t' find help?"

"Aye, this King be askin' for ye t' come visit an' talk about makin' a wee bit of trouble in here for the Thane. Be ye feelin' the right sorts for it, Eiki? I was sent here t' pull ye out so ye can make this visit. I have a friend, a scout, hidin' in that store of yers waitin' for me. From there, we go t' the camp they have outside, an' from there t' see this King."

Eiki pauses from the conversation, feeling worn from all the accusations and evocative statements. She studies the ring one more time, turning it over in her hand, then passing a painful glance around the room. She sighs deeply, trying to pull up her strength. This was a lot to bear, and it also stank of conspiracies and falsehood, much of which reflected the same opinions she so often expressed in the past.

"Fine then, Belrum," she relents weakly. "I s'pose I nay have anythin' else here t' d' with me'self. The coin here be a-runnin' too thin, an' there nay be any more wool t' weave, an' nay more cloth for me sewin' work."

"Mayhap this good King can help ye. He has gone an' helped a great many in this war."

"Help me with what, Belrum? Will he give me coin? Nay... I'll nay go askin' of a King for that!"

"He be a wise one, Eiki. Ye can be sure of it! But ye need t' come with me an' I'll lead ye out of here t' go meet with him."

"Aye, but if this be any manner of trick...!" she jabs at him strongly.

"Aye lass, I can see it in yer eyes. Ye be a good sort, an' I know why Tol would have ye as his wife. Come then. I nay be good at findin' me way through a big city like this."

The two of them pick themselves up and make ready to head out the door. Eiki flusters for a moment about her appearance, removing her apron and dusting herself off, then combing her hair hoping to make herself more presentable outside. When she was satisfied, she followed Belrum out the door and into the streets.

They wandered along the lanes and avenues, with Belrum asking Eiki to help guide them, since she knew her way around much better. They found their way up to the Thane's Hall and slowed their motion to wait until the general area was clear of any pedestrians before ducking along the alley up to the door leading into the storage room used for the ingots.

"Lad, be ye in here?" Belrum calls gently into the seemingly empty room.

Off to one side, an image appears. The sudden emergence of this unusual form caused Eiki to start, letting out a soft yelp. She studied the form of a tall man, taller than any she had ever seen before.

"What…" she hesitates. "Belrum, be this yer friend? I nay have ever seen a man so tall!"

"He nay be a dwarf, Eiki. Many of these folks be that way, an' these Daanen-Aryku…oi! It be enough t' give ye a sore neck for it."

"My greetings to you, good woman Bronzeheart," the scout announces in his form of Dwarvish. "I am very pleased to see Belrum was able to gain your faith. It took a little while, but I'll guess the story was simply a difficult one to tell."

"Aye, ehm…" she falters. "Ye speak like us, by a wee bit."

"We have a dwarven population back home, part of an ancient migration. The language has changed by now, but it still seems to work."

"Really! I wonder… A migration, ye say? I nay be one t' study these things, but how long ago was it?"

"Oh, this is ancient history to us by now, on the order of fifteen or more millennia."

"Oi! That yay be a grand long while ago. I was a-thinkin' mayhap we have some old books on this, but I nay can be sure of it now."

"It might be interesting if we could find something, but perhaps later for this. For now, I'm sure we have more than enough work to bring this world back in order. Do you think I could gain enough trust from you to bring you up to my Lord for a little chat?"

"Your Lord…this be how ye call him?"

"In my case, yes. Those of us who are citizens have grown accustomed to it. He likes to use the name Lord Thaelyn, even though he is a fully coronated King. He tells us it holds a certain nostalgia from his earlier days."

"Does he now? How nice," she titters. "But I be just a simple clothes maker. Belrum here said somethin' about makin' a wee bit of trouble, but if ye're tryin' nay t' be so open in the streets, ehm…"

"Ours is a very clever society with a lot of curious ways of approaching problems to find solutions. My understanding is you don't hold a lot of love for how things work in here. This is what we're hoping to use."

"Oh! I think I see it now. So, it be a wee bit of rumblin' ye're lookin' for. Hmm, aye, mayhap…"

"That's right, but we need to move very carefully. My Lord will give you the details of it. Are you ready?"

She glances at Belrum, and then at her clothes, which were not the finest she could possibly be wearing, but it was all she had available.

"Ye'll be a-takin' me t' see yer King, be that the one?"

"Yes, it is. Don't worry about your appearance, these are minor details as compared to our greater needs."

"Aye, for ye it may be that way, but I come from a fine family, an' goin' out like this be a wee bit embarassin'."

"Still, we need your help. Right now, there are more important demands in front of us. We will not judge you for your appearance. Maybe at another time, things will improve."

"Aye, mayhap…" she sighs. "These clothes are all I have now. Fine then, how d' we go about this?"

"I will open a portal to our camp, and we will wait there until we can go see my Lord. There is a difference in time between our worlds. It is nighttime for him now."

"Truly. That be a curious one. Another world, an' for them it be nighttime. But wait. If we have the time for it, mayhap ye could bring me up top so I can see for me'self the outside?"

"I could. I doubt we should be expecting any visitors out there at this time. But it's a long climb from here."

"Aye, fine, it'll d' me a bit of good t' stretch me legs."

They exited out the other door and began the long climb up the stairs. Even though the stairway was relatively shallow, the length was enough to offer its own workout. They plodded methodically around the spiral staircase, layer by layer rising higher, until finally they arrived at the upper door.

"Blessed Mother, that was a bit more than I expected."

"I tried to warn you," the scout ushers humorously.

"Aye, but now I need t' ask who built it an' when. I recall tales of a poundin' said t' be from the war outside. It be a-rumblin' through the rocks. Mayhap some of it could be this here?"

"Perhaps. This looks very professional to me, and likely would take some effort, maybe even to use explosives to carve out portions of it."

"Oi, that nay be somethin' t' play with lightly."

The scout escorts them out the door and onto the roadway, where the bright sunlight quickly assaults Eiki's sensitive eyes after a lifetime of living underground. She grunts as she covers her face, barely peeking through her fingers trying to see around her.

"You'll adjust in a few moments," the scout comforts. "You people live in very low light conditions down there."

"Aye, I recall a few tales now. Our people used t' go out more often, so we nay would feel this much. Give me a wee bit."

They wait as Eiki slowly removes her hands, allowing her eyes to better adjust to the light levels. Now she is able to take in the full effect of the sights. She gazes out onto the valley below, and also began taking notice of the air.

"It feels warm out here," she notes privately. "Just like ye said, Belrum. I ne'er felt it afore, but it yay does feel like a land dryin' up."

She tries walking around for a better view down below, trying to orient herself to see where the outer part of the city should be. She was just barely able to catch a glimpse of the ruins and part of a large landslide.

"An' that be what remains of our fine home," she moans. "Those devils, they nay hold any proper respect for anything."

"We should go gently on the words here, Madam Bronzeheart. The people who did this are believed to have been under a very strong control effect."

"A strong control effect... Anythin' like that poison Belrum said was in that feast?"

"Not quite like the poison. But these people can create devices for a similar effect."

"Oi, that sounds at least as bad. An' ye don'na need t' eat anythin' for it."

Eiki peruses the sights a bit more before turning and nodding to the scout to proceed ahead. He pulls out a rune and begins enchanting it for departure. Belrum encourages Eiki to touch it so she is taken away, and he follows after. The scout then re-enchants it for his own passage.

They arrive in the outpost. Eiki again notices the warm dry air, which seemed more intense here at ground level. As she steps away from the portal, she takes notice of the strange assortment of soldiers and scouts sitting around a campfire.

"Blessed be the Mother. Where be this place?"

Belrum walks up behind her.

"This be the north end of the Sungold Fields, or what be left of it after the blastin'. Every city an' every town, every farm…if it was out there, it nay be there now. I've seen a bit of it with me own eyes, an' these lads here be a-tryin' t' search the lands t' find any who still be alive out there. We've been a-movin' them t' Therinë, like I said. They be a-goin' t' work now on the local farms, workin' the land t' make coin an' food an' a new life. This land out here nay be any good now."

"Can I see it?"

"Aye, if ye like, but ye'll nay like what ye see, if ye even knew what t' expect of it."

He guides her over to the exit from the outpost, leading her through to the outside to see the barren wasteland. She looks around at the desolation, not entirely sure what she was expecting to find, but this certainly didn't meet with the general stories told in the city.

"An' there be nay more farms, nay more herdin', nay more weavers, cloth makers, nay t' any of that now?"

"There be only a few of us here an' there hidin' in the caves an' mines huddlin' together an' hopin' for the All-Father t' bless us with a miracle."

"An' these people here?" she turns to go back inside to see the soldiers again. "Be they the miracle then?"

"Aye, t' some if we can catch them in time. But we found a few out there that went too soon."

She hangs her head to consider the memory of those who have died in all this. Even though she didn't know them, they were still people who suffered.

The Captain was sitting in his officer's hut at the time they came through. He rose up at the sound of their voices, but waited for Belrum to show the distraught woman around. When he saw them come back inside, he made an effort to present himself.

"Greetings to you," he calls politely. "My name is Captain Hagmaert. Do I have the pleasure of speaking with the good woman Bronzeheart?"

Eiki turned to face the well-appointed man. She instantly took notice of his uniform.

"Dear Blessed Mother, where did ye get that armor?" she mumbles.

She pauses to look around at the others in the group, quickly glancing over their equipment. She catches herself to respond.

"Aye, the name be Eiki Bronzeheart. I beg ye t' excuse me poor dress. Times have been hard, an' the cloth t' make new ones be a wee bit short."

"Not a problem, good woman. In some ways, you're actually lucky. We have seen people in a much worse state than this. We have seen cities destroyed, worlds demolished, and people left without their worldly possessions. This war has taken a tremendous toll on many."

Eiki suddenly began to feel very foolish for her self-centered interest. The mention of worlds destroyed was beginning to settle in with the sights outside and the stories Belrum gave.

"Me pardons, I still be in a wee bit of shock. All me life, I be a-listenin' t' the tales inside the city. Tales told mostly by the Thane, an' then a few old ones left behind by others, an' things don'na always make a great bit of sense t' me. When Belrum here came an' told me his tales... Oi! It be a hard one t' swallow."

"I fully understand. No doubt this war has progressed across many worlds, perhaps more than we might know about. It may be impossible to know how many people have truly suffered."

"But now ye're fightin' back?"

"We only came into it recently, when Darumon tried invading

our home on Tae'Eladar. He sent a bunch of orcs at us, which wasn't very wise on his part, as they tend to make trouble. If he was trying to keep a low profile, he should never have used something so rough around the edges," he chuckles.

"Oi, so that be the way of it, ay?" she grins.

"At the same time, he might not have been expecting us on the other side, being so organized as we are by now. But for now, we need to proceed carefully. We believe he is using your adamantium to make a very powerful weapon. We need to find it, remove it, and disband all his work here, while at the same time not revealing ourselves to him directly."

"Great Mother, how d' ye think ye can d' that without him knowin' about it?"

"This is part of a very delicate plan we need to work out, first by studying his people here, and then to find a good opportunity for ourselves."

"Then what be ye a-makin' here so far?"

"Scouting, mostly, to study our enemies… We have plans in the works to take control of an enemy base, and then use it to take us to the next step, but it must be done very carefully. Also, there is the Thane in control of your city. We believe him to be an agent working for them. We have people out there investigating that as well."

"Fine, but what d' ye need me for? I be just a clothes maker. Yer man here said somethin' about makin' a bit of rumblin' methinks, but I nay be one t' go shoutin' in the streets. An' if ye're tryin' so hard t' keep it low, I think ye'd nay want any big noises, ay?"

"That's right. My Lord will share with you his ideas, and we can go from there. It will most likely involve some quiet gossip and a few new rumors to whisper in the alleys. Our purpose would be mostly to break the Thane's stories with a few of our own."

"Hmm, that will be a fine one. But I think I nay would want t' be the one listenin' t' him yowlin' in his Hall when he hears of it."

"Maybe so, and this is why we need to study him. If we're right, we'll try a little game where we might try to push him into a corner.

To our knowledge, you are currently mining adamantium in your city. Is this correct? What about mithril?"

"Adamant, mostly. I think the mithril veins ran out long ago, an' even the Adamant runs out on occasion. So, the Thane orders us t' go lookin' for more."

"This is useful to know. If you have a history of this, perhaps we could use it."

"Mayhap, an' then it be said we trade it for such fares up here t' serve our needs."

"We were speaking of the value of that trade once," the scout adds. "How much is adamantium actually worth, in terms of coinage. And what do you receive in return for it?"

"Oi! Aye, that would be a good one t' argue! But if there nay be a war, an' nay any people t' trade with..."

"Indeed," the Captain responds. "We actually witnessed one of those deliveries recently where your local stockpiles, and those in a nearby mine, were taken away by the Suuden-Aryku."

"Did ye now. How grand..." she smirks ironically. "So, there truly nay be a war at all. Nay a tide of point-ears ragin' across the land, nay the warriors fightin' a ne'er endin' battle t' where we need t' be a-servin' up the fare t' help them," her voice begins to escalate. "We mine our Adamant an' make bricks, day in an' day out, an' all he can d' be t' scream for more. An' he tells us his fibs about tradin' with the people up top, when there nay even be a world up here t' trade with?!"

Her face begins to flush as her obvious rage settles in.

"Further! He be a-sellin' off our finest Adamant for mere baubles that nay even serve our people..."

"And he probably has no true idea what the metal can do in a wartime scenario..." the scout offers mischievously.

"Oh! Be that the way of it?! Aye, lad, that would be a fine insult t' pile on top of things," she shouts.

"Um, Scout, was that actually necessary?" the Captain mumbles cautiously.

The scout simply smiles and shrugs.

"Well, Captain, I think any good dwarf would know better, what do you think?"

"I swear t' ye!" Eiki screeches. "Curse that Thane for all he be worth! May the All-Father, the Revered Mother, and all the other Morndinsamman, cast him in t' the eternal deep!"

"Not to worry, good woman Bronzeheart," the Captain consoles. "We will see to it."

"Aye, ye'll see t' it alright! This here be a true war now! For all the blastin' dear Belrum tells of it, there will be a grand price t' pay! Four hundred years, we've been a-hearin' of it. Four hundred years, or at least the greater part of it, our men have been a-chowin' this feast! An' four hundred years, our women have been a-goin' t' the altars prayin' for their men who be a-lyin' dead in some forgotten hole!"

"Good woman Bronzeheart... Please..."

"The name be Eiki, an' don'na forget it!"

"Right then, but please try to control yourself."

"Fine! I'll be a-controllin' me'self just as soon as I finish layin' the blazes upon a world that bears up such a foulness as t' take from us our most precious gifts an' bring us nothin' but lies!"

"Gracious, Tol must be a very strong man to keep you in good sorts," the Captain muses gently.

Eiki heard the statement and realized her outbreak. She always considered herself to be a dignified woman, but he was right, she did have a temper. She forces herself to break from her tirade and turns away, covering her face in shame for her behavior. She struggles to constrain her voice as she replies.

"Me pardons. It nay be proper for such a woman like me, what with me upbringin', t' go an' rage at ye who be a-tryin' so hard t' help."

"It is quite all right, Eiki. We know dwarves quite well. You're a very passionate people. You should've seen your husband when he first learned of it."

"Aye, we be two of a kind," she offers as she timidly tries forcing a smile into her face. "Where he be at now? Belrum said he be on another world, ay?"

"Yes, he is, but it is currently nighttime there, so we should send you forward this eve to meet with him. You can also meet with my Lord, and he can tell you the rest."

"General, do we have anything of interest to report on last night's mission?"

"Indeed we do, my Lord. We seem to have success all around, much to my great pleasure."

Thaelyn had just arrived in the WIC building for his morning review. Messages had been delivered the previous night from Morndindor with preliminary reports of the activities, and with more detail promised to be delivered later.

"And what is it we have to report?" Thaelyn asks.

"First, Belrum was able to make contact with the Chief's wife, and I suppose they are preparing to come across any moment by now. I sent word for the Chief to join us, so he should be along soon. As for Kaliya and her team, they were successful at locating several promising vantage points in both the Thane's Hall and the forward portion of the Suuden-Aryku control booth. The Commander here has already sent word to his people with some of the details to be sure we can have something ready to suit our needs."

"Good, but now onto the more serious matter of the Thane himself. Do we have word on that?"

"Yes, but Kaliya begged to present it to you in person, since it was apparently rather disturbing to her mind. She felt it needed more explanation than what she could write in a simple note. She did mention, however, that we got our theories right. He is an unmodified young Suuden'kai male who apparently uses weightlifting equipment as a hobby."

"Incredible. Mark a point down for each of us, General. That one is surely worth it."

"Yes, I feel we made a lucky hit with this one."

"As for the rest, I must wonder what that was about. Very well, we shall wait until her classes are finished for the day."

"She mentioned something about seeking some consultation to help her thoughts, so perhaps we will see what that results in."

In the outpost camp on Morndindor, the sun had set, and the camp was settling in for the evening, all except for two people who were just getting ready for departure.

"Are you ready?" the Captain asks.

"Aye, I think," Eiki asks tenuously. "Ye sure this here be safe?"

"We use these all the time, both in our military when travelling to far places, as well as our people in the cities and towns."

"In yer cities an' towns, be it? Oi…that would be a yay fine sight t' see. Fine then, well, here I go…"

Eiki and Belrum were on their way through the portal gate in the outpost camp. Since Belrum knew the way by now, he volunteered to take her across, and at the same time pay a visit to his own wife along the way, who was now living in Rolsklinde. They jump through, first with Eiki, and then Belrum, leaving the camp to arrive on their first leg of the journey into the camp on Ruuki uy'Daan.

Chief Bronzeheart was rushing through the streets of Rolsklinde after receiving his summons to report to the WIC building. He was anxious to meet with his wife after so long an absence, but his nerves were also on edge since he knew deep down the meeting would be very emotional for both of them. He arrives inside the building and hurries up to the strategy room.

"Here I be, Yer Kingship," he calls into the room. "Did they come yet?"

"Not as yet, but we are expecting them very soon, if the Captain lives up to his good name. Have a seat and rest. You look like you ran the full distance."

"Aye, but it nay be only the runnin' to cause me the hard breathin'."

"I understand. When she arrives, I think we should offer you a moment to reacquaint yourselves. I am sure there is time enough for us to attend to our discussion afterwards."

"Thank ye, Yer Kingship. Ye ne'er cease to show yer fine soul."

Outside in the plaza, Belrum and his charge arrived through the dedicated gate from Ruuki uy'Daan. Eiki was nervous, not only to meet with her husband after his departure several years before, but also from the strange manner of transport being used here. When they arrive in the city, she takes a long moment to look around.

"Blessed Mother, this be a grand one t' see. What be this place, Belrum?"

"This here be the city called Rolsklinde. Here now we be on Therinë, that one I was a-tellin' ye about with the Daanen-Aryku an' the last bit of the war the King was a-fightin'."

"But the people here! Look at them, so many kinds. Be they all fightin' this war now?"

"Aye, in a way... The war took its toll on this world, much the same as it did ours, except for the part of the blastin'. But a lot of people were lost, just the same."

"These horrid Suuden-Aryku an' their master, I hope they get what be a-comin' t' them."

"Mostly t' the Titan, though, an' the one they call Darumon. The rest be only slaves, t' me right knowin'."

"Mayhap, but t' get t' them, ye'll have t' go through his army of slaves, ay?"

"It be a wee bit hard for me t' say, but mayhap. They be a-hopin' t' save as many as they can. Anyway, here, this way."

Belrum leads them across the plaza and into the WIC building.

Thaelyn and his officers were reviewing the report given earlier by Kaliya's team on some of the details of the camp. The Chief sat and listened.

"So, these aircraft here," Thaelyn considers, "are largely as we suspected, except for this small one. We have a cargo transport and a personnel carrier, likely for moving the work crew, but this small one is reported to be more of a private transport. Are we speaking of perhaps for an individual to use?"

"My guess," Kailen suggests. "Is it might be for that Prodigy Child, maybe as a personal vehicle for his own use."

"Of course, that would make sense, so he could come and go independently."

A subtle knocking comes at the door as Belrum and Eiki

emerge into view. Eiki looks around the room to study the various people, including the officers and the exceptionally tall Daanen'kai Commander.

"Blessed Mother, what be that one?" she mumbles.

The Chief turned in his chair at the sound of the voice. For the first time in years, he set his eyes on his dearest love.

Eiki's eyes were instantly drawn to the man in the chair as he turned around to face her. She felt completely overcome with her emotions, a sudden uncontrollable wave of them.

"Tol!" she screams into the room and rushes over to him.

Tol jumps out of his chair, barely able to contain himself. He barely has time to steady himself on his feet when she plows into him. They wrap their arms around each other tightly as she buries her face into his shoulder.

"I thought I lost ye!" she blubbers. "In all these years, nay a man has ever returned from the feast. I prayed t' the Revered Mother so many a time, but nay did it ever change."

"Eiki, me dearest beloved," he soothes. "Me an' the lads who came along with me, we be the lucky few. I nay can say the more of it. If it were nay for this good an' kind King here, we would'na be here now t' speak of it."

The two of them held on to each other for many long moments. Eiki continued her sobbing into his shoulder while Tol tried to wipe away his own tears.

Thaelyn and the others in the room felt a similar reaction to the sight. Thaelyn did not practice the skill of empathy like Aelwyn did, but his inherent senses could still feel strong waves of grief and elation flowing outward from the pair. He folded his hands together and laid his head down in an effort to find his own comfort.

Belrum stood off to the side, with little else to do but to find a chair and lay his head low to find his own peace. In time, the couple was able to recover themselves enough to restore their composure.

"Eiki," Tol laments. "I missed ye so. It be many a year since I left ye. I did'na want t' go t' the feast, ye know that. But the Thane, ye know how he be when the time comes."

"I have a few choice words t' say t' that man, or whatever he be if nay a man."

"Aye, I'll bet ye d' at that!" he laughs. "But now, we have need of ye. This man here, he be the one t' talk t' about what ye can d' t' help us down there."

Eiki looks over at the table to study the various people represented. Tol turns around and directs her to make the acquaintance.

"Eiki, I'd like t' present His Kingship, the Lord Thaelyn. The finest man I ever did have pleasure t' know about."

Eiki gazes at Thaelyn as he stands up and offers a polite bow.

"I would offer you a pleasant greeting, good woman Bronzeheart."

"Grace be, his eyes. Be they made of gold?"

Tol offers up another laugh as he continues his introduction.

"An' this here be General Gabarleine, an' this mighty one here be Commander Nazég."

Eiki offers smiles at the other officers, but still couldn't help the look of astonishment at the tallest of them.

"What be that one, Tol?" she whispers in his ear.

"He be of a people called Daanen-Aryku, me dear."

"That be the folk this Darumon be a-chasin'? Oi, what be he about if he be a-chasin' a folk like them?"

Tol pats her on the shoulder and redirects her to the group for their meeting.

"Good woman Bronzeheart..." Thaelyn begins.

"Oh, please, call me Eiki, if ye will. I ne'er was one for the formal talk, if ye don'na mind."

"Very well then... Eiki, we have a situation where we need to step around things very carefully. My understanding is that our good friend over here," he directs at Belrum, "was successful in relating to you some part of the story of the events of your world, but now we must see about what we can do from this moment."

"Aye, this one ye call Darumon, an' his slave folk, these Suuden-Aryku, an' then the Thane, may the Shield Brothers drag him t' the blazin' depths! But what can I d' for ye? I be only a clothes maker.

Yer man said somethin' about makin' a wee ruckus in the streets. Be that the way of it?"

"In a very simple manner of speaking, yes. But we must proceed according to a plan, in order to achieve our best results."

Thaelyn directs the assembly to take up seating again after the introduction.

"Although we are still waiting on some important scouting reviews," he begins. "We have speculated that the Thane may be of a sort we could try playing a small ruse on. Up until now, we were trying to interpret who and what he might be. One thought was he could be a native dwarf, but badly corrupted to serve Darumon. Another was to use something to imitate a dwarf during these appearances, but this carried its own complications. Finally, we managed to gain a small amount of insight that he could be a Suuden'kai agent with a rather severe attitude problem, but also with a special skill to impersonate one of your people using what we might describe as a form of disguise."

"Ehm, forgive me a moment," Eiki interjects. "Suuden'kai?"

"Ah yes, this is a term in their native language to refer to individuals, or perhaps native possessions, in a descriptive form."

"Oh, fine then. But it must be a yay grand disguise, for all the yowlin' I hear he lays down on the poor Chancellor's ears. If he be one of this folk," she points at Kailen. "Be he usin' this thing Belrum whispered about that can change shape t' somethin' like a bug?"

"Yes, this would be the skill. We are still studying just how far this can go, but the implications are extraordinary. Now, if we are correct in our assumptions, we would wish to see if we can interfere with some of his plans. But we must proceed very cautiously, and this is where you can help us."

He picks up a report paper from the table that described the mining activities around the region.

"Within your city, we understand you are mining adamantium and producing ingots. Is this the only thing he has you mining? For instance, what about mithril?"

"I think it be mostly Adamant by now. The veins ran out on us many a time in years past, an' we had t' dig deeper t' find new ones t' keep up with the Thane's demands."

"Really! This is perfect, as we are going to see this again very soon," he grins.

"Uh oh…" she smiles cautiously.

"We also understand that the Thane conducts these feasts to call your men to service for what he apparently describes as serving this war effort, correct?"

"Aye, he has one each year."

"One? Tol described this as two per year."

"Aye, it was that, but one was stopped, an' now he charges the miners an' smiths inside the city t' double up their work."

"My Lord," the General offers, continuing in the Dwarvish tongue. "This would make sense to me, if only to explain the result of our capture of the mine to the north, where the Chief was working."

"Yes," he nods. "And with that one no longer in operation, the associated feast would be cancelled, unless he was to find another mining opportunity elsewhere, but it seems he has not. And further, I might also suggest doing so would require bringing people out of the city to conduct a survey expedition, which could complicate matters with the stories he tells."

"Aye," Eiki admits. "He tells the tales harshly. I know the tellin' goes that the Chancellor cringes at the thought of goin' in there t' speak with him. An' every time he does, the Thane be said t' scream at him for more Adamant."

"This Chancellor, what can you say about him? I ask this because we have seen close servants of this sort to be as corrupted as the ones they serve."

"Nay t' this one, methinks. He be a good sort. He be a-tryin' hard t' run the city affairs for the people, but it be said the Thane rages at him every time they meet."

"Then if he is some manner of underdog, perhaps we might be able to trust him. Do you ever speak with him directly?"

"Nay me'self. An' I nay be a-knowin' anyone else t' me mind."

"Do you think you could try, maybe to ask a few questions?"

"What sort of questions?"

"Among other things, we would like to know how the Thane is managing the city. Is it wise or unwise to the benefit of the people? He tells these stories of a vicious war but does not apparently offer your people any manner of local security from your alleged enemies."

"Aye! Ye be right t' that! An' what more, some tales say the upper part of town be smashed, an' yet we be a-tradin' our wares t' the folk up top while the doors be closed. An' more!" she wags her finger. "Yer man spoke of the coin we get for our Adamant in trade for nothin' more than a wee bit of wood an' coal for his blessed cauldrons. A fine one, that! How d' ye answer that, I say?"

"Indeed, we have asked this as well. We think he must hold some very poor leadership skills in order to be making so many errors. What about the people? Do you have enough food, and other necessary items to survive?"

"Food be fair, nay grand, but fair. The farms below be a-workin' hard, an' the herdin' folk be a-tryin' their best, but the wool we get be a mite short much of the time. With me bein' a clothes maker, the coin nay be good."

"Eiki," Tol asserts. "Be ye gettin' along well for yerself?"

Eiki ducks her head into Tol as she glances around the room at the other officers.

"Nay, Tol, the coin be so thin, I had t' ask for a wee bit from Telta. D' ye remember her?"

"Aye, I recall the two of ye have been friends for a long while now. Be her husband still runnin' his shop?"

"Aye, an' they be a-farin' well enough, but I nay be t' knowin' what t' d' for me'self. When the shearin' time comes 'round, the wool runs out quick."

"Could you use some help, Eiki?" Thaelyn asks.

Eiki looks up timidly at him before answering, her head still resting on Tol's shoulder.

"Yer Kingship, I nay be one t' ask for help unless I be on me last legs. An' I nay be a-wantin' t' ask for help from a King, if ye please. I'd feel so low."

"Nonsense, Eiki," he waves it off. "There have been many people harmed in this war, in one form or another. There is no shame in receiving help from those who fight against this. In many ways, I would describe this as either a war effort or a disaster relief effort, depending on the circumstances. This is how we are treating the people outside your city who have lost everything and need help."

Thaelyn directs her attention at Belrum who was contentedly seated on a chair across the room.

"Just take his people as an example. We are conducting an extensive search far and wide to find more survivors out there. Then we will try to negotiate with them to come here and join with us, at least temporarily, until we can bring stability back into your world. We are drawing up plans for building a quaint little village for them to settle in, including new homes, workplaces and markets, as well as land for farming and their herd animals."

"Blessed Mother, Yer Kingship, how can ye afford all this? This here be a yay grand bit of work ye speak of."

"The land is not an issue, as we have more than enough. The work is necessary, as we feel the lives of these people are more important than the cost of building such as a village to hold them. And once they settle, we will actually see a return on some of this as we begin to see trade and other forms of positive interaction. This is the strength of unity, and we cherish this quality."

"Oi..." she covers her mouth as a new gush of emotion surges upward. "Belrum said somethin' about ye an' these gods of yers comin' t' the rescue. Now I see what he be a-speakin' of."

"Indeed, Eiki, this is simply our way. We are a prosperous people, and we will use this as needed to aid others. But if you feel too self-conscious to simply ask for aid, we could easily describe this by other means. After all, we hope to put you to work for us, and surely this would fit nicely with some form of compensation, would it not?"

Eiki abruptly pulls her head off Tol's shoulder at the suggestion. This was a new twist to her previous worry.

"Compensation...payment, ye say? Yer words are as rich as yer manners," she chuckles timidly. "Aye, that would make me feel the better for it. But now, what service?"

"We would have you start by spreading some small rumors in the alleys and perhaps through some trusted friends. Also, we need you to make contact with the miners and smiths currently operating your forges. Tell them to make it seem the veins are running low, cut the production by some modest amount to start, and at a later time, cut it some more. We will make the Thane believe his tidy little operation is drying up."

Eiki begins to beam brightly at the suggestion.

"Aye! I can d' that!" she chirps.

◆ ◆ ◆ ◆ ◆

Kaliya was finishing up her classes for the day and taking a quick shower to freshen up before her meeting with Thaelyn. She still had to file her report on her observations from the night before at the Suuden-Aryku base, and while she was anxious to get this off her chest, the sights she saw in that place were deeply disturbing to her. She makes a final trip to her dorm room to drop off a few things before heading out to the gateway hub. As she arrived in Rolsklinde, her anxiety was building. She strolls briskly into the WIC building and through to the strategy room.

Thaelyn and his officers were still gathered around the room, along with Tol and Eiki. Belrum had gone to visit his wife and stay a while to catch up on his rest, while the others had been asked to stay until Thaelyn could receive his final word on the Thane before setting his plan into action. The length of time past Eiki's bedtime on Morndindor was showing its effect, but Tol helped her find a lounge to rest on for a few hours before calling her back into the room. When Kaliya arrived, Eiki turned to see the tall young officer as she entered the room and approached the table.

"Blessed be, another one?" she asks softly.

"Aye, an' this be a special one."

"My Lord!" Kaliya steps up to the table in a formal posture and salutes. "My apologies for the delay in my report, but I felt it required a personal touch, and we returned rather late in the eve."

"Not a problem. Rest at ease and let me hear what you have. This is about the Thane, or rather who he is in real life, correct?"

"Yes, it is, and the results I found have me a bit worried for what I saw in there."

"I reviewed your report that he does appear as a Suuden'kai male, unaltered and perhaps with a hobby of weightlifting, as the Commander here suggested, correct?"

"Yes, so I think we can say that Alpha Male idea is right. He looked young, and wow, what a body," she whistles enthusiastically.

"Uh huh," Thaelyn glances at Kailen for his reaction. "Four centuries, right?"

"Yes, this is to be expected," he notes with a smile.

"How old would you judge him to be?" Thaelyn asks.

"I would say within his first millennium. Probably half or so."

The General erupts in a spontaneous chuckle under his breath. He tries to stifle it, but not before he draws the attention.

"My apologies," he emits tenderly. "But when speaking of someone who is described as young, and yet by such terms as those…"

"Sorry, General," Kaliya smiles. "We're just made that way."

"Naturally, please go on."

"When I arrived, he was apparently working on his exercise equipment. I chose to investigate some other areas first, avoiding direct line-of-sight with him to give me time to check the place out. I later saw him come out of the room, and he was without his shirt, so I had a clear view to see there was no biotech seed, nor did he have the cranial implant. But he was very brawny. Kailen, you have some competition."

"I'll consider it for later," he muses.

"Very good," Thaelyn considers. "So far, this confirms a few things for us, like his emotions and a potential for his behavior issues. If he is not altered with any implants, especially the seed entity, this would surely make him feel special for his physical perfection, and especially if he likes to further augment it with his exercise routine."

"Also," Kailen adds. "If he's not fitted with that interface unit, he wouldn't be connected to a data network, like the others. Therefore, if we take any sort of action, no one should know of it."

"Indeed. But now, what part of this report has you so agitated?"

"My Lord," Kaliya continues. "I guess my upbringing, which was in such a calm, nurturing, and most importantly, a sane home, with no crazy sexual fetishes going around, didn't give me the kind of experience to identify some of this stuff. But I saw things in there which I'm interpreting to be his sex toys, and a lot of it looked more like medieval torture gear rather than pleasure instruments. I'm not even sure how to report on this, or if I want to. But I feel I should, if only to give you an idea of just how perverted this guy must be."

"Do your best, Kaliya. We should probably hear at least some part of it. It may affect how we approach him."

"He must be very abusive of his female partners. This would represent that Alpha Male syndrome gone wild. I entered the building, and it appeared as a quaint little home, maybe a two-bedroom home, with a kitchen and an entertainment room, one actual bedroom, and the other one with his exercise equipment."

"So far, this seems reasonable for a young bachelor, especially if he has a hobby and the second room could be his hobby room."

"But not one I would want to visit. Aside from his exercise equipment, there were other things in there, most of which I didn't recognize, but considering the report you received about that female, this has me deeply worried. I've spent some time trying to analyze this, and then decided to speak to Marelle to see if she could offer some insight. She has better experience in this area from her old Guard duty. I also shared a few words with Ankhia to help identify some of this from our side of it. Fortunately, she had some background knowledge to share with me."

"Ah, picking at a bit of mature wisdom, are we?" he smiles.

"Hey, if it's out there..." she shrugs. "First, in the bedroom, partially hidden under the bed, I caught a glimpse of some straps, like bondage straps, and something that resembled cuffs and a collar, almost like what I've seen in the history lessons at the academy of old prisoner restraints. Also, a whip and a baton…"

"This is not a pleasant sign, if he uses that as part of his sexual meanderings."

"Oh, this is the light stuff, so far. In the room with the exercise equipment, I found something else. According to Marelle, one of these was some sort of prisoner restraining mount, standing upright, so you could tie someone to it, maybe using those straps and cuffs."

"Oh dear…and here it goes."

"Which one?" Kailen wonders. "The perversion, or my little sister's innocence," he chuckles.

"Indeed!"

"Both, probably," she smirks. "As for the rest, I saw metal clips that were connected to a power source, and I can barely imagine where they might be going, to say nothing of how it would feel once you turned on the power. I saw several rodlike things, and according to Ankhia, these may be what she calls female pleasure sticks, for personal stimulation. But THESE examples? Uh-uh…you're not coming anywhere near me with those. I saw some with knobby or ribbed texturing, which by the way, both Marelle and Ankhia say is not so unusual, as part of an adult market. But since I'm apparently so young…and a virgin…" she sighs. "I probably never explored anything like this before."

"Perhaps, so your inexperience could be working against you, for this point."

"Maybe, but I'm not going to argue that for now. Then there were others with power cords, and some with metal rivets or plates on the surface, as if they might be powered somehow."

"I could possibly offer an idea here. I know of some of this from a few things I have learned during my lifetime with races that may indulge in such things. This is largely from the Outer Planes where we might have access to a broader array of societies and their personal interests. And even on Tae'Eladar, we have an adult market. I do not prohibit people from seeking their pleasures, so long as it is kept safe and sane, and no one takes harm from it. But when speaking of such items as what you describe, a powered item might offer a vibrational component for an enhanced effect, or some other form of animation. But rivets and plates?"

"Some of this looked like a hack job if you ask me. Those first ones might be factory-made, if you have an industry designed to make toys like this. But these others looked more homemade."

"Uh huh…then this could not be such as that. If we are speaking of a homemade item, they might be for some other purpose, and certainly NOT for the female's pleasure. They could be electrified, maybe even heated, and this would better qualify as your torture device. Powers help us."

"And finally, I saw long skewer-like tools, like you might use for piercing something, and several slim blades."

"Blades and skewers?" he grimaces.

"And lastly, I saw some rags with blood on them."

"This is intolerable!" he growls. "This would implicate him as not only perverted, but severely deranged, especially if you consider the frailty of that seed implant. I must wonder how many women he has abused, as well as killed if he was employing those blades and skewers. It is no wonder that one female was seen stumbling out of there. He probably damaged the seed entity during that encounter, and this is what killed her. This man is surely responsible for a number of crimes, even though we might not be able to provide the evidence at this time."

"Indeed, my Lord," the General responds. "But how do we approach this? We are in a state of war with those he has abused, at least technically, so we cannot simply approach them to offer our legal counsel. And yet, regardless of the situation of war, this cannot go unanswered."

"It is a paradox, General. But nonetheless, we still need to take that base, and I would wish to do so before he has another opportunity like this. We need to prepare ourselves post haste. Kaliya, how are you progressing on your team thus far?"

"We've been conducting a number of training exercises together at the guildhall, and I've also decided on a direction I would like to take with them. I've already spoken with Lady Aerlie, and she's helping arrange some new courses for us at the temple."

"Courses at the temple…" he raises his brow. "What are the two of you conspiring on this time?"

"Um, well," she grins sheepishly. "We would like to consolidate our dedication to Oghma?"

"When you say consolidate…and then the name Oghma…for a society that is not known to hold any religious practice…what is it you are hoping to acquire here?"

"Oh, that's actually really simple. In the beginning, we're hoping to gain that priest spell for the sleep chant."

Thaelyn glares at the girl for a long moment as she smiles innocently at him.

"General, will you kindly warm up my list again."

"Oh dear…" he relents. "Here we go again."

"All right Kaliya, how does this play into your training exercises? It was not my…original…impression you wanted to be a priest."

"Oh, no, a priest probably isn't the right direction for me. After all, I'm much more the soldier type."

"Yes, this was my first thought, so how do you fit in a priest… oh wait. Kaliya, you would not be thinking of…" his voice trails off.

"Paladins!" she grins brightly.

"Powers behold," he mutters softly and lays his head in his hand. "My dear young lady, do you know how much effort is involved in training a paladin?"

"Can it be any worse than what I'm going through now?" she muses satirically.

"Well, eh…technically yes, as it adds another dimension to the training. Very well, let me hear it. Why would you choose this? I may as well simply take the plunge at this point," he smiles intriguingly.

"All right, in your own famous words, consider these principles…"

"Oh! Are you now turning the tables on me?" he grins.

"Why not, you do it often enough. And you are supposed to be a teacher, so I'm just doing my duty by learning from your example."

"Indeed. General, add one more point to that list."

"Gracious, two at once!" he emits avidly.

"We're basically reinventing the Stormhooves, right?" she explains. "We're also described as an elite force, and as such, we need to rise to certain very high standards. Paladins are representative of the finest in valor, honor, morals and ethics, and other prized virtues. Naturally, everyone in the Order follows these, but the image of a paladin is special in many people's eyes for their dedication."

"This is very often true," Thaelyn admits. "They are roughly two-thirds warrior, one-third priest, and this combines some very strict conditioning."

"And then we have the Prodigy Gift. This, among all the other innate skills my people might discover, holds us to some very delicate responsibilities. For this, I need to apply what YOU said once about us resembling a new Celestial race. The blessing of the cu'Nar, the positive side of the Measure of Balance, Maker Kuroku and how she's converting us to the Estelar's side of things… I don't think I need to tell you what that means for a society. You should already know."

"Yes, this is true. But is this to say you are hoping to actually rise up that far?"

"We're already there for our breeding and skillset. Culturally, no, not even close. But my Lord, how do you condition someone for something like this? Normally, they have to evolve over an extreme amount of time for it. Just look at any real Celestial race. The Seraphim, for example. How long did it take them? What did they have to go through to arrive there? And best of all, how do you look upon them in relation to yourself? You address them with a highly prestigious title: Dame, usually, right?"

"Yes, we do, and they most certainly earned it for all they achieved in their long history."

"And here we are, like it or not, with qualities that place us in the same bracket, but we're not ready for it. Therefore, we need examples to set the standards. If we have the skills, we need to evolve ourselves as a kind of rush job for the rest. Otherwise, we're going to be tail-deep in trouble before you know it. Look at that guy, the Thane. That would be a perfect example of what NOT to do."

"Indeed, you make a good point. This is a very interesting perspective."

"And so, if we describe this as a godlike ability, it will similarly demand some godlike standards of respect, discipline, and control to govern how it's applied. And I'm not just talking about within our own. We'll need to set the example for an entire world. Did you know that?"

"Azgarén..." he muses silently. "Powers help us, but yes."

"And what else but to reinvent something that already holds a type of romance for our people, the Stormhooves. This is what I think Adalon meant when she said it will rise anew. We're going to be the parental figures to teach the rest, just like you and the Celestials teach everyone else. We must be, we're the only ones qualified."

Thaelyn gazed lovingly into the exuberant young officer's eyes for a long moment as he felt a surge of pride well up inside him. He leaned back in his chair as he considered the direction of this movement.

"General, kindly add one more...very honorable...mark to that list."

"Great gods, three..." the General mumbles. "Kaliya, I think you just made celebrity status."

"And we may need to make this one official somehow," Thaelyn notes. "This young lady has just promoted herself from a people's hero to a living legend. This is probably the finest suggestion I have yet heard from anyone. Of course, we never had such a situation as this before, but it does make a solid point. And here we are to pay witness to it, the birth of a new Celestial race, right before our eyes."

"Incredible, my Lord, but how do we give proper credit to something like this?"

"I cannot be sure, but at the very least, this new unit will need to be much more than a simple team of special operatives. It will need to be a full governing body applying itself to a world population, much like our Order of Tyr is to us. And I must admit that world population will need to take careful heed of them, for its own inherent safety. Kaliya, if you are to create such a force as this, you will need some assistance. You are still young, as ambitious as you are, therefore I must offer whatever I can to see you succeed."

"My deepest thanks, my Lord, I knew you would see it through." she smiles brightly.

"Cu'Nar help us all," Kailen shakes his head. "Did we mention innocence before this? This goes a little beyond that now. If only Father could see this, I think he would be so proud of you, he might need the smile surgically removed just so he could eat again."

The group shared a warm round of laughter.

"Kaliya," Thaelyn resumes. "One question. You mentioned the sleep chant. Why this one specifically?"

"It's a start," she replies. "But for this mission to capture that base, you spoke of using priests on a nighttime raid while they slept. If my people held this, we would be a complete service."

"Very clever, young lady, and then to develop your association to Oghma, which would provide you with a rather interesting portfolio of blessings, once you were trained. Some of you could also train as Templars, if you desired, or straight priests, if this is your fancy. You do not ALL have to be paladins, but this would surely be a fine example to start with and to set for any who would follow."

"At the same time, if we're going up against Darumon, I want him to see what we made of ourselves and know we're turning it to our favor with Oghma behind us."

"Oh, Kaliya, that is a subtle rub in the face. It would further express that you, like the others, have found favor in the Estelar, which is what drove him out of here in the first place."

"And then, we need to think of the future, which would include our actions on Azgarén, and how we approach it, then anything that comes after."

"Yes, again you are right. This military body we are developing is not a simple short-term exercise. And to approach such a target as a full world, and whatever we must do there, which will likely involve one or more large-scale operations, you will need a similarly large-scale force…an army. These skills of yours are extraordinary, and could pose value in countless other applications. But Azgarén also holds its own burdens, whether the people in the present day are aware of it or not. And for this they will need to understand these practices and procedures whether they like it or not. To ignore this could result in chaos if they should ever lose control. Therefore, they will need examples to follow, and likely a governing body of some sort to regulate it. Dear Powers, this could get complicated very quickly."

"Yeah," she sighs. "And it looks like it's going to fall largely on our shoulders, at least for now."

"Yes, so let us get you off to a good start. In the immediate term, we have that base. I need your team to be trained in Special Operations combat. General, please see about this. Assign one of our officers to run them through their paces. If need be, use the athletic field outside the guildhall for some of the practice."

"Right away, my Lord."

"Make up dummies as their targets, and tell the Mage Elders to hurry with that stun attack. They also need to be trained in at least a minimal form of urban assault tactics to infiltrate that base effectively. We can send them out to the Cormyr training fields for this."

"Of course."

"Now, Tol and Eiki, we seem to have our answer as to the Thane. Let us proceed with our plans. We will send Eiki home with her instructions. We have assembled a wagon full of goods outside to take with her."

"A wagon?" she cries. "Blessed be, how much d' ye think me service be worth t' ye?"

"We are trying to save a city, Eiki. Your service can be worth a great deal, and not only to me. Please accept this and work your finest skills for us. We all have faith in you."

Eiki felt humbled by the suggestion. She feels compelled to bow in reverence to the generous offer.

"I thank ye, Yer Kingship. An' I'll be a-tellin' me closest friends t' help me. We'll get the word out, quiet but true."

"Just remember to keep the word of our own people to yourself.

You may share it with your most trusted friends, but they must also keep the secret. It is one thing for you to know about us, but not the general public. Not until we take the next step."

"Aye. But now, how d' I get back home from here?"

"Kaliya, you are studied in this language, correct?"

"Yes, I am," she responds in the Dwarvish tongue. "Though only just recently finished, as I was anticipating something when we were closing in on Morndindor."

"Excellent, forward thinking is a good sign. You will need a lot of that from this moment," he chuckles.

"That's right, put a little more pressure on me."

"I think you already placed a healthy amount on yourself," he smiles. "Meanwhile, if you would do us a most gracious service. This woman needs to return home to Glimmerheim. I would ask you to escort her, and at the same time, we need you to follow her to her home. We have a wagon outside filled with goods to deliver there, and your method provides us with the best option at this time."

"All right, so I'll probably need to sneak in somehow, maybe under a cloak, then crawl my way through their local streets, if it's anything to scale with their people..." she chuckles.

"Aye t' that, lass!" Eiki giggles.

"...And then recall back here, then to project and deliver the goods after."

"Whatever method you deem the most convenient," Thaelyn accedes. "Please see to this now before we send you off to any other duties."

Kaliya pulls herself up to attention again and salutes. She then follows Tol and Eiki outside to examine the cart that was waiting for them.

Chapter 6

EVERY LITTLE BIT

"Eiki! There ye be!" Telta shouts as she walks up to the house. "I came by yesterday an' ye were gone, so I thought mayhap ye went out shoppin', but then I came back later an' ye were still gone. I started t' worry for ye."

Eiki was sitting in her patio going over some notes she made about the details she needed to be passing around as part of her service to stir things up in the city. When Telta came into view, she pulled her head up sharply to meet her. She jumped out of her chair and ran over to the wall to catch the woman on the arm.

"Telta!" she announces boldly. "Aye, I did just a wee bit of shoppin', an' a wee bit more of walkin' for the feel of it. Nay the more!"

Eiki pulls Telta around the wall to the gate, and almost drags the poor woman into the yard.

"Eiki! What be wrong with ye!" she complains.

"Shush!" Eiki urges quietly. "Just play with it," she then resumes her display. "Aye, me dearest of friends, I be simply perusin' the shops t' see the latest wares. Oi, ye should see what I picked up. It be right inside here!"

"Eiki, ye nay be actin' normal…"

"I said shush!" Eiki urges again in a hushed tone. "D' ye know what shush means?"

"Aye," Telta whispers. "But what be wrong with ye?"

"Ye have t' play with it…"

"Play with what?"

"Oh, bah!" she relents and then resumes her boisterous portrayal. "Here, come take a look, an' we'll share a wee cup of tea. 'Tis a grand day t' be in the city."

Eiki promptly opens the door to her home and shoves Telta inside. She briefly glances around the street to see if anyone was watching before ducking inside and closing the door tightly.

"Fine then!" Telta grumbles. "Now, what be the matter with ye?"

"Telta, me dearest of friends, ye have t' shut yer mouth an' listen hard. I need yer help."

"Help? What d' ye need help with now? D' ye need more coin already? Oi, did ye go through the last one so quick?"

Telta sighs deeply as she glances around the modest home and the tidy furnishings. As her eyes take in the many antique adornments, she catches a glimpse of something resembling a large clutter of goods in one corner. She turned suddenly to focus on it and began to count the items. She saw a heavy stack of leather sheets, a dozen thick rolls of fabric in a variety of colors, several bags of yarn and thread, and a leather pouch with rows of high-quality needles. Her eyes bulged at the opulent display.

"Blessed be! Eiki, where did all that come from?"

"Ne'er ye mind for now, just listen. I've got a tale t' tell that will burn yer ears off!"

"But Eiki! I nay have ever seen that much in all the city at one time. Where did it come from? Did that small bit of coin I gave ye grant ye all this?"

"In truth, nay, I still have most of it. In fact, I might simply give it back t' ye for yer favor. But this here, this came from the outside."

"Outside?!" she shrieks. "Eiki, ye did'na go out there, did ye? What did we say once about goin' outside?"

"We said that dastardly Thane would give a few words for it. But I have a few words for him, instead. Now, sit an' listen."

Telta gaped at her friend for the statement, but the pile-up in the corner couldn't go unnoticed, if only for the unusual variety of materials on display, none of which looked native to the city. So, she pulled up a chair and sat down.

"What was all that ye said about shushin' an' playin' with somethin'?"

"D' ye know how t' play an act? Well, if nay t' that, ye'll need t' learn."

"An act?"

"Firstly," Eiki begins. "Drop everythin' ye ever did hear from the Thane an' his hard yowlin'. It nay be more than a big pack of lies. I've seen it with me own eyes, an' heard it with me own ears, the true tales of what be a-happenin' in the world, an' it nay be even close t' what the Thane has been a-tellin' us all these years."

"What d' ye mean, ye saw somethin'? Where did ye go? An' how did ye get there? Ye've been a-sayin' for so long how the doors be closed, so did ye find a way out?"

"One at a time... A man came t' me yesterday. He be from the outside, a farmer, or what be left of him for all his years. He was sent here, nay a-comin' for a simple visit, but with business t' talk t' me. He carried a message an' a ring from me dearest Tol."

Eiki felt a subtle moment of emotion well up and she covered her mouth briefly. Telta watched and felt a sudden chill run through her.

"Eiki, be he...ehm..."

"He be fine an' good, Telta...one of the lucky few who still be alive...a lucky few...VERY few."

"A few...out of all of them?"

"Aye. But Telta, he was nay sent up t' serve any fare for any war an' t' aid any warriors with anythin'. The Thane an' his ruddy feast be a full ragin' lie."

"A lie! Then what be all his ragin' about if it be a lie?"

"It be about Adamant, Telta. That be the whole of it. Our most precious Adamant."

Telta leaned back to ponder the suggestion while Eiki continued.

"The feast nay be a call for smiths t' serve up a fare. They be a-servin' in a mine out on the barrens, makin' the same as we in here, just more of it. There was ne'er any war, save for a hand or two of years in the beginnin' t' give us the tales an' t' drive us deep, then t' close the doors an' lock us inside."

"Lock us inside?!" she shouts. "Then what be a-happenin' out there if nay any war?"

"Oblivion, Telta," she admits somberly. "Ours be the last city by now. The rest of it was sent t' the All-father when the REAL enemy showed up t' clear out anythin' that nay be a miner or a smith. An' the Thane be in league with them!"

This sent shivers through Telta, and she grimaced deeply as she continued to listen.

"This man was one of the last few survivors of a wrecked world out there," Eiki recalls. "The rest of it be nothin' but holes where once there were cities an' towns."

"What could hit the land like this?"

"What could hit the land? An enemy from a world where they be a much higher folk, an' with bigger weapons, big enough to wreck worlds," she closes her eyes and shakes her head. "It would seem, Telta, we nay be the only ones. We be a young folk, for how much knowin' we have here. But there be others, some of them older an' wiser, an' some of them nay as kind."

"Oh, how grand," she spurns sarcastically. "An' so one of these found us an' blasted the land so they could take our Adamant? What...they did'na have enough of their own, mayhap?"

"I think it better t' say they nay have any at all, an' they nay know how t' make it. First, these here be called Suuden-Aryku, an' they be but slaves, nay more than that, just slaves. They serve up t' a gnarly one with the name Darumon. Keep this name in mind, Telta, as I go on with the rest."

"Aye then, I be a-listenin'."

"The land was hit so hard, it be a-dyin' now, too hot t' grow anything, an' all the plants an' animals be a-fadin' away. This man, he came in here because Tol met with him an' gave him a message t' bring t' me."

"Why did'na Tol bring it here himself?"

"Tol could'na bring it here because the Thane sent him out on a fool's errand t' mine up Adamant, an' he nay be s'posed t' come back from it at all."

"What? Why?"

"It be the feast, Telta. It nay be a grand call t' our finest in the trade. It be a call t' any who know how t' mine up Adamant. The food they give be a poison t' put them under a spell where they d' as he tells them without a word t' argue the meanin' of it. An' this food be a poison that kills after a while. This here be why the Thane calls up for more every year."

Now Telta was going into shock, and her face showed it, as it twisted with disgust.

"That be criminal, Eiki!" she screeches.

"Ye think I don'na know this?" she grimaces. "This here be why I say me beloved Tol be one of the VERY lucky few t' still be alive. Someone found him an' saved his life, they did," she finishes with a slight tremor.

"Who found him? Be it someone still alive out there…this man, mayhap?"

"Nay," she pauses to clear her throat. "The land was blasted so hard, the few who still be alive be a-hidin' in any hole they can find that gives them shade an' cover from the fear of more blastin'. But now, t' the next part… These point-ears were nay more than a diversion. The tale goes how four hundred years ago, they came out of their portals, but like it was once said, they be sickly an' weak an' nay good fighters. This much be true, an' this man confirmed it from his side that the warriors had t' make like a mercy killin', if yay only t' defend against the magic this folk were a-tossin' at us…nay more. But that one ended quick when they stopped comin' through, an' it was nay much after when he says this pummelin' from above came down an' blasted everythin' away."

"Blasted everythin' away...just because they nay be smiths out there?"

"The way I hear of it, it be t' clear away anythin' he does'na want. All he wanted was us in here."

"So, he blasts an entire world just t' keep one wee city?" she shrieks.

"Hold yerself a bit an' let me finish."

"Aye then..." Telta huffs and shakes her head morosely.

"While our eyes were turned t' these point-ears," Eiki continues. "These Suuden-Aryku set down a military base in the mountains right over our heads," she points upward. "Ye know the store where we drop the bricks said t' be for the folk outside?"

"Aye."

"Well, the only folk we be a-speakin' of here be these Suuden-Aryku. The other side of that store has a door leading up a long stair t' a road in the middle of the mountain, an' this passes through a tunnel t' this base in a hollow behind us."

"Sounds lovely..." she relents ironically. "An' d' they have a view of the wrecked world they made?" she chuckles crossly.

"I know how ye feel, Telta. I was up there an' saw it. The air was hot an' dry, an' the outer city, what I could see of it, was wrecked an' more, with a big lump of the mountain collapsed on t' it. It got me so riled, ye should've seen me when I raged at the folk who be a-tryin' t' help us right now."

"Uh oh... There be folk tryin' t' help us? Who?"

"Aye. This man, he came t' me an' called me t' follow him out. We went inside that store, where we met with a scout. But this scout was nay a dwarf. He be from another world, one where Darumon made more trouble, but this trouble turned 'round on him an' chased him away," she smirks.

Telta now found a new interest in this story. She raised her brow at the mention.

"Trouble that chased him away?" she muses. "What kind of trouble?"

"A King of a world he tried hittin' on. But this King, he be a powerful one…one of those who be a high an' mighty sort, but also a good an' kind sort. Now, he be a-chasin' Darumon one world at a time, tryin' t' find him an' put a stop t' him."

"This be a yay better tale now. So, where does it bring us…here mayhap, if this man called ye out t' hear this tale?"

"Aye. I met with him, this King."

"Wait now! Ye met with a KING?" she gasps.

"Aye, Telta…a King, with eyes of gold, he be so mighty."

Telta gaped at her friend as she tried to imagine someone with golden eyes.

"This scout took me t' him," Eiki resumes. "I travelled t' a world they call Therinë."

"How?"

"This folk also uses portals it seems…lots of them. Methinks this be another sign of how high they be."

"Eiki, be we so far behind that we be a-missin' somethin' grand here?"

"Ye're talkin' t' the wrong sort for that," she smiles. "I be but a simple clothes maker."

"Aye! An' me a shopkeeper!"

"Anyway, this King an' his folk are out there pickin' up any survivors he can find an' givin' them new homes on this other world, at least for now, until he can chase Darumon an' these Suuden-Aryku off our mountain. Me beloved Tol be with him right now, also livin' on that world."

"Oi, Eiki!" she interrupts abruptly. "Ye saw him?"

"Aye, this King be the one who saved his life. He found Tol an' the crew he went out with workin' a mine on this other world…nay even this one, but another world entirely. This King be a-bringin' together a great many folk, all different kinds, t' go fight this Darumon, but Darumon nay be the only one. Telta, Darumon nay be but a servant t' a bigger one…one we all thought t' be a myth."

"A myth? What be this about?"

"A Titan, Telta… The old tales be true after all, but only one be still alive, an' he be an angry one. This Darumon yay be on a rampage t' take revenge on the greater gods for some old battle he lost, where…get this…he an' the others were a-makin' trouble for folk like us, an' the greater gods put a stop t' it. Ha!"

Telta stares at Eiki for the suggestion, now trying to imagine this new scenario.

"An' this King?" she inquires timidly. "How does he fit with this tale?"

"Eyes of gold, Telta… Gold! He be a kinfolk t' these others who be known as Estelar, a grand folk the size of gods. The All-Father an' his kin be a part of it. They nay be just idols in a temple, they be real folk."

Telta was feeling faint by now. She glared sternly at her friend.

"Eiki, are ye bein' true t' me, or have ye actually lost yer mind now?"

"Telta, this man…his name be Belrum, by the way… He an' Tol be a-workin' for these folks now. They be a-takin' new lessons, learnin' new things. They probably know more than any of us down here by now. They brought me out t' hear this tale, t' see it for me'self, an' all this here…" she directs to the pile-up of materials. "This be payment ahead for me t' help them."

"That?!" she points assertively at the corner.

Telta glances once again at the mound of goods, trying to fathom who might give such a wealth of material for anything at all.

"Aye, an' I have instructions t' follow, an' I need a few good friends t' help me. An' this be where ye an' mayhap yer husband come in."

"Me?" she blurts alarmingly.

"I nay can d' it all me'self, an' we need a few good folks in a tight group t' see it through."

"Oi…" she wheezes. "Well, ehm…what d' ye need from me?"

"We need t' be a-makin' just a wee bit of rousin' in the city. Just a wee bit, mind ye, an' mayhap a wee bit more later, if ye catch the meanin'. An' the forges, we need t' get their attention, but real quiet, an' make them slow it down a mite."

✦✦◆✦✦

A Suuden'kai Lieutenant enters the office of her superior at the mining base.

"Commander," she states as she approaches his desk. "We have a new supply shipment arriving."

"Acknowledged," he responds distantly.

"I have also received an inquiry from Central Command about the cause of termination for Ensign Ka'zheen."

The Commander had been sitting at his desk studying a report of statistical data from the processing site they were managing as part of their mining and refinement operations. Although his attention had been redirected by the arrival of his junior officer, his focus seemed distracted elsewhere. He paused in contemplation of his response.

"I was expecting this. Her injuries were severe, more so than the last one. They will require an explanation."

"Not simply severe, but fatal. And we both know this is not the first time, either."

"Ytani has traditionally demanded an excuse be made for the others…animal attacks, rockslides, accidents."

"Commander, with respect, how do you justify this? Not specifically you, Sir, but figuratively speaking, for the types of injuries he is inflicting. How many times can we make these excuses? For instance, how do you make an excuse for an animal attack involving rape, or a rockslide causing vaginal laceration? These excuses are simply irrational."

"I know, Lieutenant. I do not like it any more than you. Perhaps a small piece of me hopes someone from CC will actually get enough of a tail-itch to investigate above my authority."

"Above your authority?" she wonders.

"Not simply to take these excuses, but to force the issue so I can reveal what is actually occurring here. I would love to see this operation brought under investigation for what he is doing to it."

"All right," she relents. "And this would naturally follow with my next argument. How many times can we give such excuses when I feel it is quite likely someone back home is conducting autopsies that would surely yield conflicting results?"

"This is also understood, and therefore my quiet anticipation. And yet, nothing. This forces me to sit here, contemplating these issues as well. It also tends to reflect on several of my observations along the way, which only compound matters."

"How so?"

"It relates to the intercommunication of our command elements, or the lack of it. When the Marshal first organized our new military venture, he placed some very restrictive security protocols on it along the way. My observations since that time suggest no one talks to anyone to share any coordinated detail of what we are doing together."

"How nice. But is there any rational meaning to this?"

"I have a few thoughts here and there, none of them polite. Lieutenant, you have the chip the same as I. It forces us to comply with our immediate superior."

"In active mode, yes," she sighs. "Even the passive mode offers a subtle coercive effect."

"Coercive..." he muses. "Such a fascinating word."

"Sir, I objected to this when it was first shoved at me, much like the rest of it," she examined her body for the seed implant. "Why did I need it? Do they think I cannot follow instructions on my own? I did well enough in my previous occupation."

"Perhaps. I was once an officer in the old Sentinels before they arrived. You are young, Lieutenant, and as I understand it, your only service prior to this was mostly local security and administrative duties. But they sent me out there..." his voice trails off as his eyes drift away to the skies.

"Sir, I feel a need to file a complaint here."

"Proceed."

"Our working conditions are placing us at an unrealistic risk of injury and even death, and these have nothing to do with our actual work. It is all due to an individual who abuses his position of authority and makes us his victims, even to insult and debase us for complying with the clear and obvious mandates placed on us... ALL of us...by the Council. This is not only abusive, as well as demeaning, it is also prejudicial and demonstrates what I believe to be a subversive derision to the Council and their mandates. These mandates are intended to apply to all our citizens equally…his special exempt status notwithstanding. What is worse, this is a military base, and as such should be under military law, at the very least. Therefore, HE, as a civilian, should not hold such authority as to dictate life and death without any form of law enforcement, be it military or even civilian. And as someone who holds a law degree, I feel confident in my perspective."

"Understood and accepted, Lieutenant. But if I may now offer a rebuttal."

"Of course, Sir."

"First, I agree with your perspective, and I would not wish to argue your point of law enforcement. But my position is unfortunately being leveraged here. The Marshal demands the metal, and although I am willing to comply with that, I am not the one actually providing the metal proper. Ytani is. Therefore, we need his skill to acquire the metal while we simply deliver it. The Marshal placed him in a position of authority, if only due to this skill he possesses to achieve the fulfillment of our objective. My only duty is the technical management of our operations, that being this base, the processor, and the depot."

"Yes Sir. Then this is essentially to say we are being made sacrifice to him and his insults, as well as his lust."

"Were you present during my last conversation with him?"

"No Sir, I must have missed that one."

"He threatened to file a report directly to the Marshal complaining of my lack of participation to fulfill my duties to procure the metal. This is an indirect reference to not supporting his…needs…as he calls them, as payment for his services."

"Sir, with respect, how can you allow him to make such a threat? Do you not hold any authority at Central? You hold the rank of a Fleet Commander, which is a rather prominent title within our military service. In fact, it falls directly beneath that of the HC himself!"

"Yes…" he reflects. "But I also have the authority chip in my head, and I know what it feels like to have it put in active mode. Consider yourself fortunate, Lieutenant, that you never had this."

She pauses to examine him. He was a mature member of the Suuden-Aryku military, one who has seen many years of service.

"He is threatening this on you? To accuse you of disobeying the Marshal, and as such to cause your chip to be activated to ensure you no longer complain? In all the nether-space, I think I am losing my interest in serving with this military. If only I could actually feel the disgust I want to hold for this situation…which is my 'other' complaint where these chips are concerned."

"You and me both, Lieutenant," he sighs gently. "If I lose control of this, I lose everything."

"You are losing it anyway, Sir."

"Lieutenant Ti'van," he leans back in his chair. "I have been sitting here pondering a series of…alternative possibilities…to the best of my ability for these chips."

"Alternative possibilities…" she muses uncertainly. "Such as… can you give me an example?"

"As a military commander, it is my duty to ensure the safety of my crew, and I am unable to provide this under these conditions. Even under critical circumstances, where I may be forced to make a life-or-death decision, I must still weigh the values carefully. But there have been times, including here in this base, and especially with him in such a position of authority as he is, where that power has been taken away from me, and for multiple reasons, at least some of which I have no capacity to correct."

"Some of which…" she ponders. "This suggests there are others where you might hold this capacity?"

"The answer becomes problematic. For instance, these chips…" he taps a finger on his cranial interface. "If we had a diagnostic probe here at the base, or at least one with the correct program feature in it, I could order a med-tech to deprogram the thing. And then, regarding Ytani and his demands, I would be able to take my own form of justice against him for what he has done. Just like you said, even in our society, we still have laws, despite the Marshal and his wonderful…" his voice suddenly cuts off with a grunt as his face flinches.

"Carefully, Commander…the chip," she cautions.

"See what I mean?" he wheezes.

"Yes Sir, I know about that one. I have had it on many occasions, an emotional surge and the corrective feedback."

"But this does not correct the larger concern with the Marshal himself, or the Council. Even High Commander Geilv has his issues, and worse for his position."

"I have heard of that. And I recall you mentioning once or twice that he is on active most of the time."

"And he is quite tired of it by now. Last I heard, his chip was near to a failure point."

"I think I heard a few rumors that he was actively ignoring his maintenance schedule, and therefore allowing it to fail intentionally. Is this true?"

"Yes, his way of defying the Marshal's authoritarian methods."

"But Sir, he is the HC. Should this not hold enough authority to simply order a med-tech to turn it off?"

"Unfortunately, no. The Marshal was granted full authority over our military by the Council in those early days due to the crisis of these insurgents. This demotes the HC, who would normally be the highest-ranking officer in our military, to a subordinate position under the Marshal."

"This is simply unacceptable. Sir, this means our military is essentially in the hands of an alien authority."

"Yes…" he nods. "When the Marshal first arrived, I watched as our world changed from a society of intellectual pursuit to one that would employ forceful military actions to accomplish anything he demanded of us."

"But this was all in the name of assisting Sargeras against these insurgents, correct?"

"This was his underlying reason, but I was given many assignments during my career which resulted in conflicting perspectives, and this caused me to wonder about his real direction."

"What experiences, can you tell me?"

"Unfortunately, all this is classified now, but I was placed in active mode during these occasions, as was my full crew, simply to ensure we got the job done."

"Sir, my impression of you tells me you are a dedicated man in our military service. If you are given an order, I believe you would fulfill that order, correct?"

"Precisely, Lieutenant, I would, for as long as that order held reasonable definition."

"Ah, and these did not?"

"Initially, they might have, but the end result left me questioning the initial interpretation. And being in active mode, we were denied the opportunity to analyze the situation to ensure it met with our expectations."

"That sounds almost like a cover-up, especially if it was classified to the point where no one is allowed to speak of it afterwards. This might also reflect on no one talking to anyone about anything. And this again brings it down to the authority chip. Remove that, and we might have the opportunity of free thought again. Law and justice can once more prevail, except for the fact that the Marshal is apparently in control of this concept of law and justice. But Sir, this notion simply leaves us with one direction for logic to classify. You are sent out on missions with ill-defined objectives that do not meet your expectations. But who cares about that, as you are placed on active simply to get the job done? What job, Sir? This is the question to ask if your own analysis no longer matters."

"And this is also my point," he affirms. "One I have contemplated many times after I was returned to passive control and could think on my own again. But, of course, what does it matter now? The deed is done, and we are back home again."

"And now, here we are, with Ytani in control of our base, and us as his psychopathic target practice. And worse, if we argue with him, HE will turn the chip on, which causes us to lose any control of our own minds."

The conversation pauses as the Lieutenant steps across to look out the window, which had a partial view of the central roadway and the conveyor at the far end of the base. She could also see part of Ytani's house from here.

"I recall in the beginning," she muses. "He was still young, a child of only seven decades. How do you justify employing a child like that in a situation like this?"

"I do not know, and neither why any of his family might allow it."

"At first, his service was modest and benign. But as he matured, his activities became malevolent and abusive. He began to take too much pleasure out of his position."

"I think he developed a psychosis due to this skill."

"Directly or indirectly? What I mean is, did the skill itself cause it, or is it his love of himself for his abilities, to say nothing of his unmodified condition."

"Surely that, as much as anything," he affirms. "And if you add on top of that his recent bodybuilding interest…"

"Oh please, not that again. The Alpha Male syndrome, which in itself could easily be half his problem where his sexual fantasies are concerned."

"And without any proper conditioning, to say nothing of his lack of parental rearing…" he sighs. "I cannot speak for the skill as accurately, as I do not understand the full definition of what this skill is or how it works."

"He has no certified training in military affairs or management authority. Yet he is the only one capable of performing his assigned task, and the Marshal requires the metal, leaving us to accept his role despite his errant behavior."

"Either that or I attempt to argue his behavior and see myself lose whatever minor capacity I have to protect my crew, which at this moment is not much. He could perhaps place all of us on active, and then it would not matter what we think."

"Commander!" she surges, but quickly cuts off with her own feedback flinch. "Dammit…" she whispers softly. "I do not desire to be his next victim, nor do I desire to see any others. What about those alternative possibilities you were speaking of? Do you have anything useful that does not see us turned fully into machines?"

"Lieutenant..." he begins, but then halts as he glances around the room. "Ayene..." he waves her over to a chair at the desk.

She steps around and sits down opposite him. He leans over the desk, and she follows suit to meet him up close.

"This is purely off-the-record and confidential, understood?"

"Yes Sir."

"The only way for us to preserve ourselves would be to find a way out of here. But this carries a number of impediments. One would be where to go, as this would amount to insubordination. Another is who will follow us as Ytani's next victims, and I do not want to be responsible for any more injuries, not ours nor anyone else's."

"This means Ytani must be removed from the equation."

"It does, but this brings even more concerns, namely those involving the Marshal, and with him, probably the remainder of our military."

"Commander, this is backing us into a corner. The only solution I can possibly see here is to suffer until we make our full quota, and whoever is still alive at that time request an immediate reassignment to something far away from anything else."

She sighs as she tries to think of any other choices.

"Have you ever tried filing your own complaint with Central about his behavior?"

"I did a few in the past, but they were largely rejected, and I think by the Marshal so he could get his metal. No one else can do Ytani's job like Ytani."

"What job is it he is actually doing?" she asks imperatively. "He somehow portrays a local resident, and from what I hear of it, he descends down inside this mountain to scream at someone to produce more of what they are already producing to maximum capacity."

"And his behavior with them is just as obnoxious, by the reports he files."

"But how does he actually portray an alien species within their local environment?"

"And furthermore, one that is essentially one-third his physical size," he shakes his head. "I wish I could answer that, but his skill is undocumented. I cannot even recall the Marshal giving it a name when he assigned Ytani to the base."

"This resembles something proprietary. The Marshal gave him something. Is it conducted by a device, perhaps something exclusive for Ytani to operate?"

"This is an interesting question. Are you suggesting commandeering it and removing him from the equation, then we could complete our objective for the Marshal ourselves?"

"Commander, like you, I think I would not wish to place myself in a position that could result in any illegal action…"

"Ayene, you said it yourself. HE is already conducting illegal actions. Murder is still a crime in our society, despite the Marshal and his objectives."

"Yes, I agree, but if the Marshal or anyone else should find out…"

"I am the one to report the activities around here. Ytani tells me to falsify my reports on these sexual assaults, so what is the difference in falsifying one on his unexpected leave of absence."

"Interesting…" she raises a brow. "But then we will need to understand how to proceed, and likely do so quickly in order to fill in for his…unexpected leave of absence. We need to locate and interpret this device, or whatever mechanism he uses for this purpose. The trouble here is how to get inside and make a study without him noticing. He never comes outside for any reason."

"I cannot be sure; it seems like a paradox. So, unless we can entice him to come out for…hmm, what about an inspection tour of the processor, or even the depot, or both? When was the last time he did that?"

"Well, whatever the reason, I would suggest we find a way before his next demand for companionship is made."

Ayene pulls back from the conversation, stands up and offers her traditional salute before leaving the office.

The Commander observes as she makes her exit. He stares into the room as he considers these suggestions, as well as their implications, and even a few unresolved variables. Eventually, he returns to his review of the data terminal, but even though his eyes were on the screen, his mind was elsewhere. He was recalling the image of the female officer lying on the ground outside a few days before, naked and bleeding to death, and with further injury to the biotech implant causing a reflex reaction that sent waves of necrotizing impulses into her body as a sort of self-destruct signal to kill the host.

"Damn him…" he emits gently, but his face still flinched slightly from a minor feedback response of his emotion chip. "And not just Ytani, but the Marshal too, for this remarkable curative medical chip…as if I needed it. As for Ytani, he cut the seed entity on purpose. He knows what it does, and he did it on purpose. The rest could have been corrected, if only we could send her off to a medical ward fast enough. But with the seed entity injured, it is an irreversible and painful death syndrome."

He continued to reflect on the timing of Ytani's calls for his rewards.

"By the time of his next demand…the time of the next collection event. One way or another, we need to find justice. I will not let him take another. Maybe when he makes that final visit down below, but how does he do it. Is he operating something in his house, or absent to visit the city? We never see him go outside. Either way, I need to be sure I can function, and for that, I need a diagnostic probe. I wonder if I can requisition one from Central. Hmm, maybe the ARC, that way Central cannot track it as easily."

✦✦✦✦✦

It was a new weekend on Tae'Eladar, and Kaliya was preparing her team for a training session out on the athletic field below the combat hall. A series of dummies had been placed around the field for target practice. The Mage Elders of the academy had just finished up a prototype attack spell for testing on the field, and scrolls had been distributed to the team to try out on the dummies. Although this attack was intended for live targets, they first wanted to examine the effect as it was presented by the combatants to non-living targets. A later session would involve volunteers.

The practice session started out as a normal combat maneuver using martial arts techniques to attack and subdue their opponents. The team was lined up in rows, five across, which would dash forward and attack the line-up of dummies with a selection of hand and knee jabs to the abdomen and flanks, and then to the back as the opponent was interpreted to double over from the initial assault, and finishing by flipping it over onto the ground and pinning it. The team made repeated attack runs in this manner until the process became well-rehearsed.

The next lesson was to make an example of using this new attack spell. The first exercise involved a dry practice run. It did not make use of the spell as yet, just the physical motions. The team would again run up to their opponent and use either a jabbing or side kick attack, and finishing with a sturdy palm-strike to the forehead. The strike was intended to be charged with the stunning effect of the magic, thus causing a systemic ripple discharge effect of disruptive bioelectrical energy. The effect would stun and incapacitate the victim long enough to keep them until they could be collected after the area was secure.

When creating this spell, the Mage Elders had to consider several permutations of its usage, as well as the overall effect on the body. They didn't want to cause death, only to render the body inert for a period of time, taking it out of battle and keeping it there. Along the way, they had to consider the effects on the critical organs, like the heart and lungs. The final version was carefully attuned to affect only the primary muscle tissue.

After making several new runs practicing the technique, they were each given two spell scrolls. They would only get two runs to practice the magic version this time. But considering the spell had to be cast from a scroll, they omitted the attack run and simply stood in place ready for the strike.

Each member took up a position, in turn with the next, and cast first the one, then the other scroll, striking the head of the dummy for their test. The strike was firm and solid, and held in place for a brief moment to allow a full discharge. The dummies didn't show any reaction to it, of course, but it was important for the combatants to understand the application.

When the session was finished, the field of dummies was cleared, and they began practicing combat moves on each other as live opponents working in teams, trying to subdue each other in the same way as with the dummies earlier. One team would be the aggressor while the other the target, and then they would exchange places, allowing the other side a turn. At the end of the day, the team retired to the showers.

Kaliya was on her way out into the courtyard to see if Relissa and her friends were in their usual place. She found them, along with Sulíma, Túfula, and Petrith once again engaged in conversation, this time about classes and the coming school year.

"Hey there, kids!" she shouts to the assembly.

"There you are!" Relissa calls back. "We saw you and the others out on the field a bit ago and were watching that wacky tussling you were doing."

"Yeah, we had a good workout this time. I feel good about it, too. But I have to admit one thing, it's nothing like the training they give in the Sentinels."

"Aye, this one's a lot more physical. I've never seen people duke it out like that before."

"And this gives us a good advantage over the Suuden-Aryku already. They won't be expecting a physical attack like this. In fact, they might not even know how to respond to it properly."

"I've had a little of my own practice in this, by now," Marelle remarks. "Since that day Relissa and I went out with Thaelyn to study that first orcish portal, and saw him take on a group of orcs, I've been itching to give it a try. I'm not anxious to find myself running up against any Suuden-Aryku, but I'm sure it can come in handy if I need it."

"Me too, actually," Haran concedes. "Even though I'm not intended to go out on the front lines, we all need to learn at least a little bit, just in case. I'm getting some of the same combat training, and much more with a staff. But in my case, being a mage, the staff I'll end up with officially will likely be enchanted somehow."

"I don't know if I could actually go out and start hitting people," Sulíma winces. "I'm not the military type. I would be much happier with a civilian job, or something technical."

"Yeah, me too," Túfula agrees. "I'm itching to start studying all this wonderful history they have here. Then I could share stories with my father."

"Well, Túfu," Kaliya offers. "I'm sure you'll have lots to study here. The lessons I got shared some really interesting stories of the world and how it came to be as it is now, mostly because of Thaelyn."

"I'm sure my father would find that interesting, and no doubt he'll want to compare it to King Saakerav," she pauses to reminisce, and then begins to frown softly. "I just wish I didn't get my romance spoiled by Darumon playing so many roles on us."

"Easy does it, Túfu. We'll fix it, and then you'll have a whole new romance to admire…a living one."

She perks up with a gentle smile at the suggestion.

"All right, Kali, if you say so."

"Anyway, I need to get my team to go check our recorders," Kaliya asserts. "We set up a couple yesterday to watch the local scene for us, but we need to go back every so often to pull out the chips and replace them with new ones, and also to check the power cells."

"Kali," Sulíma considers. "These are physical objects you're working with. How does it apply if you're swapping out a chip or a power cell in your phased condition?"

"I need to pick it up and hold it a moment for it to phase with me, then do the work, and finally I set it back down. Not so difficult, actually. But I need to do it all in my own hands, rather than get help, since it seems we can't work in teams on something like this."

"Oh, hey," Relissa interjects. "About that… Did you ever figure out why you couldn't swap that book around your group that one day? I remember you holding it out, but the others kept missing it to grab hold."

"Yes, we did. In my time practicing this skill, I've become fairly accustomed to how it works, at least for my own actions. Working with others, however, is another thing. I asked Aelwyn and she confirmed my thoughts on this."

Kaliya prepares herself for a little demonstration to represent her thoughts.

"Say I'm holding out an object," she simulates by holding out a hand. "And another person wants to pick it up. We have an immediate problem in terms of how each of us is manifested in space. Compared to one of you, or another physical object, we seem solid. This is a matter of how we manifest ourselves in this form, due to how we perceive of our own image within our thoughts."

She reorients her hand to the side with the palm facing her.

"But in relation to each other," she continues, "while we might be able to see and hear each other, we don't fully harmonize in our phased condition, making us resemble something more like a ghost. My perception, as compared to the other person's perception, and how we guide our mental will to create our respective forms in the space around us, is not in sync, so we don't seem physical to each other."

"Um, sure," Relissa teases. "I understood it up to the point where you held out your hand, and then you lost me. So, you can't touch each other because your minds aren't working the same way."

"That's right. We would need to be in a much more precise form of synchronous harmony to do that. Aelwyn suggested we might need to evolve some more before we see this, or maybe after a long time in practice, we could learn something."

"So then, how will you manage this?" Haran asks.

"We'll just have to use a work-around in this case, pick something up, move it, set it down, and the next person takes it."

"Can you toss it to the other person?" Marelle wonders.

"That's a good question. It depends on how quickly it realigns with the local space so the next one can grab it again."

✦✦✦

"General," Thaelyn states as he studies the daily report. "I am interested in monitoring certain activities within that base."

"Which ones, my Lord?" the General responds. "Our scouts seem to be doing a well enough job reporting them as they occur."

"Indeed, but this is in relation to our scouting efforts for survivors, and the suggestion we had not long ago about employing gryphons."

"Ah, yes! I recall that now."

"Thus far, all we have seen are the vehicles they use to retrieve their supply of the metal, meaning the ground vehicle for the city depot and the aircraft for the mine. We had one recent supply delivery, but nothing else coming through the conveyor, although we did notice one of their officers apparently loading up some of those same supplies to take back through the conveyor."

"And this is what we think to be them sharing their goods with the production facility."

"Yes, so they receive a supply, and then locally distribute it amongst their own. But so far, I see no other activity, especially of a nature to scout or survey the surrounding region."

"I have noticed that as well, and in reference to our previous discussions, we may be correct if they consider there is nothing to patrol out there, with the world being so heavily devastated."

"If this is the case, we should involve some of our gryphons in the search for survivors. They can travel farther and faster, and we can also scan the terrain from high altitude to survey a larger area. The only uncertainty would be if there is another Suuden'kai base out there. But I have doubts they would go to the trouble of building two conveyors, do you think?"

"It seems reasonable on the surface, and if there was another base out there sharing the same conveyor as this one, we should see traffic of some sort."

"Correct, but still we should be careful until we can survey the area. Call up a few flights and equip them lightly to compensate for the heavy gravity. Make a series of high altitude runs and keep a close eye out for more bases. If they should find one, duck low and make note of it, but otherwise let us begin mapping this land and see where we can find more people."

"Very good, my Lord, I'll put the word out for you."

"We should also inform Belrum to solicit more help from his fellows for this. We are going large scale on this now. Just keep it away from the existing base. I would also suggest keeping the survey runs subsonic, as a shockwave might be fairly noticeable to a Suuden'kai base, to say nothing of any people down there who might be disturbed by it."

"Understood."

"Next, I wonder about that troop transport and the personal shuttle, as the Commander describes it," Thaelyn smiles at the Daanen'kai officer. "As I look forward on this, I think I would like to acquire those for our own use at some moment."

"For research, or otherwise, Your Lordship?" Kailen asks.

"Otherwise, in this case... Having a native Suuden'kai vessel would make good cover for us when we find our way to Azgarén. It could buy us just enough time to escape from the immediate area, assuming we arrive in a heavily populated zone, then to find shelter for our later operations. A troop transport could offer multiple benefits, including an invasion of the production facility, which must be our next step after taking the base."

"And the personal shuttle? That might only be good for one or two people."

"Perhaps, but I think I will take a mention from your dear Ankhia on this matter and collect it just for the sake of having one. You never know if it might come in handy."

Kailen gives off a subtle laugh at the reference to Ankhia's packrat mentality before nodding in agreement.

"But then," Thaelyn supposes. "I wonder if and when they receive any troop reinforcements or a change of work crew."

"That's a good question, but if I were a female officer, I wouldn't want to be assigned to this unit if they have a history of abuse and even death at the hands of that...man."

"Absolutely! I must wonder how the other females in that service feel about this. Even with their emotion inhibitor chips, I should think they ought to have some manner of opinion, and likely some measure of aversion to it. One does not need emotion to desire shelter from such abuse or violent death."

"It still seems so abhorrent in my mind that a man, any man, would do this. I find it unconscionable that the base commander could permit this even once, let alone on a continual basis."

"Unless this other man has some special authority to overrule this, but this creates a paradox. We know he is a Suuden'kai, unmodified, and apparently capable of projecting himself as the Thane. However, if we suggest he is a civilian, as he does not seem to demonstrate any command or leadership skills within the city, could he hold any rank at all, for instance political as you once suggested, and therefore any privilege to overrule a military commander."

"At his age? Unlikely. You need to remember how long our society has to wait for promotions."

"Of course, but with Darumon pulling the strings..."

"Yes, and then we have him."

"What if we suggest the base crew is under the full control effect of these chips, and therefore with no free will of their own?"

"Dear cu'Nar, that would be a horrible situation to serve under."

"My Lord," the General interjects. "On a curious side note, I have been trying to pinpoint him as he comes and goes from his home to their command building, or anywhere else, for that matter."

"Ah, good..." Thaelyn muses. "Do we have any indications?"

"Well, I suppose the absolute LACK of him going anywhere could be an indication. The others seem to move around well enough. There is a building that looks like a barracks, and most of the crew retires there on a regular basis. The ranking officers are not seen outside often, but the command building might also house local quarters for them."

"This is reasonable."

"So, other than that one female officer we saw, there is no other traffic coming or going to the house, save for the supply deliveries."

"This is curious. Are we saying he does not actually do any work at all, nor any other form of interaction?"

"I can't be sure if he has any form of interaction at all unless it is by remote. I suppose we will learn something once we begin reviewing those spy videos of their operations inside the booth. So, unless he does everything from his home, he seems very reclusive."

"This reminds me. I was speaking to Aerlie about this, relating our observations of the female, and Kaliya's investigation. She suggested if he is unmodified, he might feel repulsed by the others, therefore his abusive treatment of that one female. When speaking of his… ahem…toys in his house, this suggests a clear sexual fetish involving bondage and sadism. This can be compounded by his apparent youth and perhaps also be associated with antisocial behavior. Finally, his devotion to his physical prowess, as indicated by his bodybuilding equipment, when combined with the rest, might further suggest a strong megalomania complex."

"Gracious! That sounds simply awful."

"This also sounds like he took lessons from Darumon," Kailen admits. "He had to be installed there, and then given special privileges, so part of this has to come from somewhere."

"Perhaps, Commander," Thaelyn concludes. "And this may carry a possible answer. If Darumon installed him, he might hold a close relation. These people may be expendable for as long as this man holds the power to provide the metal. If he uses this as a leverage tool, he might then make demands on the rest for his pleasures. But like the General says, we should wait for those spy videos. With a bit more study, we may find our answer. We have a set of scouts observing that house now, as well as the control booth. We shall see if anything new occurs."

"What if he calls for another female before we can make a move?"

"I have asked myself this, but my answer is problematic. I would wish to preserve lives if it is at all possible. I am hoping we have enough time to make a few observations, though I cannot be sure how often he likes his pleasures. But if the last one was so recent, perhaps he might be content for a while. Commander, if I may, how often do you and your wife take your special moments?"

"We both carry busy schedules, and this often results in each of us being rather tired by the end of the day. But generally, if you're trying to gauge the average cravings we might go through, it tends to run long, like everything else in our society. Then again, we both belong to a slightly older generation by now, where some of that youthful zeal has settled down a bit."

"Of course. And if you are a young man still within his first millennium? I would imagine the cravings at this point might be stronger for the youthfulness aspect."

"They would be, especially with the Alpha Male syndrome driving things. And this is why I'm so concerned, especially if he has nothing else to do in there but work out on his machines. He's probably bored to tears if his only activity is to scream at dwarves at long intervals."

"This does not bode well for us, then."

"Either way, I think we should plan something sooner rather than later for the issue of the dwarves in that mine. Ankhia has been sending out people on a regular basis to monitor their condition. So far, they seem to be holding up, but the readings are showing high levels of toxins building in their blood stream."

"What about those readings taken once from the dwarves up north? Did she have an opportunity to compare with these yet?"

"The numbers she recorded at the time, as compared to what we're seeing now, suggest possibly a seven-month occupation. The ones in this mine here are showing a slightly less volume so far, maybe six months by now."

"Very well, if we consider Chief Bronzeheart and his crew survived seven months well enough, we might believe ourselves to have another month of fair safety. Therefore, we must try to understand that man and his timing before we see another victim."

"You know, if you were to tell me, before all this started coming out, that one day I would find myself in a position where I had to come to THEIR rescue, after all they did to us…I'm not sure which

I would do first, laugh at the idea, scream at it, or just sit blank-faced with the notion that bad deeds actually can come back to you after a while."

"Fate can drive us into many a strange turn of events. This we can be sure of."

◆◆◆

"You will simply make another excuse, Commander," Ytani issues sternly on the com-link. "I am sure whatever you can come up with will serve nicely. It always has in the past. After all, if he needs this metal so badly, surely a little payment would not be outside of reason. There are certainly enough of you back home."

"Ytani," the Commander responds coolly. "Have you ever considered the possibility that they might check to verify these statements with autopsies, and the results of those may conflict with these statements?"

"Why should I care about their opinions, Commander?" he shouts. "It's the Marshal…the MARSHAL…who runs things. The rest of you are nothing more than programmable tools, and most often in active mode to ensure you do it right."

"Ytani, we are a society of laws, regardless of the Marshal…"

"Oh! Laws, is it?" he interrupts harshly. "And who makes those laws, Commander? The Council…yes! But who controls the Council, can you tell me? I believe you were there when it happened, am I right? You sure show the wrinkles for it."

"Ytani, as for the Council," he struggles to maintain his composure. "Yes, they do seem to follow his directives. But you might also find it interesting to know our schools and universities still teach our people the principle of law, and our courts do still prosecute it amongst our population."

"I don't care about that, Commander!" he screams. "This is a military base, not some stupid civilian hoof parade! And he most certainly DOES run things here!"

"Ytani… Regardless of that minor detail, laws are still laws, and even WE have them. Furthermore, that Council, for all their tail-kissing, created directives such as for the application of the Tav'ageen Suppressor chip, which is mandated for EACH citizen, as well as the An'gamu Seed, again mandated for EACH citizen. And I believe you are classified as a citizen. As such, I suspect, once this operation is complete, and your service to procure the metal is no longer needed, your privilege to remain unaltered may also cease. I will look forward to that day."

"Really!" he laughs riotously. "Commander, I am UNIQUE! The only one of my kind in all existence! This requires special consideration, and the Marshal knows it."

"Oh yes, I am sure of it. And I wonder, once this operation is complete, how will your one and only unique skills serve a society that does not even know what they are."

"Are you sure?" he retorts brashly. "But it's not that society of dull-horns I'm serving! It's the Marshal, and he surely has higher demands that ONLY I can serve. For instance, right now, he wants the metal, and I want my pleasures. And you WILL pay me for my services, each and every time I deliver. We want all those hideously adorable rag-tails of yours to keep me in a good enough mood that I don't 'accidentally' let go that the so-called point-ears these runts down below are so afraid of are actually stealing all their precious metals. And then, oops, just look outside at that convenient little road leading up to this hidden base. How would you like that, Commander? An army of dirt-shovelers sticking their pointed little sticks in all your sensitive spots!"

"Are you now threatening me with an uprising? This would not serve YOUR position very well, either, as you would still lose your job when you can no longer provide the metal."

"Oh, don't worry about that, Commander," he gloats. "I'm sure I can probably gain control again easily enough. After all, I'm their LEADER!" he roars. "And once your groaning for your females is settled, maybe I can find someone new to take over. But next time, I may just have to call a little conference with the Marshal to discuss our staffing problems. The obedience rating around here is sorely lacking. So, unless you want to find yourself replaced, or better yet, the full staff put on active so there are no more complaints at all… oh yes! That would be such a joy. I could call on my playmates and do whatever I want, and they won't even cry about it! So, Commander, I'll say this one last time, you will stick to the program… MY program! And if you're so nether-wild upset about making excuses for people returning home in a bag, STOP RETURNING THEM HOME! In case you hadn't noticed, there's this HUGE desert out there. Bury them in it!" he screeches.

The link ends abruptly, leaving the Commander and his staff in the booth staring at each other silently and in shock.

He turned to look at the faces of each of his staff members who were present at the time. Many of them were clutching at their interfaces on the sides of their heads. He tried to resist reaching for his, but his face was still flinching from the feedback.

"Lieutenant Ti'van, Lieutenant Az'krun, come forward."

His two junior officers stepped forward from the assembled crowd, which involved a number of ensigns as well. The gathering had been called to attention as part of the Commander's plan, should he have another argument with Ytani. They would be his witnesses.

"You have observed and understood the exchange, correct?" he asks.

"Yes Sir," they both reply.

"And you are fully aware of Ytani's statements, his intentions, and his manners towards our base staff, correct?"

"Yes Sir."

"We are in a situation where we must take action to preserve our security. Ytani is demonstrating aberrant behavior to the point of becoming dangerous to the health and welfare of our staff members. His threats are a clear indication of his instability, and regardless of his function to provide his service to procure the metal, we cannot function efficiently in this manner if his demands involve the expense of our own membership."

"Commander," Ayene inquires. "Would any of this involve the discussion we had yesterday in your office?"

"It does. Lieutenant Az'krun, I will have you meet with me in my office later today for a briefing on the details Lieutenant Ti'van and I discussed. You will then share this with the other staff members. I will require everyone's participation. We must also pass these details along to the work crew at the processor, but this can wait for now. Lieutenant," he directs at Ayene. "I have an assignment for you. You will carry this out within the next hour, maybe two."

"Why an hour or two?"

"So that it does not occur too closely to this altercation, and thereby suggesting a response."

"I see, and what is the assignment?"

"I will give you a data chip with a special requisition on it. You will then go home to C.P., to the ARC Center to fill this requisition, and then return back here."

"The ARC...the medical research labs? Why not Central? We have a rather extensive medical lab there."

"Yes, we do, but it is also monitored more closely than the activities at the ARC, which is a civilian facility. Also, this requisition will require a custom order."

"May I ask about this custom order?"

"It is to order a set of diagnostic probes with custom programming. The...harsh environmental decline of this world is causing a contamination within our interface circuits; therefore, we will need a temporary override in order to conduct some special maintenance to restore ourselves to full operation. Understood, Lieutenant?"

She raises her brow at the curious statement.

"Indeed, Commander, and very well stated. Do we have a timing schedule for when we might perform this maintenance?"

"First, we will need to conduct some preparatory work to investigate our options. But ultimately, this procedure will need to occur on or before the next delivery date of the metal."

"Yes Sir. Then I will see to this assignment in perhaps a couple of hours, once I recover from my own unfortunate lapse, and also due to this declining environment."

In the ventilation duct over their heads, out of view of the people in the room, there was a small device peeking through the grill observing the conversation. It recorded the audio as well as the video of the scene below, including the reactions of the people to the voice on the speaker.

Later in the day, close to evening, a small visitor made an appearance directly inside the duct from places unknown. Its shape was strange, to say the least. It resembled a mantis, but with arms and hands. It filled the space in the duct vertically, large enough to lift up the camera unit fully and set it on the knee of one leg. The creature brought with it a small memory chip and a replacement power cell, which it set down temporarily. Once it had the camera lifted and well within its grip, it pulled out the old memory chip and power cell, and replaced them with the new ones, then reinstalled the unit back to its former position. It collected the used pieces and departed in a small puff.

❖❖❖❖❖❖❖

Morning had dawned over the guildhall and the students were attending breakfast. It was the second day of the weekend. Kaliya and her team were scheduled for another day of general combat practice out on the field. The results of the previous day's exercise using the new magical strike proved promising, and the Mage Elders who created it were ready to experiment with a live test.

When their morning meal was finished, Kaliya assembled her team for their practice session. They started their day with a series of warm-up exercises, followed by a lap around the field. When the team was ready, a group of Mage Elders arrived on the field with a box of newly inscribed scrolls, the same as what was used the day before.

A row of priests had gathered on the sidelines to attend to any injuries that may result from this test. Experimenting with a new magical incantation didn't always require live subjects, but on that rare occasion where it became necessary to understand the effects on the body, such as with a non-lethal application, precautions were always taken.

Kaliya called her team into formation, aligning them in rows to the line-up of subjects on the field. Each member was given a scroll. The process would involve every member of the team, one row after another, and then repeat a second time for the experience.

The volunteers were veteran soldiers, but dressed in common attire so that the Mage Elders and priests could make a careful study of the effects on the body as it occurred, rather than to be hidden beneath layers of armoring.

Kaliya participated in the first row. She unrolled her scroll, along with the others in the row, and called out the glyphic runes to cast the spell. The scroll erupted in its traditional flash after a successful casting and her hand became charged with a potent electrical pulse. It was not the same as a lightning charge, which would cause damage. This was a different sensation, high voltage but low current.

She looked square into the face of her opponent, realizing she was about to strike a fellow soldier, but this was required as part of the test, and they both knew it. She pulled her arm back, coiling up the tension in her muscles, then jabbed it forward into a solid palm-strike to his forehead.

The impact knocked his head backward, but that was only a minor reaction to the discharging effect. She could see the electrical sparking under her hand as it radiated through his skin. He grimaced harshly and made a weak grunting sound. The waves rocketed through his skin and the musculature just underneath, causing his whole body to clench. Arms and legs shook with tension for a brief moment of time, and then went limp. He fell to the ground inert.

The whole row of volunteers succumbed in this way. Kaliya and her group moved back to allow the priests and mages an opportunity to examine the victims. The priests made a careful check of the critical signs, the heart and lungs, and regular breathing. All seemed good. They were alive and appeared to be uninjured. They also appeared to be conscious, though unable to respond to questioning due to their muscles being rendered inoperable.

"Sorry guys," Kaliya bends low and speaks softly. "It's only business. I'll treat you to an ale later, to make it up to you."

She steps away with her row and calls up the next one. The priests carry off the first group of subjects, and the next one moves into position. The team steps up and the process repeats. By the end of the session, a long pile-up of bodies lined the side of the track, with priests monitoring how long they would stay in this condition, in order to determine an approximate duration for the effect.

✦

"My Lord, a pleasant morning to you," calls the General as Thaelyn enters the room.

"And to you, General… Do we have anything new to report today?"

"Indeed, we have our first receipt of recordings from our spy operations. The Commander and his people have been busy reviewing both recordings, the one from the Thane's Hall, and also from the control booth."

"Did we receive anything useful out of it?"

"So far, the one from the Thane's Hall is mostly empty, but then I expected this if the Thane only makes his appearance at rare intervals. However, we did record a brief tirade when he called in his Chancellor and demanded more ingots, shouting a series of accounts about how the so-called point-ears are swarming across the land and the warriors are unable to keep up the pace without more and faster supplies. He even went so far as to suggest every city on the surface was under siege."

"Such a fascinating fabrication of words. This brings me back to our earlier discussion. Does he have any true knowledge of what adamantium actually is and how it might compare to anything else he may be familiar with, that he is stating it to hold such a short lifespan."

"Yes," he chuckles. "That would be perhaps the greatest irony here. To say nothing of such a widespread siege that should leave nothing standing to send out warriors from."

"Absolutely. And what do we have in the control booth?"

"The Commander and Lieutenant Lapäli over there," he directs to another desk across the room, "were both reviewing it, and in fact I believe they have done so multiple times by now. Although I was trying to keep out of it, giving them their space, I could hear whispering, some of it rather anxious, and in the end they both want to talk to you."

"Is that so," he turns and eyes them suspiciously. "Commander, do we have something interesting?"

"Your Lordship," Kailen rises from his desk. "If I didn't know what I was looking at, I wouldn't believe it. And even if I did know what I was looking at, I still wouldn't believe it, but I suppose I would have to when you consider the parameters."

"Indeed, then how would you wish to describe this thing you cannot accept to be believable?"

"The best way is just to invite you to come over here to this terminal and see it for yourself."

Kailen waves to Thaelyn to join him at his desk as he turns a video monitor around for them to study. Thaelyn steps around the conference table, waving for the General to follow along, and they all convene at Kailen's desk as he readies the video.

"Generally speaking," Kailen begins. "I think we have a result to answer numerous questions we were asking about these people, and Great cu'Nar above, the situation over there doesn't look good. The Commander and his officers ARE very upset, as much as one can be with inhibitor chips installed, about the death of that female, along with what I'm assuming to be their military HQ. I even heard a term relating to their feelings about the Council, which was rather interesting."

"Indeed! A term relating to their Council? Which one?"

"Tail-kissing up to the Marshal."

"Oh!" he smiles. "How quaint. But then, relating to that one female, how do we explain the lack of action taking place?"

"Because the one who is responsible, named Ytani, is a fiend at least as bad, if not worse than Darumon. Lady Aerlie was right, and maybe even understating the problem. He's using his position as what I'm assuming to be a Prodigy Child to threaten and coerce the rest into serving his needs. He uses abusive language, has belligerent manners, and virtually no respect for authority or the law, as the Marshal is apparently in control of everything, including their government, at least in an indirect manner, and Ytani behaves like he's a favorite child who can do anything he wants within the Marshal's custom military, where law is apparently anything the Marshal defines, regardless of their university and court system back home, which apparently still work according to normal."

"Powers behold. Is this to say the civilian side, at least as we might understand it, is still a reasonably functioning body? How interesting. Can we see this?"

"Absolutely. Here…" he turns on the player.

The group all direct their attention to the video as it replays the conversation between the Suuden'kai Commander and Ytani on the com-link, up until the final ultimatum and Ytani cutting the link. Kailen then pauses at this point for their opinions.

"Great gods!" the General gushes. "I'm only partway through the Daanen-Aryku language course, but that is more than enough to tell me this young man has some serious social issues, as well as a god complex. If the Commander has a problem with filing accurate reports with his command, he can bury the evidence in the desert? Pshaw!"

"And more is Ytani and his perceived usefulness," Kailen adds. "The one and only, unique, at least to the Marshal, even if no one else knows what it is. This says, Darumon probably hides it from the rest. And here is where his authority comes in, to provide the metal."

"This is a very serious situation," Thaelyn accedes. "General, I want Aerlie to see this, and I think we should invite Kaliya to review it as well. Her team will ultimately need to contend with this, so she needs to be briefed."

"Yes, my Lord."

"So, this Ytani is threatening either an uprising of dwarves against the crewmembers if they do not comply, thus removing them, and if he is so fond of using excuses, he could probably fabricate anything he desires for the occasion, or else call in a favor from the Marshal to invoke what he calls an active condition. For this I am going to suggest a reference to these chips. Those people looked like they were in much better control of themselves than that occasion I had on the trans-com with Commander Geilv. Could it be these chips have something like an on-off switch to them?"

"That's what I'm thinking right now," Padriyl suggests. "And currently they're off, which might give them greater freedom to make decisions for themselves. Commander, we should show them the next scene."

"Yes, Lieutenant…this one is good."

"Is this the part you cannot believe?" Thaelyn muses.

"You tell me, Your Lordship," he smirks.

He resumes the video and allows it to continue to the scene that followed, with the Commander speaking to his two Lieutenants and giving instructions, followed by his strangely referenced excuse for the new assignments.

"Most… Interesting…" Thaelyn ponders beguilingly. "Yes, I see your point, Commander. That almost looks like they are on the edge of mutiny, not that I would blame them, but with emotion chips and these military chips installed? That would not follow expectedly."

"Not only that," Kailen admits. "But it also fully and completely contradicts our original notion of them acting like machines. They seem to hold feelings after all, and even opinions of things they're made to do."

"What were these references he used?" the General wonders. "Someplace called C.P. and ARC. And that probe he mentioned?"

"I can tell you about C.P.," Kailen offers. "But it's almost a myth to me. I know the reference only from my parents when they would sometimes talk about our old home. It's the same as you referring to your city of Bya'an Tamoranth as B.T. This is our capital city back on Azgarén, and we call it Capitol Prime."

"Ah, very good…"

"I recall that ARC once before," Padriyl considers. "It was on the shipping label of that medical box the Dean was going to use on his students. Here it sounds like it's a medical research industry, and this makes sense if you consider several of Darumon's death toys he was using. And if you can place custom orders with them, they must be capable of all sorts of things. As for the probe, I'm going to guess it's used on these cranial interfaces. I recall a mention of a port access on the unit, maybe for diagnostics, although here he is calling for something with custom programming."

"To deactivate it, I'll bet," Kailen admits. "To free himself from it completely so he can deal with Ytani before Ytani deals with anyone else."

"While I would normally applaud the man," Thaelyn suggests. "I think he is taking a number of serious risks. I am sure he probably knows this, but how he hopes to account for them, I cannot be sure. And ultimately, it could affect him, his staff, possibly also our own position and objectives, and who knows what else after that."

"My Lord," the General considers. "Perhaps we could somehow make contact and arrange something. This resembles an open door for us, at least partially."

"It does, but that door still has a few obstacles in our way. His issue is largely with Ytani. The rest remains the same, as far as I can tell. We know we want that base, and we know we want them, at least as much for interrogation to learn details about Azgarén and Darumon, perhaps also Sargeras, and how we might proceed against them. He might want Ytani out of the way, but I think we should still consider him potentially hostile for his support of the rest."

"Yes, I suppose so. But once he is in our custody, perhaps a bit like a captive audience, do you think we could soften him up to our cause, much like we did the elves or Kaliya the orcs?"

"Perhaps, if we play our words right. So, we may need to continue with our existing plans, but at least now we have a time estimate. He mentioned a date of on or before the delivery of the metal, and this reminds me of that female. It was on the same day they retrieved their shipments. This must be his cue. The supplies we tallied up suggest intervals of one month. So, Ytani uses his ability to provide the metal, and on that same day he expects some manner of compensation, in his case female pleasures. Therefore, we must intercept this before that time, and hopefully before the Commander takes action."

"And then what? How do we contend with Ytani?"

"I would like to continue our observations to see if Ytani receives any visitors. If he feels himself so close to Darumon, I will not want Darumon to discover his loss prematurely. In the end, however, he must be removed. And for this, we must be the ones to apply the justice. He is a criminal, self-convicted and unremorseful. He holds desires to repeat this at any whim, and even to remove any witnesses if they should choose to oppose him. And further, to dispose of the evidence by burying it in a forgotten desert. Therefore, our judgment is hereby passed! But in a time of war..." he sighs. "This becomes an assassination mission, as much as I hate those. And poor Kaliya, I must ask her to do this."

"My little sister," Kailen relents. "But you're right, and I'm sure she'll understand."

"Greets t' ye, lads," calls a dwarven patron entering a local tavern. "What be the tale today?"

The workday was coming to an end inside Glimmerheim, and the local men were making their visits to the taverns and dinner halls around the city. It was a routine practice for them. They would gather, sometimes with their wives, to meet in the taverns and listen to the local gossip and stories going around the city, not that there was ever anything especially new to talk about, so the conversation was often rather dull. It was simply a habit of talking to hear a different sort of noise other than the general clamoring of their usual workplace.

"Hey there, brother!" shouts another patron sitting in a group. "Come an' sit here with us, we have a fine one for ye."

"Truly? Good then, just let me get me'self an ale an' I'll be right over."

The man steps over to a bar and orders up a stein of the local brew, which was comparatively weak due to the local farming being more oriented to produce food rather than anything for brewing. The ale was a product of alternative foodstuffs to simulate the traditional drink. He takes his mug and sits down with the group to hear the latest stories circulating around town.

"Now then, lads," begins the lead dwarf at the table. "Here be a good one for ye. A new tale has been a-churnin', an' it be a-callin' up some old ones that nay a one of ye mayhap ever did think of afore. For a long while now, we've all been a-thinkin' the war be a-ragin' above. But a few have gone t' thinkin' that mayhap there be somethin' wrong with those tales."

"What d' ye mean, Angan? Did someone hear it different now?"

"It be about a good many parts that don'na fit together the right way. A few people here an' there mayhap did think of this once upon a tale, but nay a one ever really drew them together all at one time. We hear the tales about the war, an' it tends t' drown out all the rest, till our ears be a-burnin' so hot, we can'na take the tellin' anymore."

"Aye, I hear that. But then, what be this new tellin' about, if ye say someone drew it together by now?"

"Here be the parts we all be a-knowin' about from the old tales. First, there be a wave of point-ears that rages across the land above an' makes trouble for us. Then be the closin' of the doors an' we dig deep t' get away from it, since it was said they nay be good diggers. A few also say the upper town got smashed, though nay a soul has ever truly seen it with their own eyes."

"Where did that tale come from if nay a soul ever saw it?"

"It be an old one, t' be sure, so it be hard t' say, but nay a soul ever can go up t' see the truth of it. Then, we hear the callin' t' make wares for the warriors above, an' the mines are made t' pull up Adamant t' nay an' end. But lads, here be a curious one for ye. They be a-sendin' up only bricks, nay the wares for a war in the way ye might think."

"Aye, I heard this from a friend who be a-workin' down there.

But the tale was the men sent up afore be a-workin' the bricks in t' the wares for the warriors."

"Fine, but then we have these new tales t' think about. The doors be closed. How d' ye send up bricks through closed doors, an' for that matter a smashed town, if it truly be that way?"

The dwarves sitting at the table pause in silence at the thought, but before any of them can respond, Angan continues his story.

"Next be another part that ye can take home an' swing yer axe at. The men called up in the feast, they go up t' serve the fare, so goes the tellin', but nay a one ever returns back. Not even a wee word t' their loved ones t' say they be alive an' well. If the bricks can go up t' serve the war, that means someone from above be a-comin' t' pick them up from the store. Why can'na they bring word t' us in here from our men gone t' serve the fare? How hard can it be t' deliver a simple note t' a lonely wife?"

The men at the table now start glancing around at each other. This simple notion was enough to cause serious concern over the interaction of the trade being conducted above.

"An' one last one for ye," Angan continues again. "The war be said t' be a-ragin' for four hundred years, lads. I nay be a warrior, but I have t' wonder how the world above be a-farin' by this time. The tales say every city be a-blazin'. Four hundred years, lads! How long does it take t' burn a city, d' ye know? An' the warriors…if every city be a-blazin', where d' these warriors be a-comin' from? If I were a warrior, an' me home was a-blazin', I'd fight t' me dyin' breath t' save it. But if every city now be a-blazin', where yay be the warriors who go out fightin' t' save anythin' at all! It don'na make sense!"

"But the bricks we send up must be a-goin' somewhere," contends another man at the table.

"Aye, I nay be t' arguin' that. But has anyone actually seen who picks them up? Mayhap it nay be the warriors at all! An' I say this for a couple of reasons."

"What kind?"

"Think, lads. A sturdy warrior, properly fit with the fare for war, would be a hard foe to defeat in honorable battle. Any of us who knows what Adamant be about can say this, ay?"

"Aye."

"An' more, we all know how valuable Adamant be for its trade value. An' what d' we get in return for it? All I ever hear be the wood an' coal for the Thane's cauldrons t' burn. Nay more than that. We should be a-swimmin' in gold an' fine wares down here for all the metal we sent up."

The group all let out a bold round of oohs and soft mumbling for the revelation.

"An' the men who go up t' serve the fare?" asks another man.

"Nay a one ever called back t' his love here in the city, lad. If ye were t' go up an' serve for anythin' at all, would ye let yer pretty sit in a lonely room for the rest of her life?"

"Ye're right, Angan. There be somethin' foul in this."

"Now, who be it that tells these tales, lad? The tales of the war, the tales of the feast, an' the tales of some fool pickin' up bricks for a war that has been a-ragin' so long that there nay can be a world above t' be a-fightin' any more, ay?"

"Wait now, Angan. We should take care here, if ye're tryin' t' put this on the Thane."

"Aye, I'll take care for it, for a man who be said t' rage every time the Chancellor walks up t' him, callin' for more bricks, givin' these tales, an' then runs t' his room nay t' be seen till the next time he comes out t' rage again. I know one of the lasses who be a chambermaid in there. She be the sister of a good friend. She be a-tellin' there nay be any doors in there but the one leadin' out t' the Hall. If this man nay be a-goin' out t' d' anythin' but rage at the Chancellor, how can ye tell me he be a-knowin' of the war, the world above, or anythin' if he ne'er goes out t' look at it?"

"D' ye know of anyone else t' come in an' speak with him?"

"The only one t' speak with him be the Chancellor, t' the best of me knowin', an' the Chancellor nay be t' knowin' any more than the rest of us, so it be said. The smiths in the forges say they drop the bricks in the store, but then turn t' close the door an' go back t' work. Nay a soul ever stays t' see who picks them up."

"Mayhap we should pay closer attention t' it, just t' be sure? I agree…there be somethin' wrong here."

"An' another thing…" Angan continues. "There be a wee tale that tells of that wood an' coal comin' in t' burn in the cauldrons in front of the Thane's Hall, but where d' ye think it be a-comin' from? Nay a soul ever sees anyone drop wood or coal at our feet, the same as the bricks goin' out…an' once again through closed doors. So, where d' ye think it comes from, ay? Especially from a world that, by the tellin' of it, has been a-burnin' for four hundred years. Methinks there nay can be any trees left up there by now. An' further is the coal. If yer home be a-burnin', when d' ye spend time diggin' up coal t' make trade for anythin', includin' Adamant. There must be a big hole in all of this."

"Nay a soul has ever seen where it comes from? It has t' come from somewhere!"

"Aye, I s'pose, but it don'na make sense t' me straight away. That lass who works as a chambermaid, she tells of a small supply room inside the Thane's Hall. Every now an' again, she takes notice of it fillin' up with new supply, but ne'er t' see where it comes from. It be like the room just fills up by itself."

"An' this be INSIDE the Hall, but with nay anyone seen movin' it t' an' fro. Aye, that be a strange one, Angan."

"Right. So, if we say nay a soul ever did see anyone from above pickin' up the bricks or droppin' trades at our feet, as weak as those trades may be, mayhap we should take a closer look inside that store t' see where it goes."

"I'd say if ye be a-thinkin' that," offers another man at the table. "Ye should be real careful, in case the world above nay be what ye think. If there be warriors up there fightin', that be one thing. But if there be point-ears lurkin' about, we nay want them t' be a-comin' down here."

"Hold there, lad," mentions another. "In all this time, there nay be a point-ear t' come down here. As I hear it, the Thane once said we be safe from them here."

"Aye, brother," Angan admits. "As the tale was told, they nay be good diggers. Diggers, me brothers, that be the word used here. T' me mind, this tells of the city t' be buried with nay a way in or out, that ye need t' dig t' get t' it. Mayhap it be because the doors be closed an' the upper town be smashed, or mayhap another thing. But now think on this. If the war be a-blazin' so hard above, they should be everywhere by now. Four hundred years would yay be enough t' learn how t' dig, d' ye think?"

"Aye," he chuckles. "Even if ye nay be good at it, ye can learn, mayhap."

"A wee babe can learn in that much time. Then t' find the doors, pry them open, an' come down here."

"That would be a good one."

"Better yet, why dig at all. If the Thane has a way t' send the bricks an' the men out, after four hundred years, with every city blazin' above, ye might think someone would take notice of it by now."

This notion stunned the group at the table, and they each turned to gaze at one another. It was a concept most people didn't acknowledge. A way out also means a way in...for their enemies. And further would be the display of goods moving around out in the open. But why has it not happened?

"Aye, 'tis true that," responds the other man. "An' methinks this city be such a grand one, by the old tales of it, they nay can miss it."

✦ ✦ ✦ ✦ ✦ ✦ ✦

The week was well underway after Kaliya and her team finished their practice with the new attack spell. In the late hours after their classes, they were escorted to the Cormyr Training Fields by a captain in charge of running them through the drills of urban warfare. Along with her team, he also brought another team of practiced soldiers to serve as the opposition force. These would represent the resident troops that would be stationed in a mock town setting that Kaliya's team needed to infiltrate.

Although their actual duty might involve both physical as well as projected forms, in this instance, her team would use only physical form for the pure experience using conventional methods. A later training session would involve both forms to coordinate her team members with different functions.

The captain managing the exercise organized and deployed his men to their positions within the mock setting. He then gave his instructions to Kaliya and her team.

"Your objective here is to infiltrate the town, locate and acquire a prisoner being held in one of the houses, and extract that prisoner safely. You must move covertly, and take out any hostile forces silently, leaving no trace of your activities until your final goal is met. On this occasion, since this is your first trial, we'll go easy on you, where the opposing team will be in a relaxed state of alertness."

Kaliya accepts the mission and brings her team into position to begin the operation. She studies the setting a moment before giving her first orders. Even though this was a practice session, it was intended to resemble actual duty. And her nerves were tense.

The mock setting gave the appearance of a modest frontier town, with several shops and marketplaces, rows of houses, and a quaint town square. It was a simplified setting, but the critical element was an enemy occupation said to be keeping a high-value hostage. Her objective was to retrieve that hostage using any means necessary while not sounding the general alarm. To do so was to fail, as the hostage would be killed to keep it out of her hands.

"All right, everyone, go dark and go silent to the near side," she commands, directing them to the back wall of the nearest building.

The group casts cloaks on themselves and moves into position. They were not official troopers of the Order. So, unlike many of those who were, they didn't have the special enchantment that allowed them to see each other while under their cloaks. This would be difficult, as it would require them to pop into view on occasion to share reports and give further instructions. This would require finding a secure location out of view of any hostiles. Therefore, scouting would be useful here.

The group reaches the back side of what appeared to be a tavern. There were no windows on this side. She dispels her cloak and gestures for the others to follow. She then gives a series of sign language signals to her group.

She first assigns a series of scouts. She sends one to circle around the tavern and investigate the front. Scout Two would make a tour through the town square, checking market stalls and booths, and report back on her findings. Scout Three would check a neighboring building to the right on a lane facing the tavern, while Scout Four takes a workshop to the left, and Scout Five would investigate a stable across the way from that. The scouts cast cloaks on themselves and move off to their assigned tasks.

The first to return was Scout Three from the building on the right. He reported silently that it appeared as a butcher shop occupied with five soldiers behind the counters, as seen through a window, but the front door was closed.

Scout One returned with a report that the tavern was occupied with ten troops distributed around the room. The front door was open in this case.

Scout Five reported the stables had four soldiers lingering among the stalls as if waiting for something. Scout Four said the workshop had six, once again seen through a window, but this door was also closed. Any action against it under a cloak, the same as with the butcher shop, would need to find a clear entrance, since the opening of a door would constitute interaction with external objects, and this breaks the spell. Those two buildings might have to wait.

Scout Two returned shortly after, telling of troops hidden within some of the market stalls, apparently watching for approaching invaders.

So far, the easiest targets seemed to be the stables and the tavern, for the accessibility of it, but those two side buildings troubled her, and the square was a tripwire for even more. She decided to use an alternate strategy. These front buildings were an obvious trap.

She sent one more scout around the stables to see what was behind it. The word came back as an inn. There were four guards in the lobby, once again behind a closed door, but in this case, there was also a back door which led into a utility room with a window. There were no occupants inside. Kaliya made this their first target. She gave a signal to cast their cloaks and regroup behind that building.

They arrived behind the inn, and she carefully peeked through the window while still under her cloak. It was clear, so she popped into view to cast a silence spell on the door itself, in case it was squeaky, and then opened it.

The room inside was small, with a laundry tub, some tables and racks, and a cabinet. It would make a tight squeeze for her team if they all entered at once, so she called one squad to follow her while the rest stayed outside under a cloak. She would send a scout for a quick run through the halls to check side rooms before moving forward. The building was also a two-story design, and she needed to check upstairs as well.

Several side rooms were checked on the first floor, but they were all clear. It seemed the only guards on this level were in the front lobby, as if expecting the incursion to come from that side. She analyzes the report of their positioning and assigns four teammates to go under a cloak, then to sneak in and each take a specified target.

The four members comply, moving through the hall gently to keep their stealthy advance at maximum. Timing and coordination were important here. They needed to count the seconds for each of their actions, so they would know how long they have to position themselves under a cloak before making a coordinated strike. They take their positions, counting the seconds from their initial launch, then pop out, each grabbing a guard around the face to silence him while plunging a practice dagger into his chest.

The daggers were not true weapons in this case. The blade was blunt and mounted on a spring-loaded guide inside the hilt, allowing the blade to retract as it was thrust into a body.

The guards reel from the attack and fall to the ground, playing dead as their turn in this game is done. The movement was swift and silent. No indication of activity was revealed outside.

Kaliya calls the rest of her team inside from the back door. She moves into the lobby to see their handiwork, and then considers the upstairs. It was a confined space. If there was anyone up there, they had nowhere to go. She decides to send pairs of teammates to each of the rooms. There were six in all.

They carefully ascend the stairs, keeping their hoof steps as silent as can be. Each pair positions itself outside a door, with one to the side and another in front. All six doors were covered simultaneously. A signal was given for a combined strike. The member on the side gently turned the latch while the other kicked the door in, rushing into the room and closely followed by the other. Three of the rooms proved to be empty. The other three had a pair of occupants, which were summarily slammed into the floor by the rushing bodies entering the room. They were then dispatched with more blade strikes. The group reassembled in the lobby.

"All right, we have one building to ourselves," Kaliya whispers.

She discreetly peeks outside the window to survey the square.

"Those guards in the square are trouble," she continues. "There's a town hall just outside, which would be a very likely spot for more guards, and a temple across the way."

She studies the market stalls in the square.

"Those stalls don't look completely enclosed. We could probably sneak in from the opening to the rear. It looks like we have six of them: Three on this side, three on the other. The stalls should offer enough cover if we keep our heads low. I need twelve people to go dark, two on each. Work your way to the rear, sneak in low to the ground, and remove that threat."

She selects the members to perform this task and gives the positioning of the targets. They cast another cloak and exit through the back door to work their way around, once again counting seconds to reach their positions before striking. While this first squad moves out, Kaliya selects another one with eleven people for the tavern.

"Here's how you'll do it," she instructs. "Go dark, work around, and enter the building. One takes a position in the center, the rest around the perimeter. The report says they're distributed at random, so let's have three on each side, two in front and two in the rear. Give yourselves a little spacing and take your nearest targets. The center will pop first to draw their focus, the others pop two seconds after while their backs are turned and take them down."

She once again designates the positioning and sends them out.

A few moments later, out in the square, all six market stalls erupt with a subdued instance of commotion as the targets are eliminated by the first squad. The teammates then cast yet another cloak and return back through the rear entrance of the inn to the lobby. Another few moments pass for the second group, and a hushed disturbance echoes quietly inside the tavern as those targets are eliminated. The group rejoins at the inn.

"Good work," she applauds. "This gives us a little breathing room. Now, we have the stables, the workshop, and the butcher shop, plus the others out there. I need a scout on the town hall," she motions to the building just outside. "Check the windows and see about back doors. I need another scout on that temple across the way. I can see the doors are open, so check inside carefully."

Two scouts prepare themselves and venture forth, while Kaliya and the others wait. She continues peering cautiously out the window, taking notice of a row of houses lining another lane behind the town hall and extending as far as the temple.

"These houses out here will be fun. Looks like six of them. We'll need to go door-to-door looking for bad guys and saving the hostage, but we'll scout them carefully through the windows before making any moves."

The scouts from the town hall and temple return. The temple had six guards inside, some stationed along the walls just inside the door, others deeper within. The town hall doors were closed, with a few guards seen in the forward windows, but none through a side window into an office space.

"That town hall sounds like trouble," Kaliya notes. "I don't think I want to make a run through the front. All right, the temple sounds easy enough. Six of you go dark, move across, and take up positions with your targets. The hall will be tricky, but if we can gain entrance through that window… Trouble is, there's a house with line-of-sight, and I'm sure we'll need to pop if we want to open the window to get in. I need a scout out there to check it thoroughly."

Another scout casts a cloak and leaves through the rear entrance of the inn, turning around the side and up to the nearest house just behind the town hall. He makes a careful check through the windows before returning back. A squad also goes out to contend with the temple.

"Lieutenant," reports the scout. "The house is occupied; two in the front room, two in a kitchen on the side, and two more in a bedroom to the rear."

"Any hostages?"

"None visible…"

"Any back doors?"

"No ma'am."

"All right, Alpha Leader, bring them down. Go dark and get in position. Two take the door, one to open, one to storm. Follow this with four dark, two for the kitchen, two for the bedroom. They'll pop as needed when the guards go live. Keep the rest on standby."

The squad leader makes a salute and issues a command for all to go under a cloak until they arrive at their goal.

The guards that were previously occupying the inn lobby were laying on the floor behind the group listening to the orders. Although they were technically dead, as for this exercise, they couldn't help but cast a subtle glance at each other grinning at the professionalism of this team.

Kaliya waits for the current assignment to clear the way for her next move. The squad sent to the temple was successful at taking out the guards in their positions, while Alpha Squad took the house.

The squad at the house played as they did with the inn bedrooms. One gently turned the door handle while the other made a quick kick and stormed into the room, followed by the first one. The two guards in the front room were body-slammed while the others in the kitchen stepped around to engage, only to be met by a surprise attack by two cloaked figures grabbing them from out of the shadows. The two in the bedroom heard the commotion almost immediately, but by the time they made their way through the door leading into the front room, they were also grabbed by two hidden attackers emerging from either side of the doorway. When the operation was done, the squad leader stepped into view at the front door to signal a successful hit.

"Now, Beta Squad with me…" Kaliya commands. "Gamma, wait here for my signal. Your orders will be to take the stables and the workshop. Did you see any back doors on that workshop?"

"Actually yes. But no windows to see what was on the inside, so it could be anything."

"And they have line-of sight to the stables on the other side, right?"

"It sure seems that way."

"What about behind there? Anything interesting, like storage, piles of anything, something to provide cover?"

"Um, I recall some crates and piles of straw."

"All right, I have an idea. Let's see if we can offer a distraction. Send someone back there and take up hiding under something. You may need to build something with those piles of things. Then make some soft animal noises, like something injured. Let's see how they respond to that. This should cause them to wonder how and why anything is out there. If any one of them goes around to check on it, take them down with a hidden agent, then conceal him from view. Rinse and repeat for the rest, maybe to elevate the sounds of something in even greater distress until they're all down."

"Oh, you're not nice, Kaliya," he chuckles. "All right, got it."

"As for the workshop, once the stables are clear, set up a team with at least as many as you can be sure of in that front room, plus someone for the door. But send them to the REAR door, and in the absence of anyone with line-of-sight out in front, use one guy to, um, fumble with the handle."

"Fumble with it?"

"Yeah, duck down, out of sight, and gently toy with it, like someone or something trying to open it, but not really opening it, just fumbling with the handle to draw attention. Then, as they turn towards the front to greet their guests, your REAL assault hits them from behind after entering the rear."

"Ouch!"

On the floor behind her, one of the guards pipes up softly to comment.

"You know, Lieutenant, he's right. You're simply nasty on those tactics."

"I need to invent something no one ever thought of before. And like Thaelyn says, war is a thinking man's game, and I'm a woman. So yes, YOU are all in trouble," she snickers.

"Oh grand, but aye!" he chortles.

Now Kaliya takes her squad and exits the rear, casting a cloak along the way, and moving to the side of the town hall. She arrives at the window looking into an empty office space.

The window latch was closed on the inside. It was a hook latch that pivoted to one side. She tried wedging her blade between the two panels to push it up. After some amount of effort forcing the blade inside the seam and wiggling it upward, she noticed the hook pop open. She was now able to open the windows, which both swung open inside the room. She peered inside to see the office was clear, but the door leading into the hall was open. This could present a problem for the progression of sound into other parts of the building as they climbed through the window. She signaled two of the men in the group to lift her up for greater ease of sliding across the windowsill.

She twisted around and carefully lowered herself to the floor, then stepped quietly over to the door to close it, while the rest of the team made their way inside. Once they were all safely inside the room, she called a scout to run through to check the rest of the building under a cloak.

The only occupants seemed to be clustered in the main hall, nice and neat. She ordered up an assault in the same manner as the rest.

A unit under cloak goes out and quietly dispatches the guards, and with the building now under control, she leans out the window to give the signal to Gamma Squad.

Gamma leader led his team under a cloak around behind the stables, where he surveys the area carefully for any observers in critical positions. He then directs his team to move a series of crates and bundles of straw into position to create a concealed hollow, where he stations one of his people to begin making animal sounds, as if it was trapped inside the enclosure. The rest went dark again and waited.

Inside the stables, the men stood around waiting for anything to show itself. Then one of them heard the soft bleating of what sounded like a small goat.

"What the…" he mumbles. "Lads, do you hear that? Did someone leave a goat out here for some reason?"

"A what?" calls another soldier. "There shouldn't be anything of the sort out here. Where is it?"

"It sounds like it's coming from behind the wall here, out back."

"Go check on it."

"Aye. One sec."

He diverts through an opening in the wall that leads through to the storage area. But as soon as he shows his face, and is generally out of view by the others, an invisible agent pops up to silently take him down. He is then dragged off to another area of the building.

The agent with the sound effects then increases the distress calls.

"That's getting worse," notes another soldier. "Whatever it is, it's sure isn't a happy little bloke!"

"What's going on back there?" announces one of the men. "Great gods, this is surely going to complicate things. All right, both of you, get back there and see to it."

Two additional soldiers now turn to pass through the rear door to see about the noises. And once again, they are taken down by hidden agents.

The animal noises now make a frantic upturn, as if something is happening, and not in a good way. This causes the last man to become nervous. And with no obvious solution coming from the rest of his team, he decides to file through the rear access to check on things…much to his chagrin as he is soon taken down like the rest.

"Bloody hell, you people," he grunts as they drag him away.

"It worked, didn't it?" soothes one of the agents.

"Aye, granted that."

The team again goes dark and circles around to the rear of the workshop, while one agent ducks down in front and hides below the windows in front of the door. There he begins gently nudging and wiggling the door lever to generate a disturbance for the occupants inside to take notice.

"What's going on there," wonders one of the soldiers.

"Did anyone see anything pass by outside?" asks another one.

"Not in front of the windows."

"Is someone outside actually trying to open the door, or is it something else?"

"Maybe you should go look?"

"Maybe…"

But before he, or anyone else, could make any moves, the room came alive with hidden troopers taking down the full assembly from behind. When the deed was done, the group leader peeked outside and gave a hand signal to Kaliya in the town hall building to signal his success.

"Next, Beta," she announces. "You'll take the butcher shop. It's on the other side of town, so maybe we can use the same procedure. Was there a back door?"

"Yes ma'am, much like with the workshop, but no windows."

"All right, apply the same tactic, and this will finish up out here."

Beta Squad exits out the front door of the town hall under a cloak. There was no one left outside in the immediate area to see them use the door, but the cloak was important to get into position. And while they were busy, Kaliya leans out the window again to signal Alpha Squad, still waiting inside the house. She orders scouts to investigate the next two houses in the row.

With the forward buildings now cleared of hostiles, Kaliya gave a hand signal through the town hall door, first as two open palms facing out, with fingers raised to enumerate each of the squads, in order to draw their attention. Then turning them sideways, curling her fingers into fists and yanking down. This was a sign of engagement for an action. She followed with symmetric circular sweeps on both hands to point at her location, next with a curtain drawn over her eyes to go dark again. The command here was to reconvene under a cloak at her position.

Her next action was to return to the office window and check Alpha Squad for their scouting results. She leans out the window and signals for a report. The squad leader gestures back using sign language that the second house was empty, but the third one was occupied with four guards in the front room, no others. She signals to move to the empty house and scout the rest.

"Everyone, we're moving to the second house in that row. It's empty, and Alpha is closing on it. These houses will need to be handled carefully. Storming them sequentially might be overheard. We'll check the rest in the row and plan accordingly."

She leads the team out and back around the side of the town hall, now confident they can move about in the open as there is no one on this side who can see them, at least until they reach the end of the building. She gives a command to cast cloaks again and they proceed up to their new waypoint.

Moments later, one by one, the scouts return from the remaining houses in the row. There were two more with guards, and observations found one with a civilian.

"Good, this is it," she utters softly. "We need to move really carefully here. There are three houses with guards out there: We'll number them Three, Four and Six. Five is empty. Four has the hostage. I want a careful search around the perimeter for possible openings. She's apparently in the rear bedroom, which is dangerous, because there's only one door. Storming that door will trigger the guards, and she's gone."

"How do we handle this, Lieutenant? There are two guards in front, and two in the rear watching the hostage."

"We may have to hit from multiple sides. But let's get the report first."

A scout casts his cloak and runs outside to make another review of the fourth house. When he had his survey ready, he returned to report.

"Lieutenant," he calls. "We have guards in the front room and the rear bedroom, no others in sight in any other room. There is a window on the far side that might be accessible if we're careful. But it's smaller than the one at the town hall. And the close quarters make the entry problematic."

"Hmm, nasty... We need to infiltrate. Is it large enough for the females at least?"

"Barely. We'll need to lift them up so we can stick their legs through and ease them down inside."

"All right, we'll need a couple of strong men for this. They need to be lifted, inserted gently, and set down without any noise. Then they go dark. We'll send two of them inside. The rest go through the front, but only on my mark. We need to get the timing right on this. Beta and Gamma will take houses Three and Six, to clear this zone. We can use conventional bust-and-bash tactics on those."

They break the group, and each squad goes their own way, casting cloaks to sneak up to their intended targets. Kaliya moves around to the window on house Four to reconvene with Alpha Squad. Once again, she examines the window and tries using her blade to gently push up the locking hook, then carefully swinging open the windowpanes.

The room appeared as a washroom. She peeked inside to see if anything was near the window, but the immediate space was empty. She called up two females for the maneuver, and two males to do the lifting. The males took the first one at both sides, gripping her at the shoulder and supporting her at the hip. She had to keep her body rigid to fit through the opening until her legs were through and she could bend down to the floor again. Once she felt solid ground, she was able to reorient herself to a standing position. She checked the door behind her, but no one was observing.

The next one was lifted and inserted the same way, with the first female assisting with the feet. When she was in place, they both cast cloaks on themselves.

Kaliya made a gesture with her hands for the two women to count to ten on her signal, and to the rest of the squad going to the front door to count to twelve, two seconds longer for an offset. Beta and Gamma were informed to time theirs when they see Alpha going in. When everyone was in position, Kaliya made another action gesture, the open hand curling to a fist and pulling down.

The two women inside moved to the other room, lining up with their targets while the squads made ready at the front doors. As the count ran out, the women inside struck at their targets, gripping them by the head, pulling them in, and jabbing them with their practice daggers. An instant later, the other squads barged through the front doors to finish the rest.

Kaliya made her entrance to the house to examine their work. The hostage was sitting in a chair in the rear room, her two oppressors now lying motionless on the floor. The other guards were similarly inert.

The hostage was a wood elf in noble attire as her costume for the occasion. When she saw Kaliya enter, she stood up and applauded her achievement.

"Nicely done, Lieutenant," she praises. "This example is actually one of the more difficult at your level for this final stage. If I could tell you how many times I've been killed by these guards because the previous squads did not engage this step correctly..." she giggles.

"Thank you," Kaliya smiles. "But you might want to hold that thought until you brief some of the others we took down."

"Oh, did you experience trouble?"

"Me? Not a bit. Them? Oh yes, they never saw it coming. But we're still not out of it. I want to see this all the way back to the starting point."

"Very well, but at this moment, I doubt it's truly necessary."

Kaliya nods and leads them out to the front room again.

"Alpha, send out a few scouts under cloak to check those buildings along the way, just to be sure nothing has changed in this time. They might try throwing a curve at us."

The scouts go into their cloaks once more as Kaliya begins leading her charge back to the captain to receive her score.

"Angan, ye know if we get caught in this, the Thane will ne'er let us hear the end of it."

"Brother, we need t' be a-knowin' the truth of it. If we be wrong, we be wrong, but at least we'll know the better of it. But if we be right, the Thane will be the last worry on me mind."

"Aye then, but we should be grandly careful. We be only a step away from breakin' his rule here."

"Aye, mayhap, but have ye ever seen any guards on those doors afore now?"

"Nay, actually, for a set of doors leadin' t' the outside where our foes should have found us so long ago."

Angan and two of his fellows from their meeting earlier in a local tavern, were making their way through the city towards the storeroom used by the forge smiths to store the ingots made for the alleged trade with the surface. This action was in response to their discussion of the odd anomalies and inconsistencies between the various stories being passed around the city over the course of their history, combined with the more recent rumors being generated by Eiki and her friend Telta as part of their service to Thaelyn and his interaction.

Angan was Telta's husband, and he was recruited into service to assist in spreading these rumors into the local taverns to other patrons, as a means of getting the word out and raising suspicions.

They made their way along the road, casually walking along as a group, trying not to draw attention. They arrived outside the alley that led to the door of the storeroom. Angan directs the others to stop and wait for the people to clear from the immediate area.

"Now, lads," he whispers to the group. "We do this grandly

careful. If the Thane's tales be true, we have nay a worry. But if they be a lie…"

"Aye," responds another. "We could find ourselves in a deep mire of trouble."

Angan leads the others along the alley, checking one more time to be sure no one was looking, and carefully opens the door. The room beyond appeared empty, and so they entered and closed the door behind them.

"Good then," Angan announces. "Here be the store where the smiths drop the bricks. It looks well enough as a store."

"Aye, an' over there be the way out," directs the first party member. "D' ye think we should poke our noses through t' sniff the air?"

"I nay be t' thinkin' we came in here just t' turn back after seein' the store."

"Aye, but we should go slow an' careful."

"Aye t' that."

They make their way across the room to the door leading into the spiral stairs travelling up. At first, they creep along, not knowing how far they need to go to find the exit.

"Great All-Father, how long be this stair!" groans the second member.

"It be a long one, t' be sure!" responds the first member.

"We must be deeper than we thought if this be the way out."

"I nay be t' recallin' just how much we dug, but the tales nay did make it seem this far."

They increased their rate of climb, since it seemed to be taking so long, until finally they saw a door ahead.

"There now," Angan calls gently. "We be a-comin' up t' it. Move slow here."

They cautiously approached the exit. Angan lifted the latch and slowly pulled the door open to peek outside.

Angan already knew what was waiting out there. His wife, Telta, told him the story as related by Eiki about the road and the Suuden-Aryku. His purpose here was not to share it directly with the others, only to suggest something other than the common stories being spread around the city, so they could come here and make their own discovery. The revelations had to go in steps, and this was the first one. It was risky, but it had to be done in order to override the stories by the Thane.

The three of them peered through the door, the first time any citizen from the city, aside from Eiki in recent times, had set eyes into the open light in centuries. Angan and his group saw a strange road apparently winding around a mountainside.

"This nay be a-lookin' like the way t' any field of battle," comments the first party member.

"Aye," remarks the second member as he steps outside to see further into the open. "An' we nay be anywhere on the ground out here. Look, lads, an' see where we be now!"

The three of them emerge fully from the corridor onto the road. They found themselves standing on a neatly cut road high on the side of the mountain.

"Blessed be, lads. Where did this take us?"

"Nay t' any front gate, an' nay t' any war. Look down there," he points into the valley below.

From their vantage, they could just make out portions of the outer city of Glimmerheim, or what was left of it, seen in the distance below.

"Lads, can ye see anything clear down there?" offers the first member. "T' me own eyes, it looks t' be nay more than rubble."

"If that be the outer city, then Angan was right. It was burnt an' smashed, but from the looks of it, that yay be a long while ago!"

"What about this road? Why d' we have a road up on the side of a mountain?"

Angan turns to look along the road. He directs them to slowly creep up to the nearest bend curving around a crag, then into view of the tunnel further along the way.

"Look there!" calls the first member. "What be that tunnel about?"

"'Tis a big one, t' be sure. Grand wide an' tall ..."

"Mayhap we can take a closer look?"

"Mayhap so, but mayhap we be a-steppin' in t' a bad place, methinks."

"Lads," Angan suggests. "We can take a wee peek up close, but ye're right. Seein' that tunnel nay be a-givin' me a good feel."

He leads them up to the opening of the tunnel to inspect the design of it. They examine the smooth concrete walls and perfect curvature.

"Lads," Angan asserts. "Recall what I said before. The tales are the point-ears nay be good diggers. Now, four centuries can teach, but this nay be anythin' like dwarven make, either. An' I might say we be some of the best."

"Then who?" asks the first member. "If it nay be the point-ears, and nay any of us..."

Chills began tingling through their skin at the potential answers.

"This tunnel here be high an' wide," Angan declares. "D' any of us make such as this? What about the point-ears? Be they as tall as this? Mayhap if ye have a grand wagon, but it would yay have t' be double-tall t' call for this."

"Aye."

"Ye know, this brings a few thoughts t' me mind right off. Firstly, where d' ye think this goes? Here we be, way up here, nay on the barrens where ye have the cities an' towns that are s'posed t' be a-burnin'. Did someone build a new city up here? An' if so, how d' they get down below t' fight anythin'? This nay can hold any proper reason."

"I'll agree with ye, Angan. This nay fits together right of a war down there."

"Now, if we say it goes t' our people, an' if we say they have another way down, this yay be fine an' good. BUT, yay or nay t' this, if this be a secret pass t' a camp of any kind..." he pauses for emphasis to study the tunnel again. "If it were me, I'd put a watch inside, just t' see if anyone be a-comin' through, friend or foe."

"Aye!" the second member affirms strongly. "An' it could lead t' a mound of trouble for those who pass through! Even if they be friends, the Thane still forbids it, an' HE would be the trouble here."

"Hold now," the first one issues. "The Thane forbids it, aye. But forbids it for what reason. If we have warriors out here fightin', these are our kinfolk we be a-speakin' of, ay? D' we say he forbids us t' meet with our own kin now? The same kin we send up so much Adamant t' help fight? That yay be a gnarly way t' give thanks for all our sufferin'."

"Ye're right! This here be a right grand hole, an' nay a nice one at that. An' this nay gives us t' know HOW they fight, if this be way up here on top of the mountain."

"An' using bricks, nay more, just bricks."

"Aye!"

"An' if nay a friend," the first member continues. "Our trouble could be they who own the place an' built this strange tunnel."

"Aye, an' right on top of our home!" the other man yelps.

Angan steps away from the tunnel to observe the valley below. The other men follow his direction.

"An' feel the air out here, lads," he observes. "The tales say the war was a-blazin', ay? If that be true, the world may be burnt by now, an' this air feels hot t' me. But I nay be a-seein' any fires blazin' down there, so methinks the world got burnt long ago, an' it has'na settled yet. And then we have this," he directs at the tunnel. "Think now, lads. I recall tales of the old days, the point-ears were said t' be sickly an' weak. D' ye recall that?"

"Aye, in the beginnin', but then we all thought that changed somehow."

"Changed so they can burn up every city out there? Changed t' also dig better, yet nay be any trouble for us under the mountain?"

The other two dwarves stare at each other while Angan prepares his next suggestion.

"If that down below be the remains of the outer city, we were found long ago an' hit hard for it. How hard can it be t' find the doors if ye already pummeled the city proper? An' then we have this tunnel made by nay any hand we can figure. If we say the point-ears nay be good diggers, an' even if they learned a thing or two, this be better than us!"

"Aye, verily."

"An' if nay them at all, an' nay by us, then we have someone new here. Mayhap the tales of sickly point-ears be only a part of it. There be nay anythin' else, only those old tales, told an' retold. Somethin' blasted that down there, an' so long ago that time be a-buryin' it now. I see holes in the ground, nay burnt buildin's. So, unless ye now want t' tell me those sickly point-ears hit us with somethin' explodin', which is a wee bit different from simply burnin' things, I say somethin' else followed after. An' if they can dig a tunnel this wide an' this clean, I nay be a-wantin' t' see what else they can make. An' clearly, they know where we live," he points back at the door.

"But then, what d' we say about the war?" asks the first member.

"Aye," the second member adds. "An' what about the bricks? An' the men goin' up t' serve the fare?"

"That room down there," Angan mentions. "There be only one way out, an' this be it. I be a-thinkin' now whatever waits at the end of this tunnel be the answer, but I nay be a warrior if they be foes t' us. Ye're right, if the Thane forbids us even t' say thanks t' our own kin, if they be the ones. So, this reeks of somethin' else, an' nay our kin. Bricks, aye, nay the proper fare for a war. But bricks are easy t' carry, if ye want a lot of them."

"Oh grand, Angan… Thieves?"

"Aye!" the first one huffs. "An' such a fine one, that. They take our most precious Adamant an' give us back nay more than simple wood an' coal for the Thane's cauldrons. Such a fine trade that be!"

"But it yay can offer a new idea or two," Angan offers. "The way t' the ground be the other side here. This goes behind the mountain. An' since there nay be a word t' say otherwise of it, I be a-thinkin' the tales be a lie. An' now I ask ye, who be the one a-tellin' those tales, ay? A man who ne'er goes outside, t' the best of our knowin', but still calls for the bricks an' the feast. An' if they can only come up here…" he casts off into the tunnel for emphasis.

"I nay be t' arguin' this," offers the first member. "But methinks it yay be better if we can see a wee bit more t' answer these questions, afore goin' out an' makin' a big rousin' for it."

"Aye," the second one agrees. "I nay want t' travel this tunnel just yet. It nay be a-smellin' right t' me. Look up top there. D' ye see that long glowin' rod thing stuck t' the roof?"

The group looks up at one of the nearby lighting fixtures, which in this case resembles a long fluorescent tube fixture, which is completely alien to their knowledge base.

"Aye, I ne'er seen such like that afore. We dwarves don'na have such a thing, nay down below. An' if it be point-ears, that looks yay like it would take a fair bit of knowin' t' make a stick that glows for ye in a tunnel so round, an' so neatly cuttin' through the mountain. Diggers, yay or nay... Point-ears, yay or nay... This nay be a place t' visit for now. I think mayhap I would like t' see just how the Thane knows what be a-happenin' up here first. Start with that, it may be a bit safer for now."

"Aye..." Angan considers while offering up a pause. "But if he be the only true friend t' these folk..."

Angan didn't want to argue this point, but he also didn't want anyone simply to go right up to the Thane and start asking questions when he's not supposed to know what they're doing. He needed an excuse to satisfy the need, but also to remain discreet.

"Wait. Think on this here, lads," he submits. "Follow me with an idea. The Thane calls for bricks an' more bricks, ay? We'll give him a small glimmer of right an' try this now. Nay speakin' of this here, does he ever ask if the people have enough food? Does he ever ask if we have good clothes on our backs? Does he ever ask if our shops make enough coin an' the people livin' their lives as good folk in such a proud city? Nay. We think he makes trade for his cauldrons, but does he make trade for food an' cloth from all those herders an' weavers we heard so much of once upon a tale? Look at yer clothes. Look at mine! Even with the world bein' ablaze with point-ears, he still fills his cauldrons with somethin' that nay even be necessary for our folk down there."

"Aye," the first one relents. "That nay be a very considerate thing."

"Aye! An' then he forbids us t' see this up here, what we s'pose t' be our kin fightin' a war, but on top of a mountain lookin' out on a dead land, an' usin' nay more than bricks. If they be so close t' us in the city that we could simply walk up here t' give them armor an' axes, why d' they need bricks. Even if this tunnel goes t' a camp with all our men smithin' up the fares, it seems a waste that we nay be a-makin' the same down below an' savin' them the trouble for the walk."

"He has a point," the second man nods. "Bricks or fare, that walk still be just a walk."

"An' so," Angan continues. "He calls for bricks, nay the more. An' he ne'er seems happy for what he gets. He simply yowls for more. Then he yowls for even more after that. What sort of mind does that suggest t' ye for a man s'posed t' be a-runnin' the affairs of our great city?"

The other two stop and gaze at each other sternly. The clear implications didn't fare well for a caring soul you might want to go up to looking for answers.

Angan continues, "If the Thane be a-tellin' a big lie, then we don'na want t' go straight up t' him with what we think, especially if he be in league with whatever waits at the end of this tunnel. If all he cares for are bricks, we need t' ask ourselves why. Who built this tunnel with such a nice back door t' our home?"

"Worse!" the second man notes. "One we ne'er knew about, and he ne'er tells us about."

"Then, why is the outer city pummeled an' by what, an' then why not barge in through the doors that were clearly in view? Did any of ye ever see guards protectin' us from anythin'? All we have are tales of diggin' deep an' boom, we be safe from somethin', while everythin' else burned…or was pummeled," he looks over his shoulder at the ruins below.

"Then what ye're sayin'," the first man offers tepidly, "tells that he be a thief, as well as a liar. An' whoever made this tunnel be the ones takin' our bricks he rages for so much."

"An' if this be so," Angan nods. "He would be the LAST one ye'd want t' go up t' askin' questions of what he be a-makin' out here.

If whoever made this tunnel also did the pummelin', an' they clearly know where we live…" he trails off.

"Aye," the first man relents. "More pummelin', but this time, whatever be left of the city."

"But wait!" the second man asserts. "What about the men? Where d' they go an' what for?"

"Servin' up a fare, so he says," the first one growls. "So, what sort of fare be it, if all he wants are bricks? If the world be burnt already, where be those point-ears said t' be a-ragin' all across the land? I nay can see any plumes of smoke from burnin' cities, can ye? An' if they hit us already, why d' we nay see them inside the city by now?"

"Oh grand! So, I s'pose we say they're sent out t' make up more bricks, ay? But then, why don'na they ever write back, or d' we simply say they're prevented from it?"

"Mayhap. But then we should also ask about the feast. He keeps a-callin' for it."

"Only the one by now, so mayhap the one mine ran out? But then…" he pauses in brief thought. "Well, wait, that nay be right. It goes every year, man!" he shouts. "Where d' all those men go if he be a-callin' for bricks? Even if we say they be a-goin' out t' other mines, d' ye think he has so many of them out there, or be it somethin' else swallowin' them up?"

"Lads," Angan declares, trying to contain the outbreak before it gets out of control. "The first thought t' me mind, afore we go wild up here, may be t' see about a few of our own answers. This tunnel, if they be foes, he be a foe also. Better t' keep it quiet an' check around in whispers. If we be wrong, fine, nay a one will know of it, an' we can save our own skin from the Thane's ragin'. But if we should find somethin' t' tell us the truth, an' we be right, the Thane would be a villain of the worst sort for all the lies he be a-tellin', t' say nothin' about the rest of it. Mayhap the first thing t' d' should be a wee bit of askin' t' see if any of this can be answered in a slight way."

"But Angan!" growls the first member. "Who d' we ask this about? Every citizen in the city believes these tales told by the Thane. Who might there be t' d' any askin' at all?"

"Hold a wee bit," the second member offers. "What about the Chancellor? The Thane rages at him every time he walks in t' the Hall. If this be a way of knowin', mayhap he nay be a part of it. D' ye think we can trust him enough t' try talkin' t' him?"

"Mayhap we can," Angan suggests. "An' mayhap I can try. I can go at it slow an' easy t' see what he knows, an' if I feel he be worth our trust, I'll go a wee bit more."

"Fine then, Angan," the first member relents. "Mayhap this can be a fair start. But I have a cravin' now t' go diggin' through the upper town t' see what be out there. Did I see what looked like an old door on the side down there in the store?"

"Um, aye, if just barely," the second member considers. "I think I saw it, but it was filled with rubble."

"Then we should clean it out an' see where it goes! I nay be a-wantin' t' live under a mountain with nay a way out."

Chapter 7

COMING TO
CONCLUSIONS

"Chancellor, d' ye have a moment for a wee bit of kind talkin'?"

"A wee bit, aye. The pressures of this post be a-wearin' hard on me. I keep askin' me'self, time an' again, why did I take this work."

"The tales say the Thane rages at ye every time ye go in t' see him. Be it true?"

"Aye, every time… It wears on me poor nerves. What be yer name, good friend?"

"Me name be Angan Gemhand, a good greetin' t' ye, Chancellor."

Angan was making a visit to the Chancellery, which resided down the street from the Thane's Hall. He was following up on the little adventure he and his two cohorts made through the spiral stair up to the roadside the day before. He knew the details of the world outside, due to his wife and Eiki informing him, but he was going to play it slow to test the Chancellor to see what he knew, if anything.

The Chancellor was an aged man sitting at his desk in his office, busy sorting through a series of tablets, which is what they used to record the details of the city affairs. Paper was unknown in this environment, since the materials needed to make it were generally unavailable.

"Aye t' that, Angan," replies the Chancellor. "What be it ye need from me today?"

"There be a few odd tales whisperin' in the streets. Some folks be a-wonderin' the truth of it, but since so many still be a-thinkin' the ways of the old tellin', there nay be a sure way t' know what t' think of this. Mayhap ye know of somethin' t' answer these whispers, since ye be so close t' the Thane?"

"I nay even be a-knowin' what ye're talkin' about, friend Angan. The only thing I know be the Thane demandin' more bricks t' serve the fare above. He nay ever can be happy with what we have."

"An' what about the men we send up from the feast? D' any of them ever write back with word from above?"

"Nay that I ever did hear. I've asked him afore, but the Thane says they be a-makin' the fare, an' then he orders nay more t' be askin' about it."

"Hmm, that sounds a wee bit like he don'na care much for the lonely women left behind, an' I know there be a good many of those by now."

"Aye, I did think of this a time or two."

"So, he ne'er tells ye why we need t' be a-sendin' up more every year, when so many were sent up before? How many d' ye think there be by now?"

"I ne'er did actually count it. But aye, it would be a fair few by now."

"An' then we drop the bricks in the store for the warriors above t' pick up, but d' ye know where they actually go? Did ye ever see who picks them up?"

The Chancellor had been studying one of the tablets on his desk during most of this conversation, only dividing his attention casually with his visitor. At this mention, he redirected himself fully at Angan.

"What be it ye're tryin' t' say here, Angan? What be these new whispers ye be a-talkin' about?"

"Old tales, Chancellor, some of them go back t' me father an' his father. Mayhap ye know a few already."

"Aye, me father told me many of the same tales as methinks the rest of ye got. What about it?"

"For one, how can we be a-sendin' up bricks an' men t' serve the fare when some people say the doors be closed an' the upper town be smashed. This would yay be a good place t' start."

"T' start? There be more?" he muses as he sets the tablet down. "What more be there then?"

"Chancellor, what d' ye really know about the tales of old? Did ye ever ask questions on how they all fit together?"

"Fit together..." he ponders. "Angan, ye're nay t' makin' a lot of sense here. Help me t' understand what ye mean."

"Oh come now. Ye sound like the average soul on the street out there. How d' ye move anythin' through a closed door, be it men or bricks. Closed, Chancellor. That means ye can'na move anythin' through it, unless ye can somehow open it again. An' these were locked at one time, so it be said."

"Um, well, aye. I s'pose ye have a point."

"The tales say the doors were closed when the Thane made the city dig deep t' get away from the point-ears. This be one. Some say they think the upper town was smashed, though nay a one, t' me knowin', ever saw it with their own eyes. This be another. Then the smiths make the bricks an' drop them in the store for someone t' come pick up an' take t' the war outside...through closed doors an' a smashed town. So we need t' ask...how."

The Chancellor considers this notion a moment before answering.

"But friend Angan, there yay be a door in there. I did see it with me own eyes as I was tallyin' the bricks many a time."

"Fine, but did ye ever go up t' see where it leads? I still be a-thinkin' of the tales of the closed doors leadin' t' the outside, nay a small one leadin' out of a store. An' more, if t' say we closed the doors to bar off the point-ears outside, this be t' say we closed THE doors, nay just one set, but the ONLY doors. I ne'er heard of a back door leading out of a store t' anywhere outside afore."

"Aye, this yay does sound a wee bit odd, ye be right t' that. An' nay, I ne'er did follow it out. Me work was only t' tally up the bricks, but I know the bricks are bein' picked up by someone, since the store be empty now an' again."

"But nay a soul sees who it be a-comin' t' empty it? Fine, but now, what say ye t' this one? We send out the bricks for so long a time, an' our city be said t' be a right grand one, such that ye can probably nay miss it sittin' out in the open…an' sendin' out so many a fine fare for so long. If the land were a-blazin' for so many point-ears ragin' everywhere else, why d' we nay see them ragin' through that same door that leads outside, an' where we set down nay less than Adamant bricks?"

The Chancellor jerked back in his chair with a sudden chill running down his back. This one simple revelation did hold a serious note of contradiction. Regardless of anything else, this metal was a precious resource. Enough to make it worth stealing.

Angan continues, "Next would be this one… What then d' ye say about the men? The feast calls them up t' serve the fare, ay?"

"Aye…" he replies concernedly.

"They go up an' leave their wives here all alone, ay?"

"Aye…" the Chancellor now leans forward on his table, becoming even more troubled for the subject matter.

"An' now, good Chancellor, if there be people from above, as ye say, workin' this same fare, comin' t' pick up the bricks, why be there nay a single word from these men t' their wives t' give them a fair greetin' in all this time? Note that I say IF there be our people up there."

"If…?" he yips.

The Chancellor perks up in his chair, casting his glance unconsciously around the room as he ponders the suggestion in deep thought.

"Four hundred years, Chancellor," Angan asserts. "That yay be a long while for nay a single smith t' write even a single note."

"But d' ye know for sure it be nay a single note in four hundred years?"

"Well, best I can say would be for those of us who know of it in recent times, those wives who still be alive t' tell of it. An' this tells me, if nay a one ever got a note in their lifetime, mayhap it be this way from the beginnin'."

"Well, mayhap…but…"

"Let me ask ye another one," Angan interjects. "The tales say we have a war ragin' over us. By the wild tellin' of it, it makes a man think the whole world be a-blazin' by now."

"Aye, he does say every city an' town be a-burnin'."

"An' this tale has been a-runnin' through the streets, one way or another, for four hundred years, tellin' of cities an' towns burnin', an' point-ears rampagin' across the land without end."

"Aye, this as well."

"Now, let me take this in two directions for ye t' think about. One, we make trade for our wares. An' I will say it again, this be for nay less than Adamant, which yay be a right worthy thing t' trade, such that our fair city should be a-swimmin' in fine wares as our payment, d' ye think?"

"That would surely seem fair."

"An' yet, all we get be wood an' coal for the Thane's cauldrons, nay more than that. Nay any new clothes, good food, an' other treasures t' make our people happy."

"Well, um…"

"An' worse, if the world above be a-burnin' so hot, where d' ye get it from? The forests may be burnt by now, an' who would spend time diggin' up coal if their homes be a-burnin'?"

"Ugh…ye're right!"

"But then, if ye recall the early tellin', Chancellor, the first stories said these point-ears were a sickly lot, d' ye recall that one?"

"Aye, that one be an old tale. But now, friend Angan, d' ye have somethin' new t' tell, because this old head already be a-spinnin' 'round more than I need for all the ragin' I get from the Thane."

"Chancellor, I don'na mean t' put more on ye, but it should be quite easy t' figure, if only a man would put his right mind t' it, instead of listenin' t' so much wild tellin' with nay a scrap of proof t' show for it. We're ne'er allowed t' peek outside t' see it, an' we ne'er hear word of it from the outside, other than what the Thane claims for himself. So, how can we say any of it t' be true?"

"Wait now, Angan! Are ye tryin' t' say he be a-lyin' here?"

"Oh, I can go more than that! Let me ask ye this, an' then ye tell me what ye think. Did he ever ask about how our food be a-farin'? Or mayhap if we have good clothes t' wear, mayhap even if we have enough coin t' pay for ourselves? He be a-tradin' for somethin' up top, but what be it he makes trade for with all our most precious Adamant, if nay more than wood for his blessed cauldrons? Did he ever show himself up as a man who actually cared for the people here? Ye just now told me he forbids ye even t' ask about the men sendin' word back t' their pretties. This nay be a kind thing of him…as our Thane. Now ask yerself. Where d' ye think our Adamant goes if he forbids ye even t' ask about it, or any of us t' go outside t' check on things. An' those point-ears he claims t' be a-ragin' all across the land, which should include right down here through that door he forbids us t' go through t' see it."

The Chancellor now felt that chilled rush turning to a frigid spike. These words were painting a rather bold picture.

"Ye speak of him tellin' lies," Angan continues. "But did ye ever see him go for a walk outside? Or one of those phantom people visitin' the store go up t' his private chambers that nay a soul here ever be allowed t' knock on for even a wee talk? The only time he yay be seen outside be t' rage at YE, Chancellor, nay anythin' else. Some may even ask when he calls for his food, if he nay ever be seen outside simply t' eat. So, where does HE get his tales?"

"Nay ever simply t' eat?" the Chancellor muses softly. "But a man needs t' eat on occasion…"

The Chancellor was quickly realizing the error in the logic of the statement. He had to admit to himself, the Thane was never seen outside the Hall, and never conducting any other meeting outside his own. He lowers his head and covers his face for the misplay.

Angan continues, "Now think. The point-ears were said nay t' be good fighters or diggers, as they were sickly an' weak. I recall it said t' be like a mercy killin', nay a proper war. So, d' we say we dug deep t' get away from folk who were sickly an' weak?"

"I can'na say for sure if that be the way of it, but the Thane tells now they be a-ragin' everywhere, so in me mind, they grew stronger, ay?"

"Aye, if this be all ye have t' play with, mayhap…in all this time. So, then we need t' ask this. If they grew stronger in four hundred years, could they also learn t' dig better? An' this brings us right back t' them findin' us for all the Adamant an' men we send out. How hard can it be t' miss if they be everywhere up there? The Thane does'na seem t' be a-makin' a great amount of sense if he be a-tryin' t' convince us we're nay in trouble down here with an unguarded door leadin' t' the outside, an' with so many precious goods goin' through it."

The Chancellor was now clearly disturbed. He slowly shook his head as his hands fell into his lap.

"Aye, ye're right. I nay can argue it."

"I might also say, an' this would surely stand out, that as a dwarf, a man who should know the strength an' value of Adamant, that ye don'na bring down a sturdy warrior wearin' this in battle, an' neither d' ye let it go for such trifles as his wood an' coal, no matter if there be a war or nay t' that. We still need our payment for our work. An' Adamant don'na run out that quick. Ye might have suits of it that get passed down from father t' son, an' it still holds up."

"Aye! I've surely heard this much. Though nay in me own family. We be more the merchants and clerks a-workin' the offices, like this one."

"Fine t' that, I be a shopkeeper, me'self. But I know enough t' say ye don'na run through it like what he be a-tryin' t' claim. So, it makes me wonder where he got his schoolin'.'"

"His schoolin'? Hmm… Aye, this would be a good one t' ask."

"An' so, Chancellor," Angan continues. "How much d' ye really need t' fight a war against sickly an' weak folk, no matter how much they be a-ragin' in four hundred years against sturdy warriors who know how t' use it. An' then, if t' say EVERY city an' town be a-burnin', what does that say for where those warriors be a-comin' from, t' say nothin' of what be left of it in this time."

The Chancellor could feel a headache coming on, and he laid his palms against his temples trying to hold it back while still shaking his head at the ridiculous reasoning.

"An' finally," Angan concludes. "I nay have anythin' against ye as a man, but ye be the one in charge of a lot of responsibility here. An' yet, ye be a-listenin' t' a man weavin' so many wild tales, an' for so long a time, that he be a-leavin' a great many holes behind by now. It makes ye wonder how many times his tales have changed, simply t' keep folk like us buried as we are, an' nay t' askin' the questions we had t' ask long ago."

"Angan, I nay can give ye an answer t' all this, but I wish I could. All I know be what the Thane tells me, an' his ragin' makes me head pound. Now here ye be with more of it, an' what ye say makes good sense, but nay at all what he says."

"Then we find ourselves goin' back t' the beginnin'. He be a-lyin' t' us."

This caused the Chancellor to perk up sharply.

"Angan, he be the Thane, ye know."

"Aye, which makes it all the worse. A Thane. Him? Pah. A Thane nay be a god, Chancellor. He be a man, an' no less one who can lie than a burglar in a dark alley. But if ye wanted t' fool a lot of folk with yer wild tales, an' especially t' steal Adamant, who d' ye dress up like t' d' it best?"

The Chancellor glared alarmingly at Angan.

Angan continues, "Who was his father? Who be his son? Where did he come from an' how long ago? D' we have any records of the Thanes t' show his family?"

"Ehm, actually, aye! But, well..." he hesitates.

"An' how long have ye sat in this office?" Angan interjects. "How long have ye been listenin' t' his yowlin' in yer lifetime? An' then, how old d' ye think he be a-sittin' on that throne, an' then put these two together."

"Put them together?" he ponders unexpectedly. "I, ehm...well,

I've been here for a good long part of me life, since me father passed on. But..." he frowns suddenly.

"In our culture, the position of Thane be a fine an' proper place for a man, demandin' of honor an' respect by the people. An' we give ourselves t' it, trustin' the man for all he be entitled, simply for his throne. An' yet, if a Thane should ever disrespect his own place, he brings dishonor t' it, t' say nothin' of the people who look up t' it. After all, he yay be still a man, an' this one nay seems t' have a proper history or kinship t' hold claim t' it."

"Aye! An' made worse that I nay ever saw a change t' a new one in me lifetime, an' nay me father's. An' he looks t' be half me age!"

"Oh grand! An' here we have one thing we CAN prove. He sits on that chair for longer than ye've been sittin' in yers? An' then he rages at ye for one thing or another, forcin' it down yer throat, which be t' say forcin' it down all OUR throats. He denies us t' go up an' see it for ourselves, which only forces it down harder, as HE be the only one t' tell the tales, nay anyone else with hard proof t' show for it."

"All-Father help us, Angan, but I can'na argue with ye. But what ye say can yay be a dangerous thing if ye be a-thinkin' of goin' against our city's rule here."

"Oh please, Chancellor. A rule that does'na seem t' care for the health of our citizens? A rule that sends our men up with nay a word comin' back that they still be alive out there? An' more every year, the same? That nay be a very kind rule, Chancellor. Nay the sort I would want t' follow t' begin with. The same with a lot of folks. He be but ONE Thane, an' he don'na even employ a guard of any kind. How thoughtful of him in a time of war."

"Aye..." he sighs. "But what be it ye're tryin' t' say here? Be ye thinkin' of goin' against him?"

"Directly?" he muses as if in thought. "Nay me directly. If there be any sort of law here, I'll let that deal with him. But methinks that law will want t' see the proof first. What I can say of it be for a few new tales passin' through the streets out there. Folks are tired of listenin' t' the Thane rage about somethin' when we nay should even be here by now. We have a door leadin' t' somewhere, but be it t' the outside, with so many point-ears ownin' the land by now that they should be a-chargin' through that same door t' finish us in here?"

The Chancellor considered the suggestion as he tried to reflect on his lifetime experience of absolutely no activity of any kind threatening the city.

"Nay any of the men ever write back," Angan charges. "But someone DOES come t' pick up the bricks. So, who be it, if nay any of our men bringin' home notes, or any other word of the war outside, especially if it be such a grand scene t' match the Thane's tales?"

The Chancellor frowns sternly at the suggestion, as this made perhaps more sense than anything else. News of anything as serious as the war should be coming from all directions, especially those on the front lines as they report into the city.

"Where does that other door go in there," Angan asks. "D' ye know?"

"Nay me, I only tally the bricks, an' then leave. The Thane forbids goin' through that other door."

"Well, Chancellor, if the only way t' know of the outside be t' go through that door, mayhap ye should. If he be a-lyin' t' us about anythin', the truth of it be out there."

"Angan, d' YE know somethin' about all this? Because by yer tellin', I get the idea ye may."

"What I know nay be the question. It be what YE know, an' then have t' learn if ye nay know of it. Ye need t' see it, Chancellor. Me words are nay any good here."

"Have ye actually been through that door?"

"Mayhap…"

"An' now ye want me t' go through it."

"Aye, if ye please. If ye be true t' our kinfolk, nay the Thane an' his wild tellin', ye'll go look, an' then know the truth. I'll even go with ye an' hold yer hand if ye be so scared," he smirks.

"I nay be scared, Angan, just weary from me work an' all the ragin' I get."

"I nay want t' rage at ye, Chancellor, but if ye want t' know the truth of anythin', sometimes ye have t' stand up an' go look at it. An' by yer tellin', the Thane forbids all of it."

"Aye, ye're right..."

The Chancellor pulls himself together and gets up from the chair, trying to straighten his attire along the way. He steps around in front of his desk and pauses briefly.

"What did ye see out there, Angan?" he asks tenderly.

"Chancellor, I would tell ye, but ye still need t' see it for yerself, an' it nay be anythin' like what the Thane describes. After we go up, I'll tell ye what I know."

"What ye know...meanin' t' say ye know somethin' about the Thane, mayhap? About what be a-happenin' out there, mayhap?"

"Mayhap. Come, good Chancellor. We'll go for a wee walk. Ye spend too much time sittin' at that desk."

"I nay be the young fellow like I once was," he chuckles faintly.

The two of them leave the office and strolled down the lane to the alley, then up to the door. They entered the room to find several other dwarves digging out the blockaded exit on the side of the room.

"What be this here now?" the Chancellor asks alarmingly.

"Several of us have learned of it by now," Angan confirms. "An' we nay be a-wantin' t' live under a mountain with nay a way out. If the Thane says the doors be closed, but somehow, he can trade wares with the outside, this nay be the one. So, we be a-diggin' our way out t' see what it looks like. The view from the other side nay be what ye think."

"Angan, should I ask about the Thane in all this? What d' ye think he would say t' it?"

"Nothin' good, that much I can be sure of. But then, when was the last time he ever said anythin' good?" he chuckles. "Chancellor, think on this a bit. If he be a-lyin' t' us, d' ye think he would WANT us out there lookin' for the truth? An' then, if this be the way of it, would ye WANT t' tell him what ye found?"

"I don'na know how t' answer that. Show me the rest, an' I'll give ye me thoughts about it."

Angan leads the Chancellor through the door leading through

the spiral stairs. The two of them work their way along until they eventually reach the door at the top.

"Great All-Father," the Chancellor exclaims. "Who built that! We were a-goin' straight up, nay t' the outer city!"

"Aye t' that, Chancellor, that be a gnarly stair, if ye ask me. But now, what d' ye think lay beyond this door?"

"After that stair, I nay can think of anythin', 'cept mayhap the top of the mountain."

The Chancellor opens the door and peeks outside. He sees a road stretching out along the side of the mountain. He steps outside to examine the scene.

"Angan, why would we have a road up here? I can see the land down there, but nay a way t' get t' it from here."

"Nay unless ye tried t' jump, but I nay have any wings on me."

"An' who made it? This cut in the mountain yay be a right clean one!"

"Aye, I saw that. An' look 'round the bend there."

The Chancellor continues forward around the crag, then to come into view of the tunnel.

"Angan! What be that over yon?" he shouts as he starts rushing up to it.

The Chancellor approached the mouth of the large tunnel and made a close inspection of the work.

"Aye then, Angan, give me a few of yer words on this. This here nay be anythin' like I ever did see afore. Nay any marks, nay from chiselin' or hammerin'. This nay even looks like proper stone t' me."

"I can tell ye it nay be any kind of stone we dwarves would know about. It be somethin' called concrete. It starts out as a slushy mix of sand, gravel, an' a few other things, then set in a mold t' harden, an' it comes out like smooth stone in any shape ye like."

The Chancellor glared at him for the otherworldly explanation.

"An' how d' ye know all this?"

"The tale be a hard one, Chancellor. I'll give ye fair warnin' for it."

"Aye then, yer warnin' yay be heard."

Angan turns towards the valley below and orients on the ruins of the old city.

"Ye see that down there," he points. "That be whatever remains of the old city. It be smashed, burned, pummeled, call it what ye like, but it was long ago, same as everythin' else out there. D' ye feel the air? It feels warm t' the face…too warm, like a world burnt an' still hot from it."

"Aye, I can feel it, an' I think it nay feels good t' me. An' this tunnel?"

"Chancellor, the point-ears were nay the problem for us. What made this tunnel be the problem, an' the point-ears were only a wee part of it t' turn our eyes so we dig deep. We close the doors, mainly t' lock us in, while the real foes built this," he points at the tunnel. "An' then we have the Thane callin' for Adamant bricks, nay any fare for a war of any kind. He only wants bricks. An' it all goes in here," he again points at the tunnel.

"An' who be this real foe? An' then why d' they want bricks? An' also, how d' ye know all this?"

"I know of it because me wife has a friend, an' her friend has a husband who was one of those the Thane sent out on a feast. Nay long ago, she called on me wife, an' me wife called on me t' join up with a tale she received back from the outside. A man, an old farmer from one of the fields out there, found his way in with a message from her husband. According t' this farmer, four centuries ago, the point-ears came an' went in only a hand or two of years, nay more than that. So, for all the tellin' the Thane gives, the folk outside already forgot that tale."

"Forgot it? Then how d' we explain the wreck of the city down there an' this tunnel?"

"Nay long after the last of the point-ears got put down in their mercy killin', a great pummelin' came down on the land. A folk of high an' mighty knowin' from some other world came from the sky an' blasted everythin' t' the All-Father. So, if the Thane says every city an' town be a-burnin', we can say yay…four centuries ago, an' the land still be hot from it. This man said everythin' be a-dyin' out there now."

"Everythin'… An' the cities an' towns?"

"Nothin' but great holes in the land now…our city be the last of it. This folk then built a military base behind us here, an' this tunnel t' the door, an' I s'pose the stair in there. The Thane nay be a dwarf at all, but someone dressed like one of us an' callin' for nay an end of bricks. The men sent out go t' other mines an' d' the same. There nay be any war at all. These folks are stealin' our Adamant from us, an' that be the whole of it, at least from our side."

"From our side… They be a-stealin' it!" he shouts. "That yay be a right fine thing t' steal, four hundred years of it!"

"It could also explain why he cares nay a trifle about any of us down there."

"Aye! An' then t' stop askin' about it. But what be the other side if this be only ours?"

"This friend's husband was found by a folk fightin' a war with these others. This folk here be called Suuden-Aryku, but even though they may be foes, they be also slaves t' a bigger one, made t' d' his work as blindly as we are in the city. We can hate them for stealin' our Adamant, but we need t' know they also suffer for their side against this bigger one."

"An' who be the bigger one?"

"If ye recall the old tales of the Titans, ye need t' know some of them be true. There be one out there, only one by now. The rest are said t' be dead, but this one, he be a nasty one, he an' his servant, who does most of the work. That one be the one t' worry about, an' his name be Darumon. He made all this trouble for us, blastin' the land t' clear out anythin' he did'na want, an' keepin' us buried in a hole. Then he puts this false Thane in there with us screamin' for bricks, an' fillin' us with his wild tellin'. Now, nay long ago, these new folks arrived out there on the barrens."

"Be these the ones ye say are fightin' this war?"

"Aye, they only now found us. It seems Darumon made trouble on another world, an' this be his reward. They be a-chasin' him now.

They found folk like this farmer out there on the barrens, the last few still alive, an' they be a-tryin' t' save them an' move them t' new lands where they can live again. They also found us in the city, an' now they be a-tryin' t' help us, but the Thane NAY can know about it."

"Why?"

"This Darumon an' his master, one called Sargeras, be a-hidin' from some old foes, big like them. This other folk be part of it, an' if they see them comin', they might run an' hide again. We nay be a-wantin' that. We want them t' stay put, so these others can catch them. But if the Thane passes the word, it goes bad."

"Aye, I see it now."

"But the Thane, with all his tellin', be a-feedin' us a great pack of lies. The bricks, the war, even the men."

"Where be the men right now?"

"Chancellor, ye'll nay like the answer."

"Aye then, give it t' me. I think I yay need t' hear it."

"The feast be a lie. It feeds them a kind of poison t' put them under a spell where they nay speak a word, but d' whatever they be told until the poison finally kills them. This be why he keeps callin' for more."

The Chancellor closes his eyes and lets out a soft whine as he drops his head mournfully.

"Dear All-Father, forgive me for this. How could I know?"

"Chancellor, the Thane makes himself look like one of us perfectly. He be part of these folk behind us, with very long lives an' strange talents."

"Long lives? How long?"

"Long enough that he be the first an' only since all this got started."

"Uh huh…an' with nay any family t' pass through. Aye. An' also, by the tellin' of it, he nay be very good at keepin' his tales right!" he growls. "In fact, now that I think of it, he can'na even think t' change his dress in all this time."

"Aye, ye got that right," Angan chuckles. "Now, we should go

back t' yer office. I'll tell ye the rest an' what we be a-tryin' t' d' right now t' help our new friends."

"Cadet, good day to you," the flight instructor announces.

"And to you, Sir," Marelle responds. "Are we making another practice flight today?"

"Yes, we are. On this occasion, we'll conduct another flight pattern with several waypoints and return back to base."

"These flights seem rather simple. We just go up, make a few circles, and then come back down again."

"Maybe so, but you have to start somewhere, and you need the experience in the simpler skills before you go on to the more advanced ones."

"Yeah, I suppose so. I'm just anxious to get started on the combat training."

"I understand, but don't get too anxious. It's not a game, and the mechanics of it will be quite different from the more casual role. You need to become very familiar with all aspects of flying, since you never really know what you'll be doing up there and how it can affect the final result."

"Of course. All right then, so let's get ready."

Marelle and her instructor were preparing for her training exercise in one of the training vessels. She had been promoted to flying actual aircraft by now, although these were the original Daanen-Aryku configurations, not the more advanced combat designs she was discussing with Thaelyn and Chief Technician Lapäli. Still, training is training, and she needed experience no matter what she was flying.

After settling themselves in their seats, she engages the usual power up sequence, which by now was a practiced ritual, powering on the various subsystems, running diagnostics, and checking the monitors for their statistical readouts. When the vessel showed a ready condition on all the indicators, she took hold of her flight stick and slid a finger across the flux field gauge on the forward console to provide vertical lift. She then took hold of the throttle in her other hand and pushed it forward.

The control configuration was the same as in her simulator design, and she felt comfortable with the arrangement based on her previous experience, though she found herself wondering about the new combat design currently being developed at the research center. That one would be very different, and might even require her to start over on some aspects of handling the aircraft.

The concepts being created right now to involve the new technology would likely require a complete remake of the hull design. Just to call it an aircraft would no longer be accurate, as it would be a ship capable of travelling through air as well as space. No longer a simple fighter craft, it would be larger to accommodate an increased reactor size, dual-mode weapons, and a completely different form of propulsion as compared to what she was flying now.

She casually guided the aircraft on course to her first waypoint, which was laid out on her navigation monitor.

"Sir," she muses. "That new fighter design they're working on. How would we classify it as far as a vessel design?"

"I would still describe it as a combat fighter. It's still a single-man design, though a bit larger in form factor than usual."

"But no longer a simple aircraft, like this one."

"No, surely not… Not when you have a spatial inversion generator installed, and that arcanic jump drive, as they're describing it now. Unlike our usual designs, this one will be capable of travelling through space in much the same way as some of our old star cruisers once did."

"But on a smaller scale of design and using our technology to drive it, rather than your original technology."

"That's right, as much as it makes my horns sag," he chuckles.

As she made her way to the waypoint, she continued to imagine the new combat ship design. Much of the technology being developed was based on this conjoined science, using the dynamistic flows at least as much as the more common physical sciences, and the mage focus as a driving force, but here augmented with devices to relieve the pilot from some of the micromanagement aspect. Still, many elements would require new training, as well as a potent mage to operate.

She made her first waypoint and set her new heading to the next one. It was a clear day and pleasant skies, so the flight was fairly relaxed. Once aligned with her new course, she returned to her visions. The arcanic jump drive, as it was tentatively called, would function similarly to a standard rune stone in some ways. She would still need her mage studies to work the enchantment; Sixth Circle to use it, Seventh to mark a new exit point, and it would operate as a channeling orb embedded into the console, similar to the rune stone used on their gryphons where it was mounted in the saddle harness.

"But in this case," she continues. "This fighter would be larger, if only for all the goodies being put into it. It would certainly not be as large as a star cruiser, from what I've heard of those. Do you have any other names for different sizes of craft?"

"Yes, we did back home. This brings up a few memories for me, as it's mostly from a historical perspective these days."

"Of course…"

"This would date back to our old days. I remember some of our history lessons from a period when we once travelled the galaxy in a variety of exploration vessels. We collectively described them as star cruisers, although we had different sizes. These usually involved class names like Light, Medium, and Heavy, and this revolved around the overall size and capacity of the vessel."

"Are we speaking of military ships here, or something else?"

"Although I'm aware we had something like a navy, it was still the Sentinels' service, just like for us at the Naarg uy'Sodrad. We had evolved out of the military aspect of things once a long time ago…" he pauses and sighs longingly. "I suppose this relates to the story I'm hearing lately about Darumon and King Saakerav."

"I'm sorry, Sir, I don't mean to bring up bad memories."

"Don't worry about it, Marelle. It's just a little depressing that we thought we had so many credits to our name, but it might instead be nothing more than a form of manipulation to put us where he wanted us. Anyway, since those early days, our government evolved into a Council of Elders, and we became much more scientifically oriented. But still, we had to maintain a naval force for security reasons just in case something bad came our way."

"Naturally, we wouldn't want anything bad…well, um, maybe I should hold my tongue for this part, because something bad did actually come your way…eventually."

"I know your meaning, but still, we did have a number of military class vessels, including such as frigates, which are the smaller category of what we describe as capital ships, then the cruisers, and finally I believe it ranged up to the size of battleships."

"Battleships?" she wonders. "That sounds serious."

"Oh yes. Although I can't think of any specific examples right now, they were said to be large, very powerful, and often manned with a few or several thousand crew members."

"Ouch, I wouldn't want to be on the receiving end of that."

Marelle tried to imagine these large ships. Then to further imagine fleets of them in battle. The weapons they must've carried would be frightening for the sheer size alone. But she also had to apply some judgment for the defensive measures, and this led her back to the new design they were creating. It would use an application of the Infinity Shield, which has proven quite effective in the past, and might give a good edge in battles of this sort. The design used in these new combat ships would be governed by a control setting, not necessarily something she had to spend her mage focus on. You turn it on as needed, and the technology maintains it until you turn it off.

She arrived at her next waypoint and again adjusted her course. The process was fairly mundane, and something she practiced many times on the simulator. But being in an actual aircraft allowed her to feel the effects of flying, and this added a new dimension to the experience. She knew she needed this, and the more experience she had, the better she would understand the process in case she found herself in adverse conditions.

"But as far as these smaller ships," she wonders. "We have this one we're calling a fighter. You said the smaller of yours were frigates?"

"Yes. I can't recall if we ever used individual combat fighters, like what we're developing here. I know we had such like security patrol craft back on Ruuki uy'Daan, and to my knowledge this was derived from our practice on Azgarén."

"But here we're speaking of a civilian force, like me in the Guard back home, where it was basically keeping the peace on the streets."

"Right, law enforcement, and maybe emergency services. As for a military application, I can't be sure, but I think I recall a few design concepts they had on the books once."

"Really! Such as?"

"For example, you could have a light version and a heavy version. Light would mean stripped down, very fast and maneuverable, and with smaller weapons. Heavy involves stronger weapons, more power, stronger hulls, but they also tended to be slower."

"Light versus heavy," she considers. "How would this compare to what we're developing now?"

"I can't even be sure how to describe it. The old designs used a completely different power core, propulsion, and armoring. Nothing like what we're looking at here. Even the materials used, this adamantium for example, changes the definition."

"And once we get that arcanic harvester, assuming we're successful with that, it could change even more of these concepts."

"I can barely even imagine the end result, so we might need to invent a few new terms. I believe there were some philosophical design concepts once used which crossed the line between the fighter and the frigate, a kind of intermediate design, and I think the artists were describing it as a corvette class. Most of this is academic for us now, though."

"And so, with everything we're cramming into this little bugger, do you think we're actually producing one of those now?"

"It would sure look that way. And this just makes my horns sag even more when I think of you who don't even have a proper form of aircraft technology, are now jumping over several technological steps to something like this."

"Meaning this corvette, in our case, will include things only found in your bigger ships."

"That's right. A spatial inversion drive, a jump drive, advanced shields, which are probably better than anything we ever had…and these weapons of yours…" he rolls his eyes.

Marelle grinned brightly as she continued trying to picture this technological wonder. But it was still deeply in the design stage, and nothing would be ready for quite a while.

She progressed to the final waypoint and oriented for a return back to base. This exercise was easy. She quietly wished for at least a small rainstorm, just to make things interesting, but settled on this much for the early lessons.

As they arrived back home, she lined herself up with the landing pad and brought the aircraft down gently, reducing the flux gauge slowly until the landing pods made contact with the ground. She then powered down according to her routine practice, and the two of them prepared to exit the craft, when a new thought came to her.

"Sir," she calls as he gets up from his seat. "This new propulsion drive… It'll be a super way to fly as compared to what we have here, but what about take-off and landing? I would imagine it's still a VTOL design, so we still need to move up and down at zero forward velocity."

"Yes, that concept has already been considered, and they're thinking we might still need a flux field for the initial boost and settling effect."

"What about this spatial sphere? Can't it go up and down, not only forward?"

"Well, in theory, I suppose it could…"

"So, instead of the flux field, put in a control to move me directly up and down for this. Dump the flux field entirely. We could add this as a side control on…oh, say my left hand, next to the throttle, since I don't think I'll be working both at the same time, and I can certainly move quickly enough from one to the other. And even if I do need them both…" she pauses abruptly.

"Cadet," he eyes her carefully. "I think I've learned enough about you to know when you have one of your crazy ideas coming to mind. What is it this time?"

"Not just up and down, like for landing, but at any time, along with sideways. Not as a continuous movement, but only when my finger is on it, like for a quick sidestep while flying. Maybe to dodge or to duck in and out of something."

"I know what you're talking about. We call it a strafing action. Interesting."

❖

"But what about the Thane's rule here?" the tavern patron whispers urgently. "T' go outside was forbidden. The doors were closed because of the point-ears."

"Aye, that be the tale from long ago," offers another patron. "But the new tales be a-bringin' it together t' say if the point-ears were a-ragin' so hard, they should have found us by now. There be a hole here, as the tales say the whole world above be a-burnin'. Every city an' town it be, so why not here? If the point-ears were truly a-burnin' everythin', they should have burned us in this hole."

"But the doors… They be closed t' keep them out, ay?"

"Aye, but how hard can it be t' pry them open if ye've already burned the rest of it? This be another hole in the tale. The tales run for four hundred years, lad. How long d' ye need for it? It was said they be bad diggers, but that was long ago, at the same time they be bad fighters. But if they somehow learned t' be better at one, why not the other?"

"Fine then, this be a nasty hole in the tale. So, I be a-thinkin' the warriors above must be a-workin' hard t' keep them away, ay?"

"Mayhap nay t' that! If yer home be burned, where d' ye come from t' fight a war? An' if ye be a-fightin' a war, why d' ye let yer home burn?"

"Aye, another bad hole there… But the fare we send up, what say ye t' that then?"

"Only bricks, lad, nay the fare ye need t' fight a war. Warriors need armor an' weapons. Ye don'na fight a war by throwin' bricks at yer foes!"

"But the men who went up… They be said t' make the fare from the bricks, ay?"

"That be the tale, but d' ye know how t' smith a good weapon? D' ye know how t' smith armor? It nay be done with cold bricks. An' if the war be a-burnin' everythin' up there, where d' ye have forges t' make anythin'?"

"Oi, another hole!" he relents heatedly. "But then, what be a-happenin' t' the men?"

"This here would be a good one, if only it made any sense. The Thane be a-tradin' our finest Adamant for nay more than wood for his beloved braziers, nay anythin' else t' make us rich in this hole. Ye d' know how valuable Adamant be t' trade with, ay? For as much as we've seen a-goin' out, we nay even have full bellies or proper clothes on our backs. An' here be a man said t' be our most trusted Thane, where all he calls for be bricks an' more bricks, with nay anythin' comin' back t' honor us for the work. He ne'er once asked if we had good food or clothes, enough coin in our pockets, an' the like. It also be said that he rages at the poor Chancellor if he even asks about the men sendin' word back on how they be a-farin' out there. Now ask yerself, where be those men a-goin' if nay t' serve up anythin' t' pay us back for the effort, an' for a Thane that nay even cares if they be alive? He be a-dishonorin' his throne just by sittin' on it. An' THEN ask about his rule, an' if we'd even WANT t' follow it."

The man reeled back with a prominent frown. The implications were becoming evident for the Thane's motivations. He mulls the idea as the other man continues.

"D' ye know of anyone in yer family who was called t' the feast?"

"Nay in me own family, we be shopkeepers."

"Mayhap ye know a friend or a neighbor, or mayhap the wife of a man called up for it. Did any of them ever get even a wee word back from their men t' say hello? Four hundred years, lad, the feast has been a-callin' up the men, an' in four hundred years nay a one ever writes t' say hello. Now think, lad, why can'na a man write t' his pretty even for one note in all this time? Be it from the doors bein' closed? Mayhap. But if the doors be closed, how d' the people above come t' pick up the bricks we lay down for them, ay?"

"But wait now! Aye t' that, an' also how d' the men go out t' serve up anythin'? Who be it t' pick up the bricks, because I know it be said someone does."

"Aye, but nay any who also bring notes from the men, ye can be sure of that much!"

"But if they nay be the ones t' bring notes from the men, an' if everythin' else ye say be true, like there nay can be any warriors fightin' for all the cities burned, an' the point-ears havin' learned t' fight, so why can'na they also dig us out, then what say ye t' this war? Where d' the men an' bricks go?"

"Ye may also want t' ask how the Thane knows anythin' about anythin' out there, if he nay has a way t' learn of it, nay more than the rest of us with the doors closed. I hear it said he only comes out of hidin' t' rage at the Chancellor, then runs an' hides in his room again, nay more than that. Nay even t' call for food on occasion."

"But that..." he flusters. "Lad! How can a man rage about somethin' if he nay can have anythin' t' rage about? Blast it!"

"An' so, this be the reason why we be a-diggin' ourselves out of this hole, t' find the truth of it. There be a door in there, but it nay goes out t' where we think the REAL doors be. It only goes up a long stair, an' nay anythin' WE built. So, if we say our fine city has a back door none of us knew about, who built it an' why? An' then, who be it that comes t' pick up our most precious Adamant an' men without any proper trade?"

"Uh oh..."

"Aye, lad! That be the way of it for a lot of folks now. For now, we'll leave the stair be, especially if it goes up t' folk we don'na want t' meet. Instead, the lads be a-diggin' through the upper town right now, an' when we find the doors, we'll pry them open an' see the world with our own eyes. If it be as the Thane says, fine an' good. But if nay t' that..." he frowns and shakes his head morosely.

This conversation was echoing through taverns and workplaces throughout the city by now. Local gossip was spreading about the new revelations over the inconsistencies in the age-old stories and poor leadership handed out by the Thane. The contradictions and conflicts between the different stories as they developed over the centuries have finally made their mark on the minds of the people. Now they wanted answers, and there was only one way in which to find them. They had to climb out of their city beneath the mountain, open the doors and look outside.

A work crew had dug their way through a buried tunnel from the storeroom where they dropped the ingots. They emerged into a section of the old upper town district, where they noticed buildings and avenues that were fairly clean and open. The damage told by many of the stories was not apparent. Homes, shops, smithies, the place was eerily quiet, like a ghost town, but otherwise intact and still habitable. They worked their way cautiously through the streets until they found a further section that did show some collapse. This would now require more digging, as it looked like the top of the cavern fell down on it.

A set of eyes followed this new activity, peering out from under an invisibility cloak while scouting through this new tunnel and the subsequent old town. The scout was making a routine run into the store from the roadway above on the mountain, as part of a maintenance review to keep tabs on the flow of ingots. He observed the new work being made by the crew, which appeared to be digging its way through to the front doors. He knew this had to be reported.

He cautiously returned outside to the road, where he had a moment of privacy to dispel his cloak. He then pulled out a return rune and cast his enchantment on it, then clamped his hand on top to transport away.

"Captain, we have a little problem," the scout announces as he arrives.

"When you say a little problem, how little?"

"Well, if you'll pardon my pun, dwarven sized," he chuckles.

"Fine, but you should watch yourself amongst some of the others here," he grins as he glances around the camp assembly, some of whom were dwarves.

"Right!" he smiles. "I made my run into that store to check the supply of ingots again and found a group of dwarves apparently starting to dig out a side tunnel which I think leads into the upper town area of the old city. I think they're trying to make their way out into the open."

"Uh oh, we'll need to get this turned in so we can make a decision on it. If they go outside, we could possibly lose control if the Suuden-Aryku see them."

"At this point, I think it'll probably take them a while to dig through all that rubble. I followed the lanes inside up to where it seemed some of the upper town had collapsed, probably the outer area right underneath that slide."

"I hope they're wise enough to take caution in that area. It might not be very stable. But if you're right, we might have the benefit of time on our side. Surely, it'll take time to dig themselves fully out of that mess, especially what we can see on the outside. Maybe, what we can do is try some sort of effort to meet up with them, but not us personally. Maybe if we send Belrum and the others. What if we try meeting them halfway with our own tunnel?"

"You were just now speaking about the Suuden-Aryku... That would make a fair showing also."

"It would, but the road up there is on the east side of the slide. If we come in from the west, we'll be eclipsed by it, and the road doesn't seem to have that much visibility down there anyway, assuming anyone even bothers to look. Not to mention, the Suuden-Aryku don't travel that road on a regular basis."

"Right, then, Captain. Then we should submit this for their consideration."

"I'll write this up. Meanwhile, let's make a few careful surveys of that slide to see how we might approach it, just in case."

"Ah, my Lord," the General calls as Thaelyn arrives in the room. "You should know I received a curious note from none other than Adalon this morn."

"Indeed, General, as did I. I wonder what she has in mind this time, especially if she is sending out notes in multiple directions at once."

"May I ask what yours was about?" the General wonders. "Mine was to inform me to prepare a meeting of several of our active officers, including myself and the Commander. Kaliya was also mentioned, as well as our science and research directors. But curiously, she is dating this meeting to occur this following week."

"How interesting… What is our timing with the Suuden-Aryku and that pick-up date for the metal?"

"Less than half a month by now, so this meeting would occur before that."

"But we need to act on the crew before too long, so are we expected to perform this before or after the meeting? Does the meeting involve this action, or is it a consequence of it?"

"Good gracious, my Lord, and when speaking of Adalon, that does not help matters. And what about your note if I may?"

"Mine was received in my personal office at the guildhall, and it suggested we do not take any action on the weapon until we meet, or on the Dynamistic Harvester, as she calls it. This suggests to me she has something in mind."

"You were planning on a journey to meet with the Estelar on that, were you not? So, does this mean you need to postpone that plan?"

"It would seem so, and this now reminds me of the Arcanicium. I recall when I was preparing to speak with Torm on this back in the day when we had this idea of Darumon using it on his old enemies. Then, just before I could arrive on the platform, she strolls in to intercept me. She must be playing a very devious game here, and not only with us."

"I might further suggest it involves direction from the Maker, in this case, and reflecting on our previous discussions where the Maker wants a piece of the action outside the other Estelar."

"But General, I feel we should ask why she would seemingly take this unilateral action. Do the other Estelar know of her plans, and if so, are they being told to keep clear of it, or is she hiding everything and taking a personal action."

"I doubt we can answer that from where we stand except to reflect on Adalon's prophecies and what they tell us. It would seem someone, likely the Maker, has been planning this for a very long time, if she has been aware of Sargeras from the beginning."

"Very well then, I will have to make an assumption here and suggest the base can go by our own timing, but the rest must wait until after our meeting. If she is saying not to touch anything until after, this implies we are moving against the base before then."

"It surely would, and this might also give us a time frame to work with."

"Indeed, and the weapon is a clear and obvious threat, and likely a very delicate matter, so she may have some special handling instructions for it. As for the Harvester…well, if she is suggesting we wait on that, maybe this reflects on keeping the other Estelar largely out of the picture. But then I must wonder what she has in mind as a substitute, because if she is mentioning it at all, she must know we need it, and therefore must have a plan of some kind."

"Well, my Lord," he chuckles. "This is Adalon, and you know her as well as I do. I suppose we should continue to place our faith in her and allow her this game. Just like with everything else around us, we will probably see the answer only at that time it is ready for us."

"Indeed, General, but her timing is wearing on my nerves a bit."

"Meanwhile, the Captain filed a new report last night regarding the dwarves. They are apparently trying to dig their way out of that hole. The local gossip, as overheard by our team, is sending many of them into a minor fit over the Thane and his wild tales of the war outside, to say nothing of his poor management skills of their local affairs."

"While this is good, and we wanted this, at least to some degree, the fact that they are now trying to dig their way out can be problematic for the timing aspect."

"This is true, and he has a suggestion to offer. He feels we could possibly meet them halfway. Although there is a risk factor no matter how we proceed here, but if to follow his advice on the matter, it does allow us to possibly contain the risk."

"To meet halfway… Perhaps, but then what?" Thaelyn wonders. "Does he suggest using any form of diplomacy?"

"He first suggests digging through the side which is out of clear view, using some of our own people, probably dwarves as they are not only very efficient in this regard, but also less conspicuous, and then to send Belrum in as our intermediary. This could bring an exchange of information to satisfy their stories and contradictions, but it also allows us to point a finger in a direction they would not wish to immediately offend for fear of an unknown factor lying in wait."

"Very clever, and this could buy us a little time to massage the situation until we have control of the base, and anything else up there."

"I would further recommend we use some of our own construction methods, especially when you consider the unstable ground we are likely to be tunneling through."

"Indeed, this is not a good example for boring a tunnel. Send word to have our industry prepare a large quantity of concrete mix and iron reinforcement bars, and have those delivered onsite. And select our work crews to involve industrial grade excavators. We will use machines, if necessary, but try to keep it far enough to one side that it does not make that much of a showing. Maybe you can also erect some camouflaging overhangs to shelter the operation."

"This is becoming rather elaborate, but I suppose for safety's sake, it can't be helped."

"That slide would represent a lot of loose material. In the longer term, we might simply need to bulldoze the entire thing to scoop it away back down to the firm bedrock again. Next, we would need to share with them the stories from the outside, but only those pieces that should normally be available at this time, meaning whatever Belrum might have to offer, I should think."

"Most certainly, at least until we can contain the situation with that base."

"And Ytani, which also brings to mind if they should happen to travel through that tunnel above. Do you know if they have made the attempt?"

"The Captain sent a scout in to make contact with Eiki on this matter. She informs us that her friends are making efforts to defray attention to that road with suspicions it could lead to unknown dangers. Their priority is to break through to the outside and see the world as it truly is, as compared to the stories told by the Thane. Only after answering some of those questions will they start asking more about the other."

"Then our time is becoming critical here, depending on how quickly they dig. Now we have time working against us on two... no, three sides," he shakes his head. "One being the pick-up time for the metal, and thus Ytani demanding another of his payments, and this represents a fairly solid timing objective. But the other being the Commander and his intentions, and this we cannot be as sure about."

"We will need to keep a close eye on our spy recordings to see if he leaves any clues for us. I know we recorded one where that female Lieutenant...um, Ti'van, I believe is her name, returned with that special order from Azgarén."

"Yes, those devices to disable their interfaces. This is clearly a preparatory step. But I still wonder how he plans on compensating for Ytani's absence. We will need to plan our move soon. This essentially forces our hand in relation to Adalon and her meeting, so she must be speaking of after, rather than before our capture of the base."

"This makes sense to me, and then she will advise on the rest of it."

"And this also brings us back to Belrum. When he reveals the final clue to this mystery, we must have that base, and the Thane must be the last to know of it. We must then play a very careful game with him on his own turf, making him believe all is well, at least where the base is concerned, but at the same time we must attempt to contain him by restricting his interaction with Azgarén. All that remains after that is to remove him."

"And this is where my innocent little baby sister comes in," Kailen muses from his desk.

"Innocent, Commander?" Thaelyn grins. "I recall she has a history behind her."

"Yes, but we're hoping that's long past us by now."

"Indeed! And she is truly developing as a sturdy soldier for us. More so with that last exercise where she quoted my own words on war being a thinking man's game, and SHE, being a woman, is going to reinvent it for us. Powers help us for the result," he chuckles.

"I read that report, and I think I can see now where some of her…history…was trying to take her. All those wild ambitions to go out on her vendettas. She was trying to invent that warfare, but we, being so offended by the topic, simply cowered away from it."

"Yes, this is unfortunate. And while I do not care for an operation of this sort, justice must still prevail. Ytani is surely deserving of the price he must pay for his actions, and Kaliya could possibly present us with a curious method of performing it."

"What sort of method are you thinking of on this occasion?"

"First, I would not wish to leave any clear evidence locally. Therefore, the body should be removed from the area. And unlike his suggestion for the females, I am not going to grace him by burying him in a lonely desert on a world he holds no respect for. Further, I do not want Darumon to know anything, so Ytani cannot be allowed to make any form of communication home."

"For this, I would simply suggest we cut his access to the com-links."

"Very good, and we should disable or redirect that conveyor, so he cannot run from us."

"That might be a bit of a problem if their HQ is monitoring things."

"We will see if we can have Kaliya's team impersonate the base crew, and then give excuses, as best we can. This now brings us to how we might finally dispose of him, but I am tempted to wait until that last moment, after we speak to Adalon and see what she has in mind for the rest. Maybe we can combine a few things, and perhaps it can coincide with his demands," he grins mischievously.

"Your Lordship," Kailen winces. "This is my sister were talking about, remember?"

"Oh, do not worry, Commander. Even as a young and innocent virgin, I am sure she will be more than capable of managing herself. I suspect the processing and storage sites to be located somewhere very remote, and I just happen to recall we have a spare atomic left over from the mines up north."

"Cu'Nar's Pity..." he wheezes.

"All right, you tenderfoots..."

"Um, Captain," Kaliya mentions. "We actually use hooves," she grins.

"Oh, is that so," he chuckles. "All right, just for the sake of it, what term do you usually use for raw recruits in your service? That way I can be on the mark with you."

"Oh, that's easy. We use the term velvet horns."

"Really!" he laughs. "I need to make a note of that. But anyway, this time you'll be up against a real challenge. Behind me, you'll see the enemy camp. This is a capture mission. Every soldier inside is to be taken alive for future interrogation. We'll make it easy on you in one simple way. Ordinarily, you would remove your prisoners by rune transport, but in this case, we'll bypass that as an obvious step. You'll just knock them down and leave them where they lay. That should be good enough to achieve your score. Still, you don't want your enemies to find them, so your best course is to pull them to one side and hide them. The final objective is the HQ building and the base commander. Capture him, and you win the field."

The captain was organizing one more session for Kaliya and her team. This was another simulation scenario to train her team in commando combat roles. Ahead of them was a fortress set inside a wooden palisade wall. It was designed as a military base with multiple barracks, a mess hall and rec room, storerooms and depots, and a large officer's command station.

On this occasion, there would be a difference as compared to their previous exercise. The other one was designed to be solely a covert run, using their physical form, and without magic, certainly no advanced magic, except for a cloak. This example would pull out all the stops. They could now use magic, as well as their projected forms...any means necessary, so long as they accomplished their goal without setting off any alarms or taking casualties.

The toughest part for this mission, as opposed to the other one, was that the men inside would be much more aware of their surroundings. The previous operation had the men largely isolated into groups. Taking out one group would not necessarily set off any of the others. Here, there were roaming guard patrols, and people would now take notice if a building full of troops was attacked. This simulation was designed to represent a real-life wartime scenario more accurately.

"Sir," Kaliya responds. "Do we use our new stun strike, or traditional methods?"

"Since your official duty will involve that new strike, I think you should get some practice out of it while you're here."

"Yes Sir!"

Kaliya accepted her mission and assembled her people. They were hidden behind a barricade wall to conceal them from their target. From here, they had to make a careful approach to infiltrate their objective and begin their mission.

"First, we need a scout to go dark and peek inside, so we know what the lay of the camp is like. I also need to know about patrols and their routes. We need to take them down, but we also need to keep it quiet, so no one gets wise to it. And for this, we need a quiet place to begin our work. Most of all, we're going to need to improvise a lot."

"How do you mean improvise, Lieutenant?" asks one of the team members.

"Up until now, we've been practicing our projection skills based on stuffed animals and facsimiles. No longer! Now we need to do it on-the-fly. We're not going to have the luxury of time to study something a long time before imitating it. We'll need to imagine new shapes ad hoc as soon as they come up."

"Like what you did that time on Ruuki uy'Daan with the orcs?"

"Yeah, and if I can do it, so can you. We're smart enough to put this together; we just need to get the idea in our head one time and do it."

"We'll need time to project ourselves though. Do we do this here, or elsewhere?"

"Let's get a scout out there to see what we have to work with first. Maybe we can take a building with enough privacy that we can use it."

She selects a member to perform the scouting run. The member casts her cloak and takes off in the direction of the front gate.

The front gate of the base was closed, so the scout ran along the wall to the nearest corner to peek around it. She continued around the outer circumference until finally returning with her report.

"Lieutenant, the wall seems secure on the outside. The doors are sealed, and there are no other clear points of entry."

Kaliya ponders the situation, realizing access to this fortress will be her first big challenge.

"What do we have for watchtowers?"

"Four corners, one man each."

"If they disappear, the patrols inside will likely take note. And if the patrols inside disappear, I'm sure lots of others will take note. We'll need people in projected form to replace them, at least until we can gain some security. Gamma, we'll use you on this occasion. I need all of you in projected form now. Lay down here, and someone give up your lap to support them until they're out."

The squad lays on the ground with their heads resting on the other members' laps for better comfort. The team waits until the squad is able to project out of their body.

The captain was reclining in his tent as the team made its initial preparations. He watched as the squad emerged from their bodies in projected form. He couldn't help but to wince at the thought of having such strange apparitions moving against his men inside the fortress.

"Good," Kaliya offers. "Now, we need better scouting inside the wall, but not as people or animals. Our best way in, so far, might be the gate. A need a scout to creep under it as a mound of dirt, then see who's standing on the other side."

"A mound of dirt?" mutters one member. "How does something like that move?"

"Use your imagination. Think of a mini dust storm, or a tumbling rock, or just sliding along. But try not to be too conspicuous. Nothing too rhythmic, more haphazard. After all, you're just a pile of dirt," she smiles.

The squad leader selects a member, and he changes into an approximation of a clump of sand, refining his appearance as he examines himself to seem more realistic. He then began creeping along the ground like a cascading swirl blown by an invisible wind.

The captain continued to watch, with his expression now turning to trepidation as he observed an animated piece of earth tumbling along towards the gate.

"Next," Kaliya asserts. "I'll have one of you fly as a bug to one of those towers for a peek around the grounds. Land on the side, out of view of the guard. I need a review of the patrols inside. Another four make like bugs, fly up, gain line-of-sight and fold down into the camp. Then change to dried leaves on the ground in the four corners near some of the buildings. Make it look like you're blown by a breeze to move around and see inside. I want to know what's in there. The last four, more bugs, and tell me how those guards get into their towers. Be discreet. It's likely a ladder, but is it inside or outside the tower."

The captain studied the actions as the scouts altered their forms and departed the scene. He found himself trying to imagine how this might appear on the other side of it. He shuddered to think how this could be employed in an actual combat role. He sat there shaking his head in disbelief.

Inside the fortress, a small insect crawls along the lower side of one guard tower, pausing intermittently to peruse the local surroundings. At the same time, a small pile of sand rests loosely just beyond the gate, apparently inert. Two guards are standing at watch near the gate oblivious to their observers, while another four patrolled around the camp along a road circling the officer's center. The camp was laid out in a semicircle around the central building.

From different corners of the walls, a collection of old leaves blew in towards some of the buildings, stopping and starting as if nudged by a gentle breeze, curiously weaving in and out of the various buildings. On occasion they might seem as if slipping under doors, only to be blown back out onto the road and forward to the next building.

Finally, another set of insects had landed on each of the watchtowers, examining the structure to discover how the guard would find his way into his position.

The scouts didn't technically need eyes to see, as these were simply manifested images. Their perceptions would allow them to see in any direction they turned their focus, regardless of what form they took, as this was a matter of the mind directing itself, not a physical body with true sensory organs.

The guards were clearly on alert this time. This was not a game; they were behaving as if they were on actual duty. The realism of this scenario would require careful tact on Kaliya's part. This was a much more advanced training session, but it might still present its opportunities for her team.

When the scouts had seen their fill, they each returned with their reports.

"Lieutenant," calls one scout. "The guard patrols appear to make a circuit in intervals, two along a straight edge in front in opposite directions, and two along a curve circling the rear, also in opposite directions."

"Any intersections?"

"They meet in the center of each of their paths, and may encounter each other at the endpoints."

"What do we have for the towers?" Kaliya asks the next scout to return.

"The towers are enclosed with a ladder leading up inside to a trapdoor at the top."

"And the buildings?" she defers to the next one.

"Many of them hold a number of troops, but a few appear as supply depots."

"How is it arranged?"

"A semicircle around the HQ with a straight edge in front. The curve is lined with buildings while the edge has only two, one on either side of a lead-in from the gate. Everything faces the road."

"Good, so we need a way in, and those guards at the gate are our first obstacle. I need a bug to fly up to their HQ and find one of their lesser officers. Get inside somehow, maybe as an object on a table. Study him, then report back and show me what he looks like. We'll use him as our decoy."

The captain was starting to show signs of distress. It was becoming obvious as he listened to these tactics that the people inside the base were going to be subject to a form of deception unlike any they had ever encountered before. The possibilities were frightening.

The teammate flies across to the HQ building as a small insect. It lands on the side and crawls through a crack under the door, then behind some of the furniture along the base of a wall until he finds a suitable target. He moves up into view over a nearby tabletop and folds himself over to a discreet location, reshaping himself as an inkwell. There he pauses as he studies the details of a lieutenant sitting in a chair across from him at another table. He carefully records a mental image of the officer's physical appearance and uniform, as well as his voice during a moment of conversation. When he was satisfied, he recalled himself back to Kaliya.

"What do you have for me?" she asks on his return.

The team member reimagined himself into his new form to imitate his target. Kaliya studied the results and gave her approval. But the captain, who was still observing the interaction from his tent, was now in shock that his troops were being impersonated as doppelgangers to fool the others.

"All right, it's showtime people," Kaliya orders. "We'll have everyone go dark and move to the front wall. Gamma Decoy will change to a bug, fly to a convenient spot, find a nook, fold into it, and take your new form. Make it appear that you came out of a local building, but without anyone in direct sight of it. Then make your way to the front door. You'll give an order to redirect those guards. Tell them to make a quick run to check the wall for diggers. When they're out of sight, you'll open the door briefly, but discreetly, for Alpha One and Two. They'll split off to the two towers in front. Gamma One and Two will fly up as bugs and make an inspection of the guards to imitate them. When you're ready, go downstairs and take your shapes. You need to take out the old and quickly replace them with the new. When the door guards return, the decoy will move to one of the towers out of sight and fold back to me outside the door."

The team members each take their orders and cast cloaks on themselves, while the projected members change to insects. Two of them fly to the towers while Kaliya has the rest fly up to the outside wall and land on it. The one to act as the decoy flies over the base and finds a convenient location between a couple of buildings along the curve to one side, out of view of the patrols, and changes to his officer disguise. He then makes a casual stroll out along the road in the direction of the door. As he passes one of the guards crossing the straight road in front, he simply offers a confident nod in his direction and continues forward.

"Sir!" salutes one of the guards at the front gate.

"Men, we have a concern they might try digging under the walls," the officer submits.

"Wouldn't the towers see them in that case?"

"Not if they're using elementals. I want you to make a quick run to check on it for me. Check for rumbling sounds while you're at it. I'll stay here and cover for you."

"Aye!"

The two guards take off in opposite directions to make their inspection. While they were busy, the officer makes a quick scan of the other guards to make sure no one was looking. He discreetly lifts the latch on the gate behind his back and pulls it open just long enough for two people to pass through before closing it again. The two people in question were cloaked, so the operation had to be carefully managed for the timing. He counted several seconds, enough for them to move inside, and then closed the gate again. They each turned off to their respective tower assignments and waited.

The two agents sent to study the tower guards were in place and making a careful examination. Once they felt confident, they proceeded around to the door on the outside of the tower and entered through, out of sight of anyone in the camp. There they would take their new shape. Also, inside was a cloaked figure that watched and waited for the signal.

The replacement guard then gave his action gesture of a fist pulling downward. He started up the ladder and opened the trapdoor, keeping his head down and turned away to conceal his face from the guard above.

The tower guard was busy looking out for anything moving outside the walls. When the trapdoor opened, he turned to observe what appeared to be another guard, at least by the uniform and helmet, coming up for a visit.

"What's going on down there?" he asks.

"They figure two sets of eyes are better than one," the replacement replies calmly, keeping his back to the other guard as he stands up on the platform. "Rumor has it these people are clever."

"Yeah, so I hear."

"Anyway, keep watch for anything moving around."

"Aye!"

Before the guard had a chance to turn around again, a firm palm-strike knocks him off his feet. The rippling waves of stun force in the electrical attack numb his body, and he collapses to the ground. The replacement guard glanced casually over his shoulder at the stricken soldier.

"Yeah, a bit like that," he snickers.

The Daanen'kai operative from below had followed the replacement guard up the ladder through the door that was still standing open, ducking low for cover behind the wall in the tower, and taking down his quarry. The same scene was being repeated in the other forward tower, and the two replacements took over the positions as decoys to defray the attention of any ground observers, while the Daanen'kai members returned to the base of the towers and waited.

The decoy at the gate observed the action. It was quick, silent, and very efficient. When the scene settled, he waited for the door guards to return.

"Sir," offers one of the guards. "All seems clear. There's no digging on this side."

"Good," he responds. "These people are a clever bunch. Keep your eyes open. I'm going to check this tower over here."

The decoy walks over to one of the towers and closes the door behind him. He then folds himself outside the front gate to signal their success.

Kaliya now uses sign language to instruct him for his next objective. He nods and returns back to the tower, exiting through the door and walking across to the other one. He peers inside briefly as if looking at something, then turns to the gate guards and whistles gently to get their attention. He waves them over with a pair of fingers. The two make a brisk trot to investigate while the decoy glances around nonchalantly at the rest of the camp, taking note of the other patrols.

"Yes Sir?" asks one of the guards.

"What do you make of this inside here?" he directs inside the tower base.

They turn to peek inside the tower through the door, when no sooner than their heads make their appearance, two hands reached out from the shadows and grabbed them, yanking them inside and slapping them on the forehead with another stunning strike.

Moments later, another two clones emerge from the tower as more of Gamma Squad takes shape to replace them.

The decoy signals for the two attackers to return under their cloaks and take up positions at the remaining two towers, where Kaliya had another two projected team members studying the tower guards. They would engage the same maneuver as with the first set and reconvene behind one of the front buildings.

The captain conducting the exercise tried to observe the actions from his tent outside. Waves of horror shot through him as he watched his men being replaced so cleanly. All he could actually see were the activities in the towers, but he tried to imagine the rest of it. He would not know the true outcome until later, when the exercise was complete, and he conferred with the resident officer inside the base before grading the exercise.

The decoy returned back to the front gate to engage in a seemingly casual conversation with the front guards, pointing off in various directions as if giving instruction, while the guards made discreet intermittent moves with the gate to open and close it, allowing small groups to file in from the outside. The full team reassembled behind that same front building.

The new objective was now to take one of the buildings near the front. The decoy made a casual stroll along the lead-in road to the intersection with the cross street, turning towards one of the two barracks. The door in front was closed, so he peered through an adjacent window to check inside, and then opened the door for an informal visit to inspect the troops, leaving the door open as he stepped inside.

"Sir?" calls one of the members inside the room. "Is anything occurring outside?"

"All seems quiet, so far, but keep on your toes. Reports say they could use stealth to infiltrate our position, but the gate is closed, and you know how it goes if they try opening that under a cloak."

"Aye! And the tower guards would see that immediately."

"Right you are, soldier! So far, I'm not anticipating any problems..."

At this moment in the conversation, a mass of bodies appears out of nowhere in the room, followed by the sudden smacks on each of the heads of the resident troops, sending them down with a series of minor groans and muffled thuds on the floor.

"…Well, except for that little one," the decoy finishes with a smirk.

He closes the door while the team tidies up the bodies, moving them to the rear of the room and concealing them behind a set of tables covered by sheets.

"Good work, people," Kaliya declares. "This is our pattern. One by one we take them out. But we need to work those guards outside too. Gamma Leader…"

An image pops into view from a diminutive form on the wall at one side of the room.

"Assemble the rest of your team. Everyone go dark. Gamma Decoy, call in one of those passing guards for a happy little chat. I'll take him down and we'll set up another clone. We work it the same for the next one as he passes by."

The team goes into their cloaks while the projected forms take up as bugs on one wall. The decoy opens the door and steps outside briefly to wait for one of the passing guards, then to call him up to the door.

"Yes Sir?"

"Come in here quickly. I have something special for you."

The guard unwittingly obeys the command and marches inside the structure, soon to be greeted by an unexpected stunning strike and moved out of view. A clone is dispatched, and the decoy waits for the next guard on the forward road to approach, and the process repeats.

"So far, this is a cakewalk," Kaliya mumbles. "No wonder Aelwyn calls this a godlike ability. People like us shouldn't have something like this."

"You're right, Lieutenant," the decoy admits. "But for some reason, we do."

"Call it a birthright. We may not like where it came from, but cu'Nar's Grace, we're sure going to make good use of it. And we'll do so in the names of all those who were made victims of those monsters."

"Yes Ma'am!"

"You know, that actually sounds a little funny. You're three times my age, right?"

"A minor detail, Lieutenant," he smiles. "You're also the daughter of our council leadership, which sort of gives you a kind of noble station. So, I don't mind. We'll just say it harkens back to a romantic period."

"Romantic. Uh huh. If you say so. All right, we proceed systematically around the camp. Gamma Decoy, lead us to the next building and around the circle. We'll take those other two guards similar to these here. Then we'll hit the HQ last."

The decoy exits the building, along with the rest of the team back under their cloaks. They proceed methodically from one building to the next, following a similar process to the first one. Each one falls in a similar manner, with the last two guard patrols brought down by more deceptions, then replaced by the remaining projected forms.

By this time, all of Gamma Squad had been spent as projections occupying their roles as guard replacements. Kaliya needed one more to take the HQ, so she found a comfortable chair in this last building and projected herself. She considered that using the same image as the officer wouldn't work in this case, as the real one was still inside the HQ, and having two of them would be trouble. Instead, she took up the image of a local soldier.

She leads the remaining group, which had once again gone under a cloak, up to the HQ building. She peeks in through a nearby window to check the occupants inside before opening the door to enter. As she stands there just past the open door, she appears as though searching for something.

"Is there something you need, soldier?" asks the base colonel from behind his desk.

Kaliya turns her focus to him and steps forward in a formal presentation.

"Yes Sir, I have a need to speak with you on an urgent matter."

"Oh, what is it? Is there something happening out there?"

"The situation outside seems stable, Sir. This is another matter."

"Very well, but make it quick. This is a critical condition we face here."

"Absolutely, Sir! What I wanted to say is this..."

The room quickly fills with a score of Daanen-Aryku operatives emerging from their cloaks surrounding the other men and pounding their palms into each of their heads, knocking them flat on their backs before anyone knew what was happening. The surprise attack dazzled the commander, leaving him with no time to react as two agents rushed up and grabbed his arms to restrain his movements.

"...You are now my prisoner...Sir!" Kaliya finishes with a pleasant smile.

"What the..." he barks. "Who in all the nine hells are you?"

Kaliya changes her image to her own form before responding to his demand.

"Lieutenant Kaliya Nazég, Sir. I wish to report my objective is complete."

"Gods above!" he gasps. "But that's impossible! What about the guards, and the rest of the camp?"

"Would you like to make an inspection, Sir?"

The colonel looks around the room at his stricken fellow officers, then the two Daanen'kai operatives holding him.

"Indeed, I would!" he charges. "At ease, soldiers..."

The two teammates restraining him let go, and Kaliya leads him out of the building to inspect the grounds.

"Lieutenant, what about these guards out here?"

"Gamma Squad, present forward!" she shouts into the yard.

The guards patrolling the roads, the two at the front gate, and the four in their towers, all fold their images to her position, reimagining themselves to their natural forms and lining up at attention. The colonel watched in awe as all his guardsmen vanished and were replaced by her Special Ops team.

"Great gods..." he whispers breathlessly. "What have you done to my men?"

He makes a brisk stroll around the camp, carefully inspecting each building, only to discover his entire company had been disabled and were lying motionless on the floor.

"Lieutenant," he presents a modest smile and runs his fingers through his hair. "You're going to put me out of a job."

"I think I just did," she grins.

"Yes, as a matter of fact," he chuckles. "But in the longer term, I have to wonder who is the more dangerous out there. Very good then, we'll count this as a successful mission. It'll take some time for me to file my report, especially as I'll need to wait for my men to find their feet again before I can debrief them. Report back to the captain outside and inform him this session is complete, and then return home."

"Yes Sir! Thank you, Sir!" she salutes.

She then returns to her body and leads her team outside.

Chapter 8

FINAL COUNTDOWN

The Suuden'kai Commander was once again in his office reviewing a series of reports on his terminal, when an announcement came at the door.

"Commander?" Ayene calls. "Do you have a moment?"

"Lieutenant, yes, come in. Have you had any success at infiltrating Ytani's house?"

"I tried it last night, hoping to find a way in while he was sleeping, but he keeps the door locked, which does not actually surprise me, so I had to use the override key on it. I must admit, even with my Suppressor chip, I felt very nervous."

"Did you get any feedback from it? Perhaps we should disable it in your case to give you better freedom."

"I got a minor hit, twice actually, but I managed to get through it. I am wondering, however, when will we actually use those?"

"So far, I hesitate to apply them, if only due to the sensor logs recorded at the security console. If Central should ever decide to investigate anything around here, they might check those logs and see an extended lapse in the ping responder timestamps. I would wish instead to minimize the discrepancy as a means of providing cover in case we cannot find an alternate solution. But now, as for Ytani's impersonation device, did you find anything?"

"Negative, unfortunately. I inspected the front room carefully. He has a kitchen and an entertainment area with a vid-com and a holo-disk player, but there was nothing of unusual design in there. The chair looked very well-used, so I think he spends a lot of time in it, probably watching his holo-disks."

"This makes sense. I cannot think of what else he might have in there."

"He has that set of exercise equipment, which is located in a side room, and it also looks like he uses it a lot, but the other items in that room...this is where I got my hits."

"What did you see?"

"Commander, I cannot imagine where he found it, but I saw a bondage restraining mount, several female pleasure toys, a couple of which appeared electrically powered with metal contact points on the surface, as well as electrocution clips, and a set of thin blades and long piercing skewers. I am suddenly even more revolted at that man for what he has apparently been doing with our female staff members."

"Metal contact points on...a pleasure toy? Do they even make such things?"

"This looks a little like a homemade item, and if so, he is not only taking whatever deviant pleasure he can with our staff, this would also represent torture."

"Yes, I would imagine that would cause injury, probably indicative of what we saw on several occasions for those who came out and had to be sent home for medical aid. But you saw no other devices?"

"Not in that room, and I did not wish to try peeking into his bedroom, not while he was in there. I consider myself lucky I was able to sneak around the forward portions quietly enough not to disturb him. He must sleep rather soundly."

"Then we have a problem. Either the device is in that final room, or we are mistaken of the method."

"Commander, let us consider this a moment. First, let us suggest the device is in the bedroom. How do we get inside while he is at home? There is no way to get in there without passing through the rest of the house to find it."

"If this is the case, we may have no choice but to engage him on our way through. But this carries the obvious complication of his absence where we need to create an excuse."

"We would have that regardless. But this also assumes if anyone comes around asking about it. He never receives visitors, no family or friends, not that I would expect him to have friends for his obnoxious behavior."

"This could work to our benefit, but then we have the Marshal, as he does make periodic inspections."

"I do not specifically recall him visiting Ytani's house for a chat, however. Not the last time he visited, at least."

"Then this might buy us an opportunity. What other considerations did you have?"

"My other thought relates to whether we could be wrong about this device, although I cannot imagine what other method he might have for it. There is no obvious exit from that building for him to travel down some secret access to the city, and he never comes outside to stroll through the tunnel."

"But we know he must go down there. We know this from the metal he calls up, and those…" he pauses to close his eyes and takes a slow breath.

Ayene studies him a moment, watching as he seems to be trying to constrain himself.

"Commander, are you alright?"

"Yes, I am simply trying to prevent any new hits as I think of this other…atrocity…we are committing for that…creature."

"Are we speaking of Ytani here?"

"He is certainly one, and bad enough for what he does. I am actually referring to the Marshal in this case. He is the one who authorized the use of that drug we apply to these mining teams we bring out on occasion."

"Are you reflecting on more of your old experiences in the Service?"

"Yes, and this simply adds into it. He wants the metal, and those people down below are made expendable for it. He does not simply ask them for it, he drugs and abducts them into a form of slave labor. Ayene, what have we become while working for that…thing?"

"Then I suppose you are turning against his service, and for this point, I cannot blame you. I do not like it either. I have been out there, if you recall, to clean up after this on many occasions. And unfortunately, like Ytani was saying for our officers, they were buried in that desert. It was all we had."

"Then we need an escape. I do not know what plans he has for this material of his, but I suspect it is not good. It is known to be highly volatile. Why does he need something that could easily be used as an explosive, possibly a violent one, and without even a name given to it. If he is willing to sacrifice lives in the production of it, what does he hope to sacrifice in the application of it?"

"Commander, that sounds scary, even with a Suppressor chip."

✦✦✦✦✦

"My Lord," the General asserts. "We have a new report from Captain Hagmaert about a recent scouting run into the city."

"And what do we have this time, General?" Thaelyn replies as he enters the room.

It is two days after Kaliya made her last training mission. Thaelyn and his officers were waiting patiently for the report to come in from the base colonel as well as her instructor. In the meantime, they received a new message from Morndindor.

"Apparently, we were right about the Chancellor," the General continues. "Contact was made recently and carefully carried out by one of our agents inside the city. He is apparently innocent of any personal wrongdoing, being as much a victim of the propaganda as anyone else, and he is now working for us."

"This is excellent news. Having someone in such a position as that could be very useful. What is the progress estimate on the excavation inside there?"

"It's difficult to tell, actually, as we really do not know precisely how deep the doors are on the inside, and we can only guess as to our efforts on the outside. But we are attempting to measure our distances, as best we can, and some estimates are suggesting at least a week, maybe two."

"This might give us just enough time, but then we must consider the Suuden-Aryku. I want to make our move this coming week or sooner, certainly well enough before they are scheduled for their next pick-up. Once we have the base, we will send our people to that mine and rescue the miners. I will also have you send people to collect the ingots and store them for safety, possibly to shut down the operation for now until we can decide what to do with it."

"As you wish…"

"I am still waiting for that report on Kaliya's last training session. Do we have anything yet?"

"He promised he would have it ready later in the day. Apparently, he had a number of details to collect on the tactics she used."

"I would be very interested to see how she did this. Those early reviews they gave suggested she accomplished her goal in record time. Considering her use of projected troops, this might not surprise me, but then I wonder how she deployed them. Just to breach the exterior, in this case, would have been a challenge even for the best team."

"Indeed, and she apparently did it before any of them knew what was happening."

The day proceeded into early afternoon when a report finally arrived in the WIC building for Thaelyn and his officers to review. They gathered around the conference table and discussed the various details of Kaliya's latest operation. The day wore on until it was time for her class schedule to finish on Tae'Eladar, after which she received a note to report to Rolsklinde for her summary. When she arrived in the strategy room, she was presented by Thaelyn and his usual officers, along with Med-tech Tad'vaal.

"Reporting as requested, my Lord," she announces with a salute and stands at attention.

"Rest at ease, Lieutenant," Thaelyn responds. "And take a seat.

You have been called here for a number of reasons, not the least of which is the report we are studying concerning your most recent exercise."

"I am eager to hear your opinion, my Lord," she offers as she sits in a chair at one end of the table.

"First and foremost, I think it is safe to say that each of us is at once fascinated, perhaps even a bit amused, and for some, rather disturbed at the efficiency and alarming potential you hold with your team."

"That's, well, I suppose it's a good thing, right?"

"Kaliya," Kailen asserts. "I don't know if I should applaud you for your performance or run and hide in a closet for it."

"Oh, Kailen, it can't be that bad."

"Really? You took down a full company of his best men, nearly ten times your own number, and without so much as a whisper. Now I worry if the next time I sit at my desk, my chair will attack me or if my teacup is actually a spy," he laughs.

"I fully agree, Commander," Thaelyn admits. "A clump of sand, a wind-blown leaf, an inkwell... Such innocent items made to serve as disguises for a form of espionage we have no clear defense against."

"But remember, my Lord, I'm on your side," Kaliya soothes.

"And this is our only saving grace. But when we examine this report, we must next ask ourselves as to the ultimate direction for this skill. First would be the utilitarian use for it in any or all forms of service. To infiltrate hostile areas with virtually no risk to our operatives, or to gain access to people and places discreetly and without a trace. You would be at the same time the perfect spy as well as the perfect thief. But this now brings us to the other side of it..."

"The criminal applications, I'll bet, if it's used inappropriately."

"Correct, so your idea of a regulatory commission would be a superb idea, if only we could find a way to do so. This aspect of coming and going virtually undetected could be a problem for us. As for your mission here, under any normal circumstance, I would declare it an unqualified success. In your case, I think I do not even have strong enough words for it. You accomplished what any other team would likely not have been able to accomplish at all, and certainly not to the level of proficiency you did."

Kaliya beams at the commendation, glancing around the table at the other officers and their pleasant responses.

"Furthermore," Thaelyn adds. "Your instructor has given you a prominent point towards your next promotion, which is quite an honor for someone still in the academy and with such young experience as what you have within our service."

Kaliya perks up at the mention and the proud smiles from Kailen and Ankhia.

"But for as much as I will admit to your achievement," he continues. "Let us keep our heads about us and focus on our work."

"Of course! What do you have next for me?"

"Time is pressing upon us, and now we must take some form of action to keep ourselves in line with our objectives. In perhaps just more than a week from now, we are expecting the Suuden-Aryku to make another visit to their mining operations to pick up their supply. We need to take that base and hold it before that happens. We have a few complications in the form of your team being enrolled in classes, and as such still in need to continue their training, so we must carefully manage our scheduling with perhaps rotating teams to impersonate the base crew."

"Do we have those jammers yet?"

"Yes," Ankhia replies. "Our engineers have created a couple of area jammers and a few dozen personal devices. The personal versions are worn as a collar around the neck with a locking clasp. This will ensure they stay where we put them, at least until we can get our hands on these people to keep them under control. Our engineers have suggested it should not be necessary to maintain these once they are here, as the implants could not possibly have such long range as to pass from world to world. We don't know if they can communicate through a conveyor, so it may come down to a local security station or a network hub. Therefore, the personal jammers might be best used on those occasions of relocating them away from their other facilities. After that, we can remove and recycle."

"All right, area units to jam, personal ones to keep it that way when moving things around. What do we do about them afterwards?"

"We will use portal runes to move them to the outpost," Thaelyn responds. "How is your temple training coming along?"

"Aerlie has been assisting us in a crash course on putting people to sleep…you know, without the use of heavy clubs," she grins.

"Yes, that is the preferred method to use," he smiles.

"We've been trying to put in as much of our free time as we can to our new supplemental studies, and we feel we have made enough of a pact with Oghma that he is offering us a favorable stance, if only due to the imperative nature of our upcoming mission, and our new dedication to the cause we are taking for our people."

"Is this to say, he understands the nature of your decree for this skill and the examples you need to set for it?"

"Yes, we explained it to him, and he sees the greater wisdom of it, so he is supporting us now."

"Wonderful work, Kaliya…" he nods. "So, how does it feel now to take up a religion?"

"Relissa asked me this question recently. You know how she is, always yanking my tail about something. But on this occasion, I had to answer that it felt like suddenly I had a new father figure standing over me…well, in addition to my own, of course."

"Yes, naturally. This would be a new sensation for you and your people. I must wonder where it might eventually lead, not only for you but maybe others as well. Might your society of scientists and scholars take up a new belief in a holy figure or symbol that could give you a new direction for yourselves?"

"That would be a sight to see. I'm trying to imagine Ankhia applying a laying-on-hands technique in her medical practice."

"Very well, so you will use whatever combination of your stun or sleep actions to subdue your targets. Ultimately, we want them all asleep, so use the sleep chant on everyone, even after the stun."

"Got it."

"And once they are asleep, you will use portal runes to send them here to us."

"We will collect them at the Naarg uy'Sodrad," Ankhia notes. "And my team will be on standby waiting to permanently disable and try to remove those implants."

"All of them?" Kaliya wonders. "That sounds tricky, and a lot of work all at once."

"I had some practice when studying the cadavers we picked up outside the ship during the battles, and this gave me a good idea of how they're attached. It shouldn't be too bad. Most of it is on the surface with tiny probes embedded into the tissues. The interface is outside, of course, and simply attached to the cranium. We will need to use a little restoration to replace some bone and skin loss from the implantation procedure, but this isn't a problem."

"Good."

"The real problem is the time it'll take to perform the procedure across so many at once. We apparently want to keep everyone asleep until I can process each one. Then we'll move them to a detention facility to recover."

"How many people will you have working this problem?"

"Everyone on my staff, which technically isn't a large number, but Lady Aerlie and her people will assist with some aspects of it."

"This should be fun to watch," she winces.

"The fun part," Kailen suggests, "will be to see their reaction after they wake up. I would personally like to see the look on their faces when they discover who it is that captured them, though that won't come out immediately as we'll be testing them to see if we can gain any useful details out of this."

"Yeah, just imagine… Ten millennia of being pushed from one world to another, and now WE are the ones pushing. I wonder what they'll say to that."

"First things first, though. We need to capture them alive."

"Right. But now, what about Ytani? I'm still reeling from that video recording you showed me. I can't imagine someone who could be as cruel as that."

"Indeed," Thaelyn concedes. "Even Aerlie was surprised at that presentation, or perhaps I should say revolted. His is a most noteworthy example. For this, we have a number of objectives that must be declared where he is concerned. First, Darumon cannot know of it. Second, Ytani must not be allowed access to Azgarén by any means once the base is ours. This includes communications or transport."

"All right, I can already see where we need to disable the communications, but how do we do the transport? Shut down the conveyor?"

"At this point," Kailen offers. "We will probably redirect it to an alternate destination, but we need to know those destinations and if they have any secondary routing locally."

"Like the processor going to Azgarén direct."

"Right, and then choose appropriately. You will need to discover this during your initial raid."

"All right, good."

"As for Ytani himself," Thaelyn continues solemnly. "Kaliya, I must send you on an assassination mission. How does this make you feel?"

"An assassination mission?" she ponders softly, following with a cautious sigh. "Well, this is war, so we should expect there to be casualties. And this one is dangerous, a criminal, one who has broken the law before and seems to desire to do it again, if only to get his hands on someone to do it with. Justice would be a better word for it, rather than assassination, although both might apply as we are taking it into our own hands rather than bringing him into a courtroom."

"This is true, and therefore we must give you the authority to make this decision in the field, not that there is much of a decision to make, as his judgment is already made with those of us here, and I am sure the Suuden'kai Commander also has in mind to do something."

"Do you think he might do it first?"

"I cannot be sure at this point, but I feel we should move before that, if only to ensure our plans for the city follow a predictable path."

"All right, but do we have a plan for it?"

"At this moment, our thoughts revolve around isolating him on one or the other destination endpoints that represent either the processor or the storage site, whichever might seem the most convenient. You will likely need to lure him out somehow, perhaps by using his own desires against him," he grins.

"That sounds more like a job for Suli, actually."

"And use whatever means you can to bring him to your destination. I cannot necessarily advise you on this, other than to say, make it convincing," he smiles gently.

"Uh huh… Did I mention I was a virgin…a sweet innocent virgin?" she chuckles.

"I think the innocent part was lost after you visited his bedroom," Kailen muses.

"Oh, thanks, dear brother!" she grins.

"And the sweet part is brought into question for your innovation at that last testing site," Thaelyn adds.

"Yeah, maybe so. All right, I think I'll need some special lessons on this."

"That poor man," Ankhia moans. "I'm actually starting to feel for him…a little…at least in theory."

"We also need to dispose of the weapon," Thaelyn resumes. "So, perhaps we could clean up two at once in this regard."

"Are you thinking of just detonating the thing?" Kaliya winces. "What would that do to the local space?"

"In a barren fold, not nearly as much as in any other, but I suspect it would still be a lot. However, here we have a small issue, as Adalon sent out notes to us that she wants to hold a meeting regarding this, and this meeting will apparently occur before the Suuden-Aryku would normally pick up the metal, giving us perhaps a few days to plan for it."

"Am I to assume she has a plan? Hmm, this should be interesting."

"You are invited, by the way."

"Me? All right, I guess that makes sense."

"We also have that atomic left behind by the Suuden-Aryku in the mines up north. We might use that somewhere. And I think I might wish to dispose of the processor, as well, to prevent any further activities there."

"This list seems to be growing. So, what I'm getting out of this is to scout those two locations, deal with the crew at the processor, but if it's in a barren fold, we'll need to transport them manually, at least back to Morndindor, before we can use runes on them. Then check the storage site and see what it looks like."

"But do be careful not to set anything off while you are in there," he grins cautiously.

"Oh, you can be sure of that!"

The meeting in the WIC building had completed and Kaliya was sent home to rest and meet with her friends. Relissa and her group were once again sitting in the courtyard, as always, chatting about their daily classwork. Sulíma, Túfula, and Petrith were also visiting to share some details of their language studies and learn more about the other classes they hoped to take later.

"Hey there, kids," Kaliya shouts her usual greeting as she approaches.

"Kali!" Petrith calls back. "The whole academy is talking about that last training session you made. Some are even suggesting you could completely redefine the testing process."

"Yeah, shame on you," Sulíma pouts. "You're making it hard on poor little Petrith over here who needs to catch up with you."

"Well, don't worry about that," Kaliya laughs. "I'm sure there will be plenty of time for him. My team is still in the early stages. Now I need to think about what's ahead of us."

"And what might that be?"

"Well, other than an official mission, I'll be looking forward to a bigger team one day."

"Bigger? How much bigger?"

"Captain size," she grins.

"Buggers!" Relissa yelps. "Don't tell me they're getting ready to promote you again. I'm still trying to turn my head around from the last one."

"It won't be any time soon, I think, but that last mission put me a step ahead for it."

"Kaliya," Marelle recalls. "I spent years in the Allegiance Guard to earn my rank of Lieutenant, and now you're looking at Captain in just a fraction of that? I hate you," she casts playfully.

"Is this how it usually goes for people here?" Túfula asks. "When I look at the Sentinels, and how long it takes there…"

"It takes us a long time for everything, Túfu," Petrith relates. "I think it goes with the territory of living half an eternity."

"Anyway, I need to prepare for my new mission," Kaliya declares. "We're planning on taking that base next."

"Finally," Haran notes. "I was beginning to worry about that for your story of that Prodigy Child running things as he is."

"Yeah, and I also have another mission relating to that. But I need to take some special lessons to see it through right, which is why I'm here now, actually."

"What sort of lessons are those?"

"The kind I might learn from a certain flirtatious little tart I once knew," she casts off to Sulíma.

"Hey!" she protests. "Is that how you see me?"

"Well, Suli, you always did know how to tease the boys."

"How does this relate to that Prodigy Child," Túfula asks.

"He likes girls, apparently. So, I'm going to give him something to keep him for the rest of his miserable…short…life."

"Cu'Nar's pity, Kali…" Petrith moans. "Is this how you treat your men? Maybe I should go crawl under the bed whenever you make your visits," he grins.

"But that doesn't actually answer the question all the way," Túfula resumes.

"Very simply, I need to take him out," Kaliya infers. "So, I'm going to make him an offer he can't refuse, and in the end, we'll have a blast."

◆◆◆◆◆

"Well now, Chancellor, I hope ye've got some good word for me this time," shouts the Thane.

"Aye, good Thane," he submits fawningly. "I know ye've been a-waitin' t' hear word about the bricks. The forges are workin' as hot an' fast as they can burn, an' the lads down below, they be a-smithin' as best they can t' yer service."

"D' I need t' remind ye once again about the point-ears? Ye know they be a-ragin' across the land, an' the warriors can'na hold up the lines if they don'na have the bricks!"

"Aye, that be the way of it for as long as we can remember here. Those nasty point-ears, they be a hard foe t' fight, by the tellin' of it. An' in all the land, we need t' be a-servin' up our fare if we should ever hope t' see the end of this terrible war."

"Right ye be! This war be a-blazin' ever since those point-ears first be a-showin' up on our soil. Ne'er lettin' up on us, ye know this?"

"An' by the tellin' ye've given us for so long, they be a-burnin' our cities an' towns for just as long. I nay can imagine the hard tales from above."

"Ne'er ye mind those tales. The only tales ye need t' be a-knowin' be that we need the bricks! That be the only one t' be a-thinkin' about now."

"An' a fine one, t' be sure. But we have a wee bit of a problem recently."

"Nay! I nay want t' be a-hearin' of yer problems, Chancellor! Ye'll get those forges t' cookin' it up hot an' fast. I nay be a-wantin' t' hear about problems with bricks!"

"Ah, but good Thane, the miners are sayin' the fare be a-slowin' down in this time. They think the veins mayhap be a-runnin' a wee bit thin on us."

"Nay! Nay, nay, nay!" he screeches and stomps on the floor. "I'll nay be t' hearin' this tale! Ye'll tell those miners t' dig deeper, dig wider, dig harder, dig till there nay be anythin' more t' dig! Ye'll get those bricks cookin' up t' where I want them, ye hear?!"

"Right ye be!" the Chancellor offers with feigned enthusiasm. "I'll get back down there an' tell them t' work hard an' find more for ye. We nay want t' be a-slowin' down…even though we've been a-workin' these mines for so long, we may have run out by now. But mayhap not!"

The Chancellor bows curtly and retreats out of the room, leaving the Thane by himself to ponder this unwelcome bit of news. The Hall is empty now and the Thane looks around tentatively while his motions betray his innermost concerns of what this could mean. He begins mumbling to himself, but not speaking Dwarvish. It is another language he unconsciously mutters.

"Dammit! This is the last thing I need right now. First that mine on Therinë, and now this? The processor load will be cut to a fraction before we're done here."

He leaves the Hall to find his personal quarters, once again closing the door behind him and messing up his room after the chambermaids had just finished cleaning it, to give it a lived-in look before departing away in a puff.

He returns to his own body in his private home. He gets up from his chair and strolls into the kitchen to fetch a drink from the refrigerator, then returns to his chair to consider his options. His first action must be to call up the base commander to file a routine report after his visit.

"Commander Kriv'tik, speaking," ushers the cool voice on the data-com terminal.

"This is Ytani. I just finished my most recent visit below."

"What is your report?"

"Mostly the same as usual, but we may have a small issue with our supply down there."

"What has occurred?"

"Nothing major, at least not so far. I'll watch it myself. But that…creature…is now suggesting they might be running out of their mineral vein."

"This is to be expected. They have been mining that vein for almost a century. I expected this long ago."

"Yes, we had this on a few occasions before, but in the past, they were able to find new sources down there. By this time, that hole should be so thoroughly honeycombed with all their little tunnels, I wouldn't be surprised if the city fell into a pit soon. Nevertheless, I'm sure we'll find another. I'll just have them dig new holes until they discover something."

"If that mine runs out, it will severely impact our production schedule. This will leave us with only the one remaining mine."

"I thought of that, and this reminds me again of searching for another deposit. We may find ourselves doing that regardless one day."

The Commander stared at the console in the control booth where the com-link passed through. Ayene and a few other officers were present at the time. He turns to look at her briefly as he gets an idea.

"Ytani, we mentioned before the complications of an expedition. Do you recall that?"

"Yes, Commander, I'm not that empty-headed," he shoots back.

"My direction is to consider a viable option if it becomes necessary. We would need their skills to locate one, as well as their support. I do not believe the drug would work in this instance."

"Yes, I suppose. That drug wipes their senses right off the map. So, what are you suggesting, Commander, that we might actually try it? And why can't you just do it yourself? It can't be THAT hard to find a new mineral deposit."

"Normally, I would agree, and we have been through this before. This mineral contains properties we do not fully understand, and neither do we apparently have the correct technology to process it."

"Yeah, and this is one thing that bothers me the most. We can travel across the galaxy and back again, but we can't figure out how to process some backwards mineral that a bunch of primitive dirt-shovelers can do better."

"To my knowledge, our studies of it seem to indicate it contains some unknown element that our science is unfamiliar with. And I think it is native to this universe we are in."

"And the Marshal? Why can't he just explain it to you? He sure seems to know what it is, as well as this unknown thing."

"I am unsure why he would neglect this, unless we speak of some form of proprietary knowledge that he keeps to himself. Therefore, it seems to fall to us to find our own way. And right now, that requires the support of miners who can participate. But it would need to be carefully planned, and no doubt the operation to simply lead them out that door would likely complicate matters."

"Yes, they think their lovely little ingots are going somewhere useful…well, useful to them, that is. What do you have in mind?"

"We must try to maintain the flow of the metal. If, for instance, we have them try digging their way out of that landslide, it will surely delay our ability to finish this project. And since you are so often bored sitting in that house, I think you would not want to spend that time, correct?"

"Well, Commander, for once you're actually thinking straight. But then, how do we accomplish this without those complications you mentioned?"

"If my interpretation is correct, that drug has a limited duration. If we apply a smaller dose, enough to lead them out, we could transport them into the field for a survey. However, we would need to allow them time to recover first before they can function normally."

"All right, so far I'm with you."

"But simply sending them by themselves might not yield a result. They will need a leader to direct them on this expedition. This means you. You would need to use your skill to guide them on this mission. Can you do this?"

"Wait, you want ME to go out there and lead them?"

"Ytani, where do you expect them to go and what do you expect them to do unless someone TELLS them to do it. Simply dropping them in the middle of a desert is not enough, especially if they think that desert should represent a world they cannot even recognize by now."

"Oh, that..."

"Right. I think they will not follow your direction unless you are present. This must represent a type of campaign, and a campaign is typically led by a leadership figure. Consider, Ytani, they will see the landscape out there and suspect a discrepancy in your stories. You must be present to offer excuses, especially if to uphold these stories you have given and the imperative need for it."

"Of course, I see it, as annoying as it might be, but yes. So, I'll just have to yell at them some more to get them to keep moving until they accomplish something."

"I would further expect this to occupy time, but it is time we must spend if we are to bring ourselves back on schedule."

"Oh, now wait a minute! Am I sensing a delay tactic here, Commander? Are you trying to get out of delivering my next payment, since we're getting so close to the due date?"

"Ytani, a survey for resources is not something that is accomplished in one day. You do not simply pick a spot and start digging holes, and boom, there you are. Just ask any REAL mining team, like those we have back home. It requires geological studies, boreholes and mineral sampling, and other procedures simply to find a viable deposit, to say nothing of establishing the actual operation. And that is with our own industry. I cannot speak for these people, but I must assume it to be a similar process. Otherwise, if the metal ceases, our operation ceases. And if our operation ceases, your job ceases, along with your...payment. It is that simple."

Ytani went silent for a moment, as the reasoning was actually sound, although it also seemed like a lot of work he didn't actually care for, not for all those steps. In addition to this, his ego didn't allow him to believe his purpose would end with such a mundane occupation as this one job. He was worth more than that.

"Commander, even though this operation is exceedingly dull, those few moments where I gain so much joy are worth keeping it around a bit longer. We will finish this operation, whether fast or slow, and I will take my payments, ALL of them, for as long as there is still something out there to mine."

"Does this mean you are no longer interested in this plan to bring the Marshal back on schedule?"

"I'll simply explain the existing mines are running low. I'm sure he'll understand. After all, it's not MY fault the mineral veins only hold a fixed amount. And since he loves this stuff so much, I might ask him if we can extend this lovely little arrangement even longer. Then we might consider this plan of yours to compensate."

"Ytani, maybe you should also ask him why he wants it in the first place, and whether or not there is a true limit to his needs. My impression is he has this quota for a specific reason, and that number is fixed."

"I don't care!" he shouts. "After all, I'm sure you can never have too much of that...stuff...he's making."

"That...stuff...appears to be a highly volatile explosive material. Too much? For what reason. What does he plan on blowing up, and how many of them? You can only blow something up one time, and there is nothing left of it."

"Again, I don't care! That's not my problem! Unless HE tells me he needs it faster, I'll just say we get what we get out of it."

"I see," the Commander pauses to restrain his feelings. "Ytani, my base staff is not here to be sacrificed to your fetishes."

"Commander!" he screeches. "Your base staff is here to serve whatever it is you're told to serve. That chip inside your head doesn't allow you to have a personal life. The same goes for those females in there."

"These females are all trained professionals, Ytani, not prostitutes. I do not care if Central has more, it costs resources to train and condition them as soldiers and technical experts. They are not here to lift their tails to you."

"Commander, this is it!" he shrieks. "One more outburst from you and I'm calling in my own private army. I'd like to see how long you can last with a bunch of stunted spear wielders sticking their pointy things in all your sensitive spots. I'll grant you two choices, out of the immense kindness of my heart. Either you send your least valuable female to me, or you find some dull-horned civilian and bring her in here for it. I suppose one rag-tail is the same as the next. And a civilian might not cause as much groaning out of you for the loss. Then just lose her in the desert. I'm sure no one will notice."

Ytani cuts the link.

The Commander sighs and once again glances around the room at his staff.

"Well, Sir," Ayene relents. "It was a good try."

"A good try…maybe, but in the end, his mania cannot be resolved. He must be removed. Now he would dare threaten any random civilian and leave her body in the desert?"

"His attitude seems to have taken a serious boost recently."

"He felt the power of control when he had Ensign Ka'zheen in his house."

"I shudder to think of what he did to her, after seeing all those devices of his in there."

"She will be the last. But then we need to think of what comes next."

"The metal?"

"Yes, and the Marshal, maybe even Central Command if they cannot be made to understand our situation."

"Commander, maybe you should file another complaint, at least to put something on record."

"I will consider this, but if the Marshal is overriding them, it may not matter."

"You cannot direct it to someone else? Someone who can review it, at the very least, to call in third-party attention and spread the information to additional witnesses who are not so closely monitored by him? Possibly to override HIM and his authority over us?"

"I, uh…well, I suppose this is possible. There is a clear chain of command, but maybe… He tends to classify everything he does. This is one of his tools…"

"Precisely, Sir!" she urges. "One of his tools to cover up everything he does, and denying anyone ELSE to review it."

Ayene finished by clutching her interface for the minor feedback hit she was now suffering after her outbreak. The Commander took notice of this, along with several others in the room.

"Yes, Ayene, you are correct. And this might also reflect on some of my past experiences with him. All right, I will consider this as well. Meanwhile, if the mine below runs out, it will become useless to us, so we might need to close it off to prevent them from discovering our position. This leaves only the one to the south."

"And once those miners expire?"

"Lieutenant, how long have they been in there?"

"I think it is going on seven months soon…not critical but getting there."

"I am asking myself how they might feel if we should reveal ourselves to them. If we take that drug away and allow them to recover, maybe to offer medicine for their illness, could we make a deal with them to continue the work willingly?"

"That represents a very problematic question. And not simply for how they would respond to where they are, and WHY they are there. All they need to do is look outside."

"Yes…" he sighs deeply. "He did this. And he makes us do the rest. And we spend innocent lives on it."

"Oh yes! And then we have that…stuff, as Ytani likes to call it. What is THAT for. Sir, a question, if I may… I recall the original reports of this world describing a contamination effect by those insurgents. What can we say about that where this city is concerned? It has been isolated for four centuries, and my understanding of these natives is they do not live that long naturally. If there was any contamination effect down there, it should be long forgotten."

"Especially after Ytani and all his stories. I cannot be sure about that report. It sounds like too many others I heard before."

"Your earlier missions, perhaps?"

"Yes, Lieutenant, those… Something was described, but with questionable details that do not appear appropriate on the surface. And his description of those people does not sound as if they could threaten us anyway."

"Other than for the use of sharp implements," she glances at her body and the seed entity. "Yet another of my complaints for being who we are."

He gazes at her momentarily, then examines her figure, and spreads his attention to the rest of the crew, and finally himself.

"And one more reason to suspect his intentions…did we actually need this. This was related to that old symptom, but it was never resolved. And then…well…"

"So, we have a questionable contamination effect, followed by a planetary wipe, the isolation of this city, and everything we have done since. This gives the impression of stealing their local resources with the added benefit of no one coming up to us to complain about it. Sir, if I said before I am losing my interest in serving this military, I am very close to quitting now."

"You and me both… But for now, we need to stay together and try to finish this."

"All right, what is our next course of action, Sir?"

"I want you to run a few calculations. I recall once Ytani giving reports on the types of food these people eat. Do you remember those?"

"That was a long time ago, in the early days when we were first trying to stabilize the city after they bottled themselves up."

"Yes, find them and conduct some research, then try to calculate for that work crew in the mine. If we cut their existing food, we need to replace it with something normal, and this will need to be requisitioned."

"But Sir, are you saying you would do this? I mean, yes, it would be the right thing to do, but do you think they would help us or attack us?"

"Ayene, we will lose them in a few months anyway. If they turn on us, it is really no different an outcome, but at least they will survive. And if we can negotiate, maybe we can make an arrangement and explain what happened."

"That will have to be one nether-wild explanation, Sir. And what about those in the city? These people apparently live to dig, by Ytani's descriptions. Even if we try closing it off, if they should find us, and then turn on us, we will need to run, although I have no idea where, except through the conveyor, which only leads home. We do not have a ship of any kind."

"Then we need to prepare a plan for ourselves. I think we will be losing this operation soon. I do not know if... Well, maybe I can find some help. But it will also very likely bring complications."

"All right people, listen up," Kaliya shouts to her team. "In two days, we're taking that base. I want everyone to check their gear. This is going to be a nighttime raid, at least as far as Morndindor is concerned. We'll be going out next weekend in the morning. For them, that's late evening. We need to be sure we have everything in order."

The team was inspecting a new set of gear they had received and stowed in their backpacks. This included a custom-designed bodysuit in black leather, made to cover them fully from horn to hoof, including boots with insulated padding to soften their hoof steps. They had hoods sculpted to hug the contours of their heads, with pockets for their horns, and masks to cover their faces. They also received a set of specially made goggles to cover their eyes in an effort to dim their innate glow. The design was to conceal them as Daanen-Aryku, even though they might still resemble a familiar form, which in this case could just as easily be mistaken for Suuden-Aryku, minus the obvious mutation deformity. They would carry a set of area effect jamming devices and a large collection of personal collars, as well as basic combat knives in case things went bad, and lethal force was necessary.

A delivery was made from Ankhia involving a bag containing several hypo-spray devices from the medical lab, along with a large number of vials containing strong sedatives, just in case their priest sleep chant ran out on them. This might be especially useful at the production facility, since it was expected to be outside an arcanic cloud, and they would not be able to use magic to take down their foes. Although priest spells were not based on arcanic energy, as these were divine gifts, and usually transcended beyond the need for the flows, so this much should still work.

Kaliya also received a rune pointing to the outpost camp with Captain Hagmaert. This would serve as a waypoint drop-off for the collected prisoners, where they would be checked and forwarded to the medical teams at the Naarg uy'Sodrad. Since Kaliya was the only one so far with enough mage training, she would need to remain physical in order to properly enchant the rune to use it. She could not do this while projected.

After checking their gear, she had them go over the photos and recent reports of activity in the base in order to refresh themselves of the situation. She was nervous about this mission. The training exercises were just practice, even though they were to be treated as serious situations, but this had a different feel to it. She also had her team review several of the spy videos to become familiar with their targets and their general manners, so they could effectively imitate them later.

They were using the tactical planning room of the guildhall to assemble their gear and make these final preparations. This operation had to go down smooth and easy, without Ytani noticing, and without any alerts passing through to Azgarén. Among their priorities were to take control of the operations booth, including the communications relay. A team of technicians would be kept on hand to move into position to reconfigure the consoles, as well as the conveyor, as needed for their future operations.

While making their cursory review of their plans, Marelle appeared in the doorway.

"Lieutenant," she announces officially on entering the room. "I'm offering myself to your service for this mission."

Kaliya looks up to see her standing just inside the room at attention.

"Marelle, what are you doing here?" she asks.

"You're going to need a pilot to take you through the conveyor, or rather two conveyors when you consider those other locations, and I'm your pilot."

"Um, Marelle, no offence, but aren't you still in training?"

"Yes, but then so are most of us. Yet I feel I have enough experience to qualify for this mission. I've already confirmed my position with His Lordship on this matter, and he had to agree with me for my motives."

"And what motives are those?"

"First, you need to pass through the conveyor to find each of those other locations for the production of the weapon, and for this you need a pilot. Second, you need a ship, and my understanding is they have one very conveniently sitting there inside the base."

"But that's a Suuden'kai vessel. Will you be able to fly it?"

"It's all the same to me at this point. The photos I reviewed of the transport didn't look too bad. Besides, I flew that heavy transport from the mining enclave down to Firstfall well enough, and it was considerably larger."

"Well, I guess I can't argue with that," she chuckles. "Although you also scared virtually everyone in the camp along the way."

"Yes, well, minor detail," she grins. "The point is I did it with a remarkable amount of grace and style for someone who never flew an aircraft before. And I'm confident I can do it again. Besides, I'll have my instructor helping me."

"So, I'm going to have a trainee pilot and her civilian flight instructor piloting a military troop transport through hostile space to deliver my people on a covert mission into enemy territory. Well, so much for this operation!" she laughs.

"Kaliya, you should know me by now!" she teases. "Besides, I think I have an edge on this that even Thaelyn couldn't argue. And for this, I'm going to help you all the way through until you finally do away with Ytani, which by the way should ensure our full success…I hope."

"Oh, this should be good, especially considering your reputation with him. All right, what is this edge of yours?"

"Remember that time when Adalon made her appearance in the

courtyard, and she gave that new prophecy? She said I had some up-and-coming moment with her, and Thaelyn thinks this involves our final showdown on Azgarén. So, if you believe in prophecies, and she has a good reputation where this goes, I should survive whatever I do, at least long enough to meet that moment. And this is why I'm offering myself to you on this mission."

Kaliya grimaces at the absurd form of rationalization, but Adalon's prophecies were surely guiding them forward, so it couldn't be argued.

"Marelle, he's right about one thing… You have a wicked sense of mischief in you. So, you're offering yourself on this otherwise very dangerous mission, where we could possibly be transporting, or even trying to dispose of, what might be described as THE most dangerous material known to men and gods alike, only because of a prophecy saying you have something waiting for you in the end, and this isn't the end yet?"

"Um, yeah, that's about the size of it. So, am I in?"

Kaliya turns to study the blank stares of her teammates in the room, some of which can only turn away in amazement at the gall of this suggestion.

"And Thaelyn approved this?"

"Well, better to say he couldn't argue with my reasoning, so it's approved by default."

"Uh huh… And did he give you any new marks on that list of his?"

"Well, um…yeah, a little one," she coughs subtly.

Kaliya shakes her head at the notion, but she couldn't deny the implications.

"Marelle, I wonder what sort of career you're going to end up with here. All right then, you're in, but you'll need to hang back until the base is secure, and we'll go the next step together."

"Excellent! I'm sure it'll be a pleasure working with you," she salutes and leaves to meet with her instructor to inform him of the plan.

Kaliya watches as Marelle leaves the room, slowly shaking her head at the odd encounter, but feeling a subtle sense of fulfillment that with Marelle's help, this mission has taken on a greater sense of confidence.

When her team had finished organizing their packs, she dismissed them to other duties while she went in search of Sulíma.

* * *

"Unbelievable…" Kailen moans softly.

"Commander?" Thaelyn wonders. "Is there something wrong? I believe you were studying the most recent spy video, correct?"

"Yes, Your Lordship, and I'm sitting here pondering our long journey as we were chased from one world to another by these people. I recall stories of homes blasted, people killed in the streets, and the rest just barely loading up and jumping to our next destination, only to see a repeat later on. It was nightmarish, to say the least. Now, here I am looking at these officers and feeling sorry for their desperate struggle against Ytani and Darumon. It's the last thing I would've ever expected to see, especially for the history we have with them. And it makes me rethink everything, finally to wonder about the rest of Azgarén."

"What do we have today?"

"Apparently," he sighs. "Our propaganda about the mines in the city running low is paying off a little. Ytani came in with a report, but he and the Commander got into another argument. The Commander apparently tried his own little play about sending out a survey mission, using Ytani as the expedition leader, so he could make up excuses along the way of why the world isn't as it should be for all his stories."

"Interesting, and rather clever…"

"Ytani almost bought it, too. They had in mind to use that drug to pull out a team, which would sidetrack the obvious questions of that door and the road, then drop them somewhere, let them recover, and Ytani would lead from there."

"And this is even more interesting. Then, the Commander is

suggesting they need to be aware of themselves in order to successfully fulfill the mission."

"Yes, but here is where Ytani caught on to the play. The Commander suggested, and even had to explain it in baby terms for Ytani to understand, how and why it would take time, but time well spent if to put them back on schedule."

"Baby terms?" Thaelyn raises his brow.

"Oh, this is good. My first impression here might need to involve how long Ytani has been in there, and when he was originally pulled out for this service."

"Oh? And how would you describe this?"

"If he started young, he was likely still in school, maybe even as low as junior school. That doesn't give much education."

"Powers help us, but yes."

"Next is he doesn't seem to like going outside for anything physical. The Commander had to explain how these things take time to perform such as geological studies, core samples, and ultimately the establishment of a full mining operation. Something that could easily take weeks or months on a good site, based on our own tech, to say nothing of what those dwarves are capable of."

"Indeed, and so appropriate. But to explain it in baby terms might suggest Ytani thinks these people can simply sniff it out like a hound for a piece of meat. Should I ask about his reaction?"

"Violent, of course… He turned it around that the Commander was attempting a stall tactic. He said he doesn't care how long it takes, and that the Marshal will just have to accept that mines run out on occasion. He further suggested to have a talk with him about extending the operation, maybe to use this idea of surveys at a later time because, and I quote: You can never have too much of that stuff…referencing the Arcanicium, I suppose."

"Incredible. If only he knew what that…stuff…truly was."

"In reference to that, I think none of them do, only that it's highly volatile and explosive. The Commander tried to excuse it away that the Marshal may have a quota for a reason, being a fixed amount, no more, and likely to blow something up, which can only be blown up once and that's all."

"Indeed!" he chuckles ironically. "So, never having too much means he can blow something up multiple times? How interesting."

"Oh yes, this guy is a piece of work. Unfortunately for all of us, Ytani doesn't seem to care what, where, how, or why. Unless the Marshal himself tells different, its business as usual, with him getting his payments on schedule. Perhaps even to keep it going so he can take his payments indefinitely."

"Dear Powers, I cannot believe that man."

"Oh, it gets even better! The Commander then tried to protect his people by saying the females are military professionals, not prostitutes, but Ytani only countered that they're all expected to behave like trained animals due to the chips. And he's apparently tired of these arguments by now. He's pressuring the Commander with his private army of dwarves, and at this moment, I believe he might actually do it if his next demand is not fulfilled."

"This is serious," the General mutters solemnly. "Is he demanding anything now, or is he still pointing at the delivery date?"

"Nothing was mentioned immediately, so I'm guessing it still stands as before. But he also gave a new ultimatum. Listen to this. Either the Commander should sacrifice his least valuable officer or find some random civilian and import her for the job, and then drop whatever is left of her in the desert, as no one is likely to take notice."

"That's even more despicable than anything else I've heard so far! Now he is targeting civilians! This young man is turning into a serial-minded killer."

"With the only constant here being the timing for this metal," Thaelyn accedes. "But still, this could develop into any number of other permutations. Did the Commander have anything further to say about this?"

"This is where Ytani hung up," Kailen recalls. "But after the conversation ended, the Commander and that one officer, Lieutenant Ti'van, shared a brief dialog concerning their actions. This is where I'm having my issues right now with all my personal memories and feelings from our long chase. They spoke of losing the mine in the city, and potentially the need to close it off to prevent detection. Then the mine to the south, asking about the duration of the miners, this drug poisoning effect, and possibly trying to save them by taking this drug away, giving medicine, and a few carefully worded explanations to gain their support, if it is at all possible. Otherwise, they're losing this operation and may need to evade."

"Very curious… I will need to consider these aspects carefully. It would seem they hold remorse for those dwarves."

"Chips or no chips," the General muses. "They're still people after all."

"Not just that," Kailen continues. "But I heard the Commander mention something about inconsistencies in their orders for the planetary bombardment, and a vague reference to previous missions he was on. He apparently filed complaints in the past, which were ignored, likely by the Marshal, and that Lieutenant suggested passing them to others…for other witnesses to see…since the Marshal apparently classifies virtually everything to cover up for himself… and explicitly so they could NOT evaluate what he was doing."

"How very interesting," Thaelyn nods softly. "And so very typical, especially for our past observations."

"Therefore, it gives the impression he is skeptical of Darumon's intentions. And finally, that Lieutenant associated this as stealing resources with no one to complain about it."

"Indeed!" Thaelyn croons. "This is the female? She sounds like a passionate one. Yes, this could be useful. For this, I may have a few ideas on how I might proceed in my interrogation. If we could play on the illegality aspect of this operation, perhaps we could learn a few things, and then use this to break open his loyalty to Darumon. He seems like a rational-minded individual, despite the chips and Darumon's attempts to govern him. He would make a good starting point for a defector."

"So, in the end, we might actually have him working for us. That would be fun to see."

"And then it comes down to Ytani," the General spurs. "My

Lord, this is one of those occasions where I simply feel revolted over the affairs of this war."

"I must agree, General," Thaelyn nods. "But Ytani will not have his day on this occasion. First, he does not hold as much power over the dwarves as he thinks, although this might not help the Commander and his situation for the secrecy aspect. Second, the Commander and his people will be removed from the equation, and therefore Ytani will hold no more power over anything. We will reduce him down to a simple lonely young man with his private delusions of grandeur, at least until Kaliya moves in. Hmm, yes, maybe SHE could pose as our lovely young and very innocent civilian playmate. And let us also leave her unmodified, as further enticement to his virility. If this does not pull him out of that house, I cannot imagine what would."

"Cu'Nar's pity," Kailen mourns. "There goes my baby sister again."

"Commander, have your people been able to examine that detonator for the atomic and adjust it to our needs?"

"Yes, actually," he affirms. "The unit is very easy to reconfigure. We simply need to reprogram the clock mechanism. It's currently waiting for us at the Bahlaie Center, and we can input any number you need for the timing. As for the atomic itself, it's still located in a remote area to prevent accidental radioactive contamination."

"Good. If our intentions are to destroy that processor, we might use that. But then, I wonder… We should see about any remaining input material stockpiles to be found there. I see no point in destroying good adamantium along with everything else. Then we have the weapon. Adalon wants to discuss options, but I wonder if we want to leave any product at the processor or move it all to the final site. And then what…do we detonate it? Commander, what sort of explosives can you produce that are viable in a zero-atmosphere environment?"

"I am aware of a number of plastic explosives we can use. We sometimes use this in our mining operations, but in the right configuration it should work in space. What do you have in mind?"

"Just in case we do detonate something, we must have it ready for use. I think one small charge, enough to set off one quantity of product. I cannot be sure how this product is packaged, so let us make a few tender assumptions, like an air-tight container, in case we need to repackage it, and a timing mechanism, something Kaliya can activate in projected mode. Then, if we should use this site for Ytani's last stand, I am thinking of relocating this outside where she could set it down and engage it out of his reach. We will have him go down with this…stuff…he seems so fond of," he smirks.

"Oh, that's nasty. And then what, have him sit and watch the timer count down?"

"For lack of a better solution, but we cannot allow him to tamper with it."

✦✦◆✦✦

"Now remember," Sulíma instructs. "It's not only what you say, but also how you move. There's a very precise way to play with the boys, and we girls know exactly how to tickle their tails without letting them tickle ours."

"Yeah, and you have a reputation of tickling tails that dates back to our early days on Ruuki uy'Daan."

"Well, Kali, some of us just have natural talent," she giggles. "Now, let's practice that walk again. You need to get this right if you want any hope of getting him to chase you."

"Chasing is one thing, catching is another. Let's not forget, he's a violent person, and treats women as objects for his personal desires. He might just as well choose to drag me off into his house and try having his way with me."

"But you'll be in projected form, right?"

"True, but he can't know this, at least not immediately. All he can know is I'm a cute girl he wants to chase…and do whatever else he thinks he can get away with. At least up until I can corner him somewhere."

"When you say corner him somewhere, what do you have in mind for him after that?"

"Well, it won't involve tickling tails, you can be sure of that much."

The two girls shared a few laughs as Sulíma directs Kaliya into her performance. She was teaching Kaliya how to flirt unabashedly with a series of tried and tested methods Sulíma had developed over her lifetime, involving modal expressions and vocal manners, as well as provocative body language and postures.

"Here we have the follow-along strut," Sulíma demonstrates.

She begins walking a line with her hands clasped femininely behind her waist, a clear sway to the hips, and a prominent tick-tock sweep of the tail. Kaliya follows the practice, mimicking the motion while strutting across the room.

"Good, be sure to wag the tail in wide arcs," Sulíma affirms. "This says you want his attention, but you aren't actually announcing it openly. Next, we play the coy weave. This can be a circle, or my favorite, a double-circle."

She begins a casual saunter in a figure-eight pattern, looping one side to the other while passing demure and suggestive glances at her alleged suitor. At the same time, she occasionally brings a finger to press sensuously on her lower lip.

"Suli, I'm surprised you're still a virgin," Kaliya chuckles as she observes the display.

"It's a gift," she teases. "Now you do it."

Kaliya makes the effort to imitate the motion, following the same path on the floor and making the same expressions and gestures. She couldn't help but feel a certain power to the sultry moves. It harkened deep within her natural instincts.

"Not bad," Sulíma admits. "But now, in case he tries to play the game his way, we need to remind him who has the slender tail here."

"Uh huh, and how do you suggest that, Suli?"

"I have a special little trick I came up with years ago. Unfortunately, since we were stuck on Ruuki uy'Daan all that time with orcs in our backyard, I didn't really have much opportunity to try it. I'm actually jealous that you'll get the first use out of it."

"Let's just call it a practice run and I'll give you the results later," she grins.

"This is a suggestive action to keep things under your control. We'll say he wants to play it his way, but you're not going to give him that option. To reinforce the idea, you need to remind him who makes the rules here. This is your response if he says something that you don't want to lead in his direction."

Sulíma steps back and takes up her previous coy posture, then strolls slowly around with her back turned to her opponent. She turns over her shoulder seductively, allowing her mouth to part open with her tongue crossing just into view over her teeth, then lays a finger on it and drawing down, swinging it around alluringly as she speaks.

"Tail..." she croons erotically while pointing at the appendage.

"Grace of the cu'Nar, Suli," Kaliya mentions at the sequence. "If he doesn't pick up and charge at me for that..."

"Just be sure to keep your distance with room to run. Don't forget, we girls are faster than the boys. So long as you get to your ship before he gets to you, we're in business."

"Thanks, Suli. Maybe we can play this on Petrith one of these days just to tease him."

"We'll need soap for that, remember," she giggles.

✦ ✦ ✦ ✦ ✦

"Easy there, lads, that be a big one!" shouts the dwarven mining foreman as his crew works to remove a large boulder.

"Aye t' that!" calls one of the workers. "It looks like the mountain came down in here."

"But the real question t' me thinkin'," declares another worker. "Did it come down as the work of the point-ears, or be it another reason?"

"Ye mean by the tales makin' the run through the streets?" the foreman asserts. "Aye, they be a-tellin' of the old tales that the point-ears were sickly an' weak. Some say they nay even got this far. The warriors were a-cuttin' through them for the mercy of it as they dropped out of their portals. If that be the way of it, this came down for another reason."

"Fine, but what about the Thane's tales of them ragin' across the land? There yay be a grand hole in there somewhere. If they did'na get this far, or even if they did, could they actually d' this amount of harm t' the mountain? It would take a mighty blast t' knock all this rock loose."

"Aye lads, an' all the more reason we need t' be a-seein' the outside t' see what else there be."

"What about that other door in the store? Did anyone ever pass through t' see where it goes?"

"The only tale I have on that be a long stair goin' straight up. I heard one fellow say he could see the valley outside, but it be barren an' dry, with no people in sight, and bits of the outer city blasted by somethin'. Mayhap this can also explain this rock here if some kind of pummelin' came down on it. Aside from that, it nay be a-goin' anywhere I think we want t' travel right now, if it be t' places nay friendly t' us. We don'na have any warriors t' fight anythin'. An' ye can thank the Thane for this much."

"But if they nay be friends, what if they should decide t' come down through that door t' find us?"

"I think it yay be clear they know we're in here. If they be friends, it should'na matter. But if they be foes, this be where our bricks be a-goin'. So we should see what be outside first afore decidin' on the rest."

"Aye, but this makes me think now. What if they come again t' pick up the bricks? Surely, they'll be a-seein' us in here diggin', an' get wise t' us movin' about."

"That be a good thought, lad," the foreman considers. "But the last word on it be a-tellin' they don'na pick up but one time a month, an' it nay be ready yet. I be a-thinkin' of puttin' up a false door in there t' make it look as though there nay be anythin' t' look at."

"A false door?"

"Aye, one t' look like the rubble we cleared away. That should fool them well enough."

"A fine one, that! Mayhap we can get a few of the lads t' workin' on that already."

The dwarves inside the city had been hard at work clearing away debris and large rocks in the upper town area of old Glimmerheim. The loose material was being relocated into the many holes they dug previously as part of their local mining efforts, to pack in some of the older tunnels. They were making progress slowly if only for the large shards of stone collapsed into the cavern from the impact of the bombardment weapon on the mountainside above. Somewhere behind this clutter were the doors leading outside, but it was becoming obvious those doors might not be in working order due to the other damage.

Outside the mountain, tunneling inward from the western side of the landslide covering the doors was another team. This group was an excavation crew consisting of dwarves from Tae'Eladar, and a few natives to cover for the language barrier should they meet with those inside. They were making good progress so far, using mechanized tools to chisel away the slide, and wagons to haul the debris, then to shore up the tunnel with reinforced concrete. The earth they were boring through was softer and did not include as many large rocks as what came down inside, since the outside suffered the impact of the heavy weapon, and the resulting shockwave pulverized the material into smaller bits. But this also resulted in a more difficult job to build a secure passage in the loose material.

The objective here was to meet at the doors, hopefully to make their encounter as the other team from inside cut their way through. It would be at this moment when the two sides would offer their greetings and share their stories. The biggest concern would be how the people inside would interpret the strange visitors meeting them halfway, as they were not informed as yet of the nature of the outside world and what actually happened. This was still a secret only known to Eiki, Telta, Angan, and most recently the Chancellor. They were waiting on the signal from Thaelyn's side as to the situation on the enemy base upstairs.

Meanwhile, the outpost stayed busy with scouts riding out on their gryphons surveying the land in search of more survivors. Belrum and several of his fellows were still making their runs, travelling far afield from their home while other scouts charted new maps of the land, creating an ever-expanding picture of the devastation of the world from the bombardment.

"Captain," shouts a returning scout. "I have a new report for you here. We're making our way along the western coastline travelling south now. We think we found another one, maybe two new settlements. We'll be sending people out there to follow up on it."

"Good to know. Maybe this world isn't as dead as we first thought. Can you tell how well they're surviving out there?"

"We were at high altitude, so as not to make a strong showing in the sky, but we saw something outside near a shoreline, possibly a small village. They might be trying to survive by fishing the sea."

"I have to wonder how many fish are biting under these conditions, but if the settlement was evident enough to see from up there, maybe they're doing better than some."

"Possibly, but we should still make contact so we can combine their efforts with the others."

"Agreed. We'll get on that for our next run. Sit a moment and take a break."

While the Captain and his men made their work at scouting the land, back in the mining base, Lieutenant Ti'van was visiting the Commander's office again. By this time, it was late afternoon on Morndindor.

"Commander?"

"Yes, Lieutenant, what is it?"

"I am becoming increasingly worried, nearly to the point of a feedback hit, about Ytani and his threats. I have even gone so far as to equip myself with a pulse pistol in case he tries breaking into my room."

"You are becoming paranoid. This is not healthy, Ayene. You need to settle yourself. His threats are based on his reward for his service. We still have several days to go before that, and then we will take action."

"We cannot take action before that?"

"I will wait for one last full shipment before taking that action.

Unless we are able to somehow negotiate with the people below, this might be the last one from the city, regardless of their shortages. As soon as he finishes his visit and calls in his report, we will make our advance. And if he is so insensitive as to drop everything out there in the desert, we will do the same for him."

✦✦✦

"Mister Girhani, please come in," Thaelyn directs from the conference table in the WIC strategy room. "How have you been faring with your studies thus far?"

"I've been mostly involved with your language class at the academy," Petrith admits. "So, I can't say I've done much else on that side of it. But the Commander set up a team of engineers to assemble some equipment for me to play with to refresh my memory on data systems and network interfacing. We're using some computing terminals designed as testing platforms, combined with, um…" he clears his throat emphatically, "…some recently acquired communications and data storage equipment you apparently found in the last days of your war here."

"Yes, I thought that might come in handy for you, especially as it can give you an introduction on the Suuden'kai designs."

"One thing I was noticing right away is the Suuden-Aryku seem to use a lesser grade of data encryption than what we had that one time in the Security Council mainframe. The Commander suggested ours was so high-grade because we were trying to hide it from them. But in their case, I guess when you're at the top of the food chain, with no one to threaten you, who do you have to hide from?"

"This seems to be a common theme for them," the General muses. "Perhaps we can use this to our advantage?"

"Based on what I'm seeing with these units you picked up; I should be able to find a way inside with just a little practice to uncover some access codes. When we take that base, I'd like to take a close look at some of their terminals, if any are left open, and search through

458

their files locally, maybe even to see about a passive data feed from their network."

"This sounds like a reasonable course," Thaelyn agrees. "We simply need to be discreet and not allow our efforts to stand out too boldly, if at all."

"Of course, I understand, but having access to their network could work wonders for me to learn more about them."

"We will also need you to study their conveyor control panel to see how it might be operated so we can send Kaliya's team forward to the next step."

"Right, just send the word when you're ready and I'll be there."

"Good to hear. We are scheduled to make this engagement on the morrow. I would suggest you keep your schedule open to accommodate this."

"Absolutely, Your Lordship."

The weekend was dawning, and Kaliya had assembled her team in the tactical planning room of the guildhall. They were making one last check of their gear before setting out. They had already donned their new leather outfits, which hugged their bodies closely. Their hoods were pulled back to leave their heads exposed, and they were fastening their belts with their knives and several slots for potions. Finally, they hefted their packs over their shoulders and began making their way outside to the courtyard.

Relissa and her friends, along with Sulíma and her group, were all waiting outside when the team came into view. They couldn't help but ogle at the professional appearance.

"Jiggers," Relissa mutters. "You look like you're up for something serious, even though I already know it's serious."

"This is the big one, Relissa," Kaliya replies. "No more games. Now we take the fight to them, for the first time since we left Azgarén."

"And we didn't actually fight them on Azgarén," Petrith remarks. "We just left."

"That's true, this is really the first time for a lot of things, and we need to get it right."

"Good luck to you, Kaliya," Haran offers. "May the gods walk with you."

"After what she did to that practice range last time," Relissa winces. "I think they'd do better to just step out of the way."

"I will agree with Haran," Túfula adds. "May the cu'Nar guide you. We've never gone into battle like this before, so we'll all be waiting for your safe return."

Kaliya smiles at all the well-wishes and nods for the favor.

"This is actually considered a fairly small operation as compared to my practice runs, but no less critical."

"Will you be taking on that man during this trip?" Sulíma asks.

"Not yet. First the base, and we'll work him in with the timing for their next pick-up of the metal, so he won't be suspecting anything out of the ordinary."

"How long before that?" Túfula asks.

"That should be close to the end of this next week, but a nighttime operation for us so it coincides with daytime there."

Kaliya pans across the group to single out one in particular.

"Marelle, are you ready?" she asks.

"Yes, Lieutenant!" she perks up at attention.

"You don't actually need to stand in such formal posture for me, Marelle."

"Technically I do, since I don't officially carry my former rank from the Guard."

"All right then... You'll follow us to the outpost and wait until we have the base. Petrith, you too, and we'll send for you to take us to the next point."

"As you wish, Lieutenant," he answers while also forming at attention.

Kaliya shakes her head in amusement before proceeding out onto the street. She leads the group, along with Marelle and Petrith, to the gateway terminal, following through to the hub station, and then to Rolsklinde. On arrival, they made a detour to the WIC building to check in. Marelle's flight instructor was waiting for her, as well as a small group of engineers from the Naarg uy'Sodrad to assist Petrith with interpreting the Suuden-Aryku control room instrumentation.

"My Lord, we're ready," she announces. "Do we have any last-minute instructions?"

"I believe we have covered as much as can be covered for now," he confesses. "Simply keep low and remember not to cause any significant disturbance in close proximity to that house. This includes the activation of the transport. We do not know how much of a sound sleeper Ytani might be."

"And I would also mention the conveyor," Kailen adds. "Redirecting the conduit might make a disturbance as the new rift is forming."

"That as well. Let us hope Ytani tends to ignore such anomalies."

Kaliya gives a salute and turns to leave the building. She leads her troupe across the plaza to the gateway node standing on one side as a dedicated link to Ruuki uy'Daan and jumps through. As she emerges on the other side, she turns toward the node leading to Morndindor, and makes another leap. The assembly arrives in the outpost camp with Captain Hagmaert and his crew, along with several priests as backup for the sleep chant, and some dwarven forge keepers who had arrived earlier. It was late evening.

"Well now, Lieutenant, don't you look important!" the Captain declares haughtily as he studies the new arrivals. "Are we going to a costume ball this eve?"

"Yes, Captain! We hope to crash that sleepy little party and send them for a wild ride."

He laughs at the cute response before giving his final word.

"Our scouts say the base seems quiet, only a few inside the window at their forward station. If they follow their standard pattern, most should be asleep by now. We'll wait for you to bring them out and check their condition before sending them forward. Good luck to you."

"Thank you, Captain. Marelle and Petrith will stay here until I call for them. Meanwhile, I'd like for a few of my people to take up seating so they can project."

"Understood, you can use my office if you like."

Kaliya turns to her team to begin giving orders.

"I'm expecting we shouldn't need too many projected on this run. If most of them are asleep, we only need enough to draw attention and to use the jammers. On this occasion, let's have Alpha take a turn. We have two area jammers. They tell me the range is best kept to a single room for assurance. Let's have two of you go under. We'll meet on that road up there."

The teammates find a seat inside the officer's hut and begin their meditation to project outwards. While they work on that, Kaliya observes the rest of the camp.

"Captain, once the base is secure, I'll send my people back to reclaim their bodies and rejoin with us up there. Marelle and Petrith will help us travel to the next site, but you might also want to take the opportunity to move on that mine."

"Right you are. When we have the word, I'll be sending these dwarves out, along with a group of my men to take down the miners. We've got shackles over here to use on them for safety reasons until we can secure them back home. Then we'll pack up the ingots and the dwarves will finish what's left in their smelting vats before shutting it down."

"Good. Maybe we can make a deal for it later to help our war effort. Which reminds me, we might have more at the production site to bring home. Do we have any extra bags?"

"I have a pile of them in the storeroom over there. If you need any, just ask."

"Maybe we can attend to that after the people are secure. We should be able to use projected forms for that."

The group inside the officer's hut had emerged into their projected forms by this time and Kaliya made one final assessment of their equipment. She called up a local mage with a rune to the road on the mountainside and had him open it for her team. They each made their exit while the projected members recalled themselves to the location directly.

"All right, we'll move soft and swift through the tunnel," Kaliya orders. "But remember, there's a surveillance camera in there, so we'll need to go dark under it. Other than that, we'll have the spooks go forward as bugs to scout the path and make sure it's clear."

"Spooks?" asks one of the members.

"Yeah, we need to make up some new terms for our operations. This seems like a good one for the projected forms. It reminds me of my father's stories of the original Prodigy Children, and how the projections resembled ghostlike apparitions. So, it seems to fit, and it rolls off the tongue nicely."

"Uh huh..." he chuckles. "Well, it sounds good enough to me, so why not."

"Now, this tunnel is a long one. Let's find that camera first so we can sneak past it. Then we'll make a quick trot until we come within range of the other side. Let's go."

The projected members take up their new shapes and lead forward to inspect the path. Kaliya followed up with a hurried pace. They made their way through the tunnel until they spied the camera, where she halted the team and gave instructions to cast cloaks on themselves. The group all began creeping by until they were out of view before returning to normal. Then they resumed their pace, keeping a close watch for anything else that might be in their path. When they arrived at the exit, she motioned for them to stop.

"Here we are. I need the spooks to go out there and check for walkers. Take a close look at all the secondary buildings: The storerooms, the utility shed, and the vehicle ports. Make sure they're all empty. The Suuden-Aryku should all be inside their command building or the barracks at this time, so I don't want any surprises."

"What about the reactor maintenance room?"

"I'm guessing that uses a powered door with a touch-sensitive control panel to open it, and I don't recall seeing any windows last time. We may have to come back to that after the control booth is ours."

The assigned members move out to investigate the base. They peeked inside the vehicle garages and other supplemental buildings to ensure there are no people moving around the grounds outside. The area seemed clear.

"Good," Kaliya asserts. "Now, our first objective will be the command building. That booth in front has a nice big window to it, which affords them a grand view of everything. We need to take that before we can hope to do anything else."

"I only saw three people in there as I was passing by," offers one of the spooks.

"All right, that should be easy enough, but we need a way in. Let's move behind the building. They have a window leading into a restroom. We'll start with that. We also need disguises, so let's try to find one of the officers."

The team goes under their cloak and follows a path across the base to the command building, circling around behind where they found the window to the restroom, the same one Kaliya used previously to enter the building for her initial spy mission. They duck low and check for any other windows with a clear view before dismissing their cloaks.

"Spook One," Kaliya whispers. "Check the window to make sure it's clear. We'll try an experiment. I think that door in there uses a motion detector to open it. If the room is clear, go inside, change to yourself, and see if it responds."

The spook crawls up the wall in his insect form to peer inside. He then folds himself onto the floor and reshapes into his natural self. He tries walking up to the door, but there is no response. He steps back and tries again, but still no response. He tries waving at it, but again nothing. He further examines a small control panel on the side before returning to report.

"Lieutenant, the door is unresponsive to me in projected form."

"Interesting, we can appear solid to people, but not machines. We may need to find a work-around for that. At the same time, it could also be useful to infiltrate places under surveillance by devices."

"I also took notice of a panel on the side, and it appears to be pressure touch sensitive."

"That's good to know, we might be able to use that. All right, let's see about the other windows. I'll bet the officers have their own quarters rather than bunking in the barracks. Let's check the other side."

They work their way along the back wall to the other corner and up the side, taking notice of a series of windows along the wall.

"Spooks, check these windows," she issues quietly.

The projected members change to bugs again and investigate each window. Kaliya and her team kept low to the ground and silent during this time. The base appeared ghostly quiet, with the only prominent noise being a low droning hum from the conveyer at the far end. The scouts returned a moment later.

"Lieutenant," the spook reports. "There were window coverings, so I had to fold inside the pane and crawl around a bit to find a clear view. But the lights were off, so no one could see me."

"Good enough for our benefit, but could you see them?"

"Affirmative, just barely. The first three rooms appear as personal living quarters with a single occupant each. The one in front looks like an office, probably for the Commander."

"Anyone inside?"

"No ma'am."

"Good, so we can suppose these three are officers' quarters, one should be the Commander and the others are probably those two lieutenants we saw in the video. We'll have the two spooks go in and study those lieutenants. We'll use them as our marks. Then we need a clever way to get inside."

The two projected members change to insects again and crawl up to the respective windows. Each member folded inside the room and onto the ceiling, then took on a camouflaging color to match the décor. The rooms were dark, and the two lieutenants appeared to be sleeping in their beds.

The first one found a male officer in his bed, contentedly sleeping. The spook studied his face and upper body, but with the bed covers in the way, he could do no more, so he knew he would likely need to improvise a bit based on the videos they studied before. In addition, he needed to study the uniform. He saw a closet across the room, so he folded himself to the floor and took the shape of a small child to keep his size low to the ground. He crept over to it and opened the door gently to peer inside. There he saw a fresh uniform hung on a rack, so he pulled it out to make a close inspection.

The other spook found himself trying to study a female. The spook was male, so his role would be that of a cross-dresser. He rested on the ceiling as an insect staring down at her, and like the other one, tried to imagine those parts that were covered by the bedsheets. But then she began to stir.

Ayene had been restless ever since the last conversation between the Commander and Ytani. On her nightstand, she had a pulse weapon resting within easy reach. She tossed and turned in her bed but couldn't get comfortable. Out of frustration, she decided to get up. She sat on the edge of the bed staring into the darkness of the room, silently hoping there was nothing else in there with her. She tentatively turned toward the window, as if to look outside, even though the window was covered, and hoping there was nothing standing out there peering in at her. Finally, she reached over and hit a switch for a table lamp.

The illumination quickly drew the attention of Kaliya's team outside. She instantly gestured for them to go under cloaks.

The spook inside, still on the ceiling, knew he had to hide, and quick. He was in the shape of a bug, color-matched with the ceiling texture, but this might not be enough in full light. So, he folded himself to the wall behind the woman and blended as a flat surface.

Ayene sighed deeply. She was tired from her day's duties, but unable to sleep due to her distress. She rose from her bed and started for the door, but halted abruptly, then returned to the nightstand to take her weapon, along with a belt, and fastened it around her. She then continued to the door, stepping out into the hallway, and turning towards the rear of the building.

The spook chose to follow to see where she was going. At the same time, he also paid attention to this opportunity to study her full form. She was wearing short-legged pajamas, white with a delicate pink floral pattern.

He folded himself to the wall opposite her in the hallway, again taking a shape like a spot on the wall. From here he could see her strolling towards the end of the hall where he suspected the restroom was found. He folded to a more convenient location to confirm this, and as she went inside, he decided to return to the room to take a look at her uniform.

From outside, Kaliya and her team, who were still hovering around the corner of the building, could now see the restroom light turn on behind them. The window was small and near the top of the wall, so she kept low as she came out of her cloak. She made a series of hand signs for them to come out of hiding, but to stay silent and still as she waited for one or the other of the spooks to return. After several more moments, the first one arrives.

"Spook," she whispers. "What's going on in there?"

"I just finished with the male officer. But as I was coming out, I saw the light and peeked inside. The female must be awake. The room is empty."

"By the looks of it, she's in the restroom. All right, fine, we can handle that. Let's see your new shape."

The spook alters his form to match his target, including his best guess at the body and then the uniform. Kaliya studies it and gives a tentative approval. A moment later, the second spook returns.

"All right, what's happening with her?" she asks.

"She looks restless," he reports. "She rose from bed, looked around, like she was expecting something to jump out at her. Finally, she got up and went to the restroom. But Lieutenant, be aware. She's armed."

"Armed? Is she in uniform?"

"No, night clothes, but she looks nervous. She had a pulse pistol on her nightstand and took it with her on a gun belt."

"That sounds like paranoia if you ask me. She...yes...a female. I'll bet that's Lieutenant Ti'van we're speaking of from the video.

I remember reviewing that last recording we got. She's probably nervous about Ytani and all his threats. All right, people, listen up. When we take her down, be gentle. I don't want to send her to an asylum by popping in her face with all our weirdness. She's distressed enough, so we'll grab her, and I'll see if I can talk her down a little, then we put her to sleep. Got it?"

The rest of the team nodded in acceptance.

"Meanwhile, Spook, did you get her shape?"

"Yes, I did. I got a good look at her. Trouble is, if she's mobile, we can't use her yet."

"Yet... But let's see it."

He now changes himself to the new shape. Kaliya gives her approval and prepares for the next step.

"All right, I'll have Spook Ti'van go back to a bug and find her again. Be discreet and follow her. I want to know where she is and what she's doing. If she's armed, she represents a wildcard."

He nods and returns to a bug, then flies back to the window to peek inside.

The bedroom was still empty, and the door was still open, so he folded himself inside and back to the wall in the hallway as a small spot. From there, he folded himself to various points on other walls trying to locate Ayene again.

"Next, Spook Alpha," Kaliya continues. "I don't know the other guy's name, so we'll call you Alpha for now."

"That's fine, Lieutenant."

"Check that window to see if it can give us access. This could be an interesting opportunity."

He nods and changes back to a bug, then flies over for a close inspection.

Ayene was making a visit to the mess hall at this time. The spook sent to follow her, found her sitting at a table apparently trying to enjoy a glass of juice. The glass was recently filled and looked like she might be a while as she tried to relax her nerves, so he folded himself directly outside again.

"Lieutenant," he calls softly.

"Yes, what do you have?"

"She's in the mess room having a drink. I think she might be a while."

"Good, maybe we can use her room. Go back and watch her. We'll try to sneak into her room and wait. When she's mobile again, come back and report."

"Acknowledged."

He again travels off as a bug to his work while the first one returns.

"Lieutenant," he reports. "The window looks like a normal slider with a screen insert. I believe if we take the screen out, we could get inside easily."

"All right, be quick about it. Get inside, open it, pull the screen out, and feed it through to us out here. I'll take two people in with me. Now listen carefully. We'll go dark and silent, wait for her to return, and once she's inside, I'll throw a holding spell on her to keep her while the other two grab and disarm her. Then I'll try talking her down before putting her to sleep."

They all nod and go to work. The spook returns to the room, pulls the blinds aside, and opens the window, then quickly struggles with the screen to pull it out of the framework. He feeds it through to the outside while another member takes it and sets it on the ground. Kaliya and two others now climb over the sill and inside the room, closing the window behind them, and resetting the blinds to their original condition. The two assistants go into their cloaks while Kaliya waits for the spook to return.

Ayene sat casually sipping her drink, trying to settle her nerves along the way. Another crewmember entered the room and sat next to her for a chat.

"Lieutenant, are you alright?" she asks. "You are up late."

"I cannot sleep. Ytani and his threats are causing me too much distress. This situation is unbearable."

"The Commander has a plan to correct this. I am confident in his abilities."

"So am I, but it does not help."

Ayene takes another sip of her drink as she glances around the room.

"I signed up for service hoping one day I could earn a position that would gain prestige and allow me to demonstrate my value to an honorable purpose. Now here I am, assigned to this place where we drug innocent natives and force them to mine this metal until their last breath. This is not honorable. This is disgraceful."

"I have thought about this, as well. I am also worried that I could be Ytani's next victim. I see you are carrying a gun. Are you so frightened?"

"Yes, even with my chip, I cannot let go of the feeling that something is about to happen tonight. I can feel it crawling up on me."

"I think it is your imagination. You need to relax. I think even Ytani would be sleeping right now, so there is nothing to worry about. This world is empty except for us."

"Yes, of course..."

Ayene finishes her drink and walks over to a waste bin to dispose of her cup.

"I will try again," she announces. "Keep your eyes open, Ensign."

"Sleep well, Lieutenant."

Ayene now prepares to exit the room.

The spook who was watching her suddenly flashed into the bedroom.

"Lieutenant, she's coming back," he urges.

"All right, make like you're not here."

The spook vanishes from sight and Kaliya quickly gives directions for the placement of her teammates who were still under a cloak. She then casts one on herself.

Ayene returns to her room and closes the door behind her. She stands there a moment staring into the room before sluggishly moving back to her nightstand. She unhooks her belt and lays it, along with her weapon, back on the table. But as she turns towards her bed, a shadowy figure suddenly emerges into view out of the corner of her eye.

She abruptly spins around, but no sooner than she can focus on the outline of a figure in black clothing, does this figure seem to throw a strange translucent sphere at her. The object makes impact, and she can feel her body become rigid and unmovable. An instant later, two others emerge into view and rush at her, grabbing her arms and restraining her tightly.

Kaliya calmly steps forward after casting her holding spell on the young woman. Ayene's face still showed her initial fright at the sudden surprise.

"Easy now…" she soothes. "I'm not here to hurt you. I realize you're scared, maybe more so at seeing us appear out of nowhere, but let's try to keep it calm. Can we speak briefly without you screaming? I'm going to hope your answer is yes, so please cooperate."

Kaliya raised a hand with two fingers outstretched and drew a squiggly line downward in front of Ayene's face. She circles once and then snaps her fingers. Ayene could feel the sudden release of her body from the hidden force that froze its motion. At the same time, she was able to speak again.

"Let's keep it calm and quiet, all right?" Kaliya asserts gently.

"Who are you?" she mutters softly. "And how did you get in here? And what did you do to me just now?"

"How we got in was through the window. No offence, but you were walking around, and we took advantage of it. What I did, well, that one would take some time to explain. We'll just say I took some special lessons in some tricks I can play to get the job done. As for who we are, we're a military unit on a covert mission, but that's all I can say for now. We are in a state of war, and this base is our target. I have to take all of you prisoner, but I don't mean this to sound as if I have anything special against you. It's just business."

"It's just business to take us prisoner? What business?"

"Let's call it a law enforcement action. Just look outside, and then what you people are doing here with it. That would be a good place to start."

Ayene muddled the meaning briefly, but it soon came to her of the devastation.

"Wait, you mean this world, and um, us…the mining operation.

First, I was not a part of that particular operation out there. My only duty here is management of the base facilities. You know, staff assignments, supply refresh, and so on."

"All right, fair enough, but it doesn't actually matter right now. My orders still stand. We're capturing this base and everyone in it. We'll work out the details later."

"But wait. Military? What military, ours? Then why the covert thing if you are our own people. Why not just come in and say, 'This operation is being shut down for such-and-such reason,' and then bring us home, or whatever."

"Look. I would be very happy to answer some of this, but the whole thing is classified for the moment until we can secure the situation, and unfortunately, you people are on the wrong side of things…because you're following that monster you call a benefactor. We're not."

"Monster…" she mutters softly.

"As for anything else, maybe later after the situation stabilizes. But now, I need to put you to sleep for transport."

"Sleep…?"

"Yeah, but not to worry, we'll take good care of you. Unlike that young man down the road."

"You know about him?"

"Unfortunately…"

"Are you here because of Ensign Ka'zheen, perhaps?"

"That woman who died out there recently? I can answer yes, at least partially, if it makes you feel any better."

"So somebody did actually pay attention…" she mumbles.

Kaliya brought her hand up to Ayene's face. The young woman watched curiously as Kaliya made a strange circling pattern around her face, and then sliding down. This would be her last experience for the night as they lay her on the floor.

"One…" Kaliya notes. "Spook Ti'van?"

The hidden spook now forms up in his new image.

"All right, I need the rest of our people in here. We'll use this room as our starting point. And get a collar on this girl so we can send her off. I'll bet the folks back home are wondering what's taking their Pride and Joy on the practice field so long to produce our first victim…er, I mean, prisoner," she chuckles gently.

One of the teammates opens the window to let the others in while Kaliya brings out her transport rune. They pull out a jamming collar and attach it around Ayene's neck, and then Kaliya sends her on her way.

"I need Spook Ti'van to change clothes to her PJs. This is what she was last seen in, at least by those who might be walking around out there. Spook Alpha, I need a quick refresher survey. Be discreet and report back. We were waiting here for an extended period, so I need to know what's changed."

Spook Alpha goes off again as a bug, folding away to the mess hall and proceeding from there. He checked several side rooms and storage closets, the restroom, and finally worked his way forward to the front booth, before returning to the bedroom.

"Lieutenant… We have one in the mess room and two in the booth. Everything else seems clear."

"All right, Gamma Leader, assign two for each walker and go dark. Spook Alpha, you'll make a casual stroll to the booth like you're on an inspection. Bring a jammer and use it. When the unit goes live, the Gamma units move in. One hits, both carry back here… quietly. Bring collars and attach them onsite."

The spook takes his persona form and leads out the door with four hidden units behind him.

"Spook Ti'van," Kaliya continues. "You're going to make another trip to the mess hall and bring the other Gamma units with you. Take down that last one and repeat the process."

The second spook nods in acceptance of his orders and leads out the door the other way.

In the control booth, the spook appearing as the male Lieutenant enters the room carrying his jammer unit. The two officers working the consoles turn to look at him and immediately stand to salute.

"As you were," he offers.

"Sir," remarks one officer. "Are you returning to work already? I thought you went to bed."

"It is a rough night, so I thought I might investigate this item here," he glances at his jammer device.

"What is that?" ask the other officer.

"This? Here, let me demonstrate. I will set it down in front for you to observe."

He sets the unit on the work surface of the console.

"Now, this unit here holds a curious purpose. If I press this button..."

He presses the button, and the unit goes active, sending out a pulsing signal to conflict with the communication signals of the cranial interface units.

The two officers take notice of a soft static haze buzzing in their ears, but before they can comment on anything, four figures jump out of the shadows. Of the two pairs, one of them lands a firm palm strike on each officer while the second one catches him and lowers him to the floor, then attaches the collar. The first one also casts the chant to put them to sleep, and between the two of them, they lift the fallen officers and carry them back to the bedroom.

In the mess room, the spook appearing as Ayene arrives inside to find her conversation partner still enjoying her break.

"Lieutenant?" she wonders. "Are you back again?"

"Yes, it would seem that way," she responds calmly. "Do you recall that mention I made earlier?"

The spook sets down her jammer on a nearby table while she carries her conversation.

"Mention?" the Ensign replies curiously. "Which one?"

"The one where I thought something was coming for us tonight."

"Oh, that. Ayene, I am sure you are simply overreacting."

"Actually, no I was not..." she pushes the button on the unit. "It is here now," she smiles mischievously.

The Ensign glared at her for the emotional display, but before she could open her mouth to inquire further, two darkly clad figures popped into view and hit her with the stun, then a collar and a sleep chant.

Between all of them, Kaliya was now receiving deliveries back into the bedroom.

"Nicely done, people," she muses. "Now we send them forward."

She engages her rune again and touches it to each body lying on the floor.

"By the way, Lieutenant," Spook Ti'van recalls. "This might be something to ask about later. The real Ti'van was carrying a conversation in there about having a creeping feeling of something coming for her tonight. Is it coincidence, or could it be another hidden Gift?"

"Interesting…precognition, perhaps? Thaelyn has that. All right, we'll keep it in mind. For now, let's finish this. We have the other Lieutenant and the Commander, and this building is secure. Gamma, pick a team and do it…same procedure as before, soft and swift. Spook Alpha, go check that reactor to see if anyone is inside. Ti'van, change clothes to your uniform and check the barracks. I want to know the lay of it before we take action. I also want scouts to check the windows outside. Make sure everyone is in their beds. We don't want any more surprises."

The two spooks once again make their runs, both going outside with one travelling off to the reactor to investigate the maintenance room, and the Ti'van persona checking the layout of the barracks. Scouts are assigned to go under a cloak and make a circuit around the outside of the building to peek in the windows.

The Gamma teams line themselves up with the doors to the two remaining officers' rooms. Each set presses the button to open the door. One goes in under a cloak while the other sneaks in to apply the priest chant. The cloaked unit served as a backup in case the target should wake up.

The two officers were sound asleep when the team made their arrival. The first one cast the chant to put them deeply under, and they then attached the collars and carried them back to Kaliya for transport.

"Good, this building is ours. We're moving to the booth."

She leads them forward and meets with the rest as they were returning from their scouting runs.

"Lieutenant," the first spook declares. "The reactor room seems clear."

"All right, and the barracks?"

"The barracks is arranged as two parallel hallways," the second one offers. "There are rooms on both sides. I counted six in each row for a total of twenty-four throughout. And there is a cross hall in front."

"All right, sounds straightforward. Now, scouts, what about the windows?"

"We made runs on both sides," replies the first scout. "Only the outer rooms have windows, and they all appear dark and silent."

"So, the inner rooms don't have windows? I feel for those people."

"Probably for the non-coms… But the blinds are drawn, so we can't see who is inside. Likely, however, it's one person each, if to go by the numbers."

"Word to the wise, don't be a non-com in the Suuden-Aryku military. All right, everyone, to the barracks. We'll pair up and take them down in the same pattern, and our work here is done. Then we pick up the technicians and move forward to the processor."

The team now proceeds outside from the booth. There was no further need to use a cloak as there was nothing left to observe them. They entered the barracks building, which was the first one in the row, and gathered in the front cross hall.

"Now, listen carefully," Kaliya whispers. "We split into pairs like before, one for the chant, one dark as backup. Sneak in and apply, latch the collars, and carry back here. We'll proceed through systematically to clean it out."

The team once again acknowledges their orders and pairs up, each moving off to a different door. They began infiltrating the rooms one-by-one to take down the occupants. As before, the sleep chants were used, and the collars attached. The bodies were then carefully carried back to Kaliya for removal.

"Lieutenant," offers one of them. "For what it's worth, those interior rooms do seem to have skylights and ceiling vents."

"Well, I suppose that's at least something."

In the hidden outpost, where Captain Hagmaert waited for the deliveries on their first waypoint, his people were working to pull the bodies out of the portal receiving zone.

"It looks like our people up there are getting busy," he remarks as he observes the activity.

"All these new ones must be from their barracks," Marelle suggests. "A large cluster of them…"

"If this is the case," Petrith muses. "I'll bet we'll be moving in soon."

As each new prisoner was relocated, the resident priests made a quick examination to ensure they were deeply asleep before giving the approval for a mage to send them to the next destination. This would involve another portal rune leading directly to the Naarg uy'Sodrad, where Kailen, Ankhia, Aerlie, and their associated teams waited to remove them to the medical ward.

The mining base was now under Kaliya's control. She moved around outside to a concealed location to mark a new rune for a convenient arrival site. This would be their secret access from the outpost.

"Spooks, present forward," she calls softly. "Take this…" she hands over the new rune. "Report to the Captain and give this to him. Grab your bodies and bring the rest of our team up here."

They both nod and flash out of sight while Kaliya returns inside the control room.

✦ ✦ ✦ ✦ ✦ ✦ ✦

"We're getting new arrivals," Likha shouts.

"Let me see that," Kailen instructs.

The Suuden-Aryku prisoners were just arriving at the Naarg uy'Sodrad. Kailen was overseeing this part of the operation from their side of it. The Suuden-Aryku were motionless from the sleep chant. The first to arrive were the officers, followed by the three crewmen, and soon after a flood of others.

"Well, it looks like we have some new guests," he smirks. "A commander and a pair of lieutenants, a few ensigns, and a crew of non-coms. Not bad for her first time out."

"Kailen, "Ankhia notes. "I'm still thinking of taking one of the lesser members for practice, although I don't like the sound of that statement."

"Do you still feel yourself a little nervous about this?"

"Well, I reviewed my notes, and the procedure seemed like it might be fairly straightforward, although delicate. This is, after all, brain surgery."

"Ankhia," Aerlie offers. "I can offer assistance with the removal if you need. My Celestial training should be more than enough for that. This will allow us to process them with less worry, at least until you can feel more confident. And then Thaelyn can get on with his work that much faster."

"All right, if you think we can do it, then let's go. We'll start with the Commander."

"How long do you suppose this will take?" Kailen asks. "It's my understanding we'll need to keep them under until they're all processed."

"The major portion of these implants is mostly on the surface, incorporated within that interface. Then we have a series of probes leading into the neural tissues. I don't expect any serious trouble, just some delicate work."

"We can also assist with the tissue and bone restoration," Aerlie adds.

"Yeah, I heard about that regeneration stuff of yours. Cu'Nar's Grace, Your Ladyship, do you know how long it took us to develop these techniques?" she chuckles. "Good, this could cut our time in half if we rotate our teams."

"Very well, let's bring them in. We'll probably be getting more when Kaliya takes the production facility."

In the outpost camp, the spooks make their return to report in.

"Captain, this is for you," one of them reports as he sets down the rune. "It leads to a space between the command building and the barracks. The base is ours."

"Excellent work…and relay my mention to the Lieutenant as well."

"She's requesting the rest of our team to join us up there for the next step."

"Very good," the Captain turns to a mage standing by. "Mage, open this portal here," he directs with the new rune. "Marelle, Petrith, get up there and do your part."

"Yes Sir!"

The mage opens a portal with the new rune so that Marelle with her instructor, and Petrith with his engineering team, are transported away to the base. The projected team members return to their bodies and follow shortly after. The Captain then turns to his men in the camp and begins barking orders to take the mining operation.

Kaliya and her group were inside the control booth browsing the consoles and investigating the cabinets and drawers throughout the building to see if there might be anything of special interest to take for study.

"Lieutenant, look here," announces one of the members.

He presented himself with three elongated plastic hard-shell boxes. They appeared to be new.

"I found these in their infirmary. I think these could be the devices we heard about that were custom ordered from Azgarén. The labeling here says ARC, and I recall this from our briefing on that meeting they had."

Kaliya took one box and opened it to reveal a hand-held device with a probe attachment and a small readout display, along with several buttons to perform a series of diagnostic operations. The plug seemed to match the appearance of the interface port.

"Good, we'll collect these for study. Maybe we'll find a use for them one day."

She continues to survey the control booth and the various consoles, then peeking outside at the other buildings and the conveyor.

"We're going to need to maintain some form of presence here for the foreseeable future until we're ready to make our next move. In the meantime, I think it's reasonable to suggest we'll get at least a few visitors through the conveyor. Hopefully only supplies, but we'll need to simulate the actions of the officers here to receive them, and any other form of interaction they might expect."

"Lieutenant, we should also consider any kind of regular reports they might file to their headquarters."

"That as well, and I'll bet the Commander is the one to check for that. Maybe he keeps a log of his reports, and we can study that to imitate his style."

Marelle and the others were arriving through the portal. She tentatively walks around to the control booth to peek inside. When she sees Kaliya and her team, she looks for the button to open the door and joins the rest.

"Did someone call for a pilot?" she announces jovially.

"Yeah, as a matter of fact," Kaliya states impishly. "But I guess you'll do."

"Hey! You should be nice to me, or I might accidentally forget which way is up," she grins.

"Petrith, we need your people to figure out these controls, like this one behind us," she directs to the console on the rear wall. "That one looks like a monitor for their fusion reactor. Try not to blow it up, we might still need it. Here in front looks like comms and the conveyor control, so far."

Petrith takes up a seat by the front console while some of the engineers study the reactor status displays.

"These reactor controls look like a standard arrangement," advises one of the technicians. "This shouldn't be a problem, so long as we can maintain a stable fuel supply."

"I'm guessing that has to do with their deliveries. I can't imagine where they would get that stuff around here."

Petrith scanned the console for the conveyor control. He was able to make out certain critical readouts for the rift generator and containment field stability, and finally found the selection input for the conduit indexing. He began trying different parameter icons to discover what they do, hoping he wouldn't collapse the rift into a singularity in the process.

"This interface here," he announces. "It looks a bit like those we had on Ruuki uy'Daan."

"In the hands of the orcs?" Kaliya considers.

"Right, and I remember when we were examining that one pointing to Morndindor, although this one seems more elaborate."

"Makes sense, this one is official whereas the others were probably stripped-down versions."

"So far, I see a menu selection, along with status icons. These seem to show the condition of the sister units on the other side. But this readout is a little strange."

"Why is that?"

"First of all, I see three choices here, one is listed as Azgarén. So, if you ever wanted to visit the old breeding grounds, this is your ticket."

"Thanks, but I think I'll wait for the discount tour. Next?"

"One of these says Therinë on it, but it's showing a gray highlight and with this message of Inoperative."

On listening to the conversation, one of the engineers stepped over to see if he could offer any help. He studies the display over Petrith's shoulder.

"I think it's because that one no longer exists," he suggests.

"Could this have been their HQ on that world?" Kaliya asks. "They had a mine there, if you recall, so this might have been their link back here."

"Yes, I would probably have to agree, and that one was destroyed.

I think if it were simply shut down or inactive, like for maintenance, the display would show a temporary condition. But this looks like a permanent condition for a lost unit."

"Then why not simply deprogram it? Why keep old data in here?"

"Don't ask me. But this would likely be the result of the loss of the ping responder on the other side."

"All right, and the last one? I hope that one leads somewhere useful."

"The final one says Madzurki," Petrith offers. "So, if we're saying they need a dumping site for the metal, this is probably our next destination."

"What's it set for now?"

"Azgarén, of course…"

"Yeah, that's what I was afraid of," Kaliya admits. "We'll need to change that, and probably make some noise along the way."

"Hopefully not too much. So, what are your orders…Lieutenant?" he smirks.

"That's right, Petrith," she grins. "Suli might swing her tail, but I carry rank. First, let's power up. Marelle, I'll have you and your instructor head out to that troop transport and begin looking over the control configuration. Use a cloak on your way out, just in case that miscreant young man down the lane is peeking outside. In fact, let's have a scout go out there and take a quick look to see if he really is asleep in his bed."

Marelle and her instructor both nod and go outside, where she casts a cloak on both of them for their run out to the transport. A teammate also goes outside under a cloak to inspect Ytani's windows.

"I want everyone to check their gear," Kaliya orders. "Collect our jammers and bag them. We'll start moving out once the scout returns."

They waited several moments for the scout. Marelle and her instructor climb inside the transport and take their seats in the pilot and copilot stations. Shortly after, the scout returns.

"Lieutenant, I found him apparently sleeping in the rear bedroom. All seemed quiet."

"You could actually see inside this time?"

"Yes, the blinds are partly open in his case, and the window is slightly ajar, maybe for ventilation."

"What, no air conditioning in that place? I think I would complain to the management for that one," she chuckles. "Good, now once we get moving, I want to be quick, just in case the conveyor makes too much of a disturbance. I need someone on comms. If anyone calls, take a message. If it's him, just say we're making a quick visit to check on the production, or something innocent."

"Understood," the engineer replies.

"Now, let's go people. We are mobile! Petrith, hit it."

The team rushes outside towards the transport while Petrith readies himself with the conveyor control. He waits just a moment for the bulk of the team to actually reach the vessel before he hits the selection. Outside the window, they observed the rift fluctuate, and then collapse, followed by a new flash and another rift opening. The modest hum that had been droning all evening was momentarily punctuated by a roar as the rift opened and stabilized into another hum.

"Let's go, Petrith," she advises. "The rest of you stay and manage the shop. We shouldn't be long, but if anyone comes knocking, hide in a closet or something."

"Thanks…"

Kaliya and Petrith now trek outside and hurry over to the transport. They load up and find a space for themselves amongst the others.

"This thing doesn't look like it's made for a large number of people," she remarks. "We'll need to distribute ourselves carefully to balance the weight. Either take a seat or crouch low. Marelle, it's your game. Try to do this without any of those wild moves of yours. We're trying not to wake the neighbors on this run."

"Right," she smirks. "So, I should probably avoid the switch with the flashing lights and audible landing alarms, right?"

Kaliya sighs and shakes her head as Marelle powers up the craft.

A soft whirring rises up from the engine nacelles and the console status displays run their diagnostics. Marelle takes the flight stick in her left hand while pushing a lever for the flux field on the floor between the two seats to a forward position, giving lift to the vessel. She follows by flipping the landing gear switch while reflecting on her past experiences.

"This is more like that large transport from the mining camp," she recalls, "rather than the Daanen'kai designs."

"Then it should be somewhat familiar to you, I guess," Kaliya notes.

"Maybe a little more so this time… At least now I know more about what I'm doing, so it's just a case of associating with the different configuration."

"It's good to have trained professionals."

"Oh, is that a compliment…finally!" Marelle smiles.

She applies the throttle in reverse and pulls out of her landing stall, aligning with the central road which leads in a straight line to the conveyor.

"This part wasn't on my original lesson plan, though. Instructor, how do we do this, just fly into it?"

"Yes, as if flying a straight path, but instead we'll be inside the transport conduit. It's a similar experience to your portal runes. I never actually piloted a conduit before, but I hear you might need to make a few adjustments in case the conduit makes turns of any kind. And watch your speed as you come out."

"Oh thanks… And she said not to make any wild moves."

Marelle throttles forward gently, making her approach to the rift aperture. She closes in cautiously, first to pass through the containment sphere and finally to penetrate the rift.

The ship suddenly experiences an enormous rush of movement, although the sensation didn't actually result in a strong inertial jolt. They could see outside what looked like a long tunnel effect, stretching into what seemed like infinity. Outside the tunnel were shapes of unnatural proportions, some of which appeared impossibly complex. The flow of energies within the conduit carried them along like a river.

She found herself perplexed and bedazzled, almost instinctively driven to fight against the convolutions of the pipeline, but forcing herself to remain focused and keep it steady. The flow began to bend, and she had to orient herself to follow it smoothly, tilting into one curve, and then another. She strained her mind to predict the motion of the flow, ignoring the sights from outside and keeping her eyes directly ahead of her.

In the distance, she could see a membrane wall. She interpreted this from her experiences using portals to be the exit point approaching, but she still had some distance to go. The conduit turned again, and she followed it into another curve, then back in the direction of the membrane.

Kaliya and the others silently held their breath during this time. None of them had ever piloted a ship through a nether-space conduit before. Even when travelling in the Naarg uy'Sodrad, they didn't have a way to see outside, as it was mostly by instrumentation in that case with very few actual windows. On this occasion, they could see outside, and it was both beautiful and frightening.

Marelle guided the ship towards the membrane, which could be seen rapidly approaching in line with the conduit now. The flow of the slipstream rushed in as the ship made contact with real space again.

She found herself emerging through another rift into local space. She quickly checked her status for her velocity and orientation. The ship was now moving at a normal speed, the same as when she first entered, a cautious gradual pace.

Kaliya and the others let out a sigh of relief.

"Cadet," the instructor asserts. "I have to congratulate you. You handled that very well, perhaps even better than I would have on my first try."

"Thank you, Sir. That means a lot to me. Now, where do we set down?"

"Look at this place…" Kaliya croons as she peers out the window.

They looked outside to find themselves hovering above a desolate gray landscape. To the left was a large facility, resembling a manufacturing plant. It appeared to be completely enclosed inside a shell-like housing. In the starry sky above, they could see an enormous gas giant hanging over them, with wispy streaks of blue-violet clouds circling around it.

"So, this is Madzurki," she mutters. "We must be on a moon here. I suppose that makes sense, especially considering it's supposed to be making this weapon."

"Yeah, but I don't see anything out there to land on," Marelle admits.

"Down there," the instructor points. "You see that building, the wall that looks almost transparent? That's an atmosphere curtain. We need to fly inside there to land."

"A curtain? Like to someone's shower?" she giggles.

"No, not a shower," he grins. "This is an energy barrier to hold back a hospitable environment. Outside here probably has no atmosphere. Bring us down and guide us in carefully."

"This also wasn't on the simulator."

Marelle makes a casual loop to align the ship with the landing bay inside the building. She maneuvers slowly, now able to see patterns on the flooring to indicate landing pads. She selects one and lines up with it, passing through the energy barrier and into position over the marked zone. She hits the switch for the landing gear and lowers the flux field, gently setting the craft down.

"Very nicely done, Marelle," Kaliya smiles. "Now, you might want to duck down before someone sees you. Meanwhile, I need my two decoys up again. And everyone else, take note of where we are so you can project here later. Who has the hypo-sprays?"

"I do," answers one of the team members.

"Good, keep them handy just in case our sleep chants ran out on us back there. I can already feel there's no arcanic field here, so we're reduced to the classic combat methods. We'll see if we can simply grab them and put them to sleep. But we also need to shut down their production."

"How do you suppose you'll do that?" Marelle asks. "Go up and ask one of them?"

"Well, not me personally, but I wonder if one of their 'officers' could do it for us," she grins.

"Kaliya, you're starting to scare me."

"All right, we'll see if we can play a game on them. We'll make up an excuse, like the shortage of ingots coming out of the city, and if we also play on that idea of conducting a survey, we need to shut down temporarily until we can restore a full supply."

"Sounds good to me," comments one of the teammates. "Then we take them down?"

"We should use the jammers again, and I think it would be a good idea to see if we can call the full assembly into session. But then, we need to find out how many are currently working here, and it has to be casual, as I'm sure the real officers should know the answer already."

"Lieutenant?" asks another member. "Can I offer a suggestion?"

"Yes, Navina?"

"I once worked in an electronics assembly workshop on Ruuki uy'Daan. Although this might represent a very different environment, I would suggest if they're making such a volatile substance, most of it is probably automated with only a skeleton work crew."

"All right, good point."

"I would further suggest they probably have a primary control room, where they can monitor everything, and maybe a few have individual stations."

"That makes sense, but I don't want a lot of people stomping around the factory floor out there. So, let's see if we can pull them together into the control room. Once the decoys are up, we'll make a quick inspection and test the waters a bit."

They wait as the two teammates go into their meditation and emerge as their projected alter-images, using the lieutenants from the command base as their example. Kaliya then starts considering her objectives.

"All right, Spook Alpha," she orders. "Go out and make a casual saunter around. I want to know the lay of the place and see if you can find their control center. Make some casual talk, ask about their production levels, and see if you can call everyone into one place. Have them gather up and wait, then come back and report."

The first spook exits the transport and begins walking confidently across the landing bay to a door towards the rear.

"How many of those collars do we have left?" Kaliya asks.

"Only a few..." responds another member. "I doubt it'll be enough, even with a small crew here."

"Then it's time to recycle a few. Spook Ti'van, I'll have you go home and collect some extras. Go over to that corner and memorize it for your return. Bring a bag with you. You might also want to change back to normal, so you don't scare anyone."

"Aw," she moans. "You mean it's not fashionable to wear Suuden-Aryku blue with parasitic growth?"

"Ugh..."

The spook empties out the bag from the few remaining collars and leaves the ship.

The first spook walks inside the facility, strolling down a corridor, passing a mess hall and the crew quarters, and a few storerooms for supplies. He checks each room, peeking inside as if to inspect the tidiness of the compound. At the end of the hall, he finds a door leading into another room. A window set into the door allows him to see an automated factory control center inside. He finds the control panel for the door and presses the button to open it.

As the door opens, it draws the attention of two workers currently inside the room. They were overseeing the factory process through an observation booth window while monitoring several data displays.

"Lieutenant," the first worker turns with a salute.

"As you were," he responds using his practiced monotone demeanor.

The spook steps up to the window and looks out onto the factory floor, then moves nonchalantly around the room, continuing his inspection. He sees another door leading out the other side, seemingly to another section of the plant.

"Is there something you require, Sir?"

"Yes, I am assessing the production output for a report. What is the status here?"

"We are running at forty-eight percent capacity. The input supply is nearly expired. If we do not receive another shipment soon, we will be forced to shut down again."

"Understood, this is becoming a problem for us, and we expect it to get worse soon."

"Sir, what do you mean?"

"The production of the mines inside the city is dwindling, perhaps permanently this time. The Commander and Ytani have conferred about conducting a survey for a new deposit, but in the meantime, it might be necessary to shut down fully until this can be corrected."

"This will place us on standby, and the schedule will be severely affected."

"It cannot be avoided. Therefore, I must have you call a meeting. Bring all of them together into this room. Are we still at full staffing?"

"Yes Sir, all fourteen technicians are at their stations throughout the facility."

"Good, tell them to stop whatever they are doing and gather here immediately."

"Yes Sir."

"In the meantime, I have some items I need to retrieve from the transport. I will return briefly."

He turns and leaves the room while the worker issues an announcement on the local intercom network to collect the other workforce. The spook makes a brisk stroll back to the landing bay and onto the ship.

"Lieutenant," he urges. "I have them gathering in their control room. There are apparently fourteen workers at stations, and I saw two people in the control room, so we might say sixteen, total."

"Excellent. We're still waiting for Spook Ti'van to return with new collars. Meanwhile, how does it look on the way in?"

"You have a hallway leading in past a few rooms, up to a door at the end for the control center. If they're all assembling in there, the way should be clear."

"What about the production, can you get them to shut it down?"

"Yes, when I entered, I had them give me a status report. They're apparently running at roughly half-cap, and their input is running out. They even mentioned there might be a need to shut down…again!"

"Again? Meaning they've done this before?"

"If their supply keeps running out, maybe it's because of the loss of that third mine."

"Interesting. This would make a beautiful end result, nice and neat, and with minimal argument."

"I told them the mines are running out, but the Commander and Ytani are working on a new survey, so we're going to shut down until we can ensure our supply again. They seemed to accept it, so I would recommend we do this before rushing in."

"Good. Now, if we use our sleep chants, or even the hypo-sprays, we shouldn't need the jammers. Those are only really necessary if we use our stuns because they might cause a disruptive effect that could set off an alarm on a security station. So, we'll try for our chants, but bring the hypos as a backup."

Kaliya breaks from her review to look outside the transport into the hanger.

"They have another transport out there. I wonder if we should confiscate it."

"We'll need another pilot," Marelle suggests. "Maybe the instructor?"

"Maybe. And that should clean out everything we can clean out for now."

"Perhaps I could offer a suggestion for that, Lieutenant," the instructor notes.

"What is it?"

"This transport is already heavy for all these troops. If we involve another sixteen people, it might be a little too much. But if we load them in the other transport instead, I could pilot it back to base while you carry forward. I think Marelle can handle things from here."

"That sounds good to me, but I wouldn't want you to set it down in the base proper. We don't want any extra vehicles sitting around to draw attention. Do you think you could fly it all the way back to Captain Hagmaert's camp?"

"I'm not sure if I could find my way without a proper navigation signal."

"Hmm, let me think. You would mostly travel to the south, and I believe west a bit around some mountains. A signal… How about something like landing lights? I could send one of the spooks to his outpost and tell him to line up a group of scouts holding up Sparks."

"Sparks?"

"Yeah, these are nifty little First Circle cantrips we learn. It's basically a bright little light in the palm of your hand. You can even make it in different colors. Put a group of these out there in a row or a circle, and there you have it. You should be able to see it even at distance."

"If you say so…" he chuckles. "You people and your magic…is there anything you can NOT do with it?"

"Not really," she smiles.

The second spook had returned to the Naarg uy'Sodrad with his urgent call to retrieve more collars. As he arrived, he changed to his normal shape.

"Commander?"

Kailen had been waiting for more deliveries when the shape appeared out of nowhere. He nearly jumped at the sudden arrival.

"Yes…um, well, Cadet at this point, I suppose, right?"

"Yes Sir, at least under my new training. I need a resupply of collars."

"Good enough. We've been stacking them up over here on the floor. Help yourself. What's the situation out there?"

"We've arrived on a moon outpost called Madzurki. We're currently parked inside the flight hanger of a large processor facility. We have a lovely gas giant over our heads and a brilliant starscape to admire. Some of us were thinking of taking a stroll outside, but the weather report said we might be experiencing an extreme low-pressure zone."

"Extreme?" he smiles. "How extreme?"

"Zero…"

The two of them share a brief laugh as the spook loads up his bag. He then makes a parting salute and returns to the flight hanger. He arrives just outside the transport and reshaped himself back to his Ti'van image, setting down the bag along the way.

"Lieutenant, I'm back."

"All right people," Kaliya instructs. "Let's go. Instructor, get to the other transport and see how it looks in there. I want both spooks back inside and have them shut this thing down. Spook Ti'van, stand near the door and make ready with the signal. The rest of you, move slow and quiet up to the door. We'll get them to shut down, Ti'van gives the signal, we rush in and grab them, and…well, maybe we should play this a little like with the real Ti'van. We'll restrain at first, and I'll try talking them down a little before we put them under. There's no sense in causing a lot of hard feelings."

"A military raid, with love and kisses," Petrith muses teasingly.

The two spooks hurried outside again while the rest of the team arrived at the door of the hanger. The instructor dashed across to the other transport to inspect the controls. Marelle and Petrith ducked low to keep out of sight for now. Kaliya began leading them inside and along the hallway while the spooks arrived back in the control room.

The factory crew had assembled and there was some hushed murmuring going around as to the outcome of their operation and this new upcoming survey. The two spooks entered the room to find all sixteen people collected together and waiting. Spook Alpha moves in front of the room and calls their attention, while Spook Ti'van stands behind the group near the door. She cautiously waves at Kaliya and the rest to move into position.

"We have an issue with the resourcing," Spook Alpha announces. "Recent reports are suggesting a decrease of product which may result in another shutdown procedure. This report suggests the decrease may be the permanent failure of the local mining operation. Therefore, the Commander and Ytani have been in consultation for the deployment of a new survey mission. Naturally, this survey might take some time, and until then, the constant shortages and shutdown of the facility is disruptive to our efforts to maintain a stable production run. It is for this reason we have decided to shut down the facility until such time as we can correct the situation."

"What about us, Lieutenant?" asks the foreman. "What do we do in the meantime?"

"You will go on standby for now. We are considering relocating you until this situation is resolved."

"I see. Very well, Lieutenant, are we proceeding on this plan immediately?"

"Yes, we are. We feel there is no further point in struggling with such low input values as we are."

"Of course, then I want all stations to shut down immediately," he announces to the group. "Just like before, we follow the numbers. Stop the supply belts, then the plasma extractors, the conduit coils, the condensers, and finally the injectors."

"And be sure you reassemble back here when you are done," the Spook asserts. "I have a final briefing to give."

The team of technicians all exit out the side door back onto the factory floor. Kaliya and her people found they had to wait, since apparently there was no simple off switch in this place.

The two spooks inside the control room watched and waited as slowly, section by section, the factory processes came to a halt. The humming and churning sounds from the factory equipment began to die down, and soon the technicians returned inside the room.

"Are we all assembled again?" he observes. "Good. Now, the next phase of this operation goes like this. Ti'van?"

Now Spook Ti'van goes into action with her signal. Kaliya sends her team in to rush the people inside, while she follows up the rear.

The people all jerked and screeched at the sudden arrival and aggressive actions of the group fully clothed in black uniforms. Even their faces were covered, so none of them could be identified. The team grabbed the full assembly by the arms and held them in place.

Kaliya strolled inside to observe the results of her team and their new prisoners.

"Who are you people?" the foreman shouts.

"I would like everyone's attention," Kaliya announces. "We are a covert military operation conducting a law enforcement action. This is as much as I can say for now due to reasons of security. I have no hostile intentions towards any of you, but the situation demands we take affirmative action to secure this facility. I apologize for the deception, but none of us knows how to turn this blasted machine off, so we needed your cooperation."

"You could not simply ask us?"

"Well, technically, we did," she shrugs. "But the prospect of you actually cooperating with our official objective was questionable, and our needs are paramount. Therefore, with respect, we had to conduct ourselves in such a way as to assure a result."

"But we are working as a subsidiary to your mining operation. Is that not a sign of cooperative behavior?"

"With me and mine, no. I'm not part of that operation. What you are doing is working for Darumon and his desires. Our operation is breaking away from that."

"Breaking away! Why? You mentioned law enforcement, what kind?"

"Let me first ask you this. Are you people military here?"

"No, we are civilian industrial technicians. But this only confuses me more. You should know this already."

"I personally do not. Like I said, I'm not from the mining base. And while we might be military, we are not working for YOUR military. We are an outside body conducting this operation, both here AND the mining base. All of it is being brought down."

"Not OUR military, which means not Central Command?"

"Correct, as they are also working for that creature you seem to believe is doing you a favor, or something. Ours is a special operations team as part of a new regulatory body. But again, this is all I can say for now due to the extreme security we need to follow."

"And these officers here?" he directs at the two spooks.

"They are currently cooperating with our efforts. So, here's the deal. First, we need to relocate you to a secure area. Once we have the situation under control, I think we can relax ourselves and find time to answer more of your questions."

"But wait! You said something about law enforcement. Did we do something wrong? Central Command is the one managing this operation. How does this new regulatory body of yours relate to that?"

"Look, I can understand you have a lot of questions, and I would surely wish to answer them…in the right environment. But this isn't that environment. So, I will give you this much, but you'll have to wait for the rest of it, alright?"

"Well, if you say so."

"We need to operate under a very precise security situation because our opponents are exactly those people who think they own everything. We believe this operation is being conducted for illegal purposes against fictitious entities and under false pretenses. This means Darumon, and I'm not going to use the title of Marshal here because we do not believe he is deserving of it. He is coordinating actions that hold highly questionable intent. Even the Commander at the mining base admits to this from his personal career experience."

"That suddenly does not sound good."

"No, it does not. He tells people to do things without a full and complete explanation, and then classifies the result so no one can figure out what they just did. That's not nice. And what you are producing here is a highly dangerous substance. Why does someone who goes around with so many questionable directives, and with a history known by those who actually conducted some of those directives, need something like this? The only answer we can give is he is using us for something, and it may NOT be what he originally claimed it to be that brought all of you into this."

"Uh oh. But do we know what it is?"

"What we know needs to be kept silent for now. A lot of lives hang in the balance. And if Darumon has so many ulterior motives, a lot of those lives could be our own. Got it?"

"Yes ma'am. But now what happens? You need to remove us somewhere?"

"Yes. I have orders that require me to put all of you to sleep for the journey, again for security reasons. Nothing personal, but I will ask you to cooperate, and in the end, I hope we can find time for a pleasant little chat to explain why we had to do what we did."

"Then what are you going to do, hit us with sedatives?"

"Actually, on this occasion, we are using a different technique."

She now directs the free members to move in front of the captives and begin their chants. At this moment, over half of the team was occupied restraining the captives, so the few who were not immediately attended to by the sleep chant were able to observe the others who were, including the foreman.

"How are you doing that?" he asks. "You wave a hand, and they simply slump over?"

"Oh, this is a cute little trick we learned recently, instantaneous and no drugs necessary."

The team continued through the assembly until they arrived at the foreman, who fell into a deep sleep just like the rest.

"I love this job," Kaliya notes. "Especially, as Petrith calls it, the love and kisses part."

"Lieutenant," Spook Alpha offers. "I think that was a good effort you just made. I'm sure Oghma would approve."

"Thank you. I'm just trying to envision my report to Thaelyn now, and how many new marks he'll put down for it," she shakes her head. "Now, let's haul them outside. We're loading them up in the other transport. Spook Alpha, go back to Captain Hagmaert's camp and inform him of our plan with the landing lights."

"Acknowledged."

He flashes away as Kaliya begins directing the others to carry away the prisoners. The team applies the collars, and they carry the bodies out of the room and back to the ship.

"Landing lights?" Spook Ti'van wonders.

"Yeah, while you were gone, we decided to commandeer the other transport to carry these people, with Marelle's instructor piloting it home, but not to the base to keep things clear."

"Ah..."

"Meanwhile, since you're not corporeal, maybe you could look around out there on the factory floor and see about what kind of metal they have left over. We'll want to try to reclaim it if we can."

"Understood."

Kaliya made a brisk strut back to the flight hanger and called Petrith out of the transport.

"I want to check the depot. I'm going to need to study that place so I can go back to it one day."

"Go back to it?"

"Yeah, we're thinking of killing two birds with one stone…or as it turns out, one psychopath and a lot of nasty stuff with one bomb… or whatever it is Adalon has in mind for it. But I'm thinking of using one or the other of these places to corner him, and so I need to check both."

"Uh huh…so you're going to maroon him on a lonely moon in the middle of cu'Nar-knows-where so you can have your way with him? Hmm, can I watch?" he grins.

"Um, Petrith, I don't think this is the sort of thing for sweet young boys to look at. And it won't be involving soap, in this case," she giggles.

"Oh please, not another one."

"Anyway, let's go take a look at the conveyor control."

They return back inside to find the conveyor controls on the console to the rear of the factory control room. It held a similar configuration to the one at the command base, and Petrith was able to identify the necessary components quickly this time. He found the index directory and began to read it.

"It looks like we have only two options here. Interesting, didn't you mention once something about possibly going to Azgarén? I don't see that here."

"Well, it was a suggestion, and a reasonable one at that, if they ever exchange work crews."

"Maybe they go through the other base, instead. We have one to Morndindor and another to someplace called Ooduan."

"Well, we know about Morndindor, and we were assuming there should be a link to a storage depot. Could Ooduan be it?"

"Don't ask me, I'm just the kid with the computer skills."

"All right, let's wait for Marelle's instructor to finish up, and then we'll hit it. Wait here. I'll go check on him."

She makes another quick stroll out to the hanger to check the loading of the second transport.

"How are we coming in here?"

"We're just about ready," responds one member.

"Instructor, are you confident with the controls?"

"Yes, this is very similar to the other one. It shouldn't be a problem. Do we know anything about the conveyor yet?"

"Yeah, Morndindor and another one called Ooduan, which we're guessing to be the storage site for this material. I'm going forward to check it out before returning back, so we'll send you on your way with your passengers. These people are civilian industrial technicians, so tell the Captain to handle it gently. I already had a little chat with them, just enough to settle their nerves. They probably have no idea what they were doing, just like all the rest."

"Wonderful. The Marshal has them building a superweapon and probably tells them it's just a holiday fireworks display."

"Could be… But one thing I noticed, they behave like ordinary people, just clueless as to what Darumon is doing out there, like a lot of other people."

"So, other than for the seed thing, and that unit on their head, they really aren't any different from the rest of us? Interesting. This changes a few perspectives for all of our miseries."

"Yes, it does," she nods. "And it makes me wonder what he did over there."

The last of the teammates finished packing the bodies on the floor of the transport and Kaliya pulls out. She signals the instructor to settle himself, close the door and power up. He engages the engines, applies a little flux to lift off the pad, and begins backing out of the hanger. On the tarmac outside, he pulls around and begins gliding into the conveyor. In another moment, he flashes out of sight.

"Good luck to you," Kaliya mumbles. "All right spooks, back in your bodies, we're going forward. Everybody, load up."

She makes her way back to the control room and Petrith.

"We're ready, hit it."

"I hope you don't get us lost on the far side of the universe."

"Petrith, we're already lost on the far side of the universe, and on top of that, it's a different universe than where we came from."

"Yeah, and it actually feels a little scary, if not for these conveyors taking us around."

"Even with the conveyors…"

Petrith selects the new configuration and the conveyor outside changes course.

"We'll need to stop back here on the return trip to reset this," Kaliya mentions.

They return to the ship and settle themselves in.

"Marelle," Kaliya notes. "You're solo now. Make us proud."

"Yeah, solo and suddenly a little nervous."

"Just keep your cool and work the problem. You know how to do it."

"With or without my crazy stunts," she grins sheepishly.

She powers up the ship and lifts off, again putting it in reverse to back out of the hanger. She pulls it around on the tarmac, just like the instructor, and proceeds forward into the conveyor.

They emerge on the other side to a new sight. It appears as a small rocky moon around another gas giant with clouds circling in orange and red hues and a prominent set of rings around it. In the distance, they could see an orange dwarf star.

"Ooh," Marelle coos. "This is interesting."

"Don't get used to it, though," Kaliya intones solemnly. "Depending on what Adalon has to say, all this might be gone soon."

"That seems like such a shame, but I guess there's not a lot we can do about it. But one thing is for sure, she was right. I am going places and seeing things I never imagined before."

"That's right, Marelle, for all of us, I would think.

This facility was much simpler in design. From the outside, one could see only a few buildings, and they looked much more like warehouses, rather than anything else. The hanger sat on one end of a central lane running between four buildings, two on either side. Except for the hanger, everything appeared to be covered in a natural dust layer from the surrounding lunar surface as a form of shielding from the native radiation fields and solar winds.

Kaliya studied the layout.

"Bring us in to that hanger, Marelle. Gently... EVERYTHING here gently..."

"Right, got it... You don't need to shout."

"I need spooks up. I want a quick survey inside there just to be sure there are no people...not that I could imagine any loose-horn wanting to spend time in this place."

Marelle circled around to line up for the hanger. She oriented to pass through the atmosphere curtain and entered inside, settling down neatly on one of the pads.

The two teammates once again went back into their meditation to project themselves. Shortly after, they were out wearing their previous disguises.

"Go out there and make a brief survey. Check those large buildings, that control booth, and anything else you pass along the way. But for the love of the cu'Nar, do not touch anything!"

"Yes Ma'am!"

The two spooks leave the ship and part in different directions along the walkways to investigate the various buildings. Kaliya and the others waited.

Marelle studied the sights, looking up through the windowed hanger at the planet overhead and off to the oddly colored star.

"Is it just my eyes, or is that thing orange?"

"What, the local star?" Kaliya responds. "Yeah, it's what we call an orange dwarf."

"Aw, it didn't grow up right?"

"Almost correct," she laughs. "There are different types, in size as well as color. You can have such as red, orange, and yellow, like the one we have back home, and you can even have up to a kind of blue-white."

"Well, at least they come in all colors, but what about the size?"

"Size often relates to their overall mass. Some are dwarf stars, while others can be super massive."

"How does that happen? They eat up a lot of little ones?"

"While that may be possible, it more likely depends on how much material was present when they first formed. There can also be a few other factors. Like, for instance, some can erupt in a type of explosion we call a nova, which can jettison some of the material. This might reduce the size somewhat. And then you might have a supernova, which most often only happens with the really big ones. This is a type of explosion that leaves a huge cloud behind usually referred to as a nebula, and whatever might be left of the original star might not even be normal anymore."

"So much to learn out there," she reminisces.

"Yes, Marelle," Kaliya reflects. "Even for those of us who might have seen so much already."

The spooks returned quickly after their little jaunt to report what they found.

"Lieutenant, there doesn't appear to be anyone present here. There are four warehouses, but they appear as automated storage facilities."

"Interesting...and maybe very appropriate... Use automation rather than manual labor to prevent accidents. Good thinking."

"You might want to take a look. The situation seems stable enough."

"All right, Petrith, go up and take a look at that conveyor booth. See where it goes. As for the rest, if you want to take a peek at Creation's most terrifying superweapon, do so with extreme care. Don't bump into anything, don't even breathe on it. Does anyone have a camera?"

"Yes, actually," Navina affirms. "I have my trans-com, but in mute mode."

"Leave it to a girl..." she chuckles. "All right, let's take a few shots and maybe some video for the folks back home to enjoy. This may be the one and only time we'll ever get to see something like this. Just remember to be careful."

They leave the ship and Kaliya strolls along one of the walkways to the first warehouse. She comes up to an archway entrance, which leads inside a large building.

The warehouse appeared to contain an automated transport network of trays moving along a series of tracks. To one side was a retrieval station, where one would deliver or retrieve a unit from the facility. This unit would then be shuttled along the belts to a storage slot inside the vault.

She tried peering through the transparent wall into the vault, where she could see many rows stacked several layers high and running deep into the building.

"Great cu'Nar above!" she mumbles breathlessly. "There must be hundreds of them in there.

On the near side, she could see one of the units. It was packaged in a large transparent cubical case. The case looked like it might be glass, but it was more likely a dense polymer. Inside she could see what looked like a translucent gel-like substance, and embedded within was a strange spiky crystalline material.

"That must be it, right there. And it's held in a neutral buoyancy gel, I'll bet. Good, keep it nice and happy."

The material radiated a soft glow and seemed to undulate. The spiky projections pulsed, occasionally retracting inward, and with new spikes stretching outwards.

"I don't like that," Kaliya mutters. "Is that thing alive, or simply experiencing a kind of metamorphic transition?"

Navina approached next to her.

"Lieutenant?" she whispers.

"Yes, Navina, what is it?"

"I'm videoing these things, and trying to look inside to see if I can get an idea of how many are stored here. Unfortunately, it's a little difficult to see all the way back. But I'm thinking we might want to make some kind of tally."

"You may have a good point."

Kaliya turns to find the retrieval station, which included a terminal console.

"All right, so if Adalon says Marelle should survive for some period of time, let's put that to the test."

"Um, Kaliya," she asks timidly. "Didn't you say we shouldn't breathe on anything?"

"Well, the Arcanicium, yes. But this terminal should be safe to play with. Let's see…"

Kaliya studies the display and locates an icon to give an inventory status.

"Here we go, look at this. I'm showing a full inventory of five hundred here. Let's check the rest."

They move across the way to the opposite building and check the inventory there, then up to the next one.

"Full, full, and full…this isn't good…"

They continued to the last warehouse. Kaliya checks the terminal at this station.

"This one shows two hundred twenty-four. Navina, do you have a calculator function in that thing?"

"Yeah, what do you need?"

"If their goal is to fill up everything, five hundred each, that's two thousand total, which sounds bad no matter what it is you're making, but here they have, um…" she mentally adds up the numbers. "Seventeen twenty-four, so what percentage of max is that?"

Navina makes a quick calculation on her trans-com.

"I'm showing eighty-six-point-two percent. That sounds pretty close if you ask me."

"A little too close, and depending on how fast this stuff loads up…"

Navina runs another series of calculations.

"All right, this is very rough, and doesn't account for shortages, shutdowns, that one mine on Therinë closing, and so on. But if to consider four hundred years of constant production, with this much product being the result, then to determine how much per year, and what's left to fill up, we have more than six decades yet to go. By the way, this roughly translates as twenty percent per century."

"Interesting. Well, that's not critical, but bad regardless. Worse, if you consider the losses along the way."

"Yeah, that number could change by a small margin if he didn't lose that one mine."

"And this means we were probably right. He was getting close to the end and everything else was becoming expendable, including us."

"I don't like the sound of that, but I'll have to agree."

"And even with what he has now, he could do a lot of damage with it. I don't know how much of this stuff you need for any one application, but the way it sounds to me, if you divide this into quantities, and distribute over distance to create a broader effect..."

"Wow, Kaliya, that could be devastating. If we say just one of these units is enough to create a broad effect within an arcanic cloud, he could send them out in multiple directions, and maybe not just in one universe. If he has in mind to kill them ALL off, he might try jumping all over Creation, in a literal sense of the word, and dropping these things everywhere."

"Cu'Nar's pity, Navina, he must be insane."

"This is clearly a terrorist weapon. I can think of no other word for it."

"All right, I guess if we're finished here, let's pack it up. I'll check on Petrith."

Kaliya walks along the lane to the control booth, where she finds Petrith studying the console.

"What do we have in here?" she asks.

"This arrangement seems simple by comparison to the rest. We have a basic com-station, although who you're supposed to talk to, I have no idea."

"It's probably a standard feature in case someone is over here and needs to call something in."

"Maybe, and then the conveyor with only one choice. This setup looks like its set to automatically ping and configure when linked by the other unit."

"The one at the production facility... So, from here we have a one-way trip back to where they make the stuff. That makes it simple. They make it, bring it over here and drop it, go back, make more, rinse and repeat."

"Right, so now what do we do?"

"Now we go home. Our work is done for now."

They return to the ship and pack up. When everyone was settled, Marelle powers up and brings them back to the production facility, where she lands just long enough for Petrith to change the conveyor indexing, and they continue forward to the base. After landing, Kaliya gives one final review.

"Marelle," she offers. "You've done us a great service. We're not finished, though. We still have Ytani, but for today, this is it. You too Petrith, it looks like you'll have your work cut out for you. And thanks to everyone here, now let's go home."

Chapter 9

TURNCOATS

“My Lord, I need to speak with you.”

Thaelyn and his officers were convening for a meeting in the WIC strategy room. It was still morning, and at this time, Kaliya was still engaged in her mission, having moved to Madzurki and Ooduan by now. But as a curious result of some heretofore unknown action, Vonafel was arriving at the door.

“Archivist?” he calls. “Normally, I would say it is good to see you, but lately, whenever you arrive, it means something dire has occurred. What do you have for us this time?”

“Yeah, something has occurred. I was actually going to ask you about that. I’ve become a little obsessive with these prophecies lately. It seems every five minutes when I’m at my desk, I turn to look at the book I have there to see if anything new has turned up.”

“Vonafel, I know this may seem important, but at the same time, you should try to relax. I am sure whatever it is can wait long enough for you to catch your breath on occasion.”

“Yeah, you’re right. But anyway, is there something going on right now that might be justifiable cause for an event to occur?”

“This is difficult to say with any amount of accuracy, especially when you factor in Adalon and her manners. She is using some very peculiar methods here."

"Well, what is happening out there right now that could be important?"

"The most important is a raid on that Suuden-Aryku military base and the associated facilities. Does this help?"

"Maybe it does."

She approaches the table and takes a seat, while setting down her pile of books on the table. She separates one out containing Adalon's prophecies.

Thaelyn and the General, along with Padriyl, were the only ones in attendance at this time. Kailen was still at the Naarg uy'Sodrad overseeing the arrival of prisoners. They gathered around to observe the elder historian as she prepared to present her latest findings.

"We have a new quatrain that revealed itself just a short while ago. So, if our focal point is that raid mission, something must've happened to trigger this."

"Good gracious," the General whispers. "Her encryptions are applying to such things even across such distances?"

"This is most abnormal," Thaelyn notes. "I would expect this to involve some very complex wording, rivaling and perhaps even exceeding some of the examples I have observed in Sigil of the masters of curses and other applications of meta-spatial manipulation. She is able to imbue an object with the authority to incur an action based on a change in condition of another object located elsewhere, and apparently even across dimensional bounds. I would expect such a thing from no less than the Estelar themselves, and even at that, I should think this would require some effort."

"That sounds scary," Padriyl winces. "And I can just barely understand what it was you said."

"Indeed, even my own teachings would regard this as extraordinary. Vonafel, what do we have on this occasion?"

"This one fills in a space between two others, and follows after the last one in the sequence, the one with the Children of Breed, the slumbering gift, and that reference to the Hooves of Storm. I called in a couple of my assistants to glance over it with me, and we all agree this looks like a logical continuation of where we are in the timeline, but your mention of this raid is interesting. Listen to this…"

She opens her book and prepares to read her latest discovery.

"It begins with… 'In a place of pits and people stout.' From what I've been hearing of that world, it's pitted with all sorts of blast craters, and it's also the home of the dwarves, who are often described as the Stout Folk."

"Indeed, so we must be speaking of Morndindor in this case."

"Then, it continues with… 'a foreign Child is found.' This must refer to your raid."

"Indeed! Then we must have found someone important. The Suuden-Aryku would surely be regarded as foreign to that world, and this individual might therefore play a special role. What else do we have?"

"My Lord, I'm wondering about that term right now…a special role. Listen to this as I give you the whole thing…" she clears her throat to recite the passage. "In a place of pits and people stout, a foreign Child is found; her gift revealed, a journey made, the corruption in rebound."

"Cu'Nar's pity," Padriyl moans. "Another Prodigy Child? Are we speaking of another example like Kaliya and her prophecy?"

"Fascinating…" Thaelyn muses. "But it refers to this person as a female, so we cannot be speaking of Ytani in this case."

"Thank the gods for that," the General sighs deeply. "Then it must be one of the base staff, or perhaps the work crew in the processor."

"Yes, and so now we need to understand who it is and what this role might be. Dear Adalon, are you going to give us any more hints, or is this another of your games of wait-and-see?"

"I don't know if I could answer that for you," Vonafel relents. "But this next one should stir the pot a little bit. This is the last open passage before we hit that blank page in the end…except for that one that popped up when Kaliya met with Adalon in her chamber."

"Meaning all the rest are encrypted for some special occasion. Very well, proceed."

"With vivid thoughts and talents found, a dreamy path they'll seek; the unshackled mind will show the way, to shores where others peek."

"Uh huh… That sounds like Adalon," he grins and nods. "She is back to her original tricks, probably due to this one being exposed."

"But now," the General wonders. "How do we interpret this?"

"Right away, I might suggest the unshackled minds refer to the base staff being relieved of their burdens relating to these chips."

"All right, good, this is reasonable."

"And if we are speaking of a foreign Child, this is certainly understandable. Vivid thoughts and a dreamy path… If we are speaking of Prodigy Children, well, many things become possible, since they are essentially in a sleeplike condition during this time. But now I believe we are speaking in plural here, which means this unshackled mind is sharing something with others. She is showing the way, and together they will peek in on…ooh, Adalon, thank you most graciously," he beams broadly.

"My Lord?" the General smiles expectantly. "Do we have something?"

"The term 'shores' again… I think we just found our ticket to Azgarén, much like Kaliya did with Ruuki uy'Daan. This is where we make landfall."

"But how do we use it if only this one person carries the memories of it?"

"Keeping in mind, this might be a universal talent, so they should all be capable of serving. But if only this one is discovering herself, she must be our center of focus. Therefore, her memories would need to be shared with Kaliya and her people, as they would be the ones to make this journey…to shores where others peek…scouting operations. Vivid thoughts and talents found… General, we need

Aelwyn in here to examine this. Once this new Prodigy Child is found, we may have more work to do."

✦✦✦✦✦

"Greets to ye, Yer Kingship, how ye be today?" the Chief asks as he enters the strategy room.

"I am quite well, thank you," Thaelyn responds. "We are just about to review a few details and wished to include you since you will be involved in some of our future efforts."

"Aye to that! I've been itchin' to hear about that raid ye made on the base. Do ye have any news on it yet?"

"Indeed, we have several favorable reports recently handed in. Take a seat and let us begin."

It was midafternoon on Therinë, and Thaelyn was convening another meeting in the WIC building with his officers, this time including Kailen, who had left the affairs of the prisoners in the hands of Captain Lapäli at the Naarg uy'Sodrad. Chief Bronzeheart had been called in for a consultation concerning the dwarven miners and the future interaction with the people of Glimmerheim.

Among the group was Kaliya, who had recently returned from her mission and was now giving her report on the raid of the Suuden-Aryku base earlier in the day. She had presented her results, as well as a collection of photos and videos downloaded into a data-pad for review by the group.

"First, I must say I am pleased," Thaelyn admits. "Technically speaking, one could say this mission should not have been especially difficult. But Kaliya, since your team is still fairly new, I must say you did a fine job with it. I would also wish to make a special mention as to what your beloved Petrith said about the love and kisses aspect."

The group erupts into a burst of laughter over the imagery.

"You mentioned that one officer appearing jittery," Thaelyn continues. "Restless, paranoid, wandering around the base carrying a weapon...this represents a clear danger if she should lose control of herself. Your handling of that situation was very thoughtful and considerate."

"I didn't want to send her into a worse panic," she reflects. "In fact, she seemed almost as if she was relieved it wasn't Ytani coming for her. One of my teammates mentioned, while he was spying on her in their mess room, that she was in conversation with another about a creeping feeling of imminent danger approaching. I was thinking of asking Aelwyn if this could mean anything. Because she was right."

"Curious…it would seem your people may be showing signs of a number of hidden talents. I wonder where this could lead in the end. These could easily fall further into that category of Celestial skills."

"Yeah, and this complicates things for us in the longer term. We might have a full society with this, and none of them know how to handle it. Then we have the crew of the processor. They're all civilian, by the way, and they actually seemed to accept my explanation of why we're conducting this operation."

"Oh? In what way? How did that one proceed?"

"First, we played a little trick on them with my projected teammates playing like the two Lieutenants. I wasn't taking chances on them being uncooperative, so we made up a story based on the recent events at the base of supply shortages and the suggested survey mission. We told them we're shutting down until that survey finds something, and we can ensure our supply again. Apparently, they were running at only half-cap and occasionally running out of input materials, then being forced to shut down anyway."

"Really, so this would fit nicely into that scenario."

"Once they had their people shut down all the various pieces of equipment, they reassembled back in the control room for a final review. That's when we pulled it. But like before, I decided to excuse myself for our actions and talk them down a little. The conversation was very interesting."

"What did you say?"

"Well, naturally, security was a top priority, so our message had to be short. I simply explained how we were a covert military operation, but without names, and serving a law enforcement operation. There were some questions of what they did wrong, the mention of them being civilian industrial technicians working in cooperation with 'our' mining operation, and so I had to reveal that WE were not part of that base, but an outside body taking all of it into custody based on false pretenses and illegal actions being conducted by those authorities who put it together. This naturally reduced it down to Darumon and his questionable acts, where even the Commander agreed to something from his history. This offered a little credibility."

"How interesting, and quite appropriate to demonstrate a point."

"After that, I generally had to leave it for a later review where we might have better stability, as lives could be at stake here. And although they weren't happy about the idea, they sounded as though they actually accepted it."

"Interesting. Then it might seem the civilian population is under even less affirmative authority than their military."

"They behaved more or less like normal people to me, except for the flat monotones of their speech, which suggests more of those inhibitor chips. And I also took notice they had the seed entities."

"There must be something special about those if even the civilians have them."

"Anyway, I might actually suggest those people could be revived early so we don't have as many limp bodies lying around. They could offer us some background on Azgarén, and we could queue them up after the more critical military members are processed. They might even thank us for it."

"Very well. Commander, perhaps you could pass the word and we can see where this carries us. They would not represent the same high priority security concern, and if we can keep them reasonably contained until a proper explanation is given, I believe this should work well for us."

Thaelyn now picks up the data-pad to study the photos brought back from the mission.

"And then there is this," he muses. "The famous Agent of Unmaking. I must wonder how many eyes have ever set themselves upon this material during the long course of history, if even the Estelar are so averted to it. It is as much a mystery to me as it is to so many others, and yet I must admit, for all its extraordinary destructive potential, it is a curious spectacle to behold.”

“When I was inside there,” Kaliya admits. “I was watching it undulate, almost like it was alive inside those cubes. It was a little bit creepy.”

“No doubt. I would probably feel the same, for this point.”

“And then, Cadet Lar’akan assisted me in tallying up their stockpile. They used an automated retrieval system to move the cubes around, and the data terminals told us three of the four warehouses were full, at five hundred each, with the last one at two hundred twenty-four.”

“Interesting, as well as disturbing… This comes very near to their full capacity.”

“We figure about eighty-six-point-two percent. She suggests a rough estimate of six decades to finish it off.”

“Indeed. But it also exemplifies how close the rest of it must be. And then with us coming into this picture when we did, Maker Kuroku is playing on thin ground here.”

“But now, what comes next for it?”

“Adalon is calling a meeting in only a couple of days, so you should keep your schedule open in case we need to make any movements. In the meantime, Vonafel came to us this morning with another prophecy. It would seem your actions out there invoked another event.”

“Uh oh… What kind?”

“For our purpose, a good one, I think. This one revolves around Morndindor, the Suuden-Aryku occupation, and you discovering another Prodigy Child somewhere.”

“Really! Hmm, and what do we do with it? Who is it, do we know?”

“No, and Adalon is playing one last trick on us. She says this Child, whoever SHE might be, so we are speaking of a female here, will probably experience an awakening, for lack of a better word, and her knowledge will likely give us access to Azgarén, like you did with Ruuki uy'Daan."

"So, it might be a little like me when I had mine. Interesting…"

"Then, the following quatrain, one last exposed one, tells of this knowledge being shared with others. Her memories of Azgarén must be given to you and your people. I called Aelwyn earlier and she says we will likely need to expand your telepathy training to a higher level where you can absorb other people's memories as if they were your own."

"Grace of the cu'Nar! How much more training can I possibly hold? My horns are already drooping down to my knees."

"Perhaps," he grins. "But I think this should not be too difficult. She tells me you took to the previous training well enough, and if your kind is exhibiting so many additional traits, we should not worry about it."

"Your Lordship," Kailen begins. "Regarding the processor and the depot… We are expecting to be disposing of this material in some manner. My main question is how to cover it up in case anyone comes looking. I would imagine someone might wish to make an inspection from time to time."

"For now, we will need to provide excuses and cover, perhaps using our projected team members to simulate their actions. If we borrow from Kaliya's idea of the shortages, we could say the operation is on standby until the situation is corrected. I cannot be sure as to the delicate nature of that processor and its operation, but I should think the constant startups and shutdowns would not be good. Then we must consider the base itself. This is where we need to perform at our best to cover for our actions. We will need a crew present at all times to simulate the base staff, or at least some portion of it to meet our needs. This staff will need to simulate interaction with their headquarters as well as their supply deliveries. But we also need to simulate their food consumption. Therefore, the supplies must diminish as the new ones come in."

"So, are we supposed to eat it now?" Kaliya winces.

"I would expect this to be your native food, so it ought not to poison you," he smiles. "But my thoughts are instead to pass it on to the base commander and his people, since this represents a diet they are most accustomed to. They might not be immediately accommodating to our food here."

"All right, this is reasonable. And this leaves us with Ytani, and the final direction for the base, I suppose, if we want Darumon out completely."

"We will need to sour the milk for him in such a manner as to forfeit that world as a lost cause. My hope is he will simply walk away from it. But along the way, he will surely take notice of his missing weapon, so I hope Adalon has some suggestions on how to contain this. After that, we have perhaps two possibilities, of which I hope the first will be the most likely."

"And those are?" Kailen wonders.

"First would be he returns home to sulk for a time before taking his next move. This would represent a heavy shock to him, to lose four centuries of work. I think even he might wish to take a rest before attempting it again. If you combine this with our interactions here on Therinë, he might not be quite as eager to pursue it immediately."

"This would be a favorable choice. But the other?"

"At some moment, I would expect he will indeed make another attempt, it is only a matter of timing…to do it sooner or later."

"Got it, and the second choice is sooner rather than later…no sulking, just do it."

"But it might take time for him to find something, and then decide on his course of action on how to approach and interact with it. And we might also wish to consider his other objective, and that being his intention of releasing the others from their prison. Recall he once said 'they' would be a Power once more, and this is a plural term that surely cannot be limited to only him and Sargeras."

"Right, have we received any word on that from Sigil?"

"Nothing yet, but the Lady knows to send something if anything is sighted on her streets."

"How will we handle that when it occurs?" Kaliya asks.

"This is a question I am still considering, and at this moment the answer depends greatly on variables I do not yet understand. I think, after our chat with the base commander, perhaps I can feel around for a few of those and gain a better focus. Speaking of which, Commander, what is the word from the Naarg uy'Sodrad?"

"The last report from Captain Lapäli says they're still working on removing the implants from the base commander and his two lieutenants. Lady Aerlie was assisting Ankhia and her team, and together they were taking a cautious approach due to their inherent value. Since this is the first time we've ever done this on a live subject, she wants to get it right. She suggests the next ones might go quicker once they develop the technique."

"And the others? The non-coms and those civilians?"

"So far, all the others are still asleep from Kaliya's team, including those from the processor. Although if we consider Kaliya's suggestion, we might try waking up that one crew and sit them down for a chat. I don't think a bunch of civilians would make too much trouble for us."

"Good, but next we must ask where to detain them. We do not have any substantial prisons in our world, as crime is largely absent. We have a small detention center under the guildhall, but it does not have the capacity for forty-three people, each held in isolation."

"Do you think you would want to keep each of them in isolation?"

"The lead officers, surely, at least for now, until we have time to make our initial interrogations. I think the isolation might work to our benefit to gain any private or sensitive knowledge. The Commander and his two Lieutenants were making their plans for a rebellion, and I am assuming they had the support of the rest. So, we should consider if they could be turned into defectors. It is largely an image we are trying to portray in those first moments. As for the rest, well, perhaps we could group them together for efficiency. And to keep things calm, we could have one of our officers make occasional rounds to share some conversation, maybe a little of Kaliya's love and kisses technique," he smiles. "We can assure them that we are pursuing a responsible course of action for their own safety."

"All right," Kaliya grins. "I can see I have a new reputation unfolding."

"This sounds good to me," Kailen notes. "But I would be very interested in observing this interrogation. Will you be conducting this in the prison itself, or take them out somewhere?"

"Some of our detention rooms involve special windows into a darkened viewing room, for observers like you. We could use this. Then you can see out into the detention room, but they cannot see through to you."

"Dear cu'Nar, you have those too? One-way mirrors?" he chuckles.

"In a certain sense, but ours are enchanted, so the image on the inside seems to reflect another scene. It is part of our illusionary school of magic. In this case, it shows an outdoor garden."

"This I need to see," he grins. "All right then, so when you get ready for your little chat, I'd like to be present inside the booth."

"Of course..." he nods. "Now, I believe the next topic should be the dwarves, and this is where you come in, Chief. Captain Hagmaert informs us we have control of that mine. The miners were removed and brought here, where they are being held in a temporary tent camp just outside the city. We have guards as well as priests watching over them, though we do not technically expect any trouble. This is only for security once they wake up."

"Aye, I understand the need for that," the Chief agrees. "If they be anythin' like me and the lads when we first woke up, ye'll have a few words goin' around for it."

"And this is where you and your fellows can offer help. These are essentially citizens of Glimmerheim. And, in fact, they might even know you, so this familiarity could gain control of the situation very quickly for us. I would ask that you make yourself available for this."

"Aye, ye have me word on it. I'd also like to take a wee gander at them while we have them this way, so I can see how they look for this drug. It can help me to know how we were when ye first found us. We dwarves are a sturdy folk. For a drug to do this to us, it must be a hard one."

"Indeed, and we will also provide medicines to help them recover. Next will be Glimmerheim itself. The Captain will deliver word of our success to your wife and her agents inside the city. Our people are working to dig through to meet with yours on the inside, and once done, we will begin opening up our secrets of the mining and the Suuden-Aryku. But we still have Ytani to deal with. To our benefit, we have control of the base, and therefore the conveyor, to limit his movements in case he should get any ideas about leaving."

"When will be the time ye'll think of goin' after him?"

"The scheduled retrieval of the metal was expected to be by the end of this next week. I feel confident this gives us time to prepare."

"And that's when I go into my greatest performance of all," Kaliya muses. "Swinging my tail like there's no tomorrow, all for the joy of a man in his last moments."

✦✦✦✦✦

"Telta," Eiki calls to her friend as she strolls up the lane. "Come quickly lass, I've got a few words for ye."

The two women were gathering for their usual meeting in Eiki's home in the city. Telta had been making ritual visits since the news from outside arrived, so she could relate it to her husband and assist in spreading the new rumors in the streets. The two of them retreated inside the house and closed the door.

"What be the tale today, Eiki?" Telta asks.

"I just had a visit this morn from the scout sent by the good Captain out there. His people have taken that base over our heads, an' so there nay be any more Suuden-Aryku t' bother us, at least nay directly."

"Nay directly, but what else be there?"

"Our friends have hold of the base an' they'll put up a good show if anyone else comes along. Also, they say the mine t' the south has been taken an' the miners moved out t' safety so they can rest an' recover from this poison they've been eatin'.'"

"Oh, thank the Mother for that," she sighs.

"Aye, but it be a sad thing t' think of all the others gone t' their maker in these past years."

The two women pause to lower their heads in memory of the previous mining groups sent out from the feast.

"Now, the people outside," Eiki continues. "They be a-diggin' through the slide that came down over our doors, an' we've got the people inside diggin' their way out. I don'na know where they'll meet, but Belrum…ye recall him, ay?"

"Aye, he be the one who came t' ye first off."

"Aye t' that. He'll be there, so they say, t' make our meetin'. Then we start letting out about the mine an' the men under this spell, along with the blastin' outside, which will be Belrum's new tale."

"Fine an' good. They'll learn the point-ears nay be a-ragin' outside, there nay be a war, an' the men sent up nay be a-servin' up any fare, instead slavin' away in a mine."

"An' ye can be sure this will send a fair few of them stormin' up a fury for it. An' who d' ye think their fury will be a-stormin' at?"

"Aye, but we need t' give our friends time t' d' away with him, ay? We nay can be a-fightin' him ourselves."

"Right ye be, but I be a-thinkin' of how the timin' will work for when they be ready up top. Then we have a new task, an' this will be a hard one. We need t' let the people know about the Suuden-Aryku, but only so much as what Belrum saw that day when they were a-pickin' up from that mine outside."

"Nay about our friends yet?"

"Nay so far, as they be a-thinkin' of more Suuden-Aryku comin' t' look at us. There be that one gnarly cur t' be wary of, an' he be of a worse sort than the Thane. He can change shape an' check up on us down here, an' if he hears tales in the streets of our friends…"

"Aye! There goes the war again."

"So, until we can be sure he has nay more mind for us, we still need t' keep quiet, unless somehow we can get all the people t' line up the same for this part, which I nay be so sure of right now."

✦ ✦ ◆ ✦ ✦

"My Lord, he's awake," shouts a guard entering the strategy room.

"Very good," Thaelyn submits. "Return to your post. I will be there shortly."

"Here we have our moment of truth, my Lord," the General considers. "How will you proceed, I wonder?"

"I ask that of myself, as well. Commander, it is time, if you would wish to participate."

"Absolutely, I wouldn't miss this for anything. What about Kaliya? I'm sure she'd like to see this too. And maybe we could invite Ankhia, to observe from the medical side of things relating to these implants, and see how they're recovering."

"This is reasonable. Is she currently available?"

"I think she was taking a short break after the recent group they processed."

"Very well, send word for her to meet with us in B.T. at the guildhall."

"Thank you," he responds as he turns to find Padriyl at his desk on the other side of the room. "Lieutenant, this would be an excellent occasion for you and your video recordings. I want to save this for later review."

Thaelyn checks the table one last time, scanning over the reports and photos from his scouting runs and selecting a few in particular for a final review, as well as the data-pad recently delivered with Kaliya's mission photos. When he finishes, he leads his delegation of officers out of the WIC building and through the gateway network to the guildhall. The Suuden-Aryku Commander and his two lieutenants had been relocated there after the surgical procedure to remove the implants was complete.

Along the way, a messenger found Kaliya in a practice session on the upper mage field and brought her down to join them. Ankhia was also just arriving from the Naarg uy'Sodrad, and together they proceeded through the guildhall, travelling along a hallway to the rear on one side. They navigated two more side corridors to find a set of stairs leading down into a lower level that served as the detention hall. As they moved along a passageway leading to the holding cells, Thaelyn paused to give directions to the group.

"We will see about the Commander first, in this case," he declares in a hushed voice. "He is in the first cell here, behind this door," he gestures to one of two in a set. "The detention chamber is a room with a table and chair, allowing someone to sit while in conversation with the prisoner, who is most often held within a confinement cell to one side. This door adjacent here leads behind the room to the viewing booth. Enter here and remain quiet while the session is in process."

The group splits with the officers passing through the door to the viewing booth while Thaelyn prepares to enter the detention room. He checks his attire and straightens his garments for a better presentation, and then opens the door and steps inside.

The Suuden'kai Commander had only recently woken up from his sleep enchantment, having been one of the first to pass through surgery. He was groggy and disoriented, and struggling to understand where he was and what happened to him.

Thaelyn casually strolled into the room and stood near the table and chair. He waited for the Commander to pull his wits together well enough to respond to his presence. The Commander looked up at him, appearing perplexed at the strange being standing in the room with him.

"Who are you?" he asks in a subdued voice. "Do you speak our language?"

"Indeed, I do, I am well-studied in it. But for the moment, with apologies, I must refrain from answering certain questions. We are in a delicate situation of security. My people are in a condition of war, and therefore we have some restrictions placed upon us. Until I can settle myself as to where we stand presently, I feel we should proceed carefully during this interview to understand one another."

"I see, and I thank you for your polite conduct, but..."

The Commander pauses to study his cell and the window on one wall, which appears to hold a view of a small flower garden.

"...Where are we?" he muses quietly. "This world cannot be the same one..." he tries lifting an arm, as if testing it for the weight due to the local gravity. "You must have relocated us somewhere."

"You are very observant. But of course, I suppose this particular aspect might stand out a bit."

"Yes, it would. To be honest, it feels good to be away from that place. Over the course of time, I became used to it, but in the end, the local environment, the temperatures, the dry air, among other things, were all very depressing...if only I could..." he halts his statement as he began to realize a new sensation arising.

He held his position as he tried to interpret this new feeling within his conscious perceptions. He impulsively lifted a hand to the side of his head where he formerly had the interface unit attached. He gently felt around the bare patch left behind by the removal procedure.

"If only...I could feel it..." he emits distantly. "The interface is gone. You removed it? But wait a minute..."

He continued to gently probe the area with his fingers, trying to determine if there were any bandages or scars left behind. The area was clean and only felt slightly tender by now.

"I do not understand this. It was there, and now it is not, and there are no surgical patches or anything else I can tell after the procedure. How long have I actually been here that it is fully healed by now?"

"Actually, not as long as you might think. We have a few special procedures where this goes that allow us to repair and restore injuries quite rapidly. The procedure to remove the device was carried out very carefully, of course, and then a restorative method was applied to regenerate the tissue and bone loss left behind by it. You were kept asleep during this time, but overall, it is barely more than a day since we brought you in."

"Only a day? Amazing. You must have some very advanced medical techniques."

"I suppose the term may be appropriate, but perhaps also subjective, depending on how you look at it. Still, they are certainly noteworthy for how they are applied."

Thaelyn takes a seat in the chair to relax into the conversation.

"As for the interface," he continues. "We had some time in which to study you, and we discovered a number of anomalies, such as those devices within your neural tissues that gave the impression of a governing effect. Therefore, we took the initiative to remove them. We deemed this might be necessary if we wanted to learn anything from you."

"All right, I will not argue. In fact, I would even thank you for this. I hated those things."

Inside the observation booth, the others watched. Ankhia glared at the interaction.

"Hated them?" she whispers intriguingly.

"But excuse me," Thaelyn considers. "How is it you would have such devices at all if you are so revolted by them?"

"It was a mandate by our local government. There were two devices, one is a medical implant and the other a military grade authority chip. I did not…did not…did-n-t…"

The Commander again halts as he begins to feel another sensation occurring. It echoed from something very old and deeply rooted. He frowns as if recalling something long forgotten. Finally, he lays a hand over his brow as he realizes what it is.

"Didn't… In all the nether-space, I can actually say it again. Didn't!"

"Huh?" Thaelyn inquires curiously. "My apologies, but I am lost on your meaning. What are we speaking of here?"

"The word…didn't…" he begins to form a tiny smile as a subtle flow of neurological relief relaxes into him. "I can say it again! How long has it been?"

Thaelyn was visibly perplexed by the strange reaction, and he casually glanced in the direction of the window before returning to the prisoner.

"I apologize," the Commander resumes. "You probably think I am going crazy now."

"The thought passed briefly," he smiles cautiously. "But if you can help clarify."

"I can, and for this one little gift alone, I must thank you again. That interface, and those chips…" he scorns softly. "As I said, one of them is a medical grade application, and it causes an unfortunate anomaly in our language center. It...it's...supposed to correct for a medical issue, but the focal point in the tissues is too inconveniently located in the same cluster as our emotion center, therefore it has the effect of dampening our emotional output. There is also a side effect of interfering with some of our linguistics, like contractions and other shortcuts, causing us to spell everything out verbosely."

"Fascinating..." Kaliya mumbles. "Just like what Geilv was saying, but inconveniently? Or is this simply a story by someone. Having no emotions would certainly offer a nice control effect if you're sending out killing machines to wipe whole planets."

Thaelyn studied the Commander as he was clearly experiencing a moment of delight over the removal of his chips.

"This is a rather interesting mention. Could this be a design flaw, or simply an unfortunate coincidence?"

"It's described as a coincidence, as the two are closely linked within the cortex."

"I see, well then, I suppose I should congratulate you on receiving some relief from it, but a medical implant you say? Were you ill in some manner?"

"No, but it became a mandate as a preventative procedure. The illness was appearing at random, and it posed a fatal threat, so we mandated this procedure as a control mechanism."

"This is a rather curious form of control over something described as an illness. We cannot be speaking of something as mundane as a simple biological infection, could we?"

"We don't know what it is or where it came from. It's called the Tav'ageen Anomaly. It was originally found in a series of children many millennia ago, before the Marshal and Sargeras appeared..."

Inside the observation room, several people all gasped at once.

"You bastards!" Ankhia scorns silently. "What did you do?"

The Commander continues, "At the time, our medical teams couldn't understand what it was, as it defied all our attempts to analyze it. Fortunately for us, the Marshal came along when he did, and his advanced knowledge helped us to find a solution for it, even though it also dulls our emotions along the way. Personally,

I'm not so sure I would agree with this, as I never experienced the symptoms, but it became one of those mandates simply for reasons of public safety."

"Public safety, my crinkled tail!" Ankhia growls with an angry swipe of her tail.

Kaliya reaches over and places a hand on her arm to settle her.

"It would seem you have a few delicate dilemmas back home," Thaelyn accedes.

"I…would say it goes deeper than that," the Commander affirms solemnly. "But I can't be precisely sure how deep. Anyway, what is this condition of war and how does it relate to us? Did we do something to you? And how did I get here? You must have hit us while we were sleeping or something."

"Yes, with apologies, but a nighttime operation gave us a decisive edge to capture your staff with minimal opposition or collateral damage."

"Now that's a new approach. You essentially attack us, and then you apologize for it."

"Indeed," he smiles gently. "One of my operatives nicknamed the approach as a love and kisses technique," he chuckles. "I find it rather quaint, so I thought I might give it a try."

"You must have some very unusual people working for you," he attempts a tiny smile.

"Unusual would be a good word for it, but clever and considerate also fits nicely. And of course, yes, we should move forward. By the way, may I know your proper name? From our observations, I suspect you hold a command rank, am I right?"

"Yes, of course, my apologies. I suppose we became distracted. My name is Fleet Commander Lajivi Kriv'tik, and I serve a military authority we call Central Command on our home world of Azgarén."

"Very good, Commander, and thank you," Thaelyn nods. "A Fleet Commander, is it? That seems like a rather prestigious title for someone working in what appears to be a resource acquisition operation. How did you manage that one?"

"I'm basically on reserve station from my former service role. They once called for a mission team to serve in what they described as a high priority operation to serve the Marshal as part of our promise to assist him in his personal affairs. This became that mining base. Although, if you were to ask me if I'm very happy with our experiences, I would have to say no. We've seen a few things we don't necessarily care for during this time."

"I see. Perhaps we can go into this more as we continue. Now, as to your questions, for instance this condition of war and what you may have done to us. Technically speaking, those of you in your base did nothing, at least not to us. But we are a society of laws, and some very determined moral standards. During the course of our war, we have been stepping from one world to another, until we came upon that one where we found you. And, well, if you know the condition of that world, I think it speaks for itself."

"Oh great," the Commander sighs and glances around his cell. "So, the deed is coming back to us now."

"You were expecting something of this sort?"

"No, not personally, and neither by other means, not after this long a time. There's probably nothing left out there to argue about it, and we were under the impression our actions were not noticed by anyone who would take an interest. But it does carry a certain irony to it now that you're here."

"An irony... This is an interesting term. I suppose it might be appropriate, within a certain context. But Commander, the loss of life and devastation on that world is unimaginable. And then we found you there taking up the local minerals. How would an irony play into this? It gives the impression that you are responsible for it, or at the very least, opportunistically taking advantage of it."

"All right, wait, before you go and accuse me of anything, allow me to try to explain a few things which might change your perspectives a little."

"Very well, Commander, out of fairness, I will listen. But I hope you will accept that we are not at all pleased by what we saw. An entire world made virtually lifeless is a very high crime for some."

"I'm sure of it, and I'm not happy either. This is one of those things I spoke of a moment ago that I didn't like about our operations. This, and a number of other things I've seen during my career."

"Other things in your career?" he muses. "Might there have been other occasions of a similar sort?"

"Yes," he sighs. "But here it gets complicated, and I suppose we're deserving of this, if only I could qualify the reasoning behind it, and this eludes me on many occasions. Um, before we begin, allow me to ask about the rest of my staff, where are they? I hope you can understand this is still my responsibility, and I need to know."

"Naturally. We took everyone in your command building and the barracks captive, and we further proceeded through your conveyor to your processor facility and found a crew working there. We took them as well."

"Those people are civilians, and essentially blameless of anything relating to the planet. They were hired only to work in the processor."

"Yes, one of our agents had a small discussion with them briefly and learned of this, so we will treat them kindly for their position."

"All right, good, and thanks again. You seem like a very even-tempered and compassionate society."

"Indeed, we believe in understanding the circumstances around us as best we can before we come to any conclusions," Thaelyn smiles.

"This is actually a good policy, and I'm thankful for it. I just wish we had as much opportunity. As for me and my staff, we are not personally responsible for the planet. We were assigned later to operate and manage the base. So, if you are looking for the ones responsible for the bombardment, you would need to contact our military headquarters on Azgarén. I don't know who was assigned to that duty, but they would, assuming it wasn't buried in more of their bureaucracy. The only problem is, I'm not sure what sort of response you'll get out of them, and neither would I be able to accurately describe the crewmembers as truly guilty of these actions, given my own experience for how these missions tend to play out."

"This is a very curious statement. How do we define this?"

"How do we define it?" he sighs again. "This represents part of my recent issue with my command, and also why I cannot be sure how deep it runs or what it truly means. My experiences came with definitions, but some of those definitions did not fall within my expectations. Forgive me, but I must ask one more question. You mentioned you took the command building and the barracks. There is a house at the far end. Did you investigate that one?"

"We do not generally attack houses, but in this case, I know of the one you speak. Perhaps if I come forward one step with you... his name is Ytani, correct?"

The Commander stared at Thaelyn for a brief moment, and then formed a cautious smile.

"You must have been watching us before you attacked."

"As any good military operation goes," Thaelyn returns the smile. "The first order of business is intelligence gathering."

"Fair enough, I'm not offended. Maybe this is a good thing, as you might understand some of our local issues. Do you know of his manners? Did you happen to see one of our officers stumble out of there some time ago?"

"We did, and we were shocked by it. We also listened in on some of your communications with that miscreant young man, and I sent a spy in there to investigate his home."

"A spy? And what did you find?"

"A typical home, as one might expect, except for one room with a number of devious implements one might use for torture and rape. So, the question is, who is he and how could he rule over you with such manners as threats and coercion?"

"Good, let's begin with this, and then we can move to the planet, as they might be related."

"Related?"

"I'm beginning to suspect you know more than you're actually letting on, especially if you've had enough time to study us...to know our language, to know how to use our technology, like the conveyor, to know we might have a processor one jump away and you would wish to shut it down. You mentioned laws and determination, then a war. Why would you be on that world to begin with if it didn't involve us somehow?"

"You are a shrewd intellectual, Commander. Do you have an answer to this?"

"Would it involve the Marshal, maybe also Sargeras?"

"This is an interesting question, as I do not believe you have given a full introduction to them as yet."

"I think you already know. Your manners suggest a form of familiarity."

Thaelyn smiled at the clever reasoning.

"That rank you gave earlier sounds like a rather fashionable one, and now I think I understand how you earned it. Very well, I will admit that when we first arrived there, we had many questions, a number of suspicions, and even a few uncertainties. But when we found you, we found curiosities instead. Let us travel this path of discovery together. I suppose your nearness to mutiny, along with your staff, has pushed you very close to the edge by now. Maybe we can find some common ground together."

"Mutiny…yes, this would be a fine way to describe it. Ytani and his demands, the Marshal and his… Normally, it would be shameful for a man in my position to admit to something like this, but my base staff was being made sacrifice to that young tyrant in there."

"Could you not report this to your command authority?"

"I think the Marshal has been overriding my complaints, he wants his metal so badly."

"Do you actually know what he is making with it?"

"All I know is, it is extremely volatile and needs to be handled with extreme care whenever we move it to the depot."

"And you have a substantial quantity over there, so I can imagine all your tense nerves along the way."

The Commander glared at him again.

"You went there?"

"We visited the site and took photos, but did not touch anything."

"My advice, don't. Not that I would tell you to keep out of it, but for safety's sake."

"I understand, but Commander, it does not actually end there. That material is a form of weapon, and one of such destructive power as to frighten even the most supreme of societies. It therefore falls upon us to dispose of it in order to deny him his pleasures."

"Pleasures? That's a strange term to use here. And then to say a weapon to frighten even the most supreme of societies, that's also a strange reference."

"Perhaps, if you are one such who has never encountered any. But there are those out there who are much higher than yours."

"All right, I can accept this, and I suppose I can also accept that they might hold technologies, some of which might relate to weapons, and these might be truly frightening. But then, I need to return to what role you play in it. They told us there are insurgents chasing them. Are you related to those?"

"Whether or not we might be described as insurgents is irrelevant for the moment. Our arrival is circumstantial to a number of incidents we encountered along the way. So, allow me to approach it this way. Treat me as an unbiased observer for now and tell me your story. We will take this in steps. Let us begin with Ytani."

"All right..." he nods. "Insurgents or otherwise, you don't match the descriptions we were given, like so many other things. About Ytani... First, he's a civilian. The Marshal placed him into a position of authority over obtaining this unusual metal they have on that world. Our science doesn't provide us with an accurate description of what it is or how to process it, so the Marshal chose to use local labor..." he pauses to glare at Thaelyn once more. "I'm going to guess you know about the city down there, right?"

"Indeed, this was one of our objectives, to see if anything was still alive out there, and that city was an important target. We also found a few clusters of survivors out in that wasteland, and we have been trying to gather them up in a sweeping rescue effort."

"Really! Where are you putting them? That world is experiencing a global meltdown."

"We know this, and we hope to correct it, once we can turn Darumon away from it."

"Darumon? Just Darumon, not Marshal Darumon?"

"I do not personally believe he is deserving of a title, not for all he has done. So, I choose to call him simply by his given name."

"Interesting," he raises his brow. "But this hints even more at familiarity."

"Perhaps it does, to some degree. As for the people, we have a world located elsewhere we are using as a temporary shelter."

"Good, I'm happy to hear that. This reminds me of one other aspect of our operations. As part of our…mutiny…we were considering trying to save one last mining crew we were managing to our south."

"We overheard that discussion with your Lieutenant. This represents one of those curiosities I mentioned, for a military operation using this drug of yours to acquire what is essentially a form of slave labor. We were previously aware of them, and when we took your base, we took them also. They are currently in our custody and will soon be receiving treatments to help them recover."

"Wow, you're good. All right then, back to the story. Ytani was trained to use some special skill the Marshal taught him to somehow impersonate the local leader of that city and have them produce this metal for us, and also to pull out mining teams on occasion. We don't know how he does it, but some of us have suggested it to be a strange device he keeps in his home."

"Is this to say Darumon did not actually explain it to you?"

"We don't even have a name for it, much less an explanation."

In the observation booth, the listeners watched.

"Incredible…" Kailen whispers. "They're completely oblivious."

"Still, this is a curious mention," Thaelyn notes. "He uses this skill to impersonate a dwarf. Commander, just for the sake of clarity, have you ever seen a dwarf personally?"

"Yes, I have, many times when those mining teams come out."

"Of course, and as a man who can surely tell the difference in appearances, you might have noticed there is a slight discrepancy in your physical proportions," he smiles tenderly.

"Yes!" he grins. "And Ytani apparently works out a lot. From what I recall of him, on those few occasions I actually met him, he carries a very robust physique, which only exacerbates matters."

"Indeed, so to say he could impersonate someone who is literally a fraction of his size must be a very disturbing image."

"I wish I could understand how he does it. We were hoping to confiscate whatever device he uses and manage it ourselves, or else try to reveal ourselves to them and see if we could appeal to their compassion, if they have any. Maybe to excuse ourselves for the mess we made and see if we could get them to understand it from our side."

"While the idea is a fair one, under the circumstances, for what you left in your wake, I might find that difficult, to say the least."

"Yes, so do we."

The conversation pauses as the Commander reflects on his discussions with his officers in the control booth and his office.

"Um," he begins again. "As a society of laws, do you have any plans for him? Where is he right now?"

"Still in his house and unaware of our actions, but yes, we do have plans for him. But our plans must be very discreet, so we do not leave anything for Darumon to discover."

"So, you are some sort of enemy to him."

"He became an enemy to me before I became one to him. But let us come to that in a moment. Please continue with your story for now. You mentioned a relation, I believe."

"A relation...yes, the planet... According to the information we were given when we were assigned this duty, we were told the planet was under conversion by these insurgents. This is the reason I suspect you are here now. How else would you know of us?"

"In truth, Commander, until that creature attacked my home world, I did not even know you existed."

"Is that so. So, am I shooting myself in the hoof here?"

"Not at all. As I said, perhaps we can be of some assistance together. Please continue."

"Well, since the time Sargeras and the Marshal first arrived, these insurgents have been making incursions into our space and elsewhere, trying to deny us the ability to return Sargeras back home. While this makes sense to us, if we say they wanted him out and to stay out, I can tell you from a few of my own experiences, the numbers don't add up nicely."

"Oh?" Thaelyn leans forward. "How so? Does this relate to those experiences you mentioned during your career?"

The Commander hesitates in his response, appearing suddenly very self-conscious and sighing deeply multiple times as he appeared to fight with himself to answer.

"If you're a society of laws," he responds solemnly. "You'll probably lock me away in here until my last days. While I wasn't responsible for that one planet, I am responsible for a series of others."

Thaelyn gazed at him, realizing this might hold a key element to answer a few old questions.

"I would wish to hear more of this. I recall a vague mention during one of your conversations of some sort of missions, correct? Would you be willing to offer something like a confession?"

"A confession?" he balks morbidly. "To simply admit that I'm responsible for the destruction of so many other worlds like that one. How would that make me appear in your eyes? Mutiny or otherwise, I can't run from this."

"I can be a reasonable man, if the explanation holds merit, or some other condition to justify the action. But if you did this simply for the joy of it, that is another matter."

"No, not for joy, this much I can assure you."

"Very well, let us try to approach this from a perspective of chronology. Commander, I know enough about your people to know you are a society of scientists and scholars. Therefore, as a man born of a society of thinkers, let us see how well you can demonstrate yourself."

In the visitor's booth, Kaliya and the others continued to watch.

"Oh dear," she whispers. "He's going into his inquisitor mode."

"A society of thinkers," the Commander muses. "All right, this sounds like an interesting perspective. I'll play along. Where do you want to start?"

"I think we should start at the only appropriate place we can…

the beginning. Tell me, how old are you? How far back do you actually go?"

"I'm one hundred twenty-two, and I actually go back to before they arrived, which was roughly ten millennia ago."

"Commander," Thaelyn grins. "If you will excuse me for one moment, I am actually much more accustomed to working with societies that measure their ages in individual years, but I am suspecting yours is centuries, correct?"

"Yes. Our lifespans travel as much as two hundred centuries."

"This is a rather extreme number for any mortal society."

"Mortal?" he raises his brow.

"Yes, recall my mention of those supreme societies out there. Some of them no longer even hold corporeal form, and so the pressures of time no longer affect them. For this, we can say they have achieved true immortality. Then we have a number of secondary races, which we often refer to as Celestials. Mine would be included in this. Some of us are natural races, having evolved into a supremely high station, while others, like mine, are a hybridized form with what we often describe as the Child Races, which is to say people like you."

"Why would they do this?"

"The purpose here is most often to create an intermediate form that might bridge the gap between the two. The reason being these others, whom we address as the Estelar, find it either too difficult or too inconvenient to conduct a common form of interaction with the younger races. Their extreme nature leaves them in a class by themselves, and the Child Races are simply not ready for it."

"Fascinating, so they send someone like you to do the work for them?"

"In a manner of speaking," he affirms. "But there are rules we must follow. We believe the Child Races must follow a path of growth and learning, so unlike what some might wish for, the gods do NOT simply give their secrets away."

"Gods..." he draws back in his seat. "We're not a religious society, did you know this?"

"It matters not if you hold a religion, as THESE gods are real.

One might describe them as the grandfather society above all the rest."

"Right…" he wheezes. "In all the nether-space, if you really are those insurgents, just what have we gotten ourselves into?"

"This is a good question, but to answer it, I believe we need to continue forward in our discussion. Tell me about the first arrival of Sargeras and Darumon. How did it occur?"

"Um, yeah…" he gulps tenderly. "But if you don't already know, um…"

"Gently, Commander, one at a time. I only came into this recently."

"Uh huh. Well, it all began as our people were greeted with a visitation by a pair of beings from another society. They claimed to be refugees from a terrible crime committed against them and needed asylum. Naturally, we responded to this and inquired as to what happened. They identified themselves as one named Sargeras, who was described as the leader of this other society, and his military advisor, Marshal Darumon."

Once again, inside the viewing booth, Kailen and the others watched.

"You must be kidding me!" he whispers sternly.

"Well, it does offer up a bit of humorous appeal," Kaliya smiles gently.

"At that time," the Commander continues. "Sargeras appeared very weak, and the Marshal requested we provide space for a special habitat for him to heal and recover. His kind apparently has some very unique medical requirements that our science doesn't support."

"How interesting…" Thaelyn reflects.

"Does any of this sound familiar to you?"

"I could probably account for certain elements, but your story would be outside my personal knowing. So, when we finish with yours, I will give you mine as fair reciprocation."

"All right," he nods. "Anyway, since then, the Marshal negotiated with us a number of exchanges for our service. One of these was to request military aid to retake Sargeras's former home and position of authority from a body of insurgents he claimed overthrew him illegally. In return for this, the Marshal would provide us with some of their advanced teachings, which could elevate our society's science and technology to an entirely new level."

"This sounds like a very rich offer."

"Yes, to our society, it is. As you already know, we are a society of scientists, and an offer like this would be very desirable."

"But in this case, you would need to turn at least partially militant to serve this purpose. A society of scientists does not, in my mind, make a good army."

"No, it doesn't. At that time, I was a young officer in our old Sentinels' service, which was mostly a law enforcement and security service."

"When did this change to a more formal military?"

"The Marshal essentially took control of our service to reshape it, as he described it, into something more appropriate to the need. We developed a new and extensive industry to support the design and construction of a large navy. This involved new ship designs, new technologies, many of them involving more powerful weapons, propulsion, more efficient energy cores..."

"Everything you need to represent yourself as a formidable power in the face of what might be unknown opponents."

"Right. And since Sargeras was represented as a member of a very sophisticated society, our opponents were similarly described as highly sophisticated."

"Indeed. Such that you must reach even higher if you would wish to oppose them at all."

"Exactly, but then came a series of reports. They started out as sightings in our local space and surrounding star clusters. We interpreted these mostly as scouting efforts to locate us and Sargeras. After all, it's a big galaxy out there."

"Of course, as they often tend to be."

"It would be a few centuries before the first of the serious engagements actually occurred, when we began to hear of them trying to establish their own outposts and military bases as forward fronts. By this time, we had an opportunity to develop some of this new tech and were ready to test it. We would put down one instance only to find another. They seemed to chain together after a while in clusters at rough intervals on the order of a couple to perhaps several centuries as we continued to scout the surrounding galaxy where we lived."

"This is a curious pattern. But it could also afford you time to test and redevelop your technologies to improve upon things along the way."

"Yes, and it did provide us with opportunities to make design changes and refinements. After a while, we became concerned that these insurgents were trying to establish a hidden base for a surprise attack. This is where my career came in, along with others I know of…or knew of. Some are no longer with us."

"Killed in battle, perhaps?"

"Yes, I think so. By the reports I heard, some of these battles were rough. But in my case, I had a number of experiences that I would reflect back on later in life."

"And no doubt, this relates to the mention you made earlier."

"Yes, it does. During my career, I was in charge of a task force component of our space navy. We kept receiving these reports from our scouting patrols of these insurgents attempting to establish bases on this world or that one, and this was too close for comfort, so we felt obligated to defend ourselves and Sargeras. The Marshal was also pursuing a group of defectors at the same time, and they were apparently joining forces with these others to conspire against us."

"Why am I suddenly getting a chill," Kaliya mumbles softly.

"And so," the Commander continues, "as a means to contain the situation, whenever we found one of these base camps, our military was sent in to destroy it. But the instructions we often received were not simply to make a pinpoint strike of a base facility. Instead, it was a blanket effect of the entire planetary surface."

"That seems a little excessive, Commander," Thaelyn admits. "How do we explain the justification for this?"

"A global contamination and conversion of the local society…

It was said these insurgents were attempting to use something to modify the full population such that they would become infectious and spread out to other worlds. This resulted in an irrefutable demand to purge the full planet as a way of cleansing it, to say nothing of watching our own tails as we moved forward."

"That sounds very serious, as well as malevolent. And how did this appear once you arrived?"

"From our perspective, it appeared as a society that didn't even know what hit them."

"What?" Kailen gasps. "Whole worlds blasted without even knowing what hit them?"

"Commander," Thaelyn accedes. "This does indeed sound as bad, if not worse, than what we saw on that one world."

"Yes," he responds softly and ducks his head. "Some of our scans indicated energy signatures and pollution levels much more indicative of a lesser-evolved society than our own. But the orders suggested this conversion was changing that somehow. And I was not the only fleet commander conducting these operations. Some of the worlds were blasted to dust, others not as much, only to reduce them down to a minimal capacity."

"I see, and then you mentioned something about defectors in this."

"Yes, a group that was led by a former member of our government body..."

"So, we're defectors, are we?" Kaliya grumbles under her breath.

The Commander continues, "All I recall of it was he turned against us shortly after Sargeras arrived and ran off with a large group of loyalists. They were aided by someone or something, the reports were never very clear, but an unknown entity that provided a huge vessel of unknown design and from unknown origins."

"This represents a lot of unknowns," Thaelyn notes. "But go on..."

"The Marshal gave chase, and we had occasional reports of discovering his hiding places, but before we could launch a full-scale assault, he escaped again. Our advance patrols were only able to take a few shots at him, but never anything to bring him down."

"Only a few shots?!" Kaliya grits through her teeth.

The General now lays a hand on her shoulder to reinforce her calm.

"He sounds like a very elusive one," Thaelyn reflects.

"Yes, but I heard a recent report where he was apparently…and finally…discovered and eliminated."

"Oh!" Kaliya grunts harshly. "Finally, is it?"

"I see," Thaelyn muses. "It would seem you have a number of curious stories to tell. Does this bring us roughly to the present day and Morndindor?"

"Generally so, as far as that part goes. The Marshal was recently conducting some exercises on a world he was using as a staging post to launch his attacks from, but I heard that was cancelled."

"Aw, too bad…" Kaliya whispers. "It was cancelled… Bye-bye."

"Most interesting," Thaelyn affirms. "But now, we should try to analyze some part of this. You mentioned these inconsistencies, and this seems an important topic to resolve. The first question to ask is how a society of scientists and scholars, who ought to know how to analyze empirical data much more effectively than this, might mistake that which never saw you coming for a society even more advanced than you, especially if it was high enough to overcome one such as Sargeras."

"That is a very good question," the Commander considers. "Other than for suggesting it was still in a conversion stage, I don't have an answer. I was under the active mode of my military chip, as was my full crew, so we didn't have the opportunity to make any sort of assessment. All we could do was follow orders."

"Oh dear cu'Nar," Ankhia moans. "Is that what it does?"

"One moment, Commander," Thaelyn interjects. "Help me to understand this chip you mentioned."

"It's a horrid little piece of technological nonsense someone invented once because they apparently didn't think we could follow orders on our own."

Thaelyn pulled back into his chair and raised his brow.

"Indeed!" he intones enthusiastically. "And by your tone, you must hold a deep revulsion to it, am I right?"

"I think many of us do. That, along with the seed entity," he thumbs at the growth on his back.

"So, none of it is truly voluntary," Ankhia mumbles to herself. "But cu'Nar help us, how could they even allow it?"

"Is this something used in your entire military?" Thaelyn asks.

"The seed is universal, same as that medical chip, but the authority chip, as we call it, is only in our military. I recall once it was described as a controversial piece of technology, but it was quickly classified and hidden, then mandated as standard equipment for all our military personnel."

"Oh, how convenient," Ankhia murmurs disdainfully.

"This represents a rather surreptitious act," Thaelyn accedes. "Especially if it is conducted by a government authority, and then used in such a manner as this."

"And I believe it was invented, or at least designed by the Marshal, like everything else."

"And this would further suggest some manner of underhandedness, especially if you involve these worlds you were told to obliterate that apparently knew nothing of your existence. Let us consider something..." he waves a finger figuratively.

Thaelyn stands up and now begins his classic pacing as he composes his thoughts.

"Here it goes, folks," Kaliya mutters expectantly.

"You have your service where you were tasked to perform certain actions. You say this was as a countermeasure to these insurgents who were claimed to be pursuing Sargeras and Darumon. They are described as a superior form of technological society. Therefore, you might expect that any outpost or other form of presence, if properly established, ought to provide some reasonable measure of defensive capability, as well as some reasonable level of discretion to remain concealed, especially if they are supposed to be assembling for a surprise attack."

"Yes, this would be my assessment as well," the Commander agrees.

"Now, we can suggest you might get lucky a few times during this period. But ten millennia, Commander, is a rather excessive measure of time for them to make so many attempts and fail on each occasion. After a while, you might think they would learn their lessons, and either NOT make any further attempts, or do so somewhere well outside your capacity to locate them so conveniently."

"Boom..." Kaliya notes.

"Yes," the Commander considers. "I would need to agree with that."

"Furthermore," Thaelyn continues. "We might ask ourselves why they would bother establishing themselves on worlds that gave the appearance of ignorance to your very existence, unless we suggest those worlds were being used as a form of distraction for some other action they were preparing."

"Maybe."

"Instead, I would put it to you that if they knew enough to find you at all, and for this we must assume they know where you are if you are suggesting these worlds were being used as hidden bases for a surprise attack. And if we further reflect on their nature as a superior form of technology, and with such determination to hunt and destroy Sargeras, why not simply arrive on your doorstep as he did? Why spend so many worlds along the way?"

"I...uh... I don't know if I have the answer to that, or if I would want to suggest one."

"On the surface, it would seem the military prowess of these people is poorly lacking. This therefore represents a paradox, if they were so successful in ousting him in the first place."

"Yes, I suppose it does."

"Then you mention this traitor. Let us examine this briefly, since it seems to hold a relation to these others. He turned against you in the beginning. Do we have any details on this?"

"Let me see... He was a member of our government at the time, but I recall people say his division wasn't a very highly regarded one to begin with. It was granted a voice mostly to quell any protests that might be generated by the faction he represented."

"Father won't be happy to hear that," Kailen admits. "I know his wasn't a favorite for the radical nature of it, but..."

"Propaganda, Kailen," Kaliya replies. "An empirical society that doesn't believe in mysticism. And even at that, given what we've learned since then, this would change very quickly."

"A faction..." Thaelyn muses. "Describe to me how your government appears."

"It's described as a Council of Elders," the Commander explains, "which is a body of statesmen where the title of Elder represents the leading authority in one or another of the scientific factions our people support for research. It's a representative body, chosen by an election that occurs every decade. Therefore, if it represents any kind of true science that allows us to evolve as a society, they govern our direction in it."

"This is a rather interesting form of government...a technocracy. A representative government is not so uncommon, but one made up of statesmen reflecting a spectrum of varying fields of professional or scientific specialization, as opposed to one concerning political, cultural, or ethnic divides, is surely an unusual one. So then, we might say, to declare one as a traitor in this environment is to say one who rejects or rebels against the acquisition of this knowledge."

"Essentially, yes... As the story goes, our Elder Council, along with the Marshal, condemned them, saying they were turning against Sargeras and his misfortune, as well as his offer to us, which would have been very beneficial to our society. This apparently prompted the Council to proclaim him a traitor to our people and all of our philosophies."

"All right, let us examine this word...philosophies..."

"Uh oh..." Kaliya grins. "Round Two coming up."

"Let me first ask about this faction of his," Thaelyn offers. "What did it represent to your society of scientists?"

"His was one describing something he called Metaphysics, I believe," the Commander responds. "Which didn't seem to hold any clear definition, to say nothing of empirical evidence to support any of his crazy theories."

"Ah, I see..." Thaelyn nods. "And so, by this statement, one could easily suggest that his position was expendable. No one cared enough about it to begin with, therefore, who cares if he is suddenly a traitor, regardless of Sargeras, this ship you mentioned, or anything else. You mentioned how Darumon began to pursue him during this period. This coincided with your pursuit of these random insurgencies that were coming forward, and I recall you also mentioned they seemed to occur in clusters at intervals of some number of centuries, one stringing into another."

"Cu'Nar help us," Ankhia mumbles. "Is he taking this where I think he is?"

"You're very good," the Commander admits. "Yes, I did say that. I might also add that on many occasions, these closely followed the rediscovery of that traitor."

"How interesting," Thaelyn considers. "Therefore, if I were to interpret this, you might discover this traitor, and along the way take notice of...what shall we call it...a spillover effect, perhaps?"

"This is how we interpreted it. Our fleet would then move in to clean things up, describing it as preventative measures before it had time to climb our tails."

"Your fleet of shiny new military technology in need of testing..." Thaelyn concludes.

"Ba-boom..." Kaliya emits softly.

The Commander was stunned by this suggestion, as the pieces were suddenly falling into place for the inconsistencies.

"And there you have it," Ankhia mumbles. "Why the attacks happened at the timing they did."

"That external influence," Kailen agrees. "A distraction, as he once called it, where they were wiping up anything in the local area to test this new tech of theirs."

"So, we basically led the way to destroy anything and everything in our galaxy? And I thought I felt bad before."

"Keep in mind, Med-tech,'" the General reassures. "It is not you who is doing this. It is that beast who was directing you."

"Thank you, General, but it doesn't really make me feel any better for all the loss."

The Commander took a long moment to recover from his shock, but then he felt a need to understand the reasoning.

"So, we were sent to essentially demolish whole worlds…who never saw it coming…mainly to test our new tech?"

"And in active mode so you would not argue the point," Thaelyn adds.

"Argh!" he screams and grabs his horns. "Of course! It has to be! Why else would he use it? If we had the possibility to question it, we would've seen they weren't technologically capable of doing anything. In fact, we might even have a chance to understand what was really happening down there."

"And if we suggest any measure of underhandedness, you might find whatever it was that did not meet with your expectations."

"Naturally!"

"And at this moment, Commander, I would dare refer back to the beginning of our conversation. If you did it for a merited cause, this is one thing. But if for joy…"

The Commander seems to delay as the image sinks in, then he screams again, and his voice bellowed around the room as he doubles over in his lap. Thaelyn paused to allow the wailing to fade before continuing.

"Commander," Thaelyn resumes. "At this moment, I think we should refer back to this traitor of yours. You mentioned he was carried away by a ship of unknown design and by unknown entities, correct?"

"Yes," he moans weakly. "Do you have something to suggest for that now?"

"Let us add a few pieces together if we can. These unknowns clearly knew where you were found. If you are suggesting they could be associated with these insurgents, this also infers that they too should know where you are found. Therefore, this cannot be a secret, and it simply brings us back to the original question of why they did not attack you directly. What about this ship; how did it appear?”

“It was huge, and I’m talking huge! It dwarfed anything we owned, even our space stations. And it made a big showing in our skies. It was all over the news media, and it also caused quite a stir in the streets. It arrived in ultra-low orbit, in this case a powered orbit…”

“A powered orbit?”

“Yes, in such a low orbit as this, you would need to apply power in order to maintain your position and altitude. In fact, to use the term ‘orbit’ isn’t even accurate anymore, but we apply it as a term to represent the station-keeping aspect of things.”

“I see, how interesting.”

“And this position put it within range of any civilian transport that could reach the upper atmosphere.”

“Indeed! This sounds as if it held a purposeful intent. But this also represents a paradox, at least on the surface.”

“And another one…” Kaliya mumbles privately.

“If these were the insurgents proper, and this vessel was so immense, it would represent a rather significant technological display in your skies. And if Darumon and Sargeras were right under it, I doubt we would be having this conversation right now, assuming the vessel was of a military design to launch an attack.”

“Yes!” the Commander relents. “I must agree with you.”

“Then why are we here? What did this huge vessel of unknown origin and unknown design do, other than to position itself within easy reach of civilian transports, and thereby pick up some number of passengers. Did it attack you along the way?”

“No, it did not. I think I recall a statement by some of our security patrols, and a couple of Sentinels’ vessels that arrived higher in orbit, that the scans showed it to be unarmed.”

“Unarmed, let us keep this statement in mind a moment. Then, we can say the ONLY thing it did was to take away these people who did not otherwise agree with the remainder of your government about helping Sargeras. Then you have this pursuit, and along the way you…discover…pockets of these insurgencies that did not seem to see you coming. The traitor manages to escape from you on each occasion, but your military has plenty of new targets to play with in each of these local star clusters. Then someone calls your attention to a new discovery, and the cycle repeats."

"So, what you're saying is he was being used as an excuse to locate new targets for us to practice on."

"Commander, by your own words, this vessel was huge and unarmed. How could you possibly miss it on so many occasions whenever you actually did discover it, especially with a shiny new military that was improving over time? Furthermore, what was stopping you from parking directly on top of it to make sure you actually hit it?"

"Set them up, and knock them down," Kaliya finishes. "Woo!"

The Commander ducks his head and feels an irrepressible chuckle rising up.

"Yes, you're right. So, are we now saying the shots were intentionally misfired to make him run, just so we could continue the chase?"

"Ten millennia, Commander," Thaelyn shrugs. "This is a long time to chase someone if you really wanted him dead. We can say what we will of these insurgents being so technologically questionable or militarily foolish, but surely YOU should learn something in this time. For example, how to approach a prime target using stealth, or simply not to make the attempt until you had a proper fighting force on hand to ensure he did not escape."

The Commander was growing visibly weary from the debate and so many obvious discrepancies. He closed his eyes and sighed heavily.

"You carry a very strong point there. I wasn't present on any of these occasions where he was discovered, so I don't know precisely how it occurred. But yes, you would think whoever it was wouldn't just light up the sky with a holiday display before calling it in."

"Indeed, this is not how a proper military should behave when tracking a wanted criminal. And if this ship is not military in design, it would not represent a threat to begin with. It could just as easily have been a large colony vessel, or some other platform to transport large volumes of people. And again, civilian, whose only real crime here, if we dare use the word, is to disagree with your government. Is your government so restrictive that it does not allow for independent opinions?"

"Not that I'm aware of. We're supposed to be a free society in the open pursuit of knowledge. And I can't believe the rejection of that pursuit would be a true criminal action. This now brings us back to these insurgents again. Are there any at all, or is it just a story for our shiny new military to play with?"

"Let us consider one more aspect to see where it takes us. This traitor, where did he go and what did he do when he arrived there. If these other worlds never saw you coming, it could be said they were entirely unaffiliated. If all he did was run, he was not posing any true threat to you. Worst case, he simply did not care for your government's popular opinions. But he was not ON your world at this time, and therefore he could not pose any real threat to start uprisings or any other havoc within your society. Therefore, why spend so much of your time and resources chasing a man who was simply running away from a situation that was unfavorable to HIM if he should remain. Perhaps we cannot describe him to be truly criminal for holding an opposing opinion, but he WAS, however, undesirable, and he probably knew it. What do you expect HIM to do, stay and listen to your government berate his perspectives?"

"Wow!" Kaliya smiles. "That was a big one!"

"That was a solid hit," Kailen nods.

"That is a very fine perspective to point out," the Commander accedes. "I must fully agree with you. We are scientists, and it's even in our Charter of Laws, where we declare ALL forms of knowledge to be our domain for equal study. And his was being tossed out, even WITH all his crazy theories."

"Perhaps so," Thaelyn concludes. "Your society of purely empirical thought might not care for such as…mysticism," he smiles tenderly.

"Oops," Kaliya muses. "He's setting something up for later."

"Therefore," Thaelyn continues. "Under these circumstances, we could possibly say someone did not care for him personally. And as he began to realize this, or whatever the reason may have been to cause him to vacate his station, they simply took the opportunity to close the book on him."

"And declare him a traitor to add further insult to his position," the Commander infers.

"But..." Thaelyn waves a finger for emphasis. "If he were associated with any true insurgents, I think they would have brought him far away from your assaults during this time. If for no other reason, than to protect what was likely a large number of civilians trying to escape persecution from those same authority figures who cared so little for them in the first place."

"This doesn't sound good for our government body and their opinions. He was vilified almost immediately, and we were chasing them halfway across the galaxy and back again."

"This might also suggest some level of familiarity. Someone anticipated this. They sent an unarmed colony vessel to lift away a large number of otherwise innocent people out of a situation that was unfavorable to them, only to see this body that held this unfavorable opinion give chase. And, along the way, blast anything else out there simply for target practice. Tell me, Commander, how do you describe these two beings that came offering their gifts to you?"

"Uh oh..." Kaliya moans. "Here it comes."

The Commander hesitated in his response. He closed his eyes and turned away a moment in morbid consideration.

"Uh huh...I can see where this one is going already. I am guessing something here. You know what word I'm likely to offer, am I right?"

"Well," Thaelyn considers. "If they came bearing gifts, this is a beneficial action, is it not?"

"Yes, and therefore, we call them benefactors."

"How curious..." he intones enticingly. "And I wonder how... beneficial...you were to all those worlds who never saw you coming."

"Ba-Boom!" Kaliya mumbles. "That one hurt."

"Ouch, Kaliya," Ankhia nods. "I have to agree."

Thaelyn continues, "This now requires us to reflect on these unknowns. Who were they? They arrived at roughly the same time as Sargeras, apparently made contact with this individual, and called him out, along with some number of people to come away on this ship. Why? Well, one potential reason is right there on your back. Another was removed in a surgery room," he points at the right side of his head for emphasis. "A third is what that heathenish creature is calling your shiny new military to play with all across your galaxy. Fourth would involve Morndindor and the mining operation, as well as the production of that weapon. And fifth involves me and mine."

"And ba-blammo..." Kaliya whispers avidly. "Full point!"

The Commander gapes at Thaelyn for the laundry list of possible reasons why someone would want to disagree, and therefore escape from Sargeras and Darumon, as well as their local government, which was partly to blame for much of it.

"Does this now bring us to your side of it?" he inquires cautiously.

"I suppose it does," Thaelyn shrugs. "As SOMEONE out there knows who Sargeras and Darumon actually are, and that someone is not you. This so-called traitor was not trying to escape from you. He was being evacuated by these others for a reason."

"Evacuated..."

"At this moment, I must now live up to my promise, Commander," he sits back down again. "Allow me to introduce myself. My name is Lord Thaelyn, and I am the King of the world we are now standing on, known as Tae'Eladar. Do these names hold any meaning to you?"

"Um, no... Should they?"

"I suppose that largely depends on how much your beloved 'Marshal' actually tells you of his exploits. But my experience with him tells me he does not tell his..." he coughs subtly, "...minions... anything more than what is necessary for them to perform their immediate function."

"Really! Minions... Well, yes, this would certainly fit the way we've been behaving lately. He has us building a superweapon and doesn't even tell us. He gives us orders to blast worlds, but without the capacity to analyze it. In fact, if I compare this to those poor dwarves we pull out using that drug, we're in no better condition for these chips."

"This seems to be a common theme for him. We once observed another minion society under his influence and with a similar lack of grander knowing. They were a society called elves. Do you know this name?"

"Not personally. Why do you ask?"

"Perhaps you would know of them if I used another reference. Point-ears."

"What? That's the name Ytani uses in his illusions of a war outside. Who are they?"

"In the modern day, they are the remains of a once proud society found on Therinë, where your Marshal was conducting his staging post operations."

"Oh wonderful. So, how do they fit in, and then his explanation where that operation was cancelled?"

"The elves were once coerced into serving Darumon, and he spent a large portion of their population in a distraction effort on Morndindor while your people set down your base. This was then followed by the bombardment, likely to clear out everything else to prevent interference with your mining operation."

"Much like what Ti'van said once. Yes, this much I think I can understand."

"From here, we should step back to an earlier moment, to begin at our beginning...or at least one of them, as there are multiple entry points here. Many years ago, our world entered a war with a local race that once arrived here long ago as part of some kind of migration. We did not know where they came from, but they were not at all friendly to the other societies already existing here. We managed to keep them in check over the course of our history, but then came this new occasion where things turned very serious. I decreed that we must finally eliminate them completely in order to preserve our people and cleanse this world of all that would interfere with our mutual progress together."

"Mutual progress...how do you mean?"

"Our world was once populated by numerous nations and other independent societies, at least until I came along and began gathering them up into one global kingdom. Many came to my side willingly, due largely to the philosophies and ideals I was teaching. Others, which we might better describe as criminal or corrupt, chose to oppose me, much to their misfortune. My purpose to come here was to quell these disruptions and unite this world together for a common good."

"You know, this actually sounds a little like a historical story of our own. And so, now you are the King over all of it?"

"Yes, and for several centuries now. The people of this world are not as technologically advanced as yours, at least not yet, but as a member of the Celestial family, I am encouraging them to grow in an orderly pace."

"Where are you now with it?"

"We might describe it as an Early Industrial stage, with a few interesting exceptions where certain discoveries are concerned. We possess some very ambitious talent, and some potent resources here that allow us to solve problems that you might not normally expect for such a young society. And, by the way, using a few principles from a science you might describe as…oh, perhaps we could use the word Metaphysics," he smiles.

"Kablam!" Kaliya giggles softly. "There you go, folks."

The Commander's face dropped as he listened to the suggestion. For a moment, he was speechless as he reflected on the previous debate over the subject.

"So, his crazy theories aren't actually so crazy?" he mumbles timidly.

"To a society of empirically minded scientists like yours, they might be," Thaelyn infers. "But to people who actually DO pursue all forms of knowledge, and furthermore in those places where it might be a part of their heritage, your common laws of physics are mundane to us. Such beings as the Estelar live by these principles. The power of the mind is the driving force here…enough to actually override your laws of physics."

"Oh great!" he groans. "And our Council tossed him out."

"I might actually suggest Darumon tossed him out, as HE would know of this also, and likely to cover it up for YOU."

"Oh! So that's how it works. He comes offering the secrets of the universe to us, but forgets to tell us those secrets belong to the one faction he chased away."

"I might further suggest this one individual might be ahead of his time amongst you, if he was attempting to explain something you simply were not ready for. You need a certain background for it, and if he was unable to provide his evidence, his position might seem weakened."

"All right, I suppose I can accept that. But as for yours being Early Industrial, I might still have a problem with that for how you could find your way to another planet, unless it involves one of these unusual discoveries, like space travel."

"This is indeed an interesting story. Allow me to continue. This war involved a hidden incursion by more of the same of this one race, arriving as the result of Darumon making an attempt to use an ancient rift conveyor, which was likely built by him during a much earlier visit to spy on us."

"An earlier visit? What was he spying on?"

"We found some evidence in the form of what I can only describe as a research journal, telling of a variety of lifeforms to be found in those places in the surrounding dimensional planes near our core. We are currently in yet another universe from where we found you, if you wish to add further confusion to your quandary," he smiles. "And these realms are a series of higher dimensional folds as compared to us."

"Wow, this is beginning to sound complex."

"This journal was found in the possession of another of his servants and confiscated by us. But it represents a clear desire to identify what is out there. And this rift aperture could only be built by a being of some rather elaborate teachings, and only for one purpose...to send your shiny new military to places beyond this world, and for reasons that might involve that superweapon of yours."

"Uh oh... Who lives there?"

"His old rivals, the Estelar, and the reason he is now hiding on your world, it would seem."

"Hiding?! Is that what he's doing? But then, how do we explain the rest of it?"

"Let us come to that briefly. This new incursion brought with it a sort of corruption of the local body of this race, and therefore the reason for my war. We had them under control. He broke that by sending in new ones to corrupt things. Eventually, our war led us to destroy them as a body on this world, up until we found the last few trying to escape from us using what we call portals…which is essentially the same idea as your conveyors, but generated by different means."

"Conveyors…interesting… All right, I'm starting to see something here for travel to other worlds. You can make these?"

"Yes, we can, but our methods differ from yours, as they would involve some aspects of our studies here, but such that you and yours might simply describe as magic. In this universe, we have an ambient energy source we call the Dynamistic Flows. It exists in the universe with Morndindor, as well. For those of us who are native here, we learn how to use it, but it does not follow any form of science you would be familiar with."

"Just for reference, why wouldn't we be familiar with it?"

"Commander, I happen to know you come from yet another universe completely, and we describe that one as a barren fold, meaning to say a dimensional body that is absent this energy layer. Therefore, you who are native to that fold would be unaware of it."

"Got it. All right, go on."

"The flows are a byproduct of some very unusual creatures that inhabit a different layer of dimensional bounds as those of us here. It is generally regarded as organic in nature and therefore responds to conscious will. Using this, those with the right training can conduct what people like you would normally lose your horns over, as you like to say, as it is precisely that sort of mysticism you tend to reject. With the power of our thoughts, we can overcome many aspects of what you might spend great lengths of time in empirical study, and simply because someone has a desire to bend the rules to their needs. Due to this, some societies might focus more on this than anything else."

"That sounds truly amazing, and also a little scary. So, this means you CAN travel between worlds using these portals of yours. But don't you still need an endpoint index to target?"

"We do," he nods. "This much is still a requirement, so now I must continue my story. These beings, called orcs, ran from us to Therinë, using one such portal. I followed and brought my army there to finish my war, knowing that if such beings as these could open portals, this would represent a severe security threat to my home."

"Yes, I believe I can understand that."

"I used one of their own portals to follow them, and my arrival granted me the opportunity to make my own index mark."

"Ah, good..."

"But I also found that world in a similar condition like Morndindor, though perhaps not as bad for the environmental damage."

"Oh great... What happened to it?"

"Darumon and your shiny military, directed by your High Commander Geilv, whom I believe is probably under the active mode of his chip."

"Yes," he hangs his head and sighs. "He's like that quite often. I feel for him."

"As do I, at the moment. I regard myself as a master in the art of war, so I played a very careful game to keep a low profile in the face of so many unknown elements in that world. Among these was the governor of one surviving city, populated by a society we call humans. He did not seem to be behaving as a man in a world filled with so many hostiles he should be at war with."

"Really! What was he doing?"

"Pretending it was not an issue. In fact, he seemed rather disturbed at my arrival and subsequent interference in the local affairs."

"Oh great, that doesn't sound good for who's side he's on."

"No, it does not, and this is one thing that puzzled me. Between that city, another one filled with another clan of elves, this being in addition to those Darumon was playing with, and that final one with his servants, I learned these were all immigrants, and apparently stolen from Tae'Eladar a long time ago."

"Wait! Stolen?"

"Yes, I will describe them as stolen, and by Darumon. The elves kept some old records of their travels, which mentioned a stranger calling for a migration to fresh new lands, at least in part to escape from the recent discovery of some undesirable new arrivals, meaning those orcs, plus a recent war that occurred, and using a strange portal device of unknown origin and function. Now, to me, by this description, this portal device sounds like a creation of a form of technology that would be alien to Tae'Eladar. It is much more indicative of a technology that a Celestial might use, or someone amongst the Estelar, or at least on their level."

"Meaning, someone like the Marshal, I suppose."

"Yes, he would surely know how to do this. This, combined with the arrival of the orcs, all occurred at around ten millennia ago, which is a number with an unnerving level of recurrence in these affairs."

"That would coincide with his arrival on Azgarén."

"Yes, it would seem he was becoming active. Therefore, I say these people were stolen, because my war brought me to Therinë due to MORE orcs arriving, this time being discovered with their owner, Darumon, and a portion of our people on a world they should NOT have had access to. This is a coincidence I cannot accept. Therefore, it must have been staged to provide for his future needs."

"Oh wonderful."

"They had a rather robust civilization on that world by this time, at least until he returned roughly four centuries ago and reduced it down to a single city for each race."

"That sounds just like what he did on Morndindor. And the timing fits, too."

"And he was oppressing them in one form or another, as well. At least, until I arrived," he smirks.

"Oops!"

"Clearly, to discover all this, and further to learn of the original home world for those orcs, which was yet another world entirely, and for them, completely out of the question to find their way off of it, it became clear that HE owned them for a long period of time and was making these incursions for a reason. Why? This was a mystery at first, but it did hint at a direction, and that direction involved Tae'Eladar somehow, or at least our local space. This was unacceptable."

"I would agree."

"I recall a conversation with one of those so-called point-ears, which is a race more appropriately called High Elves. I liberated them along the way and learned he had an interest in this ancient portal rift again, therefore this recent incursion of orcs was a mission to find it and drop one of your nether-space beacons into it for your military to track. This would lead you back to our space, which at this point is beyond Tae'Eladar, but no less acceptable for the implications, as it now reflects on the Estelar, some of whom make their home here."

"Uh oh..."

"What this now tells me is he has an interest in attacking them. The trouble is, the two of them alone, Darumon and Sargeras, would never be able to stand up to them, as the Estelar are a vast society, and likely have been even from the last time they met. So, the whole idea is ludicrous."

"Yes, I think it would be under those conditions."

"At least, not unless they had an immensely powerful weapon to back them up."

"Yeah, I was afraid that was going to come into this. And we were making it for them. Um, what sort of relationship are we actually speaking of here? You describe these others as gods, whatever that actually means, but, um..."

"Sargeras and Darumon are leftover remnants from an ancient battle with the Estelar, their natural rivals, and apparently their successors to own what we most often refer to as the Seas of Creation, meaning every universe and open space out there."

"Whoa, hold on..." he jerks back and holds up his hands.

"Suddenly, that's a little bit bigger than what he told us about. Are we saying he's more like a refugee running from a governing body?"

"At this point, yes, and certainly NOT something you could blast away as if they did not see you coming. More likely, they would do this to you."

"In all the nether-space, I'm suddenly very sorry we ever got involved."

"I think it was likely outside your control, Commander. If your Council was so easily seduced by this offer of superior knowledge, he probably knew just where to hit you for the best result. But now, we need to reflect upon another starting point to this story."

He shifts his position in his chair as he prepares for this next part.

"We have stories handed down to us by the Estelar, although I will admit not many by now, as it reflects on bad memories and unpleasant feelings, such that they do not like to talk about it anymore. They date back to what the Estelar describe as an epoch ago. The actual numbers are either lost to time, or intentionally hidden, perhaps simply to erase it. It was an unpleasant moment that no one wants to remember. But those of us who try to study this generally agree that an epoch, as a term, at least where the Estelar are concerned, may refer to a period approximating a billion years."

"A billion…" he gasps. "That predates his arrival on Azgarén by a bit. Even our full species and a lot of other things."

"I am sure it does. From my own teachings, I know of these beings, such as Sargeras, by the name of Primordials, with Darumon apparently representing a servant creature under him. The Estelar are known to have numerous servants amongst the Celestial races, who take up in a form of apprenticeship. How Sargeras and Darumon relate is not entirely known, but it certainly does appear as a master and servant relationship."

"He does behave like this in a lot of ways. I suppose this is also where you don't like using a title for him. If he's simply a servant, he might not even use a title."

"We have some spy recordings of conversations he held with one of his assigns on Therinë where he did in fact admit he did not use titles as a common habit. But in your eyes, if to use this one, it would need to resemble a rather prestigious example. After all, would your shiny military choose to follow someone named Darumon the Flower Salesman?" he grins.

The Commander glared at him and couldn't help but erupt in a bold laugh. In the visitor's booth, the others were also laughing, but trying to cover their mouths to hold it back. Once the Commander regained control of himself, he reflected on this most welcome experience.

"Thank you," he offers congenially. "It's been so long since I felt anything like that."

"Absolutely, Commander!" Thaelyn affirms. "So, in this time, within our local fold of the great Seas of Creation, we had a society of these Primordials. We cannot be sure what name they used for themselves, so I must assume this is an interpretation by the Estelar to suggest an ancient precursor race. I might even go so far as to say, by the way I have heard a few using it, it is applied in a derogatory fashion."

"Derogatory. I take it they didn't get along."

"Not in the least."

"And a precursor race? So, in a manner of speaking, it could be said these others took something away from them."

"I suppose it could, but here under legitimate reasons, and not a theft. And through some of my spy operations, and a bit of research, I have learned they did once represent a vast race of beings that preceded the Estelar, but fell into decline at some moment, allowing the Estelar to rise up and ultimately replace them."

"This is actually quite interesting, one society rising up to replace an older fading one."

"And I think it is not the first time, but the history behind this would be quite vague by now, to say the least. We are speaking of time frames so immeasurable; the evidence would be impossible to find by now. But anyway, these Primordials were a rather unpleasant sort. According to my sources, the Estelar made a discovery at some moment, perhaps early on, and maybe even before they rose fully to power. They found these Primordials conducting their manners in unacceptable forms and with belligerent attitudes relative to other forms of life."

"Like blasting things that never saw it coming?"

"Something like that, I am sure. They might take pleasure, even sport, out of the experience. They seem to be rather elitist, even supremacist, loving their positions of authority over everything else. And it is said they did not like competition in any form."

"That doesn't sound good…for anything else out there."

"Due to this, the Estelar took it upon themselves to enact their own form of justice by exterminating the former and replacing them, along with a new philosophy they call the Measure of Balance. This rule defines all living things as deserving of respect, within the polarities of positive and negative influences, which ultimately govern our development as independent bodies."

"That's a fascinating perspective. It's like saying we might have good things and bad things that can happen to us, and we need to grow as the result."

"Exactly. Very good, Commander. So, here we have the Estelar, still apparently in an exploratory stage, as they were crossing the many Folds of Creation, until one day, they found this place. This reminds me now of a curious piece of history we were blessed to receive once."

"And what was that?"

"This reflects on those spy recordings again. One of our spies in that human city made a recording of their governor during some of his conversations with his agents. We were trying to find out why he was so opposed to fighting a war everyone else was suffering from. He turned out to be Darumon in disguise. It would seem your illustrious Marshal is a shapeshifter, able to alter his form on demand to suit the need."

"A shapeshifter!" he winces. "That sounds scary, like a vid-com horror show. Does he use something for this, or…"

"This would likely be an innate skill, as his kind would represent a nearly godlike species with some rather extraordinary abilities. I would suggest his corporeal body is not what it seems on the outside, as beings like these are not entirely manifested into physical space as a whole entity. Therefore, his manifested form becomes configurable, and governed by his mental influence."

"Yeah, that's a scary thing to think of."

"Indeed, and the implications are dangerous no matter how you apply it. We saw him impersonating a human in that city, and we suspect he used this at one time or another for any of a multitude of other occasions elsewhere. This would likely include your own people at some moment, to observe and perhaps to direct some of your actions during this time. For instance, those scouting reports of insurgents. It could just as easily have been him falsifying the reports to send your shiny military out for its target practice."

"Oh great!" he throws his hands up. "And at such timing to allow us to make our improvements along the way."

"Precisely. But this recording gave us a curious piece of history to open up a few details. Darumon admitted how he and Sargeras were the last of their kind, formerly of a proud race of overseers that fell into a long decline. They took the position of deciding the fate of whole societies based on THEIR idea of who was worthy or not, but never to allow them to progress any higher than what suited their interests or pleasures."

"Uh huh, that makes me feel so much better now. And not simply for such as Morndindor, and anything else out there, but for us, as well."

"Indeed, Commander. And here we have the Estelar hunting them into extinction due to these bad manners, perhaps based on previous memories or experiences. And Darumon expressed a strong revulsion of their policies, which does not actually surprise me."

"Based on what you said a moment ago about this Measure of Balance, I can certainly see it. This would otherwise deny them these…pleasures."

"Absolutely," he smiles. "So, the Estelar discovered this last pocket of Primordials and found them committing even more atrocities on lesser life forms. And we are speaking on the scale of the Child Races, using them as a form of expendable entertainment."

"This is starting to sound a little like the Marshal and all those worlds he had us blast for him."

"Quite possibly. I would imagine he was wanting a little side entertainment after so long an absence. They hold no proper respect for life on this scale, since they can apparently create it at a whim and then spend it, only to create more."

"And now I'm getting really angry about what that…creature… has been doing with us all this time. I once served an honorable role in our old Sentinels, and I recall one of my officers recalling the same desires for her career. She was near to the point of quitting the service due to our experiences in that base."

"Yes, we heard a few of these conversations about your displeasures. I am sorry for that, but as I said, perhaps we can come to an agreement of some sort. Meanwhile, you may find yourself pulling your horns out and tossing them across the room before this is done. So, try to contain it a bit longer," he shrugs mildly. "Naturally, the Estelar were once again offended by this, but the Primordials enjoyed their pleasures so much that when the Estelar approached and demanded them to stop, they refused. Thus, we have this final war, which we call the Celestial War, perhaps the last of a long series."

"A war…" the Commander muses. "And here is where the last of them likely fell, with Sargeras and Darumon probably running away to hide from it, right?"

"Correct, as far as we can tell, and much to our misfortune in the modern day. We are also aware some of them were simply captured and imprisoned."

"Wait, I remember something about a search to find people held in a prison…loyalists to Sargeras or some such."

"While this may be true, at least in part, we are not speaking of Sargeras being a leader of any kind, and these being citizens under him. They are other Primordials like him."

"All right, this sounds like trouble, especially when you consider the Marshal and all he's doing."

"Here is where we return to this weapon of his. I should probably also apply a few definitions along the way. If we say Sargeras ran to your universe, otherwise known as a barren fold, it is to say a place absent of these dynamistic flows. But here we have a problem, perhaps one of several. Such beings of this sort are often described with the term Divine, meaning to suggest a being of such evolutionary development as to have long since cast off its original corporeal form, and now existing in a much more ethereal state, as what you might find in higher dimensional domains."

"Ouch! That just stretched my horns a bit for the sheer science of it."

"I am sure it would. Evolution does not stop in a three-dimensional universe. Life may begin here, and we describe such beings as Primes, meaning to come from a Prime Material fold. However, once you begin to realize there is more out there, and your society SHOULD know this by now as you use your jump drives, because you are passing through it each time, then you can realize there is something else yet to explore."

"In all the nether-space…and literally so. So, this actually represents a valid destination to travel to?"

"We often refer to it as the Fourth Fold, four-dimensional space. And this is still not the end. You might ultimately find it useful to relocate into that space as a society, thereby evolving through the first of what we might call two ascension stages. Your new evolution will involve the native materials, which are no longer your classic three-dimensional examples. Here you begin to transcend your living essence beyond your physical form as an extradimensional being."

"Extradimensional beings," he croons. "This sounds like science fiction."

"It may sound this way, but here is where we find the Celestial races. The corporeal component begins to fall back as a vestigial body. The mind is now what mostly evolves forward. And also, this is where your famous Metaphysics would start playing a more prominent role for you."

"Uh huh…wonderful."

"The second stage, the Divine one, will simply carry you to the final goal in yet another dimension higher. Whatever remains of your original corporeal form now falls away completely, and you take on a very different form, as alien as anything you could possibly imagine relative to where you are now, with a fully ethereal body and a lot of mental prowess."

In the visitor's booth, the others listened and watched. Ankhia was leaning forward to hear this part.

"That definitely wasn't on my university class schedule," she chuckles.

"I don't think it was on Father's either," Kailen admits.

"On their way up," Thaelyn continues. "And as they change their physical forms to meet the local environments, they begin to absorb some of this ethereal mass. This can affect their biology, and one aspect of this is to reduce the aging effect, as primal matter is no longer the deciding factor here."

"Really!" the Commander intones. "And here is where you might find immortality?"

"Yes, it begins here. Ethereal mass is not as susceptible to the effects of time. And so, we can say the first ascension is an intermediate form. From here, they will continue to evolve, but the evolutionary process will take much longer due to the longevity effect, ultimately to find that second ascension, and here you have gods, the highest form of evolution we are aware of."

"That is a very unique perspective," the Commander muses. "And I can think of at least a few science factions back home that would kill for lessons like those."

"Perhaps so, but we Celestials take the same policies as the Estelar, as we are also their students. Most importantly is to allow a young society to evolve at its own pace, not simply to give out so many secrets that it could unbalance them."

"By the sound of it, this would represent another crime by Darumon in the eyes of these Estelar."

"It most certainly would. And here is where we must now return back to him and Sargeras. While Darumon might be better described as still having some corporeal essence, thereby he can persist in a Prime environment, Sargeras cannot. As you might expect, to evolve by such elaborate measures would also include your dependencies on the local environments."

"Yes!" he snaps his fingers. "That would certainly make good sense."

"And so, we have our first problem. Divine beings require the dynamistic flows as their natural support layer to survive, much like we who might still hold corporeal form need air to breathe."

"Uh oh…" the Commander pauses to consider the suggestion. "Wait a moment. This must be the reason! His condition when he first arrived. He appeared ill, or something."

"Yes, this might be a good cause for it if he is basically suffocating. We suspect Darumon must be importing something or supplying him in some way to support him in that environment."

"Possibly. He doesn't ever come outside of his sanctuary building, so it's probably inside there."

"The next issue is that he seems to have run off specifically to this barren fold to evade from the Estelar. This would likely be the last place they would look for him."

"Yes, I can certainly understand that. It would make a good tactical retreat, although an unfortunate one for him."

"Meanwhile, Darumon seems to be moving in the shadows, and I am sure for good reason. If he were detected, I think it would go very badly for him, very quickly."

"Absolutely."

"Then we have his weapon, which is easily a terrorist weapon for its potential. And for the quantity you have in there, if he were to spread this out in a multiple deployment tactic…" he whistles emphatically.

"What does that weapon actually do, other than blow up?"

"I only know of a few details, as this is a form of knowledge restricted mostly to the Estelar. It is a very privileged form of knowledge for the devastating potential it holds. They call it the Agent of Unmaking. I am told such societies as we, those who may be so privileged to know anything, would use a name like Arcanicium. It is an explosive material that is normally produced out of the flows, as they provide a rich medium for it. Other sources can be substituted, but with a much lower yield, usually due to only trace elements involved."

"Like that metal."

"Yes. But now, as I understand it, from how it was explained to me, if you took a quantity and detonated it in a barren fold like yours, it will likely erupt in a fantastically devastating explosion, perhaps even ripping apart the foundation of three-dimensional space along with the blast wave. I do not know the numbers associated with this, and a part of me does not actually want to know," he chuckles faintly. "The real potential is to detonate it in an environment WITH the flows. Here, it would cascade with a chain-reaction, erupting the entire envelope, which could easily scale on the size of a full universe, perhaps more if it touches anything else out there."

The Commander's face froze, and he nearly forgot how to breathe. His eyes drifted off as he tried to imagine the scene.

Thaelyn continues, "As an example of this weapon, if you were to look in our nighttime sky, you will see what it does, as these Primordials made a last gasp effort in the final moments of that war to dispose of their attackers by dropping one of those in our local space. The result was absolute devastation of everything out there. The entire dimensional fold ripped apart right down to the fabric of space itself."

"You're kidding me..." he whines.

"Tae'Eladar is therefore a survivor of that period. We are only alive because the Estelar constructed a shell around us to keep it out. This shell encompasses our entire star system and is constructed of a material unique to their science."

"Incredible, and it sounds so implausible. How many planets are we speaking of here?"

"Although our society is not yet space-capable, we do have some astronomy sciences which have struggled to understand the mechanics of it. As for me, my Celestial teachings tell me the Estelar managed to arrange six worlds in this space, the other five being scavenged from somewhere else. But they occupy only two orbital rings. If you were to imagine the life-giving belt around a star, in our case a yellow star, one of these would be towards the inner range while the other is towards the outer band. There are three planets per ring, all in perfect equidistant mathematically balanced orbits."

"That sounds artificial, for sure."

"And I suspect there is an external force monitoring this to keep it that way. We do not have anything else in here with us, like asteroids or other debris, so this is all we have to worry about."

"Any moons?"

"Yes, actually, some of them do have moons, as far as we can tell. We have one here we call Selûne."

"I would love to see this from the outside. To go up and investigate that shell, for instance."

"Well, I think there are possibilities for us that one day we may do just that. But naturally, we do not want to see this occur again, anywhere. And this once again brings us back to the quantity you have on Ooduan. If to deploy this in multiple locations…a great many of them…"

"Oh no!" he waves it off. "I don't want to be a part of that. Is there any way to diffuse this stuff?"

"We are asking ourselves that same question. There is one among us named Adalon the Silver who is requesting a meeting soon for what I assume to be this purpose. I am very anxious to hear what she has to say."

"Is there any possibility that I could attend? I'd like to know how you intend to do this. I feel a responsibility for it since I'm responsible for making it in the first place."

"Perhaps we can find an opportunity for that. Meanwhile, let us continue with our discussion. So, the Primordials are thought to be completely destroyed, and with Sargeras and Darumon escaping, presumably unknown to anyone, they were largely forgotten. Except, this is not actually the case."

"Uh oh…did someone actually see them?"

"We suspect so, but she has been keeping a very low profile for some reason, and we suspect this to be personal, although what relation she has, we do not know. She is a VERY elusive one," he chuckles. "Our history in this world has been a curious one, and SHE is behind much of it. First and foremost, Tae'Eladar was recently reengineered."

"Reengineered? A whole planet? How?"

"I cannot be entirely sure of the methods used, but I would imagine this would be a fascinating thing to see. Not a fast one, mind you, but surely one for study. This one individual, a local member of the Estelar whom we address as Maker Kuroku, refurbished Tae'Eladar not long ago, at least on a geologic scale, from a frozen world in a deep ice age, to the lush habitat it is today. It was then seeded with new life, resulting in what we see here now, and this includes the human population."

"Fascinating, to take a dead world, rehabilitate it, and seed it with new life. This represents a theory to us, and even a bit of fantasy."

"Perhaps so," Thaelyn smiles. "We believe she called in a society of beings to do the actual work, and they left behind a time capsule for us to find one day which identified who they are. They go by the name of Sarrukh. I must assume here that they are probably a race on par with a Celestial society, because the time capsule included some documentation both in their native language and the Celestial common tongue."

"Yes, that would surely suggest a relationship, to hold that knowledge."

"Sometime later, on the order of many millennia, we saw the arrival of several immigrations of elves and dwarves, among others, and we believe this was invoked by one or another careful study they made, or maybe with a bit of help by the Estelar who watch over those particular societies. This further embellished our world with multiple races now cohabitating together."

"Now there's a concept. Did they get along well?"

"There were a few rough areas here and there, as you might expect, but in time they found their territories and settled into a reasonably peaceful standing. At least until I arrived and united everyone officially."

"And now here you are, the king of an entire world."

"This is correct, but I was installed in this position. I did not know of it initially, as the Maker seems to behave with some very surreptitious manners. You once asked how and why a hybridized Celestial might be made. Well, I am one example, and Tae'Eladar is the reason."

"Ouch! Isn't that a little like overkill, for what I'm hearing of you people."

"You know, Commander," he grins. "You are not the only one to ask that question, and some of those who asked are also Celestials. My only answer is, yes, and probably for good reason. No mortal can oppose me. Therefore, if my purpose was to unite this world, despite any opposition by they who would otherwise argue the point, it would become moot very quickly, as I literally held a divine mandate to do so."

"Yes, by the sound of it…immortality, and who knows what other sorts of abilities you might have, being part god."

"They certainly did apply their value on numerous occasions," he nods. "But now we must move forward in our story. We will return to the war with these orcs due to this corruption and a new uprising."

"This is from Darumon and this most recent incursion, right?"

"Yes. We pursued them back to Therinë, where we discovered Darumon imposing himself as a local governor. We had your people with Geilv on one side, and a large incursion of orcs on another side, coming in from their home world using what was apparently some custom-designed mini conveyors he must have ordered at some moment."

"Mini conveyors? That's a new one. How mini?"

"Single-man size."

"That's simply tiny!" he winces.

"Indeed, and using some exceptionally miniaturized technology, along with what we think has to be a bit of proprietary design he invoked himself, and arcanic in nature, more like what we might use here with our magic."

"You can make a form of technology out of it?"

"If you have the right people behind it, yes. We have some of our people studying this, and a few of my scientists, who are much more familiar with the arcanic sciences, have already identified a few things. Although I will also point out, HIS design work is a bit more elaborate than our…Early Industrial efforts," he grins.

"Uh huh, and there goes hundreds of millennia of scientific struggle for us," he chuckles.

"I am sure you earned your achievements no less than we did ours. Perhaps the day may come when we can share a few teachings. But we need to contend with our more immediate problems first."

"All right, I'll look forward to that day."

"Anyway, in addition to these hostile forces on that world, facing against the native inhabitants, we also had one more entrant which was rather curious."

In the visitor's booth, they continued to listen to the extended history lessons.

"Here it comes, people," Kaliya whispers expectantly.

"Oh?" the Commander wonders. "Who was that?"

"To begin with," Thaelyn replies. "They were not native to that world. And, in fact, by the story they gave, they had most recently been living on that same world with the orcs."

"Sounds like travelers of some kind. Now they're in the middle of what sounds like a warzone. Did they make a wrong turn somewhere?"

"It would indeed be an unfortunate one if they did. But I regret to say, it was not, in this case. They had saboteurs on their ship directing them there intentionally."

"Saboteurs!" he shouts. "Who? And for that matter, why?"

"Why is likely to maroon them there, crashing their ship so they could no longer move around. As for who…well, this is the curious part. They apparently made a wild jump to arrive on that other world."

"A wild jump!" he screeches and grabs his horn. "In all the nether-space, they must be insane!"

"Indeed, I would tend to agree," he admits passionately. "Those of us who may be familiar with such forms of travel would normally say to make such a maneuver as this would likely prove suicidal. You would need to consider yourself extremely lucky simply to find yourself in a valid location of space, to say nothing of right outside a conveniently habitable planet."

"Huh?" he blurts incredulously. "But...but... That doesn't even make sense! The odds of something like that happening would be... ugh..." he covers his face.

"Oh, absolutely! Especially if you are travelling from a completely different universe!"

The Commander gaped at Thaelyn for the impossible suggestion. He was speechless, and only able to emit a few groaning sounds.

"But not to worry, Commander," Thaelyn emits confidently. "As they apparently had a very knowledgeable navigator punching in the codes. After all... He OWNED that world," he glares sternly at the Commander.

"Ka-pow!" Kaliya grins. "Direct hit. I love this guy."

The Commander was stunned for a long moment as he tried to analyze the statement. But then, a sudden jolt knocked him out of his shock.

"Darumon..." he wheezes. "Who are we speaking of? I'm tempted to guess here, but I'm suddenly afraid to say the word."

"Yes, Commander," Thaelyn ushers smoothly. "Your traitor, and what remained of those loyalist followers of his, now many generations removed from the original excursionists as they were decimated so often by your shiny new military taking pot shots at them in-between blasting half your local galaxy away. Each time they landed, they tried desperately to repopulate, only to be blasted again. But never to kill, only to frighten them into moving again. He was simply toying with them."

The Commander's face turned to shock and horror. He began to wail. He buried his face in his hands and doubled over. His wail escalated into a mournful bellow, at least until his breath ran out.

"That monster!" he whimpers. "And all the stories he gave us... he and that horrid Council!" he blasts.

He pulls up feebly to glance around the room.

"What condition are they in? Who's still alive and how many?"

"You will not like the answer to that, Commander," Thaelyn responds solemnly.

"All right, fine, hit me with it."

"Velen and his wife are the only two original excursionists still alive. Everyone else is multiple generations away, after so many efforts to replenish their numbers, and then losing them again on each hit. They tell me they started with something like three hundred thousand people on that ship."

"Three hundred thousand?!" he yelps. "It can hold so many?"

"It is apparently designed as a large-scale colony transport, and from the stories, they packed themselves in tight. But with each hit, their numbers were cut to some fraction, then to repopulate, cut again, and so on, until they arrived on the world with the orcs, which they called Ruuki uy'Daan."

"Land of Exile," he winces. "How nice. Should I ask why they would use that name?"

"For the same reason they now call themselves Daanen-Aryku. They regard themselves to be in exile from their ancestral home, and the rest of you as monsters with this strange mutation effect, along with this emotion-disabling chip, and your military chip turning you into remorseless cold-blooded killing machines. And this is your reward for following Sargeras. From their perspective, their proud civilization of scientists and scholars was dead."

The Commander closes his eyes and turns away in shame. He made another series of whines as he was softly weeping and nearly ready to lose control again.

In the observation booth, the people all watched and felt his pain.

"The poor man," Ankhia submits. "But then, all of us, and all because of HIM."

"At present," Thaelyn continues. "They number only around ten thousand, after losing a large number on Ruuki uy'Daan, which I am told was roughly a hundred thousand or so in their city, and then more in the crash."

"That's a hefty loss, all in one shot," the Commander moans.

"I am currently taking care of them, assisting in rebuilding a comfortable setting for them on Therinë, which will act perhaps as a new colony site. Some of them are even taking classes with us on our magic, and they seem quite excited for the prospects."

"Really! Well, I wish them the best, and I am truly sorry for their losses. If only we could've known the real story."

"I think that goes for a lot of things. But here is where a prominent element of our curiosity comes into play. They were expected to arrive here."

The Commander's eyes briefly bulge as he tries to interpret the statement.

"Expected?!" he shouts.

"Yes, much to all of our surprise, and this reflects on that ship of theirs...and those unknowns who arrived with it."

"Uh oh, suddenly I'm not so sure if I want to hear this. Who were they?"

"In a word, spies. Velen's people told me about a form of life that was found on their ship, which by the way they named the Naarg uy'Sodrad."

"Pursuit of Freedom...such an ironic and unfortunate name."

"Yes, but in the end, they did find it once they met me. But I will admit, it was a costly one. Anyway, this lifeform was a strange entity composed largely of energy and light. Incorporeal, and entirely abnormal to see in a place like this."

"I'm still trying to envision what kind of entity it is, but why do you say abnormal to find here?"

"To my people, we would identify this as a form of elemental being. There are different kinds, depending on what sort of dimensional fold they might come out of. This one would be described as positive energy. The issue here is, elementals usually do not travel outside their native homes, so why is this one here...and THEN, why is it interacting with corporeal lifeforms like these, as this is not their usual practice."

"All right, you got me, and not simply that I have no idea what you're talking about."

"Yes, these were some very curious questions we had. The type of entity we are speaking of here is VERY different from yours, so interacting for any reason becomes problematic, simply for communication, to say nothing of delivering a ship which could NOT be of their own design. They would not need a ship for themselves, neither would they likely be the ones to build it. And as you said, this thing was huge. It would take a serious amount of effort, as well as resources and motivation to build something like this, and then to simply hand it over to complete strangers? There is something wrong here."

"Yes! This much I CAN understand. I can't even begin to estimate the cost of it, to say nothing of the engineering effort to design and build it."

"But here we are. Velen and his people call them the cu'Nar. They initially delivered a warning to stay away from Sargeras and his offers. They described him as belonging to an ancient race, one that should be dead by now, and they gave a word which Velen had to interpret into your language, but it held no real meaning to him."

"What word?"

"The word was Titan. Apparently, they must have made a special effort to deliver this word, above all others, to identify Sargeras."

"That sounds intentional, but for what purpose if it means nothing to us?"

"Because it DOES mean something to me."

The Commander's eyes suddenly bulged as he started making a connection.

Thaelyn continues, "The cu'Nar, as an elemental race, would likely date back to those ancient times, and as such, carry some of that ancient knowledge, as well as wording. So, to someone like me, or the Estelar, and maybe some of the other Celestial races, that word, especially coming out of an elemental being, would reference the Primordials."

"Uh oh…"

"Velen tells us he tried to pass this warning to your Council, but apparently they were already drunk on the idea of Darumon's gifts, so he had no other choice but to run, as per the instructions of these cu'Nar."

"Uh huh, figures. This isn't anything I recall on the daily news."

"No doubt, and therefore the convenient excuse to call him a traitor. Now we have your pursuit. My understanding is this continued for something like eight millennia until that wild jump."

"Oh! Eight, is it?" he blasts. "So, how do we explain the continued insurgents in our backyard, and with HIM running from one world to another over there? Because that's where he was supposed to have been killed recently."

Thaelyn lets out a modest chuckle and shrugs.

"Darumon has become famous in our eyes for his propaganda and misinformation. You should have seen some of the chaos he invented on Therinë and elsewhere that I had to unravel. This seems to be a theme for him to persuade people to follow his lead. But there was never any mystery to Darumon where Velen was, as we believe he was travelling with them as a spy on their ship, impersonating one of Velen's advisors…his shapeshifting skill working for him again. We also believe he can fold space, which is the ability to transport himself around directly, no ships necessary."

"Oh, that must be a fun one to have!" he retorts brashly. "So, today he's in his office, tomorrow he's off on some other world destroying somebody's homes."

"Just about. I know the Estelar can do this, and many Celestials as well. I have a very close friend who can do this on occasion. Then, he simply calls in the location, and here comes your splendid scouting report, but oops, he just left. Meanwhile, look at all those new worlds out there so unfortunately corrupted by this insurgency."

"Yes, and here comes our shiny new military to clean up."

"They tell us your shiny new military appeared out of nowhere and took only a few shots to disrupt their lives and send them into a panic. These people are generally very pacifistic, which I can only interpret to be your usual manners from your ancestral origins."

"Yes, I might have to agree, before Darumon came in and 'modified' our military."

"They would jump, and you find them. They jump again, and you find them yet again. There should not be a way for you to so easily track a ship using a jump drive, correct?"

"No, not under normal conditions. Once the envelope closes, that's it, they're gone. I was often amazed by our…shiny new military…that we were able to find them at all amongst all those billions of stars and their associated planets."

"As I thought. Then we have that wild jump to Ruuki uy'Daan, and according to your Commander Geilv, he claimed they found them yet again due to some odd beacon probe sending out a tracking signal as it followed behind."

"Oh, now there's a delightful excuse. I wonder who dropped that on their tail. And so conveniently it helped us make this world-shattering discovery of a new universe. If only the people back home were allowed to know about it."

Again, inside the visitor's booth, the people gasped at this new revelation.

"They don't even know?" Kailen moans.

"I swear…" Ankhia shakes her head. "He must have them tied up by the tails."

Thaelyn continues, "Yes, and further that you would choose to follow yet again when he truly should not be a bother for you anymore. Now, they arrived on Ruuki uy'Daan, and spent about fourteen centuries there, then got pushed to Therinë and struggled for an additional three and a half there. Then I arrived as part of my campaign against those orcs. Here is where our two sides meet. As they shared this strange story passed down by these cu'Nar, who were serving as messengers for this point, I took immediate notice of that word. And being a Celestial, and not something you are going to cross paths with every day, I figure there is a special meaning to this junction…Maker Kuroku again."

"Uh oh…" the Commander groans. "So here we come around to her again."

"That individual I mentioned earlier, Adalon the Silver, works for her. She is also a prophetess, and she wrote a couple of books which have been carefully chronicling the affairs of this world since the time I and my wife each arrived, and everything we were…fated… to do along the way."

"Prophecies? Or are we speaking of more engineering?"

"Maybe a bit of both, as some of it was surely a matter of consequence for the timing of events."

"Possibly."

"This leads us up to the present moment with our recent war. Here, we see her speaking of people from places unknown…to us, at least…arriving and passing this message to us. We believe the Maker was watching Darumon and Sargeras during this long period of time, and she was the one to send those cu'Nar to Velen, along with that ship. So, Commander, if you are hunting insurgents, be aware…they DO know where you live," he smirks.

"Yeah, thank you, and they're gods, on top of things."

"We have speculated that ship may be another product of those Sarrukh if she was using them once before. This could easily give you an idea of the technological level of such a race, and this would place it on par with where Darumon might be, at the very least."

"Yeah, so our shiny new military might need a little more target practice to meet that challenge."

"Indeed! But this also speaks of an intent to remove Velen and his people and bring him to us with this message of Sargeras. This is likely as an extension of why I am here to bring this world together, as we are the answer to sneak up on him as he has been trying to sneak up on the Estelar. He had to cross my doorstep to reach this place, and I am a trap for him."

"Oops! That doesn't sound good."

"And as unfortunate as it is, Velen got caught in the middle. So now, here we are. But the Maker left a number of clues for us along the way with Adalon's prophecies, which resembles some back history for us to relate to. And some of it is truly fascinating, while other parts are, well, disturbing for some."

"Back history, interesting. What kind?"

"Some of it we are still investigating for its ultimate potential, and our results so far are astonishing. If any of your science factions could realize just what we are discovering, I think their attitude with Velen's undesirable faction would turn fully around, because HIS faction relating to metaphysics is exactly what you need to understand this…no one else."

"Oh great! Yeah, I'm sure that'll go over wonderfully with the Council."

"But to understand what this is and where it comes from, we need to go into a few of those details. The Maker was apparently watching them for a long time, perhaps even since the time of that ancient war, which may offer a clue as to why she seems to hold something personal in this. She saw them go into hiding, she saw them come out, and then find you. Adalon's prophecies continue with this chase, with Velen's people arriving with us, and now us pursuing back."

"This sounds like a very clear form of prophecy. I'm not one who understands this sort of thing much, but if she's giving out such details, it's like she's almost directing the show here."

"This is very likely the case, but in a rather indirect manner. We follow our most apparent direction, and she might drop a hint for something. Then we follow that, and we might find another. It is the classic manner of an Estelar to encourage growth and learning along the way."

"Wow, now there's a way to fight a war," he chuckles.

"But she also gave us a few clues as to something else during this time, and I believe this directly relates to something you mentioned earlier."

"Oh? What was that?"

"That medical chip of yours."

The Commander glared at him for a moment before responding.

"Do you actually know of something about this thing? It's said to be a preventative device for something that was killing us at one time in our history."

"Essentially, what we learned of the chip itself is that it resembles a torture device, more than anything."

"Yes, this much I'll agree to."

"We had that situation of war on Therinë, with your people harassing Velen's people for three and a half centuries. They were launching minor skirmishes just to keep them bottled up inside their ship, never to come outside for someone shooting at them."

"Unbelievable. He has them pinned and simply torments them."

"When I arrived, I reinforced their defenses, and we turned that around. We discovered rather quickly that you have no idea what magic is, and therefore no defense to it. This became a strong advantage on our side. We have a type of shield to block your pulse weapons, and after that, almost anything will kill you, even a simple bow and arrow. This seed entity of yours..." he points at the Commander's body.

"Yes, I can understand that easily enough."

"The resident med-tech had a chance to finally examine a few bodies, and for the first time began to realize what you people did to yourselves...not that she enjoyed the experience by much."

"I believe it. None of us like it either."

"We also saw this military chip of yours and speculated it might offer a controlling effect, and for this, I decided the best solution was to push your forces completely off that planet, rather than give you the chance to finish it like you did everything else."

"Understood, although I think I would like to point out, Commander Geilv is not very happy for his own reasons over a lot of these...inconsistencies...we are experiencing. Go gently on him, he's not a bad person."

"I actually had a brief moment to speak with him using a lost trans-com I found once, and I could hear his voice as he apparently suffered one or more of those feedbacks during our conversation. My experience here suggests he held a fair amount of cognitive capacity, so I will keep this in mind for next time."

"Good, but what did you actually do to push them off? And then the Marshal, what did he have to say about it? As I said before, from my side, it was said the operation was simply cancelled."

"Cancelled… So convenient an excuse. As if to say, nothing bad happened here, go back to your previously assigned tasks."

"Yeah…" he throws his hands up.

Inside the visitor's booth, they glanced at each other and reacted similarly.

"I had finally come to the conclusion who the governor in that human city actually was, meaning to say Darumon, and what he was doing over there. So, rather than move directly against him, leaving your military in an undetermined state, I made a casual threat to call in the Estelar to investigate why we have these stolen people over here and who was responsible for all the carnage. Naturally, he was not happy for this, so he ran away."

"Oh! He ran away, did he? That's a laugh. He blasts whole worlds apart, and finally he gets his tail spanked for it."

"Yes, but unfortunately not without a final goodbye. You had some of those dwarves over there. So, he equipped them with what one of Velen's technicians called plasma mortars, and had them march on that city."

"What?!" he blasts. "In all the nether-space, dwarves carrying PMs, and still under that drug effect? I don't think I want to hear the end result of that."

"The city was indeed leveled, but I had my people watching them, and we saw him bring these devices in. So, once Darumon made his exit, I ordered my people to assist in evacuating the city. We let the dwarves have their fun, and once they ran out of energy…or things to blast…we moved in and took them down."

"Any losses?"

"We recorded only a relative few who were unable to escape, those who were otherwise incapacitated by other means. It was largely every man for himself at this point, and we picked them up outside the city. Since that time, we have rebuilt the city, and I inherited a new world out of it."

"Inherited? So, you're a king of two worlds now?"

"By this time, we also have Ruuki uy'Daan, after resolving the issue of the orcs and relocating them far away from Darumon's influence. We also discovered one of those mini conveyors had an index to Morndindor, which gave us access to that one."

"Unbelievable, travelling across worlds by use of conveyors alone."

"It is certainly an unexpected turn. Our people were not ready for it by the more conventional means, but fortunately, they are very progressive, and adapted to it rather easily. But now, we find ourselves needing to explain a few things. For instance, that chip again."

"Right, the medical wonder chip."

"Darumon thinks that with Velen's ship destroyed, and his navigation logs wiped, we are trapped on Therinë as an endpoint. But I am not so easily deterred. And it would seem Maker Kuroku also knows of a few tricks still in the wait."

"It would seem that way, especially to see you find us in our base."

"Velen's people carried some interesting history with them…well, mostly Velen at this point, as he was original to Azgarén. I made a most curious discovery amongst his people, a young lady with a very unexpected Gift. And as it turns out, it was not the first time he had seen this. Apparently, she once demonstrated this as a young girl, but that attack on Ruuki uy'Daan played a role on her and she was traumatized for a long while."

"I'm sorry to hear that, but what sort of gift is this?"

"One to which I suspect is the REAL reason for that medical chip in your head."

The Commander again glared at Thaelyn for the evocative statement.

"But this is something all the way back on Azgarén."

"Where you said something was killing you, correct?"

"Yes, it was described as some sort of bizarre alien parasitic thing causing a similarly bizarre death syndrome."

"How interesting. But with respect, Commander, the only word out of that statement which would apply correctly is the word 'bizarre'. Well, maybe that, and the word alien, as I am sure it still applies here. Where did you hear this definition?"

"This is what the…" he halts and begins emitting a sour grumble from his throat.

"…Marshal said?" Thaelyn offers inquisitively.

"Yes," he groans. "Is this one of those moments where I pull my horns out?"

"Quite possibly, but do take care. Our janitorial crew has a hard-enough time with Velen's people," he smiles tenderly.

"Oh, thank you…" he shakes his head ironically. "Actually yes. Thanks for trying to soften it."

"Good. But I will admit, this would require something special to interpret, if only you had the right science faction working for you. Unfortunately, your wonderful Council chased it away."

The Commander closed his eyes as he struggled to contain his rising temper. He huffed and clenched his fists, softly pounding them into the bed while attempting to take several deep breaths to calm himself.

"So, HE and his unappreciated faction might know how to analyze this, while the rest of our Council, under the advisement of the Marshal no less, would want to discredit him. Yes! Naturally! And here we have our traitor, along with his full faction. And the rest of us…" he huffs again.

"Maybe you would like to explain this part of your history, how it got started? I know part of it already from Velen."

"Which part is that?"

"He carried only the earliest moments, I think, before he departed. His faction was part of those early studies of one or more children found with this strange condition, but before they could find any answers, those children died of something which seemed entirely unnatural."

"Yes. Good. We call it the Tav'ageen Anomaly, named after, I suppose, one of the early victims. It actually began BEFORE they arrived, so this made it seem like something else arrived and the Marshal so conveniently arrived shortly after to give us the answer."

"How nice of him for the timing," he smirks.

"Yeah. A series of children were discovered with this seemingly ultrarare condition. They were spaced out over the course of many years, and only a very few that I'm aware of being publicly announced. But almost as soon as they were discovered, they died, and with VERY strange symptoms. There was an initial sensation in the news, but this quickly turned to worry. Then Darumon and Sargeras arrived with their stories. And along the way, he offered his superior wisdom to help us understand what it was and to find a solution."

"The chip, I suppose?"

"Actually, no..." he huffs crossly and sets his hands on his knees to lean forward. "It was the seed first!"

"The seed?" Thaelyn also leans forward.

Again, inside the visitor's booth, they listened, and collectively leaned forward as they tried to reconcile this association.

"What did you people do over there?" Ankhia demands silently.

The Commander continues his thoughts.

"His first suggestion said it was some kind of alien parasitic thing that our science was never able to identify. He claimed it was SO alien, our science wouldn't know HOW to identify it, or measure it. And it was settling into our native environment such that we might not be able to get rid of it by now."

"How convenient," Thaelyn muses. "He fabricates an alien you cannot detect and instills fear of a global pandemic out of it."

"Exactly. It was easily demonstrated, too. Those children were said to be exhibiting some kind of ghostlike thing in the room with them, and I know there were plenty of witnesses to back this up. And not one technician was able to measure it."

"All right, so you have your empirical data, or maybe the lack of it, but visual evidence to show something was there and your science could not otherwise measure it."

"Right. This turned into a public panic after a while…we called it the Tav'ageen Scare for what it did to our population. More of these cases were turning up, which is to say these death syndromes. At first children, but then it moved to adults, seemingly at random throughout our population, everywhere, and with no apparent pattern to it."

"Cu'Nar help us," Ankhia whines. "That'll do something to them."

"The people were demanding answers," he continues. "But all Darumon could say was to run away to any planet that can take us, and use the seeds as an emergency procedure to allow us survivability on arrival."

"Grace of the cu'Nar!" Ankhia screeches under her breath and covers her mouth.

"And so, we have the seeds on everyone," Kaliya surmises. "That's one way to force-feed someone a load of nether-bilge. But why would he actually WANT those things if it's all a ruse?"

Thaelyn sat there trying to fathom these same questions, and he could sense the inquiries being made behind the window, but he had to focus on his interview.

"I recall a mention that these seeds were made a mandate by your Council, correct?"

"Yes, and later the chips," the Commander affirms. "The timeline went from this mad rush to push the seeds at us while our young military was desperately searching for any partway habitable world. But soon after, we started hearing of these insurgents rushing our scouting patrols, hitting outposts, and other things, and here is where we go building up our shiny military. The evacuation was put on hold during this time, but of course people are still dying in the streets. I recall hearing reports of people being found in alleyways, in homes, usually behind locked doors, and all with this horrible death syndrome. They were alive and healthy one moment, and the next time anyone saw them, they looked like a shriveled-up husk."

"That would surely frighten a good many, especially as it seems to defy logic as to how it might occur."

"Yeah. Eventually, as it became clear we were not going anywhere, Darumon brought together a team of our best experts and devised the chip, claiming it would neutralize a unique location within the brain that this alien thing was presumably targeting to find its victims."

"Oh, grand!" Kaliya mutters. "Now there's an excuse."

"Well," Ankhia shrugs. "You have to admit, it certainly sounds effective. And if you're panicking, I guess you'll take anything."

"That is a very unusual solution, to be sure," Thaelyn considers. "And this is what brings you to where you are now?"

"Yes," the Commander nods. "Once the population was given the chips, the deaths seemed to slow down until finally they ceased."

"I see, and this seems to explain two paradoxical items with one dilemma. You have the Scare, the application of these seeds, and finally, his superior alien wisdom gives you the chips, which seems to be a better solution than the seeds you never made good use of. But now, allow me to ask you one little question if I may. How long have you been a spacefaring society?"

"Oh, wow," he leans back as he ponders the notion. "I think this easily dates back two or three hundred millennia by now, at least the interstellar portions."

"All right, this is fair enough, and in this time, I suppose you had many opportunities to explore your local space, investigate new worlds, perhaps discover a multitude of life forms and such as this, correct?"

"Oh yes, I'm sure of it. It's said we've literally been across the galaxy and back again by now."

"That is quite an achievement. And let us also ask if during any of these moments, you ever had an occasion to discover something especially bizarre, such that your science had difficulty identifying it."

"I don't personally recall anything. I recall a lot of dead worlds, barren or frozen, molten, gas giants, and so on. There were some which had deep oceans under thick ice layers. We did discover some lesser lifeforms in these areas, and then there were some worlds with better environmental conditions and higher lifeforms. But nothing our science ever came up empty on, that I can recall. They all fit the expected parameters."

"Very good. But then, I suppose we must involve the possibility of other forms of life, like those I was speaking of earlier, perhaps of an ethereal nature. But these tend not to inhabit three-dimensional spaces anyway, and this one was certainly in your space. Also, I should probably reiterate their need for the flows, and the unlikelihood to find comfortable habitation in your space."

"All right, I think I'm with you so far."

"Let us then move to another aspect of this. Did you ever set down such as outposts, space stations, colonies and such?"

"Outposts, yes. Space stations, yes. But we never actually spread out with new colonies to my knowledge. I think our government never really held much interest in spreading our civilization to such far extremes."

"That seems like a rather constricted attitude for a society as old as yours. I would think you might want to expand yourselves at some moment to new centers in order to grow more. Perhaps you were keeping to one world where you might feel more at home?"

"I can't be sure the reason. I've heard of other worlds that were discovered and would make good colony examples, but no one ever did it."

"Staying at home?" Kaliya mumbles.

Ankhia glances at the younger woman for her private musings.

"That would make us the first time we really left home, I guess."

"Yeah, and look at what happened to us."

Thaelyn continued his interview, "I see, but ultimately, what we are saying here is with all your experience at travelling around out there, even to build such as outposts and space stations, you must have a fair amount of technology to live in what is otherwise unfavorable conditions, even without these seeds."

"Um…all right," the Commander notes. "I can already see where this is going. The answer would be yes, and if you're going to suggest why we didn't think of using this as opposed to the seeds…don't ask me. It was the Marshal and the Council making the decisions, and apparently out of panic."

"And there's those seeds again," Kaliya notes softly. "He wanted them for some reason, above all other things, including established tech to do the same job."

"Kaliya," Ankhia offers. "Are you thinking of something special here?"

"Wait a moment..." she leans forward to listen in carefully.

"All right," Thaelyn continues. "I suppose this is the best we can do for that. But as for the REAL issue behind this Tav'ageen Anomaly of yours, it is not a disease, or an alien...whatever. It is simply you."

"Um..." the Commander flusters briefly. "I think you're going to need to elaborate on that a little."

"I am sure I will," he smiles. "Let us reflect on Velen and his undesirable science faction for a moment. His was the 'science' of Metaphysics, as your people might refer to it. Where the term 'science' in this case, is very loosely applied. Your society of scientists and scholars does not seem to care for anything outside your clearly defined empirical data. No magic, no mysticism, no religion...all this is nonsense to you. Therefore, it goes without saying his faction would be very controversial."

"Yes, you got that one right."

"He tells us that among these early children, there were a variety of scientists trying to identify this condition. The medical and biology people were clueless to find anything to measure. But his people, thinking outside the box, were trying to interpret if this could be something fantastic. When all else fails, use your imagination, even if it defies rationality. You cannot tell me you know everything that is out there, and neither can you tell me that everything out there can be measured by rational numbers. For instance, define this, if you can..."

Thaelyn stands up and turns to the table next to him. He extends his hand with a pair of fingers outstretched.

"Watch out, people," Kaliya grins.

Thaelyn applies his telekinetic power to lift the table off the ground and well into the air. There, he holds it, much to the amazement of the Commander, as well as some of the people in the visitor's booth.

"Can you offer a name for this, Commander?" he asks.

The Commander gazed uncertainly at the spectacle.

"Uh-uh…" he grunts. "Levitation comes to mind, but not the way you're doing it."

"Does the word telekinesis mean anything to you?"

"Yeah, but it's a myth to us."

"Perhaps, but this would be part of Velen's field of study. A Celestial might own such a power, but this is a form of power that might normally be well above where you are. Telepathy is another one. This is what a mind, so empowered that it now becomes extradimensional, and therefore extends beyond the cage-like parameters of a corporeal body, can perform on external objects."

In the visitor's booth, Ankhia smiles contentedly as she listens.

"So that's how it works," she emits softly.

Thaelyn lowers the table and sits down again as he prepares another one. This time, he waves a hand in an elaborate circle, jutting it upwards and erupting with a ball of flame forming within his palm.

"And this, Commander, is an application of our magic, based on the flows. My perceptions define it, my mind directs the energies, and through this, the reality of space around me follows my will to create something essentially out of nothing."

"That would normally be regarded as impossible. But in all the nether-space, if I didn't just see it."

"You and me both, guy," Ankhia croons.

"You should've seen me on that first day," Kaliya recalls. "Cu'Nar help us for what he did out there in the Badlands."

Thaelyn clears his hand of the effect and returns to his lecture.

"Velen's people speak of a curious riddle they like to play with, but until they met me, they were unable to fully realize it. It apparently has two parts, the first of which goes like this, a theorem: Perception enables recognition, existence demands definition, and from this, substance becomes reality."

"That doesn't make any sense to me. It's no wonder the Council had such a hard time with it."

"I suppose Velen was well ahead of his time. I suspect, somewhere during his lifetime, he must have experienced something to open his mind to the idea. But in your barren fold universe, he might not have had the means to fully realize it."

"So, this is to say, we are handicapped for this point?"

"Technically, yes. The second part is even more intriguing. An axiom: In a metaphysical reality, nothing unknown exists. It only exists AFTER it is known. How do you like that for backwards thinking?" he grins.

"Yeah, that twists my horns nicely. So, how do we interpret this?"

"He is truly outside his element in your universe for this part, and probably outside any common three-dimensional domain. This is how the gods work, and the flows are their toolbox. What all this means is the mind, under the right conditions, and if we are speaking of a powerful enough mind to start with, can alter the reality of space around them. We Celestials have a concept we describe as to Know of a thing. To Know of a thing is to define it within our minds FIRST, and from this, we can apply our perceptions onto the space around us. Magic works the same way, so a young race can learn this much, using the flows as their energy source, until one day they grow up to work even larger miracles."

"That is simply amazing, and not just for the implications of it. And this is what he was talking about in his faction that everyone ridiculed? I can't say I blame them for this point. I doubt we hold the power to do anything like this."

"In your universe? Much of this would be difficult, to say the least. But, my dear Commander, I must beg to differ with you on one aspect, as I have one young lady who HAS demonstrated this. She is Velen's daughter, as it turns out, and she is pioneering the study for us."

"Really! So, they did finally figure it out?"

"They had to arrive here first, and then meet with me to help them find their answers. Much like the rest of you, if it did not involve that classic empirical data, it was still mysticism. It is a bit ironic, actually. They were trying to understand the aspect of mysticism while at the same time denying the aspect of mysticism."

In the visitor's booth, Kaliya let out a sturdy giggle, clamping her hands over her mouth to hold it back.

"Yeah, now there's a tail-yanker for you."

"They were stuck in a rut due to our old habits," the Commander considers.

"It would seem that way," Thaelyn nods. "But now that they are over that initial hump, I would expect a few interesting turns out of them. We have a group currently in study to develop a number of skills we are examining right now. It would seem we are discovering a series of potential traits to explore. And the crowning achievement is what we call the Prodigy Child gift."

"And what is that? It sounds important."

"Oh indeed, that would be an understatement for this example. This is a skill I would not normally expect to see in a species like yours at all. This surely qualifies as a high-ranking Celestial ability. But it would seem you do have it…as a species."

"Huh? Wait!" he blurts abruptly. "As a species? Are you saying this isn't something for Velen and his people, but all of us?"

"And we can apply a recent example, if not for his unfortunate psychosis. Ytani."

"Him!" he shouts. "Is THAT what he was using? And the Marshal taught him how to use it!"

"And it went straight to his head, it would seem."

"Oh, it sure did! But what exactly is it, and how does it work?"

"For this, we should reflect on those original Tav'ageen children. Velen and his people began to imagine a possible scenario, but unfortunately those children died before they could gain any conclusive data. The child was seen with a ghostlike apparition in the room, right?"

"Yeah, this is how they described it."

"That apparition was a projection of their spirit consciousness. The child was asleep, but its mind was active and outside the body."

The Commander grimaces as he tries to fathom this bizarre scenario.

"Is something like this actually healthy?" he wheezes.

"Well, yes, I might say it should be, if properly governed. There are those who practice what some call astral travelling, where they do something like this intentionally to travel to higher-dimensional realms for exploration and learning. What is so unusual about this one is you are projecting an image in physical space right alongside your body. Furthermore, this projection can be made tangible, such that it can interact with other objects or people, almost as the original body would. But here is where it diverges. You can move to any location you can recall in your mind by folding space. You can also alter your form to anything you can imagine."

"And here we have Ytani changing into a dwarf and jumping into that city under the mountain. No devices, just the power of his mind. In all the nether-space, this is a dangerous skill."

"I would tend to agree, Commander. We have people in study who have learned how to use this quite fluently by now, whereas Ytani might be described as an amateur by comparison."

"Oh! This I would love to rub in his face. He, for all his gloating, is an amateur."

"Yes," he chuckles. "I think he would not appreciate that one. Our examples have taken forms ranging from clumps of dirt to a variety of insects and animals, plants and other inanimate objects, and even god-sized images. They can also change to a simple spot on a wall for spying purposes."

"That's bad, from the security standpoint!"

"It is, but again it largely depends on whose side you are on. For my part, we were using this on you in your base," he grins.

"Oh! Well, of course…why not?" he chuckles. "So, here I am in private conversation with my people, and the water stain on the ceiling is actually a spy!"

The two of them share a laugh, as do the people in the visitor's booth.

"And we still are," Thaelyn submits. "As we are now impersonating you and some of your officers, just in case anyone comes around to check on things."

"Oh dear! So, what does this mean about me and the real officers?"

"It means you will need to take up occupancy elsewhere for now. We are training an army of these people, Commander, and we intend to use this on Darumon, in return for all he has done to others. This represents a dark little secret of his."

"Uh oh…a secret? What kind? Or should I guess if to consider those chips. That represents a cover-up of some kind."

"Indeed, and here we come back to Adalon and her prophecies. It would seem between her and Maker Kuroku, they know a little something about this, and they shared it with the rest of us, so we could make our preparations. It has to do with your evolution."

"Oops. Suddenly, I'm not so sure I want to hear this."

"I would imagine you are not alone. We learned the story of your extraordinarily exceptional evolution of the Eracyodines from Velen's people. But for us Celestials, we would think this to be highly improbable to evolve even this ridiculously long lifespan of yours in that time, to say nothing of the Prodigy Gift. You would need at least a few orders of magnitude more time, even under normal conditions, to earn any of this. Having lifespans measured in tens of millennia is abnormal for a common mortal species. It would be far more reasonable to measure them in decades, or at best, a few centuries."

"You know, I'm actually aware that there has always been a big controversy in the biology and archeology factions on this, and for a long time in our history. No other species in our world has ever demonstrated anything like what we have. We seem to have held this extreme longevity for a long period in our history, and with no reasonable explanation on how we got it, as compared to other native species."

"Interesting. Then it would seem the evidence may be missing, or perhaps covered up."

"If you were to ask me," Kaliya mumbles. "I would say covered up, like everything else he did."

"And yet," Thaelyn continues. "You seem to have lifespans already more becoming of a Celestial…an early Celestial at least… along with telepathy, that we are sure of, and we suspect a few other things might be possible as we continue to study this. And then we have this Prodigy Gift, which would count as a much more advanced skill. Commander, from my perspective as a Celestial, this puts you on MY level, not that of a two-million-year-old mortal society. Evolution does not work that fast, and we should know."

"All right, so how do you figure this?"

"Two words, Commander…outside interference."

The Commander lowers his head and sighs deeply.

"Should I guess who or what was interfering? Or do you just want to rip my horns out again."

"My apologies, Commander, I am not trying to do this intentionally. Velen's people are no happier for it, but the Maker saw the whole thing, and then chronicled it for us to review later."

"All right, so what happened?"

"Darumon. According to her notes, he found you back in the days of the Eracyodines. He is said to have spurred a nascent species into sapience. This is to say, he uplifted you to where you are now. And since we know the Primordials have a history of creating life, or at least modifying something to fill their needs, we have to suggest he did this to you so you would be his servants later on."

"So, the whole story of him arriving with his problems is just a cover, and for what?"

"Taking revenge on his old rivals, but we also think to cover up something he does not want you to have…this Gift. His kind likely would not appreciate a young species like yours with such elaborate gifts. Those first children did not die by accident, but they did die by something alien…him. His kind can manipulate energies your science might not be able to accurately measure…spiritual energies. Just look at those ghostlike apparitions you could never measure. They do not represent physical quantities to the conventional sciences. Suck that out in a kind of vampiric action, and there you go."

"So, he killed our children to keep this a secret. Then he stuffed these chips in our heads to shut it off."

"And those seeds, guy…" Kaliya groans under her breath.

Ankhia turns to examine the girl.

"Kaliya, you seem to be obsessed with that. What is it?"

"They still have them, Ankhia! Ten millennia, and they STILL seem to be applying those seeds. It's not about an evacuation, that was a simple excuse."

"Kaliya," the General offers. "Perhaps you would like to inquire on this?"

"Let's wait a little more to see what else comes out first."

Thaelyn continued his interview with the Commander.

"You describe those chips by what term was it?" he asks.

"They're called Tav'ageen Suppressor chips," the Commander replies. "The principle is to shut down whatever it was this alien thing was supposed to be targeting to find new victims. So, what are we actually saying here, it shuts down that part of the brain to enable this skill?"

"I would probably describe it that way."

"And the feedback effect?"

"I cannot be sure of that one, unless we are speaking of a form of reinforcement."

"Yeah, I like that term, reinforcement. Keeping us locked up like an animal in a cage."

"Let us go gently, Commander. Now that we are learning of these details, we must work positively to correct it. But with him hanging over the scene, we must move delicately."

"I agree."

"He has likely been watching over you during your long history. We have suggested a few potential moments where he has essentially interfered with your history in one form or another, probably using his shapeshifting skill to impersonate those in key positions to feed you false information about everything else."

"Yeah, that skill is certainly a dangerous one to have. But then, I feel a need to ask what he did to the Eracyodines to create us with powers we're not otherwise supposed to have. It sounds like he fouled up somewhere."

"This was a question we asked as well, especially if he is in a barren fold, and the flows would normally serve as a tool for this.

In the absence of that, and when looking at who and what you are today, we can only come to one conclusion."

"Oh dear," Kaliya moans. "Watch out people. Horns will fly soon."

"He is your father," Thaelyn asserts.

"Our father..." the Commander gasps. "As in what...a biological father?" his voice escalates. "For all he does to us, he is our FATHER?!" he screeches. "Just how much of a father is he?"

"Your species is interpreted to be half Eracyodine, half Darumon. In the absence of the flows in your space, he apparently had to resort to the most fundamental of methods to create a sentient form of life."

"Ew..." he frowns and shudders visibly. "But it must've been fun to watch HIM lower himself to this level. Mating with animals? Ugh...but is such a thing possible?"

"We suspect his body might hold some flexibility for this point. If the Estelar can intermix their essence with another species, like a mortal species to create a Celestial, he might have something similar. But here is the good part...if you can call it that. You have ridiculously long lifespans, as some of us describe them. You have such gifts as telepathy, perhaps clairvoyance and precognition, and of course, the Prodigy Gift. These are all easily Celestial grade gifts, Commander, therefore we cannot say anything less than you qualify on that level, even though you are much too young to realize the implications of holding that station."

"Wow... That's like...wow..." he croons. "All right, maybe I'll pick up my horns again."

"Yes, many of us are saying the same," he chuckles. "This naturally carries a great many demands, and we are already planning ways for how to use this. But this also demands that your entire society may need a crash course to learn the discipline associated with it."

"In all the nether-space, I'm thinking of Ytani now. And then a full society of people like him."

"Exactly. A properly evolved society of Celestials learns how to control themselves much better. What goes one way, can travel back again. We teach this to our people here for the aspect of magic, but it would be no different for a Celestial society and such things as telepathy and other skills."

"Yes, that might be easy for you to say, but how do WE do it? We don't even know what it is, and especially if you consider Velen's faction and how people treated it."

"I will offer to help, if you desire it, but we already have a body of Velen's people, led by this same young lady, who are taking up this role on our behalf. She is a very progressive individual who realized this a while ago and is working on a solution to it."

"All right, I hope she is successful. I might wish to speak with her sometime and listen to her ideas."

Inside the visitor's booth, Ankhia nudges Kaliya on the shoulder.

"You're developing a fan club, kid."

"Oh, please, Ankhia, as if I needed even MORE pressure?" she giggles.

"So, he comes in," the Commander surmises. "He modifies our ancestors to create us. He directs our history, covering his own actions along the way. He likely replaces or removes anyone who is otherwise interfering with his efforts. Then, one day, we have these children come up, and by this time now showing some of these strange abilities that are apparently part of our natural heritage. But like the dull-horns we are, probably because he bred this into us, it doesn't fit with our empirical sciences, and the one person who is bold enough to think outside the box, as you described it, is shunned by the rest. It's no wonder those beings carried HIM away, as he would probably be next on the list for Darumon to set things back to normal."

"This is very sound reasoning," Thaelyn nods. "It can easily be said the Estelar tend to play some very elaborate games as a way of seeing a means to an end. He apparently served an important role, if not for you, then for us. And now, here we are, returning back to you."

"Right, but in the meantime, here we are in a world panic due to that Tav'ageen Scare he pushed on us. He claimed it was a big scary alien thing, and to run away. And then, oh yes, the seeds!" he tosses his hands up. "We give ourselves to his superior alien wisdom, the Council bows down and kisses his hooves for his grand promise of new science to uplift us to who-knows-what, but on the other side of it, his solution to the Tav'ageen Anomaly was NOT a curative procedure. It was to infect us with these horrid little parasites… real ones this time…saying: Here, take this, it'll help you survive in places you'll never see in your lifetime. As if we ever had such motivation to leave home before this…"

"That's it," Kaliya announces determinedly. "General, do you think I could go in there and start asking questions?"

"I do not have anything against it," he responds. "But I would confer with His Lordship first."

"Fine."

Kaliya lifts a hand to her temple and focuses her mind at Thaelyn. The others in the booth study her as she attempts to use her new telepathic skills to commune her message.

The Commander continued his rampage, "And therefore, we have the panic. It was not until AFTER we had those seeds when he invented this miraculous medical chip with the livestock containment feedback circuit."

Thaelyn suddenly perks up and turns towards the window with the illusion of a garden outside. The action was quickly noticed by the Commander, who turns to follow his gaze. But to him, it appeared as just a window with a garden outside.

"What?" he asks. "Did something just happen?"

Thaelyn pauses his response a moment, then nods and waves at the window, as if offering someone or something to come hither.

"Are you speaking to those flowers out there?" the Commander smiles delicately.

"Yes, we have some rather unusual foliage around here," he smiles back. "Surely, as a man in your position, you might suspect an interrogation room to involve a side room for observers. That window is a false image, and behind it is one such room."

"I see, and now they want to come in here. But you reacted like you heard something."

"Telepathy, one of our skills."

"You people are seriously dangerous with those skills. But then, I suppose any of us would be too if we had such skills over a younger race."

"This is most often the case, Commander. But it really comes down to how you apply them. Responsibility is the most important factor here."

A moment later, a knocking comes at the door, followed by a congregation of observers. Kaliya steps forward into view, and as she presents herself, the Commander takes quick notice of her body and her eyes.

"In all the nether-space, I haven't seen anyone walking around without the seed other than young people. And what happened to your eyes?"

"The eyes are a bit difficult to explain," she replies. "Let me first introduce myself. My name is Lieutenant Kaliya Nazég. My father is Velen. I'm the one Thaelyn mentioned a few times with all the bright ideas…and a rapidly developing reputation around here, for better or for worse," she grins as she glances at Thaelyn.

"You look rather young for a Lieutenant."

"Yes, well, things here work much faster than they do back home. This here," she directs at Kailen, "is my brother and our resident HC, Kailen Nazég."

The Commander immediately perks up at the mention of rank.

"A High Commander?" he rises as best he can in the cramped quarters and salutes. "A pleasant greeting, Sir."

Kaliya continues, "Following is Thaelyn's top military advisor, General Gabarleine, and then we have our chief Med-tech, Ankhia Tad'vaal."

"Where is Lieutenant Lapäli, in this case?" Thaelyn asks.

"He's still back there with his camera."

"That young man is developing as an aspiring military journalist."

"Yeah. As for the eyes, Commander, we received this from the cu'Nar as what they called a type of protection or cleansing, and we have since interpreted this as a way of purging Darumon's

Primordial essence and converting us away from him towards the Estelar, probably at the request of Maker Kuroku, to make us more compatible with the Celestial societies."

"Are you already moving to take up that role?" he wonders.

"We have to, it's a demand for us now. When you combine all these Gifts, we need to make a very concerted effort to realize who we are, and then to form a regulatory body to teach and set the standards for the rest. We even took up a religion, if you can believe it, offering ourselves to one of the Estelar we call Lord Oghma, who presides over scholarly wisdom and the pursuit of knowledge. This is what they do, to offer guidance for young societies like ours to help us grow…much better than Darumon might ever promise."

"So, you actually did find enlightenment out here."

"It was a hard ride, but yes, and now we're bringing it home. But the reason for me being here is I have a number of issues I was hoping to ask about. My Lord, do you mind?"

The Commander winces at the strange reference.

"You call him, 'my Lord'?"

"Yes, I'm a citizen here now. As such, I serve under a King. Life is funny that way," she chuckles.

"By all means, Kaliya," Thaelyn offers. "I have probably taken this far enough for all other purposes. What do you have for us?"

Kaliya steps further into the room and begins unconsciously pacing across the floor. Thaelyn glares at the action as he begins to recognize his own manners.

"General," he muses. "I think this young lady is developing a few unfortunate habits."

"But of course, my Lord," he responds gleefully. "After all, she has a most remarkable role model to follow."

Thaelyn raised his brow bemusedly as he now glares at the General.

The Commander watches the interaction and finds himself intrigued by the strange behavior.

"Commander," Kaliya begins. "You once said this seed…what was the name again?"

"It's called an An'gamu Seed."

"All right, and this was mandated at one time by your Council. This was at the time Darumon invoked this plague on you as his first brilliant solution to this alien infestation he claimed."

"That's right."

"So, we have a world panic to take the seeds as his solution to evacuate by any means necessary, and using anything they could get their hands on, if not all the wonderful technology our society has been inventing for so many hundreds of millennia."

Thaelyn gazed at her and frowned almost immediately as he began to notice a direction in her statements.

"Yeah..." the Commander sighs. "It doesn't paint a very nice picture for us, does it?"

"Hardly that!" Ankhia groans. "Commander, as a medical technician with half a horn to spare, taking that horrid piece of antiquated rubbish is the last thing I would think of during an evacuation."

"I would tend to agree, but I wasn't the one making the decisions. The Council did."

"Right," Kaliya muses. "A Council that was likely under his control to begin with. Therefore, what Darumon wants, the Council simply gives it to him. And here we now see a mandate to apply this to every citizen...everyone, right?"

"It becomes necessary as you make your second centennial, so yes."

"Oh, how nice!" Ankhia moans. "They give you a grace period to grow up first!"

"But this all began as part of this Scare you mentioned," Kaliya continues. "Then you have these insurgents, which stifle the evacuation effort, assuming you ever had the REAL intention of leaving at all, as you say we NEVER held such an interest in all our history of space travel."

"Kaliya," Thaelyn leans forward. "How do you mean this?"

"He plays Saakerav to bring us out of the chaos of the Old World, and you think he would want his little playthings to run off all across the galaxy?"

"Indeed! You do hold a point. Then the evacuation was clearly a ruse, but to what end?"

"The seed!" she points assertively at the Commander's body. "This was his first solution, not to cover up the Prodigy Gift with the chip, but to apply something entirely unrelated…USING the Prodigy Gift as an excuse."

"Wait," the Commander issues. "You're moving too fast for me. What do you mean, and what was this mention of Saakerav?"

"We think Darumon played King Saakerav in the old days to bring the world together. It doesn't serve Darumon to have all his toys fighting each other. So, guess what, here comes Saakerav, and our incredible romance over how he did such a wonderful thing to promote our modern civilization."

"Oh please," he moans. "Did you really have to do that?"

"Yes, well, with apologies, but you're not the first one. And then we go out, find all sorts of fascinating worlds to colonize, but we never do. If we say he was basically controlling us during this time, likely with the Council as a proxy, this is to say we find places to colonize, but HE doesn't want us going out there. After all, we're his pet species to do as he tells us, not wander away from home. So, the real question is, why the seeds. If he simply wanted to cover up the Prodigy Gift, he would've used that superior alien wisdom of his to give us an instant solution."

"All right, I see it. But then, like you said, why the seeds?"

"Let me ask you again about this timeline. You have the children, and you have the initial sensation, as my father once said, about this discovery. This turned to worry, and then to a panic, right?"

"Yes, as we started seeing these bodies."

"Then Darumon arrives with his convenient alien wisdom, takes one look, and sends you into a further panic, causing you to apparently forget you have all sorts of nether-wild tech to do the job. This reminds me of Therinë and the city of Rolsklinde, where he took control not simply of their government, but also their education system. We might also say the media, for this point, for all his propaganda, and thereby overriding the people's ability to realize we're a society of smart people with smart ideas."

"Kaliya," Ankhia wonders. "Not that I would argue this, but seriously, how do you turn a society of scientists into such dull-horns that they don't even remember the tech they've been inventing for so many hundreds of millennia?"

"If you never go out there and USE it, what's to remind you of having it."

"Oh, I swear to you!" she growls.

"So, what we need to ask ourselves, if his first priority is NOT the Gift, what is it that he wants those seeds for, because you're STILL using them, right?"

"Yes, but, um..." the Commander hesitates as he glances at Ankhia, who was clearly fuming by now. "We actually do have a justifiable reason for it these days. But you're not going to like it, and I'm afraid I'm going to get my tail chewed by this woman if I say anything."

Ankhia glares at him briefly as she realizes her temper outburst. So she tries to back down.

"I'm sorry, Commander, go ahead. I'll try not to chew on it too hard...but don't quote me on that," she wags a finger at him sternly.

"Right, well, here goes nothing. When he took control of our military, he also instructed us to build up a rather extensive industry to support it."

"Oh dear..."

"And, um, since we were in an evacuation state of mind..."

"You must be kidding me..."

"It was rushed into service to help us against those insurgents, which were described at the time as very dangerous for what we had to protect ourselves."

"Oh! Naturally! Start a new panic, why not."

"So, the priority was to simply get something up and running, using the simplest tech we had. After all, we're not staying here long enough to, um, worry about it..." he glances at Ankhia and cringes as she gets ready to explode.

"I swear to the cu'Nar!" she screams. "I'm ashamed to be part of the same species as you people! Are you saying you polluted your OWN environment so badly that you now need these seeds simply to survive there? In all the nether-space! How could you possibly do that? And THEN..." she emphasizes with a finger. "Ten millennia... TEN! Count them..." she fumbles with her fingers to hold up the count. "...And you couldn't figure it out that you're poisoning every living thing, including yourselves, evacuation or no evacuation, that you couldn't go back and revamp it during this time to fix it?!"

The whole room had turned to watch her tirade as she grabs her horns and lets out a painful roar. Kailen and the General both stepped back to give her room. Kaliya was on the other side, conveniently out of range, while Thaelyn leaned back in his chair and crossed his arms.

The Commander pulled away from the fit, silently wondering how sturdy the bars were around the prison cell.

Kaliya turned to glance quickly at the window, where Padriyl was still sitting in the visitor's booth with his camera.

"And that, folks," she animates. "Is what we mean when we say, horns will fly."

"Indeed!" Thaelyn affirms. "Powers help us. Commander," he glances up at Kailen. "I feel for you and your home life. Is she like this often?"

"She has her moments," Kailen replies. "But not quite as bad as this. Although, I will admit, our women are very passionate."

Ankhia was panting by this time as she tried to regain her composure.

"Commander," she begins again. "Can you give me one good reason why our civilization of intellectuals could not, at the very least, figure out how to build clean industry in all this time?"

"Well, as I said," he reflects. "It was a rush job to get it up and running. After that...well, I think the only thing I can say about it is we were in a constant state of war thinking, any day now, our shiny military will finish with these insurgents and the evacuation plan will go forward. The chips were described to be temporary, along with the seed, until that time."

"That's just another propaganda story!" Kaliya declares firmly. "Any day now! Oh yes, turn those horns down some more with so much repeated rhetoric. He WANTED you to have the chips to cover up this Gift, and he WANTED you to have those seeds for something else, and the rest was simply to give justification to that civilization of intellectuals who would probably, and eventually, figure it out if they had enough opportunity to do so."

"You think?" Ankhia mutters cautiously.

"Ankhia, I can't imagine our people would go along with this nonsense unless someone was feeding them a continuous line of OTHER nonsense to keep up the image. So, we come back to those seeds. This was his first priority on arrival. What was his motivation at that time? He takes advantage of the Prodigy Gift as an excuse to describe something alien arriving…other than himself, that is…"

"He and Sargeras…" the Commander adds.

"Right. By the way, what is Sargeras doing during this time?"

"I have no idea, other than resting in that sanctuary building of his."

"A sanctuary building?"

"Yeah. Remember when I said he appeared very weak and in poor health. Well, Darumon ordered us to build a special sanctuary building for him to recover in. No one goes in there, except Darumon himself on occasion, so I hear, and maybe a few building maintenance workers. He told us Sargeras's condition required special treatment that our science wouldn't understand, and therefore he would do it personally."

"Using what?" she halts and slaps her head. "Hold on…yes! HE would do it. After all, Sargeras is a Primordial, what would YOU know about how to treat something like that. And he's in a space without the flows, so Darumon must be the one to offer assistance, and in this case, he has to be feeding him with something… Ugh…" she suddenly grimaces. "Oh, Kali, you didn't really have to think of that just now, did you?"

Kaliya stumbles back and covers her eyes as she clearly seems affected by something.

"Kaliya?" Thaelyn intones uncertainly. "What is it?"

"I feel suddenly ill. I think I hit on something, and I don't like what it implies. But, like you said, maybe one crazy idea can lead to another."

"I have said this in the past, but I dread to imagine what you just came upon."

"Yeah, and poor Ankhia over there will lose what's left of her horns from it."

"Does she still have anything remaining, after that last bout?" he chuckles softly. "Very well, but give it to us."

"Give me just one moment. I had a quick cascade of images hit me. Ankhia, you did a study on those seeds once, right?"

"Yes, I did," she responds. "What about it?"

"I think I recall hearing you found some really bizarre genetic coding in there once. Did you ever figure out what it was?"

"Not entirely. The computer was having a hard time trying to analyze it."

"But it wasn't part of the old records we brought with us, right?"

"Yeah, this was something new, I think."

"New... Naturally, it was new, and so alien that we don't have a definition for it. All right, my Lord, let's test your knowledge on this. That panic. He needed to drive them to take his seeds. This was his first priority to serve a need. And who do you think would be his first priority to serve, but his sick and weak master in a barren fold."

"Oh, Powers pay pity, Kaliya," Thaelyn lurches forward. "But then, how would you define this?"

"Those seeds must offer a substitute for the flows, maybe something like an empathic funnel effect...spiritual energy, a directed flow of it. And he drove an entire planet to take them."

"Oh dear."

"He's using them as FOOD?!" Ankhia screeches. "That abominable beast!"

"Yeah," the Commander affirms. "On this note, I would agree. That makes me feel just wonderful, as if I didn't feel bad enough," he examines his body for the seed entity.

"But it gets worse," Kaliya notes.

"Kaliya!" Ankhia blasts. "How can it possibly get any worse?"

"Those death syndromes. More vampiric actions, and all during the time of that panic, and continuing up until the seeds and chips were installed."

"Oh no, you can't mean."

"Yes," Thaelyn muses solemnly. "I think she can. She has enough education in her by now to teach her of such things."

"Yeah," Kaliya nods. "This is where it went."

"This is simply deplorable!" the General scorns. "Utterly and definitively the WORST part of all our experiences with that creature."

The Commander was feeling pale as he listened, but he wasn't completely aware of their full meaning, not holding this sort of background knowledge.

"Um, can one of you explain to me what you're talking about now."

"Commander," Kaliya explains. "You said the Tav'ageen Scare was based on what seemed like random deaths, the bodies were dried up like something sucked the life out of them. This is what we call a vampiric action, to suck the life energies out of a body. If Darumon was causing this, and he is the best place to point a finger, he might actually be absorbing this into himself, at least temporarily. Once he has this, he might then use it as a temporary feed into Sargeras until you got all those seeds to offer what might be a trickle effect to support him in that sanctuary building for his recovery. This is Darumon's method to help his master recover in that place after his long sleep."

The Commander grimaced at the horrid imagery. He closed his eyes and turned away.

"I'm currently training in Thaelyn's academy here," Kaliya adds. "The lessons I'm learning are amazing. These people might be ONLY Industrial Age from the technology side we understand, but the other side of the tech tree they use here is based on magic and their relationship with the Estelar, and what they might learn from that side. If you think the people back home would ridicule the idea of my father's science faction, the things I've learned in just a few years here, which is actually a huge amount so far, because their education system crams it down your throat like there's no tomorrow, it could rewrite a lot of the books back home. For instance..."

She alters her posture as she prepares to illustrate.

"The lessons we receive in the academies here teach us about the flows, how they work and how to use them. Such beings as the Estelar would need this as a type of support layer. This would likely include Sargeras. However," she raises a finger for emphasis. "We refer to the Estelar as gods, and as gods, we might offer worship to them. This is a bit like a give-and-take relationship, where we offer our piety in the form of thoughts, feelings, and dedication of mental energies. This would be transmitted along the flows into their image as we envision them in our minds. These energies serve as a form of empowerment to them, and we can actually use this a little bit like currency, where we can ask them to bestow upon us one or another blessing or ability to use elsewhere."

"A form of currency? Thoughts?"

"The energy of thoughts, meaning emotions, empathic energy, the living essence of the mind donated to them, which can make them stronger. We produce bioenergy in our bodies, and our minds can channel this. We describe this as Favor. We give them our Favor to empower them, and they might return it back as gifts of one kind or another."

"Like a form of exchange. That must be a truly fascinating relationship. How do you tend to use this?"

"As for me, I'm in training as a paladin, which is a kind of holy warrior, and part priest. It's regarded as a very righteous profession around here, and befitting of someone who wants to set a high standard for others to follow. So far, I'm still a little raw, but I had enough practice to do my job in your base, which was to capture your people and put them under a kind of sleep spell to hold you until we could process you. Other people, such as full priests, can often use this for healing and medical applications, among other things. For instance, your surgery. They took that thing out, and a priest did a laying-on of hands to instantly close up your injury."

"That sounds about as crazy as everything else around here, but if my head is telling me anything," he feels around where his interface used to be. "I think this could potentially revolutionize the medical profession."

"These are just examples, of course, a small taste of it. But if any of our people could spend even just a little bit of time here, I think most of the factions back home would be eating their words."

"And of course," Thaelyn adds. "This naturally brings us back around to our forward direction. We are moving to Azgarén to bring Darumon and Sargeras down. We would wish to help your people as much as possible, but we must move carefully so as not to cause Darumon any suspicion that he is being stalked by his old enemies."

"How do you expect to arrive there?" the Commander asks. "If you try using the conveyor in our base, you'll arrive in Central Command, which is right under his nose."

"As we suspected. We will try to avoid that and look for an alternative. One of Adalon's recent prophecies, which we found as we were bringing your base crew in, suggested we might find another such example as Kaliya here, where she was able to bring us to Ruuki uy'Daan using her Prodigy Gift. If this is so, that will be our path to Azgarén, and using projected images, rather than physical bodies, at least in the beginning."

"Ugh…" he winces. "I'm trying to imagine an invasion of ghosts hitting us now. To all the nether-realms with Darumon's insurgents, this is really bad. Well, I can tell you this much. I want to see that creature removed from my home. If I was close to mutiny before this, consider me jumping in with both hooves now. I suppose defecting over to the other side isn't any different. And considering everything that's been said, I want to try to make up for all the things I've done in my life…or been forced to do. I want him to know we're not going to take this anymore."

"This is very encouraging, Commander. I may need some time to find a good position for you, but for now, I think education would be a good place to start. We will need to bring you up to date on where we are and what we already know."

"What about my staff? Can we bring them all in?"

"I think that is surely within reason. I can bring you together with your officers for a conference, and we can proceed from there."

"Good, and then, what are you doing with our base right now? And what about Ytani?"

"As for the base, we intend to hold it until we are ready to make our move, but we are waiting on a number of things as part of our preparation. Where Ytani is concerned, I will need to send dear sweet innocent Kaliya here on an assassination mission."

"Dear sweet and innocent?" he muses uncertainly as he studies her. "All right, maybe I should ask this. How old are you?"

"Four," she responds cutely.

"Uh huh, I thought something like that. He's not a nice guy where the ladies are concerned, do you know this?"

"I know, I saw the recordings of your conversations with him, and I was spying inside his house to see his toys."

"That was you? And he calls you sweet and innocent?" he glances at Thaelyn.

"Well, figuratively," she smirks. "But I'm trained in a variety of combat methods, most of which our people wouldn't know anything about, and I'm a mage of the Seventh Circle, which is rather dangerous by itself."

"A mage?"

"Someone who studies magic. It's a type of profession around here. There are nine Circles of study, and I'm on my way up to the Eighth as my goal."

"Maybe one day you can explain to me what that actually means."

"Maybe. But I'll actually be projected at the time, not physical. So, he can't actually hurt me. My plan is to play a frisky young tail-swinger and entice him to either Madzurki or Ooduan and maroon him there while we blow the place up. This might take care of two issues at once."

"And removing the evidence, as you said, so Darumon has no

idea of what you're doing. Clever. By the way, he's responsible for two other deaths. He claimed they were accidents…injuries to the seed entity during rough play or some such. I don't think I believe it, but he demanded everything to be excused regardless, to cover it up."

"This is surely good enough cause for suspicion," Thaelyn considers.

"Maybe also his psychosis," Kaliya offers. "He got away with it before, so why not again."

"Good point. But in those cases, we might not be able to find our evidence. In this one, we have witnesses and recordings of your conversations."

"And then, it's on to Azgarén," the Commander concludes. "I don't know how you intend to do this, but you know, as for trying to teach a world full of dull-horns," he flashes a brisk smile at Ankhia before returning to Kaliya. "No offence, but aren't you just a bit young to serve as a role model that could revolutionize a world philosophy?"

"We'll see about that, Commander," Kaliya winks. "Especially as I'm reinventing the old Stormhooves."

"The Stormhooves!" he gasps. "Why would you do that?"

"Adalon has predicted their return. Darumon once created a romance for our old history, and I'm turning it into reality and giving it a new twist. We'll be leading a new crusade to bring our people out of darkness. But this time, we'll be here to stay."

TO BE CONTINUED